God's
Mirror

by

C.N. Glina

A catalogue record for this book is available from the National Library of Australia

Publisher:
ASPG (Australian Self-Publishing Group)
P.O. Box 159, Calwell, ACT Australia 2905
Email: publishaspg@gmail.com
http://www.inspiringpublishers.com

National Library of Australia Cataloguing-in-Publication entry

Author: C.N. Glina

Title: **God's Mirror**

ISBN (Print): 978-1-922920-40-9
ISBN (eBook): 978-1-922920-41-6

Author's Foreword.

This is a work of fiction, loosely based around a historical event, and some historical figures. While the historical event and figures have been researched for the purpose of giving some weight and realism to the story, they are by no means definitive descriptions of what actually occurred. The author sincerely hopes that no offense is caused by these representations.

PART 1

$$\diamondsuit$$

Chapter 1
If a tree falls in the forest...

The day her life changed drastically for the second time was drab and overcast, just the way she liked it. It had started out ordinarily enough, with just a few clouds dotting the sky. By noon however, a thick blanket of cloud stretched across the heavens, blocking out the harsh glare of the sun. With nothing else to do as she trudged along the dirt road carrying her small, pathetic collection of belongings over her shoulder, she watched the steady gathering of clouds. "Honestly Mel," she sighed to herself, wincing at the pain in her feet, "you really shouldn't ask so many questions." Her stay in the last village had been cut shorter than usual, due to her unwelcome probing of strange phenomena in the area.

"Why would you be askin' 'bout such things miss?" the craggy-faced inn-keeper had asked, raising a bushy eyebrow at her. She had huddled over her bowl of watery stew and stale bread, looked about to check that no one was in earshot.

"My only living relative has disappeared under mysterious circumstances," she had explained in a low voice. "I am searching for any place where strange things are reported to happen. Perhaps it will lead me to my brother..." The well-practised story had flowed smoothly out of her mouth. It was only a slight twisting of the truth.

"Now missy, there are some strange happenings in this region," the inn-keeper had admitted, looking uncomfortable, "but it's best you don't query folk about it. It's a touchy subject."

"People have disappeared?" she had asked, pouncing excitedly on the suggestion.

"No no young miss," he had hissed, looking suitably annoyed. He softened slightly as the gleam of hope in her eyes faded. "All I can say is that there is," he paused, struggling to find the right words, "an evil presence in these parts. It changes people..."

"Changes people?" she repeated softly. "In what way?" she asked, hanging off his every word.

"Er hem," the inn-keeper had cleared his throat, leant over the bar. "I don't know the full story mind, but there was a woman from a neighbouring village, worked at a big fancy house on the edge of the wood. Something there drove her mad, so mad she eventually killed herself," he said in a hushed voice, making the sign of the cross.

"Really?" she had cried, excitement creeping into her voice. "Can you tell me where this house is? This could be what I'm looking for..."

"No it isn't," the inn-keeper had hissed, grabbing her wrist, "there's nothing there but madness, dished out by a tall, cold-hearted man and a red-haired girl-witch. If you know what's good fer yer, you'll head straight out of this region tomorrow and go south, where the strange goings ons are less...strange." With that, the stout man had released her and moved on to another customer, studiously ignoring her for the rest of the evening. Feeling keen eyes upon her, she had turned her head to survey the smoky crowded pub, catching out of the corner of her eye several heads swivelling away from her direction.

After an uncomfortable sleep in a barn, she had set about getting directions for the infamous house which no one seemed willing to name, much less describe its location. Finally the stony, cold-eyed stares got to her, and she left. As she shuffled dejectedly along the dirt road, she made a mental note to try and find work in the next town before snooping around. She was down to her last three copper coins. Luckily she'd managed to buy some dried meat and biscuits to take on the road with her. The woman hadn't looked too happy about serving the nosy stranger, but she wasn't going to refuse her trade. Her ruminations were rudely interrupted by an extra large rut in the road catching her foot.

"Bloody dirt roads," she mumbled, trying in vain to hold back tears as she picked herself up off the uneven track. Every stone and hardened dirt clod pushed against the thin leather soles of the shoes the farmer's wife had grudgingly given her. Shoving a pouch of coins into her hand, the ruddy-faced woman had ordered her to take her things and leave. Eric had shown growing interest in the strangely dressed woman he'd discovered in their paddock one frosty morning, too much for his wife's comfort. After some haggling, she'd convinced the sour-faced woman to give her some shoes.

"Ow," she hissed as a sharp little rock penetrated the leather and bit into the tender flesh of her arch. Cursing loudly, she limped to the side of the road and bent over to take a look at the affected area. It was just a small cut, but it hurt like buggery when she gingerly put her weight on it. "Another perfect day for Melanie J Barrett in the year 1812," she muttered sourly as she straightened up and shifted the hessian sack back onto her shoulder. She had just started to hobble down the road when the clang of steel on steel reached her ears. After her own laboured breaths subsided, she was able to pick out raised male voices somewhere to her right, accompanied by a more desperate, high-pitched cry. Feeling oddly reckless, she entered the forest, creeping tensely from tree to tree until she came upon the scene. A band of four men ranged menacingly around a red-haired girl, who was now backed up against a tree clutching her right arm. Blood oozed out of a slice in her upper arm, dripped onto the hilt of the rapier dangling weakly from her hand. Judging by the three prone bodies on the ground, the girl had fought well against impossible odds. "She couldn't be more than fourteen years old," she murmured as she crouched behind a fallen tree, taking in the girl's slender, underdeveloped body. Laughing nastily, one fierce-looking character knocked the blade out of the girl's hand and lunged for her. Her shrieks were cut off by his large brutal hand clasping her throat while the other hand roughly squeezed her bosom. "Come on lads, there's enough young crumpet 'ere for all of us," he called out raucously, shifting his hand to investigate under her skirts.

Swallowing back a wave of nausea, she tore her eyes from the repulsive scene and looked around for a weapon. Finally her eyes settled on a long knife sitting next to one of the dead bodies several feet to her right. She crept over the forest floor, grimacing at every twig that snapped underfoot. The ugly sound of the girl's dress being torn spurred her on, and she ran the rest of the way, falling in a heap next to the body. Setting her bag on the ground, she grabbed the knife and quietly snuck up behind the man standing furthest back from the others. Perhaps if she held the knife to his throat, threaten to kill him if they didn't stop harassing the girl, maybe that would be enough to convince them it was more trouble than it was worth. They'd already lost three men, surely they wouldn't risk another, she rationalised nervously at she stumbled over the uneven ground, the knife barely held within her sweaty grip. She was almost in position to grab the man, her heart firmly lodged in her throat, when she tripped over a rock concealed within a clump of grass. With a painful jolt she crashed into the man, the knife finding its way between his ribs. They sprawled noisily on the ground, drawing the attention of the other men. "Aggh!" the man screamed, scrambling out from under her flailing limbs. "Who the hell are you?" he gasped, groping for the knife sticking out his back. She struggled to her feet, looked on in stunned horror as he staggered around trying to reach the knife, reminding her in a grotesque way of a puppy chasing its own tail.

"Ah, I'm sorry," she stammered, "I didn't mean to ah, do that." She stepped unsteadily back as the others glared at her, their bodies stiffening with anger.

"Hold on Roger," one of the men urged, steadying the man's shoulder, "I'll pull it out." Without any further warning, he grabbed the hilt and swiftly pulled out the blade, causing Roger to sink to knees screaming with renewed vigour.

"Don't worry Roge, we'll deal with this one," the largest man growled, eyes alight with hatred.

"No, she's mine,' Roger muttered, a fine spray of blood escaping his mouth. "You'll pay for this bitch," he snarled, stiffly standing up. Summoning his remaining strength, the man charged at her, sent her crashing into the ground amid cheers of encouragement from his colleagues. His hands found their way to her throat, the thick strong fingers crushing the delicate windpipe. She desperately wriggled a hand free from beneath his weight, clawed feebly at his red snarling face. Just when she thought her lungs would explode, he coughed up more blood, losing his grip on her throat in the process. Gasping for breath, she tried to get out from underneath the crushing weight as Roger choked noisily on his own blood and with a final shudder fell still.

"Poor Roger," murmured the largest man, solemnly rolling the corpse off her with his foot.

"That wasn't very nice," another man said in a low, dangerous voice as he swooped down to grab her shoulders and roughly propel her towards the tree.

"Yeah, what did poor Roge ever do to you?" the large man asked bitterly, swinging his fist into the side of her head. Suddenly her head felt like it was on fire, her vision swimming blurrily before her as she staggered into the tree. She sunk to the ground, the rough bark of the tree pressing into her back. "Don't worry Roge, we'll make her and the little tart pay," the large man promised, making the sign of the cross as he and the other two men approached the tree.

"I'm sorry," she gasped, willing the world to stop swirling before her with such sickening speed, "I didn't mean to kill your friend."

"Oh, you're sorry, are you?" one man sneered, grabbing a handful of her hair and yanking hard. "It's a little late for that," he breathed into her agonised face, slamming her head against the tree. The back of her head seemed to explode, intense pain drowning out the rest of her senses. She slumped even more against the tree, unable to move her limbs. At best she could move her head slightly from side to side, as long as she resisted the pain behind her eyes. She let her head loll to one side, and caught a glimpse of the red-haired girl only a foot or so away before she was forced to close her eyes against the pain. The girl was struggling to keep her eyes open. "Father," she groaned, and then slumped unconscious. She jumped slightly as cruel fingers dug into her flesh, clawed at her clothes. At the edge of her blurry vision hovered the unfriendly faces of the men, their foul breaths fanning her face.

"This is the end, Melanie J Barrett," she thought with a numb sense of finality. They were going to have their fun and kill her and the girl in the process, of that she was certain. "Sorry, red-haired girl," she mouthed, her voice unable to penetrate the lump in her throat. She twitched at the sound of her skirt being savagely torn. "Sorry farmer's wife," she thought sadly, squeezing tears out of her eyes. Poor woman didn't have many clothes to spare, and yet she had given her a set of clothes to replace the tattered rags she'd been found in. She swung out her arm half-heartedly when someone parted her legs. She was punched in the head for her efforts. The blow made her hallucinate, for she thought she heard a horse neighing. Like someone is going to rush in and rescue us, she thought bitterly. That sort of thing only happens in books, or in movies.

Suddenly the cruel mean faces were gone, their obscene jeering calls turning into startled screams and grunts. The sound of steel slicing through air and bodies filled her ears, to be replaced by the sounds of men dying and finally silence. There was a jiggling of stirrups, and she looked up to find a well-dressed man dismounting a horse, his feet touching the ground lightly. He turned towards the tree and froze as his eyes fell upon the unconscious girl. Crying out, he ran to the girl's side, frantically checking her pulse and breathing as he crouched beside her. He looked like a man who was normally in complete control of himself, she mused as he desperately shook the girl and shouted her name...Sarah...over and over again. Sarah must have stirred, for she heard a soft voice haltingly explain what happened. It was then he looked at her, his stern, scowling face hovering above her. The skin between his eyebrows wrinkled in concern as his light brown eyes considered her sceptically. Then the pounding pain in the back of her skull intensified, and the world went black.

She awoke to the irritating sensation of someone dabbing the back of her head with a wet cloth. "Ow," she whined, prying her eyes open.

"Don't move," a firm voice commanded.

"We just have to clean and dress this wound," the voice continued calmly.

"Where the hell am I?" she asked, finally deciding as the stinging intensified that she was in fact alive and not in some sort of spiritual wonderland.

"That's hardly important right now. Rest assured you are safe in the home of the girl you rescued and her grateful foster father." The smooth voice oozed refinement, and she instantly felt miles out of her league. She gritted her teeth against the pain and stared at the sparsely furnished room, trying to recall what had happened. The last thing she remembered was slouching against a tree, barely conscious as some men attacked her. They had been so angry, their faces full of hatred as they tore her clothes. Slowly the pieces started to fall into place in her fractured mind, especially as she became increasingly aware of all the aches and pains in her body. "Aghh," she cried as an evil ointment was applied, her body jerking violently on its own accord.

"I'll finish up, if you like Father," a soft feminine voice offered. The man grunted and moved away from the bed, and more gentle hands applied the final dressing to her head. "There," the girl breathed, a note of satisfaction in her voice. Mel took that as her cue and gingerly rolled onto her back. "Please be careful, try not to move your head too much," the girl cautioned. She stared up into blue eyes framed by dark red hair, a handful of cute freckles scattered across a small, perfect nose.

"I know you," she declared hoarsely, recognition painfully dawning upon her as she slowly sat up. "You were being attacked by those men..."

"Yes," the girl blushed, brushing away sudden tears, "I am in your debt, brave stranger."

"We are both in your debt," the man interjected, stepping closer to the bed. She dragged her attention away from the teary-eyed girl to stare up at the tall handsome man. "My name is Raphael Blythe," he introduced himself, extending his hand. She stared at the hand, awkwardly shook it. His lips twitching with amusement at her confused look, he released her hand and turned to the girl. "And this is my foster daughter, Sarah." Sarah curtsied, shyly nodded her head.

"Ah, well, if you hadn't turned up when you did, Mr Blythe," she said haltingly, finally recognising the light brown eyes and well-shaped lips, "we would have both died." He raised an eyebrow at her, seemingly impressed by her modesty.

"It was the least I could do, after my fool-hardy ward wondered off without an escort," he said tightly with a dark sideways glance at Sarah. The girl shrunk away from him, looking suitably contrite. "I hope you can find it in your heart to forgive Sarah for her thoughtless behaviour," he added pointedly as he turned to the bedside table and started to pack away the bandages and ointments. "She's normally a much more sensible girl."

She opened her mouth to say something placating, thought better of it when she noted the stiffness of his shoulders as he roughly shoved the first aid items into the case.

"Oh, my name is Melanie Barrett," she awkwardly introduced herself, the words sounding strange to her ears. She didn't hear her own name said too often these days.

"Melanie," Sarah repeated carefully, dragging her eyes up from her contemplation of the floor.

"But you can call me Mel, if you like. The fewer syllables the better, I say," she added hastily.

"Hmmph," Raphael breathed, a wry grin crossing his face despite his evident displeasure. He snapped the case closed and headed for the door. "You can call me Raphael," he announced from the doorway. "The more syllables the better, I always say," he retorted with a slight nod before disappearing down the hall.

Mel stared at the empty doorway for a few moments, unsure how to take his comment. "Ah, did I offend your father?" she asked, slowly turning her attention to the girl. "He seems angry..."

"Oh, he is," Sarah reassured her, wringing out the cloth and wiping the table. "With me," she added with a weak smile. "Don't worry, he'll get over it soon enough. How do you feel?"

She carefully swung her feet off the bed, set them gingerly on the cool wooden floor. "Not too bad, considering what happened," she finally responded, wriggling her toes to encourage blood flow. "How are you?" she asked, glancing up from her frowning inspection of her battered-looking toes.

"Good, thanks to you and father," Sarah answered shyly, dropping the cloth back into the bowl.

"You've recovered quickly," Mel observed with a guarded look at the girl's wounded arm. She could have sworn the cut had been longer, deeper...

"Not unless I've been out of it for days, weeks?" she proposed as the alarming thought crossed her mind, her eyes wide with concern.

"No, you've only been unconscious for under a day," Sarah hastily assured her, resting her hand on Mel's stiff shoulder. "I must be a fast healer," the pretty girl offered vaguely, removing her hand. "Ah, would you like some water?"

Nodding vigorously, Mel suddenly noticed that she was wearing a long, ill-fitting night shirt. Gratefully accepting the cup Sarah held out to her, she greedily gulped down the cool water, felt the pain of her parched throat ease somewhat. "What happened to my clothes?" she asked more smoothly.

"Unfortunately, your clothes were ruined. The men were quite rough..." Her voice trailed away as she stared out the window, remembering the attack. With a shudder, the girl returned her attention to the bed, specifically the trunk at the end of the bed. "You must help yourself to a new outfit," she offered with forced brightness.

"Oh, no, I couldn't," Mel mumbled as the girl opened the trunk and flung out several dresses.

"Don't be silly," she chided with a shake of her head. "You must at least take something to replace the clothes you lost," she continued distractedly, selecting two dresses from the pile. "I'd say something dark, to go with your pale complexion," she suggested, standing up and holding one and then the other against Mel.

"Ah, this is all very...generous of you," she said gently, watching in bemusement as the girl fussed over the choice of dresses, "but I need to ask, did anyone pick up a hessian bag when we were taken from the clearing?"

Sarah stopped comparing the garments, looked at her earnestly. "I don't believe so, Mel," she answered with a frown. "Father was in a hurry bringing us back to the manor..."

"Of course," Mel murmured past the sudden lump in her throat. "It's just, everything I own is in that sack, and as pathetic as that may sound, I really need to have it back..."

"Ah, I'll just go and check with Father," Sarah offered, dark blue eyes wide with concern, and she hastily exited the room.

"Oh, now look at what you've done," she muttered to herself, getting up slowly off the bed. "It's not like you have anything of value," she chastised herself, easing out of the night dress. "Well, maybe one thing of...interest," she corrected, selecting the plain brown dress Sarah had left on the bed. She was just doing up the buttons at the front when Sarah rushed back into the room, Raphael hot on her heels. She squeaked in surprise, quickly turned her back to them. "Oh, I'm so sorry," Sarah apologised, blushing furiously, "I should have knocked..."

"What's this about a hessian sack?" Raphael asked curtly, seemingly oblivious to her state of semi-dress.

"Ah, I was just asking sir, if you or anyone else had come across a sack. I dropped it on the edge of the clearing before charging in," she stammered, struggling with the small buttons.

"I didn't exactly have time to scour the area," Raphael pointed out, a hint of sarcasm in his voice.

"Well, of course not," she conceded tightly, grunting with the effort of pushing the hard little buttons through the holes, "I'm quite prepared to go back and find it myself, if you'll just give me directions..."

"What? Are you serious?" Raphael demanded incredulously, stepping towards her. "You're in no condition to go anywhere, Mel."

"Well, aren't you going there to bury the bodies anyway?" Sarah interjected, placing her hand on his shoulder.

"Yes," he snapped, shrugging off her hand. "We have to go now, so we can be back before nightfall."

"Can't you take Mel with you, then?" she suggested innocently.

He eyed his ward suspiciously, shook his head. "No, not possible. Just give me a description of the bag, what's in it, and we'll search for it while we're there..."

"No," Mel said firmly, finally turning to face them, her fingers grappling with the top button. "Look, I have a good idea where the bag is. It would waste more of your time looking for it than if I tagged along."

"Oh, for goodness sake," Raphael muttered, heading for the doorway, "I don't have time for this."

"Please," Mel cried, stumbling after him, "everything I own is in that sack. It's not much, but it's all I have…"

He stopped in the doorway, his hand on the door handle. She took a steadying breath, willed her voice not to tremble. "I don't know if you can understand what it's like, to be reduced to so little," she said in a small sad voice, her eyes fixed on the dusty floor boards just beyond her feet. To her surprise, he muttered something incomprehensible and spun on his heel. "All right then," he snapped, "get some shoes on and meet me in the yard."

Before she could stammer her thanks, he stormed out of the room. "Oh, my shoes," she cried, happily brushing tears off her cheek as she searched the room for her moccasins.

"You can't wear those," Sarah lamented, eying with distain the worn leather slippers that sat on the floor by the foot of the bed. "Let me get you a pair of mine," she offered, a gleam of excitement in her eyes.

"There's no time," she panted, hurriedly pulling on the smelly moccasins and heading for the door. "Your father's bound to leave me behind if I'm not there when he's ready to go."

"Wait, I'll take you there," Sarah groaned, following her out into the corridor. Gritting her teeth against the pain in her head, she allowed Sarah to take the lead. They made their way down the dusty corridor past several closed doors to a long flight of stairs at the end of the passageway. "It's mostly bedrooms in this corner of the manor," Sarah explained, catching her curious look of all the closed doors. "Except for the library, of course," she added as they started down the stairs, and Mel belatedly caught sight of the large library at the head of the sweeping stairway. She made a mental note to investigate the library later as they walked briskly down a short hallway to a large kitchen, where two women were busily preparing food. The older woman looked up from kneading bread dough and eyed her suspiciously, her wrinkled face dusted with flour. From her place at the sink, the other, much younger woman smirked in their general direction, the brush in her hand briefly coming to a stop before she resumed scrubbing potatoes. Nodding awkwardly at the women, she gratefully followed Sarah through a large thick door to the courtyard, where Raphael and two other men were preparing to leave.

"Father! Wait!" Sarah called out, running up to the imposing figure. He flung a saddle over the back of a magnificent black horse, glowered up at them briefly as he fastened the buckles.

"This is madness," he muttered as he adjusted the bridle. "You're risking further injury," he admonished, shooting her a speculative look. When she didn't answer, he sighed, turned to the younger of the two men. "Simon, get a horse for Mel here," he said with a note of resignation. The young man nodded and with a sideways glance at her went off to fetch another mount.

"A horse?" she repeated, looking up sharply from her inspection of the ground.

"You can't possibly walk there, not in your condition," he said distractedly, mistaking the reason for her surprise. He swung up onto the black horse's back, frowned down at her. "You can ride, can't you?" he prompted as he settled into the saddle.

"Ah, not really," she croaked, clearing her throat.

"How terrible," Sarah breathed, shuddering at the thought.

"Oh for the love of...Can you sit on a horse and not fall off? Can you manage that?" he demanded impatiently, stroking the thick muscular neck as his horse started to act restless. "I don't have all day..."

"Yes, fine," she said with more confidence than she felt, turning to Sarah for support. The girl grinned sympathetically, looked up at her slowly simmering foster-father. "Ah, maybe I should come along, help Mel with her horse?" she suggested casually, her face a picture of innocence as she took a cautious step towards him. Raphael gave her a look of flat denial, and she coughed nervously, stepped back. "Maybe not," she conceded, bowing her head.

Mel waited anxiously for Simon to come back with the extra horse, only too aware of the other man watching her guardedly as he bundled two shovels together. Dark brown eyes glinted from within a swarthy, bearded face. She shifted her feet awkwardly, suddenly wanting to back out of this deal. Before she could change her mind, Simon returned with a fine pony. Sarah's face fell for an instant, her hand automatically reaching out for the pony's neck as it passed.

"Be good Moonbeam," she whispered to the horse. "Don't worry, she's a good-natured pony," Sarah informed her, lovingly rubbing the patch of white hair between its ears. Moonbeam snuffed her neck in turn, the muscles under its skin twitching in anticipation of being riden by its mistress. Mel gulped nervously, feeling worse by the second. Not only was she creating a huge fuss, she was now borrowing the poor girl's horse. She awkwardly hoisted herself up into the saddle, only too aware of Raphael growing displeasure.

"Finally," he breathed, grabbing Moonbeam's reins. "Let's go," he ordered curtly to the mounted men. As they formed a solemn procession heading for the trees, Mel chanced a final backward glance at Sarah, to find her waving them farewell. She waved weakly back before the horse's movement jerked her forward and she had to concentrate on staying on Moonbeam's back.

It wasn't long before they were riding gently through the forest. Even at a normal walking pace, the up and down motion caused her head to ache, and she had to focus her vision on a fixed point in order not to get dizzy. "You look as though you're about to be sick," Raphael commented, his eyes staring straight ahead into the forest as he followed a vague path between towering birch trees and bushy undergrowth.

"I'm fine," she grunted, gritting her teeth against the pain in her stomach. Moonbeam whinnied, tossed her head as she slumped in the saddle.

"Whoa Moonbeam," Raphael crooned, tightening his hold on the reins.

"Uh, I could swear this horse doesn't like me," she said with a groan, forcing herself to sit up straight in the saddle.

"Moonbeam isn't used to other riders," he explained, glancing across at her briefly before studying the forest again.

"Oh," she said lamely, struggling to find an adequate reply. When he didn't say anything, she fell into a contemplative silence, cataloguing the various sources of discomfit she was experiencing at that moment. The pain in her head didn't seem to be getting any worse, but then she wasn't sure if it could. Her back was starting to ache from the effort of sitting upright on a moving horse, and she could swear she already had saddle sores.

"So, Mel," Raphael began, clearing his throat, "where do you hail from?"

Startled out of her reverie, she looked up to find him watching her, a faint frown etched around his mouth. "Ah, up North," she replied vaguely, "somewhere outside of Nottingham."

The frown intensified, and he quickly turned his attention back to the forest. "You're a long way from home then," he murmured, his face an unreadable mask.

"Yes," she agreed simply, looking away.

"And you don't have any travelling companions, any family with you?" he pressed. She took a steadying breath, forced herself to meet his penetrating gaze.

"No, I'm completely alone," she answered honestly. To her surprise, his eyes softened, and he hastily returned his attention to picking out the path.

"May I ask why?" he finally ventured after a few moments of heavy silence.

"Why what?" she prompted with a hint of irritation in her voice.

"Why have you travelled so far from home, on your own?" he expanded with surprising patience. "Your family must be very worried about you. We could send them word of your whereabouts…"

"I have no family," she stated over his suggestion, her pain-filled eyes briefly meeting his before sliding away to stare unseeingly at the trees. He coughed uncomfortably and abandoned all further attempts at conversation. They wend their way through the still forest, the midday sun beating down upon them through gaps in the high, thick canopy. She squinted her eyes against the stark patches of light, the intensity causing her tender head to ache even more. Apart from the odd bird call, and the men behind them softly debating which local pub sold the best beer, the forest was surprisingly quiet.

"Ah, I believe we're getting close," Raphael declared, wrinkling his nose at the stench of decomposing flesh that now wafted across their path. "This way," he murmured, steering their horses toward the smell. They pushed their way through low lying branches to enter a clearing. The smell of rotting carcasses was overwhelming as they cautiously crossed the uneven floor. It didn't take long to locate the source of the stench, with seven fly-encrusted bodies strewn about the tree enclosed area. Animals must have been worrying the corpses in their absence, the grotesque remains barely recognisable. She almost threw up when one of the bodies was disturbed by their movement, and the flies flew off the carcass to form a temporary cloud above the purple mottled flesh before settling back on the cold skin.

"Urgh," Simon gagged as they entered the clearing behind them.

"Start digging a ditch, at least three feet deep," Raphael ordered, swinging his leg over and dismounting in one fluid movement. He pulled out a large handkerchief and tied it around his head, making sure his mouth was covered.

"Be nice Moonbeam," Mel murmured, carefully leaning forward and heaving her right leg around. To her surprise, she managed to lower herself to the ground without falling in a heap. With only a few awkward hops, she extracted her other foot from the stirrup and managed to stumble away from Moonbeam, who was already unconcernedly munching on a clump of grass.

She carefully picked her way around the clearing, picturing in her mind the events that had unfolded just over twenty four hours ago. Looking hastily away from where Raphael checked the bodies for valuables, she wandered over the large fallen log at the other end of the clearing. She had entered from this side, she recalled with increasing clarity as she spotted a particularly bad corpse. That must have been the body she stole the big knife from, so her sack had to be on the other side of the log. Breathing heavily from the effort, she rounded the log. Her body went limp with relief at the sight of her sack resting against the rough bark. She crouched beside it and quickly checked the contents, a weak smile crinkling the corners of her mouth. Rising up, she hefted the sack onto her shoulder and went back to join the others. Simon and John were heartily grumbling about the hardness of the ground, and how long it was going to take them to bury so many dead bastards.

Raphael studiously ignored their lamentations, turning a body over with his foot, swatting away the cloud of flies that arose as a result. With his face lined with displeasure, he bent down and extracted the small leather pouch from the man's belt. He stepped back from the mottled stiff body, jiggling the pouch in his hand. "Here," he called, tossing the purse at the whining men. "A little extra for your trouble, gentlemen," John picked up the pouch, felt the hard round coins through the worn leather. "You'll find your way back to the castle, I trust?" Raphael asked distractedly as he gathered up the small collection of purses and knick-knacks. His tone suggested that it was a rhetorical question.

"We'll be fine sir," the older man replied with a subtle nod to Simon, who in turn raised his eyebrows and resumed digging with renewed vigour.

"Come on Mel, let's go," Raphael barked, dumping his findings in the saddle bag, patting the glossy black coat of his horse's back as he fastened the buckle. She mumbled agreement and hurried over the rough ground. She had almost reached Moonbeam when she stumbled over a fallen branch. One moment she was observing the silent exchange between John and Simon, the next she was down on her hands and knees staring into the face of the man she'd killed. She yelped, the purply blue face bringing back vivid memories. This must have been where he tackled her to the ground, his crushing weight squeezing the air out of her lungs while his hands clenched angrily around her throat. A wave of nausea rose within her, and she lurched forward, her upper body almost hitting the ground as her trembling arms threatened to give way. The sudden movement made her head throb, and she struggled to lift her head up. As she wobbled about on all fours, her bleary eyes focused on the dead man, and for a second she could swear that his grotesque face moved, that the glazed eyes popped even more out of their sockets. She screamed and fell away from the corpse.

"Mel!" The impatient voice cut through her panic like a knife through butter. She tore her eyes away from the object of personal horror to find Raphael watching her, clearly unimpressed by her display.

"Come on, I'm going back now, unless you want to stay with your friend there," he offered waspishly. She gawked at him, waiting for the multiple Raphaels to merge into one.

"Right," she finally croaked, getting to her feet.

"Mel," he said as she stumbled towards him, "your sack..." She stupidly stared at him, finally looked down to where he pointed.

"Oh of course. Excuse me," she uttered, promptly turning her head away and throwing up. The thick bile burnt her throat as it surged out of her. Coughing and gagging on the bitter after-taste, she rubbed the back of her hand across her mouth and retrieved the sack. "Don't pass out now," she told herself sternly. How unimpressed would Raphael look then? He'd probably leave her here to be buried with the other lifeless bodies. He gruffly ordered her to stuff the sack into one of his saddle bags.

"Are you sure you can sit on Moonbeam?" he asked sceptically as she struggled to lift her pathetic load into the leather bag. His heavy gaze bore down upon her like the merciless rays of the midday sun as her clumsy fingers fumbled with the buckle.

"No, I won't be a burden," she replied resolutely, straightening up to walk unsteadily to Moonbeam's side. Mustering her strength, she somehow managed to haul herself up onto the horse's back.

"A little late for that," Raphael muttered as he tightened his hold on Moonbeam's reins and urged both horses forward. "So, what was all that about then?" he asked when they were out of the clearing.

"What was what about?" she asked distractedly, her attention focused on not falling out of the saddle.

"The way you acted back there, when you saw that body..."

"That was the man I killed," she explained, her voice thickening with emotion. "It was an accident, I didn't mean to kill him..."

"You accidentally stabbed him?" Raphael quizzed with a hint of sarcasm.

"No," she cried, shaking her head, "I mean yes, well sort of. I was just going to threaten him, try to make them think twice about hurting Sarah, but I tripped, the knife was in my hand..." Her voice trailed off at the memory of that awful moment when the knife plunged into his unsuspecting body, found its way between his ribs. "I've never killed anyone before," she added unevenly, her heart heavy with guilt.

"Really?" he prompted when she didn't continue. "It's been a long time since I could claim that," he confessed with a shake of his dark blonde head. "But you mustn't beat yourself up for what you did, Mel. Those men were savages, they attacked Sarah without provocation," he said sternly.

"I guess you're right," she mumbled. "I can still see his face hovering above me, red with anger..." Her voice trailed off as her throat closed up, and she blinked back tears.

"You didn't answer my question earlier," he pressed after an uncomfortable silence. "Why are you travelling on your own, and so far?"

She took a steadying breath and launched into the well-rehearsed story, her voice only wavering a couple of times during the telling. He didn't respond immediately to her story, apparently mulling over the information. "Have you found any clues yet?" he finally enquired, as though out of polite interest.

"Not really," she confessed, bowing her head dejectedly. "I've heard the odd story of so-and-so disappearing without a trace, but there's seldom any useful information to go with the story."

"But why travel so far from home? Wouldn't it be better to focus your search around Nottingham?" he persisted doggedly.

Shaking her head, she struggled to keep her voice even. "I've tried that already," she said with a nervous cough, remembering the early days of her search, and how she had almost ended up in prison. Of course, she hadn't constructed the careful fabrication she now wore like a badge. No, she had recklessly told people the truth, or at least what she thought was the truth, and they had naturally considered her mad. "Look, I realise my brother could be anywhere by now, I've been searching for so long, but it's all I have," she explained past the growing lump in her throat. He cleared his throat, his body stiffening in the saddle.

"Well, you're welcome to use the library," he offered, glancing over at her.

"Really?" she blurted, hope lighting up her grimy face. Murmuring something affirmative, he firmly fixed his attention on picking out the path, and they rode the rest of the way in awkward silence. She was just about to make another attempt at conversation when the light grey roof of the manor appeared above the trees. As they pushed past the trees fringing the property, she promptly closed her mouth to concentrate on the imposing structure coming into view. Austere stone walls greeted her, the thick glass windows glittering in the midday sun. The main building was a plain rectangular box with a gently sloping roof, two large chimneys jutting up along its spine. If she tilted her head slightly, she could just see the corner of a small balcony poking out from the furthest side of the roof. A more ornate balcony with marble balustrade nestled beneath it, though this extended around the corner of the house. Protruding out of either side of the main building were smaller rectangles made from the same pale grey stone.

"Wow," she murmured as they entered the yard. "It's beautiful," she added with a hint of awe in her voice, her eyes drinking in every detail of the manor.

"Thank-you," he said grudgingly, swiftly dismounting. "We like it very much," he continued, walking around to help her out of the saddle. She looked down with foreboding at the ground, grudgingly accepted his hands about her waist as she swung her leg over the broad back. As she rediscovered her legs, he extracted the sack out of the saddle bag and gravely handed it to her. "I hope you enjoy your stay Mel," he said stiffly, maintaining his hold on the sack, "but be warned, I will not tolerate any mistreatment of Sarah."

She gawked up at his solemn face, opened her mouth to protest her innocence, when a breathless voice called out. "Mel! Father!" With a final glare, he released the sack and turned towards the source of the voice.

"Did you get your things Mel?" Sarah asked, skidding to a halt next to Raphael.

"Yes, thank-you," she answered in a subdued voice. Sarah's eyes narrowed slightly as she looked from face to face. "Well, I'd better take you back to your room Mel," she declared brightly, taking her arm.

"I'm sure Mel will be able to find her own way back," Raphael argued, gently guiding her away from Mel's side. "Besides, you can take Moonbeam back to the stable," he added, handing her the reins.

"Yes Father," she said resignedly.

"Now for goodness sake Mel go and get something to eat," he ordered. "And ask Mrs Habiston to show you to the wash room," he added, wrinkling his nose. "Come on Monty," he murmured to large black stallion, grabbing the reins and stroking the long face. She watched as he led the horse away, Sarah reluctantly falling into step beside him. From the tension in her young face, she expected an uncomfortable conversation to unfold once they were alone in the stables. The sudden pang of her stomach convinced her to take his advice, and with a final glance at the retreating pair, she slung the all-important sack over her shoulder and hobbled to the kitchen.

"Here you go miss," Mrs Habiston said stiffly as they stopped at a plain wooden door just a few feet from the kitchen. She opened the door and entered the simple room, feeling the older woman's keen eyes upon her. "Do yer want me to fill the tub?" the woman asked, a definite lack of enthusiasm in her voice.

"If you could just show me how," she offered, staring at the pump hovering above the tub with a small amount of trepidation. Grumbling softly under her breath, Mrs Habiston worked the handle, grunting with the effort. After a couple of strokes, brown-tinged water spurted out of the opening to fall with a splash into the tub.

"Ah, that will be fine, Mrs Habiston," she assured the woman, not wanting to incur more disgruntlement. With a grudging nod of her head, she left the room to return to the kitchen.

Sighing her relief, she set her sack on the floor and quietly padded across the cool flagstone floor to close the door behind the grumpy woman. The large metal tub set against the far wall was illuminated by slanting rays entering the room through a long horizontal window set high above the tub. A wooden bench rested against the adjacent wall, with an odd assortment of buckets and basins stored underneath. A chipped old mirror hung from the wall next to the bench, with an old crate littered with toiletries set beneath it. She carefully set her clean clothes on the bench and began to fill the tub. Despite the cloudy quality of the water, she watched the tub fill up with growing excitement. The best she had managed lately in terms of washing was the odd basin of water, or a quick chilly dip in a river. Opportunities to wash and dry her clothes had been equally rare.

No wonder Raphael had looked at her so sceptically as she lay semi-conscious against the tree, those cold eyes studying her like she was a filthy sewer rat that had just done something out of character. Of all the things to think of, she mused as she tore off her clothes and slid down into the water. Pushing aside such thoughts, she concentrated on scrubbing her skin and hair, watching with fascination as weeks of dirt seeped into the water. When she was sure most of the dirt had soaked off, she clambered out of the tub and dried herself with a nearby cloth. Frowning at her thin body, she quickly changed and dragged a comb through her hair, the dark bags under her eyes stark against the pale skin. She tossed the dirty dress into her sack, and with a final grimace at her reflection left the washroom.

"Ah, now that's much better," Sarah cooed with pleasure as she spotted Mel ambling up the stairs. She bounced eagerly on the balls of her feet, hands clasped together as she waited at the top of the stairs. "Can I do something with your hair?" she asked excitedly, deep blue eyes gleaming.

"What do you have in mind?" Mel asked warily, slowing down as she neared the top of the staircase. The girl smiled at her cautious tone, put her hands up in a warding gesture. "Nothing drastic, I assure you," she responded more calmly. The gleam was still there, Mel noted as she reluctantly allowed herself to be led off.

"This is my room," Sarah informed her as she dragged her into a modestly decorated room. A single bed sat in the far corner, while a dressing table with in-built mirror lined the opposite wall. A simple wooden chair was set before the table.

"Sorry about the mess," Sarah fussed, picking up the pile of clothes hanging over the chair. "Here, take the seat," she offered, quickly dumping the clothes onto her bed and pulling out a small stool from the foot of the bed.

Mel sat down and looked grumpily into the mirror. The mirror in the washroom hadn't fully captured her gaunt appearance, she decided as she turned her head. Her cheekbones were starting to show far too sharply beneath the pale skin, making her hazel eyes look sunken. "Ow," she grunted as Sarah started to brush her hair. She hadn't noticed the girl settle down on the stool behind her.

"Sorry," Sarah mumbled, concentrating on untangling a clump of knotted hair.

"So, ouch, what's your story Sarah? How did you come to live with Raphael?" she asked casually, watching the girl's reaction with interest. "Of course it's none of my business. Just tell me to butt out if you want," she added hastily as Sarah's face blanched at the question. Their eyes met in the mirror, and the girl shook her head shyly, a small smile playing on her lips.

"No, that's alright. It's just, I haven't been asked about that in some time..."

And so she told the story of her years living on the streets of London, begging and stealing to get by. When she was about eight years old, she'd been sent to the city by her parents. They were pig farmers, struggling to maintain their livestock through a hard winter. With too many mouths to feed, they sent her and her younger brother Tim to a supposed Uncle Joe in the city. Instead of finding a loving, caring relative however, they found slavery and cruelty. Their parents had sold them to a textile factory as workers. The long hours and meagre food portions, combined with easily-provoked beatings from the foreman, took the life of her brother.

Sarah paused for a moment, abruptly turned away as tears gathered in the corners of her eyes. With a mumbled curse, she brushed the tears away and turned back to face the mirror. She cleared her throat and continued the story, explaining that she somehow escaped the factory and joined a gang of street kids. She quickly learnt how to pick pockets and subtly lift items from street stalls.

"Street urchins also know the best hiding places," she said distractedly as she brushed out the last tangle. "One day I was scoping the stalls in a street market when I saw Raphael running for his life. He gave me a desperate look as he ducked into the alleyway behind me and hid behind a cart. Moments later a handful of guards entered the market and started asking everyone if they'd seen a tall blonde man with a fancy sword run through. Luckily everyone else had been too intent on selling/buying to notice such a gentleman." She looked up to study her handiwork, nodded her satisfaction.

"So you helped him to escape?" Mel prompted as she began to braid the fine, smooth hair.

"What? Oh yes," Sarah continued in a far away voice, "I told the guards that he'd run past me to the next corner and then disappeared. To be honest," she said, lowering her voice, "it was more to annoy the guards than anything else. It's the street urchin's code."

Mel snickered at her admission. Something about street urchins living by a code struck her as funny. "I then helped him to get out of the city, via the alleyways and rooftops," Sarah continued, her eyes fastened on the bunches of hair she was weaving together. "I was just hoping to get a coin for my trouble, one way or another," she frowned as she carefully selected strands of hair to pull into the growing braid. "Instead he invited me to run away with him. He said he owed me his life, and that he'd take care of me for as long as I wanted..." Her voice trailed away as a strange, unread-able expression crossed her face. Her fingers came to a stop mid-braid. "Anyway," she said with a start, "it just so happened I was thinking about leaving town, seeing as I owed the thieves' guild some money. They were making life very hard for me...Damn, I'll have to start this one again," she muttered, grabbing the brush and straightening the section of hair.

Mel refrained from asking further questions, leaving the girl to concentrate on her hair. Her deft hand movements as she parted and wove the strands were quite relaxing.

"There," Sarah declared with some satisfaction as she tied off the last braid. "What do you think?" she asked anxiously as Mel turned her head to inspect her handiwork. Two thick braids encircled the crown of her head, her hair all neatly tucked away into the intricate network of strands.

"You know, I've always wanted to have my hair done like this," she confessed with a smile, carefully touching the tight tidy weave. Light bounced off the smooth, dark brown hair. "Wow, I almost look human," she murmured at the mirror.

"You're much too modest Mel," Sarah chided mildly from the bed, where she was putting away the stool. "I can't wait to see Father's face when he sees you at dinner..."

She wasn't sure she liked the underlying excitement in the girl's voice. "I doubt your Father will be impressed," she argued, frowning at her reflection. Sarah's garbled response from the bed made her swivel around in her chair. The girl's bottom wiggled wildly from under the bed as she crouched on the floor and strained to reach something.

"A-ha," she grunted triumphantly, carefully reversing out from under the bed. "Try these on Mel," she ordered breathlessly, brandishing a pair of boots.

"Oh, I couldn't, you've already been too kind..."

"Don't be silly, these are way too big for me anyway," she countered flippantly, placing the boots at her feet. "Come on, we've got just enough time to take a tour of the manor."

With a sigh of resignation, she tried on the boots, and was surprised how well they fit. "Ooo, they really suit you," Sarah cooed, hands clasped together. "How do they feel?"

"Um, good," she answered cautiously as she got out of the chair and walked around.

"Then it's official, they're yours. Now let's go." With that she grabbed Mel's arm and firmly steered her out of the room.

After dropping the sack off to her room, Sarah proceeded to drag her throughout the manor, the tour punctuated with discussions about the boots. Leaving the familiar territory of her room, they headed down the corridor, Sarah insisting she was more than entitled to the boots, considering what had happened. "At least let me do some work about the place. Raphael saved me too after all," she pointed out, nodding acknowledgment at Sarah's comment about the door to Raphael's room. They followed the corridor around the corner, past another spare bedroom and a sitting room. "What if I help out in the kitchen or stables for a week?" she offered as they rounded another corner and crossed the wide corridor diagonally to enter the ballroom. Her words dried up as she looked around the cavernous room, the only sound being the click of their heels against the hard tiled floor. The smooth black and white tiles reflected the grey-purplish veins of the marble ceiling that arched overhead. Padded chairs were haphazardly arranged around the edge of the dance floor to her right, while a raised platform sat half-way along the wall to her left, cluttered with chairs and music stands. In the soft golden light that streamed in through the glass panelled doors at the far end of the room, dust disturbed by their movement swirled lazily into the air.

"Wow," Mel said softly, stumbling slightly as a result of her awed inspection of the room. "What was I saying?" she asked distractedly.

"Something about the boots," Sarah said. "Don't worry, we can settle it later."

Something in her tone made her faintly apprehensive. "Good," Mel replied doubtfully.

"So, what do you think of the ballroom?" Sarah asked, quickly changing the subject.

"It's amazing," she answered sincerely as they pushed through the twin doors and walked out onto the balcony. She moved from end to end, fixing in her head the details of the courtyard and surrounding area. Across the dusty yard sat the stables, the clop of hooves against the stone floor reaching her ears.

"The men must be back," Sarah observed, resting her elbows on the wide marble railing.

"Hmm," she responded distractedly, straining her eyes to make out the collection of smaller structures on the far side of the yard. "Is that some sort of barn?" she asked, deciding that the moving specks must be poultry.

"Yes," Sarah said with a yawn, "we have poultry, cows, goats, some sheep. We try to grow our own food where possible."

"I guess you have to, being in the country," she reasoned, spying a sprawling vegetable patch beyond the barn. At least, she assumed it was a vegetable patch. There seemed to be more weeds growing in it at the moment.

"Come on," Sarah prompted, growing restless with the view, "let's go to the look-out point. You get an excellent view of the valley from there." She grabbed her hand and led her towards the balcony doors. She quickly glanced up as they approached the doorway at the smaller outcropping platform above them. "Is that the look-out point?" she asked, suddenly recalling her earlier observation of the two balconies.

"Sure is," Sarah replied, steering her back inside and through the ballroom.

"I take it this room hasn't seen a lot of use," she commented breathlessly as they sped past the raised stage area. The thick cobwebs in the corners caught beautifully the afternoon light.

"No," Sarah admitted shortly, pulling her along out the door.

They walked to the end of the corridor, where an inconspicuous door sat flush with the wall, the only tell-tale sign of its presence a tiny keyhole and its thin outline. Sarah muttered something under her breath as she fumbled for something in her pocket. "Ha," she breathed, willing her eyes to follow the faint dark line as Sarah pulled a key out of her pocket and inserted it in the keyhole, "I totally missed this when we walked past."

Sarah looked up from jiggling the key in the lock, grinned at her. "That's the idea," she said cheerfully, finally turning the key to unlock the door. Mel pulled a face at the girl's back as she opened the door and started up a small set of stairs that were built into the end wall. She followed Sarah carefully up the cramped stairs, straining to make out the edge of the steps in the dim light. At the top was a plain door held shut by a thick wedge of wood. Sarah lifted the bar out of its cosy home, grimacing as the wood scraped against the metal hooks that held it snugly in place. "I keep telling Father those clasps are too close to the frame," she muttered, pushing open the door. She stepped out onto the small balcony and rested the bar against the wall.

"Wow," Mel breathed, squinting into the late afternoon sun as she settled next to Sarah. Gripping the thick iron railing, she leant over slightly and drank in the view. She hadn't realised that the manor was built on the edge of a gently sloping valley. A lush carpet of trees rolled out before them, stretching to the horizon. Mel caught glints of light through one large patch of trees. "Is that a lake behind those trees?" she asked, pointing to the patch.

"Yes, Lake Burchell, it's gorgeous there at sunset."

"Is it good for fishing?" She had never been interested in fishing until it became a matter of survival. The last few months of travelling from town to town had forced her to develop rudimentary angler skills.

"I believe Simon and John fish there a fair bit," she answered, wrinkling her nose cutely. "They always stink out the yard with their smoked fish," she whined, rolling her eyes.

She laughed at her droll expression, returned her attention to the view. Her eyes searched for signs of farming or settlements in the area. Finally she discerned faint trails of smoke drifting up through some trees on one side of the lake.

"Is that a settlement over there?"

Sarah followed her finger and squinted into the distance. "Yes, there's a small village on the shore of the lake, Burchellton. We trade with them every now and again," she answered, her tone guarded.

"Do you have any friends there?" she asked absent-mindedly as she tried to figure out which direction she'd come from. Somehow she'd completely missed the lake during her travels, even though she must have come down from the North East. She looked forward to drawing a map for herself from the charts in the library. With a bitter grin, she remembered the simple map the farmer's wife had drawn in the dirt outside the house. Shivering in the pre-dawn mist, her pathetic sack of belongings on her back, she had strained to make out details in the grey half-light. Unfortunately, she hadn't done much better since.

"Ah, not really," Sarah murmured, turning her head away. She tore her eyes away from the horizon, peered around at Sarah's blushing cheeks.

"Not really eh?" she gently teased. "Looks as though you know at least one person down there, possibly a boy…"

"I do not," Sarah protested, shooting her a querulous look. "I don't know him, really," she added grumpily, "I just saw him at the blacksmith's one day, helping with Moonbeam's new shoes..." Her voice trailed off as she remembered the dark curly head bent over the hoof, the smooth gentle face set in a mask of concentration. He had looked up as if sensing her eyes, and given her a shy smile, brown eyes crinkling at the corners. "Anyway," she said, shaking herself out of her reverie, "we'd better go and finish the tour, it's almost time for dinner." She turned to the door, pointedly held it open for her.

"Okay," Mel murmured with a knowing smile, averting her eyes as she passed through the doorway. Sarah closed the door behind her, slid the wood back into place.

"That's most of the upper floor covered," she announced as they entered the corridor. "There's a little music room next to the ballroom," she said distractedly as she locked the hidden door, "but there's a much more interesting room downstairs you've got to see."

With that declaration, she grabbed her hand and tugged her along the corridor and down the stairs. She briefly glimpsed a cosy room at the end of the corridor, simply furnished with some over-stuffed chairs and a piano set against the wall, before trotting down the curved staircase. At the base of the stairs, she got her bearings back as she looked across the hallway space and recognised the matching set of stairs on the other side. "Aw, I didn't notice there were matching staircases," she mumbled, nodding at the doorway of the library on the upper level.

"It's no wonder Mel, you've barely had time to notice anything," Sarah reasoned as they walked down a wide passageway that ran down the middle of the bottom floor. To her left was the main dining room and servants' quarters Sarah explained, casually nodding at the relevant doors as they passed. "Storeroom, linen closet, yet another sitting room to your right," she continued over her shoulder, guiding her relentlessly to the large room at the end of the passageway. She gave up trying to peek into each room as they sped past, and just focused on not tripping over her own feet as Sarah tugged her along. "This is my favourite room in the house," Sarah announced, pushing the door open.

They entered a huge rectangular room which seemed to be largely empty. Light streamed in through generously sized windows, illuminating the thick grass mats that covered most of the floor. "This is the weapons training room," Sarah gushed, skipping over to the racks of weapons lined against the wall. "Come here and choose a weapon, Mel," she ordered cheerfully, picking out a solid blade and swishing it through the air.

"Er, I don't know if that's a good idea," she murmured, drifting over to the neat row of swords hanging off the wooden shelf built into the wall. She peered down at the waist-high shelf, observed the little slots cut into the solid wood, a slot for each sword. "Huh, clever," she mumbled, idly grabbing the hilt of the nearest sword and sliding it out of its snug home. "I've never used one of these before," she explained sheepishly, looking up from her inspection of the battered edge.

Sarah's face lit up, a beatific smile curving her features. "I could teach you, if you like," she offered excitedly. "Father's been teaching me how to use a sword for almost two years now, I could at least show you the basics..."

She frowned at the sword in her hand, bemused by the girl's eagerness to offer fencing lessons. "I guess it can't hurt," she admitted, remembering how easily she'd been overpowered in the clearing. "It might at least give me a fighting chance," she muttered, hand tightening around the leather-bound hilt.

"Excellent," Sarah cooed, clapping her hands together. "We'll have to try and squeeze in some training tomorrow," she said thoughtfully, staring at the grass mat by her feet as though it contained her daily schedule. "Just light exercises, don't worry," she added when Mel coughed nervously, looking up from her study of the floor. "We have special armour too, so you won't get too bruised and battered," she said as an afterthought. She smiled weakly at the excited girl, uncertain whether to be comforted by that last statement or not.

"Oh goodness, look at the time," Sarah suddenly fretted, noticing the lengthening shadows on the floor. "We have to get ready for dinner," she declared, returning her sword to the rack.

"The tour's over then?" Mel prompted as she slid the blade back in its slot.

"That's most of the house covered," Sarah replied, ushering her out of the room. "I'll show you the cellar later."

"What's in the cellar?" she asked as they bustled down the passageway.

"Oh, just a lot of beer and wine. That's why Father calls it the best room in the house," she grinned.

"Hmmph," Mel murmured in agreement. Maybe she had more in common with Raphael than she originally thought. As they entered the hallway and turned towards the stairs, she cleared her throat. "Ah, I'm no expert, but shouldn't there be more servants?" she asked awkwardly as they trudged up the stairs.

"We've had trouble recruiting workers," Sarah answered stiffly, her lips compressed into a thin line of displeasure. "It's hard to win the locals' trust," she added, as though that explained everything.

"Oh," she murmured, frowning at the niggling sensation at the back of her mind. Something about this situation seemed familiar, but she couldn't quite put her finger on it...

At Sarah's urging, she changed for dinner, into a light blue dress especially picked out by the fussy girl. The dress fit her perfectly, perhaps a little too perfectly she decided as she tried to pull the bodice up whilst walking down the corridor. Sarah emerged from her room dressed in a dark green gown just in time to witness her attempts to adjust the front. "That's how it's supposed to sit," the girl assured her as they trudged down the stairs.

"I feel so exposed," she muttered, giving the square neckline a final tug before giving up in disgust. The smell of roasted meat hit her nostrils as they turned the corner, and she quickly forgot her misgivings about the dress. They entered the dining room and took their places, their eyes glued to the large roast chicken sitting in the middle of the table. Raphael strode in shortly after and took his place at the head of the table, frowning at the naked hunger in their faces. Mrs Habiston and Wendy solemnly sliced up and dished out the chicken and roasted vegetables, both women sneaking guarded glances at the dolled-up stranger in their midst. Mel largely ignored their curious looks, her attention firmly fixed on the plate set before her.

"Thank you ladies," Raphael said dismissively. With a nod they left, closing the door behind them. "Well, let's tuck in, shall we?" he declared without further preamble, picking up his cutlery.

It took every ounce of self-control to not gorge the food set before her. She forced herself to chew thoroughly each mouthful, peering up from the plate every now and again to make sure no one was glaring at her. Thankfully the conversation largely buzzed around her, with the occasional question batted her way. Apart from a tense discussion about Sarah's failure to complete her homework, the meal passed uneventfully. For the first time in months, she ate until fully sated. With her stomach pleasantly full, she sat back and sipped her wine, quietly absorbing her surroundings. Portraits adorned the walls, the unfamiliar faces staring out faintly in the yellow light from the sconces. Not completely unfamiliar she corrected, spying a painting of a red-haired girl with dark blue eyes. The girl gazed out impassively, hands folded neatly in her lap. How could someone so young look so serious? Being sold off to a factory by your parents would change your perspective on life, she reasoned. Despite the massive gaps in her memory, she was decently sure her upbringing had been relatively normal. If she closed her eyes, she could see a modest white house raised off the ground on stumpy stilts, a pink concrete path leading to a short set of stairs, a car parked in the driveway...

"Mel!"

The image vanished abruptly as she woke up with a start, opening heavy eyelids to gaze blearily at Sarah's flushed face sitting across from her.

"Oh," she breathed, feeling her cheeks reddened, "Sorry about that," she said sheepishly.

"Perhaps you should go to bed," Raphael suggested with a frown.

"I should help clean up," she offered half-heartedly, stifling a yawn as she began to pick up her plate.

"No, don't worry about that for tonight," Sarah told her flatly.

"Tonight?" Raphael quizzed, raising a well-shaped eyebrow at her.

"Just a little business arrangement between Mel and I. Of course, I'll need to discuss it with you before anything is finalised..."

"Of course," he drawled, picking up his cup and draining the contents. "After you show Mel to her bed we can talk about it," he suggested, a hint of steel in his voice.

"Yes Father," the girl said meekly, scraping her chair back.

"Oh, right," Mel mumbled as the girl helped her out of her chair. "Ah, good night, sir," she said awkwardly as Sarah started to lead her away. The girl hastily grabbed a lit lantern from the side table on the way out.

"Good night, Mel," he returned, rising to his feet and politely bowing his head.

When they were alone in the corridor, she cleared her throat. "Sorry about falling asleep," she finally apologised, glancing across at Sarah's pinched face. Grinning weakly back, the girl shook her head.

"That's alright. The look on Father's face was precious," she giggled as they entered the hallway.

"Damn, I shouldn't have touched the wine," Mel groaned as she began to lumber up the stairs, her limbs feeling heavier with each step.

"Don't worry about it," Sarah said gently. "You've had a big day. It's perfectly understandable that you're tired."

"Thank-you," Mel sighed, reaching the door of her room. She gratefully turned the handle and stumbled through the door. Sarah followed, holding the lantern out before her.

"Here, I'll light the candle for you," she murmured. Mel blinked at the candle now sitting on the bedside table, struggling to remember if it had been there before. Sarah pulled out a slender stick from the top of her boot and dipped it into the fiery bowl of the lantern.

"Thank-you," Mel yawned, collapsing on the bed as the girl hovered over the bedside table and transferred the flame.

"There," Sarah said triumphantly, shaking out the fire on the end of the stick. "Well, good night Mel," she bade with a weak smile, picking up her lantern. "I'm off to have a pleasant chat with Father," she sighed, pulling a face.

"Oh yeah," she murmured, slowly remembering the brief exchange between guardian and ward as they left the table. "Will you be okay? He looked decidedly annoyed..."

"Oh, I might have to sweet talk him a little, promise to work harder on my lessons, that sort of thing," she said with a shrug of her shoulders. "It's all part of ongoing negotiations," she laughed, heading for the door. "Good night," she bade a final time over her shoulder.

"Good night," she returned to the closing door.

"Finally," she breathed, crossing the room to latch the door shut. On her return to the bed, she grabbed her sack and set it beside her as she sat down to pull off her boots. Tucking her sore feet beneath her, she opened the sack and tossed out the dirty dress to reveal her small collection of belongings. A battered pot and tin cup, a rusty knife, a bundle of string, a flint, a couple of coins, some other odds and ends she'd picked up along the way. it was all there. Nodding her satisfaction, she felt about the bottom of the bag, her fingers searching for a fold she had sewn into the material near the seam. "Ah," she croaked as she felt the groove, followed it to the edge. The furry crinkled paper jutted out of the concealed pocket as she fiddled with the opening, her tired fingers struggling to get a purchase on the surface. Carefully she extracted the boarding pass, gazed at the faded printing in the yellow candlelight. She could just make out the "Melanie J Barrett" at the bottom of the card. "Flight 207 Melb to Syd," she mouthed, fingering the crinkled line. Apart from the tattered clothes on her back, this piece of paper was the only thing she'd had on her person when the farmer discovered her in the field.

On regaining consciousness, she'd idly put her hands in her pockets, her fingers encountering the folded-up piece of paper. Moments later the farmer's wife had bustled into the room, ordered her to change into more "sensible" clothes. Sliding the paper under the pillow, she had complied, only too happy to shed the rags on her back. She hadn't counted on the stout woman placing them straight on the fire. It was only later she realized that the strange clothes had made the woman uncomfortable, driving her to burn the garments as soon as possible. Sometimes she wished the boarding pass had found its way to the fire before she ever laid eyes on it. What it implied was too horrible, too unbelievable for her mind to grasp. If she didn't have the boarding pass, she could have discounted the nebulous visions she sometimes experienced as meaningless dreams, rather than as fragmented memories of her own life in the twentieth century. "Damn stupid piece of paper," she muttered, her fingers tightening around the edges. It wasn't going to last much longer, she decided sadly, the paper soft and worn beneath her fingers. She'd been caught out in the rain too many times, the coarse hessian material offering only so much protection from the elements. At least the boarding pass had given her a name, assuming of course she hadn't picked up someone else's pass...

"Don't go there, Mel," she cautioned herself, reverently smoothing out the creases. "18 October 200..." she read for the umpteenth time, squinting at the fuzzy blob where the last number had been. Something must have been spilt on that particular spot, for the printing had worn clean off, even before she'd shoved it into her pocket. With a sigh, she slid the pass back into its special pocket and closed up the bag. She reluctantly got off the bed and set the sack at the foot of the bed, then quickly got ready for bed. "Ah," she sighed as she finally sank into bed and pulled the blankets over her. It was the most comfortable bed she'd lied on since arriving in this world. She just managed to reach over and blow out the candle before collapsing into a deep, dreamless sleep.

"Mel, Mel!" Sarah called as she burst through the external kitchen door. Mel groaned inwardly as she looked up from the bread mixture she was endeavouring to push a wooden spoon through. She'd only excused herself a short while ago, claiming that standing out in the yard on such a sunny day was giving her a headache. There was only so much equestrian prowess she could admire while maintaining the facade of polite interest. It didn't help that Moonbeam seemed to stamp the ground extra hard every time they passed her, sending dirt and dust flying. Finally, as a particularly big cloud of dust drifted over her, she had made her excuses and left, only too aware of Sarah's concerned yet injured eyes following her back inside.

"Yes Sarah," she responded, feeling the edges of her patience steadily fray. It was only four days after the incident in the forest, and already she was running out of good, feasible hiding places.

"You've got to help me with my homework," Sarah cried urgently, her eyes frantic.

"Aw, not again Sarah," she sighed, tiring of these last minute homework sessions.

"I'm sorry," Sarah cried, shifting her feet nervously. "I promise I'll do my homework on time in future. Please Mel, Father will be back from his morning ride soon…"

"Oh alright," she gave in with an exasperated sigh. "You run up and start, and I'll be up in a minute," she ordered, pushing strands of hair behind her ear with a floury hand.

"Thanks Mel," she gushed, letting out an expectant breath. With a vague nod of acknowledgment to Mrs Habiston, she scampered out of the kitchen.

"I'll just finish mixing the dough," she announced, moving the spoon through the increasingly thick mixture.

"Thank you," Mrs Habiston said quietly, drying her hands on a cloth. "Wendy's taking her sweet time coming back with the mushrooms." Mel stared at the old woman for a moment, surprised by her unsolicited comment.

"I guess it's a long way to the mushroom field," she suggested, tossing more flour onto the table.

"Aye, a long way that passes by the stables, and Simon Trenchard," she drawled, her voice thick with innuendo.

"What!? Wendy and Simon?"

Mrs Habiston grinned wickedly at her startled response. "She thinks I don't know what's goin' on between them two," she snickered as she poked the fire in the belly of the stove.

"What, you mean she's sleeping with him?"

"She's doing a bit more than sleep with him, lass," the old woman said dryly, tossing another log onto the fire.

"Isn't she a bit young to be, er, sexually active?"

Mrs Habiston turned away from the oven to eye her curiously. "Too young? She's nearly nineteen, miss. All her sisters and brothers have families of their own, and she's not even the youngest."

"Oh," Mel breathed, silently kicking herself for not thinking nineteenth century enough.

"You really are an odd one missy, but at least you help out," she conceded, gently nudging Mel away from the bowl. "You'd best be goin' up, before the mistress seeks you out," the older woman pointed out. Mel groaned and wiped her hands on her dress.

"Are you sure you don't want help with something else, Mrs Habiston?" she offered desperately, reluctantly making her way out of the room.

"Oh, call me Margaret," the older woman said generously as she sprinkled flour onto the table.

"Can I help you with anything else Margaret?" she repeated hopefully, her hand on the handle.

"No. Now get going," Margaret growled, scooping the dough out of the bowl. Groaning, she left the kitchen, catching out of the corner of her eye Margaret's smirk as she closed the door.

She wondered what homework delights awaited her as she made her way to the library. Raphael was certainly a thorough educator, she conceded, pausing at the door to collect herself. "Don't look grumpy," she told herself sternly. Just because Sarah was a lonely girl wanting to monopolise her time, that was no reason to be resentful. Maybe if Raphael didn't go out so much, leaving the girl to her own devices... "Right," she muttered under her breath, "whatever you do, don't look grumpy." Taking a deep breath, she relaxed her facial muscles, and pictured a dark solid rock in her mind. "I am the rock," she mouthed. Hold the rock up to the light, and all you'll do is blot out the sun. A faint smile tugged at the corners of her lips as she finally pushed the door open and entered the room. Sarah looked up innocently from her papers and frowned.

"Is something the matter?" Sarah asked, eyes full of concern. Mel felt her face fall as the rock vanished and was replaced with a piece of glass.

"No," she protested, taking her place at the table, "nothing's wrong."

"I'm sorry about the homework," Sarah pressed, obviously convinced otherwise. "I just lost track of time."

She had to bite her tongue and focus on the book before her. That had been Sarah's excuse every time so far this week.

"It's not that, well, not exactly," she admitted, quickly realising the girl wasn't going to let it go. "I'm almost completely recovered from that nasty encounter in the forest," she pointed out, folding her arms protectively over her chest. "I'll have to move on soon, and I've discovered very little through my research."

"You don't have to leave straight away," Sarah protested, sitting up in her chair.

"I'm not sure your father agrees," she mumbled, distractedly running her finger over the edge of the table.

"Why do you think that?" Sarah asked earnestly, her brow wrinkled in bemusement.

"Oh, I don't know," she muttered with a sharp intake of breath as a splinter of wood entered her finger. "He never looks happy to see me," she stated flatly, squinting at the sliver of wood jutting out of her skin.

"Father can be a quite prickly character," the girl confided with a sad shake of her head. "He finds it hard to trust anybody, even me sometimes."

She frowned as she pinched the end of the splinter between her fingernails. "I guess I can't really blame him," she murmured, yanking out the splinter with a grimace. She had been correct in her assumption that Raphael was from an upper class family. He had led a pampered life, wanting for nothing, in complete contrast to his young ward. Something had happened to change all that, and make his family turn against him, something that involved being betrayed by someone close to him.

"He obviously cares a great deal about you though," she added, flicking the splinter away.

"I know," Sarah sighed, "but even I find him difficult at times." She almost spluttered in response to that, looking up in disbelief at the girl. At times? They had clashed on a daily basis since she regained consciousness, the underlying tension between them so thick it could almost be cut with a knife. She couldn't help but think it had something to do with her presence in the manor, despite Sarah's flippant, evasive replies whenever she broached the subject.

"Look, how about I ask Father if you can stay on a bit longer?" Sarah suggested coyly, tapping her pencil against the paper.

"Oh no, I couldn't allow you to do that," she hastily replied, imagining how well that would go down, "especially when he's going away next week." She couldn't see Raphael wanting her to hang around while he was away on business.

"Why are you so convinced Father doesn't like you?" Sarah quizzed, her brow wrinkling in bemusement.

"Let's just focus on your homework, shall we?" Mel pressed, a note of finality in her voice. Frowning, Sarah bent her head over the paper, while she started drawing a map from one of the nearby books. They were both engrossed with their respective work when Raphael entered the room. "Ah, doing homework are we?" he enquired, startling them both.

"Oh, yes Father," Sarah replied a little breathlessly, cheeks reddening under his questioning gaze. "I'm just about finished..."

"Well then," he drawled, leaning over the table slightly, "I may as well take a look." With that, his hand darted out and snatched the paper.

Sarah looked on in shocked horror as his eyes scanned the pages, his face an unreadable mask. She turned to Mel for support, a pained expression on her face. Mel shrugged helplessly as she set her pencil down and cast a critical eye on the map she had just copied. "Hmm," Raphael finally murmured, reaching for the pencil resting precariously between Sarah's slack fingers. "You made a mistake in question five. Mary has a quarter of the number of apples that Susan has, not a third. And you made a mistake subtracting 87 and 36 from 180," he added, pointing to a triangle at the bottom of the page.

"Oh," Sarah said in a small voice, her face relaxing.

"Not bad at all," he rumbled, handing her back the paper, "assuming it's all your own work..." Mel coughed nervously, her eyes sliding away from Raphael's challenging stare.

"Of course it is," Sarah assured him indignantly. "Mel's been hard at work copying the map." He peered over the pile of books in front of her to admire her reproduction.

"Hmm," he murmured thoughtfully, rubbing his chin. "So, no help today then?" he asked casually, a smirk tugging at the corners of his mouth. Sarah opened her mouth to protest, faltered in the face of his knowing gaze. "Not today, no," she admitted meekly, lowering her eyes.

"Ha," Raphael barked, his composure briefly shattered by Sarah's admission. He reached out to playfully ruffle her hair, a broad smile on his face. "Thank-you Sarah, that's enough homework for today," he said generously, withdrawing his hand as she whined and ducked her head defensively.

Mel swallowed hard at the pang of envy she suddenly felt. "Go and wash up for lunch," he ordered with a smile.

"Yes Father," she agreed eagerly, jumping out of her seat. "Coming Mel?" she prompted as she pushed her chair in.

"Um," she began, looking at the carefully copied map and picking up her pencil, "I'll be down in a minute. There's just a few more features to add."

"Don't take too long, I'm famished," the girl warned as she strode out of the room.

"Okay," she called to her vanishing back. She bent her head and resumed work on the map, assuming that Raphael would follow suit. The sharp scrape of the chair penetrated her concentration, and she looked up to find him sitting down at the table directly across from her.

"So," he started casually, hands behind his head, "how long have you been helping Sarah with her homework then?"

"Ah, pretty much from day two," she confessed sheepishly, putting the pencil down. "It is mostly Sarah's work, though," she added hastily as his eyes narrowed, "I just point out things she might want to try again."

"Really?" he probed.

"I eventually offer more help when it's obvious she's stuck on a problem," she supplied anxiously, bracing for an explosion. He had made it abundantly clear that he didn't want Sarah to solicit help from others when it came to doing her homework.

"Your guidance is producing results," he conceded, tilting his head back to contemplate the oak beams of the ceiling. "As you know," he continued before she could respond, "I am leaving for town next week. I'll be away for over a week…"

"You want me gone by the time you leave," she guessed aloud, her voice ringing with resignation. He stared at her in astonishment, his hands falling away from his head. "No," he drawled, leaning forward in his chair, his light brown eyes fully upon her, not allowing her gaze to drift away. "I want you to guarantee that you'll stay at least until I get back."

Now it was her turn to stare. "But, I thought you didn't like Sarah being around me…"

"I had concerns," he said distractedly, picking up the pencil Sarah had left behind. "I still have concerns," he murmured, rolling the pencil between his fingertips, his eyes drawn to the rotating lead. "Anyway," he said with a start, looking up as he straightened in his seat. "I've come to see that there is more to you than meets the eye." Her eyes slid away from his at the subtle compliment. She willed her cheeks to stop flushing.

"Thank you," she mumbled, her eyes fixed on the map before her.

"So you'll stay?"

"Yes," she answered, struggling to keep the relief out of her voice. "As long as it doesn't cause any trouble," she said pointedly, glancing up at him.

"Why would it be trouble?" he asked, idly grabbing the map out from under her unsuspecting hands.

"It's just, things seem to be tense between you and Sarah," she explained awkwardly, her fingers tightly gripping the pencil. "I've asked Sarah if it's because of me, but she wouldn't give me a clear answer..." Her voice trailed away as he pulled the original map closer and turned it around.

"It's true your presence is causing tension," he admitted distractedly, his fingers tightening around the pencil as he scanned the two maps. He added the final features to the map, put the pencil down. "However," he said, raising his eyes to fully meet her questioning gaze, "it's not your fault. The problem exists between us, and we'll just have to work it out," he explained, passing her back the map. "Now let's go to lunch." She stared at the completed map, opening her mouth to argue as he rose from his seat and headed for the door. The sudden pain in her stomach convinced her to accept his pronouncement for now. "Coming," she blurted, hurriedly scrambling to her feet. With an embarrassed nod, she preceded him out of the room, his face unreadable as she passed him in the doorway.

Raphael tightened his grip on the reins and gently pulled back Monty's head. "Whoa Monty," he bade the powerful stallion. The large sweaty horse was only too happy to oblige. They'd been pushing hard for the last hour, rider and horse alike sensing they were nearly home. He could just make out the dark grey slate roof of the manor above the tree line. Noting the foam oozing out of the corner of Monty's mouth, he mentally chastised himself for pushing the horse too hard. His general irritation with how the trip had gone was affecting his judgment. He disliked going to town at the best of times. It had been more crowded than usual this trip, the streets clogged with farmers and traders haggling over produce. Then he had met Troughworth, the prospective buyer. On its own accord, his nose wrinkled in distain at the memory of the man. A flabby, balding bulk in ill-fitting clothes, he struggled to make up his mind about anything. If William Troughworth had been on his own, he surely could have persuaded him to buy all three artifacts at premium prices. Unfortunately his dear wife Catherine had tagged along to keep a sharp eye on proceedings. The stout, rosy-faced woman had made sour, disapproving faces throughout his presentation, quickly overriding her husband whenever he started showing interest in the pieces.

If there was one thing he hated, it was being treated like a dodgy dealer. He prided himself on selling only genuine artifacts, all personally acquired during his travels through Europe and the Middle East. Of course he tried to keep the best items for himself, but he had been forced to relinquish some of his more prized pieces over the years, due to the fluctuating competition of the market. He was fortunate Sarah had only picked out a few modest trinkets for herself. After such a hard upbringing, she could be forgiven for being greedy. The thing Sarah hungered for the most was a family, he thought with a grimace, which brought him to the subject of the woman Mel.

He hadn't believed Sarah that day as she whispered hoarsely to him, her wounded body slumped against the tree. "It's her," she had panted, her hand resting weakly on his arm. How she recognised the thin, dishevelled woman slouched beside her he'll never know. She had lost a lot of weight, the dirty, tattered dress hanging off her frame like a sail off a mast. Her face and hair were so smudged with dirt he had a hard time telling her apart from the men he'd just cut down. Only when she managed to open her eyes and gaze blearily up at him did he think it was possible. He hadn't seen those murky hazel eyes for months, but he recognised them immediately.

"Sarah, what have you done?" he croaked softly as he entered the yard and stiffly alighted from his saddle. He subconsciously braced himself for the usual running hug from Sarah that almost bowled him over every time he returned from a trip.

"Welcome back sir," a rough voice called from the stables. John ambled over, wiping his hands down the front of his shirt. "Good trip was it sir?" he asked as he took Monty's reins from his hand.

"Not as good as I had hoped," Raphael answered with a sigh as he unbuckled his saddle bags. "Where's Sarah? She's normally out here by now..."

"Ah, I'm not sure sir. She did say somethin' 'bout giving Mel some sword handlin' lessons," the swarthy-faced man recalled, idly stroking Monty's long nose.

"Really? Thank you Mr Morley," he grunted, hauling the bags over his shoulder and making his way to the house. Funny, he'd been encouraging her to practise with the rapier for the last couple of weeks with infrequent success. Now she was enthusiastically teaching Mel some moves.

With this annoying observation in mind, he pushed through the kitchen door to a scene of domestic bliss. Mrs Habiston was sitting at the table, nipping stalks off beans, a cup of tea set beside her. Wendy was scrubbing pots while a stranger slid a mound of dough into the oven. "And then I told him he could kiss my...oh, Master Blythe," the older woman broke off her seemingly raucous story to stand and greet her employer.

"Mrs Habiston, ladies," he returned, emphasising his use of the plural, his sharp gaze falling on the young woman standing near the oven.

"Ah, this is my niece, Jane Smith," Mrs Habiston explained nervously. The young woman, who looked about the same age as Wendy, curtsied awkwardly, bowing her mousy brown head.

"She's just visiting for a few days, although Miss Sarah did suggest she might stay on, with your approval, of course," she added hastily when his face darkened.

"I thought I told you people no visitors without my express permission," he grated, fists tightening at his sides. He was just about to order the girl to leave immediately when the aroma of freshly baked cake assailed his nostrils.

"Would you like some cake sir? Miss Sarah made it herself," Mrs Habiston offered, correctly reading the change in his facial expression.

"Sarah's been...cooking?" he uttered, almost choking on the last word. He thought Sarah hated cooking.

"Well sir, with Mel helping out in the kitchen so much, she started hangin' around, and well, one thing led to another," she explained as she cut the cake.

"We'll discuss this later," he interjected impatiently, accepting the generous slice she held out. With a final glower at the three women, he bit into the sweet sponge and exited the room. As he turned into the long corridor and made his way to the training area, he catalogued the changes that had taken place in his short absence. Someone had gone mad and cleaned the floor along the passageway. The thick dust that normally lined the edges was gone, along with the cobwebs on the ceiling. The tapestries looked more colourful than usual, as though someone had gone to the effort of shaking the dust off them.

His irritation grew with each step. It had to be Mel, he reasoned. Sarah had never shown any interest in cleaning, and what staff he had were too busy with their main duties. He would hire more people, but news of the curse had spread far and wide, so only people completely down on their luck ignored the rumours and accepted positions in his household. Just because of that one idiot girl… The sound of clanging sticks and laboured breathing broke into his thoughts. He wiped his mouth with the back of his hand and brushed the cake crumbs off his shirt. Taking a steadying breath, he pushed through the door to see Sarah and Mel engaged in combat. Neither seemed aware of his arrival, Mel struggling to deflect a flurry of blows from Sarah. Even though they practised with rounded sticks, and she wore a leather vest and helmet, Mel was obviously gritting her teeth against the pain of some successful blows. He felt a twinge of pride to see Sarah standing so confidently without any protective gear, bouncing lightly on her well-placed feet. She darted forward suddenly and landed a firm tap on Mel's hip.

"Ow," she cried angrily, the strands of her patience clearly fraying.

"That was for not returning to the ready stance," Sarah informed her primly. "At the end of each move, you should return to the starting position, like so…" She proceeded to illustrate her point, with Mel just managing to block the advancing stick. "See how I'm standing, sword at the ready for the next strike?"

"Yes, I get it," Mel muttered, holding the stick more firmly as she suddenly realised it was drooping in her hand. They turned as one towards the sound of Raphael's slow claps.

"Father!" Sarah cried, flinging down her stick and running to him.

"Oh, so you did miss me," he teased, returning her hug.

"Of course," she replied, looking up at him with those dark blue eyes.

"Really? Sounds like you kept busy enough, baking cakes and training Mel here." He shot Mel an accusing look over Sarah's head before returning his doting gaze to her. Groaning inwardly at the dark look, Mel set her stick down and peeled the helmet off her sweaty head. "I'm in for it now," she thought with a mental sigh as she watched him lovingly smile down at his ward.

"Welcome back sir," she said formally.

"Thank you Mel," he replied with equal stiffness, levelling his unwavering gaze at her. "I take it you have been busy too, trying to clean this place."

"Oh yes Father, she's been working like a demon," Sarah answered excitedly for her, stepping back from him. "That's why I dragged her in here for weapon training."

"I see," he said thoughtfully. "Well, I'll leave you to it then," he continued pointedly, turning to go.

"Oh, we're finished for now," Sarah hastily interjected with a questioning glance at Mel. Despite his anger, he almost laughed aloud at the relief in the woman's face as she wordlessly nodded. Draping his arm protectively around his young ward's shoulders, he guided her out of the training room amid goodbyes. As he answered a question about his trip, he made a mental note to have a private talk with Mel about how she had overstepped her bounds.

Cursing softly under his breath, he stepped away from the kitchen door and strode purposefully towards the stairs, droplets of water falling down the back of his shirt. All the tension that had left his body during his soak in the tub began to build up again. "That's what you get for eavesdropping, Raphael," he told himself sternly. He had started to reconsider his attitude towards Mel, and acknowledge that he was being irrational. She was just upholding her end of the bargain, earning the right to keep those blasted boots. Sarah hanging out in the kitchen with the workers was just a by-product of that process, he reasoned as he ascended the stairs. With Sarah's full-throated laughter still echoing in his ears, he stomped into the library, flinging the door noisily open. Mel looked up from the book she'd been reading, her face suitably startled.

"We need to talk Mel," he started without preamble, his frustration erupting to the surface. He closed the door behind him and strode to the table. Mel gulped nervously and pushed the book aside, nerving herself to meet his agitated gaze. While on some level she had expected this confrontation, the strength of his feeling still caught her off-guard. "What's wrong?" she asked guardedly, willing herself not to cower beneath his looming form as he leant over the table.

"I go away for a few days, and you turn everything upside down," he explained, his voice strained.

"Look, I know I might have gone a bit far with the cleaning," she admitted, looking suitably contrite. "It's just when you clean one thing, you invariably clean another, and so on and so forth..."

"What? That's not what I meant," he snapped, gripping the back of the chair. "I mean, thanks to you, Sarah has obviously taken to hanging around the kitchen and talking to the staff..."

"What's wrong with that?" she asked, her brow wrinkling in confusion.

"They could be a bad influence on her," he replied, the volume of his voice increasing on its own accord.

"A bad influence? Give me a break," she snorted derisively, rising to her feet. "Sarah isn't exactly a delicate flower. She could probably teach John and Simon new swear words."

"That's the point," he returned heatedly, straightening up, "I'm trying to push her beyond all that, show her there's more to life than cruelty and crudity."

"So who is she suppose to talk to when you go away?" she demanded, stepping away from the table.

"She can still talk to the staff on a certain level," Raphael explained, slowly rounding the table. "But a certain distance should be maintained..."

"Oh, I see," she interjected sharply, indignation rising within her, "she can talk to the lowly servants to order them around, but she can't have fun."

"That's the way it works," he grated, coming to a stop in front of her. "Clear boundaries need to be set..."

"Oh come on, she's just a kid," she scoffed, glaring up at him.

"That's no excuse," he snapped, his hands bunched into tight fists. "I had to learn such things as a child."

"Because you were born into that world," she argued. "Sarah doesn't care about that stuff, she just wants someone to talk to."

"How dare you," he uttered, gripping her shoulder roughly as his eyes bored into hers. "How dare you stand there judging me," he growled softly into her face, his long fingers digging into the soft flesh around the base of her throat. "You don't know me, and you don't know Sarah, so just mind your own business." He gave her shoulder a final squeeze before releasing her in disgust. She stumbled back a few steps, her hand creeping to the affected area as she stared in shock at his dark angry face. She opened her mouth to protest, but no sound found its way out past her stunned vocal cords.

"Father!" Sarah called from the stairway, "the cart's arrived from town with our supplies."

"Coming," he called back, his glare never leaving her injured face. Without another word, he turned stony faced to the door and left the room. She waited until the sound of his footsteps faded completely before slipping out of the library. Thankfully she didn't pass anyone in the corridor as she scurried to her room, her face beet red. Once safely in her room with the door latched behind her, she promptly collapsed on the bed and sobbed into the pillow.

Carefully readjusting her sack, she peered around the edge of the doorway. Raphael sat in the large, overstuffed armchair in the far corner of the library, his head bent over a book. Gathering her nerve, she padded softly across the doorway, watching the dark blonde head out of the corner of her eye. It didn't move at all as she made it to the other side. Trust Raphael to be up at this time of night, she thought with disgust. The first conscious thought she had when she stopped crying pathetically on the bed was to leave. She had quickly decided to leave under the cover of darkness, in order to get a comfortable distance between herself and the manor. Sarah would want to search for her, of this she was certain. It was therefore with great relief she had spied the large, almost full moon through the window as she went down to dinner. At least she wouldn't be stumbling about in complete darkness.

Dinner had been difficult. Sarah had asked her immediately about the scarf around her neck, of course. Her hand creeping to the strip of material covering the darkening marks at the base of her throat, she'd explained she was trying to avert a cold. She thought she saw a hint of guilty concern in Raphael's eyes as he hastily turned his attention to the food being served. She had studiously ignored him throughout dinner, while every fibre of her being wanted to smash every plate and serving dish over his fat, arrogant head. After several failed attempts to drag her into conversation, Sarah had contented herself with discussing the latest fashions Raphael had seen during his stay in town. Finally she'd been able to excuse herself and head for bed, all too aware of Sarah's frown as she left the room.

Packing up her gear had taken little time. Feeling only a twinge of guilt, she had picked out two sets of spare clothes from the chest. Luckily she'd found an old pair of trousers and hose in the bottom of the chest, along with a couple of musty, over-sized shirts. Peeling the dress off her suddenly sweaty body, she had quickly taken stock of the rest of her possessions. Maps, notes, those blasted boots, she had mentally ticked off as she pulled on the baggy trousers. "Well, you're slightly better off Mel," she had reassured herself as she waited for the household to fall quiet, her bulging sack at her side. After some deliberation, she had decided to write a brief note to Sarah, explaining her reasons for leaving, some meaningless crap about not wanting to be a burden and needing to continue her search. She must have drifted off to sleep while waiting for the others to retire for the night, Sarah's timid knocking on her door startling her awake. "Mel?" she had spoken softly to the door, "are you awake?" After a couple of seconds of waiting, the girl had grunted and continued on to her room. More footsteps had passed her door, most probably Raphael's, his boots ringing loudly against the hard wooden floor.

So now she crept along the corridor, stealthily making her way to the kitchen. She'd grab some supplies on her way out, she decided. Hell, she'd helped out enough in the kitchen, she was entitled to some of the food. After a cautious knock on the door, she eased it open and entered the room. The ladies had called it a night by the looks of it. Wendy was obviously planning to finish washing up in the morning, she noted with a grin at the sink full of greasy pots and dishes. Wrinkling her nose against the smell, she ventured into the pantry in the corner. She grabbed a small loaf of bread and a handful of small honey cakes. Her first attempt at baking in the century, she thought with a small smile. Maybe Raphael will choke on one, she ruminated, the smile widening. With a final addition of some apples and a small kitchen knife, she went to the table and sat down, setting the sack carefully on the floor. Straining her eyes as a cloud passed in front of the moon, she pulled on her boots and fumbled with the laces. Nodding her satisfaction, she rose carefully from the table and grabbed her bag. Treading softly over the flag stone floor, she made it to the door and turned the door handle with agonising slowness. With a prolonged click it opened, and she stepped out into the mild, moonlit night, feeling faintly victorious. She closed the door behind her and heaved the sack over her good shoulder, smiling at the gentle breeze that caressed her face as she started to make her way across the yard.

"Going somewhere, are we?"

With a yelp she spun around, her heart hammering wildly in her chest. Raphael leant nonchalantly against the wall, arms crossed. His narrowed eyes and clenched jaw belied his casual stance.

"What do you expect?" she shot back, her anger bubbling to the surface.

"So you are just going to run away?"

"You hurt me," she cried unevenly, a hard lump forming in her throat. His eyes widening with concern, he gestured for her to keep her voice down.

"Don't order me around, you stuck-up arrogant toff," she spat out disgustedly.

"For goodness sake, keep it down," he hissed, moving away from the wall.

"Like I care," she muttered, turning her back on him to continue her trek through the yard.

"Now wait a minute," he grunted, quickening his stride to catch up to her. "Can't we talk about this?"

"What's there to talk about?" she panted, not slowing her pace. "You obviously don't want me around. I've got the marks to prove it..."

"That's what I don't understand," he broke into her bitter mutterings, grabbing her arm and forcing her to stop.

"If you're so mad at me, why did you wear this scarf..." He picked at the material moving gently in the breeze, rubbing it between his fingers.

"Stop that," she snapped, yanking the cloth out of his grasp. "I wore it for Sarah. The girl idolises you. I didn't have the heart to show her your uglier side." With that she shook off his hand and trudged towards the forest.

"Wait, Mel," he called, running up to her. "Please Mel, don't go. I humbly apologise, I shouldn't have hurt you like that..." Despite her anger, her steps slowed at the awkward apology. She slowly turned and faced him. In the moonlight, his handsome face appeared suitably contrite.

"Look, whatever it takes to get you to stay, I'll do it. Just name it..."

"Help me find answers," she blurted without hesitation. There was a moment of heavy silence as Raphael stared at her, his jaw working silently.

"You're welcome to keep searching for your answers here," he finally said, clearing his throat.

"Ha," she scoffed, shifting the sack on her shoulder, "you say that now, but how long will it last? I'm not going to wait around for you to lose it with me again."

"Wait," he bid her as she turned back to the forest. He solemnly pulled a gold band off his left index finger and held it out to her. "This ring carries the symbol of my house. It's one of the few things from my old life I've managed to keep." She cautiously picked up the ring and examined its plain exterior. As she turned it over, she spotted an elegant engraving on the inner surface.

"An albatross?" she prompted, squinting up at him.

"Yes," he sighed, raking long fingers through his hair, "it's been the symbol of my family for many generations."

"So, if this got into the wrong hands, it'd be bad news for you, wouldn't it?" she guessed, closing her hand around the innocent band of gold.

"Yes," he stated simply, his fingers creeping on their own accord to the indentation left by the ring. Despite the danger, and everything that had happened, the precious heirloom rarely left his finger. He remembered with a sad smile his father gruffly handing it to him on his fifteenth birthday, his lips twitching beneath the neatly trimmed beard in a brief display of emotion.

"If I ever hurt you again, you can go freely, and take the ring with you," he proposed hoarsely, his eyes finding hers in the murky moonlight. "Of course, if you leave on your own volition, I expect to get the ring back."

"Of course," she murmured thoughtfully as she squeezed her hand and felt the hard edges pressing into her skin. "You're really serious about this, aren't you?" she pressed, a hint of awe in her voice.

"I over-reacted to your comments," he admitted stiffly, looking down at the slightly scuffed toes of his boots. "I have to make amends." He glanced up from his inspection of the ground to find Mel watching him critically.

"I want it in writing, the agreement I mean," she said carefully. "I would need some sort of proof that you gave me the ring, under those conditions."

"Of course," he agreed, sounding relieved. She protested half-heartedly when he took the sack out of her hands and hoisted it effortlessly over his shoulder. "You know," Raphael began as they headed back to the manor, "I had to get you to stay. Sarah would have made my life a living hell."

"It would have served you right," she grumbled.

"Yes, I know," he mumbled with a sideways glance at her closed face. "I was jealous, I guess," he admitted awkwardly, unaccustomed to baring his soul. "When I overheard her laughing in the kitchen, so at ease, I resented it. I'm not used to sharing her with others..."

She plodded on in silence beside him, feeling treacherous cracks forming already in her stony facade. He solemnly pushed open the kitchen door and held it open for her. A small sigh of relief escaped her lips as she stepped into the house. Out of the corner of her eye, she saw Raphael smirk as he closed the door behind her. "Glad to be back then?" he pressed as he handed her the sack.

"Life on the road isn't very glamorous," she admitted stiffly. "It's nothing at all like the books I've read. They make it sound so...adventurous and fun."

To her surprise, he laughed freely at her admission. "I know only too well what you mean," he said heartily, nodding in agreement. "One of the biggest disappointments of my life was going on the run and living like a vagabond."

Despite her resolve to remain frosty towards him, the corners of her mouth started to relax on their own accord.

"Right, I'll be in the library writing up the agreement," he declared with a yawn, stretching his tired body as he ambled over to the inner door. "Meet me there, please," he added, looking at her earnestly. She mumbled an affirmative and started to unpack the food, barely hearing his departure with her head bent over the sack. Suddenly feeling very tired, she hastily returned all the items and raced up to the library. Raphael glanced up from where he sat at the table, pen in hand. "Oh good, I'm almost finished," he mumbled to the table, pen scraping against the thick paper. "There," he breathed, straightening up. "If you could just look it over, give me your thoughts..."

She plopped down in the chair and dragged the sheet across, straining her eyes in the wavering lamp light. "Sword of my choice?" she asked, frowning up at him.

"You need a weapon," he stated flatly, stretching his arms over his head.

Shrugging, she continued reading. "A copper coin for every week I stay, on top of a ten pound reward for helping Sarah," she murmured, raising her eyes from the paper. "It's a generous offer."

"I wanted to give you more," he volunteered with a grimace, "but the trip didn't go as well as I would have liked. That was the other reason I wanted you to stay until I got back," he explained awkwardly. Frowning, she turned her attention back to the document.

"I imagine you'd expect me to do some work for this amount..."

"No more than what you're currently doing," he said firmly, raising his hands in a warding gesture. "Look, this is still an open-ended arrangement, you can leave whenever you want," he reassured her, leaning forward in his chair. "But it obviously wouldn't hurt to earn some money, for when you hit the road again. I just hope you'll stay long enough for me to redeem myself," he added earnestly, his eyes settling on the scarf fastened around her neck. Swallowing past the sudden lump in her throat, she stared at the uneven scrawl and slowly signed her name at the bottom of the page.

"Thank you," he mumbled, rising out of his chair. He rounded the table in a couple of long strides and added his signature to hers. "Do you have a safe place to keep this?" he asked as he handed her the agreement.

"Yes," she murmured, thinking of the special pocket sewn into the base of her sack. She carefully folded up the paper and tucked it into the waistband of her trousers.

"Good," he sighed, rubbing the back of his neck. "Oh, and can we just keep this between us for the time being, until things settle down around here? I've still to make a decision about Jane," he muttered tiredly, letting his hand fall heavily away.

"Of course," she agreed, getting stiffly out of her chair. "Well, I'd better go to bed..."

"Wait Mel," he bid before she could turn for the door. "Would you take off that horrible scarf for a minute?"

"Why?" she asked defensively, her hand creeping to the base of her throat.

"I can make the bruising heal more quickly," he told her evenly, stretching his hand out towards her.

"What?" she asked sceptically, stepping out of range.

"It's an ability I have," he explained carefully, lowering his hand. "How do you think Sarah recovered so quickly?"

"You did that? That explains a lot," she murmured thoughtfully, eying him warily as he stepped closer to her.

"Please Mel, let me do this for you," he implored. "I don't know if I can handle you wearing that awful scarf much longer," he added with a straight face.

She blinked at him, her hand reaching on its own accord to the edge of the coarse wool. "It won't hurt, will it?" she fretted as she scratched the itching skin.

"You'll feel a tingling sensation in the affected area, that's all," he answered, shrugging his shoulders.

"What, like pins and needles?" she pressed, tensing up as he closed the distance between them.

"That's a fair analogy," he murmured, his eyes fastened on the opening her shirt.

"I hate pins and needles," she grumbled as her clumsy fingers unfastened the scarf. His breath caught noisily in his throat as he pulled away the cloth and surveyed the darkening bruises. He muttered something in French, raised guilty eyes to hers. "Just stand still," he instructed, slipping his hand under the material of her shirt. She flinched slightly as his hand settled on the tender flesh around the base of her throat. The pain quickly faded away as warmth spread from his fingertips and penetrated her skin. She swayed unsteadily on her feet as her neckline tingled pleasantly under his hand. Without lifting his eyes from the pale skin, he reached out with his other hand to steady her.

"There," he sighed, his hands dropping heavily away. "How was that?" he asked, stepping back.

"Hmm, nice," she breathed, craning her neck to look down at the faded marks. She lifted her hand to cautiously probe the faintly tender area.

"I couldn't heal it completely," he offered ruefully, running a trembling hand through his hair. "I use my own energy to speed up the body's natural healing process, so it's quite taxing. We could try again tomorrow, when I'm rested..."

"That shouldn't be necessary. The worst of it is gone," she marvelled, looking up at him with renewed respect. "That's amazing. Have you always had this ability?" she asked, eyes wide with curiosity. He looked away from her avid face, fatigue lines etched around his mouth.

"Ah, it's a long story, and I'm about to pass out," he answered with a yawn, shuffling over to the table to fetch the lantern.

"Right," she murmured, biting her tongue. "Another time, perhaps," she suggested, bending down to grab her sack.

"Thank you Mel," he sighed gratefully as he followed her out the door. They trudged in silence down the corridor, their shadows dancing over the dark wood walls in the flickering lantern light. "Well, good night Mel," he mumbled, handing her the lantern as they reached the door of her room.

"Are you sure?" she asked with a nod at the lantern.

"Positive," he breathed, stretching his neck, "I'm just going to stagger to my room and collapse onto the bed."

"Very well," she murmured, setting down the sack to fumble with the door handle.

"Oh, where are my manners?" he muttered, hastily stepping in to open the door for her. She stumbled into her room and unceremoniously dumped the sack on the floor. "Well, good night Mr Blythe," she bade, her hand on the handle.

"Please, call me Raphael," he bid with a tired wave.

"Goodnight...Raphael," she uttered, the name sitting oddly on her tongue. With a final glance at his weary gait, she stepped back and closed the door. Trying desperately not to think about his warm hand on her neck, she quickly dumped all the clothes back in the trunk. After stuffing the agreement into the concealed pocket of her sack, she stripped down to her underwear and crawled into bed. Extinguishing the flame of the lantern, she laid back in the darkness and huddled under the blankets. As she drowsily closed her eyes, she could have sworn that the skin around the base of her neck still tingled from his healing touch.

Wispy cirrus clouds stretched across the blue sky like ghostly fingers. She gazed out of the tiny window, wishing that long distance flights weren't so tedious. Sighing, she returned her attention to her novel, willing the obnoxious kid two aisles down to suddenly lose his voice. "I'm bored, I've finished all my games," the bratty boy whined.

"We'll get you a new one at the next stop," his mother promised, with all the backbone of a jellyfish.

"Why do we have to go visit Grandma anyway? I wanted to go to the amusement parks..."

"Oh shut up, you little brat," his father suddenly snapped.

Her quiet cheering of the father's outburst was interrupted by a pretty hostess offering her coffee. She gratefully set her cup on the tray. The hostess was carefully pouring the dark brown fluid when the plane jolted violently. Hot coffee splashed onto her lap, but she hardly noticed being scalded as an explosion tore through the wing only a couple of metres in front of her. The deafening roar of wind as the plane quickly depressurised filled her ears. Bodies were sucked out through the jagged, burning hole. The hostess who had just served her so intently now clung to an armrest for dear life, her screams swallowed by the howling wind. Her struggles were ended by a laptop striking her head on its way out of the plane. A few feeble hands made a grab for her unconscious body, but the pull of the atmosphere was too great.

She stared about in disbelief. This couldn't be the end, could it? The pilot's absurdly calm voice faintly reached her above the roar. Engine difficulties? That was one way to put it, she thought bitterly as the plane began to lose altitude. The whole right wing was gone. What a horrible way to die. Surrounded by strangers, utterly helpless, everything beyond her control. Almost everyone was crying or screaming uncontrollably by now, her own gut-wrenching sobs adding to the deafening cacophony. The man next to her was praying ardently, his hands clenched together tightly. She glanced out the window, hastily looked away. The ground was coming up fast. It wouldn't be long now, she decided, bracing herself for the inevitable impact. Her body ached from the vibration of the plane, and the ferocious tug of the racing wind. The background roar was suddenly replaced by a loud crashing sound. Metal and plastic crunched and cracked as the underside of the fuselage bounced along the ground. Damn good pilot, she noted as they spun dizzily towards the trees at the edge of the field. They could all now scream heartily for a few seconds more as large sections of plane were sheared off by its chaotic passage through the forest. With that cheery thought in mind, she stared up grimly as the roof above her head creaked loudly, the high-pitched whine of tearing metal cutting through the background noise. "This is it," she croaked as the roof fell towards her. She instinctively raised her arms protectively over her head, closed her eyes as she waited for the inevitable end...

Mel opened her eyes with a jolt, her heart hammering wildly in her chest. "Damn stupid dream," she muttered, closing her eyes against the early morning sun creeping in through the window. She'd been having the same dream on and off for months, with only minor variations. A few nights ago, the hostess had actually been John dressed up like a woman, facial hair and all. She had struggled not to giggle when she saw him in the yard the next morning. Hopefully there would be a version with Raphael playing the hostess, she thought with a wicked grin. He'd make a good-looking woman, she decided as she rolled over and snuggled into the blankets. As always, she catalogued the familiar parts of the dream, saw the vivid images in her head. It felt real, so real that she always woke with a heart-thumping start. A million thoughts raced through her head as she shaded her eyes against the increasing light in the room. Perhaps what she experienced as a dream was actually a memory, and the only way her scattered mind could access it was during deep sleep. But if it was a memory, then what had happened? Why hadn't she died in the plane crash? In that final moment, as she waited for the ceiling to fall, had she somehow fallen through a crack in space and time? Or was she just mad as a loon? She caught herself falling asleep, forced her heavy eyelids to open. Gathering her strength, she propelled herself out of bed, her feet curling up against the cold hard floor. Her stomach growled, informing her it was definitely time for breakfast. She quickly dressed and made her way to the dining room.

"Morning Mel," Sarah greeted through a dainty yawn, "sleep well?"

"As well as can be expected," she answered vaguely, helping herself to a bowl of porridge. "What about you, feelings of guilt didn't keep you awake?" she returned archly as she sat down at the table.

"Hey, I won all those games fair and square," the girl retorted as she smeared jam over her bread.

"I'm starting to wish I hadn't found those cards," Mel growled as she sprinkled sugar over her porridge. She had innocently shown Sarah a dusty deck of cards she'd discovered in a long-forgotten cupboard, never suspecting that Sarah was a poker fiend from hell. While they only played for twigs and buttons, the girl's unbelievable winning streak was becoming irritating. She glowered at Sarah's smug little face, mumbled something under her breath.

"What was that Mel?" she asked sweetly around a mouthful of bread.

"I said you must have learnt more than how to pick pockets while you were living on the streets," she repeated grumpily, spooning porridge into her mouth.

"Oh, don't be such a sore loser," the girl scoffed, lifting her cup to her lips. "I can't help if I've been incredibly lucky."

Mel muttered something else under her breath, and this time Sarah didn't ask for clarification. Clearing her throat, she lowered her cup. "I take it things are getting uncomfortable in the kitchen," Sarah ventured, eager to change the subject.

Mel grimaced as she poured herself a cup of tea.

"Wendy's convinced I'm trying to steal Simon from her," she supplied with a groan.

Outside the dining room, Raphael's steps slowed as her words caught his attention. He'd been sensing something was wrong between Mel and one of the staff, but no one seemed willing to talk about it. "Reduced to eavesdropping," he muttered softly, placing his ear against the door.

"All because I helped Simon write some letters to his family," Mel lamented.

"You weren't to know that Simon would become infatuated with you," Sarah protested. Making a low guttural sound in his throat, Raphael straightened up and entered the room.

"Finally," he declared as he approached the table, drawing startled looks from both Sarah and Mel, "I have some idea of what is going on."

"Father," Sarah croaked, almost choking on her bread.

"Ah, good morning," Mel added, hastily swallowing a lump of porridge.

"Good morning indeed," he retorted, grabbing a handful of bread slices from the serving tray. "So how long has this been going on?" he demanded as he sat down at the table.

"What?" Mel asked defensively, still reluctant to discuss it with Raphael.

"The situation between you and Wendy," he elaborated patiently as he reached for the butter. After a moment of gloomy contemplation, she grudgingly answered.

"It's been building up over the last couple of weeks," she explained. "I keep trying to convince Wendy that I'm not interested in Simon, but she doesn't believe me."

"Do you want me to talk to her?" he offered.

"No, no way," she replied strongly, gulping down a spoonful of porridge. "She'd really hate me then."

"Well, what do you want me to do?"

"Nothing," she told him bluntly, carefully skimming the surface. "I just hope this all blows over soon," she continued glumly, blowing on the porridge, "otherwise I may have to leave…"

Sarah spluttered noisily, spraying the table with droplets of tea. "Leave? Are you serious?" she cried as she set down her cup.

"That's a drastic step to take," Raphael grumbled, his face darkening.

"I don't see what choice I have," Mel insisted. "It would be unfair for Wendy or Simon to leave, they were here long before I arrived on the scene, and if things don't improve, I don't think I'll want to hang around…"

"No, I won't accept losing any member of my household through a silly misunderstanding," Raphael declared, his jaw clenched determinedly. "Just give me some time to ponder this predicament," he murmured, thoughtfully sinking his teeth into the thick buttered slice. A heavy silence fell over the table as they all concentrated on the task of eating, punctuated only by the clank of utensils and crockery. Finally Raphael grunted, drained the dregs of his tea.

"Are you teaching today Mel?" Raphael abruptly asked, setting down his cup.

"Yes," she answered cautiously, fully aware of his reservations about her teaching the local children. If the villagers hadn't offered such a generous discount on locally produced goods, she was certain he would have protested more vigorously to her conducting classes in the old shed just outside his land. All this came about when she visited the village on an errand for Mrs Habiston. She'd encountered a little girl sitting in a doorway struggling to read a word, her dirty cheeks streaked with tears. Unable to stop herself, she had helped the girl to sound out the word. Before she knew it, the girl was rushing for her story book and demanding more help. Gradually a number of children congregated around the doorway, drawn to her like moths to a flame. Some of the parents eventually approached her, asked if she'd be interested in teaching the children part-time. For some reason, she had accepted…

"Good," he said simply, stuffing the final corner of bread into his mouth.

"You have an idea?" she prompted, hope creeping into her voice.

He swallowed the bread, glanced over at her anxious face. "Perhaps," he answered mysteriously, a wicked glint in his eye. He promptly turned his attention to Sarah, quizzed her on her plans for the day. She tore her sympathetic gaze away from Mel's expectant face, vaguely answered the question. Mel let the conversation drone on around her, struggling to contain her impatience. Trust Raphael to hold her in suspense, she thought bitterly. He had a knack for pushing her buttons, and then calmly walking away when she was about to explode, but at the same time doubting her stance. Studiously ignoring his smug, confident face, she finished her breakfast in gloomy silence.

She hastily excused herself and took her bowl and mug to the kitchen. Exchanging pained looks with Mrs Habiston and Jane, she deposited the dirty crockery on the table. Wendy turned her head and gave her the evil eye, her hands slowly scrubbing a plate in the water. With a garbled, hurried "good morning" she quickly exited the kitchen and made her way to the library. It was one of the few safe places for her these days. Going outside generally involved evading Simon, who was somehow capable of detecting her movement the moment she set foot out the door. The kitchen was a painful place to be even when Wendy wasn't there, as Mrs Habiston and Jane walked the precarious tightrope between divided loyalties. The weapon training room was a place of physical torture, and the ballroom too cold and lonely. Even venturing to the lookout for some peace and quiet was fraught with danger, as Simon's keen eyes would invariably pick her out, resulting in an embarrassing exchange of bellowed greetings. She grimaced at the memory of her last foray to the lookout as she sat down at the table. As luck would have it, Wendy was out in the yard at the time, glowering up at her as Simon cheerfully yelled out to her.

Apart from her own room, the library was a book-filled sanctuary. For some reason, it seemed to be off-limits to the rest of the household except for Raphael, Sarah and herself. Odd how she had been afforded the privilege of using the library whenever she wanted, when she was still relatively new to the manor. Even now after almost three months of living within its stern, grey walls, she felt like an interloper at times. Firmly pushing these negative thoughts aside, she reached for her note book and began working on a lesson plan. "Maths," she murmured to the crowded shelves, a wicked grin tugging at the corners of her mouth. The kids were going to love it.

"Red wine, Mel?"
She looked up from pushing a piece of roast beef around her plate to find Raphael watching her, a bottle of wine held expectantly in his hand. The slight emphasis he placed on "red" didn't escape her. It was the secret signal they had arranged earlier that day. "Yes please," she replied demurely, pushing her glass towards him, effectively committing herself to his plan. He carefully topped up her glass, his eyes briefly meeting hers in the candlelight.

"Can I have some more, Father?" Sarah asked hopefully, lifting her empty glass.

"No," he said flatly, sitting back in his chair and replenishing his own glass.

"Not fair," the red-haired girl grumbled, setting her glass back on the table. "I never get to have any fun."

"That's not true," he argued, wagging a finger at her sulky face. "We went for a ride today."

"Which reminds me," the girl said with a start, "where did you go afterwards Father?"

"What do you mean?" he asked gruffly, sipping his wine.

"I saw you ride off again shortly after we returned," she disclosed archly, her eyes narrowing suspiciously.

"Oh that," he said offhand, cutting a portion of meat and enthusiastically putting it in his mouth. After a few moments of chewing, he answered. "I had to go and get some nails from the village. There are a few loose boards in the stable that need fixing."

"Really? You went by yourself?"

"I did," he answered truthfully. He had decided to kill two birds with the one stone, and visit Mel on the way back from the village. Standing at the back of the old shack, he had been able to catch her in action for the first time. The look on her face when she finally turned away from the make-shift blackboard had been priceless. Hastily setting an exercise for the children, she had ushered him out of the classroom, only too aware of the curious little faces that followed them to the door.

"No one came out with a pitchfork?" Sarah pressed, bringing him back to the present. Mel glanced up from sipping her wine, watched the exchange with interest. She was aware that the locals generally distrusted Raphael and his young ward, believing them to be cursed. There was some incident when they first moved into the manor, involving a young local woman they hired. The woman went berserk one day while cleaning and ran from the manor babbling incoherently. She eventually took her own life, but not before she told everyone in the area that the master of the manor was an evil sorcerer, and his ward a red-haired witch. According to Sarah, the woman hadn't been the most stable of mind when she started to work for them. When she'd asked what could have thrown the woman off the deep end, Sarah had shrugged her slender shoulders unconcern-edly. "Who knows? Maybe she saw something while she was cleaning, an apocalyptic vision made by the dancing dust." The flippant reply had seemed a little too well rehearsed to her puzzled ears.

"Well, thanks to Mel here, and her deal with the locals," he said warmly, waving his glass in her direction, "we're no longer the evil cursed ones of the manor." He paused, took a sip of wine. "We're just strange. Apart from making the sign of the cross when he thought I wasn't looking, the blacksmith sold me the nails without any unpleasantness." He gazed at her over the rim of his glass, a faint smile tugging at the corners of his well-shaped mouth. "That wasn't possible before you came," he told her solemnly. "I was always forced to send one of the workers on such errands," he admitted sourly, taking another sip of wine. She shifted uncomfortably in her seat, not enjoying all the praise and attention being heaped upon her. "Um, it was nothing really. I just happened to be at the right place, at the right time," she mumbled, referring to how she landed the teaching job.

"Oh please, don't be so modest," he rumbled, topping up their glasses. "I propose a toast," he announced, setting down the bottle.

"To Mel," he said seriously, raising his glass, "I don't know how we got by without her."

"Here here," Sarah chimed in, lifting her glass.

"Ah, thanks," she mumbled as they waited expectantly for her to respond.

"To Mel," he repeated, promptly draining the contents of his glass.

After dinner, Raphael suggested that they play poker in the library, to Sarah's delight. While Sarah raced to her room to fetch the cards, he pulled her aside, glancing around to make sure they were alone. "Here's the plan," he said soberly, despite the strong smell of wine on his breath. "After losing a couple of hands to the card shark from hell, I'll excuse myself and go to the stables. It won't take her long to clean you out," he whispered conspiratorially, guiding her towards the table. "Then you come down to the stables, we keep an ear out for the lads, get caught in the act, and hey presto, problem solved. More wine?" he added as he opened a fresh bottle.

"Sure, why not?" she muttered, not sharing his confidence in the plan. "I don't know if I can pull this off, I'm not much of an actor," she admitted shyly, admiring his graceful movements as he poured the wine.

"All the more reason to drink up," he suggested cheerfully, handing her a full glass. Pursing her lips thoughtfully, she accepted the drink.

"I just hope this works," she sighed, sipping the dark red shiraz. "Everything was going swimmingly before this Simon situation developed. I'd hate to have to leave."

"Have faith Mel," he murmured, moving closer to her. "I want this to work as much as you do." She gazed up at him, surprised by the sincerity in his voice.

"Sorry I took so long," Sarah declared stridently as she entered the room, making them both jump and move apart.

"Stacking the deck were we?" Raphael drawled with a grin, pulling out a chair. Sarah stuck her tongue out at him as she settled down at the table and began shuffling the deck.

"There's no need Father," she stated calmly as she split the pile and smoothly ran her thumbs past the corners, causing the halves to overlap perfectly. She pushed the interspersed cards neatly together and started to deal. "Regardless of what some people think, it's mostly skill." Mel and Raphael exchanged rueful looks, hunkered down for a battering.

She made her way across the yard, her feet slightly clumsy. After several disappointing hands, she had made her excuses to Sarah, and quietly slipped out of the house. At least the wine softened the blow this time around. If only she could drink something alcoholic whenever they played cards, she wouldn't feel so decimated by the girl's ruthless style. "You're just not bloodthirsty enough, Mel," she muttered, straining to make out the outline of the stables against the dark grey sky, the sliver of moon affording little light. As she neared the large rectangular building, she could just make out the faint glow of a lantern seeping out through the high-set window. The chill, fresh air cleared her head a little as she stumbled towards the entrance. Raphael had been over-enthusiastic topping up her glass, she decided as she waited for the edge of the doorway to stop moving. As an afterthought she glanced over her shoulder at the manor, half expecting to see Sarah's head silhouetted in one of the windows. The girl had paused in mid-gloat to eye her suspiciously as she yawned pointedly and declared she was going to bed. Sighing with relief at the absence of any obvious onlookers, she groped her way past the bales of hay stacked against the wall.

"Hello?" she called out hesitantly, peering into the dimly lit space. As her eyes adjusted to the light, she recognised Raphael's head bent over a book, his legs stretched out along the bench. He looked up from where he slouched against the wall. "I was starting to think you had backed out of the plan," he commented, returning his attention to the book.

"Who, me?" she squeaked, stepping nervously past the stalls. "No, I just had trouble getting away from Sarah," she said truthfully, peeking enviously at the horses sleeping so peacefully in their compartments, the smell of fresh hay hitting her nostrils. He obligingly shifted his legs so she could join him on the bench, his eyes still glued to the page.

"So," she drawled, rubbing her hands together, "we just wait here then," she confirmed.

"Yes," he

"How do we know when they've come back?"

"Don't worry, we'll hear them. They don't exactly creep quietly home," he assured her with a grimace. "We should have enough time to, er, position ourselves," he said delicately, lifting his eyes to hers briefly.

"Right," she murmured, bouncing her thighs anxiously against the wooden bench. It was a good plan, she reassured herself for the umpteenth time. As Raphael had explained when they were a safe distance from the classroom, the problem was that Simon saw her as being available. All they had to do was reverse this impression, by allowing him to catch them "in the act", so to speak. Swallowing nervously, she craned her head around to admire the polished leather tack hanging from pegs above their heads. This must be where John and Simon clean up all the tack she reasoned, noting the table next to the bench laden with rags and bottles of oil. Even before the uncomfortable situation with Simon arose, she had managed to stay largely away from the stables. She somehow doubted she had spent much time with horses in her previous life, unable to share Sarah's enthusiasm. Casting a baleful eye at Moonbeam's stall, she restlessly stood up and started to pace back and forth.

"Will you stop that? It's very distracting," he grumbled, lowering his book in frustration.

"I'm sorry, but I'm a little nervous," she cried, crossing her arms defensively over her chest.

"Well, you should have brought a book with you," he retorted with a shrug of his shoulders, pointedly returning his attention to the book.

"How can you be so casual about this?" she demanded, leaning back against the wall.

"It's no big deal Mel, we're not getting married or anything," he murmured distractedly, determined to keep reading. "It's just a kiss, for goodness sake," he grunted to the page.

"But, are you sure about this?" she fretted. "I mean, won't this be bad for your reputation?"

"You have to be linked with someone above Simon's social ranking, otherwise he'll think there's a chance of winning your affection," he stressed, reluctantly looking up from the page. "Come on Mel, we've been over this already," he added.

"Damn," she swore as she resumed pacing. He was right of course. Simon wouldn't be deterred by mere rumours. He would have to see the evidence with his own eyes, and that meant staging a performance where he was most likely to "catch" them in the act. "I just wish I had more time to prepare," she muttered. "It's been a long time since I've had that kind of contact," she admitted, feeling her cheeks burn with embarrassment. Every fortnight, John and Simon borrowed a couple of horses and went on a pub crawl, invariably returning in the middle of the night singing raucous songs and telling tall tales of that night's misadventures. Tonight they were in for a surprise, if she didn't completely lose her nerve and run screaming from the stables.

"Well, we could postpone it for another two weeks, but I thought you'd prefer to resolve this situation as soon as possible," he offered, putting down his book with a look of resignation. "It's been a while for me too," he confessed, getting up stiffly from the bench. "Perhaps we should practice, seeing as we both appear to be rusty," he suggested smoothly, taking a measured step towards her.

"Ah, I'm sure it'll be fine," she croaked past the sudden lump in her throat, bumping against the door of Moonbeam's stall. "Just talk to me about something."

"What do you want to talk about?" he demanded crossly, resting his hand on the beam supporting the door.

"I don't know, tell me about your life as a noble," she suggested carefully, shifting awkwardly under his intense gaze.

"What?" he asked, his body stiffening. "Why do you want to know about that?" he pressed, his face darkening as he loomed over her.

"I'm just curious," she answered defensively, shrinking back. "I've been here for nearly three months, and I hardly know anything about you." He grunted, his arm falling heavily by his side.

"I don't really like to talk about it," he muttered darkly, moving moodily to the bench. "It's not exactly a happy story," he added, idly fingering a piece of leather tack hanging from the wall.

"I guess you must miss your family..."

"Are you kidding?" he interjected vehemently, turning away from the wall. "I barely knew my family," he told her flatly, "and the one person I was close to betrayed me." She hastily looked away, her cheeks reddening.

"I'm sorry," she mumbled, wandering over to the table. "It's none of my business."

He noted the tension between her shoulders, mentally kicked himself for being so prickly. Sighing, he lowered himself onto the bench. "Take a seat Mel," he ordered, patting the bench, "and I'll tell you about my glorious upbringing." Eying him warily, she settled down beside him, hands folded neatly in her lap. "As you know, I was born into a family of high social standing. My father was a noble in the French court, dividing his time between the royal court in Paris and the estate in Rouen. I was quite the precocious, pampered brat," he explained with a wry grin, slowly warming to his subject. "I'd spend my days running through the vineyard, exploring the forests around the castle, or burying my head in a book. It was a good life," he sighed, his eyes staring into the distance.

"Then at the tender age of eight I was sent away to live with my aunt and uncle in London," he recounted bitterly. "But at least I didn't go alone. My brother Sebastian was sent away too."

"That's horrible," she breathed, imagining how hard that must have been. "Why did they send you away?"

He shrugged his shoulders, leant his head against the wall. "They said at the time it was to keep us safe from the French revolution. Truthfully, I think we were too much of a handful for mother," he grinned, stretching his legs out before him. "I imagine many noble families were able to offload unwanted children during the revolution."

"And your aunt and uncle didn't mind?" she prompted, her eyes wide with curiosity. His eyes fixed on the far wall, he slowly shook his head.

"No, they didn't mind. My parents paid them a handsome allowance for our upbringing. We saw most of it, I think, even though my uncle was known to gamble a little too heavily when playing poker." Noticing the way she started to rub her bare arms, he casually draped his arm over her shoulders.

"It's okay," she protested, stiffening under his arm.

"Don't be silly," he chided, squeezing her shoulder, his fingers brushing the bare skin beyond the short sleeve. "Your skin feels so cold. Why didn't you bring a coat?"

"I was warm enough from the wine," she confessed, cheeks reddening as her treacherous body pressed against his. "So, your aunt and uncle were good guardians?" she asked, trying to ignore the effect his proximity was having on her.

"They were...adequate. What Uncle Bruce lacked in care and guidance, Aunt Sophie more than made up for." She watched as he reminisced, his face softening.

"You see, Aunt Sophie had lost her only child to disease a couple of years beforehand, so she was only too happy to care for her sister's excess children. I got over the change fast enough, but Sebastian resented it. Being a couple of years older than me, I guess it was harder for him to adjust."

"So you didn't see much of your family?" she guessed, feeling the tension leave her body as alcohol and fatigue combined.

"Not for years. I must have been about thirteen the first time we returned to the family home. It was awful, we both felt like outsiders. It then became a yearly ritual for us to spend the summer in Rouen. I guess we were less troublesome by then," he grunted. "But enough of me, what about you?" he asked suddenly, shifting the subject. "Tell me something about yourself." She stiffened under his arm. "What about your brother?" he added recklessly. "You're supposedly searching for this man, and yet you never talk about him."

She abruptly shrugged off his arm and stood up. "There's not much to tell," she mumbled, walking stiffly to the table. Keeping her back to him, she picked up a bottle and studied the label in the pale lantern light, her hand trembling slightly.

"Oh come on, there must be something you can say about him, being your only relative and all," he urged, feeling something deep inside him start to break.

"Just let it go," she growled, her hand tightening on the bottle.

"Fair's fair," Raphael persisted, getting up from the bench. "Hell I don't even know the man's name..."

"That makes two of us," she snapped, spinning around to face him, the bottle slamming into the table. He tore his eyes away from her glaring face to notice with a start the blood oozing out her hand. Muttering something in French, he strode over to the table and pried her hand off the jagged glass. "God Mel, what do you think you're doing? This isn't going to help our cause," he muttered, grabbing a nearby rag and pressing it against her hand. "The lads will be back any minute now..."

"Don't you understand?" she murmured, staring into space, "I don't remember anything about my life."

He stared at her blankly, his jaw dropping. "You don't remember anything?" he asked.

"No," she said hoarsely, finally raising her eyes to his shocked face. "I woke up four months ago in a field with nothing but the tattered clothes on my back."

"Mel, I'm so sorry," he murmured thickly, his throat going dry. She nodded mutely, winced suddenly as he pressed on a particularly tender spot. Without another word, he removed the rag and started to heal her hand. "Why didn't you mention this before?" he asked, rubbing his thumb over the severed flesh.

"The last time I openly talked about it, I almost ended up in prison," she answered bitterly, shuddering at the memory. His eyes widened at the mention of prison, recalling his own close escape from incarceration. "I managed to escape the guards before they could put me in chains. Since then I vowed to be more careful," she said softly, swallowing past the sudden lump in her throat.

In the distance, he heard the men's raucous voices as they entered the yard. Holding her hand in both of his, he drew her close. "It would seem," he said thickly, reaching a hand to her cheek, "that we have more in common than I first thought." She watched in fascination as he lowered his head towards hers, his eyes fixed on her parted lips. She was vaguely aware of a loud noise in the background and slurred male voices cursing as their lips and bodies pressed together. After some more inventive curses, the voices abruptly stopped. Several moments later Raphael pulled away, leaving her flushed and breathless. She belatedly looked round to find Simon and John gaping at them, their horses shifting impatiently behind them.

"Ah," Raphael broke the stunned silence, snaking his arm possessively around her waist, while his other hand grabbed the bloody rag behind his back. "Did you have a good night out, lads?" he asked casually, as though nothing out of the ordinary was going on, subtly shoving the rag into his pocket.

"Yes sir," John answered as soberly as possible. Simon stared silently at her, his ruddy face a mixture of shock and hurt. "We had a good night, didn't we Si?" the older man prompted, nudging him.

"Yes," he croaked, swallowing painfully as his stony-faced gaze flitted over Raphael's smug face. "A good time was had by all," he said in a small voice, his words thick with added meaning.

"Good," Raphael responded briskly, turning to the bench to retrieve his book. "We'll leave you to it then. Goodnight," he bade, taking her arm and guiding her past the men and their horses.

"Goodnight," she added hastily with a final guilty look at Simon as they hurried out of the stables. To her surprise, he kept hold of her arm until they were back inside the manor, his feet navigating the dark yard with ease.

"Well, I think that will do the trick," he commented as he closed the kitchen door behind them.

"Yes, if the devastated look on Simon's face is anything to go by," she said ruefully, wringing her hands together. She hadn't considered how strong his reaction would be.

"Sorry if I got a bit carried away," she added shyly, looking up from her hands. He coughed nervously, raked his hand through his hair.

"Well, I didn't exactly hold back either," he admitted sheepishly, turning to the inner door. "I don't know about you, but I'm exhausted," he abruptly declared, his hand on the handle.

"Yes, it's been a long day," she agreed, following him out of the kitchen.

They silently made their way up the stairs and past the library. "Well, goodnight then," she stammered awkwardly as she came to a stop before her room.

"Good night," he said with a nod as she opened the door. "Wait, Mel," he added, clearing his throat. She stood in the doorway, watching him expectantly. "You're not really looking for your brother, are you? That's what you meant by being more careful," he ventured, resting his hand on the door frame.

"I had to construct a cover story, to explain why I was travelling alone," she answered truthfully. "I could have a family out there somewhere, I don't know. It's like the hand of God picked me up and dumped me in that field," she muttered darkly, suddenly eager to talk about her mysterious entry into this world.

"Well, thanks for confiding in me," he said earnestly, raising his eyes to hers.

"Ah, sure," she mumbled, looking away. "These things have to come out some time, I guess. I keep meaning to tell Sarah, but it's so hard to talk about..."

"I understand," he muttered, struggling within himself not to blurt out the truth. "She won't hear it from me," he assured her belatedly, digging his fingers into the wood.

"Thanks," she sighed with a tired smile. "Well, good night," she added, backing into her room and closing the door.

"Good night," he said softly to the door, forcing himself to move away before he did something rash. "It's too late for that," he told himself sourly as he staggered to his room. Stumbling through the door, he felt the familiar fingers of cold air brush his skin, the faint voices calling from beyond the cold, disused fireplace. He just had to close his eyes, and he could see the many jagged shards sitting innocently on the dusty floor of the concealed room. "What have we done, Sarah?" he uttered darkly to the cluttered room as he pulled off his boots. "That poor woman," he sighed, shedding his clothes and dropping them to the floor, with most of his other clothes. "Shouldn't have kissed her," he finally mumbled as he collapsed onto the bed and passed out, the mirror's disjointed song lulling him to sleep.

Sarah gave the dough an extra hard thump, sending a cloud of flour into the air. Margaret frowned, her calloused hands pausing momentarily over the pot. "What's the matter, Sarah?" the old woman asked, returning her attention to the soup as she gave it a final stir.

"Oh nothing," the girl muttered, pressing hard on the dough with the flat of her hand. "Father's just giving me a hard time about something," she admitted guardedly.

"Oh," she replied weakly, not knowing what to say. She was sorely tempted to joke that it was business as usual then, but managed to hold her tongue. It was a mixed blessing, having young Sarah help out in the kitchen. While she welcomed the extra pair of hands, she had to take care with what she said around the girl, even if she appeared to be trust-worthy. "I'm sure he means well," she offered lamely, getting a tea pot from the draining board.

"Hmph," the girl grunted distractedly as she sprinkled more flour onto the table.

"Are you upset about the Master and Mel?" Margaret asked, her curiosity getting the better of her. It was day two after the stables incident, and they were all still coming to terms with the unexpected development. Poor Simon had looked most upset when relating what he and John had interrupted in the stables. "Lord knows what we would have walked in on if we'd been any later," he'd added gravely, visibly shuddering at the thought. Her imagination running wild, she had patted him sympathetically on the back. Wendy of course had been quick to offer him a shoulder to cry on. Judging by the way they had walked off hand in hand at lunch time, it was more than just a shoulder, she decided with a wicked grin.

"Ha, are you kidding?" the girl laughed, breaking into her brazen thoughts. "It's about time Father had more than one female in his life," she mumbled, lifting her hands out of the dough. "No, it's not that," she murmured, blowing the hair out of her face.

"Then what is it?" Margaret prompted as she spooned tea leaves into the pot.

"It's complicated," the girl answered vaguely.

"Oh," the older woman murmured when Sarah didn't elaborate. "How about a nice, simple cup of tea, then?" she offered, wrapping a thick rag around her hand.

"Yes please," Sarah sighed as she set the dough onto a board and carried it to the window, where hopefully the sun's feeble rays would help it to rise. Margaret carefully lifted the kettle from the stove top and filled the pot. Sarah set out the cups and then gratefully sank into her chair. They both fell silent as they concentrated on the serious business of pouring tea. "So Mrs Habiston," she began, idly stirring sugar into her tea, "what do you think of Mel getting involved with my father?" The older woman eyed her warily over the rim of her cup before taking a sip.

"I really don't know miss," she replied cautiously, lowering the cup to the table. "It's going to take some getting used to, but at least Wendy isn't giving Mel the cold shoulder anymore," she admitted, absent-mindedly brushing crumbs off the table.

"No, I imagine she's very supportive of Mel right now," she murmured.

"Yes, well, no surprises there," the older woman conceded sheepishly, taking another sip of tea.

Sarah had almost finished her tea when she thought she heard Raphael's irate voice outside the kitchen door. Preparing for flight, she hastily drained the rest of her tea and made for the door. With a garbled farewell to Margaret, she yanked the door open and flew out into the corridor, a triumphant grin tugging at the corners of her mouth. "Ha ha," she breathed, hurtling round the corner, only to have the laughter die in her throat as she skid to a halt before Raphael, who stood waiting in the hallway. "How, how do you do that?!" she cried in dismay, her breath ragged.

"A magician never reveals his secrets," he declared sternly, uncrossing his arms. "We need to talk," he stated flatly, taking her arm.

"Yes Father," she croaked as he guided her towards the weapons training room at the end of the hall.

In heavy silence they entered the large rectangular room, Sarah waiting anxiously as he closed the door behind them. He spun away from the door, his face grim. "I take it Mel has told you about her memory loss?" he probed as he strode to the centre of the room.

"Yes," she answered hoarsely, reluctantly moving away from the door. Yesterday morning, after the exciting news had circulated round the manor, she had taken Mel aside to interrogate her about the incident, suspecting it was a ruse. After they had discussed the sordid details, Mel had awkwardly told her the truth about having no memory of her life beyond when she woke up in a field six months ago. The only clue she had was a name on a piece of paper she found in her pocket. Swallowing painfully past the sudden lump in her throat, she had thrown her arms around Mel, as much to hide the guilt in her own face as to offer comfort.

"You know," he murmured, running tired fingers through his hair, "I've clung to the slender hope all this time that we were wrong. You of course recognised her straight away, under all the dirt and grime. I couldn't believe it, didn't want to believe it," he muttered, shaking his head. "I can't deny the truth any longer," he sighed, resting his hands on her shoulders. "We have to tell her Sarah." She stared at his solemn face, swaying slightly as the room began to spin about her.

"No Father," she cried, tears welling in her eyes, "she'll hate me."

"It's not like you knew what you were doing," he reasoned, idly brushing the hair away from her face. "If we explain to her it was an accident, that you just wanted to save her..."

She took a shuddering breath, shaking her head. "She's been through so much Father. I mean, it's a miracle she's survived so long on her own. To think that I'm responsible for all that pain and suffering..."

"All the more reason to tell her the truth," he croaked, staring intently into her eyes.

She dejectedly nodded, knowing deep in her heart he was right. She just didn't know if she could do it. Over and over again she played the events of that fateful day in her mind, seeing herself sneak into the secret chamber in Raphael's room to watch the Mirror. Giggling inanely, she'd settled down in front of the ancient artifact, to watch images of Mel saying goodbye to her family. The strange silver screen showed Mel climbing into a large metal bird, showed the large metal bird climbing into the sky. She was just about to leave the stuffy, dusty space and go for a ride on Moonbeam when one of the wings exploded. Shuddering at the loud sound, she'd froze in front of the screen to watch in horror as the metal bird plummeted towards the ground. What was left of the metal monstrosity careened into a field, bounced violently into the bordering forest. Torn asunder by its passage through the trees, the battered fuselage slid across the dirt floor towards a massive tree. Just before the side of the craft ploughed into the thick trunk, she grabbed the mirror and screamed, every fibre of her being willing Mel to be spared from the final crushing blow. The Mirror had emitted a high-pitched screech of its own, shattering in her hands. The next thing she knew Raphael was crouching beside her in the tiny room, his eyes dark with concern as he treated the many cuts on her body.

"This is all my fault," she murmured hoarsely, staring blankly at the toes of his boots as she hung her head in shame. He tightened his hold on her shoulders, gazed down at the tightly drawn-back hair. "I broke the Mirror, dragged Mel through time,.." She lifted her head to peer at him through a curtain of tears and hair. "I somehow caused you to lose control of the Mirror," she sobbed. Clenching his jaw, he drew her shuddering body close and awkwardly patted her back until the sobs subsided.

"I shouldn't have let you use it as a plaything," he muttered darkly into her hair, feeling the old anger rise within him. "But it made you happy..."

"Father," Sarah croaked, slowly backing out of his embrace, "please, I need more time. This is the hardest thing I've ever had to do..."

"Sarah, the longer we leave this, the harder it's going to be," he said with a hint of desperation in his voice.

"Father, if we tell Mel the truth now, who knows what she'll do?" she cried, her hands clutching at his shirt sleeves. "At least wait until she's properly trained, so that she can defend herself if she chooses to leave. Please Father," she implored, gazing up at him through fresh tears, "I just want a chance to make it up to her." He studied her through narrowed eyes, his brow wrinkled in thought. Finally he sighed, hung his head in defeat.

"All right Sarah," he grunted, lifting troubled eyes to her red, teary face, "you've bought yourself some time. But be warned," he added, wagging a stern finger at her, "I don't know how long I can withhold the truth."

"I know Father," she said meekly, releasing his sleeves to rub the salty water off her cheeks. "You don't like to live with lies and deceit."

"Ha," he laughed bitterly, "that's because I've been forced to live a lie. Now get out of here before I change my mind." She smiled weakly at his growling face and quickly exited the room, feeling his heavy gaze upon her.

As though the hounds of hell were hot on her heels, she raced down the corridor and ducked into the washroom to splash cold water over her face. Once her cheeks returned to their normal colour, she took a steadying breath and nerved herself to leave the room. Maybe she should lie low in her room for a while, she decided, suddenly feeling quite worn out. Just as she was about to clamber up the stairs, Mel emerged from the library, a satchel slung over her shoulder. "Oh, there you are," she said brightly, plodding down the stairs, "I've been looking for you."

"Hello Mel," she croaked, her throat clammy. She nervously pushed her hair back, her other hand gripping the handrail.

"I was going to ask you at breakfast, but you disappeared before I got the chance. Do you want to help me with the class today?" The unexpected question penetrated the fog of guilt and dread that clouded her mind. "What? Why? You've never asked before…"

"Relax petal," she laughed, resting a hand on the girl's tense shoulder. "I just thought you might want to come along, that's all. No particular reason…" Something in her voice suggested otherwise.

"What is it?" Sarah asked, her eyes narrowing suspiciously.

"You'll just have to come with me to find out, won't you?" Mel suggested mysteriously.

"You're going now?" she pressed, her eyes falling on the satchel. "Just let me get my coat," she added hastily when Mel nodded. Muttering under her breath about how much she didn't like surprises, she raced to her room and grabbed her coat. She jogged down the stairs, pushing her arms through the sleeves as she went.

"Let's go then," Mel murmured, a smirk tugging at the corners of her mouth.

"Come on, just tell me what it is," she whined, skipping impatiently at her side as they made their way out of the manor.

"Where's the fun in that?" Mel asked with a straight face. Sarah divided her attention between watching where she was going and gawking at Mel, almost tripping over her own feet several times in the process.

"Aw, what can it be?" Sarah whined as they finally entered the forest.

"Just wait and see," Mel sighed, rolling her eyes.

"Hmph, it's not fair," Sarah grumbled, kicking the dirt in disgust. "I'm still grumpy you didn't let me in on the plan," she added sourly, glancing over her shoulder to make sure no one was around.

"I told you, we needed you to be genuinely surprised by the news," Mel explained, shifting the strap of her satchel.

"Good job," she snorted derisively, blowing the hair out of her face. "I almost dropped my plate when Jane told me the story."

Mel laughed at her growling face, the sound reverberating in the still forest air.

"It's not funny," Sarah cried indignantly.

"Yes it is," Mel said breathlessly. "I can't believe people are falling for this. I just went along with the plan out of desperation."

"Well, it must have been a very convincing kiss," Sarah suggested tartly, giving her a sly look. "According to Jane, John's cheeks went red when he talked about it." Mel blushed at the memory of their bodies pressed tightly together, their lips locked in surprising passion. She coughed self-consciously, striding ahead so Sarah couldn't easily see her cheeks. "It must have been all that red wine," she muttered thickly, studiously ignoring the smirk on Sarah's face as she caught up to her.

"Hmm, that must have been it," Sarah agreed sarcastically.

"We had to make it convincing," Mel protested. "The success of the plan depended on it..."

"Well of course it did Mel," Sarah teased, enjoying the sudden turn of tables. "And I'm sure it was a real chore, having to cuddle up to Raphael like that."

"Hmph," she grunted, walking stiffly ahead.

Eventually the shack came into view, the children's voices already ringing across the clearing. "Sounds like they're all there," Mel noted, wincing at a particularly strident voice cutting through the babble.

"Ah, I'm not sure about this, I'm not very good with kids," Sarah mumbled, her steps slowing.

"Oh no you don't," Mel cried, gripping her shoulder and gently guiding her towards the shack. "You don't want to miss this..."

"No, really Mel, I never really fit in with the other kids when I was living on the street. That's why I got into so much trouble..." Mel opened the door, the general din settling down to a dull roar as she entered the simple building. Sarah reluctantly followed Mel into the room, looking with foreboding at the excited faces. "I'm not even sure...what you're teaching," she croaked, belatedly finishing the sentence as she came face to face with the biggest brown eyes she'd ever seen in her life. Dark curly hair and smooth tanned skin framed the dreamy brown pools, which stared back at her with equal admiration.

"Sarah, this is Daniel. He's just joined our class," Mel explained with a broad grin. The distracted girl dragged her eyes away to give her a dumbfounded look.

"Oh," she breathed, trying to regain her composure.

"Oh, please Miss," Daniel said with a start, reaching out for the satchel.

"Thank you Daniel. If you could hand out the sheets of paper, please." He awkwardly took the bag, nodded shyly to Sarah as he turned towards the main table, almost tripping over his own feet in the process. Sarah watched him lug the heavy bag away, her face still dazed.

"See, wasn't that a nice surprise?" Mel murmured beside her, making her jump.

"He works at the smithy shop, doesn't he?" she asked in a dreamy voice. Mel smirked as the girl's gaze wandered back to the boy passing out work sheets.

"His father is the resident blacksmith. You've seen him before?" she prompted casually as she moved towards the head of the class.

"Ah, once or twice, when I've gone with John or Simon to get Moonbeam shod," she answered vaguely, following Mel to the blackboard.

"Well, that's why I asked you along. Daniel is a bit more advanced than the other kids, so I was hoping you could sit with him and go through this book," she proposed, her head bent over the satchel. "Here," she breathed triumphantly, digging out the book. "Unless of course you still don't want to help out," she added thoughtfully, holding the book away from her outstretched hand.

"No, that's fine Mel," Sarah said hastily, grabbing the book and moving to the table in the far corner. Daniel looked up and smiled at her as she approached, an extra stool already set beside him. Grinning at the girl's eager face as she sat down next to Daniel, Mel turned her attention to the restless class. Raphael wasn't going to be very happy with her of course, playing matchmaker with his young ward. Hopefully she'd be able to convince him that Sarah needs to mix with people her own age. Plenty of time to thrash it out with Raphael later, she decided with a sense of foreboding. Taking a deep breath, she launched into the lesson, firmly pushing aside such thoughts.

"Did you know that Daniel is the blacksmith's son?" Sarah asked excitedly as they made their way back to the manor.

"Ah yeah, I believe I mentioned that," Mel replied with a hint of sarcasm, stepping around a patch of soggy earth.

"He remembered me from the times I've gone with the men to have Moonbeam re-shoed, can you believe that?" the girl ranted, skipping happily beside her.

"No kidding," she murmured. Daniel had shyly asked her about the red-haired girl who lived at the manor, explaining he'd seen her at the smithy shop with a grey dappled mare.

"He even remembers Moonbeam," she sighed dreamily. "He said Moonbeam's one of the most intelligent and spirited horses he's handled." Mel eyed her sceptically as the girl stared off into space, a ridiculous grin on her face. She had no idea Daniel was such a sweet talker. "Spirited" and "intelligent" was one way to describe Moonbeam. She preferred to use words like "haughty" and "difficult".

"Well, you seemed to get on well together," she commented, lifting her skirt to navigate a narrow section of path that was almost overtaken by shrubs. Sarah belatedly followed suit, barely noticing the branches tugging at her dress.

"Yes, but then you knew we would, didn't you Mel?" she asked warmly as they stepped out of the undergrowth, vigorously flinging her arms around her neck and planting a big sloppy kiss on her cheek.

"Er, I had an idea you two might have things in common," she replied with a grimace, wiping her cheek.

"He's sooo dreamy," Sarah sighed to the forest canopy, hugging herself.

"So, does this mean you'll be joining me more often for class?" The starry-eyed girl blinked at the brilliant scraps of blue sky showing through the canopy, turned her attention to Mel.

"Are you kidding?" she asked incredulously. "I'll be tagging along every opportunity I get. Although father might get suspicious..."

"Just say it's a way to reinforce what you've learnt," she pointed out.

"Mel, you're a genius!" the girl exclaimed, thumping her enthusiastically on the shoulder.

"Ow, thanks," she grunted, rubbing her shoulder. "Perhaps you should tone down your excitement before we get to the manor," she cautioned the bouncing girl as the grey slate roof appeared above the tree line.

"Right," she conceded, reluctantly restraining her steps, struggling to turn down the intensity of her smile. "So," she started casually, forcing her hands to stay at her sides, "are you going to mention this to Father?"

"Hmm," Mel breathed thoughtfully, rubbing her chin, "maybe we should play that one by ear. There's no need to worry him about it yet, you're just helping me out with the class."

"Thanks Mel, you're the best," the girl gushed, sounding relieved.

They strode out past the trees, their steps slowing as they spotted Raphael and John talking urgently outside the stables. With a look of foreboding in her eyes, Sarah raced across the yard, Mel following more slowly, the heavy satchel bouncing uncomfortably against her side. "Hmm, we may have to put on more men," Raphael said thoughtfully as she lumbered towards them.

"I never would have thought they'd be so bold as to hit Middleton," John muttered gravely to the ground.

"Yes, the raiders have never gone so far inland before...Don't you have family in Middleton, Mr Morley?" he asked sharply.

"Yes sir," the distraught man croaked, shuffling his feet.

"What's wrong Father?" she asked breathlessly, coming to a stop beside him.

"What have I told you about running across the yard like that?" he snapped irritably, spinning towards her.

"I'm sorry Father," she panted, "but you both looked so serious, I couldn't help but be concerned." He glowered at her briefly, annoyed as ever by her ability to combat his overbearing manner with reason.

"We just received word that raiders hit Middleton two days ago," he stiffly informed her, swallowing back his irritation.

"What?" she cried, glancing at John's sombre face. "They don't normally go beyond coastal towns," she protested.

"Raiders?" Mel echoed as she finally joined the party.

"That why we have to take this seriously," Raphael replied solemnly, sparing Mel a sideways glance as he turned back to John. "Mr Morley, pack what you need for a quick trip home. You mentioned some of your brothers are looking for work..."

"Yes sir," he stammered, hope creeping into his voice. "My four younger brothers, Mr Blythe. They're good lads, and handy in a fight..."

"I'll have to take your word on that," he said reluctantly, seeing his options dwindle before him. "Bring them back with you, if they are willing."

"Yes sir," the older man said hoarsely, nodding his gratitude, "I'll start making the preparations." With a final, awkward bow, he quickly took his leave, heading for the kitchen door.

"Goodness, this is serious," Sarah murmured, clearing her suddenly clammy throat.

"There's too much fighting going on abroad," he explained with a sigh. "There are always people ready to take advantage of a bad situation," he muttered bitterly as they made their way to the main entrance.

"So I take it these raiders are bad news," Mel said anxiously, struggling to keep up with his long strides.

"They're ruthless, cold-blooded killers who make a habit of setting the towns they raid on fire," he informed her bluntly, holding the door open for them. "We'll have to start a rotating watch duty," he mused as he followed them into the manor. "And we'll have to step up your weapon training Sarah," he decided, his eyes flicking to Mel's shuffling steps, the satchel sliding slowly off her shoulder. "You too Mel," he added as she wrestled with the strap.

"What?" she cried, stopping in her tracks.

"What's wrong Mel?" he asked, overtaking her.

"Ugh, I'm already a mass of bruises," she groaned.

"It's true," Sarah volunteered helpfully, grinning over her shoulder. "She's been making excellent progress."

"Great," he rumbled as he started up the stairs, Sarah close behind him. "See you in the training room in fifteen minutes."

"What?" she cried, staring up at his back in dismay. "I can't train with you, I'm not ready," she whined, jogging to catch up with him.

"Oh, you're ready," he told her calmly, noting with satisfaction the sheen of sweat that had suddenly broken out on her brow.

"No I'm not," she panted, "Sarah beats me to within an inch of my life each training session..."

"Ha ha, very funny Mel," Sarah snorted, opening the door of her room.

"See you in fourteen minutes," Raphael declared, disappearing into his own room. She swallowed nervously at the sound of Sarah's door closing, looked about the deserted corridor.

"Aww nuts," she cursed, her sweaty hands fumbling with the door handle. "I'll be a smear on the wall by the end," she muttered, stumbling into the room and dropping the satchel on the floor.

She'd never trained with Raphael before. She barely managed to fend off Sarah's furious blows, she thought with a grimace. In a mad flurry she dug out a pair of leggings and a loose cotton shirt. Wrinkling her nose at the musty smell, she hastily changed and tidied her hair, pulling it into a tight ponytail. After a quick knock on Sarah's door, she hurried down the stairs, assuming the girl was already there. "That was fast," she muttered as she raced down the hallway, to burst noisily into the training room. Raphael turned around sharply at the sound of her entrance, frowning as she stood in the doorway catching her breath.

"You know," he drawled, turning back calmly to the rack, "for a moment there I mistook you for a herd of elephants."

"Ha ha," she panted, closing the door behind her. "Where's Sarah?" she asked belatedly as she walked gingerly to the weapons rack, hand pressed against the stitch in her side.

"She said she had too much homework to do," he answered distractedly, picking up a weapon and squinting along the blade.

"Homework?! Hey, that's not fair, I've got stuff to do as well..."

"You need more practice than she does," Raphael informed her bluntly, experimentally swinging the sword. Her eyes widened in alarm as she realised he intended to use a real weapon.

"Ah, Sarah and I have been using sticks," she pointed out, her throat going dry.

"I assure you the raiders won't be so considerate. You must start learning how to handle the real thing," he insisted mercilessly, unmoved by the blanching of her face.

"Right," she grunted, pulling on a battered leather vest, "be sure to have that engraved on my tombstone."

"If you insist," he murmured, gracefully slicing the air as she twisted around and tightened the leather thong dangling against her hip, pulling the two sides together. "When you're ready," he said pointedly from the centre of the practice area, "pick out a weapon, and we can perhaps start training within the next hour." Noting the growing impatience in his voice, she hastily pulled on the leather gloves and selected a sturdy-looking sword.

She half-heartedly swung the sword back and forth as she slowly approached the middle of the room, the hilt slipping in her nervous grip. "Ready?" he asked, getting into position. At her slight nod, he swung his sword at her in a tightly controlled arc. She felt so clumsy and lumbering in comparison, fending off the blows with crude strokes of the well-used blade. He moved lightly back and forth, side to side, his feet always well-placed, while she stumbled and lurched about, struggling to recover in time from each blow.

"Come on Mel, try to hit me. You can't just defend all the time, you have to be offensive," he hissed as his blade darted out and tapped her on the ribs. She gasped at the sharp pain, felt anger rise within her. Gritting her teeth, she lashed out with her weapon, swinging aggressively at his smug, controlled face. The self-assured mask slipped briefly, his eyes widening in surprise as he suddenly had to work a little harder to fend her off.

"Good, use your anger," he grunted, stepping up the pace of his strokes. He punctuated his advice with a firm tap to her thigh, causing her to hobble painfully back.

"Ow, you pompous, arrogant son-of-a-bitch!" she shouted ferociously, launching herself at him, her sword aimed at his torso. He easily side-stepped her attack and followed through with a tap on her hip.

"But don't lose control of yourself," he warned, casually resuming his stance. Swearing profusely, she leant over and pressed where the flat of his blade had found her hip. "That's not what I meant when I said you had to be more offensive," he clucked, shaking his head in dismay. She looked up at him, pure hatred burning in her eyes. Snarling deep in her throat, she hobbled back into position, her face set in a grim, determined mask.

"Perhaps we should take a break," he suggested, frowning at her painful gait.

"No," she said hoarsely, shakily raising her sword, "I have to learn how to fight. I don't want to be weak and defenceless." He stared at her for a moment, then simply nodded, his eyes full of approval.

They practised and sparred until every muscle in her body ached and she could barely hold up her sword. Every attempt made to break through Raphael's defences was effortlessly deflected, the room blurring around her until all she could see were their blades dancing and clanging together. She caught glimpses of his cool, impassive face in the background between strokes. He had hardly broken into a sweat, while she was uncomfortably aware of the sweat trickling down her brow and neck. His calm voice grated against her nerves as he pointed out weaknesses in her form throughout.

"Don't reach out so much with your sword, it leaves you vulnerable."

"Watch your footwork woman, you're about to trip over your own feet."

"Tighter arcs Mel, you're swinging like a drunk sailor."

"Take advantage of the space Mel, there's heaps of room to move about, attack me from different angles."

With that last gem of advice, he circled to her left and struck the sword out of her hand. "Ugh," she cried out, clasping her hand as the sword clanged loudly against the floor.

"Are you alright?" he asked, setting his sword down.

"Ow, there's a bloody splinter in my hand, went right through the glove," she explained gruffly, gingerly easing the glove off.

"Let me see that," Raphael ordered, reaching for her hand.

"Get away from me," she sulked, holding the hand protectively to her chest.

"Don't be silly," he chided, stripping off his gloves.

"No, it's fine," she hissed, wincing as she bumped the splinter. While she was busy moaning, he grabbed her hand and took a close look. "Ow, stop that," she protested, shooting him a venomous look as he held her hand firmly, steadily ignoring her attempts to snatch it back.

"Hmm," he murmured as he spotted the long sliver of metal embedded in the fleshy mound of her hand. "Stop pulling, or this will really hurt," he told her bluntly, his eyes glued to the splinter as he closed his fingernails over the short protruding end. She reluctantly obeyed, willing herself not to pull away as he gripped the end firmly and yanked.

"Ouch," she cried, flinching as the metal was torn out of her flesh. "Thanks," she muttered, moving to reclaim her hand. He continued to hold her hand, studying the bleeding hole left in her palm.

"You have worker's hands," he stated critically, shaking his head as his eyes moved over the rough, chapped skin.

"Alright, that's enough," she protested softly, half-heartedly pulling her hand back.

"Not the hands of a lady," he continued undeterred, turning the hand over. "All these little scars and nicks," he breathed distractedly as his fingers traced the fine network of lines.

"I like to be useful," she said defiantly past the sudden lump in her throat, willing her hand to stop trembling in his grasp.

"Useful," he repeated thoughtfully as he reached for her other hand. "There's no need for you to be this useful, Mel," he told her sternly, raising his eyes to hers. Without another word, he ran his fingers over the rough skin, extending his energy into the cuts and abrasions. Her breath caught noisily in her throat as the skin tingled warmly under his fingers. Finally he rubbed his thumb over the tear in her flesh, filling the stinging hole with energy.

"Wow," she whispered, watching in awe as the skin grew back before her eyes. "That's incredible," she breathed, cautiously probing the shiny pink flesh as he released her hands. "I wish I could be a healer like you," she added wistfully, glancing up at him shyly. Clenching his jaw, he swooped down to collect his sword and gloves.

"It's a limited ability," he pointed out stiffly as he moved to the rack. "I only encourage the healing process, the body still does the hard work." His words sounded overly bitter to his ears as he grabbed the nearby stone and rubbed it against the blade, frowning at the new nicks marring the edge.

"Has that ever not been enough?" she asked, forcing her tired limbs to move and fetch the neglected sword and gloves. His hand slowed over the battered steel, his fingers tightening around the stone. Uncle Bruce used to say, the best way to tell a lie was to make it as close to the truth as possible. In explaining the origin of his healing ability, he had practically told her the truth, with a few minor alterations. She had accepted his story with only a faint clouding of the eyes, a vague shrug. "Sounds like you got more than you bargained for with this archaeology business," she had concluded, touching the faded bruise at the base of her shoulder. "That must have been some artifact you cut yourself on. Shame it was destroyed." He had mumbled something in agreement, thinking of the strange, shattered glass gathering dust behind his fireplace.

With a start he returned to the present, the stone almost falling from his listless fingers. "You really didn't have to heal my hands," Mel was saying awkwardly, returning her weapon to the rack.

"I like to fix things," he murmured with a shrug, hanging his sword between the long pegs, the base of the hilt nestled against the rounded wood. "Speaking of which, how are things in the kitchen now?"

"The kitchen?" she echoed as she untied the knot at her side, "oh, fine. At least Wendy isn't likely to poison my food anytime soon." He watched the loose material of her shirt rise up as she pulled the leather vest over her head, his eyes glued to the pale smooth skin of her stomach.

"But there's a problem?" he pressed, meeting her gaze innocently as she finally lowered her arms and looked up, the offending garment held triumphantly in her hand.

"It's worked a little too well," she explained ruefully, stretching up to hang the vest on its usual peg. "Now that I'm linked romantically with you, all the staff are being cautious around me. I guess they're afraid I'll divulge their secrets when we're, you know, together," she said carefully, gesturing expressively with her hands.

"Things will calm down eventually," he assured her, his eyes moving on their own accord to the opening of her shirt as she bent over to pick up a glove. "Although I don't think we're out of the woods yet," he murmured distractedly.

"What?!" she asked sharply, straightening up.

"Simon and Wendy still aren't completely back together," he informed her gravely, averting his eyes. "I overheard Simon and John talking in the stables...It sounds as though he's beginning to suspect it was a one-off fling."

"Are you serious? He's barely looked at me since that night, except to glare at me from the shadows," she stammered incredulously.

"I guess he's had time to cool down and think rationally," he offered casually, moving away from the wall. "Look, we just have to maintain the illusion that you're not available for a little longer, until Wendy works her magic." Her eyes narrowed suspiciously as she turned to face him.

"How do you propose we do that?"

"Nothing drastic, I assure you," he said silkily, running long fingers through his dishevelled hair. "We just have to give the impression we're spending time together. Tell me, do you play chess?" he asked, rubbing his chin thoughtfully.

"Ah sure," she answered hesitantly, surprised by the question. "I'm a little rusty..."

"That's fine," he interjected, heading for the door. "See you at dinner, Mel. I have to make arrangements with Mr Morley."

"Alright," she mumbled to his rapidly disappearing back, wondering what she had gotten herself into this time. Shrugging her stiff shoulders, she slowly limped out of the training room, feeling new pain with each step. Blushing furiously to herself, she wondered idly if Raphael could take away all her physical pain, imagining his hands roaming over her body. "Get a hold of yourself Mel," she muttered derisively, shaking her head in an effort to dispel the arousing images from her mind.

The only thing that was going to help relieve her aches and pains was her messy, unmade bed, she decided with an inward groan as she hobbled to her room.

Raphael rested his elbow on the table and took a long sip of wine, his attention firmly fixed on the board in front of him. Mel watched him anxiously, her face tense with anticipation. She obviously had a big move planned. Did she have any idea how transparent she was? he wondered. The instant she castled her king, he knew something was up. She normally resisted castling, admitting she found it too restrictive. When he queried her about the move, she had looked at him blandly, thrown his own words back at him. "You said I should be more aggressive," she had pointed out, her voice edged with sarcasm.

"Hmph," he had snorted, promptly taking one of her pawns. That had been several moves ago. The board was now sparsely populated, with losses on both sides, although his collection of captured pieces was clearly bigger than hers. Without the slightest flicker of emotion, he finally made his move. A sharp intake of breath answered his move. "Something wrong, Mel?" he asked innocently.

She looked up sharply at him, her mouth pressed into a thin line of displeasure. "Not at all," she replied stiffly, tapping her fingers against the ceramic mug in her hand.

"It's a very interesting strategy you're using here Mel," he drawled with confidence as she hastily took a gulp of ale. "Sacrificing your knights and bishop like that, I'm sure it's all part of some diabolical plan..."

"Ha ha, very funny o mighty chess master," she retaliated sourly to his teasing as she set her mug down, eyes fastened on the board.

"By the way, checkmate in two moves," he informed her casually, leaning back in his chair.

"By the way, checkmate in two moves," she mimicked, pulling a face at him. "No wonder Sarah won't play chess with you, you're a complete monster."

"I think she prefers the simple brutality of poker, especially the way she plays," he murmured into his glass, watching his opponent out of the corner of his eye. Aware of his guarded scrutiny, she smirked and moved her queen two spaces.

"Check," she stated with barely contained excitement. He spluttered noisily, hurriedly leaning forward as droplets of wine sprayed the air.

"Why, you little sneak," he exclaimed, setting his glass on the table. His remaining pawns were too far away to protect the king, and she now had a clear path to eliminate the last pawn in the area without endangering her queen. From there it was checkmate, as she was nicely backed up by a bishop and one lonely pawn that had limped its way across the board.

He studied the board desperately for a way out. All his available pieces required at least one move to be effective against her queen. The only thing he could really do was move his rook into position to take out the queen. Cursing under his breath, he moved his rook in line with her queen.

With a smile as brilliant as the sun, she moved her queen diagonally to stop two spaces in front of his king, removing the pawn with a flourish. "Checkmate," she uttered softly, her eyes checking and rechecking to confirm she was right.

"Argh," he cried in disgust, knocking his king over. She sat absolutely still for a moment before abruptly cheering loudly, thrusting her arms into the air. "Woo," she finally gasped, collapsing back into her chair. "I can't believe I've finally won a game," she gushed, slowly straightening up. "I thought it was all over with that last move of yours, I thought you were on to me," she explained cheerfully, picking up her mug and triumphantly downing the rest of her beer. "Ahh," she breathed, setting down the empty mug, wiping the back of her hand over her mouth.

It had become a nightly, after-dinner ritual whereby Raphael ordered Jane to take wine and ale to the library, always ensuring they were there when she arrived. The plan was working beautifully, with Simon apparently abandoning all hope of her becoming "unattached" any time soon, if Wendy's salacious stories were anything to go by.

"I suppose congratulations are in order," he said grudgingly, extending his hand. She eagerly took it, gave it an enthusiastic shake.

"Thank you," she sighed, a broad grin pasted across her face. "And to think it only took two weeks of intensive playing," she added cheerfully.

"Hmph," he grunted, looking away before he smiled back. "Another game?" he suggested as he started to reset the board. His sour demeanour finally penetrated her euphoric cloud, her eyes narrowing.

"You're not grumpy about losing, are you?" she asked incredulously, leaning forward in her chair.

"No, of course not," he murmured, his head bent over the board.

"Ha," she barked, slumping back into the chair, her mind pleasantly fuzzy from the beer and her chess victory. Watching his shoulders tense up under the dark fabric of his coat, she decided to let it go.

"So, John's brothers have settled in well," she commented casually.

"Yes," he responded distractedly, his head still bent over the board. "The manor is starting to get a bit crowded." She grinned at that. The whole village could move in, and they'd still have plenty of room.

"I think John enjoys having his brothers around to boss about," she mused. Ever since his return, he'd kept the younger men tightly organised. Ted, Peter, Gerald and Cedric seemed happy enough to follow his orders, despite their token grumbling.

"It's a relief to have more men around the place," Raphael murmured grimly. They had received reports of raiders hitting the roads past Middleton, gradually making their way south.

"There's a good chance they'll attack, isn't there?" she asked solemnly. He clenched his jaw, face set in a grim mask as he finally looked up at her.

"Yes," he answered gravely.

"But why?" she asked plaintively. "Why are they going so far inland? Shouldn't there be troops or guards to stop them?"

"Ah Mel," he sighed, eyes staring off into the distance. "You're right of course, but the most influential nobles are busy fighting Napoleon in Europe. The raiders are taking advantage of the fact that troop numbers are down."

"Napoleon?" She stiffened as the name triggered long-buried memories.

"Yes," Raphael said slowly, eying her quizzically. "He's the emperor of France. Thanks to his aggressive leadership, the French empire now extends throughout Central and Western Europe. Word is he and his armies are planning to invade Russia..."

"Don't worry, it won't last," she murmured, staring at the board as more history lessons percolated her fuzzy brain. Another great war over a century later spreading across Europe, spilling out into the world, only this time it's the Germans attempting to invade Russia, eventually forced to retreat in the midst of a harsh Russian winter...

"Mel."

She jumped at the sound of his voice so close to her. "Are you alright?" he asked, leaning over the table to peer at her flushed face.

"Oh," she breathed, lurching slightly as the room spun around her. "I just, remembered things, when you mentioned Napoleon. Things I learnt in school..."

"Learnt in school?" he echoed, his brow furrowed in concern.

She opened her mouth to elaborate when Gerald burst noisily into the room, the sheen of sweat on his brow emphasising his urgency.

"Sorry to disturb you Master Blythe, ma'am, but several buildings have just been set on fire at the village," he gasped, holding his side.

"Damn," Raphael cursed, springing to his feet, "I had hoped for more time...Gerald, rouse the men, tell them to get their battle gear and meet me outside the stables."

"Yes sir," he responded hastily and disappeared from the doorway.

"Mel, go and wake up Sarah and the other women. I want you all down in the cellar. You should be safe there, but take your weapon, just in case," he ordered rapidly as he strode purposefully out of the library.

"But we can help you," Mel protested, hastily getting out of the chair. "You'll need all the help you can get fighting the raiders at Burchellton," she panted as she struggled to keep up with him.

"Burchellton?" he questioned sharply, stopping in his tracks. "I'm not going to Burchellton. The men there will just have to do their best. No, we have to bolster our own defences, patrol the forest..."

"But there are women and children down there," she stammered, imagining the sweet, cheeky faces of her students contorted in fear.

"There could be raiders encircling the manor right now," he hissed, grabbing her arm, "and I have only six men at best to fight God-knows-how-many-raiders..."

"We have a little more protection in this huge house than those poor people huddling in their simple homes," she protested, anger building within her. "At least send someone to help..."

"I don't have time to argue about this woman," he snapped, giving her arm a final squeeze before letting go. "Just go and organise the women," he barked over his shoulder, striding down the hall.

She glowered at his back for a second, waves of resentment radiating from her dark, hard eyes. A plan started to form in her mind as she forced herself into action. Sarah emerged blurry eyed and rumpled at her violent pounding of the door. "What is it?" she asked with a yawn.

"Raiders have hit Burchellton," she said without preamble. "Get dressed and grab your weapon, then go down to the cellar. I'll wake up the other women and meet you there."

"Down to the cellar? But I could help them with the fighting..."

"Look, I just had this argument with your father. If you want to convince him, be my guest," she informed her, frustration creeping into her voice.

"Alright," the girl muttered, retreating into her room to hurriedly change, well imagining how that conversation might have gone.

"See you there," Mel shouted through the door before tearing down the stairs to the servant quarters next to the kitchen. Odd, she thought as she skidded to a noisy halt in the narrow passageway behind the dining room, she'd never been to the servant quarters before. Amid grumbles about the wisdom of making them hide in the cellar, the women made their way to the pantry, where the trapdoor to the cellar resided.

"Margaret," she said in a lowered voice, touching the woman's arm as she slowly started to follow the younger women. "I have to go and do something, I'll join you all later..."

"Don't be doin' anything rash, young miss," the older woman cautioned sternly, catching her off-guard.

"What do you mean?" she asked defensively.

"Come on Mel, you're like a sheet of glass. I can see it in your eyes you want to fight," Margaret informed her with a knowing nod.

"I am not going to fight," she denied hotly, her cheeks reddening with indignation.

"Just don't get yourself hurt. The master would be mighty cranky," she overrode her denial with annoying self-assurance.

"He'd get over it," she muttered, leaving the woman before she could dispense any more pearls of wisdom.

She ran into Sarah on her way to the armoury. "Where are you going?" the girl shouted as she hurried past, her sword glinting dangerously in her hand.

"I forgot to grab a weapon," she shouted back. "I'll see you there," she added. Sarah moved as if to join her, changed her mind as she sped down the hall.

"Just don't take too long!" she yelled back. With a wave of acknowledgment, she entered the training room, wishing she could involve Sarah in her plan. The girl could certainly handle a sword she mused, remembering with a shudder the dead bodies that had littered the forest floor on the fateful day of their first meeting. "No," she mumbled, shaking her head. Raphael would never forgive her if anything happened to his precious ward. She wasn't sure which would be worse, facing a band of savage bandits or facing one angry Raphael. Grinning weakly to herself, she grabbed a scabbard and strapped it around her waist. A quick scan of the pegs above the weapon rack revealed one remaining leather vest. It had been left behind for a reason, she decided as she pulled it on, the leather worn through in several places. With a sigh of resignation, she tucked a dagger into the top of the scabbard and cautiously left the room. As she snuck up the hall towards the main entrance, the men's voices rang out from the yard, where Raphael was already busy shouting out orders.

"Damn," she swore, stopping in her tracks. She couldn't get out that way, and the women were probably still clambering down into the cellar. "Of course," she cried softly, making her way to the ballroom. It'd be a bit of a drop, but if she could hang from the bottom of the balcony, she should be able to fall to the ground without breaking her leg. With that cheery thought in mind, she entered the grand room, her boots clicking loudly against the hard floor, despite her careful foot placement. Finally she made it to the doors, opening them with a nerve-jarring creak. She stood tensely in the doorway for a few moments, her heart hammering wildly in her chest as someone stirred above. The flickering light of a flame torch danced over the ground beyond the balcony, followed by a disgruntled grunt and silence. Just as she gave up hope of clambering over the balustrade without arousing suspicion, another voice could be heard overhead. Simon had come to relieve Gerald on the lookout platform. While they exchanged notes, she quickly lowered herself over the side, to hang from the bottom. "It's now or never," she whispered to her trembling arms as the men finished their discussion. Biting her lip, she let go.

"Did you hear something?" she faintly heard Simon ask at the sound of her fall.

"What?" Gerald responded slowly. There was a moment of silence as Simon strained to pick out the noise. "It must have been one of the cats," he finally said.

Surprised that they couldn't hear her pained breathing, she gingerly got up and crept to the corner of the building. Peering round the stone wall, she saw that the yard was momentarily deserted, the men obviously out on patrol. Taking a deep breath, she limped across the yard to the stables. Feeling light-headed from the fall and the nerve-racking race across the yard, she giggled as she entered the stable. She didn't think she'd make it this far. Her triumphant giggles died in her throat when she gazed at the stalls and registered the lack of horses. She hadn't counted on that. It made sense of course for the men to be on horseback. The only horse left was an old mare called Plodder. She had ridden Plodder a few times at Sarah's insistence, the stubborn old thing refusing to go above the speed of, well, plodding. Normally she didn't mind, but tonight was different.

She hastily heaved a saddle onto the dozing horse's back and tightened the straps. "Plodder," she whispered gravely, drawing the bridle over the horse's head and doing up the buckles. "I know that after so many years of faithful service, you deserve to rest, but just this one night, I need you to run like the wind, old girl." As she stared into the huge brown eyes, she imagined something flickered in those dark orbs, almost as though the mare understood. Grabbing a riding crop off the wall, she eased the mare out of the stall and climbed up into the saddle.

Flicking the reins, she guided the mare out into the yard. "Come on Plodder, ride like the wind," she urged in a low voice, conscious of the torch moving overheard. Wincing in anticipation, she dug her heels into the horse's smooth brown flanks. Plodder whinnied and moved off at a pedestrian pace. "Oh, you stubborn horse," she cried, bringing the riding crop down hard on the mare's rump. She almost fell off as Plodder reared up on two legs and tore off through the trees, Simon's voice briefly following them into the forest before fading away. It was only then, as she grimly clung to Plodder's back, that she recalled John saying something about never using a crop on Plodder. Hunkering down in the saddle, she managed to steer the galloping mare in the general direction of the village. The smell of smoke met their nostrils as a warm orange glow appeared through the trees. She would have carefully come to a stop and dismounted, but Plodder ignored her urgent tugging of the reins, recklessly racing past the trees and into the open. The devastated village stretched before them, fire and smoke steadily engulfing the pathetic collection of buildings. Women and children ran out onto the dirt track bisecting the settlement, escaping the fire only to run into the raiders as they moved from house to house. The men, armed with crude, makeshift weapons, were fighting off the raiders as best they could, with the bodies of locals and raiders alike littering the ground. Despite their heroic efforts, the men were still outnumbered, their haggard faces set in grim determination as they pushed their exhausted bodies on.

Straying too close to the flames, Plodder suddenly panicked and reared. This time she wasn't so lucky, and tumbled off the horse's back. She rolled away from the mare's nervous feet, getting up in time to stare helplessly as Plodder ran off into the forest. Groping clumsily for her sword, she staggered down the broad dirt track, not knowing what to do. Her bleary eyes fell upon a raider holding an ugly weapon aloft, ready to deliver the final crushing blow to an injured man kneeling helplessly on the ground. With sweaty, anxious hands, she drew her sword and ran towards the raider, the point of her blade finding its way into his unsuspecting back. The ugly spiked club fell from his hands, and he slowly stumbled around to see his attacker, his eyes wide with shock as he fell forward onto his face. Neville the blacksmith looked up from the slumped, twitching body, gave her a grateful smile as he staggered to his feet. "Thanks Mel," he gasped, holding his side.

"Do you want help with that?" she asked, nodding at the patch of blood above his hip.

"No, I have to find Daniel," he hissed, gritting his teeth against the pain.

"I'll help you," she offered, backing away from the spreading pool of blood, the raider's body now completely still.

"You've done enough Mel," he said warmly, briefly gripping her shoulder before limping away.

She moved to follow him when she heard frightened voices to her right. Tightening her grip on her sword, she cautiously tread towards a large gap between two buildings. In the orange glow, she saw four bandits grouped around a woman standing protectively in front of her children. The woman brandished a pitchfork at the jeering men, her arms trembling as they lurched towards her, their weapons drawn. They made a pantomime out of evading her desperate swings, toying with their victim before swooping in for the kill. Running out of patience, the man who appeared to be the ringleader effortlessly knocked the pitchfork out of her hands, swiftly closing the distance between them and wrapping a massive hand around her throat. As the woman frantically clawed at his meaty paw, he tore at her skirt, ordered the men to hold her legs apart. One of the children charged at the bearded brute, only to be flung aside like a rag doll. As the men gathered around the woman's struggling body, she finally found her nerve and sprung into action. "Leave her alone," she screamed behind them, her sword held firmly before her. The men looked around, roughly dropped the woman to focus their attention on her, their lips curled in cruel sneers.

"Ooo, look what we have 'ere then," one dark haired man purred through a long, matted beard, his beady brown eyes travelling lewdly up and down her body.

"A girl with a sword, now that gets me goin'," another joined in, blue eyes gleaming as he made a move for her. Swallowing nervously, she side-stepped his clumsy attack, lashing out with her blade as he stumbled past. He abruptly screamed, collapsing to his knees as blood squirted out of his side. She wouldn't get another easy shot like that, she realised as the remaining three men watched their comrade clutch the hole between his ribs, his breath coming out raggedly. Swearing loudly, the ringleader barked savagely at the other men, rushing to the gasping man's side. They turned stiffly towards her, all traces of humour gone from their faces. She barely had time to draw out her dagger before they rushed at her, the ringleader watching from the sidelines, his face darkening as the man's shuddering breaths stilled.

All her training sessions now culminated into this one moment of truth. She could almost hear Sarah's voice coaching her as she narrowly ducked a wild blow and drove her dagger into the attacker's soft belly. With surprising grace, she lightly stepped out of the way as he pitched forward clutching his stomach, his agonised screams adding another discordant note to the general cacophony. There was an explosion of pain, and she stared down at the blade biting into her side, the dagger falling from her slippery, bloody grip. She staggered backwards as the snarling man brought his sword around for another bite, his eyes glittering dangerously in the amber glow of the still-raging fires. Gritting her teeth, she fended off his furious blows, losing precious ground with each thrust of her sword. Suddenly her feet gave way beneath her as she tripped over a body, her impact with the ground jarring the air out of her lungs. Gasping painfully, she desperately scrambled out the man's path, grabbing a handful of dirt as she struggled to her feet, her sword held weakly at her side. The man quickly regained his balance, shifted his feet in preparation for a final attack. With the last of her strength, she hurled the dirt into the charging man's face, lurching sideways as he stumbled blindly past, her sword swinging wildly into his head. There was a sickening crunch of bone and skin, and the man collapsed unconscious to the ground.

She barely had time to catch her breath when a huge fist connected with her head, knocking her clean off her feet. The world spun around her as she struggled to sit up, the ring leader's beady eyes swimming blurrily above her, a vicious-looking club hovering over his head. "This is it," she thought grimly as the rough, studded wood fell towards her, her heavy limbs refusing to move. Squeezing her eyes shut, she waited for the final blow. There was a horrible squelching sound followed by a startled cry, and the club fell with a dull thud onto the ground beside her. She warily opened her eyes to see blood dribbling out of the ring leader's mouth, his eyes rolling back into his head as he slowly slumped forward. Scrambling hastily away from the bleeding corpse, she looked up to find the woman holding a bloody knife in her hand, her torn skirt swirling round her legs in the gentle night breeze. Her eyes fastened on the dead body at her feet, she absent-mindedly held out a hand to Mel.

"Thank-you, Judy," she grunted, wincing against the pain in her side, finally remembering the woman's name. Judy took a shuddering breath and tore her dark eyes away from the still body.

"Thank-you, Mel," she returned unevenly, squeezing her hand briefly before letting go. The sound of a building collapsing nearby jolted them into action. Rounding up the children, they scurried out of the area, the heat of the spreading fire propelling their steps. Finally they made their way to the lake, where other families were gathering round makeshift bonfires set up on the sandy shore. "Now there's a bit of irony," she mumbled as they joined the others, shakily wiping the blood off her sword before returning it to the scabbard.

Raphael swung his leg over Monty's twitching rump and dismounted. "I'm just going to check on the women," he told John breathlessly as he handed him the reins. John shifted in his saddle, grunted agreement as he wrapped Monty's reins around his free hand, his tired, blood-splattered arms resting against his thighs. Raphael turned away from the battle-weary man, making a mental note to give him a rest as soon as possible. They had encountered two groups of raiders moving stealthily through the trees towards the manor. Some of the men were still out there mopping up the dregs, chasing down the blighters who had turned tail and fled when it became evident it was going to be a fair fight. His limbs trembled with the excitement of battle as he approached the kitchen door, the fresh night air hitting the various cuts and grazes on his body, making them sting. He and his men had made a considerable dent on their numbers he thought proudly, grinning at his blood-stained hands. Suddenly the door opened with a violent thud, and he had to quickly step back as Sarah hurtled out of the building.

"Father," she cried, gripping his arms, "Mel never came to the cellar. She just woke us all up and told us to meet her there..."

"What?" he asked in a low, dangerous voice, his face darkening with anger.

"She said she had to get a weapon. I went and told Simon as soon as I realised she wasn't coming, but you'd already left with the men…"

"She must have gone to the village," he muttered, his shoulders tensing up under the thick material of his coat. At that moment Plodder trotted smartly into the courtyard, nodding her head agitatedly. "Damn," he swore, shaking her hands off and striding towards Monty.

"I'm coming too," Sarah asserted, jogging up to Plodder and grabbing her reins.

"No," he grunted, hoisting himself up into the saddle. "There are still raiders out there, and I need you here in case any get through our net." He grabbed the reins off John, his eyes flitting to the man's exhausted face. "You stay here and take the horses back to the stable John. Then get the women to prepare for the others' return, in case any of them are injured," he ordered.

"Aye sir," John croaked with a grateful nod. He stiffly dismounted and gently took the reins out of Sarah's hand.

"But what if Mel's hurt?" Sarah asked plaintively, tears welling in her eyes as she looked from one grim face to another.

"Please Sarah, let me handle this," he said firmly, nudging Monty around. "I promise to bring her back in one piece," he muttered, before racing off into the night.

She kicked the ground grumpily as John started to lead the horses away. "It's not fair," she grumbled, resting her hand on the hilt of her sword. "I'm a competent fighter, why won't Father let me fight?" she wondered aloud. John turned his swarthy face to her, eyes crinkling sympathetically.

"You'd understand if you'd seen him that day you were attacked by those men miss," he told her gruffly. "Never seen a man so scared to lose something he cared about," he added, a hint of awe in his voice.

"Hmph," she grunted as she turned to go back inside. He smiled as he led the horses back to their stalls for a well-earnt rest. He hadn't missed the softening of her eyes as she turned away.

Raphael sped through the moon-lit forest, his mind a cauldron of simmering anger. How dare she defy him? he silently raged, digging his heels into Monty's side. If she survived this insanity, he swore he was going to throttle her. As he entered the village and absorbed the destruction and death, he began to doubt he would find her alive. What had possessed her to run off like that? Did she care for these people that much? A handful of raiders remained, searching the bodies of locals and colleagues alike for valuables. He quickly cut them down before they could flee into the forest. He looked around for signs of activity through the smoke and flames, finally spotting a group of local men carrying buckets of water into the street. One man spotted him as he approached, hastily emptied his buckets onto the nearest fire. "Thank-you Master Blythe," he rasped, nodding appreciatively at his handiwork. "They must have come out while we were fetching water," he mused, nudging one of the bodies with his foot.

"Hopefully they're the last," Raphael growled, wondering how his men fared with their hunt. "You're the blacksmith, aren't you?" he asked, suddenly placing the thick-set shoulders and wispy brown hair. He belatedly noticed a dark patch on the man's shirt roughly the size of his hand.

"Yes sir, Neville Dempsey's the name," Neville replied with a grin, following Raphael's eyes to the alarming stain on his side. "Don't worry about that sir, it's just a scratch," he offered with surprising good humour. "It would have been a lot worse if your Mel hadn't arrived when she did," he added, his eyes bright with admiration.

"Really?" Raphael murmured, taken aback by the man's fervent testimony. "Ah, speaking of Mel, have you seen her around?"

"She's at the lake, sir," Neville answered.

"Thank-you Neville," he said gratefully, turning Monty towards the lake. Murmuring assurances to the agitated horse, he walked between two smouldering structures, steam still rising from the blackened wood.

Beyond the burnt-out buildings sprawled Lake Burchell, her near shore ironically dotted with bonfires. Small, frightened faces huddled round the flames while the older children helped their parents with the fire-fighting effort. After some searching, he spotted Mel standing knee-deep in water, filling buckets and carrying them back to shore. Leaving Monty to nibble on a clump of grass, he strode across the shore, vaguely aware of people hurriedly moving out of his way. All he could see before him was Mel, who in turn seemed oblivious to his approach. He didn't even register the chilly water lapping his calves, he was so enraged. She finally turned toward the sound of his sploshing steps, jaw dropping in surprise.

"What are you doing here?" she asked, almost dropping her buckets.

"What am I doing here?!" he exploded, grabbing her arm. "I'm here to take you home, that's what I'm doing here. How dare you disobey me woman. You're lucky to be alive."

"But there's still work to be done," she protested weakly as his eyes were drawn to the spreading patch of darkness at her side. He reached out and touched it, squinted at the blood coating his fingertips in the faint orange light. "You're bleeding," he cried, staring at her in disbelief. "What the hell are you doing hauling buckets of water around when you've got a bloody big gash in your side?" he demanded heatedly, tightening his hold on her arm.

"Ow, let go of me," she whined through chattering teeth as he half-dragged her back to shore.

"For goodness sake, drop those buckets woman," he shouted over his shoulder as she stumbled after him.

"So...cold," she mumbled as her legs gave way beneath her. The sound of her body collapsing into the water coupled with the sudden dead weight pulling on his arm forced him to stop.

"Mel!" he cried, bending down in the shallow water and rolling her over. After draining the water out of her airways, he placed his ear next to her mouth, heard her faint, shallow breaths. Gathering her up in his arms, he staggered to his feet and walked back to shore.

"Is she alright?" one woman asked concernedly, rushing toward him as he laid her down on the shore.

"She's passed out, lost too much blood," he muttered, peeling the blood-soaked material away from her side. "Ugh," he groaned, blanching at the deep ugly wound. He turned to the woman standing anxiously beside him. "Get me some bandages woman," he ordered tersely. Nodding her head, she mumbled "yes sir" and ran off. Looking around to see if they'd attracted any more onlookers, he placed his hand over the wound. "Damn," he cursed as he extended energy into the gash, feeling a wall of infection block its path. It was going to take a lot more energy to burn out the infection. At least he had managed to stem the flow of blood, he thought grimly as he sat back on his heels, blinking back his fatigue. Hopefully it would hold until he got her back to the manor.

"Here you are sir," the woman panted, bandage in hand. Raphael looked up in surprise. He'd more sent her on the errand so she wouldn't witness his healing efforts.

"Thank-you," he murmured sheepishly, accepting the wad of material and pressing it over the wound. "That was fast," he added as the woman struggled to regain her breath.

"She helped me. Me and my kids was surrounded by raiders, and she just threw herself at them. That's how she got hurt so badly," she explained, her voice catching.

"What's your name?" he asked as he gathered Mel up in his arms.

"Judy Cahil, sir," she answered, tears welling in her eyes.

"I want you to do me a favour Judy," he grunted as he rose to his feet and made his way back to Monty. "Just worry about yourself and your family. It's what Mel would want," he added with a backward glance. She nodded gravely, her feet tumbling to a halt.

"Please sir, take good care of her," she implored before turning away, her torn skirt billowing in the wind. He lifted Mel up into the saddle and hauled himself up behind her.

"I'll be taking care of her alright," he muttered darkly as he took up the reins and dug his heels into Monty's shivering sides.

The fiery remains of the village blurred around him as he galloped towards the silent, dark forest. Gripping Mel's unconscious body tightly to him, he weaved through the network of trees, straining his eyes to pick out the shadowy branches against the dimly lit night sky. With a sigh of relief, he spotted a glimmer of light above the tree line, and soon found himself pulling up in the yard, Sarah running towards him. "What happened?" she asked breathlessly, eyes wide with concern as he dismounted.

"She's got a nasty cut in her side. She's lost a lot of blood," he grunted, easing Mel out of the saddle. "On top of that, it's infected," he added as he carried her inside, Sarah hot on his heels. Jane and Wendy waited anxiously in the hallway, their arms loaded with bandages and a basin of clean water. "Good work ladies," he panted as he clambered up the stairs. "Sarah, can you bring those up with you?"

Grimacing at the young women, she wedged the bandages under her arm and juggled the basin in her hands. "Thank you girls," she sighed as she carefully negotiated the stairs, "you'd better go and see to the men."

"Is she going to be alright, Sarah?" Jane asked, her eyes drifting to Mel's unconscious body lolling against Raphael's chest.

"I don't know," Sarah answered truthfully, shivering despite the beads of sweat on her brow. Over her laboured breaths she heard their footsteps recede in the general direction of the kitchen.

Better that they stay away, if what she suspected was true. Biting her tongue, she followed him along the corridor to his room. "Father," she started in a low voice, her mouth going dry as she set down the basin and bandages, "you're not going to use the mirror, are you?"

"Get the key out of my pocket, will you?" he grunted, shifting Mel's body to expose his coat pocket. Frowning, she dipped her fingers into the deep pocket, cold metal brushing her skin.

"Please Father, it's so dangerous," she protested as she opened the door.

"I don't think we have a choice," he muttered, entering the room. Staring despairingly at his stiff back as he strode to the far corner of the room, she shook herself into action and brought in the water and bandages, closing the door firmly behind her.

He carefully set Mel down on the bed and went to the nearby chest of drawers, grabbing his old medical case from the bottom drawer. Waving her over, he quickly set about cutting away the blood-soaked material, exposing the deep, dirt-encrusted wound. Taking a moment to admire his handiwork, he knelt stiffly beside the bed.

"Oh my God," Sarah croaked, her hands trembling as she wrung out a cloth and handed it to him, her eyes barely leaving the gruesome gash.

"It's not pretty," he concurred distractedly, gently cleaning the surrounding skin. "How are the men? Any serious injuries?" he asked casually, putting aside the bloody cloth and holding his hand out for another.

"A few minor cuts and bruises," she reported unevenly, hastily preparing another washcloth.

"Good," he grunted, giving the wound a final wipe. "I'm not going to have much energy left after this. Okay then Sarah," he began, tossing the cloth aside and shifting his body closer to the patient, "I need you to open the wall behind the fireplace..."

"No!" she cried, backing away from the bed. He looked up and saw the anguish in her face, his heart lurching painfully in his chest. "Please Father, the voices," she said hoarsely past the sudden lump in her throat.

"There's no other way," he assured her, shaking his head. "All sorts of nasty germs have made their way into her system. Mel will die without the mirror's power."

Staring at Mel's pale, still face, she merely nodded and moved to the disused fireplace, positioned herself awkwardly in the dusty pit. "Ready?" she croaked as her fingers found the edge of the recessed stone tablet that formed the back of the fireplace. She glanced over her shoulder at Raphael, saw dread in his face that matched her own. He nodded bleakly, his hand hovering over the wound. She pushed, and the stone tablet slid sideways on a set of well-oiled wheels built into the floor beneath it. The instant the panel slid away, musty stale air crept out of the secret chamber. Wrinkling her nose at the smell, she shifted to other side of the firepit in preparation for sealing off the concealed space. Already faint voices whispered in her ear, while cold fingers of air brushed her arms, giving her goosebumps. "Think of Mel," she uttered softly, her eyes drifting to the unconscious body on the bed. No matter what the voices made her see, she had to be strong.

Raphael shivered as the dank fingers of air travelled over his body, penetrating his clothes with ease. "Right," he croaked hoarsely, focusing on the wound. He closed his eyes and saw behind his eyelids energy flow out from his hand, diving into the cells of Mel's body. In his mind, he could see a gathering darkness against the backdrop of healthy red blood cells, his breath catching in his throat. The infection was worse than he had expected, the edges of the growing wall of bacteria breaking off to spread itself throughout her body. "Come on Mirror, lend me your strength," he pleaded, opening his mind to the strange fragmented voice humming around his ears. The voice snatched greedily the projected thought, channelled images into his mind. "Everything dies," a silky voice whispered as scenes of life and death flashed through his head. The world spread out before him like a blanket of shifting lights, each light representing a life. New lights twinkled into existence while others winked out, the emotions behind each event washing over him briefly, leaving him increasingly hollow with each passing.

Pushing aside the vivid image, he extended the mirror's energy into the wound, felt the infection melt away under the strengthening onslaught. Just feeling the Mirror's presence in his mind filled him with power. The greater danger was losing himself in the seductive mix of power and detachment, seeing the universe through an alien consciousness he couldn't hope to understand. "He tried, you know," a sour voice grumbled in his ear, and the pictures in his mind dissolved, to be replaced by images of an ancient city. People ran through the streets of the city as a silver-suited form walked calmly amongst them, firing a gun-like weapon at the fleeing crowd. As the intense beam of the weapon came into contact with the frantic people, they turned to steam. When the steam cleared, all that was left were piles of white powder on the ground. The image focused on the dark shiny visor of the suited figure's helmet, where reflections of the desperate crowd running through the ghastly steam could be seen. Beyond the shiny curved surface, he could just make out a hard angular face which looked largely human, except for the third eye situated above the bridge of the nose. Abruptly the third eye opened and stared straight at him, the deep purple orb piercing the crude matter of his body and seeing right into his soul.

"Ugh...close the panel, Sarah," he grunted through the pain in his chest. Now the suited alien sat in a padded seat, surrounded by screens and illuminated buttons. A large glass window opened out to space above the cluttered board, through which he could a blue planet shrouded in thick dark clouds. The alien touched various controls on the board before him, changing the view on one of the screens into an odd picture of green lines and dots against a black background. Several dots were shown to be in position around a large circle in the middle of the screen. The alien nodded and checked the other screens, which showed wooden boats in different locations being loaded with animals. Behind the visor, a lone tear glistened on the alien's cheek as the rain started.

"Sarah! Close the panel, for God's sake," he cried, clutching his head.

"Timmy," replied a small frightened voice from the fireplace, "please don't leave me." He lifted his aching head, squinted through bleary eyes at the cowering figure lost in her own world of painful images. "I tried to save you Timmy, please don't hate me," she sobbed, stretching out her arms to the other side of the fireplace.

"Aww," he gulped, resting his weary head on the bed next to Mel's hip. Now the Mirror seemed to tear away at the tightly wrapped images of his own life, flashing them mercilessly through his mind. "No," he whispered as he saw himself stumbling through the front door of his old London apartment. Lurching about unsteadily in the moonlit shadows of the room, he'd crashed noisily into his Uncle's body as it lay still on the floor, blood trickling out of the hole in his chest. His head muddled by wine, he'd pawed the body clumsily, trying to stop the bleeding, but it was already too late. Leaning back in despair, he had felt something hard press into his knee. With trembling hands he'd picked up the knife, studied it intently in the pale moonlight streaming in through the window. The door then opened, and Aunt Sophie stood frozen in the doorway, Sebastian close behind, a lantern held before him. Try as he may, he could never forget the look of pure dismay on her face as they stared at each other over the body of her husband. Behind her back, Sebastian had looked equally shocked and repulsed, except for the briefest twitching of his lips as their eyes met. He knew in that instant that Sebastian had set him up, the realization leaving him colder than the dead body on the floor. He couldn't begin to imagine the extent of his brother's betrayal...

Screaming hoarsely, he lifted his head off the bed, looked down at the unconscious body. Staring in horrified disbelief at the pale form, he saw at first his uncle, the gaping hole in his chest glistening with dark, congealed blood. Then the features melted away, to reveal Sebastian's smug, sleeping face. He saw the eyes abruptly open, and he sprung onto the bed to wrap his hands around that scrawny throat. A weak voice penetrated the Mirror-induced fog of his mind, and he suddenly saw Mel's face before him, his hands closed around her neck. "Raph," she croaked weakly, looking up at him through fluttering eyelids, "what are you doing?"

He gazed helplessly at her, trembling hands easing off her throat. Behind him, Sarah closed the panel. "That's better," Mel sighed, closing her eyes. For the longest time he knelt over her sleeping body, oblivious to Sarah's cautious approach until she timidly laid a hand on his shoulder.

"She made the voices stop Sarah," he muttered thickly, finally tearing his eyes away from the innocent face to look solemnly at his young ward. "Mel controls the mirror."

"Coffee?"

She looked up from the novel she was trying to read. It was hard to concentrate on the words with the little girl a couple of rows down screaming her lungs out. The hostess waited expectantly, silver pot held at the ready.

"Yes, thank-you," she replied, placing her cup on the waiting tray. "See if you can stop that kid from screaming, will you?" she jokingly asked the pretty woman as she poured the coffee. The hostess grinned sympathetically and extended the tray to her.

"The raider was a little rough when he stole her lunch money," she answered with a rueful shake of her head. "She'll stop soon." And with that, the blood-curdling screams died away to a faint, sobbing whimper, and then stopped altogether.

"Thank God for that," a gruff voice said beside her. She turned her head and found herself staring into familiar beady eyes. "That kid was really starting to get on my nerves," the ring-leader raider confided to her through his dirty, knotted beard.

"Name's Erik," he supplied cordially, offering his hand. She half-heartedly took his hand, her eyes falling to the dagger in his lap. "And now," he continued, calmly picking up the dagger and holding it to her side, "if you could just give me all your valuables love." She fumbled for the attention button in the armrest as she bent forward to pick her wallet out of her bag. "Thanks love," he murmured, taking her wallet and tucking it into his leather vest. Without warning, he deftly ran his knife along her side.

"What was that for?" she cried vehemently, desperately pressing her hand over the deep cut.

"That's for pressing the help button," he answered evenly, wiping the blood off the blade and returning it to his belt. "I'm in for it now when the hostess comes back this way," he added gravely, picking up the in-flight magazine and thumbing through the glossy pages, studiously ignoring her pained gasps and gushing blood.

"Damn," she breathed, watching as the hostess continued up the aisle serving coffee, oblivious to the red angry light glowing in the bulkhead above her head. Suddenly there was a loud explosion as the right wing violently blew apart, leaving an ugly gaping hole in the side of the plane. "Come on Mel, it's your move." She tore her eyes away from the hole to gaze stupidly at Raphael who now sat before her, a chess board balanced on his lap.

"What are you doing here?" she asked, watching distractedly as a raider was sucked out of the plane. The hostess was clinging desperately to an armrest as vicious air tugged at her body, urging her towards the hole.

"What's it look like?" Sarah asked, now occupying the seat next to her.

"Where'd Erik go? He's got my wallet," she asked absurdly, looking around for the tall, hairy bandit.

"Will you just have your go?" Raphael demanded as the plane started its rapid, uncontrolled descent.

"Do you really think this is the time for playing chess? We're about to crash, and I'm bleeding all over the place…"

"Excuses excuses," Sarah chided, rolling her eyes.

"You just don't want to lose again," Raphael surmised shrewdly, his attention firmly fixed on the board.

The bone-jarring shuddering of the plane as it careened through trees prevented her from responding. "It's too bad. I was really starting to like you Mel," he said sadly, running his fingers down her cheek. Then he and Sarah vanished, and a large hunk of the plane's roof broke off and was falling towards her…

"Ugh," she breathed, opening her eyes to a dimly lit room. As grainy early-morning light filtered in through the window, she looked around and slowly recognised the interior of her room. "What happened?" she croaked, closing her eyes against the gentle light, her brow wrinkling as the dull pain in her side finally penetrated her foggy brain. With her eyes still closed, she probed the tender area above her hip, encountered a thick cotton bandage. "Oh," she breathed, remembering with a flash the raider's blade biting into her side. What on earth had possessed her to run off and play heroics like that? she wondered groggily. Raphael was going to give her grief for months over this, she decided with a groan. "Raphael," she uttered with a start, prying her sticky eyelids open. The image of his enraged face looming before her over the dark water suddenly popped into her mind. The last thing she remembered was being dragged back to shore, his fingers digging mercilessly into her arm as he stormed through the shallow water. He must have brought her home and healed her wound.

"Oh no," she moaned, struggling to get up out of bed. She managed to raise her head and shoulders off the pillow before collapsing weakly back. "He's going to kill me," she cried to the ceiling, her voice barely scraping past her parched throat. Just then there was a sharp knock on the door, and the object of her terror waltzed in, with Sarah close behind him. "Good morning," he said briskly as he approached the bed.

"Morning Mel," Sarah echoed, carrying a tray of food and water to the little bedside table.

"Ah, good morning," she replied cautiously, trying once more to sit up.

"Wait, let me help you there," he muttered, positioning himself behind her. His hands slid in under her unsuspecting arms and lifted her gently up.

"Ow," she grunted as her side protested at the movement. "Is this the part where you say "I told you so"?" she asked through gritted teeth.

"Oh, there'll be plenty of time for that later," he assured her, handing her a cup of water from the tray. She wordlessly accepted the cup and greedily gulped the contents.

"How do you feel Mel?" Sarah asked anxiously, taking away the empty cup.

"Like a mad raider got his sword stuck in my side," she answered distractedly, her eyes straying to the bowl of porridge on the tray.

"You can eat in a moment," Raphael said firmly, catching the naked hunger in her face. "I need to check the wound."

She pulled a face and carefully swung her legs over the edge of the bed. Leaning heavily on Sarah, she stood gingerly on numb feet as he removed the dressing and studied the blood-encrusted gash. A large scab was already forming over the straight, horizontal line of red naked flesh, spanning at least three inches along the curve of her waist. He placed his hand over the gruesome line and closed his eyes. His roving tendrils of energy encountered no secondary infection in the area. With a sigh of relief, he opened his eyes and continued the examination.

"How much do you remember?" Raphael asked casually as he gently prodded around the raised edges.

"Ah," she hissed as his finger found a particularly tender spot, "not much. I remember everything up to you dragging me back to shore, and then feeling really cold. I guess I passed out."

"You didn't just pass out, you almost died," he snapped, anger flashing in his eyes as he looked up at her. Returning his attention to the wound, he poked another spot, his lips twitching with satisfaction as she cried out.

"It's sealed, and there appears to be no further infection" he concluded thoughtfully, giving the laceration a final scrutiny before replacing the dressing. "Be careful not to bump it," he warned as he stood up stiffly.

"Yes, Raphael," she murmured, her eyes sliding away from his.

"I'd also appreciate it if you downplayed the severity of the injury when discussing it with staff," he added.

"Of course," she acknowledged meekly, stumbling back onto the bed. "Raphael," she cried desperately as he turned to leave the room. "Thanks for saving my life," she stammered to his impatiently waiting face. He glowered at her, his eyes briefly softening at her awkward display of gratitude.

"Hmph," he grunted, turning back towards the door. "Sarah, can you help Mel wash up and change her clothes?" he asked, wrinkling his nose at the smell permeating the room.

"Of course father," she agreed, bowing her head. With a final grumpy look, he stormed out the room.

"He's mad with me, isn't he?" she asked in a small voice, pushing herself back onto the bed.

"He's not the only one," Sarah grumbled, crossing her arms sulkily over her chest as Mel reached for the bowl of porridge. "What were you thinking Mel, running off like that to play heroics? You're just lucky Father was able to heal you…" Her voice trailed away at the memory of Timmy glaring at her with hate-filled eyes as she cowered in the corner of the fireplace. Why did the mirror make her see such a horrible thing? Timmy wouldn't resent the fact that she was still alive, while he was nothing but a distant memory. She had tried so hard to save him from the cruelty of the factory, she told herself adamantly. Surely Timmy had known that? She looked up to find Mel watching her intently, a frown tugging at the corners of her mouth as she slowly ate her porridge.

"Are you alright?" she asked, dipping her spoon into the bowl.

"Not really," Sarah answered truthfully, perching on the edge of the bed next to Mel's feet. "Please promise me you won't do something like that on your own again," she croaked, lifting teary eyes to Mel's guilty face.

"I'm sorry Sarah," she said with difficulty, swallowing past the sudden lump in her throat. "I don't know what came over me…"

"Just don't leave me behind next time, okay?" the girl interjected gruffly, rubbing her eyes. "I don't know what hurts more, the fact that you excluded me, or how close you came to dying," she complained.

"I doubt I would have survived Raphael's wrath if I had let you tag along, Sarah," she pointed out gently. "It's one thing for me to risk my own life, quite another to risk yours."

"You wouldn't say that if you had seen how frantic Father was, racing back to the manor holding you to his chest."

She almost choked on the food in her mouth at the mental picture those words evoked. Her cheeks reddening, she wolfed down the rest of her porridge and then with Sarah's help selected a set of clothes to change into.

"Really Mel, you're not going to wear those awful breeches, are you?" she asked for the fourth or fifth time as they carefully made their way to the washroom.

"I told you, I'll need to expose the dressing with ease," she explained breathlessly, her concentration fixed on the stairs. The world swayed slightly with each step, her legs feeling as though they might give way beneath her at any moment. Sarah had offered to bring up a basin of water, but she had stupidly insisted on going to the washroom. "Not one of my better ideas," she muttered under her breath, gritting her teeth against the sharp pain in her side. Finally they were on the ground level, and she hobbled along more easily, the pain subsiding to a dull roar.

"I'll just take this tray back to the kitchen," Sarah said, rushing ahead of her.

"Right," she panted weakly after her, watching enviously the girl's light, fast steps. She had just made it to the door of the washroom when Sarah came marching purposefully back, a kettle of steaming water held carefully before her. Her lips twitching in a sympathetic smile, Sarah opened the door and stepped inside.

"Aww, I feel so helpless," Mel whined as she hobbled past.

"Serves you right," Sarah retorted, closing the door behind her. She quickly set about preparing the water, lifting the basin onto the bench. "Margaret thought you might want some warm water to wash in," she grunted as she emptied the kettle.

She glanced down at herself, grimaced at the dirt, soot and blood caking her skin and clothes. "That woman's a saint," she said sincerely as she limped to the bench. Draping her fresh clothes over the end, she gratefully collapsed onto the wooden seat and shuffled closer to the basin.

"Well, I guess I'll leave you to it then," Sarah suggested tactfully as she topped up the basin with cold water.

"I think I'll manage," she answered with more confidence than she felt. She started undoing the buttons of her dress, wincing at the movement. "This dress is ruined," she said ruefully, taking in the gaping hole around the waist and the numerous tears throughout the material. Pursing her lips together, Sarah picked up the kettle and headed for the door. "I'll ask Margaret if she wants any more rags," she offered.

"Ah Sarah," she stammered as the bright red hair disappeared through the doorway. "Thanks... for everything," she said awkwardly, feeling slightly ashamed of herself. The girl smiled and slipped quietly away, her sensible boots clicking faintly down the hallway.

Despite the pain of twisting around, she managed to clean away most of the dirt and grime. The pleasure of being clean again more than compensated for the discomfit she experienced. She carefully pulled on her new clothes, grinning at the anticipated stir she was going to cause dressing like a man. "What a mess," she muttered to her reflection, eying with dread her unkempt hair. She picked up the comb that lived on the stool next to the mirror and started to drag it through the mass of knots. After what felt like an age, she put down the comb and left the washroom, holding the dirty, ruined dress with distain before her.

"Mel!" a familiar voice called out as she headed for the kitchen. She turned around to find Simon anxiously approaching from the main entrance. "Mel, how are you?" he asked, concern lining his tanned face.

"Simon," she uttered in surprise, staring at him in bewilderment. "Oh, well enough I guess," she answered, gingerly touching her side. "How did you fare with the raid?" she asked in turn, eager to be back on speaking terms.

"Me?" he asked, surprised by her interest. "Oh, I'm alright. A few cuts and bruises when I did a sweep of the forest with John. A handful of raiders were still prowlin' around, but we got them," he explained, his chest swelling with pride.

"Good," she said with a smile. "Hopefully they'll think twice before attacking us again."

"Yes," he agreed, shoving his hands in his pockets. "Ah, should you really be up and about? I heard you got hurt pretty bad..."

"Oh no, it wasn't as bad as it looked," she answered flippantly, as per Raphael's request. Why he wanted to keep his healing abilities a secret mystified her, especially as he used to study medicine.

It did seem rather selfish, to keep such a glorious gift to himself. He must have his reasons, she told herself with a mental shrug.

"Thank goodness for that," Simon said, relief evident in his voice. She broke off her reverie to study him more intently as he flushed guiltily, shifted his feet nervously.

"Something wrong, Simon?" He looked up from inspecting his boot, mumbled something.

"What?" she asked with a frown.

"If I tell you, you have to promise not to tell anybody," he answered more clearly, looking around to see if anyone was in earshot.

"Um, okay," she murmured uncertainly, following him as he drifted to the other side of the hall-way, away from the kitchen. Glancing about anxiously a final time, he ducked into the space under the stairs. She squeezed in beside him, idly wondering how often these stairs were used. The only times she had personally used them was during the tour Sarah had given, and last night when she snuck out through the ballroom. Finally satisfied they were alone, he turned his tortured gaze to her. "I saw you ride off Mel," he confessed thickly, his feelings of guilt seeming to reach out and close around his throat. "I was on watch, I saw you ride off on Plodder, but I didn't raise the alarm," he explained, his face darkening with shame. "I just stood there, watching the spot where you had disappeared into the trees..." His voice trailed away for a moment as he ran trembling fingers through his dark, unkempt hair. "Then before I knew it, Miss Sarah was clambering up the stairs to the lookout, yelling that you hadn't turned up at the cellar, and I just played dumb...I'm so ashamed," he finished, his shoulders shaking as she stood listening in stunned silence.

She took a deep breath to steady herself, leant heavily against the wall. "I'm so sorry Mel," he croaked, shaking his head as he stared at the floor. "If you had been more seriously hurt, or killed, God, I wouldn't be able to live with myself..." A bitter laugh almost escaped her lips at that. It was just as well she'd downplayed the severity of the wound, or the man would surely be twitching at her feet by now, in a fit of self-recrimination.

"Well, I got what I wanted," she murmured, resting the back of her head against the wall to gaze up at the cobwebs arcing gracefully overhead. The fine threads were coated in dust that sifted down through the gaps in the wood, the tiny particles catching the slanting light.

"You have to understand Mel, I was a broken man after I saw you and Master Blythe in the sta-bles together," he explained awkwardly, raising injured eyes to her closed face. "I thought you were making a big mistake, that the Master was just using you. Anyway," he changed tack, not wanting to go into detail, "that all changed last night."

"What?" she asked, tearing her eyes away from the cobwebs to gape at him. He grinned sheep-ishly at her, shuffled his feet.

"You should have seen the look on his face as he rode off after you," he said, a hint of awe in his voice. "He was so mad and...worried. I knew then that the Master actually cared about you." She bit her tongue, held back the scornful laugh that would normally follow a remark like that.

"Well, I'd better get back to work," he said, glancing in the general direction of the kitchen. If Wendy caught him talking to Mel, there'd be hell to pay. For a second he thought he heard her strident voice from across the hall, his heart missing a beat as he waited for his possessive girlfriend to swoop down upon him like a bird of prey. The voice faded away, and he relaxed slightly. "Again, I'm really sorry Mel. I hope you can find it in your heart to forgive me," he said hurriedly, edging out of the space.

"Hey, it was my idea to sneak away and risk my life," she pointed out, tiring of his guilt. "If you take this stinking dress off my hands, I'll say we're even," she offered, holding out the ruined garment. He looked at it warily.

"Are you sure? It'll be torn up and used for rags," he warned, eying it with vague interest.

"That's all it's good for now," she assured him.

"Alright then," he murmured, taking the dress and stepping out of the shadows. "See you round Mel," he said with a nod of his head. She waited until he was gone before hobbling out from under the stairs.

As she limped across the hallway, she caught snippets of conversation through the main door. Simon didn't make the clean getaway he was hoping for, with Wendy now quizzing him about the dress. She grinned sympathetically as he groped for the right words, his tongue becoming increasingly tied. Their voices faded into the background as she started to climb up the stairs, the sound of her ragged breathing drowning out even Wendy's high-pitched cries. That was punishment enough, she decided as she neared the top of the stairs. Maybe things could return to normal, now that Simon had bared his soul to her. Funny how people kept telling her that Raphael had raced off after her for reasons other than pure rage, and the need to keep his ward happy. Tightly gripping the handrail, she made the final laboured step and waited for the library doorway to stop lurching before her eyes. Gritting her teeth against the sudden flare of pain in her side, she reassured herself she was just a few steps away from a comfortable chair and a book. She could even close her eyes for a couple of minutes, rest her head on the table...

"And just where do you think you're going?" a stern voice demanded behind her, making her jump. She carefully turned around to find Raphael jogging up the stairs.

"Ah, I thought I might spend some time in the library," she answered as he slowed to a stop before her. "What have you been up to?" she asked, keen to change the subject. His eyes travelled up and down her body, an unreadable expression on his face.

"Checking the men's progress with finding and burying the bodies of the raiders," he supplied distractedly. "Why in God's name are you wearing such horrible clothes?"

"It's easier to check the dressing this way," she said defensively. Without thinking, she lifted her shirt in demonstration. "See?" she said smugly, her triumphant expression fading fast as his eyes narrowed. She looked down and saw with dismay the spreading spot of blood.

"I see what you mean," he murmured dryly, gripping her upper arm and ushering her towards the library.

"Damn, I must have bumped it," she muttered, grateful for the pressure of his hand as she swayed slightly on her feet.

He guided her into the overstuffed chair in the corner and knelt beside her, his hand reaching for the wound. "No," she cried with a start, catching the hand in mid-stretch. "You must be exhausted," she said earnestly, raising guilty eyes to his bemused face. "It's my own stupid fault," she added roughly, her body rigid in the seat. "I should have listened to you," she croaked, tears beginning to spill unchecked down her cheeks as shock set in. "By all rights I should be dead," she cried hoarsely. He awkwardly put his arms around her and drew her trembling body close.

"Mel," he murmured as her tears soaked through the material of his shirt and onto his shoulder. He idly stroked her arm, while his other hand pushed the hair away from her face. "Honestly woman, what are we going to do with you?" he asked, his arms tightening around her. "What are we going to do?" he croaked softly under his breath, struggling to control his emotions. This could be the final straw, he thought grimly. There was so much more at stake now. Somehow the Mirror had bonded itself to Mel when it dragged her through space and time. How could they tell her the truth now, and risk her leaving them forever, or worse?

"I'm sorry," Mel mumbled, breaking into his morbid thoughts. She pulled away from him, raising a trembling hand to her tear-streaked cheeks. "You've done enough for me already," she said with a weak smile. "I don't know what I was thinking, running off like that…"

"Don't be so harsh on yourself Mel," he interjected, sitting back on his heels. "You saved at least two lives that I know of," he pointed out, recalling Neville and Judy from last night's misadventures.

"Neville and Judy?" she uttered, taking a steadying breath. "You saw them?"

"Yes," he answered, shifting his knees closer to the chair. "They told me what you did," he murmured, reaching out once more to the wound.

"I was lucky," she said modestly, grudgingly allowing him to lift up her shirt. "I'm sure if you or Sarah had been there to see me fight, you could have pointed out heaps of faults in my form." Despite everything, he grinned at the sardonic remark, placing his hand over the wound.

"You'll have to give us a demonstration, when you're fully recovered," he suggested calmly, closing his eyes to focus his energy on the jagged, bleeding gap in her flesh.

He opened his eyes to find her watching him intently. "You must be exhausted," she said huskily, her voice barely scraping past her sore throat.

"I'm alright," he assured her, hastily retracting his hand. "I've had enough time to recover. Now you take it easy," he warned her sternly as he got stiffly to his feet, eager to change the subject.

"Yes sir," she said with a tired salute. He stood still for a moment, glowering down at her cheeky face. Abruptly, he took her raised hand and brought it to his lips.

"Take care Mel," he grunted, releasing her hand. She watched in stunned silence as he turned tail and stormed out of the room, distractedly brushing her fingers over the skin that had been touched by his lips. Shaking her head in an attempt to dispel her confusion, she gingerly got up from the chair and hobbled over to the bookshelves.

"He's not exhausted, he's delirious," she muttered under her breath, selecting a book and taking it to the table.

$$\diamondsuit$$

Chapter 2
Alyce Means Truthful.

"Mel, Mel, guess what?" Sarah cried excitedly, running to catch up with her careful steps. Almost three weeks after her foolhardy heroics, her side was largely healed, but the area still protested whenever she overstretched it.

"What, finished talking to Daniel already?" she teased breathlessly as she made her way through the forest. She had left the starry-eyed pair chatting outside the school shack, as it was now affectionately called. It had become standard practice since lessons recommenced for Sarah and Daniel to linger outside the classroom after all the other children had gone home.

"He had to go back to the shop," she explained, shifting the strap of the satchel. "His father is still really busy trying to catch up after all the repair work."

"Hmm," Mel murmured thoughtfully. She could well imagine Neville sweating over the anvil, chopping up long strands of glowing hot metal to make more nails. With almost half the buildings needing some sort of repair after the raiders' attack, his stock would be seriously depleted. "Are you alright with that?" she asked as Sarah continued to grapple with the wayward bag.

"It's fine," Sarah grunted, finally slinging the strap across her body and onto the opposite shoulder. "Hey, you're supposed to guess the news," Sarah whined, jumping up and down at her side.

"Calm down princess," she laughed, playfully ruffling her hair. "What's the news?"

"Daniel says he'll be able to work in the stable again." He had worked briefly in the stable while John was away. Raphael had talked about keeping him on part-time, once the new staff were settled in. The raiders' attack had put that plan on hold.

"Really? Neville can spare him?"

"Only two afternoons a week," Sarah admitted sheepishly, her excitement toning down somewhat to a bubbly half-step.

"Well, you can tell Raphael the good news tonight," she pointed out, trying to ignore the growing anticipation she felt at his expected return. She had missed him more than she cared to admit over the past week.

"Hmm, I hope he's in a better mood this time," Sarah murmured, her merriment diminishing further. Raphael seemed to be crankier each time he returned from a business trip of late. Dealing with clients took every ounce of his patience, the irritation he stored away during these taxing encounters building up as he rode back to the manor. It took a few glasses of red wine before he unwound sufficiently to let go of his annoyances. "Hopefully he's had a better trip," Mel panted as she stepped over a patch of ground still damp from the recent rain. "Don't worry, he'll cheer up when he beats me at chess," she added gloomily. Even though there was no longer a need to maintain the charade, they still settled down in the library each night to match wits over the checked board.

Sarah looked across at Mel's face, noting the slight tinge of colour in her cheeks. Something was happening between Mel and Raphael, she just knew it. She should be delirious with joy at the budding friendship, yet she couldn't help but doubt Raphael's motives, now that he knew Mel controlled the mirror. As they emerged from the thinning trees to approach the manor, she silently promised to muster up the nerve to discuss it with him next chance she got. "Father's back already," Sarah exclaimed with a start, spotting Monty being led into the stable by Cedric. Judging by the foam oozing out of the black stallion's mouth, and the glistening sweat on his twitching rump, Father had been riding hard. "Something's wrong," she stated flatly, her legs quickening on their own accord. They hurried to the manor, almost running into Jane as she bustled down the hallway, a bundle of clean bandages and cloths in her arms.

"Jane, what's going on?" Sarah cried, running after her. The harried girl slowed her steps so they could catch up.

"Master Blythe found a young woman on the road. The coach she was travelling in was hit by raiders," she explained breathlessly as they ducked into the narrow passageway that led to the servants' quarters. "She's badly wounded," Jane added, coming to a stop before a door at the end of the passageway. Mel hastily opened the door for the burdened girl, and they followed her into a small room, to position themselves between two sets of bunks arranged along opposite walls. A single long window let in the lengthening rays of the afternoon sun. In the bottom lefthand bunk a young woman lay unconscious, her pale face almost matching the colour of her fair hair. Raphael knelt beside the bed, his brow furrowed in concentration as he cut away the fabric of the young woman's dress to expose a deep wound in her abdomen.

"Jane, good," he said gruffly, looking up from his grisly task as she set the bundle beside him. "Sarah, Mel," he greeted, sparing them a fleeting glance before returning his attention to the woman.

"Are you alright Father?" Sarah asked as she knelt beside him. Without thinking she grabbed a cloth and dipped it into the basin of water by his knee.

"Yes, the raiders were long gone by the time I arrived on the scene. She was the only survivor I could find," he answered, accepting the moist cloth she held out.

"Raiders?" Mel repeated, her body stiffening. The tension in her voice did not escape him.

"Don't worry Mel," he murmured, his attention firmly fixed on cleaning the gruesome sword wound. "Judging by the remote location of this attack, I'd say the raiders are focusing their efforts on the road, preying on poorly defended coaches."

"Oh," she mumbled, her cheeks reddening with shame at her selfish concern.

"Okay Jane, that will be all for now," Raphael informed the girl hovering anxiously in the background. She dragged her eyes away from the pale silent face on the pillow and wordlessly nodded. "I've stopped the bleeding as much as possible," he explained when the door closed behind her. "From what I can tell, it's a deep wound, but miraculously no organs were damaged." He paused, placed his hand over the site. "There's no sign of infection," he added pointedly, his eyes flitting over Mel's face as he set down the cloth. She hastily looked away, her cheeks reddening further. "So hopefully, if we just sew this up, and give it a final dose of energy, her body will do the rest," he suggested, reaching for his battered medical kit. "Mel, can you hold the sides together?" he asked distractedly, his eyes searching the neat compartments for needle and thread. She blanched at the request, but obediently pressed the flesh together. Swallowing back a wave of nausea, she watched with a sense of sick fascination the sharp curved needle dip in and out of the skin.

"Only five stitches?" she croaked, sitting back on her heels as he trimmed off the final thread. "I thought it would need more than that," she remarked, wriggling her stiff fingers. Sarah murmured agreement beside her, dragging her eyes away from the neat row of knots to frown at Raphael.

"I'm sorry to disappoint you girls," he retorted, eying them quizzically in turn. "You should be glad it's only five," he added, setting the needle and thread carefully on top of the case. "Sarah, can you please prepare a bandage?" Noting the tension in his voice, she tore her troubled gaze from the polished black stone that dangled from the young woman's dark blue choker and selected a long, wide strip of cotton material. "Right," he sighed, suddenly feeling very tired. "A final dose of energy," he murmured with a note of self-derision, placing his hand lightly over the stitches. He closed his eyes and saw in his mind the faintly glowing energy delve into the torn tissue, penetrate the cells. He followed the energy's passage through the area, nodded his satisfaction at the body's healthy reaction. With a relieved sigh, he prepared to pull away, when something strange brushed against his consciousness. Frowning, he moved his hand over the young woman's body, his eyes still tightly shut. The energy radiating out of his hand was drawn to something, sweeping over her stomach, racing through her lungs and trachea, speeding relentlessly towards her brain. Suddenly an angry misshapen face appeared in his mind. Grey, scarred lips peeled back to reveal sharp, yellow teeth, and the face roared, the black pools of the creature's eyes gleaming with hatred...

With a startled cry, he opened his eyes and jerked away from the young woman, gripping his hand as though he had touched a burning ember. "Father?" Sarah cried, dropping the bandage to rush to his side. Mel placed a steadying hand on his shoulder as he reeled back, bumping his head against the bunk behind him.

"Ow," he groaned, clutching his head.

"What happened?" Sarah asked, staring earnestly into his wincing face.

"Err, I thought I saw something," he croaked, waiting for the multiple Sarahs to merge into one. Gazing up into her puzzled, concerned face, he started to doubt the vision in his head. "Ah, I'm just tired," he muttered, slowly clambering to his feet. "Sarah, can you put a bandage over that?" he asked weakly with a wary glance at the young woman. "I have to...go and rest," he said, his words slurred.

The room tilted before him as he lurched forward, stumbling into Mel as she stiffly got up. "Thanks Mel," he breathed, leaning heavily on her.

"Maybe you should help Father back to his room, Mel," Sarah suggested innocently from the bunk.

"Er, sure," she mumbled, wedging herself under his arm. With a final glance over her shoulder at Sarah's smug face, she teetered out of the room, struggling to stay upright under his weight. "Geez Raph, you made it all sound so simple," she grunted as they hobbled down the passageway, looking about to make sure they were alone. "Just a final dose of energy," she mimicked, tightening her arm around his waist.

"It took more energy than I expected," he mumbled, a blurry, ghastly face surfacing the muddy waters of his mind, only to slip away again. Suddenly his eyes narrowed as he gazed down at her. "Did you just call me Raph?" he asked.

"Sorry, it just slipped out," she apologised breathlessly as they started to stagger up the stairs.

"Just make sure it never happens again," he warned sternly, leaning heavily on the handrail.

"Whatever you say, Raph," she wheezed as they clambered to the top of the stairs.

"Hmph," he grunted. Finally they stumbled to a stop before his door, and he released her shoulder to grope his pockets for the key. "A-ha," he breathed, triumphantly extracting the key. "Well, thanks for your help Mel," he said as he unlocked the door.

"Ah, do you want to be woken up for dinner or something?" she asked.

"No, I'll be awake for dinner," he assured her. Eying him doubtfully, she turned away and started to make her way down the corridor, hearing the creak of the door behind her. She shivered momentarily as cold fingers of air brushed over her skin, and a faint voice murmured her name. Her heart hammering wildly in her chest, she spun around as Raphael closed the door firmly behind him. "Hmph," she murmured, shrugging her shoulders to the empty, quiet corridor. Shaking her head to dispel her irrational fear, she hurried back to the servants' quarters, to see if Sarah needed any more help.

Alyce Luana Kensington carefully adjusted the bodice of her dress, nodding with satisfaction as a generous amount of cleavage spilled over the low neckline. Peering past the slightly opened door, she spied Raphael already sitting at the head of the table. The glorified peasant girls were seated as well, giving guarded responses to Raphael's questions. Giving her smooth, pale hair a final pat, she centred the smooth black pendant of her choker and pushed open the door. "Good evening, sorry I'm late," she gushed sweetly as she hobbled into the dining room, wincing at the movement in her side.

"Alyce," Raphael said warmly, leaping out of his chair. "You're looking lovely as usual," he complimented, rounding the table to pull out her chair.

"Thank you Raphael," she responded demurely as she carefully lowered herself onto the chair, bending over slightly to afford him a better view of her bosom. Out of the corner of her eye, she noted the way his eyes widened before he hastily straightened up. "If it wasn't for you, it would have been a different story altogether," she admitted shyly, gazing up into his eyes.

"I just wish I had arrived on the scene earlier," he muttered, shaking his head. "Perhaps I could have averted bloodshed altogether..." Sarah coughed delicately as his voice trailed away, bringing him back to reality. With a faintly disapproving look at his ward, he returned to his seat and started to pile food onto his plate, signalling the start of dinner.

"So, you must be looking forward to receiving word from your family, Alyce," Mel suggested politely, glancing up as she carefully lifted a large slice of beef onto her plate. Despite her attempts to conceal it, Alyce could see the tension in Mel's face. Her face had been particularly drawn during her little display to Raphael.

"Yes," she sighed, her deep blue eyes clouding momentarily. "My parents must be sick with worry."

"Hmm, the letter must be there by now," Raphael mused, his head bent over his plate. Alyce had barely regained consciousness when he urgently asked for her name, keen to send word to her family as soon as possible. That had been just over a week ago. The Kensington family would no doubt send someone up to escort her home. Despite his long absence from the social scene, he was vaguely aware that her father William Kensington owned large plots of land in and around Dover.

"Will someone from your family come to escort you home?" Sarah asked casually.

"I imagine Father will send a small army to retrieve me," Alyce answered lightly, sipping her wine.

"It's a shame you weren't travelling with a small army in the first place," Sarah commented evenly.

"Sarah!" Raphael snapped, shooting her a dark look.

"What? I only meant Alyce should have been better protected," she said innocently, waving her hand expressively.

"No, she's right," Alyce interjected before Raphael could further reprimand the girl. "We had heard word of raiders hitting the road, but didn't take it seriously. If only we hadn't been so complacent, then my companions might still be alive today..." She took a steadying breath, blinked back tears that threatened to spill down her cheeks.

Raphael studiously turned his attention to his meal. The day after he had rescued Alyce from the road, he had gone with Gerald and Simon to retrieve the bodies of her less fortunate companions, only to find the site deserted. The only remaining traces of the attack were the bloodstains on the ground. It was possible, he reasoned, that another party had come across the bodies, and done the proper thing. That section of road was travelled well enough. Still, he found it unsettling that the bodies could disappear so completely. Whoever was responsible had done a very thorough job...

"I don't know what I'm going to say to their families," she said in a small voice. They had of course sent letters to all affected parties, explaining what had befallen their loved ones. He didn't look forward to receiving the replies. They continued eating in solemn silence, the scraping and clunking of cutlery the only sound in the room.

"I'm sure Father will offer some sort of reward for saving my life," Alyce finally spoke around a mouthful of wine.

"That's really not necessary," Raphael said obligingly, even though the idea of a reward was appealing. Business hadn't been brilliant of late, and his funds were being steadily depleted.

"Don't be silly," she chided, setting her glass on the table. "No doubt Father will want to give it to you in person."

"What, your Father will come here?" Sarah asked, taking a bite of her bread roll. Alyce shook her head as she delicately cut up her meat.

"No, more likely he'll send a formal invitation for you all to come and visit Kensington Mansion."

Sarah almost choked on the bread in her mouth. "What? In Dover?" she spluttered, thumping her chest.

"Of course," Alyce said, looking up in surprise. "It's the least my family can do."

Raphael exchanged guarded looks with Sarah and Mel, his face tense.

"That's a generous offer Alyce, but I don't think it's possible for any of us to leave the manor anytime in the near future," he warned.

"Of course, it's entirely up to you," she said smoothly. "It is a beautiful area though. I hope you'll at least consider it. You too, Mel," she added, in an attempt to drag her into the conversation.

"Who, me?" Mel blurted in disbelief, setting her glass on the table. "It sounds very inviting," she responded with as much sincerity as she could muster, "but my classes have already fallen behind by a couple of weeks." Alyce pursed her lips thoughtfully as she studied the reticent woman sitting across from her. There was definitely something odd about Mel. Her accent was like nothing she had ever heard before, the nasally undulation of her voice difficult to understand at first. She appeared to be intelligent and well educated, and yet she was not at all pretentious. Most perplexing of all was her relationship with Raphael and Sarah. She seemed to be part staff member, part family member in this already bizarre household.

"My, you're certainly dedicated," Alyce remarked, her voice only slightly condescending. "But don't you worry Raphael, that the locals will become too educated for their own good? They could start developing ideas above their station."

"Ah," Raphael sighed, his eyes flitting over Mel's tense face, "Mel assures me she won't turn them into revolutionaries. I made her promise before she started teaching."

"Oh good," she said with a pretty laugh, only too aware of the growing colour in Mel's cheeks. "Well, it's very commendable of you Mel," she concluded sweetly, a faint smirk tugging at the corners of her well-shaped mouth.

"Thank you Alyce," Mel said through stiff lips, struggling to contain her indignation.

With a brief concerned look at her rigid face, Raphael steered the conversation to safer ground, leaving her to simmer quietly. She quickly finished her meal and excused herself from the table, exchanging meaningful looks with Sarah as she rose stiffly from her chair. Murmuring pleasantries, she left the room, all too aware of Raphael's disapproving gaze following her out the door. "Damn trollop," she muttered as she marched into the hallway. She could have sworn she saw those full painted lips twitch with amusement as she left. Her rebellious mood led her to the kitchen. "Evenin' Mel," Margaret said calmly as she stormed into the room. "Have they finished dinner already? The tea's not ready yet..."

"I left early. Can I help you with anything?"

Wendy eyed her suspiciously from the sink, her hands slowly scrubbing a pot submerged in the dirty water. "What has our honoured guest done this time?" she asked tartly. Despite her outwardly gentle demeanour, Alyce had a knack for ruffling everyone's feathers. Everyone except Mr Blythe, it seemed, she thought with a frown.

"Nothing really," Mel muttered, walking around to the sink and grabbing a tea towel from the rack. "It's her attitude I find so annoying. She looks down on everyone except Raphael."

"You shouldn't let her get to you Mel," Jane advised distractedly from the table, where she was sprinkling sugar on a freshly baked teacake.

"God, is that for dessert?" Mel asked, her mouth watering as her eyes fell on the steaming cake. "It's not fair," she groaned ruefully, absent-mindedly grabbing a plate to dry. "We never bothered with desserts before."

"Mr Blythe is just being a courteous host, is all," Margaret suggested as she hobbled over to the stove.

"He wasn't this courteous with me," she grumbled, setting the dried plate on the shelf.

"Well, no," the older woman replied hesitantly as she bent over and tossed more wood into the fiery belly of the stove. "That was different though..."

"Yeah, I wasn't half falling out of my dress all the time," Mel snorted scornfully, reaching for another plate. "The polished little tart, turning on the charm like that. You should have seen the way she was bending over while she sat down, all for his benefit."

"Well, you know the old saying Mel," Jane murmured as she cast a critical eye over the glistening cakes. "Fight fire with fire," she supplied, a devious smile stretched across her face as she glanced up at her.

"What? Act like a tart?" she stammered, almost dropping the plate in her hands. "No way, I won't stoop to that level..."

"Oh come on Mel, you can't take this lying down," Wendy said sternly, looking up from the sink. "You have to fight for what you want in this life." She didn't miss the added meaning in her words, remembering with grimace their awkward love triangle.

"But I shouldn't have to compete," she protested, leaning back against the counter. "Why can't he see she's a nasty piece of work?"

Margaret grinned sagely as she heaved the pot onto the stove. "Men are easily blinded love," she sighed, shaking her head. "And you're too nice. Wendy's right, you need to be more aggressive if you're going to regain the Master's attention." She gazed thoughtfully at the older woman's crafty face, slowly nodding to herself.

The conversation moved on to other subjects, and after an hour or so of helping out in the kitchen, she gratefully retired to her room. As she clambered up the stairs, she heard gruff laughter coming from the library. Sidling up to the open door, she huddled against the wall and cautiously peered into the room. Raphael sat in the overstuffed chair facing the door, taking a long sip of wine. In the gentle lantern light, she could see a soft feminine hand waving expressively, an empty wine glass held delicately between thumb and forefinger. "I swear it's true," Alyce insisted, "father was completely mortified." Grinning, he set his glass on the table and wiped the back of his hand over his mouth.

"Did they have much trouble getting the pony to leave?" he asked, turning his attention back to the chess board. Abruptly he looked up, as though he could feel her heavy gaze upon him. With a start she retreated from the doorway, scurrying like a startled bug to the safety of her room.

She had just changed into her night dress when there was a knock on the door. "Mel, it's me," Sarah hissed through the door.

"Where have you been?" Mel quizzed in a low voice, noting the sheen of perspiration on the girl's brow as she entered the room.

"I just got back from the stables," she answered breathlessly, brushing the hair out of her eyes.

"Another night-time rendezvous with Daniel?" she guessed with a frown, closing the door behind her.

"I was just checking up on Moonbeam," Sarah said defensively. "If he happens to in the stables working late, it's not my fault."

"Wow, you say that with such a straight face," she murmured, moving past the flushed girl to sit down on her bed. "Sorry for leaving so early at dinner," she added sheepishly.

"It was probably for the best," Sarah sighed, sinking down beside her. "I don't know if you could have taken any more patronising remarks without exploding."

They both felt as though they were treading on treacherous ground. From the instant she regained consciousness, Alyce had treated them with polite distain. Her clear blue eyes seemed to pierce their outer casings, seeing right through to the chewy class centre. Despite their obvious association with Raphael, it was clear to Alyce they were not his social equals. When they confronted Raphael with their misgivings about Alyce, he had reasoned that she couldn't help being a snob. "Don't worry, she'll soon be out of our hair," he had reassured them, his smile not quite reaching his eyes. He didn't relish having a stranger in the manor either. While he fended off Alyce's subtle probing about his past with vague answers, and skirted personal topics as much as possible, the strain of being so evasive showed occasionally when his mask slipped.

"God, the sooner Alyce leaves, the sooner things can return to normal around here," Mel muttered, finding the edge of the top blanket and rolling it between her fingers. Even though Raphael had expressed reservations about their guest, he wasn't immune to Alyce's more obvious charms.

"Well, the letter should be there by now, surely," Sarah suggested with forced brightness.

"Hmph," Mel grunted, standing up abruptly from the bed. "I don't know Sarah, there's something about this woman that just doesn't seem right. The bodies of her companions disappearing completely like that, without any clue as to who took them, and where. I mean, look at this map," she continued, moving to the dresser in the corner. "There are only three main towns within practical travelling distance from the site of the attack," she pointed out, showing Sarah a carefully drawn map. She frowned at the roughly drawn cross pencilled in along the wavy line representing the road that ran south of the manor.

"But Father scoured the whole area," Sarah pointed out, waving her finger over the section of map surrounding the cross, "including those towns. He couldn't find anything. Hell, no one seemed to have a clue what he was talking about," she added sourly, recalling his frustration when he described his fruitless search.

"Exactly," Mel said, standing back from the bed. "Isn't it just a little strange that no one noticed a cart full of bodies going through town?"

"What's strange is the way she always wears that funny black stone around her neck," Sarah murmured with a shiver. "Have you noticed the weird writing on it?"

Mel nodded, rubbed her arms against the chilly night air. "It's certainly an odd piece of jewellery," she agreed, sinking down onto her bed with a despondent thud.

"You know Mel," Sarah started carefully after a moment of contemplative silence, "you shouldn't let Alyce elbow you out of the way so easily."

"What are you talking about?" Mel asked in a deliberately offhand manner.

"Join in on the chess games again," Sarah suggested encouragingly. "I'm sure Father misses your input," she added coyly, a smirk tugging at the corners of her mouth. Mel coughed, turning away as her cheeks blushed furiously.

"I don't know about that," she mumbled, wiping the back of her hand over her mouth. "He doesn't seem to mind Alyce's company that much, apart from fending off her questions." Sarah shook her head as she rose stiffly from the bed.

"No way Mel, he misses you, I can tell." She smiled weakly in response to the girl's assertion, patted her warmly on the back.

"The only thing he misses is beating me soundly at chess 95 per cent of the time," she joked, following her to the door.

"That's not true Mel," Sarah protested as she opened the door.

"Good night Sarah," she bade with a tired smile, leaning forward to give her a peck on the cheek. "I'll see you tomorrow for more fun and games." Sarah opened her mouth to further press her point, only to be overtaken by another yawn.

"Good night Mel," Sarah conceded as she trudged down the corridor to her own room.

With a final glance at the girl's slouched back, she closed the door gratefully behind her and started to make final preparations for bed. She had just settled under the covers and was about to blow out the candle when there was a soft knock on the door. Muttering sourly under her breath, she threw off the covers and stomped across the room. "This had better be good Sarah," she grated, opening the door with a violent tug. Her body froze as she stared up into Raphael's stern face. Raising a finger to his lips, he silently strode past her to stand tensely in the middle of the room. Her suddenly numb hands fumbled with the door handle as she closed the door. "What do you want?" she croaked, folding her arms self-consciously over her chest, feeling vulnerable in her thin night dress.

"I ah, just wanted to say thank you," he started with uncharacteristic awkwardness, his eyes briefly sweeping over the long shapeless dress covering her body. "I could see you were biting your tongue during dinner," he continued, running long fingers through his hair. "Anyway," he sighed, glancing over at her bemused face, "I appreciate your... restraint."

"Thank you," she murmured, moving stiffly about the room. "I just keep telling myself she can't help being a self-centred prig, with her upbringing and all," she added solemnly. He grinned at the gentle jibe, his shoulders losing some of their tension.

"So, how have you been? Alyce has been monopolising my time so much lately, we've barely had a chance to talk," he muttered, settling down on the bed.

"Ah, I've been okay," she answered cautiously as she approached the bed, struggling to accept the strange phenomenon she was witnessing. Raphael had never casually visited her room before, only seeming to enter in cases of medical emergency. "Classes are going well," she volunteered, perching on the other end on the bed. At his interested look, she sprung into an increasing animated explanation of the exams she was currently working on. "We have to make sure the kids are at least getting the basics down pat," she ranted as she paced the room. "At the moment I'm just focusing on maths and language, but I'm hoping to expand the program to include science and history next year..." She caught herself waving her arms excitedly, looked across at Raphael's smirking face. "Well, you get the idea," she mumbled, returning to the bed.

"You really care about those kids, don't you?" he asked, stretching his long legs out before him. She watched in fascination as he rested his elbows on the bed, his torso reclining over the lumpy blankets.

"Well, yeah, they're cute little scamps," she responded distractedly, her eyes guardedly following the rise and fall of his chest.

"It warms my heart to see Sarah so concerned about their education," he commented, his voice heavy with added meaning. She looked up in surprise at his sarcastic face.

"She's um, become very attached to the children," she said, looking away as her cheeks blushed.

"Hmm, one pupil in particular, I'll wager," he murmured, straightening up. "Were you planning to tell me eventually, about Sarah and Daniel being so chummy?"

"Didn't I mention it? It must have slipped my mind," she said innocently, willing herself not to flinch away from his unwavering stare.

"That really is a shame, Mel. It could have been useful information to have in mind when I rehired the lad," he suggested, his eyes faintly disapproving.

"Oh," she breathed, looking away in shame.

"Don't worry, I've spoken to the boy, and I'm sure he'll be on his best behaviour, even during their nighttime rendezvous."

"Ah," she sighed, her shoulders further slumping in defeat. To her surprise, he laughed, casually reaching across the bed to ruffle her hair.

"Don't worry Mel, it's not the end of the world," he reassured her, his fingers lingering on her hair. She looked up shyly to find his eyes studying her intently, an unreadable expression on his face.

"Well, I'd better go," he mumbled suddenly, heaving himself off the bed. "It's late." She mumbled something appropriate in turn as she followed him to the door.

"Raph," she blurted awkwardly as he put his hand on the handle. "I'm sorry I didn't say something about Daniel and Sarah. I wasn't sure how you'd react, and they seem to be good for each other," she offered lamely when he looked up expectantly.

"Hmph," he grunted, opening the door. "Good night, Matchmaker Mel," he bade with a tired grin.

"Good night," she said softly, watching him stride down the corridor. Shaking her head in confusion, she retreated into her room and closed the door firmly behind her. She clambered into bed and blew out the candle, her limbs moving slowly as though she was in a dream. "That's it," she sighed, closing her eyes. "It was just a weird dream," she whispered, smiling at the memory of Raphael's fingers brushing against her hair.

Mel wiped down the table, grimacing at all the crumbs she collected in her hand. "What the hell is taking Jane so long?" she asked crossly as she moved to the bin and shook her hands, watching the flecks of food fall off the cloth. Despite her efforts to ignore Alyce's subtle barbs, she had left the dinner table in record time, surprising everyone except perhaps Alyce with the speed of her departure.

"Well, Miss Sarah isn't the only one having secret night-time meetings," Wendy supplied suggestively from the sink.

"What? You mean, she's meeting someone?" she stammered, her eyes wide with shock.

"She sure is," Wendy confirmed cheerfully, wiping her hands on a tea towel and turning towards the table.

"Who is it?" Mel cried, tossing the cloth in the sink.

"Wendy," Margaret warned, looking up from her sweeping of the floor. With a devious sideways glance at her mother, Wendy leant over and whispered into Mel's ear.

"Gerald?" she cried, staring at Wendy in disbelief. "Really? How long has this been going on?"

"Oh, now you've gone and done it," Margaret growled, giving the floor an extra-hard sweep. "I knew I shouldn't have told you. Jane will never trust me again…"

"Oh come on Mother, I would have figured it out eventually, the way those two look at each other," Wendy retorted, pulling out a chair and sitting at the table.

"How long's this been going on?" Mel repeated, settling down next to Wendy.

"Only a couple of weeks, serious that is," she explained, reaching over and grabbing a jar of biscuits from the side counter. "It'd been obvious that they liked each other for ages, but it wasn't until the night of the raiders' attack that things really started to cook, if you know what I mean," she said suggestively, nudging Mel gently with her elbow. Mel giggled in return like a school girl, dipping her hand into the jar.

"Hey, don't you two be eatin' all the biscuits," Margaret grumbled, propping the broom against the wall. She eyed them warily as she sat down. "Hmph," she breathed, snatching a biscuit out of the jar.

"You know, I had no idea," Mel confessed around a mouthful of crumbs. Wendy and Margaret exchanged significant glances, coughed politely.

"Well, you have been a bit…preoccupied of late," Margaret pointed out gently. Mel opened her mouth to protest, only to close it again at the knowing gleam in the older woman's eye.

"You don't miss a thing, do you Margaret?" she accused with a sigh.

"Not really miss, no," the older woman admitted, a hint of pride in her voice. Funny how she had found the woman's weathered face and dark beady eyes totally unappealing at that first, uneasy meeting. Now she found Margaret's lined face and sharp discerning eyes comforting.

"Alyce's continued presence is making things difficult," she conceded gloomily, brushing the crumbs off the table. Since Raphael's surprise visit to her room almost a week ago, Alyce had become increasingly demanding of his attention, stretching his good intentions to their absolute limits. If an escort didn't arrive soon, she suspected Raphael would send the young woman packing, judging by the growing weariness of his smile.

"She's making life difficult for everyone," Wendy muttered, breaking into her bleak thoughts. "Just the other day she went off at my poor Simon, demanding he do a better job of polishing her saddle," she related bitterly as she reached for another biscuit.

"You would think there'd be word by now," Mel murmured, staring at the dirt caught underneath her nails. Alyce probably never had dirty, chipped nails in her life, she thought sourly.

"Poor Si, he'd just got back from checking the chicken coop too," Wendy continued, shaking her head.

"The chicken coop? Wasn't that repaired only recently?" Mel quizzed, her body stiffening.

"It was," Wendy confirmed as she delicately bit into her biscuit, "but foxes are still getting in."

"I don't how the little buggers are doin' it," Margaret grumbled. "John reckons they can't find any breaks in the fence."

Mel felt her skin break out in goose flesh. Some of her students claimed to have seen a monster in the woods around Burchellton. "A big ugly man in rags," Lucy Cahil had told her earnestly, her eyes wide with fear.

"I saw it too Miss," her brother Luke had confirmed, clear blue eyes unflinching as he nodded solemnly. When she suggested they may have seen a vagrant, or a surviving raider, they had both adamantly shaken their heads. "It was a monster Miss, easily twice the size of a normal man, with grey skin, and a funny hat that covered his eyes," Luke had insisted. Someone else in the class had complained about foxes getting into their chickens, despite the erection of a new, high fence around the old coop...

"There must be a hole under the fence somewhere," Margaret was insisting doggedly, her wrinkled hand brushing crumbs off the corners of her mouth. "There are too many weeds..."

Her theory was cut short by a blood-curdling scream coming from somewhere outside the manor. They froze for a moment as the scream shattered the calm night air, sending chills down their spines. "Jane!" Wendy cried, springing out of her chair. With speed born of fear, they raced out of the kitchen, heedless of their own safety as the scream died abruptly. Limbs trembling from the surge of adrenalin, they came to a halt outside the stable. "Jane! Jane!" Gerald shouted desperately, emerging from the stables with a lantern in one hand, and a pitchfork in the other. They followed him as he rounded the building. "Jane!" he called frantically, shining the lantern over the area.

"What happened Gerald?" Wendy asked.

"Uh, I just went to check on the horses, they were upset about something. Jane was right here, and then I heard her scream..."

"What's going on here?" Raphael demanded as he arrived on the scene, sword in hand. Gerald swallowed nervously, nodded at Raphael.

"Jane's missing sir," he reported unevenly.

"Hey, over here," Mel cried. She had wandered a couple of feet away, squinting at the ground in the patchy moonlight. "Tracks," she stated, pointing to huge footprints on the dusty ground. The other men were now jogging across the yard, the light of their lanterns bouncing towards them.

"Good spotting Mel," Raphael murmured, grabbing the lantern off Simon. "Margaret and Wendy, return to the manor and prepare the medical supplies," he ordered, glancing over at their drawn, ashen faces. Wendy opened her mouth to protest, but changed her mind as her gaze fell upon the massive footprint. Stiffly, the women turned to make their way back to the kitchen. "Mel, go with them," Raphael added as he started to follow the prints.

"No way, I'm coming with you," she asserted, falling into step beside him.

"Damn it woman, can't you ever just do as I say?" he snapped, lengthening his strides.

"There's no time to argue," she pointed out breathlessly as she struggled to keep up with him. "Say, where's Sarah?" she asked, finally registering her absence.

"I ordered her to stay with Alyce," he answered tersely clenching his jaw.

"I bet she didn't like that," Mel murmured. He grunted in response, his attention firmly fixed on the ground. Just then they heard a distant crash directly ahead of them. Without any further prompting, Gerald sprinted into the forest, the lantern swinging madly before him.

"Gerald, wait!" John and Ted called after him in vain. With a muttered curse, Raphael chased the desperate man into the shadowy forest. The odd footprint in the dirt kept them on track as they raced through the trees, the sound of crashing being drowned out by their own footfalls and ragged breaths.

An anguished cry greeted them as they came upon Gerald kneeling on the ground, clasping Jane's still body to his chest. As the light of the lantern fell upon him, they could see tears glistening on his cheeks. "Jane, Jane," he sobbed into her shoulder, rocking back and forth. John and Ted knelt down beside their brother, tried to console him. Even in the lanterns' flickering light, it was obvious Jane's neck had been broken. Three ugly red marks showed against the pale skin of her neck.

"Come on, let's find the monster that did this," Raphael ordered darkly. "John and Gerald, get the body back to the manor..."

"Wait," Gerald interjected with a sniffle, gently disentangling himself from Jane's limp body. "I'll come too," he said, his tone brooking no argument. Raphael wordlessly nodded and moved on into the forest, leaving John to carry Jane back to the manor.

They continued on in tense silence. The night air was so still, she jumped halfway out of her skin when someone stepped on a branch, causing the crisp wood to snap loudly. Her heart hammering wildly in her ears, she took a steadying breath and nerved herself to keep walking. "Damn, we're out of footprints," Raphael cursed, his steps slowing as he moved the lamp around. The massive footprints trailed away from the dirt track, the distinctive treads disappearing into the grassy ground to their right. In the eerie glow of the lanterns, large spiderwebs stretched between the trees, the sticky silk threads gleaming only inches above their heads as they cautiously made their way further into the forest. The undergrowth seemed to steadily thicken with each step, the branches clawing at their legs. She shivered in the chill night air, wishing she could have grabbed a coat on the way out.

"This place gives me the creeps," she mumbled to no one in particular as they broke out of the undergrowth to enter a small clearing. The hairs on the back of her neck rose on their own accord as she suddenly felt as she was being watched.

"If you want to go back, be my guest," Raphael muttered distractedly, squinting at a spot on the ground.

"What is it?" she asked, following him towards the glint of white that protruded the low- lying grass.

"Ugh," he grunted as the stench of rotting meat hit his nostrils. "I think we just found our missing chickens," he murmured, prodding a pile of bones with the toe of his boot.

"Ugh," she echoed, clasping her hand over her nose.

"I'll be damned," Cedric breathed as he shone his lantern over the sizeable collection of bones. "Whatever did this, it's been attacking more than our chickens," he remarked, spotting the half-eaten carcass of a pig.

"Hard to believe foxes could drag an animal that size," Ted said with a nervous glance at the surrounding trees, as though he expected a monster to leap out at them.

"Someone or something has been camping here for some time," Raphael mused, turning his head sharply as he saw something move at the edge of his vision. He was cautiously approaching a particularly large oak tree when a high-pitched scream shattered the heavy silence. "Damn," he cursed, turning around to run back towards the manor.

"But we're onto something here," Mel protested to their retreating backs. There was no reply as darkness gathered around her, and the feeling of being watched intensified. "Shit," she swore, tearing off after the bobbing lantern lights. Stumbling over the uneven ground, she hurtled past the now sinister-looking trees to burst noisily into a clearing not far from where they'd found Jane. The men stood tensely in a semi-circle, their weapons drawn as Raphael draped a protective arm around a trembling Alyce. Sarah stood stiffly before him, her hands bunched at her sides.

"I'm sorry Father," she was saying in a tightly controlled voice. "I only left for a little while, to help them with the body..."

"Oh, you mustn't blame Sarah," Alyce interjected unevenly, looking up at him with large, dilated eyes. "I did wander off to investigate the noise. It's my own fault for being so nosy..."

"What did you see, Miss Kensington?" Gerald asked urgently, his knuckles whitening around the handle of the pitchfork.

"It was a huge man, dressed in rags," she related hesitantly, shivering under Raphael's arm. Mel swallowed back the wave of jealousy she felt at seeing his fingers brush against Alyce's bare arm.

"Which way did he go?" Gerald pressed, his body obviously ready to sprint recklessly into the forest.

"I, I don't know," she croaked, dashing tears from her eyes. "When I screamed, he ran off in that direction," she answered, pointing to her left.

"That's in the opposite direction to what we were following," Mel pointed out. Raphael looked sharply at her, his mouth a tight line of displeasure.

"It's possible our quarry doubled back," he suggested gruffly, giving Alyce's shoulder a final squeeze before withdrawing his arm. "Mel, Sarah, escort Alyce back to the manor. The rest of us will split up and do a sweep of the forest," he ordered.

"But Father..."

"No arguments!" he snapped, his tawny eyes flitting across Sarah's flustered face to include Mel in its fiery glare. With a final glower in their general direction, he stormed off towards the forest, the men warily following in his wake. Jaw clenching as she bit back any response, Sarah turned away and walked stiffly back to the manor.

"I'm sorry Sarah, I didn't mean to get you into trouble," Alyce panted, half-jogging to catch up to her.

"Well, you bloody well should be," Sarah muttered darkly without looking at her. "God, I turn my back for one minute and you rush out to investigate a noise? Didn't you see what that, that monster did to poor Jane?" she continued more stridently, rapidly losing control of her voice. Tears gathered in the corners of her eyes at the mention of Jane.

"I didn't really think about it," Alyce stammered, wringing her hands as they entered the yard.

"So ah, what happened exactly?" Mel asked, falling into step beside Sarah.

"Like I explained to Father, I just went to help Wendy prepare a place for...the body. I was only gone for a couple of minutes, and then we heard Alyce scream..."

"I was trying to help," Alyce blurted, tears rolling down her cheeks. Sarah stopped dead in her tracks, turned slowly to face her.

"You want to help, do you?" she asked in a low, dangerous voice. "Then just go home and leave us alone!" she roared into her face.

"Sarah!" Mel cried, grabbing the girl's shoulders and pulling her back. "Come on, let's just go and help Wendy and Margaret," she suggested, rubbing the girl's tense shoulders. Sarah reluctantly allowed Mel to pull her away, her hate-filled eyes never leaving Alyce's shocked face until she was physically turned around. "Be careful what you wish for, little tramp," Alyce murmured to the still night air as she slowly, unconcernedly followed Mel and Sarah back to the manor.

Alyce felt the urgent tapping against her consciousness, nudging her out of sleep. "Mistress, mistress," the deep adoring voice spoke inside her mind.

"What?" she snapped, both mentally and verbally, forcing her eyes open to the dark room.

"I have come, as you ordered," the voice explained patiently, as always seeking approval from its cranky mistress.

"Right," she muttered, struggling to sit up. "Just don't kill anyone else until I get there," she commanded waspishly, pushing herself off the bed. Already largely dressed, she donned her cloak and picked up her boots on the way to the door, her stockinged feet padding softly against the floor. The door opened with an obligatory creak, and she crept out into the corridor, wincing as she eased the creaky door shut behind her. She carefully made her way past the disused ballroom and down the stairs, her heart firmly lodged in her throat. Once outside the manor, she put her boots on and marched stiffly towards the forest, where the still night air now carried a blanket of fog. Must have drifted in off the lake, she surmised, shivering slightly as the chill dank air penetrated her clothes.

Thankfully Raphael had decided against putting anyone on watch. That would have made it a lot harder for her to sneak out undetected. She glanced nervously over her shoulder, half expecting to see Sarah or Mel spying on her from their respective windows, their suspicious faces illuminated in the faint moonlight. The wall of dark empty windows stared back at her, and she sighed with relief. Mel and Sarah were certainly tenacious in their paranoia. If only they knew how well-founded their suspicions were, she thought with a smirk.

She followed the tug of the brutish consciousness until she came upon a clearing. Greasy bones littered the floor, accompanied by the stench of rotting meat. "Ugh, it stinks around here," she muttered, walking clear of the debris. "Clay?" she called out. There was a rustle in the bushes behind her. She spun around, and slowly backed away as a huge golem emerged out of the trees. Unnaturally long arms swung by his sides as he approached, pale grey skin gleaming in the moonlight. A leather cap sat on top of his bald head, the dark glass inserts that normally hung over his eyes glittering above his forehead. She stared up at the black pools that served as his eyes, the huge pupils framed by stark white, with no mitigating membranes. Dirty, tattered clothes hung loosely from his enormous frame.

"You'd better clean up that pile," Alyce ordered, nodding at the collection of bones on the ground.

"Yes mistress," the giant rumbled, moving towards the mess.

"Not now," she hissed, hand going to the pendant swaying above her cleavage. The rectangular block of polished stone felt surprisingly warm against the clammy, cold skin of her hand. She rubbed her thumb over the strange words engraved on its glossy surface. Clay gasped as fiery splinters suddenly pierced his skull, the matching stone embedded in his brain ringing painfully.

"No mistress, stop," he croaked, clasping his head. "I'm sorry about the woman," he added desperately, collapsing to his knees.

"What were you doing, skulking about so close to the manor?" she snarled, giving the pendant a final rub, wincing slightly at the echoing pain in her own head. The psychic link that existed between them wasn't completely one way. In order to control Clay, it had been necessary for a similar stone to be implanted in her brain. Uncle Henry had reluctantly agreed to do the operation, his eyes darkening with fear at his niece's fervour. Despite his reassurances that Clay would follow her to the ends of the earth without the special stones, she had insisted on having full control of the golem, whatever the cost.

"Ahh," Clay groaned, pressing his fingers to his temple, "please mistress, I was hungry. I was just on my way to get a chicken, when the woman saw me…"

"That's another thing," Alyce interjected, letting her hand fall away. "You've got to cut back on the chickens. People are getting suspicious."

"Alright, mistress," he stammered hoarsely, clambering unsteadily to his feet as the pain in his head abated.

"That was a close call, Clay. If I hadn't distracted them, they would have discovered you for sure."

"I know," the golem mumbled, remembering with a shudder the anxious faces drifting past him as he huddled behind a giant tree.

"Damn, we're running out of time," she muttered as she began to pace the forest floor. "Jenkins will be here within a week, and we're no closer to confirming we have the right man. Raphael is too wiry to let anything slip, despite my persuasive efforts. No," she mused, staring at the backdrop of moonlit trees, "Mel is the key."

"The schoolteacher?" Clay prompted. He had caught glimpses of the woman walking through the forest, the pretty red-haired girl skipping happily by her side.

Alyce turned to study intently the large, grey man. Images of the sewn-together monstrosity lying on the huge metal table in her uncle's laboratory floated to the surface of her mind. The smell of blood had permeated the air as her uncle drew elaborate symbols on the floor around the table, his hands covered in chalk dust. "A blend of science and magic," he had told her excitedly, the magnifying glass attached to his head band falling down over his eye in his excitement. The rumble of distant thunder sent him dashing across the lab, checking the connectors and wires that hung down from the ceiling and entered the patchwork body at various points. He had only just finished tightening the connectors when lightning struck the conductor rod. The air had cracked and popped sharply in her ears as electricity surged through the wires and into the waiting vessel. She had watched in frozen terror as the massive body shuddered violently on the table, her uncle ranting madly beside her. Abruptly the eyes of the creature opened, and the dark pools stared directly at her, a faint, adoring smile forming on the monster's misshapen lips. In that instant, a bond had formed between them. a bond she was only too happy to exploit.

"That would be her," she said, disgust creeping into her voice. The woman was such a bloody do-gooder it made her sick, so much so she found herself looking forward to seeing Jenkins again. She could just picture his cold, bland face staring dispassionately at her as she gave her report, never giving away his feelings until the very end, filling her heart with doubt. With a simple twitch of his facial muscles, he could make her feel as though she was ten feet tall, or make her want to shrink away and hide in the shadows like a cockroach. "If we just give Mel a push in the right direction, I'm sure she'll lead us to the truth," she said distractedly, remembering the day she had spied Mel standing stiffly outside Raphael's room. She had been on her way to the library when she spotted Mel in the corridor. Ducking hastily back behind the corner, she had peered cautiously past the wall as Mel hesitantly reached out to touch the door. Her fingers were just about to rest on the smooth wood when Sarah's voice called out from the stairs. With a start Mel had jumped away from the door and rushed down the corridor, as though the hounds of hell were at her heels. "There's something in Raphael's room that Mel's attracted to, and I'm not just talking about Raphael," she murmured with a smirk.

"Don't worry," she reassured Clay, squaring her shoulders as a plan started to form in her head. "We'll have what we need by the time Jenkins gets here," she declared with growing confidence. "Then you can do what you like with the girls," she added, her lips curled in a sneer.

"The red head is very pretty. I just want to play with her," Clay rumbled wistfully, shifting his feet.

"Ugh, I don't want to know," she declared, raising her hands in a warding gesture. He started to protest, not liking the insinuation in her voice.

"No, it's not like that…"

"So what, you were just playing with Jane too?" she asked sarcastically.

"Jane?" he quizzed, his brow wrinkled in confusion.

"The woman you killed tonight," she supplied impatiently.

His face crumpled under her angry glare. "I didn't mean to," he croaked, his throat suddenly dry. "I was just trying to stop her from screaming. I tried to tell her I didn't want to hurt her, but she wouldn't listen…"

"Oh shut up you big oaf. I don't care how it happened, or if you meant to kill her or not," she snapped, turning away. "Just don't do it again, not until we have what we need." She stared out into the fog as it drifted through the forest like an ominous ghost. So much was riding on this mission. Her family would be tripping over each other in a race to fawn before her. Even her father would bow to her by the time she was finished, his stern, proud face broken and humble. "Sanctimonious old fool," she muttered, her body stiffening with anger at the memory of her father.

"What, mistress?" She jumped at the deep voice so close behind her.

"Never mind," she said dismissively, walking past him. "Now don't be surprised if you're required to stop another message from reaching my family. Raphael is bound to send another letter soon."

"Yes mistress," he mumbled, smiling faintly in the shadows. He had managed to remove the letter from the last messenger without bloodshed. Amazing what one well-aimed rock could accomplish. The horse had reacted brilliantly to the rock hitting its rump, throwing the courier to the ground. While the man staggered after his horse, he had rushed out and sifted through the leather satchel left unattended on the ground until he spotted Alyce's neat, sloping writing. Despite his brutish appearance, he didn't really relish violence. He had a bad habit of inadvertently killing people. In the case of Jane, he had just placed a massive hand around her throat as he urged her to be quiet. When he heard the man call out from the stables, he had taken flight into the forest, dragging the woman's increasingly limp body behind him. He must have pushed just a little bit too hard against the fine bones at the base of her neck...

"In the meantime, stay low. Alternate from one hiding spot to another, starting from now. Don't come back here for at least three days, they're bound to search this area tomorrow."

"Yes mistress," he sighed, eyes drifting to the giant oak tree that had become his home the past couple of weeks. The dense bushes at the base of the tree offered enough cover to conceal even his prodigious bulk from the outside world. After following the tenuous trail of psychic breadcrumbs left by Alyce for two days, he had come upon the tree and promptly crawled under the thick blanket of bushes to fall into a deep, dreamless sleep. He had never felt so afraid in his short, unnatural life as he struggled to pick up the faint signal, his lumbering steps through the countryside becoming more desperate. The wound he had inflicted had been deep, almost too deep.

"Don't forget, you'll have to start going to the rendezvous point every night next week..."

"How's your side, mistress?" he asked suddenly, breaking into her stern relaying of orders. She looked up at him in annoyance, jaw clenching at the memory of the sword being driven into her body. "Stop asking that Clay. It's fine," she answered tersely, her hand going on its own accord to the bumpy, tender scar tissue above her hip.

"But I almost killed you," he cried, stepping towards her. Killing all the other people in the coach had been hard enough, their faces contorted in fear as he crushed their windpipes, Alyce watching tensely from the sidelines. With the last passenger falling lifelessly to the ground, he had turned towards her, his hand groping for the sword at his side. Her face blanched with fear, she had urged him to run the blade through her, her fingernails digging into his forearm as she braced herself for the piercing blow. The clatter of the coach being dragged away by the panicked horses echoed in his ears as he drew back the sword, to be replaced by Alyce's high-pitched scream.

"Shush," she bade, putting a finger out to his dark grey lips. "It had to be done," she told him gently, touching the side of his guilt-ridden face. She traced the long scar running down his cheek, a faint smile tugging at the corners of her mouth. "I told you I'd get into the manor one way or another," she continued, letting her hand fall away. "Unfortunately, extreme measures were required. Now," she declared briskly, steering away from the subject, "I'd better head back, it'll be daylight in a couple of hours."

"Yes mistress," he acknowledged, bending down to pick up the bones.

"Good," she murmured approvingly, wrinkling her nose at the smell. "I'll be in touch, Clay."

She felt his adoring gaze upon her as she made her way out of the clearing. "Imprinting" her uncle had called it. Some animals form an instant bond with the first animal they see. It was no accident that she was there that night, standing by Clay's twitching body as he came to life. Uncle Henry had made sure she was in the right place at the right time. The ultimate gift from a doting uncle who knew he didn't have long to live, the cancer in his body slowing killing him. She still felt a sense of awe when she remembered all the work Uncle Henry did to create the golem, the months of research and experimentation building onto a lifetime of medical study. To think he did all of that for her, so that she would be protected in his absence. "Don't worry Uncle," she spoke softly to the night sky. "Our revenge will soon be at hand."

Mel opened her eyes with a start. Heart pounding wildly in her chest, she stared out into the darkness, hands gripping the edge of her blankets. The cold fingers of air that had stirred her from slumber dropped away, leaving her filled with doubt. "Must have just imagined it," she croaked to the ceiling, swallowing painfully past the dry walls of her throat. "Like all those other times," she added hoarsely, chills running down her spine. Deciding she needed a drink of water, she propelled herself out of the bed and hastily pulled on the over-sized coat she'd found in a cupboard recently. Wrinkling her nose at the musty smell, she stumbled about the room in search of her thick wool-len socks. After much groping of the cold hard floor around the bed, she felt the familiar knitted texture under her fingers. She pulled them on and padded softly out of the room, wincing with the squeaky opening and closing of the door.

As the corridor fell silent, she felt the familiar pull, and before she knew it she was standing before Raphael's door, straining her senses to catch a trace of whatever it was that called to her from within his room. Faint memories trickled through her mind as she rested her forehead on the cool surface of the wooden door and closed her eyes. Huge chunks of metal tearing off a plane as it crashed through trees, a cacophony of screams and crunching fuselage filling her ears, having the air forced out of her lungs with every gut-wrenching jolt. Against the murky backdrop of her mind, she saw herself hunkered down in the seat, waiting for the end as the ceiling crumpled above her head. Fingers of intense white light tugged at the corners of her tightly-shut eyes, and she looked up in time to see a jagged hole in space opening before her. The light intensified, and suddenly the hole engulfed her...

With a start she opened her eyes, jerked back from the door as she felt another presence in the corridor. Swallowing nervously, she turned to find Alyce studying her intently, her pale hair catching a stray column of moonlight that penetrated the shadowy corridor. Alyce put a finger to her lips, beckoned her to follow as she quietly slipped around the corner. As if in a dream, she reck-lessly followed the blonde woman to her room, hesitating briefly at the doorway before entering. She had not visited the room since Alyce claimed it as her own. In the faint moonlight, she could just make out the selection of borrowed clothes strewn over the two padded chairs in the far cor-ner. Some of her personal effects had survived the attack, a leather bag concealed within her skirts miraculously escaping the attention of the alleged raiders. The various bottles and trinkets were scattered across the top of the dresser, along with a silver-handled hairbrush.

The abrupt creak of the door closing behind her made her jump and spin around. "A bit jumpy, are we?" Alyce suggested softly as she released the handle and moved to the centre of the room.

"What do you want?" she hissed, struggling to keep her voice low. Even in the pale blue moonlight, she could see the woman's lips lift in a smug smile.

"Ah, I think it's more a question of what you want Mel" she purred, her hands tucked neatly behind her back as she walked over to the dresser. "That's the second time I've seen you standing before Raphael's door with a rapt look on your face," she murmured distractedly, picking a gold bracelet off the little table. In the mirror set above the table she watched with satisfaction Mel's guilty reaction. She wondered briefly if Mel realised how transparent she was. "Of course, it could just be that you're infatuated with Raphael…"

"Could you just get to the point?" Mel snapped, resting her hands on her hips. Her smile slipped at the woman's insolence. Putting down the bracelet, she turned towards Mel.

"Look, believe it or not Mel, I want to help you," she grated, walking stiffly to stand before her. "Something is drawing you to that room." With a sharp intake of breath, Mel looked up at Alyce's solemn face, her treacherous cheeks darkening in the moonlight. Alyce took a steadying breath, her heart beating more rapidly as she prepared to gamble.

"I can arrange for the door to be unlocked while Raphael and Sarah are out riding with me." she suggested hoarsely, throwing all her chips on the table.

"What?" Mel croaked, her mouth suddenly dry. "How? Raphael keeps his room locked tight whenever he's not there," she pointed out, her fidgeting fingers settling on a coat button.

"Please," Alyce scoffed, "I've been picking locks since I was ten. It was the only way I could have fun at night," she explained truthfully. Her neurotic father had insisted on locking his daughters up at night from an early age. She had fast learnt how to open the tumblers of the barrel lock, to sneak out of her room when the castle fell silent.

"But why would you do that for me?" Mel asked doggedly.

"For a start it'll stop this ridiculous trend of yours to linger around Raphael's door like a lovelorn puppy," Alyce sneered. "I'm sure Raphael would be mortified to find you snooping outside his room."

"Cramping your style, am I?" Mel suggested tartly. Alyce smiled, nodded as she turned away to inspect the clutter on top of the dresser.

"You have no idea," she murmured gratefully. If Mel wanted to think that, that was quite alright with her.

"It's an awful big risk you're taking, just to get me out of the way," Mel pointed out, her narrowed eyes never leaving the sleek blonde head as it bent over the dresser. Straightening her features, Alyce spun on her heel to confront the wary woman. "Raphael is of extreme interest to me," she admitted, taking meditative steps towards Mel. "If I make a big enough impact, perhaps he'll correspond with me once I'm safely home. He's not without assets," she reasoned, secretly enjoying the hurt look in Mel's eyes at her words, "and he would have much to gain by courting me…"

"All right, you've made your point," Mel muttered, stepping past her smug, beautiful face. "Answer me this then," she demanded, turning back to level hostile eyes at her. "Why are you up at this hour, fully dressed?" Her gaze drifted over to the glistening wet boots sitting in the corner by the door. "You've been out, haven't you? Did you have a secret meeting or something?" she asked archly.

"Ah, ever the detective Mel," Alyce sighed, picking hair off the shoulder of her musty coat. "I couldn't sleep, that's all," she offered with a shrug, "so I went for a little walk."

"Weren't you just slightly scared, going out with a murderer possibly lurking about?" she asked, irritably shaking the woman's hand off. With an injured look, she withdrew her hand.

"I'm sure whoever or whatever was responsible for Jane's death has left this area by now," she offered truthfully, imagining Clay striding through the forest, his lengthy steps taking him speedily away from the manor.

"You sound remarkably unconcerned," Mel observed, tugging the coat tighter around her body as a cold draft crept into the room.

"Look, do you want my help or not?" Alyce snapped, suddenly feeling very tired.

"What's the price of this help?" Mel countered, her shoulders rigid under the dark, coarse material of her coat.

"There's no price," Alyce cried, fast losing her patience. "Just get in that room and settle this once and for all, so you can stop haunting his door. I don't care what you find, if you find anything. I just want you out of the way." Her heated words hung in the air between them as they stood glaring at each other, their shared animosity breaking free of its constraints.

"What's to stop me from going to Raphael and telling him all about your little offer?" Mel finally asked, her voice struggling to escape her clammy throat. Alyce's arms hung stiffly at her sides as fear of failure reached out and squeezed her wildly beating heart.

"Do that, and you'll lose your best chance to get into that room," she warned, closing the gap between them. "Stop thinking about everyone else for a change Mel," she implored with a hint of sincerity. "It's time you started thinking about yourself."

"Fancy you saying such a thing," Mel muttered as she turned away and headed for the door.

"At least think about it," Alyce urged, taking an impulsive step towards her retreating form. "The door will be unlocked while we're gone. The rest I leave to you," she sighed.

Mel paused in the doorway to study Alyce's beautiful moonlit face, trying in vain to read the smooth, neutral mask. With a final grunt of disapproval, she left the doorway to trudge back to her room, alarm bells clanging noisily inside her head. "Alyce can't be trusted," she muttered softly as her coat fell heavily to the floor. But why would Alyce encourage her to enter and search the room if she's capable of unlocking the door herself? Maybe she did just want her out of the way. "Like I'm a serious threat," she sneered as she crawled into bed. Raphael barely had time for her these days, with the exception of that one night… "Damn," she cursed, staring out into the grey shadows, the first rays of dawn nudging at the darkness. As her mind buzzed with questions and possibilities, she gradually succumbed to sleep. In the depths of her uneasy slumber, cold invisible fingers brushed over her cheek, the familiar invitation defeating all logic and doubt in her mind.

Mel brushed her hands down the front of her skirt, frowned belatedly at the floury smudges left on the dark fabric. She had spent a large part of the morning helping a pale-faced Wendy in the kitchen. With Margaret opting to help return Jane's body to her family, Wendy had been left to run the kitchen by herself. They had stood in the yard to watch the solemn party make its way into the forest, Gerald stiffly guiding the buggy onto the dirt road, his hands tightly gripping the reins. Margaret had waved weakly from inside the carriage as it passed, her tired eyes sliding off their grim faces as she pulled away from the window.

Mel shuddered at the thought of Jane's body lying across the seat of the carriage, the flaccid flesh bouncing and rocking with every bump and pothole. "Poor Margaret," she murmured as she made her way up the stairs. The sound of her boots striking the steps seemed overly loud in the gloomy silence, the manor unusually empty for this time of day. Nevertheless, she glanced nervously over her shoulder as she entered the corridor, half-expecting someone to jump out and catch her in the act. Drawing back her shoulders, she moved determinedly past the library, only vaguely registering the familiar features of the passageway as she approached Raphael's room.

Whatever she thought of Alyce, she had to concede the woman was brilliant. Her earnest suggestion over breakfast that they all ride out with Raphael to see the carriage safely through the forest was a stroke of genius. Sarah had eagerly agreed, rubbing the back of her hand over bleary, dark-rimmed eyes. With a brief glance in Alyce's direction, she had made her excuses, wincing inwardly at the hurt look in Sarah's eyes. Raphael had merely frowned at her over his mug before urging Sarah and Alyce to hurry up and finish breakfast. Her purposeful steps finally brought her to Raphael's door, her sweaty hand reaching for the handle. With painful slowness, the smooth metal gave way under her hand, and the thick wooden door swung inwards. Alyce must have slipped away while Sarah and Raphael were preparing their horses to pick the lock.

Moving as though in a dream, she stepped into the room and softly closed the door behind her. Dusty air tickled her throat and nostrils as she took in the piles of clothes, books and bottles scattered throughout the room. Resisting the urge to cough, she tread cautiously past the dusty tomes that had apparently escaped the confines of the large bookshelf sitting against the wall. She hastily averted her eyes from the large bed in the far corner, the twisted mass of sheets and blankets mirroring the state of her own bed. In the opposite corner sat a desk covered with books and empty wine bottles, the dark glass catching the midday sun that streamed in through the grimy windows. Completing her scan of the room, her eyes fell upon two stuffed chairs sitting before the disused fireplace, clothes draped over their backs.

She stood in the middle of the room, straining her senses to catch a hint of the ghostly presence that had beckoned to her so many times before. "Oh, come on," she cried to the unassuming walls.

Nothing. No icy tendrils brushing against her skin, no whispers teasing her ears. No new memories. "I must be going mad," she muttered, turning to leave in disgust. She had just reached the door when there was a loud clang from the fireplace. She spun around, her heart hammering madly in her chest at the abrupt sound. An old rusty poker that had been leaning against the wall beside the fireplace now rested on the floor. Frowning, she walked to the fireplace, knelt before the cold, blackened stones of the fire pit. As she returned the poker to its customary spot, something at the back of the fireplace caught her eye.

Staring intently at the stone block, she crawled into the firepit, the hard rough floor biting into her hands and knees. Gritting her teeth against the pain, she shifted awkwardly to kneel before the soot-coated panel. Something made her reach out and investigate with her fingers its pitted surface. To her surprise, the stone slid back under her fingertips, and stale air rushed out to meet her. Gagging slightly at the smell, she pushed the stone back completely to reveal a small dark space behind the wall. Familiar dank fingers brushed past her, settled on her back like a determined hand pushing her towards discovery. "Ah, now that's more like it," she murmured, crawling forward.

Wrinkling her nose at the musty, mouldy smell, she squeezed through the opening. As her eyes adjusted to the gloomy half-light, she stiffly rose to her feet, half-expecting to bump her head on something. "It's not a cave, Mel," she muttered to the shadows. Apart from its concealed entrance, it was an unassuming room. Some light managed to enter the room through small holes in the mortar, the slender shafts faintly illuminating the thick blanket of dust that covered every-thing. In the far-left corner was a simple wooden chair, a stack of leather-bound books arranged haphazardly on the seat. On the floor next to the chair sat a thick, half-molten candle, sticky cobwebs stretching out from the bumpy sides. An old wooden stand stood in the opposite cor-ner, slivers of glass scattered evenly before it, the jagged edges glinting up at her from the floor.

She tread cautiously through the maze of glass fragments to the chair, picked up a book from the top of the pile. With a lot of squinting she could just make out Raphael's hurried scrawl travelling across the page. She was in the process of deciphering his writing when a movement on the floor caught her eye. A particularly large piece of glass gleamed by her feet, its shiny surface somehow piercing the gloom. Setting aside the book, she bent down and carefully picked up the shard. Her grimy face stared back at her as she stood up, the sharp edges digging into her hand.

"Mel, you look like shit," she grunted to herself, turning the piece over. The backing was smooth, pitch black. Not completely smooth she discovered on closer inspection, discerning a complex network of fine lines imprinted on the surface. Oddly the intricate pattern of intersecting lines seemed familiar. "A circuit board?" she whispered, an image of herself hunched over a circuit board filling her mind. Beneath her tense hand, a tiny resistor sat innocently on the board, the tip of her soldering iron wavering above the resistor's metal leg. The vague memory acted like a switch in her head, giving the piece of glass in her hands new meaning.

"What the hell is this?" she croaked softly, seeking reassurance from her own bemused voice. She jumped as the glass suddenly became warm in her hands, almost dropping it in her surprise. Re-establishing her hold on the edges, she watched in shocked fascination as the glass lit up, and pictures flickered across the shiny surface. A boy and girl sat at a dining table, their heads bent in concentration as they drew pictures, the felt pens staining their small hands. A dark haired man entered the room, set his mug on the kitchen counter. With a brief smile at the children, he started talking to someone out of view. The image widened, and a woman could be seen standing at the sink. At the sound of the man's voice, the woman reached out and flicked the switch on the electric jug. An unintelligible cry was torn from Mel's lips as she saw herself turn away from the sink to wrap her arms around the man and bury her face in his broad shoulder. Clutching the shard desperately, she watched as snippets of her past were replayed before her hungry eyes. Slowly she sank to her knees, losing herself completely in the precious images, even as the sharp edges of the glass bit into her hands. Blood oozed out of her palms and fingers, making the glass slippery. Tightening her grip on the fragment, she continued to stare at the animated surface, eagerly absorbing the lost memories of her life.

"Come on Monty," Raphael muttered, tugging on the reins as he urged the giant black stallion to turn around and re-enter the forest. Sarah looked up from her morose inspection of the ground, stiffly encouraged Moonbeam to follow suit. With a final backward glance at the carriage, she guided Moonbeam into position alongside Monty, carefully keeping her tear-streaked face averted from his. "Are you sure they'll be okay?" she croaked as the sound of the carriage creaking over the open road receded into the distance. Jaw clenching, he looked across at his bleary-eyed ward.

"They'll be safe enough," he assured her hoarsely, guiding Monty around a pothole in the dirt track. "How are you faring, Alyce?" he asked as her sleek blonde head entered his field of vision, peering past Sarah's concerned face to gaze at her earnestly.

Lines of tension around her eyes and mouth belied her answering smile. "I'm fine," she lied, gritting her teeth against the dull pain in her side. Every jolting step agitated the wound, making it difficult for her to maintain her balance in the saddle. It took every ounce of her will power not to lower herself to the ground and lie down. It had better be worth it, she thought darkly, silently willing Mel to take the bait she had so carefully laid out.

Raphael frowned, turned his attention back to the forest path. He made a mental note to accelerate his plans for returning Alyce to her family. With Jane's death, and the temporary lost of two more staff members, he couldn't comfortably play amicable host for much longer. More and more he found himself looking forward to having the manor back to normal, without her politely prying eyes examining every aspect of their lives. "I still don't understand why Mel didn't want to come along," Sarah muttered sourly, cutting through his ruminations.

"I guess she felt sorry for Wendy," he offered lamely, shrugging off his own misgivings about Mel's decision to stay behind. He could have sworn he saw Alyce briefly stiffen in response to Mel's mumbled answer.

"Hmph," Sarah grunted, clearly unimpressed with the situation. They continued on in gloomy silence, despite the sun shining down from a perfect blue sky, sharp fingers of light penetrating the thick forest canopy above their heads.

"Oh," Alyce murmured, swaying slightly in the saddle as the pain in her side intensified. A wave of nausea swept over her, and the forest swirled before her weary eyes.

"Are you alright?" Raphael asked sharply, swinging his head around in response to her weak cry.

"I said I'm fine," she snapped, gripping the horn of the saddle, beads of sweat forming on her brow. "That stupid bitch," she muttered, turning her face away as Raphael guided Monty to her side.

"Perhaps we should stop," he suggested, reaching out for her reins.

"No," she growled, tightening her hold on the reins. "Let's just get back to the manor," she added crossly.

His eyes narrowing at her curt tone, he opened his mouth to reply in kind, when the piercing scream of the Mirror rang through his mind. "Ugh," he groaned, swaying forward over Monty's thick neck.

"The Mirror," Sarah whispered beside him, clutching her head.

"Is something wrong?" Alyce asked innocently, watching closely their tense faces.

"We have to go," Raphael croaked, wincing at the pain in his head. Nodding at Sarah, he gathered his reins and kicked his heels into Monty's sides. "See you back at the Manor Alyce," he barked over his shoulder. She gazed at their retreating backs, a smug smile lighting her features.

"Oh, don't worry about me," she murmured, sitting up straight in the saddle. "Suddenly I'm feeling much better."

Raphael swung a long leg over Monty's shivering rump and dismounted. Cedric rushed out to take the reins, a mixture of astonishment and concern on his face. "What's wrong, sir?" he asked, reaching out to soothe the restless stallion.

"Nothing," Raphael grunted as he turned towards the manor, the mirror's mad song filling his head.

"Father, wait!" Sarah called as she galloped into the yard. She pulled Moonbeam to an abrupt halt and hastily dismounted, all too aware of the dread in his eyes as he waited stiffly for her. "How did this happen?" she panted as they stormed through the yard. "I thought you always locked your door..."

"I do," he snapped impatiently, yanking the door open. "Someone has broken into my room," he stated flatly, his face set in a grim mask.

"It's Mel, I can feel it," Sarah said unevenly, tears pricking the corners of her eyes. "The Mirror's been reaching out to her more and more since that night…"

"I know," Raphael panted, taking the stairs two at a time. Fortunately, there was no one else about to gawk at their dramatic passage through the building.

"We should have told her," Sarah croaked, her voice struggling to slip past the sudden lump in her throat.

"It's a bit late for that now," he told her ominously, his long strides slowing as they reached his room. He grabbed the handle, felt the smooth round metal give under his hand. "Are you ready?" he asked before wrenching the door open, his shoulders tensing under the thick fabric of his coat. Sarah nodded meekly, her face pale and drawn. "Right," he murmured, taking a deep breath and pushing through the doorway.

After all their frantic hurrying to get there, their steps were slow and measured as they entered the room. Funny, he thought as he approached the fireplace. This kind of scene should take place on a stormy night, with crashing thunder and flashes of lightning punctuating the drama, all with the background noise of rain lashing the windowpane. Not on a fine sunny day, with cheery sunlight streaming in through the window, and birds chirping outside. He bent down in front of the fireplace, squinted into the dimly lit space. "Mel?" he called hesitantly to the kneeling figure. He gazed at Mel's unmoving form, feeling his heart sink. With a sigh of resignation, he crawled through the disused fire pit to the room on the other side. Wincing against the mad song reverberating in his mind, he rose awkwardly to his feet in the cramped area, remembering too late to keep his head low.

"Mel?" he repeated, rubbing the back of his head as he carefully tread around the broken glass. He hadn't actually entered the secret room since that fateful night. It had been hard enough to drag Sarah out without coming back to clean up the mess, the Mirror's tormented cry creating an effective barrier. The only reason he could venture into the dusty space now was Mel's apparent control of the Mirror, turning the deafening shriek to a dull roar. He shuffled around her still body, looked down at the absorbed face. She stared at the piece of mirror in her hands, seemingly oblivious to his presence. His eyes widened at the blood dripping from the shard's sharp edges.

"Mel!" he cried, kneeling down before her.

"Is she alright?" Sarah asked through the opening.

"Not really," he answered gravely, his concerned gaze travelling over the stony, impassive face. "Mel," he called softly, cautiously touching her hand. She flinched at the contact, head snapping up. Murky hazel eyes bored into his, pupils moving back and forth as she searched his face.

"You knew," she croaked, fingers tightening around the glass.

"Mel, your hands," he cried, covering her hands with his own as more blood oozed out from beneath her fingers.

"I saw the whole thing," she whispered, looking back down at the shiny surface. "The mirror showed me."

"What's going on?" Sarah demanded, crouching down in the firepit to peer through the opening.

"Wait, we're coming out," he barked, looking past Mel's shoulder. "Come on Mel," he implored, putting his hands on her shoulders. "It's not safe in here."

She tore her eyes away from the silent pictures to study him coldly. "It's not safe for you," she uttered in a low, dangerous voice. With a slight nod of her head, the mirror's scream intensified, drawing a pained groan from his unwilling lips. He vaguely registered Sarah's high-pitched squeal in the distance as he reeled back from Mel.

"Please, Mel," he croaked, stiffly raising his head to squint at her through pain-filled eyes, "let us explain. Then by all means...punish us both," he panted, sitting back on his heels. The mad song abated, and he forced his tired limbs to move.

"Fine," Mel muttered, sliding the glass into her pocket as she staggered to her feet. The room swayed alarmingly before her, the floor rushing up to meet her.

"Mel," Raphael grunted, lurching forward to steady her collapsing body. "You've lost too much blood," he panted as they stumbled together towards the opening.

"Nonsense, I'm fine," she mumbled sleepily, slumping over his rigid arm.

"Of course you are," he grunted, setting her gently down on the floor. "So be a good girl and crawl out of here," he suggested, brushing the hair out of her eyes.

She opened her mouth to protest, belligerent eyes glinting in the grainy half-light, when she heard Sarah's anxious footsteps beyond the fireplace. "Sarah," she growled, her head snapping forward.

"Mel, wait," Raphael called desperately, following her frantically through the opening.

"Are you okay Mel?" Sarah asked unevenly, stepping back from the fireplace as she clambered out of the fire pit.

"It's all your fault," Mel croaked, rising jerkily to her feet. "You dragged me through time and space, dumped me in this hellhole, completely and utterly alone," she cried, her voice ragged.

"I didn't mean to," Sarah croaked, tears streaming down her cheeks. "I just, didn't want you to die," the wretched girl sobbed, looking away from her hate-filled face.

"Didn't want me to die?" she echoed, bloody hands bunching up at her sides. Gathering her strength, she launched herself at Sarah's cowering figure, sent her crashing to the floor. "Do you have any idea what I've been through?" she roared as she straddled Sarah's prone body and seized her neck.

"I'm sorry," Sarah rasped, clawing feebly at the thumbs pressing into her windpipe. "It was...an accident." The faint confession barely scraped past her vocal cords as Mel tightened her hold.

"An accident!" Mel shrieked, knuckles whitening with tension against the blue-tinged flesh. "Let me go!" she screamed as Raphael dragged her off Sarah's struggling body. She spun about, thumped her fists into his chest. Grunting with the effort, he grabbed her wrists, held them against him. "Let me go, you bastard!" she screamed, trying in vain to pull away from his steely grip.

"Shush," he murmured, drawing her close, feeling her trembling body through his clothes. She swore vehemently into his chest, her tears soaking into his shirt as she gradually stopped struggling and sagged against him. "Sarah," he called, scooping up Mel's unconscious body and setting it in one of the chairs, "get me some water, please."

"Did you see the hate in her face?" the girl asked softly, absent-mindedly rubbing her upper arm. Raphael looked up from Mel's pale face to where his ward leant heavily against the wall, her bleary eyes glued to a spot on the floor.

"Sarah," he repeated more firmly, raising his head above the back of the chair. She pried her wretched gaze from the floor. "Get some water please love," he ordered gently.

The girl nodded wordlessly, moved to the bedside table. He turned his worried gaze back to Mel's slumped form, reached out for her slashed hands. Running his long fingers over the lacerations, he healed the torn skin. "Come on Mel," he murmured, checking her weak pulse, his eyes darting across to Sarah's weary face as she returned with a cup of water. "Wake up Mel, you have to drink some of this," he urged, taking the cup from Sarah's nerveless grip. He dipped his fingers into the water and rubbed wet fingertips over her lips. She stirred, licked her lips. Eyelids fluttering open, she eagerly accepted the cup he held to her mouth. With much spluttering, she gulped down most of the water. "Were you ever planning on telling me?" she asked hoarsely, weakly rubbing the back of her hand across her wet chin.

Raphael looked away in shame. "Yes," he sighed, rising stiffly to his feet, taking the cup with him. "Though I'm not sure when we would have mustered up the courage to tell you," he muttered as he moved to the bedside table.

"You must have found it pretty funny, offering me the use of your library, when you had the answers all along," Mel spat angrily, her flinty eyes following him about the room. He looked up sharply, his face darkening.

"I assure you, there's nothing funny about this situation," he grated as he refilled the cup.

"Please, don't blame father," Sarah whimpered, taking a timid step forward. "He would have told you months ago if it hadn't been for me." She swallowed past the sudden lump in her throat, shrank away from Mel's loathing glare. "I kept waiting for the right time to tell you, like a true coward," she croaked. "But I was so scared of losing you..."

"What am I to you? A pet?" Mel demanded, struggling out of the chair.

A firm hand pressed down on her shoulder, guiding her back into the seat. "Please, drink this before you launch another attack," Raphael advised dryly, handing her the cup. Muttering darkly under her breath, she took the proffered cup with a trembling hand. The room fell deathly silent as she carefully sipped the water. "So," Raphael began awkwardly, sitting stiffly down in the other chair, "how much did the mirror show you?" Mel lowered the chipped ceramic cup to her lap, intently studied its glazed surface.

"It showed me everything up to the night of the plane crash," she answered unevenly. "Showed my old life, my family, everything that I've lost."

Sarah swallowed nervously as she perched on the armrest of Raphael's chair. She had known this day was coming, had dreaded it since that fateful day when Mel stumbled to her rescue. Her fertile imagination had painted many vivid pictures of how this confrontation would play out. Try as she may, she could never picture it ending well for anyone. She forced herself to look up from the floor and meet Mel's intense glare. "Why Sarah?" she rasped, pushing the scratchy sound out of her clammy throat. "Why did you pick me and my family? The mirror showed you people from all over the world, from all walks of life. Why focus on my ordinary life?"

Her eyes flitted over Raphael's solemn face, saw the deep concern hidden through tiny cracks in his grim facade.

"The Mirror shows you what you most want to see," she answered with a shrug, remembering Raphael's lectures on the artifact. Out of the corner of her eye, she saw Raphael's lips twitch briefly with amusement at being virtually quoted. "I don't remember much about my life before Timmy and I were sold off to the factory. When the mirror showed me you and your family, I suddenly real-ised how much I yearned for a normal family." She glanced apologetically at Raphael, hastily looked away from his stony face. "You have to believe me Mel, I had no idea this could possibly happen," she said huskily to her lap, unable to meet Mel's penetrating gaze.

When finally she forced herself to look up from her fidgeting hands, Mel's eyes were drawn to a distant point of the room, a strange, unreadable expression on her face. The intervals between each frantic beat of her heart seemed longer than the last, until time seemed to stop completely as they waited for Mel to say something. Even the cheery chirps of the birds outside had fallen away to grave silence, as though the tension of the room had leaked out into the surrounding forest. "Tell me everything you know about the Mirror," Mel finally commanded, her small calm voice breaking the horrible stillness. "Everything," she repeated, blasting their heads with the mirror's disjointed song. Shaking his head to dispel the song's lingering echoes, Raphael rose stiffly from the chair, his hand settling briefly on Sarah's shoulder before launching into the story of the mirror.

Alyce shifted her weight against the tree trunk, closed her eyes so she could better focus on Raphael's voice. The voices faded from time to time as the players moved about the room, but she was able to discern the gist of the unfolding drama. Hopefully no one would notice the small, pol-ished stone sitting behind one of the fallen books near the bookcase. Uncle Henry's final gift to her, an innocuous stone that matched the one in her head. It picked up vibrations from the surrounding air, projected these sounds to the matching stone. As long as she was roughly within a mile of the listening stone, she could hear whatever it "heard". "Come on Raphael," she muttered, wincing at the dull pain in her side as she straightened her legs out. "Get to the point," she sighed, leaning her head back. Clay moved beside her, his massive bulk shuffling awkwardly around as he stood watch.

That was the main problem with using the listening stone, she was vulnerable to attack while she concentrated on the faint sounds drifting through her head. Sweat trickled down the side of her face as she made out Raphael's scratchy words. His shock expulsion from the ranks of nobility had forced him to find other, more subtle ways to make a living. With the few valuables he'd been able to take with him, he and Sarah had fled to Europe. Between Sarah's deft fingers and Raphael's academic background, they managed to carve out a niche for themselves as treasure hunters, selling their finds on the lucrative black market. They were doing pretty well for themselves until a chance meeting changed their lives forever.

While scoping out possible projects in Turkey, they ran into Gunthar Bliesch, an archaeologist down on his luck. Gunthar had spent most of his family fortune procuring a scroll that detailed the location of a religious relic. Raphael agreed to fund an excursion to the Middle East, for part-ownership of the relic. After months of searching through long-forgotten tombs and catacombs, they finally located a walled-off chamber in the bowels of an extensive underground cave. Laboriously digging their way into the still space, they discovered the simple pane of glossy black material under a thick layer of dust. A bleached skeleton sat next to the artefact, its twisted bony hands fused to a stone tablet by centuries of dirt. Prying the fingers away, Raphael had managed to free the flat stone. Inscribed on its surface were the Arabic words, "Beware the Mirror of God." Alyce stiffened at the mention of the mirror, her eyes squeezed tightly shut in concentration.

"The Mirror of God?" Mel echoed slowly, her hushed voice only just discernible over the sound of Raphael's restless feet.

"There was also a picture," Raphael said with growing enthusiasm, his footsteps drifting away from the listening stone. "Engraved on the bottom of the tablet," he continued distractedly amid a faint rustling of paper and pen. "It looks like some sort of ship, but I doubt it's for the water," he offered, his footsteps returning. "I drew it as best I could from memory..."

"From memory?" Mel prompted, her voice muffled by the rustle of paper presumably changing hands. "What happened to the tablet?"

"We had to leave the cave in a hurry," he explained ruefully. "There was an earth tremor, shortly after we removed the mirror. We barely got out of there alive..." His voice trailed away as an expectant silence fell over the room.

There was a creak of leather and wood as Mel got out of the chair. "So, how come you have the mirror now?" Mel asked, her voice gaining volume as she approached the bookshelf. Alyce forced herself to breathe, straining to hear Raphael's muffled voice over the wild beating of her heart. Time to hear his side of the story, she thought with a smug smile.

"It didn't take long for us to realize the Mirror was special. The moment we touched it, it seemed to come alive, its voice ringing in our heads," Raphael explained.

"So far so good," Alyce murmured, recalling Gunthar's fevered account of their introduction to the mirror. She could see the wild, clear blue eyes and bedraggled, blonde hair as he waved his arms around, the thick German accent rising and falling like a ship on rough seas.

"It started well enough," Raphael said with a sigh. "While it was only about the size of a dinner plate, the mirror was surprisingly heavy, so Gunthar and I agreed to take turns carrying it. With each turn however, Gunthar became increasingly bad-tempered and paranoid, muttering under his breath, twitching, giving us dark looks. I should have seen it coming," he added, his voice thick with self-derision. "Anyway," he continued, his boots striking the hard wood floor, "we were making our way through some rugged mountains in Turkey when he completely snapped. He grabbed Sarah and threatened to push her over the edge if I didn't relinquish the Mirror to him. I agreed, and was preparing to hand it over, when he doubled over, screaming in pain. Sarah managed to get away as he lost his balance and fell down the mountainside. It was a long drop…"

Alyce frowned. In Gunthar's version of the story, it was Raphael who became increasingly possessive over the Mirror, culminating in him pushing an unsuspecting Gunthar off the narrow path. She shook her head, unsure which story to believe. She somehow doubted Raphael was as innocent as he claimed. Nevertheless, it was difficult to take Gunthar's word for anything, except perhaps during those rare lucid moments. All those bumps to his head had done bad things to his memory. They'd staked out several suspects based on vague, shifting description of his nemesis. If Gunthar's last description had led them on another wild goose chase, she imagined Jenkins would have arranged for Gunthar to suffer one final blow to the head.

"Curious," Mel murmured, the scrape of her boots against the floor ringing loudly in her ear. She must be standing right next to the stone. Absurdly, she found herself holding her breath until Mel's feet moved away from the bookcase. "So, what happened then?"

Raphael carefully summarised their journey back to England and settling down in the manor. While researching the artefact, a splinter of glass had somehow broken off and found its way into his hand. Too late he noticed the tiny fleck of dark glass disappearing into his blood stream. Over the next couple of days, he felt the build-up of alien energy in his body, stirring beneath his skin, pushing at the crude barrier. Agitated by the burgeoning energy, he accidentally cut himself during a practice session with Sarah. Without knowing exactly why, he extended his hand over the deep gash, and they watched as the lacerated flesh healed before their astonished eyes.

"Ah," Alyce breathed as a large chunk of the puzzle fell into place, opening her eyes to dappled sunlight kissing the ground at her feet. She had been pleasantly surprised with the speed of her recovery, putting it down as a side effect of her uncle's tinkering, never suspecting that Raphael's first aid efforts went beyond sewing her back up. "I owe him my life," she whispered to the brilliant patches of blue sky showing through the thick forest canopy, her smug smile slipping. Clay stirred at the faint sound, moved into view.

"Is everything alright Mistress?" he rumbled with the sort of instant attentiveness that always set her on edge.

"I'm fine," she snapped, closing her eyes pointedly. When Clay's shuffling steps had moved away, she took a steadying breath and shrugged her slender shoulders. It was too late to turn back now. "That's what you get for taking in strays, Raphael," she muttered sourly, pushing away her sudden feelings of guilt.

"That wasn't the only gift, was it?" Mel asked tensely, her restless footsteps returning to the bookcase. Alyce winced at the harsh sound of Mel's boot slamming into the book that covered the listening stone, struggling to hear the woman's strained words through the pain in her head. "That day in the forest, you'd cut down four large men before you were overcome by the others..."

Sarah coughed nervously, her heels clicking sharply against the floor.

"When the mirror shattered, a piece found its way into me," the girl explained sheepishly. Another blast of sound assailed her mind as the stone was violently scraped along the floor. Alyce jerked upright, breaking contact with the stone. With surprising speed, she clambered to her feet, heart pounding wildly in her chest. "Damn," she swore hoarsely, blinking up at Clay's scarred features. "Our client isn't going to be happy about that," she croaked, limbs trembling with dread.

"What is it, Mistress?" Clay asked, his massive paws automatically reaching out to steady her as she stumbled away from the tree.

"Come on, let's go," she ordered briskly, shaking off both his question and his helping hand. "We've got the information we need. Now it's up to Jenkins what happens next." Clay watched her storm off, his dark grey lips twisted in bemusement. With a shake of his head, he adjusted the thick leather band of his goggles, making sure the dark glass sat protectively before his light-sensitive eyes. Sometimes he didn't know which was the greater mystery, his creator's decision to give him such specialised vision, or the perpetual cloud that seemed to enshroud the Mistress' mind. It seemed wrong to him that such an intelligent, beautiful woman should be so troubled. Bending down to scoop up his simple bag of belongings, he lumbered after his moody mistress, who was already climbing into the saddle and bringing her horse around. Keeping a safe distance from the nervous animal, he set off through the trees towards the rendezvous point, Alyce's pale hair a bouncing beacon amid the growing shadows.

Raphael tapped on the door, waited for the frantic rustling to die down. After their tense discussion about the Mirror, Mel had left the room in a hurry, her intention to leave written plainly on her face. With a sympathetic look at Sarah, he had rushed to his cupboard, unlocked the bottom drawer. "She's going to leave, isn't she?" Sarah had murmured behind him as he hastily scooped coins into a pouch.

"Of course she is," he'd grunted, rising awkwardly to his feet. "Do you really blame her?" Sarah's stricken face filled his mind as he jiggled the pouch of coins in his hand, his palms slick with sweat. "Mel," he called out when the door didn't open. "Please Mel, we need to talk."

"Go away," she shouted through the door. He sighed, struggled to be patient.

"At least let me pay you the money you're owed," he pointed out hopefully. The rustling stopped. There was a soft click as the bolt reluctantly slid back, and the door swung open. Her back firmly turned to him, Mel stiffly bent over the bed. He slowly entered the room, carefully stepping around the various items of clothing strewn over the floor. For someone with few possessions, she'd managed to make quite a mess.

"So, you're leaving," he observed, idly picking up some under-garments off the chest of drawers.

"I can't stay here," she barked tersely, shoving spare stockings into her hessian sack.

"Well, take whatever clothes and bedding you need," he offered lamely. She straightened up, turned away from the bed.

"Thank you," she mumbled, snatching the pants out of his hand.

"This is for you," he sighed, setting the pouch on the smooth wooden surface. Her eyes flickered over the small cloth bag sitting innocently on the chest of drawers, flitted across his face.

"You're not going to try and talk me out of leaving?" she snapped, plucking up the pouch and shoving it into her coat pocket.

"There doesn't seem to be any point," he answered truthfully, leaning heavily against the chest.

"Hmph," she grunted, turning back to the bed. "Oh, that reminds me," she muttered abruptly, dropping to the floor, her fingers grappling with the long material of her dress. She finally pulled back the skirt to reveal an old woollen scarf tied around her leg, the long ends tucked down the top of her right boot. It slowly dawned on him as she tugged at the tight knot that it was the same scarf she wore to hide the marks on her neck the night he begged her to stay. With a grunt she straightened up, shaking a gold ring out of the folds of fabric. "You'd better have this back," she said solemnly, dropping the ring onto his outstretched hand.

"My family ring," he murmured, turning over the simple band of gold, the engraved albatross catching the light. "No, the ring is yours now," he protested, holding it out to her. "It was part of our agreement..."

"I can't keep it," she cried, backing away from his extended hand. He stared at her in bewilderment, glanced down at the ring glinting on his palm.

"Why not?" he demanded, feeling anger stir within him.

"I just can't," she croaked, tears spilling down her cheeks as she continued to stuff her sack with clothes. Reluctantly closing his hand around the ring, he shoved it into his pocket.

"Look, you don't have to go," he suggested softly, taking a tentative step toward her. "If you need some space, we can try and keep out of your way..."

"It wouldn't be enough," she interjected, roughly rubbing her hand over her wet cheeks. "I have to get away, give myself time to sort all this shit out," she continued breathlessly as she resumed her frantic packing.

He watched her rigid shoulders rise and fall with each stiff, angry movement, feeling his tenuous hold on her steadily slip as the sack filled up. "Mel," he sighed, crossing the floor to stand beside her, his eyes desperately seeking hers, "just promise me you won't go too far away. We both want a chance to make it up to you somehow," he offered lamely. Stiffening at his nearness, she slowly turned to face him.

"Is that it?" she asked in a hushed voice. "Or do you just want a chance to regain control of the Mirror?" He opened his mouth to protest, to offer words of reassurance, yet the tiny grain of truth behind her accusation stopped him. Telling her about the night of the raiders' attack had been harder than he imagined. Try as he may, he couldn't keep the tension out of his voice as he described how the Mirror's chaotic song had entered their heads, pushing them to the edge of their sanity. Just when the Mirror's madness had almost consumed them both, she had stirred and casually told it to be quiet. Regarding him through narrowed eyes, she had walked stiffly to the fireplace, leant forward to rest her forehead against the smooth sandstone. The hurt that crossed her face as she abruptly straightened and turned away had made him want to crawl into the nearest man-sized hole and pull the earth in over his stupid head.

"I can't deny," he said thickly, looking away in shame, "that when you successfully ordered the Mirror to be quiet, I felt unbearable envy. The things it showed me, the sensation of power coursing through my entire body, it's so addictive…" Words deserted him as she blinked back fresh tears and returned to the lumpy sack on the bed.

"Well, at least you're being honest," she muttered bitterly, carelessly shoving her battered pot into the sack.

"Damn it Mel," he cried, gazing in frustration at her rigid back, "that's not the only reason, and you know it. We care about you. You've become a part of our strange little family…"

"I had a family!" she snapped, spinning around to face him. "I still have a family, but I'll never be with them again," she cried hoarsely into his face, her hot, angry breath fanning his neck. "Do you have any idea how utterly alone I felt in those first few months, how many times I wished I were dead?"

Heavy silence fell over the modest bedroom as they gazed at each other, broken only by the stirring wind outside carrying leaves and dust past the thick glass of the window. "And yet you survived," he finally spoke, pushing past the sudden lump in his throat. "You didn't give up," he added, placing his hands on her shoulders. "You clung to hope that there was still something to live for."

Her lips parted as his fingers stroked the crumpled material of her sleeves, brushed the bare skin at the nape of her neck.

"What are you trying to say?" she demanded huskily, silently cursing her treacherous body as the ice within her began to melt under his silky touch. Sighing, he slid his hands down her arms, catching her fingers in his.

"Running away is not the solution Mel. When you're ready, I hope you'll come back, and give us a chance to redeem ourselves."

With a muffled cry of frustration, she snatched her hand back. "You're a fine one to talk," she snapped as she stubbornly resumed packing. Out of the corner of her eye, she saw his face darken, the wide, well-shaped lips pressed into a thin, angry line. Stiffly he spun on his heel and left the room, slamming the door behind him. She jumped at the sound, promptly sunk to her knees. "Sanctimonious bastard," she muttered as she waited for her limbs to stop trembling. How dare he lecture her about running away from problems. Mumbling sourly under her breath, she returned her attention to the bulging sack on the bed, the desire to get away from the manor before sunset driving her exhausted body onwards.

Raphael stormed up the passageway, his hand furiously extracting the key from a coat pocket. "That was a stupid thing to say Raphael," he admonished, voice full of disgust. With a savage thrust and twist, he opened the door to his room. Yet another mistake to add to his growing list, he thought snidely as he strode into the room and closed the door behind him. Of course, he had known this day was coming from the moment he reluctantly acknowledged that Mel was the same woman they'd watched in the Mirror. Saw it coming, and did nothing. Grimacing at the musty smell now pervading the room, he crouched down in front of the fireplace, leant across the cold dusty stone pit to close the back wall. As he strained against the thick stone, he idly wondered what Mel would do with the Mirror. "Damn," he grunted. He didn't get around to thanking her for ordering the Mirror to be quiet. After months of having the Mirror subtly gnaw at his consciousness through the thick stone wall, she had miraculously quelled the worrying voices. The resulting silence had washed over him like a cool, gentle breeze, soothing the frayed edges of his sanity.

With all the words flying between them, somehow he had failed to ask the crucial question of how she had gotten into his room. He couldn't believe for a second he had left his door unlocked, and while Mel had received a few pointers on picking pockets from Sarah, he somehow doubted she'd be capable of picking the lock. She must have had help. A chill ran down his spine at the thought of someone breaking into his room. Finally the stone slid into place, and he carefully reversed out of the cramped space. His face fell as he took in the state of the room. A trail of blood crossed the floor, with an especially big puddle by the chair. His clothes were scattered all over the place, and clumps of dust from the secret chamber dotted the floor and chairs.

"Great," he muttered, grabbing a rag from the mantle and dropping it on the puddle of blood. While moving it disconsolately through the congealed mess with the toe of his boot, his eyes wandered to the fallen book. The mid-afternoon sun streamed into the room, its position in the sky causing the shadows to lengthen. As he bent over and retrieved the tome, he spied a smooth, black stone nestled against the base of the bookcase. Frowning, he placed the book on the shelf and picked up the stone. A network of fine white veins patterned the polished surface, slicing through the pitch-black stone. He stared at the stone sitting so innocently on the palm of his hand, feeling his flesh crawl. Taking a deep breath, he reached out with his mind to the highly polished surface, felt something familiar meet his probing consciousness.

Closing his eyes in concentration, he followed the trail of psychic energy out the window, over the dusty yard, through the forest until a huge grey bulk came into view, lumbering determinedly along the over-grown path. The dark glass of the creature's goggles glinted as the massive bald head abruptly swung around. Dark grey lips peeled back to expose finely chiselled teeth, the monstrous man seeming to sense his presence. Swallowing nervously, Raphael prepared to pull back from the scarred angry face when a pale spot moving amongst the shadows caught his attention. Doggedly following the trail of energy, his consciousness approached a woman on horseback, blonde hair bouncing about her hunched shoulders. "Oh no," he breathed, hastily withdrawing from the determined face as it suddenly turned to look directly at him. "Alyce," he croaked, opening his eyes with a start.

"It must have been Alyce," he growled, clenching his hand around the stone. She had come down to the yard behind everyone else, her breathing a little ragged, a few strands of pale hair uncharacteristically out of place. Accompanying the carriage to the edge of the forest had been her idea. Suddenly all the pieces fell into place as he remembered Mel's stiff refusal, her eyes sliding away from his questioning gaze. "She set me up," he cried, throwing the stone across the room. "How could I be so stupid!?" he roared, kicking the chair over in rage. Waves of anger crashed over him as he wrenched the door open and stomped out into the corridor. The hall swam about at the edge of his vision until he came to heavy stop before Mel's door.

At the sound of his urgent knocking, Sarah opened her door, rubbing a sleeve over her tear-streaked face. "Father?" she called out unevenly to his stiff back.

"Mel, are you in there?" he said shouted at the door.

"She's left already," Sarah croaked, finally penetrating the fog of fury clouding his awareness.

"You were right to be suspicious of Alyce," he muttered darkly, turning away from the door to glare at her. "Our sophisticated guest from the South appears to be a spy."

"What? How do you know that?" she asked bewilderedly, stumbling after him as he strode down the hall.

"I'll explain later," he said brusquely, taking the stairs two at a time. "Right now, we have to warn everyone."

"Warn everyone about what?" Sarah gasped, awkwardly tramping down the stairs in his wake.

Registering the exasperation in her tone, he reluctantly slowed down and allowed her to catch up. Glancing over at her frightened face, he rested a hand on her tense shoulder, hoped she didn't feel it trembling through the fabric of her dress. "We have to expect an attack Sarah," he explained grimly, giving her shoulder a brief squeeze before letting his hand fall heavily away. "Alyce will be back, and she won't be alone." Gaping helplessly at his rigid back as he stormed out of the manor, she stood indecisively in the hallway. In the space of a day, her whole world was falling apart, and all she could do was watch on helplessly as the fabric split and fray about her.

"I'll go and help Wendy," she murmured to the silent walls, forcing her stiff limbs to move. One look at her bleak face as she trudged into the kitchen, and Wendy was rushing to her side, asking her what the matter was. Amid choked explanations and restrained sobs, Wendy guided her to the table and into a chair. "I always knew there was something funny about that Alyce," Wendy mused as she scooped heaped teaspoons of tea into the waiting pot. "Sounds like everyone will need a nice cup of tea before the day's out," she continued sagely, frowning into the empty tin. Sarah nodded mutely, finding her practical words soothing as she prattled on about the wonders of tea. "Don't you worry miss, the Master won't be caught unawares by that nasty piece of work," Wendy declared confidently, her voice slightly muffled as she bent down and fished another tin out of the cupboard. "Mark my words, miss, he'll have that tart on a spike by the end of the day," she continued, her hands smoothly opening the tin and spooning in extra leaves.

"I hope you're right Wendy," she mumbled with a shuddering sigh, watching the tiny black leaves fall into the pot. The smell of tea wafted across the room to meet her nostrils. "Ha, already I feel better," Sarah murmured, rising from the chair to help Wendy with the tea.

Mel tore her eyes away from the animated surface of the shard in her hands, looked up at the shack door. "Who's there?" she barked irritably, stiffly pushing away from the table. "Ah, it's Daniel Miss," a familiar voice answered.

"What do you want?" she snapped, sliding the shard into her pocket.

"Um, I just wanted to make sure you're okay. I saw you through the window, and you're obviously not teaching..." With a sigh she opened the door. Daniel cautiously entered the shack, brown eyes full of concern as he took in the crumpled clothes and tear-streaked face.

"What are you doing here Miss?" he asked, closing the door behind him. Swallowing past the sudden lump in her throat, she returned to the old wooden desk that resided at the head of the classroom.

"Did you have an argument with Master Blythe, or Sarah?" he persisted doggedly, slowly making his way between the rows of makeshift desks.

"You could say that," she finally grunted as she leant back against the edge of the table and crossed her arms tightly over her chest. "I really don't want to talk about it."

"Oh," the boy murmured haplessly, shifting his feet awkwardly. "Do you have food and water? I could go and get you some from home..."

The fretting tone in his voice broke through her dark mood, a faint smile tugging at the corners of her mouth.

"I'm alright for the next day or so," she grudgingly reassured him, remembering with a shudder the fanfare that had greeted her departure. Wendy had hovered about anxiously as she stuffed bread and hunks of dried meat into her sack, asking questions she couldn't easily answer. Then on the way out she had encountered Simon and John as they emerged from the stables, tiredly brushing the straw and dust from their clothes. As she stood in the yard vaguely responding to their questions, she gave up all hope of a discrete getaway, glimpsing Ted's curious face poking out of the barn. After a few more yelled good-byes, she managed to escape, all too aware of the many eyes following her into the forest. "What are you doing out here anyway?" she asked impatiently, glancing up sharply at him.

The young man blushed furiously, hastily looked away. "Ah, I was just passing by," he mumbled sheepishly, pawing at the ground with the toe of his worn boot.

"Hmph," she grunted, shaking her head, "meeting Sarah, are we?"

Daniel nodded, nerved himself to meet her knowing gaze. "Well, we were supposed to. She didn't turn up," he supplied, his voice heavy with concern.

"Well," she sighed, pushing away from the table, "she's had a busy day." His eyes widened at her bitter tone.

"What is that supposed to mean?" he asked defensively, his eyes fastened to her pinched face as she paced before him.

"It means your little girlfriend is great at keeping secrets," she spat out angrily, thumping a nearby desk with her fist. "I lost everything because of that bitch, and she didn't have the guts to tell me," she roared, kicking a battered crate across the room. Daniel winced as the crate smashed into the wall, splinters flying off the shattered grey slats.

"Perhaps I should go..."

"She knew Daniel," Mel shouted over his suggestion, grabbing him by the shoulders. "She knew from the very beginning, and she never told me," she sobbed, her hands trembling as she shook him.

"Miss," he croaked, lungs rattling in his chest. With a look of disgust, she released him, stepped slowly back.

"I'm sorry," she said hoarsely, grimacing at the obvious pain in the boy's face. Gingerly rubbing the tender area, he cleared his throat, his eyes sliding away to the floor.

"Whatever the reason miss, you don't have to stay here," he rasped. "You would be more than welcome to stay with us. Hell, you could probably stay anywhere in town, after all you've done..." His words faltered as tears slid down her cheeks.

"Thank-you," she murmured, turning back to her perching spot at the head of the classroom. Suddenly she felt so tired, and she just wanted to curl up on the dusty floor and stare at the shard...

"How long do you plan on staying here anyway?" Daniel demanded. "It won't be very comfortable..."

"I've endured worse," she muttered darkly, hugging herself protectively as she remembered those early painful months of life on the road.

"And yet you survived." She looked up with a start, hearing Raphael's voice in her head. Daniel blinked at her startled face, stepped back nervously.

"Look Daniel," she began, clearing her throat, "that's very sweet of you, but I really just need time alone. I have a lot to think about..."

Nodding weakly, he turned away and headed for the door. She stared at his slumped shoulders, winced at his heavy feet as they shuffled along the ground.

"Daniel, wait," she called, springing from the table. Stumbling slightly, she rushed after him. "Maybe you could drop by tomorrow, to see how I'm going?" she suggested awkwardly, playfully nudging his arm.

"Sure," he responded, his face brightening, reminding her of the sun breaking through thick cloud after a thunderstorm. With a tired smile he opened the door and left the shack. Her relief was palpable as she closed the door and slumped against the wall. The cluttered room swirled about her as she staggered back to the table and collapsed onto its smooth, worn surface. Daniel was bound to tell Sarah that she was staying in the school shack. Hopefully he'd describe in detail her wretched state. Bitterness welled up inside her like a bad case of indigestion, the emotional equivalent of bile scorching a path through her soul. "Suffer bitch," she whispered, rolling onto her side, and reaching for the shard in her pocket. She imagined Raphael hovering before her, his voice desperate as he reassured her for the umpteenth time that Sarah had just wanted to save her from the plane crash.

"I'd be better off dead!" she screamed, willing the grave face to disappear as the glass bit into her hands. Tiny images skimmed the surface before her bleary eyes. "I'd be better off dead," she whispered to the shard, eyes fastened on the smudged, grinning faces of her children as they played with a stranger. The slender, dark-haired woman grabbed the little boy's hands, swung him around. "Kai," she croaked, rubbing her thumb lovingly over the giggling boy as he sailed through the air. A young girl jumped up and down in the background, obviously impatient for her turn. "Karen," she breathed, fresh tears rolling down her cheeks at the sight of those bright blue eyes wide with excitement.

Panting, the woman smiled as she set Kai gently on the ground and took Karen's waiting hands. Being two years older than Kai, she barely lifted off the ground, but laughed her head off never-theless. "Who are you?" Mel whispered to the woman, straining her memory for a clue. Judging by the size of the children, it was about two years after her disappearance. "No, I don't know you," she murmured, shaking her head. She had glimpsed the willowy stranger in her last session of Mirror watching. It seemed intent on showing her, in fast forward, what had happened in her absence. The woman now seemed to be a permanent fixture in their lives. Perhaps Gary was hiring her to care for the children during work. Swallowing past the sudden lump in her throat, she watched as her husband entered the scene, tugging at his tie. The woman stopped spinning Karen around and disentangled herself from the dizzy girl's flailing arms. He leant forward and kissed her lips, arms snaking around her waist.

Her mouth went dry as she gawked helplessly at the happy couple. They separated as Kai and Karen tugged urgently at their clothes. Fingers tightening around the jagged edges of the glass, she watched her husband and his new partner chase the children about the yard. "But I'm not dead," she croaked to the beaming visage of her husband. "I'm not dead," she repeated with more force, this time seeking the ecstatic faces of her children. She moved groggily off the table, lurched unsteadily around the room. "I'm-not-dead!" she roared to the intruder as she stumbled into a desk, her shin connecting with its sharp edge. "Agh!" she yelled, kicking viciously the offending furniture. "Ugh," she grunted, a wave of nausea rising within her. She doubled over suddenly and vomited, the shard slipping out of her bloody grip.

Spitting the bitter bile out of her mouth, she staggered to the main table, trembling hands groping for the water-sack. Through the dust and tears, she glimpsed the oval-shaped bag, fumbled for the stopper. In her haste, she knocked the bag off the table, causing water to spill onto the floor. A cry of dismay was torn from her lips as she dove to her knees, her clumsy fingers grappling with the water skin's slender neck. Cradling the shrivelled leather bag in her arms, what was left of her composure crumbled away, her shuddering sobs filling the small room. Together her blood and tears flowed out onto the floor, to mingle with the lengthening shadows.

John Morley sighed, sipped his tea. Grimacing behind the mug, he forced himself to take a large mouthful of the tepid contents. "Bah," he spat sourly as he lowered the chipped mug onto the bench. Not only was it cold, it tasted strange. With all the rushing around following Master Blythe's little speech, he'd barely had time to touch the steaming cup of tea he'd so carefully carried to the stables. "We need at least one man on watch at all times," the Master had declared, eyes darkening dangerously at the resulting moans. "Ted, you can go on first watch," he had ordered curtly, piercing gaze picking out the source of the loudest moan. Red-faced, Ted had mumbled consent and shrunk back into the small crowd that stood before Master Blythe.

"Ha, that'll teach Ted to grumble in front of the boss," John murmured, reluctantly pushing his tired body up off the bench. Being doubly short-handed, it had taken him longer to clean out the stalls. Simon should be here by now, he thought irritably. Something must be keeping him. More likely someone, he corrected himself with a salacious grin as he walked stiffly over to Monty's stall. Despite her attempt to subtle, he had spied Wendy's hand desperately groping for Simon's during the meeting, her eyes dark and needy. "Probably taking some time to "comfort" her," John snickered to Monty, reaching out to idly rub the great stallion's head. Suddenly his vision blurred, and there were several pairs of black, glistening eyes swimming before him, the horse's sleek face seeming to float away from his outstretched hand. "What the hell?" he uttered, stumbling back. He managed to glance at the half-empty mug sitting innocently on the bench before collapsing heavily to the floor. Monty whinnied at the unconscious figure, pawed the fresh straw beneath his hooves in protest. When none of the other horses paid any attention, he shook his great head and turned his attention to the bucket of grain sitting in the corner of his stall.

Jenkins stroked his moustache, pulled out his watch. Squinting against the slanted rays of sunset, he could just make out the time. "Right," he announced casually, closing the engraved silver cover over the watch face with a sharp click. "Showtime," he murmured, sliding the watch back into the pocket of his waistcoat.

"What if they're not all knocked out?" Alyce asked anxiously, hovering tensely by his side. The sleeping herbs she had so carefully mixed into the new tin of tea could knock out a herd of elephants. Still, they couldn't be sure that everyone had drunk the tea before noticing its adverse effects.

"Then we'll just have to subdue them the old-fashioned way," he replied with a sideways glance at Clay. The golem shifted his feet in response, his googled eyes glued to the windows of the manor.

"I can't hear any movement," Clay growled, his grey lobes twitching.

"Handy beast your dear uncle fashioned for you Alyce," Jenkins commented, light blue eyes full of admiration as he looked back at her.

"Clay's enhanced hearing has saved my life several times," she admitted stiffly.

"Ah, it's here," a hooded figure next to Clay whispered. They turned as one to the tall gangly man staring intently at the manor walls. Oblivious to the attention, his glassy eyes remained firmly fixed on the building. "It calls to me," he purred. With a faint look of disgust, Jenkins turned away from the man.

"Let's go," he ordered, drawing his sword. He willed his palm to stop sweating as he led them through the trees. Being so close to his prey enflamed his senses, made every sensation more vivid. For the last hour he had felt the tension build within him as they waited near the edge of the forest, safely beyond the sentry's sight.

Alyce's decision to initiate the plan before first consulting him hadn't helped his mood. As they stepped out of the trees and approached the empty yard however, he had to admit she'd made the right decision. Raphael had been fast to act, if the unconscious sentry on the lookout was anything to go by. Squinting up at the roof, he noted with satisfaction the slumped unmoving body on the small balcony, legs dangling over the edge, a heavy hand resting on the warning bell. Fortunately for them, there obviously hadn't been time for Raphael to check all their food for possible doping. Fingering the hard smooth case of his watch through his waistcoat, he imagined the women busily preparing the afternoon tea, the threat of attack making the daily ritual more urgent than usual. Now that's irony, he thought with a smug grin, his neat moustache almost sinister in its twitching.

Like a silent death cloud, they drifted from one building to the next, checking for unconscious bodies. At the entrance to the barn, they discovered Cedric collapsed over a bale of hay, a pitchfork laying just beyond the reach of his outstretched hand. In the hay loft of the barn, they found Simon and Wendy clasped in each other's arms, their loose clothes and dishevelled hair suggesting they had more planned than just a nap. On the floor next to the hatchway sat their half-empty cups of tea. Moving onto the stables, they spotted John's slumbering form on the floor. "That leaves at least one more person, beside our targets," Alyce hissed, her heart still firmly lodged in her mouth despite their unchallenged approach.

"I didn't think it would this easy," Jenkins said aloud, his voice booming against the stillness of the yard. Alyce winced at the comparatively high volume of his voice, gave him a dark look.

"Let's not count our chickens yet," she warned, her voice strained. "Raphael and Sarah have both been exposed to the Mirror. They could be more resistant to the drug..."

"Clay, do you hear anything yet?" Jenkins interjected, deliberately turning his back to her. The golem looked sheepishly at his mistress, mutely shook his great bald head, dark lenses reflecting their expectant faces.

"That's good enough for me," Jenkins said impatiently, surging on ahead to the kitchen door. Gritting her teeth together, Alyce stiffly followed, her dark blue eyes attempting to bore through the back of his arrogant head.

Tightening his hand around the hilt of his sword, Jenkins cautiously opened the thick wooden door. Alyce waited tensely for the faint creak of the hinges to end before peering past his shoulder into the deserted kitchen. Don't worry mistress, I'll protect you. She jumped at the adoring voice that she alone could hear, swung around to glare at the bulky golem as he squeezed in through the doorway. Damnit Clay, you scared the crap out of me, she projected fiercely, hastily turning back to the search. Sorry mistress, Clay mumbled in her mind, his sullen, unspoken apology accompanied by the sound of his large body bumping into the table and chairs. With the high-pitched scraping sound setting her teeth on edge, she doggedly moved into the familiar hall. Funny how Jenkins seemed to know where he was going, even though he'd never set foot in Blythe Manor before, she mused, shifting her grip on the handle of her dagger. It suddenly occurred to her that she should be leading the party, being the only person in the group with knowledge of the building.

She opened her mouth to protest when the hooded figure swept past her, the flaps of his cloak brushing against her. "Up here," the accented voice grunted, long legs pumping as he raced towards the stairs.

"Wait you fool!" Jenkins cried, reaching out and catching the man's shoulder, knuckles turning white as his fingers dug painfully into the flesh. The man cried out, sunk to his knees. "We have to take care of the others first," he hissed into the man's ear, giving his shoulder a final squeeze before releasing it with a look of disgust. Swallowing hard, the man nodded, his hand creeping to his shoulder.

"Yes, of course," he wheezed, struggling to his feet.

Alyce inwardly cringed at the fear and madness in the man's face as he shrunk back into the shadows and waited for her to past. They moved into the long corridor. She sighed with relief as she spied Peter's unconscious body at the end of the corridor, his outstretched hand reaching for the door of the training room. As they passed the entrance to the dining room, Clay stiffened, signalled for everyone to stop. "Movement," he whispered, pointing at the training room. Jenkins nodded, pale blue eyes meeting hers.

"Let's do this," he murmured, raising his sword. Nodding gravely, she held her dagger at the ready and slowly advanced up the corridor. This is it, she thought, her boots tapping sharply against the hard floor despite her timid steps. She could only just hear it over the sound of her wildly beating heart. Swallowing past the sudden lump in her throat, she willed her limbs to stop trembling, the memory of her father coldly sending her away spurring her on. You will be sorry Father, she silently vowed, her face a mask of grim determination as she followed Jenkins up the corridor. You will beg for forgiveness before the end, she promised, her lips twisted in a faint, sick smile.

As he neared the punchline, he paused to finish his wine. He set the empty glass on the table, looked up at the expectant faces around him. "So then I asked him, what do you do with the other end of the hose?" he said breathlessly, struggling to finish his own story. He faintly heard the girls' delicate giggles through his own raucous laughter, their faces blurring before him as tears streamed out of his eyes.

"A toast," Mel announced suddenly, tapping the side of her glass with a teaspoon. "To Raphael, and his wonderful ward, for bringing me to this hell hole."

His laughter died in his throat as Alyce leant forward to refill his glass, his eyes drawn on their own accord to her generous cleavage. Something about Mel's toast seemed inappropriate, he mused lazily as he raised his glass. Shrugging, he sipped the dark red wine. "Ugh," he groaned, knocking his glass to the floor as he doubled over in pain. He looked down to see if someone had actually driven a knife into his stomach.

He straightened up to see the girls watching him dispassionately, their glasses untouched. "Don't fight it Raph," Mel told him with a yawn. "It'll all be over soon."

"You poisoned me? I thought you had forgiven me," he spluttered through the bloody froth that was filling his mouth.

"Forgive you? Never," she told him flatly, jaw clenched in anger.

"But, what about Sarah? She's responsible too..." Sarah coughed nervously, looked at him sheepishly.

"Sorry father, but it was the only way to make it up to Mel," she confessed, her dark blue eyes sliding away from his stricken face.

"Really Raphael, it's for the best," Alyce offered, idly sharpening a small, curved dagger. Mel and Sarah murmured agreement, calmly resumed eating.

"You just never learn, do you Raphael?" a familiar voice purred softly behind him as cold steel pierced his body. His screams are drowned by the blood gushing out of his mouth, and all he can do is look down as the tip of a sword emerges out his gut...

"Ugh," Raphael gasped, waking with a fright. He stiffly raised his head, looked about the dimly lit training room. "Sarah," he cried hoarsely, clambering to his hands and feet. "Sarah," he croaked as he crawled unsteadily to where her unconscious body lay a few feet away. "Come on girl, this is no time for sleeping," he muttered, shaking her gently. Her forehead glistened with sickly sweat, her breathing shallow and laboured. Swallowing back the wave of nausea that swelled up within him, he lay a trembling hand over her heart, felt the faint, steady beat of pumping muscle. Closing his eyes, he followed the Mirror's energy as it radiated out from his hand into her body. "Of course," he murmured, sensing the strange chemical in her blood. Taking a steadying breath, he extended more energy into her system. Her eyelids reluctantly fluttered open, and he gratefully sank back onto his heels.

"Ow," she breathed as she sluggishly sat up. "My head throbs," she groaned, pressing a shaky hand to her temple.

"We were drugged," he explained, staggering to his feet. His gaze wandered about the room in search of clues as his memory slowly reformed itself. He'd hurriedly finished his tea before coming here to prepare their weapons, Sarah following close behind. Judging by the small pile of weapons in the corner, he hadn't gotten very far before succumbing to the drug. "Something in the tea, I suspect. Damn, I didn't think of that. She must have mixed the drug into the tea leaves before she left," he concluded, his voice thick with disgust. "God, I'm a fool."

"Who are you talking about?" Sarah asked grumpily, eyes full of pain as she looked up at him. He stared at her scrunched-up face, feeling his heart grow heavier with each frantic beat.

"Alyce," he whispered, his mouth suddenly dry. From somewhere in the hallway, a strange male voice faintly reached them, turning their blood cold. Raising a finger to his lips, he grabbed her hand and led her to the window.

"What are you doing Father?" she hissed as he desperately pushed open the stubborn window.

"You go and get help, or just run to safety, whatever comes first," he hissed back, urging her to climb out through the opening. He darted away and grabbed a sword. "Take this," he told her, his tone brooking no argument. She took the proffered weapon, looked up from the battered steel, her eyes bright with unshed tears.

"What about you?" she asked unevenly.

"I'll buy you as much time as I can," he answered grimly. The creak of a nearby door opening spurred him into action. "Now go," he grated, pushing her out of the window. With a small squeal and backward glance, she was gone. He shut the window in time to catch the squeaky turn of the door handle. Scooping a sword up from the floor, he raced to the door and pressed himself hard against the wall.

Time seemed to slow down as he waited for the door to open, his hand tightening around the hilt of his sword, his heart firmly lodged in his mouth. Suddenly the door swung towards him as a man strode into the room, sword held warily before him. In his cautious wake followed Alyce, her face stiff with fear as she scanned the room. Anger bubbled to the surface as he stared at her beautiful, perfect face from behind the door. Whatever ideas he had for dealing with the situation rapidly evaporated in the blinding white glare of his hatred, and before he knew it he was charging out and knocking her savagely to the ground, his hand firmly wrapped around her delicate throat. "You filthy little spy," he spat, squeezing her windpipe. "I saved your life, God damn it!" he roared, raising her head and bashing it against the floor.

Suddenly a huge hand grabbed his shoulder and hoisted him off her struggling body. He glimpsed a long thick arm attached to the great paw as he twisted about to see his attacker before being flung across the room. Struggling to his feet, he tried to focus on one of the angry grey faces floating before him. "What the hell?" he gasped as he leant heavily against the wall and stared up in horror at the seven-foot golem. Clay glared down at him as he ominously approached, his massive fist pulled back. "Don't kill him Clay," the moustached man warned, hovering behind the giant. The golem's scarred face clouded momentarily, regret etched in his ashen features.

Raphael straightened at the man's careless words. They weren't planning on killing him straight away. Suddenly a flicker of hope burned within him, like a tiny dancing flame in a dark cavern. Groping behind him, his hand met cold hard steel, the sharp edge biting into his fingers. Inwardly rejoicing at the pain, he shifted his body slightly to hide the blade as his fingers followed the steel. "What do you want?" he snarled at the man, his hand tightening around the hilt.

"Don't play dumb please, we know all about the Mirror," Jenkins answered, his voice distinctly bored.

"So, that stone was a listening device," Raphael muttered, subtly shifting his weight. The man raised a slender eyebrow, moustache twitching with amusement.

"Our Alyce is full of surprises, Mr Blythe," he purred, tapping her stirring body with the toe of his boot as he approached the wall.

Frowning at the peculiar inflection of the man's voice, Raphael sprung out from the wall and swung gamely at the golem's calf muscle.

At the least, he suspects "Mr Blythe" is an alias, Raphael mused as he narrowly missed Clay's flying fist, air rushing past his ducking head. The edge of his blade found the golem's calf, slicing through muscle and sinew. Clay screamed, clutching the severed flesh, dark red blood oozing out between his sausage-like fingers. That was just what he needed, he decided as he lurched sideways to avoid a measured strike from the moustached man. Inadvertently revealing the existence of the Mirror was bad enough, he ruminated darkly, gritting his teeth together as the tip of the man's sword scraped past his arm. So many things to be aware of, he mentally cursed, glancing at the blood dripping down his arm. Alyce was slowly clambering to her feet to his left, the golem was leaning heavily against the wall behind him, its rasping breaths setting his nerves on edge. The man with the moustache is a half-decent swordsman, he conceded, grunting with the effort of deflecting his rapid strokes.

"I told you he'd be harder to restrain," Alyce croaked as she stood unsteadily, her dagger drawn.

"Just hold your ground," the man barked as he circled menacingly, his pale blue eyes never leaving Raphael's face. "He can't get away from the four of us." Involuntarily the man's eyes slid to the doorway. In that fraction of a second, Raphael flicked out the tip of his sword, drove it into the man's arm.

He ran for the door, the man's agonised scream ringing in his ears. Steel sung in his ears as the moustached man swung angrily at him, the blade's edge slicing the air only an inch or so from his ear. The hard steel connected painfully with his shoulder on its way down, causing him to stumble. "No!" Alyce cried, hurtling after him, the golem's heavy steps close behind. Just when he thought it was all over, there was a loud crash, and he was in the clear. Not daring to look back, he propelled himself through the doorway. At the back of his frantic mind, something niggled. "Four of us," he breathed, remembering the man's words. Suddenly a hooded figure appeared before him, and he collided haplessly into the stranger. Gasping for air, he desperately disentangled himself from the stranger's arms and legs and clambered to his feet. The hooded figure sat up, leant back to gaze up at his face. "Raphael?" a familiar voice asked. Raphael froze, stared helplessly as the hood fell back.

"Gunthar?" he croaked incredulously, unable to tear his disbelieving gaze from the pale blue eyes and wiry blonde hair. Light glinted off a patch of bumpy scarred skin on his forehead, an ugly legacy of his fall down the mountain. "I thought you were dead," he uttered. There was a dull thud, and Gunthar watched dispassionately as Raphael crumpled to the floor.

"Well done Gunthar," Jenkins purred, lowering his sword. "I knew you'd come in handy for something, other than locating the Mirror," he murmured, cleaning a spot of blood off the pommel. Must have broken the skin when he hit Raphael's head he mused as he slid the sword back into its sheath. "Right," he announced, turning back to Alyce and Clay, who were hobbling out into the hallway. "Let's get to work."

Mel woke with a start, shivering with cold. She waited for her eyes to adjust to the gathering gloom before clambering awkwardly to her feet. Chalk dust stirred as she moved, filling her nostrils. She sneezed, stumbled over to the table. Groping about the cluttered surface, she found her water skin and pulled out the stopper. Tipping the shrivelled skin into her mouth, she squeezed out all the water. Wincing, she gulped down the mouthful of water and dejectedly replaced the stopper. "That's just brilliant," she muttered darkly, tossing the water skin onto the table. Just over three hours on her own, and she uses up all her water. "And it's almost dark," she murmured to the growing shadows, her eyes struggling to discern the outlines of the makeshift desks and stools. "Damn, I should have set up a fire or something before having an emotional breakdown," she chided, looking about the room for her bag.

While cautiously stumbling around the table, her strained eyes picked out a feeble finger of light stretching across the floor. Crouching down in front of an upturned desk, she spotted the shard poking out from under the desk's rough edge, its smooth surface gleaming. Grumbling softly under her breath, she reached out and pulled the shard free, her lacerated hand protesting at the movement. With a hard lump of dread forming in her throat, she gazed down at the animated surface.

Like an expertly directed movie, the shard showed an establishing shot of Blythe Manor, its grey walls looming ominously against the darkening sky. Then the view moved in, wandering from building to building, zooming in on the unconscious bodies, barely discernible in the half-light of dusk. She gasped at the image of Wendy and Simon lying in each other's arms, sighing with relief as she finally detected the steady movement of their chests. The Mirror's view drifted out of the barn, glided over the yard and through the open door. Through the kitchen and out into the hallway, her eyes followed avidly every twist and turn of the Mirror's floating consciousness. Halfway down the corridor, Peter lay face down on the floor, his outstretched hand reaching for the door of the training room.

Swallowing nervously, she waited tensely for the image to gradually shift to the room at the end of the corridor, her heart creeping further towards her mouth with each frantic beat. Despite her anticipation, she jumped half-way out of her skin when the door suddenly opened and a huge grey-skinned man limped out, Alyce trailing behind. He turned to her, nodded solemnly as she talked, her hands moving expressively. With a clumsy bow, he turned and walked down the hallway. The view then followed Alyce back into the room, where Raphael could be seen bound and unconscious on the floor. A moustached man spoke curtly to her, pointed at Raphael. She nodded meekly, watched guardedly as he and a gangly blonde man left the room.

"Raphael," she croaked, trailing her finger over the image of his vulnerable figure. From the pools of blood on the floor, and everyone's injured stance, he had put up a good fight. Just then Alyce shuddered, spun around as though she sensed the Mirror's spying presence. She shrank away as the deep blue eyes in the glass seemed to look directly at her. Shrugging her slender shoulders, Alyce returned her attention to Raphael, tentatively testing the ropes binding his hands and feet together. Like a startled animal, the Mirror withdrew from the manor, zooming out along the corridor and through the main door. The scene rapidly shifted to the forest surrounding the manor. In the mottled darkness, she could just make out the figure of a girl staggering to her feet. As she stood up, her dark red hair caught the patchy moonlight. "Sarah," she breathed, noting the lines of pain etched on her face. Sarah looked anxiously about, started hobbling through the trees, sword dangling listlessly by her side. Trees blurred as the Mirror's consciousness sped over the forest floor, to where the golem entered the trees. A meaty grey hand settled on the goggles covering the creature's eyes, slowly lifted the leather strap. She almost dropped the shard as unnatural black pools stared back at her. "No," she cried, watching the golem cock its head and move off in Sarah's direction.

She lowered the fragment, turned her head to stare bleakly out the grimy window. "Damn," she swore softly, her hand clutching the jagged glass. The deep rumble of distant thunder answered her curse, dark clouds spreading across the moonlit sky. This had obviously been Alyce's plan all along. "Damn," she breathed, slipping the shard back into her pocket. Fumbling about in the thick gloom, she found her sword and coat. She had wanted Sarah and Raphael to pay for what they had done, but not like this, not at the hands of Alyce and her cronies. "Besides, I can't let that blonde bitch win," she grunted, pushing her stiff arms through the sleeves of her coat. With a sigh of resignation, she grabbed the sword and made her way into the waiting night.

Raphael pried his gritty eyes open, blinked at the dimly lit wall while he waited for his head to stop ringing. Outside the training room window, the few stars that glimmered in the night sky were gradually smothered by dark clouds. Having his deep dark secrets dragged out into the harsh glare of day had been bad enough, he thought grimly. Now he was trussed up like a helpless animal, ready for the slaughter. He gingerly tested the ropes wrapped around his wrists and ankles, the resulting creak breaking the thick silence. "Ah, you're awake," a familiar voice drawled. He gritted his teeth at the sweet, refined voice, felt his blood start to slowly boil.

"Alyce," he grunted, stiffly rolling over so that he could face her. "I should have left you to die on the side of the road," he spat.

She nodded agreeably as she approached, hands tucked neatly behind her back.

"Oh, I know love," she sighed as she paced thoughtfully before him. "Still, don't feel too bad. Who but your paranoid little bitches would ever suspect such a thing?!" she exclaimed, coming to a stop within kicking distance of his bound feet. If he could just swing his legs around, knock her to the ground, he thought with longing, eyes straying to the dagger in her belt. "Honestly Raphael, you seem surround yourself with cagey individuals," she continued cheerfully, drifting out of range. Stifling a groan of frustration, he strained his neck to glare up at her. "Your agent in Plymouth was most evasive. What was his name?" she pondered aloud, tapping her chin.

"James," he croaked, his mouth suddenly dry. Despite having the sharp brown eyes and long nose of a rat, the man was surprisingly trustworthy.

"That's it, James Millington," Alyce cried, snapping her fingers. "Goodness, I've never seen an agent so reluctant to make an appointment with a potential buyer."

"He's a good judge of character," Raphael growled, straining his fingers against the ropes, his fingertips just touching the edge of a knot...

Her lips formed a thin angry line as she glared at his belligerent face. "I'd step down from that pedestal if I were you, Raphael," she sneered, stepping closer. "Despite what you told Mel, you're not as innocent as you claim."

"What are you talking about?" he snapped, feeling the rope give slightly under his fingertip. She tilted her head to study him, her eyes bright with mischief.

"Oh come on Raphael," she purred, squatting down before him. "Don't tell me it didn't cross your mind to let Gunthar fall down the mountain that day. To have such a perfect opportunity fall into your lap like that..."

"If you want to believe that German crackpot's story, that's your problem," he grunted, shifting his body to conceal his busy hands. "Sarah and I know what really happened."

"Ah yes, the pick-pocket," she murmured disparagingly, rising to her feet. "I hear there's a price on her head back in London. Seems she short-changed her former gang, and street gangs take the paying of tithes very seriously."

He gawked at her smug face, feeling more vulnerable with each passing second. "I guess you learn all sorts of interesting things when you move in the right circles," he retaliated coldly.

Her smile slipped in response to his barb. "Amazing how you can look down your nose at me from your position on the floor," she muttered, moving away in a huff.

Heavy silence fell over the room as he contemplated his situation. If it wasn't for the fact that they needed him alive, he was sure the tea would have been laced with something more lethal than sleeping powder. He would have to share this with the staff if they all came through this alive, he mused. Hopefully they would appreciate the irony as much as he did. "So," he croaked, coughing to clear his throat, "you staged that whole scene by the side of the road for my benefit then?" She idly picked up a sword from the rack, stared at its fine, smooth edge.

"Yes," she finally answered in a small, far-away voice, swinging the sword back and forth before her. "It took months of research and planning of course. Luckily for us you're a creature of habit," she supplied distractedly, her gaze fixed on the glinting steel. "The fact that you use the older, less-travelled road out of Plymouth made it a lot easier for us to pick a site, set out the bodies..."

"Ugh," he groaned, wanting to throw up. "You did all that?" Tearing her eyes away from the blade, she blushed, turned back to the rack.

"Of course not silly," she said with a faint smile, returning the weapon to its resting place. "Clay did most of the work..."

"Does that include running a sword through you?"

Her hand froze on the hilt at his sharp question. She almost flinched at the memory of hard steel entering her body, her agonised face reflected in those round, dark goggles. "Yes, yes it does," she uttered huskily, willing her hand to stop trembling. "I almost didn't go through with it," she admitted thickly, slowly turning to face him. "When Clay stood over me with that bloody sword in his hand, I..." With a shiver she shook her head, firmly steered away from such disturbing thoughts.

"What's keeping Jenkins?" she muttered darkly, crossing her arms over her chest.

"So, I take it the message never got to your family," Raphael mused aloud, tucking the muttered name away for further reference. The more pieces of this puzzle he could gather together, the better. Her dark gaze flitted across the floor to where he lay, a faint smirk tugging at the corners of her mouth.

"Clay saw to it the message didn't get through to my parents, not that they would have cared."

"What?" he asked, confusion clouding his face. Despite all the clues, he was still surprised by her bitter words, and their implication. Must be the remnants of the drug, he thought derisively as he suffered her snorts of laughter.

"You're not the only ostracised person in the room Raphael," she managed to squeeze out between shuddering breaths. His jaw loosened, almost reaching the floor.

Before he could get her to clarify, the door noisily swung open, making them both jump and turn their attention to the entrance. Jenkins marched into the room, with Gunthar moving excitedly in his wake. Shifting the hessian sack on his shoulder, Jenkins eyed her suspiciously. "We have the Mirror," he told her curtly, glancing down at Raphael's pathetic figure. "How's the prisoner been?"

"Oh, fine, no problem," she answered hastily, drifting over to where Raphael lay to check on the ropes.

"How is Clay's chase coming along?"

Her hands paused over the knots, her head cocked slightly to one side as though listening to a distant voice. "He's still tracking the girl down. Shouldn't be too much longer," she reported, giving the ropes a final tug. "He warns there's a storm on the way," she added as she rose to her feet. Another ability sewn into the golem, involving a membrane stretched across the right ear canal, half an inch before the ear drum. How that tiny flap of skin detected changes in barometric pressure, she'd never know. That particular section of Uncle Henry's notes was missing when she finally became the sole custodian of his research material. Perhaps he suffered one of his infamous paranoia attacks, and destroyed them himself, she mused.

"Sarah? You can't be serious, she's of no use to you...ugh," Raphael cried, his protest cut short by Alyce's boot in his ribs. Jenkins menacingly wandered over to where he lay in agony, cold eyes studying him intently.

"I agree Mr Blythe, the girl means nothing to me," he said calmly, crouching down before him. Suddenly his other hand lashed out and grabbed his hair, yanked his head up off the ground. "But she obviously means a lot to you. One word to Alyce, and she can order the golem to kill rather than retrieve." His face contorted in anger, Jenkins slammed his head into the floor. "So you'd better co-operate," he finished gruffly, roughly releasing his head. "Help him up," he grunted to Alyce as he rose stiffly to his feet. "We don't want to keep our client waiting." Something in his voice made him look up, and through a haze of pain, Raphael saw something that turned his blood to ice. Across Jenkins' cold, bland face stretched a full, dazzling smile. Wincing against the pain in his side, he clambered awkwardly to his feet, his eyes darting to the darkening window as he stumbled. Don't worry about me, he silently projected through the glass to his young ward, picturing her slender frame hurtling over the forest floor. "Just run," he whispered hoarsely to the night.

Sarah jumped, whirled around. Odd, she thought with a shiver, staring into the oppressive darkness that seemed to swallow the world whenever her back was turned. She could have sworn she heard someone call her name. Shrugging uneasily, she gingerly continued her trek through the forest. Clawing the air fearfully, she stumbled over the uneven ground, her eyes desperately searching for shapes and outlines against an increasingly dark backdrop. It had been bad enough finding her way in the patchy moonlight. Now thick clouds gathered overhead, accompanied by the faint rumble of thunder. "Great," she muttered, almost twisting her ankle as her foot settled on the edge of a rock. "That's just what I need," she mumbled, wincing against the pain in her knee.

"God, I don't even know where I'm going," she cried out in frustration. As far as she could tell, she was headed toward Burchellton. She would have to circle the village and head for the lake, she decided solemnly, although her heart ached to see Daniel's reassuring face. "Damn," she swore, suddenly remembering their arranged date. "Poor boy," she whispered, her feet changing direction on their own accord. Maybe she could just stop by the blacksmith shop, tap on his window... "No," she croaked resolutely to the darkness, stopping in her tracks. Can't get him involved in this, nor anyone else for that matter. Her thoughts strayed to Mel. Mostly likely she was staying in the school shack. No one would begrudge her using it as a refuge. "Definitely stay clear of Mel," she told herself sternly. She had done enough to that poor woman.

"Just keep moving Sarah," she breathed, setting out once more. She shuddered as thunder rumbled loudly overhead. A flash of lightning briefly sliced the darkness, the sharp crack making her jump half-way out of her skin and stumble painfully over a fallen branch. Fat raindrops splashed down onto her head and cheeks as she sunk to her knees. "Father," she sobbed, her tears mingling with the rain. She doubled over at the thought of Raphael being captured. From the racket coming out of the training room as she led Moonbeam out of the stable, he had put up a good fight. She'd almost gone back to help him when she heard movement from within the manor. Something big was making its way through her home, and she had a feeling it would be coming after her. Swallowing back her fear, she'd guided Moonbeam into the trees and quietly mounted the nervous pony. One last backward glance had revealed a huge, silhouetted figure emerging out of front door.

That must have been almost an hour ago, she reasoned, rubbing her hand roughly over her cheeks. While she had managed to put a healthy distance between herself and the manor, she still expected that monstrous creature to step out of the shadows at any moment. It would have been a healthier distance if Moonbeam hadn't thrown her off. The dappled mare didn't like storms at the best of times. It was just a matter of time before the pony was spooked by something. "Should have taken Monty," she muttered, her tired limbs trembling as she staggered to her feet. Of course, whatever advantage she had gained was being eaten into, her progress painfully slow now that she was reduced to hobbling in the dark.

Still, at least she couldn't hear anyone crashing through the forest after her. Apart from the steady patter of rain, and the occasional growl of thunder, the woods were quiet. Perhaps too quiet, she realised, the hairs on the back of her neck suddenly standing on end. The chorus of frog song that greeted the rain had faded away. It was then that the faint sound of laboured breathing reached her. Tightening her grip on the sword, she turned towards the sound. Too late to run now, she thought grimly as a huge, grey man burst into the clearing. A perfectly timed flash of lightning illuminated his bald, scarred head and glittering black eyes. She grinned at the surprised look on the giant's face. "Well, there's something," she murmured, flinging herself blindly forward as her eyes slowly adjusted to the abrupt darkness.

As her blade met flesh, and she scrambled about in the mud to regain her balance, she felt oddly exhilarated. All her life she'd been running away. From the cruel factory owner, from angry gang members, from Raphael's past, all the time running. Most of her dreams seemed to involve her running away from something or someone. She backed ungainly away, narrowly missed being hit as the golem swung his meaty paw at her. The force of his blow stirred the air near her face. Too much running, she decided, feeling surreally calm in this moment of truth. "Mirror, don't fail me now," she whispered, summoning the alien energy that coursed through her body. Raphael didn't like her using her power. "It's an ace tucked up your deceptively delicate sleeve," he would say whenever she begged to help out in a real fight. Blinking the rain out of her eyes, she deflected another lumbering blow. A sudden flash of lightning exposed the golem's vulnerable position, and she flicked her blade around to find a space between the monster's ribs.

A horrible, gurgled cry exploded out of the golem mouth, and he twisted around to glare at her with those unnatural black orbs. So much for the ace up my sleeve, she thought grimly, swallowing anxiously as the golem started advancing towards her, the wound she inflicted barely slowing it down. Typical, she thought dryly, sliding in the mud to swing her legs under the charging giant. She finally decides to stand and fight, and her opponent is a seven-foot golem with super-human strength. As the golem leapt over her legs and quickly regained its footing, she began to suspect it could also see in the dark. Smiling sickly to herself, she clambered to her feet and faced her enemy. Her wild, high-pitched laughter, sharply followed by the sounds of battle, punctuated the stormy night, until the heavens opened, and the drizzling rain became a heavy blanket smothering the forest.

Mel crouched by the side of the stable, peering round the corner at the silent, dark house. Squinting through the thick curtain of rain, she studied the windows for any sign of life. She could just pick up the soft glow of a lantern moving along the bottom level. Taking a steadying breath, she raced around the building, scrambling over the wet ground until she found the entrance. She gratefully stumbled to a stop inside the stables, crashing into the wall as her sopping boots threatened to give way beneath her. Wheezing painfully, she straightened up and walked gingerly past the wall of hay bales. A lone lantern burned from a hook on the opposite wall, its flickering light dancing over John's sprawled figure.

"John," she croaked, rushing to his side. She giggled softly as his faint snoring reached her ears, her body going limp with relief. Without thinking, she reached out a wet, trembling hand to his shoulder. Suddenly an image of the grey golem filled her head, and she hastily withdrew her hand. "No," she whispered, shuffling back from his slumbering form. "It could be safer for you guys to remain unconscious," she muttered, rising awkwardly to her feet. If Alyce and her cronies encountered resistance on their way out, they surely would not hesitate to use lethal force.

The sudden, distant creak of the front door penetrated her morose thoughts, and she crept to the entrance in time to see a familiar party emerge from the manor. The slender, moustached man she'd seen in the Mirror fragment led the way, a large sack slung over his shoulder. Raphael trudged along behind him, his feet tethered by a short rope, his hands tied behind his back. Alyce and the gangly blonde man brought up the rear, the blonde man holding aloft a lit lantern. Undeterred by the teeming rain, the moustached man marched purposefully across the yard, glancing over his shoulder occasionally to check the progress of the others and offer curt words of encouragement.

Tightening her grip on the sword, she eased out of the stables, pressing her body against the wall. "Where are they going?" she murmured as she watched their dreary procession into the trees, her voice swallowed up by the rain. Thunder and lightning crashed overhead, making her jump. Steeling her nerves, she ventured out into the yard, training her eye on the bobbing spot of light. While the splashing created by her clumsy steps seemed overly loud to her nervous ears, there was no reaction from the group as they surged ahead. Stumbling from tree to tree, she followed them into the forest, struggling to keep up with their urgent steps without crashing noisily into the ground. Finally, they came to a clearing, where a large carriage waited, its black body glinting dully in the wavering lantern light. They converged around the doorway of the carriage, the moustached man barking orders.

Shaking her head as the storm drowned out his words, she slowly circled the clearing until she found a clump of bushes growing near its edge. Her heart firmly lodged in her mouth, she crawled into the bushes, wincing as thorny branches raked her arms. Gritting her teeth against the pain, she concentrated on picking out the moustached man's tense words. "Where the bloody hell is that over-grown pet of yours?" he yelled, waving his arms at Alyce.

"He'll be here shortly," she reassured him distractedly, her eyes combing the darkness beyond the dull glow of the lantern. "Apparently the girl put up quite a fight," she added with a frown, turning her attention back to his impatient face.

"She'd better not be hurt," Raphael growled, straining against the ropes.

"Aw, shut up!" the moustached man cried, swinging a fist into Raphael's chin. With his hands and feet bound, Raphael had little choice but to stagger sideways and lose his footing in the mud. As he lay on the ground gasping for air, the moustached man snickered and sunk his boot into his stomach.

"I guess I should have mentioned," he declared cheerfully, circling Raphael's stricken body like a shark. "While our client wants you alive, there was no requirement for you to be intact." He punctuated his statement by placing a foot on Raphael's back and roughly pushing him face first into the mud. "That's just a taste," he shouted, bending over his flailing victim. "So if I were you, I'd keep my big trap shut. All right, enough fun, let's get ready to go," he bellowed, straightening up. "Get him into the carriage. Where the hell is Travis?" he demanded.

"Travis?" Mel breathed, shrinking back into the bushes.

"Wasn't he checking the horses?" Alyce grunted as she helped Raphael to his feet.

As Mel huddled down between long thorny branches shivering with cold, she felt a presence behind her. Suddenly someone crashed through the vegetation, a claw-like hand digging into her shoulder. Screaming at the top of her lungs, she struggled desperately to free herself as she was hauled to her feet. "Hello, what'd we 'ave 'ere then?" a gravelly voice rumbled, its owner turning her around. A perfectly timed bolt of lightning slashed the sky, and she found herself face to face with a tall thin man, his craggy features and dark eyes frightening in the harsh light. She belatedly swung her sword at him, only to be met with laughter as he shoved her back.

With a sharp cry she tumbled out of the bushes, her sword clattering uselessly along the ground. Grappling with the slippery surface, she clambered unsteadily onto her hands and knees, to find herself staring at Raphael's stunned face just over five meters away.

"Mel, no!" he shouted in dismay, pulling away from Alyce. "For God's sake, run!"

"Well well, who's this then?" the moustached man purred, kicking Raphael's legs out from beneath him as he approached her rising form. Travis emerged out of the bushes to grab her from behind, his long fingers encircling her neck.

"I saw her moving in the bushes while I was checking on the horses, Jenkins sir," Travis explained, pressing against her trachea until her struggles subsided.

Almost passing out from lack of oxygen, she blinked slowly at the multiple Jenkinses hovering before her. "Mel, is it?" the Jenkinses asked rhetorically, studying her with cool detachment. She focused on the nearest moustache, moved her lips with great difficulty.

"Yes," she finally answered through stiff lips.

"Damn it Jenkins," Raphael cried as he staggered to his feet, "just let her go. She's got nothing to do with this."

"Ah well, that's where you're wrong," the moustache corrected snidely, fat drops of rain falling from the bristling hair. Fascinated, she watched the thick band of hair move up and down. "You really should have stayed away Mel," the moustache told her sadly. "We can't have you running off and getting help now, can we?"

She nodded in agreement, unable to find fault with the moustache's logic. Suddenly the moustache disappeared from her blurry field of vision, and she looked down to see Raphael wrestling desperately with Jenkins, their bodies writhing in the mud. Despite having his hands and feet bound, Raphael managed to kick Jenkins hard in the stomach as the other man was staggering to his feet, sending him reeling back towards the carriage. In that brief lull, he twisted around and looked up at her through matted, muddy hair, rain coursing down his face. "Run Mel," he managed to gasp as Jenkins grabbed the collar of his shirt and yanked him back.

"Oh, right," she murmured, suddenly realising that Travis' hands had lost their vice-like grip on her neck, his attention drawn to the fight. Mustering her strength and courage, she dropped to the ground, rolled ungainly to her left, her hand groping for the sword. She just managed to get a finger on it before he dove onto her sprawled figure, driving the air out of her lungs. Wheezing painfully, she twisted around and slammed the hilt into his temple. "Argh," he screamed, clutching his head.

"Damn it, she's trying to escape!" someone yelled as she clambered to her feet and started to run.

"Alyce, after her," Jenkins ordered. There was a sickening crunch of flesh and bone, shortly followed by Raphael falling down again, an agonised groan escaping his lips.

Her clumsy feet thumped heavily over the wet ground, sword drooping in her hand. She listened frantically for the sound of Alyce's pursuit, but all she could hear was her own desperate panting. If I can just make it to the trees, she thought with a glimmer of hope, making for the dark gap between two massive oak trees. Freedom beckoned from beyond the broad, smooth trunks, spurring her feet on. Feeling oddly light-headed and confident, she glanced over her shoulder, wondered why no one was bothering to chase after her, when she crashed into a solid wall of grey flesh. The world jolted around her as she collapsed to the ground, sword flying out of her hand. Her eyes slowly focused on the golem's huge feet, big toes poking through the worn, stretched leather of his boots.

"Well done Alyce," Jenkins said smugly, his sploshing steps getting louder in her ringing ears. She gawked up helplessly at the grey giant, his black eyes filling her field of vision as he bent down to grab her arm. A shrill voice inside her head urged her to get up and run, but her legs refused to co-operate. "Well done Clay," Jenkins added as the golem hauled her roughly off the ground. "You have the girl I see."

"Yes sir," Clay rumbled, shifting the unconscious body slung over his shoulder.

"Right, we've dallied here long enough. Dump the red head in the carriage," Jenkins ordered, digging his fingers into Mel's arm and dragging her back into the clearing. "When you're finished with the girl, get this heap loaded," Jenkins shouted over his shoulder, kicking Raphael's prone body on his way to the centre.

"Yes sir," Clay grunted, his voice muffled by Sarah's body as he limped towards the carriage.

"Now," Jenkins said coldly, pulling her around to face him, "what are we going to do with you, Mel?"

"Nothing," she croaked, her bleary gaze firmly fixed on his moustache. "I'm not a threat," she sobbed, wincing as his fingers dug further into her flesh. His pale cold eyes seemed to soften slightly, or maybe it was just an effect of the rain. Whatever emotion flickered there, it was gone in the blink of an eye.

"Hmph," he grunted, releasing her abruptly. Without his support, she promptly lost her balance and fell to her hands and knees. Shakily sitting back on her heels, she gazed up through pain-filled eyes to find Alyce walking ominously toward her. Despite the steady rain, she noticed the meaningful exchange of looks between her and Jenkins as they passed each other.

"How could you Alyce?" she cried hoarsely, struggling to find her voice. "Raphael saved your life."

"All part of the plan," Alyce answered calmly as she stepped over his unconscious form. "The greatest risk, for the greatest prize."

"And what would that be?" she spat back, feeling all her hatred rise to the surface. A cruel smile tugged at the corners of the other woman's full lips.

"Revenge," she said simply. "My family will sorely regret expelling me." Clay lumbered up behind his mistress, gingerly bent over to wedge his massive hands under Raphael's arms. Judging from the lines of pain around the golem's eyes and mouth, and the dark glistening patches on his clothes, he had sustained injuries during the stormy night.

"That monster's yours?" Mel prompted, tearing her eyes away from the grey head bent in concentration over Raphael. "That's why you were up that night. You'd gone to see him."

"Ah, the pieces finally fitting together, are they?" Alyce said with a delicate nod of her head. "Honestly, when Clay killed Jane, I thought it was all over. But thanks to you Mel," she continued, drawing her knife, "we have the Mirror."

Travis was suddenly behind her, grabbing her arms and yanking her to her feet, merciless fingers squeezing the tender flesh with renewed vigour. "You really should have stayed away," Alyce sighed, shaking her head. "I would have spared your life, in gratitude for not dobbing me in," she confessed, reaching out to push the dark hair out of her eyes. In a futile-yet-satisfying act of defiance, Mel spat at the other woman's face. Alyce frowned, let her hand fall away. "But that's not possible now," she murmured, distractedly wiping away the glob of mucus from her cheek. On their own accord, her eyes wandered past Alyce's shoulder, to where Raphael was being dragged backwards through the mud. Following the movement of her eyes, Alyce smirked, leant forward to whisper conspiratorially in her ear. "Don't worry about Raphael and Sarah," she whispered cheerfully. "They'll be dealt with by Sebastian. It's going to be a sweet, if short, family reunion."

Her eyes widened as the ugly words sunk in. Before she could utter any sounds of surprise, Alyce drove the knife into her chest. She stared in shocked horror into Alyce's cool, detached eyes, her hands, now free, leaping to the gaping hole in her chest. "Let's go," Alyce sighed, eyes fixed on the bloody blade of her knife as she turned away. Other than pausing to sink his boot into her rib cage, Travis passed her collapsing figure without a second glance. Jenkins pushed away from the carriage, stifled a yawn. "Somebody wake up Gunthar," he sneered, cold gaze flitting over the wiry-haired heap at the side of the clearing. With a jolt Raphael pried his eyes open, blinked at the kneeling figure in the mud. "Mel?" he croaked in disbelief. She slowly sunk back onto her heels, eyes fastened on the steady stream of blood oozing out of her body. "Mel, no!" Raphael cried, reaching out to her, long legs desperately kicking the ground.

She dimly registered his voice through her own blood-curdling screams, lifted her head to seek out his face amongst the disinterested bodies moving about the clearing. It was as though they were frozen in time, staring at each other in utter despair while everyone else carried on normally, making preparations to go. Then Clay hauled Raphael to his feet and roughly shoved him into the carriage, pushing him into the shadows. She gaped at the empty space, the taste of her own salty blood filling her mouth. Alyce nudged the wiry-haired man in the ribs as she passed, a look of distaste on her face. The man stirred, his nose twitching. With a final cursory glance at her victim, the blonde woman climbed into the carriage.

Well, this is it, she thought as darkness gathered before her eyes to blot out all the joy and pain of living. Her hand feebly reached for the Mirror fragment scraping her leg through the material of her trousers. The last link she had to her old life shifted reassuringly under her hand as she slumped face first into the mud. There was a brief flash of pain as the shard entered her body, and then nothing.

Gunthar's gritty eyes widened in surprise as he suddenly sensed the Mirror fragment, sharply turned his attention to the dead body lying pathetically in the mud. Getting awkwardly to his feet, he limped over to the unmoving lump of humanity, cautiously prodded its shoulder with the toe of his boot. He could sense something, an alien presence akin to the Mirror, scratching at his consciousness. He bent over the body, extended his hand over the still flesh...

"Gunthar, come on!" Jenkins shouted from the carriage door.

"But there's something here," he protested, gesturing at the body.

"Don't think I won't leave you behind!" Jenkins warned before heaving himself into the cabin.

Muttering curses in his native tongue, he withdrew his hand. Whatever it was, it was gone now anyway, he thought despondently as he stood up. With a final backward glance, he trudged back to the carriage and clambered through the door. A curt order from Jenkins, and the carriage moved forward through the trees, Travis guiding the horses onto a disused track. The clopping of hooves and jiggling of reins faded into the night, and Melanie Jacinta Barrett was completely and utterly alone once more.

PART 2

$\diamond$

Chapter 3
The End, and then some.

"**Y**ou just have to be different, don't you?"

"Huh?" she responded with a start, tearing her eyes away from the unmoving lump on the ground. "Aunty Jan?" she breathed in disbelief as she focused on the familiar round face and curly black hair. "What are you doing here?"

"Not much," the woman answered with a sad smile. "Being dead and all," she added pointedly.

"Oh yeah," she mumbled, turning her attention back to the dead body lying in the mud.

"So that's you then?" her aunt prompted, waving down at the deserted clearing.

"Yeah," she sighed, only then realising they were floating several meters above the ground. "Whoa, what's going on here?" she cried, feet frantically kicking the air. "Why am I up so high, looking down at my own body?"

"Hey, settle down pet," Jan projected over her panicked reaction. "Haven't you been listening? You're dead."

"What?"

"Aww, you're dead Mel," she groaned, rubbing a ghostly hand over her face. "Don't make me say it again, please." She opened her mouth to protest, closed it again. She was floating above the ground with her long-departed aunt, watching the rain pass through her body, while her old, discarded shell lay unmoving on the ground below. Stringing these clues together, she was forced to reluctantly accept the truth. Odd, her body looked solid enough, she mused as she studied her arm. "So, we're ghosts?" she ventured, feeling strangely calm about her own death.

An unreadable expression crossed Jan's face. "For a while," she finally answered, looking away. "Like I said, you have to do things differently," Jan reiterated, swivelling her attention back to her confused face. She shifted uncomfortably under her aunt's direct gaze. "Honestly, you couldn't stay in your own time and live out your life there, could you?"

"It's not my fault!" she cried, surprised by the bitterness in her aunt's voice. "Sarah dragged me to this wretched time and place. Dying in the plane crash would have been less painful!"

The stunned, injured look in Jan's eyes reduced her to mumbled apologies. "It's just, I've been so lonely Aunty," she finally squeezed out when she finished tripping over her clumsy, contrite tongue.

"What about Sarah and Raphael? They seem to care about you a great deal, despite their guilt. And stop calling me "Aunty". Here I am simply Jan." She blinked dumbly at the older woman as she slowly absorbed her words.

"How do you know Sarah and Raphael? Have you been watching me all this time?"

"Oh goodness no," she laughed, curly ghost hair bobbing. "No, you're leaking thoughts all over the place. There are no secrets in the afterlife, you know."

"Oh," she breathed, suddenly feeling naked and vulnerable before her aunt.

"Don't worry love," Jan purred reassuringly, putting an incorporeal arm around her stiff shoulders. "There's nothing to be embarrassed about. We've all been through it, having our dirty laundry hung out to dry in the open."

"Right," she murmured with a weak smile. "I'll try not to leak so much," she mumbled sheepishly. Snorting contemptuously, Jan grabbed her hand.

"Don't be silly," the older woman chided gently, dragging her along at giddy speed through the rain. "I'm enjoying the show, especially the saucy bits between you and Raphael," Jan said conversationally over her shoulder as they hurtled towards the thick forest canopy. Despite their incorporeal forms, she cried out, squeezed her eyes shut in anticipation of the inevitable collision. With a faint grin Jan pulled her through the network of branches, her dark eyes fixed firmly on some distant point.

She was just starting to enjoy the ability to pass through solid objects, when the scene rapidly changed, and she was suddenly standing in the doorway of a bedroom. Diagonally across from her sat a man, his large frame resting on the edge of a queen-sized bed, his back to her. Even without seeing his face, she recognised her husband. "What?" she uttered with a start, cringed at the loudness of her voice. "Why did you bring me here?" she hissed when he didn't stir, wrenching her eyes away from his downcast head.

"You don't have to whisper," Jan advised, her voice sounding overly loud in the quiet room.

"Right," she said with a nervous cough, still lowering her voice.

"Where else would you want to go?" she countered, shrugging her round shoulders as her eyes wandered about the room.

"Is it real?"

"Of course it's real," Jan snapped, turning towards her. "Do you think I'd go to the effort of creating this scene just so you can get all warm and fuzzy?"

"Geez, sorry," she murmured, her tone injured. "What's with you?"

Jan shook her head, studied her feet, her ghostly toenails jutting out through the opening of her favourite sandals. Funny, she could have chosen the visage of any footwear she fancied to clad her non-existent feet. For the first time ever, she could wear high-heels without the excruciating discomfit. Try as she may though, all she could picture were the tan leather sandals she had worn day-in, day- out. Frank would often tease her about it, pointing out the numerous pairs of shoes she had in her wardrobe, gathering dust...

"Seeing you brings back a lot of stuff. Makes me wish I had a second chance...How's Frank?" she asked abruptly, finally meeting her worried gaze.

"Uncle Frank? Uh, he remarried, about four years after you, er, died," she answered awkwardly, afraid of her reaction.

"Four years?" she repeated incredulously. "Four years..."

"I'm sorry Aunt, I mean Jan, it must be hard to learn such a thing..."

"What took him so long?!" Jan demanded, thumping her fist against the wall.

She gaped at her aunt, stunned by the outraged question. "You're not upset?" she stammered, scratching her head.

"Of course not! What sort of sad, twisted soul do you take me for?" the older woman cried, waving her arms expressively. "You'd have to be a complete arsehole to expect your partner to pine away and spend the rest of their life alone," she concluded with a hint of haughtiness in her tone. Her indignant words hit home, and Mel's eyes strayed to the man perched on the edge of the bed.

"Doesn't it hurt though?" she asked softly past the sudden lump in her throat.

"Perhaps a little," her aunt conceded gruffly, rubbing her chin. "But I guess it's all part of letting go."

"Ah, Gary?" a questioning voice called directly behind them. Jumping half-way out of her skin, she whirled around to find herself face to face with the dark-haired woman who had taken her place. Before she could move out of the way, the woman stepped right through her and entered the room. "Ugh," she groaned, furiously brushing down the front of her shirt, her hands trembling. To her dismay, Jan laughed openly at her horrified reaction, patting her on the back.

"Oh yeah, I remember the first time someone walked through me, big fat slob of a man turned the corner while I wasn't watching," she recalled breathlessly. She glared at her raucous aunt, shook off her heavy hand. With a sheepish grin, Jan stopped giggling, fixed her attention on the unfolding scene.

"Yes?" Gary responded glumly, not looking up from the object in his hands.

"Ah, I just came to apologise, for what I said, I mean. That was a... harsh thing to say," the woman said unevenly, her voice faltering as she groped for the right words.

"Harsh but true," he interjected, standing up to face her. Mel baulked at the framed picture in his hands.

"That's from our wedding," she murmured softly, reaching out a ghostly hand to the slightly faded photo.

"See, he hasn't totally moved on with his life," Jan pointed out, resting a hand on her shoulder.

"Still," the woman replied, looking away from the picture in his hands, "it can't be easy to leave this place, with all its memories."

"What?" Mel asked, stepping forward to stand beside the woman.

"Hmm," Gary murmured thoughtfully, turning his attention back to the photo. "We had a lot of good times here, it's true," he admitted, running his finger over her image. "Some good yelling matches too," he grinned, ruefully rubbing at the greasy fingerprint he'd left on the glass with his shirt.

"Hey!" Mel protested, stiffening beside her replacement.

"But I don't need this place to keep those memories alive," he said softly, lowering the picture to gaze upon his new wife. "It's all up here," he told her, tapping his head.

"So, does this mean you'll consider taking the new job?"

"New job?" Mel repeated like an over-grown parrot, moving jerkily to stand before her husband, her arm brushing his. He shivered, rubbed his bare forearm. "Better close the window," he mumbled, leaning over the bed to check the sliding window.

"Ah, sweetie?"

Frowning at the already closed window, he turned back to his new wife. "Sorry?" he asked distractedly, slipping the framed photo back into the top drawer of his bedside table.

"Are you thinking about taking the new job?" the dark-haired woman repeated, tension creeping into her voice. He noted the tightness around her eyes and mouth.

"It means a lot to you, doesn't it Christine?" he asked, a knowing glint in his eye.

Christine sighed, pressed her hand to her brow. "Yes," she confessed, sinking to the bed. "I think it would be good for us, moving to a new town, a fresh start and all that. But if you don't want to move, I'll understand..."

"Of course," he teased gently as he sat down beside her.

"It's not easy for me, you know," she blurted, crossing her arms. "Mel's a hard act to follow..."

"Sweetie..."

"I mean, she obviously had the patience of a saint to put up with your model train obsession..."

"Ha," Mel snorted sympathetically, remembering the gradual accumulation of miniature engines and tracks during their seven years together.

"It's not that bad, is it?" he asked defensively, pulling away from her.

"Not that bad?!" they cried in unison.

"You'd have trains set up on our bedroom floor if I didn't keep you in check," Christine accused.

"He did have trains set up on the bedroom floor once," Mel murmured, shaking her head. "I was bloody stepping over train tracks for a week..."

"Look, do you want me to take the job or not?" he demanded, throwing his hands in the air.

The room fell deathly silent as Christine's jaw slackened, her eyes growing bright with gathering tears. "Yes," she finally answered in a small, wavery voice. "But only if you want to, I don't want you to resent me over this..."

"How can I resent you?" he broke into her rambling rationalisation, lifting a hand to her face. "If I hadn't found you, I don't know what I would have done."

"Perhaps we should go," Jan prompted as they leant forward to kiss.

"What?" Mel murmured distractedly, struggling to tear her gaze away from the tender embrace.

"Come on Mel, we don't belong here," Jan pointed out more firmly, grabbing her arm.

Just then Kai and Karen rushed into the room, totally oblivious to the romantic moment they were shattering with their noisy presence. Amid the children's garbled requests for food and computer games, they reluctantly separated to grin ruefully at each other. With a minor rebuke for bursting into their room, Gary and Christine herded the children out the door. As their collective voices trailed down the stairs, she stood unmoving near the bed, her eyes fixed on where Gary and his new partner had sat. "Did you hear Kai call her "mum"?" she croaked.

"Come on matey," Jan said gently, tugging at her hand.

"Why'd you bring me here?" she asked numbly, resisting her aunt's urgent tugs.

"To teach you the hardest lesson of all," Jan grunted, pushing her forcibly out of the room. "That life goes on without you," she continued bitterly as they flowed out through the wall.

"Well I'll be sure to remember that while I make my way through the afterlife," Mel snapped, swatting at her claw-like hand.

"Hmph," Jan snorted contemptuously, grasping the flimsy material of her sleeve tightly, her glassy eyes focused on some spot in the sky. "Give me a break kid," she muttered, somehow gathering speed without appearing to move at all. Mel marvelled as the edges of her vision blurred, clouds and sky merging into one stretched smudge of colour. Abruptly they skidded to halt, the smudge resolving itself into a long, white corridor.

"This is a bit cliched, isn't it?" Mel commented, looking around at the sea of gleaming white.

"Huh? Oh yeah, this place," Jan murmured dismissively, studying a small plaque on a door. It was only as she followed her aunt's searching gaze that she realized the walls were lined with doors, the two neat opposing rows of doorknobs stretching as far as the eye could see.

"Not this one," Jan muttered, continuing up the corridor.

"So, is this where we're going to hang out?" she pressed, tripping over the perfectly smooth floor as she trailed after her preoccupied aunt.

"Hang out?" Jan echoed, a bemused look on her face. "You still don't get it, do you?" she marvelled, shaking her head as she examined the next door.

"Get what? I'm dead, what else is there to get?" she sulked, crossly crossing her arms.

"Like I said," Jan drawled, a grin spreading lazily across her lined face, "you just have to do things differently. Ah, of course," she cried abruptly, snapping her fingers. "Come on matey, this way," she declared briskly, seizing her arm again.

"I don't do things differently," she protested, stumbling after the black curly head so beautifully silhouetted against the stark white world.

As she was guided towards the centre of the passageway, the light intensified, drowning out most details of colour and form. Jan's body, clothed in simple trackpants and t-shirt, was swallowed by the glare, until all that could be discerned was the bobbing crown of glorious hair. "Hey, what happened to all the other doors?" she yelped belatedly, her panicked gaze travelling up and down the corridor. "There were doors all along the walls," she remembered aloud. "Jan?" she called when there was no response, quickening her step. "Jan?!" she yelled more stridently, fear gripping her as she lost sight of her aunt.

"Here we are," Jan announced brightly, suddenly appearing beside her. "All the other doors vanished because you're not truly dead, my dear," she explained breathlessly.

"Not truly dead?" Mel repeated carefully as her eyes gradually adjusted to the dimming light at the edge of the passageway. They were standing before a single door, Jan resting heavily against the gleaming white panel.

"That alien shard you so conveniently had in your pocket found its way into your body," she explained, lines of tension forming around her eyes and mouth. "Right now as we speak, it's merging with your body, repairing the damage. Almost done, by the look of it," she murmured, nodding at her niece's fading body.

"Aww," she breathed, holding up her arm, blinking in confusion at Jan through the now completely translucent limb. How could she lose so much substance when she barely had any to start with? "What's going on Jan?" she cried, fear creeping into her voice.

"This isn't your time, dear girl," Jan answered cheerfully, the doorknob squeaking under hand. "Unlike so many of us, you're getting a second, no, third chance. Don't waste that chance by moping about Gary and the children. They've moved on with their lives, time for you to do the same." With that she calmly opened the door to a swirling black void. Mel stared at the pitch darkness, her fingers groping for the door frame as a great vacuum tugged at her body. "Aunty Jan!" she screamed as her body was sucked through the doorway, fingers desperately digging into the jamb.

"It's alright Mel," Jan reassured her, gently brushing the wind-blown hair away from her terrified face, seemingly unaffected by the great force on the other side of the doorway. "Now go back and get that bitch Alyce," she ordered cheerfully, watching her fingers slowly lose their grip on the gleaming white frame.

"Aunty Jan!" she cried, fingertips actually sliding through the edge of the doorway. "Jan, no!" she croaked, scrabbling for her aunt's wrinkled hand, "I'm scared." Jan gripped her hands, smiled down into her pale face.

"Goodbye Mel," she said thickly, "we'll meet again, the universe willing." With a final squeeze, Jan released her hands and stepped back into the corridor. As she was sucked down into the void, she twisted her head around, eyes searching in vain for any sign of a doorway against the impenetrable blackness. Gasping in despair, she turned back to face the void. After an indeterminable time, pinpoints of light pierced the darkness a foot or so before her eyes, drew together to form familiar shapes, faces.

"Aww," she groaned as she watched herself give her parents a hard time about something, her lips puckered like a sulky princess. The dancing light flickered, and the scene shifted to her standing by the library shelves during lunch hour, an ill-fitting school skirt swimming around her waist as she avidly read the back of a book. Another blur of the light, and she was watching herself meet Gary for the first time, a mutual friend making the awkward introduction. With increasing speed, the disjointed images flowed before her hungry eyes. Ordering her younger sister out of her room, giving birth to her first child, kissing Gary, Raphael angrily grabbing her arm as she stubbornly carried buckets of water back to shore.

Teasing a starry-eyed Sarah about Daniel, helping Margaret and Wendy in the kitchen, avoiding Simon and his injured sideway glances. Watching on in wonder as Raphael healed her hand, his fingers warm and soothing against her skin. The plane smashing to pieces all around her as it hurtled along the forest floor, Jane's unseeing eyes staring out in frozen horror. Alyce smirking as she drove the knife into her chest, her poisonous words ringing in her ears. Waking up in the field, her body covered in frost, the farmer's curious, concerned face hovering above her. Staring across the muddy clearing at Raphael's stricken face, disinterested bodies moving about at the edge of her blurring vision. The intense cold filling her body, the slowing of her heart, time stretching more impossibly between beats, until there were no more.

The dancing patch of light faded away, and she was left in complete darkness again. "So, what happens now?" she croaked to the void, her voice swallowed by the wind rushing past her free-falling body. The void answered with a single spot of light gleaming far below her. As she fell towards it, the light took shape. Two figures with their hands bound tightly behind their backs sat on the floor of an old, abandoned barn, arms stretched uncomfortably around a single post. "Sarah, Raphael," she cried hoarsely, reaching out to their downcast, unconscious faces. She floated past them, to where Alyce paced anxiously, tapping impatiently the watch in her hand. "Damn it, they should be here by now," she muttered darkly with a sideways glance at Jenkins. Jenkins stirred from where he leant nonchalantly against the wall, ambled across the floor.

"Relax," he purred, placing his hands on her restless shoulders. "They'll be here soon, and then it'll all be over. You'll be on your way back to nobility, and I'll be back in London, picking up another dodgy assignment." He ran his fingers over the naked skin at the base of her neck, light blue eyes darkening as they followed the neckline of her dress.

"I guess you'll have to find a new assistant," she retorted huskily, moving stiffly out of his grasp. "How do you think Sebastian will deal with the prisoners?" she asked abruptly, eyes staring into the distance.

Jenkins smirked, ran his fingers through his greasy hair. "I don't think he'll be very imaginative. He'll probably just give a little victory speech and then have them executed," he answered, stretching his arms out before him. "Don't tell me you're feeling guilty?" he crowed, breaking through her pensive mood.

"It doesn't matter what I feel," she snapped, spinning on her heel to glare at him. "There's no turning back now," she added thickly.

Mel pulled away from the scene, flowed out into the night. The rain had stopped, moonlight escaping the thick blanket of cloud. Not that it mattered to her. With or without the moon's pale glow, she knew where she was going, knew where she wanted to be. Like an arrow fired straight and true, her consciousness flew over the wet, silent forest, in a suddenly urgent race to be reborn.

John Morley grunted as he shifted the lantern, dark brown eyes trained on the tracks in the mud. Thankfully the rain had abated somewhat, so he only had to blink every twenty seconds or so in order to see as he made his way through the yard. The light drizzle settled on his thick woolly coat, the tiny droplets catching the pale moon light that had started to break through. He grimly followed the collection of footsteps, head throbbing with each careful step. An after-effect of the drug, he imagined, judging from everyone else's groggy reaction.

Ted had been the first to wake, shivering violently from the cold rain seeping into his clothes. "Poor sod," John muttered under his breath. It must have been difficult for him to extricate his heavy limbs from the cramped sentry platform. He had wanted to come along, his solid body tensed for a fight, but he had somehow convinced his younger brother to stay and get dry. "They'd hear you a mile away, with those chattering teeth," he'd teased, firmly guiding him towards the oven, where a few feeble tongues of flame still licked the wood. Grumbling sourly under his breath, Ted had reluctantly settled down next to the fire, his hands automatically reaching out to the heat. With his reaction still muted by the drug, Cedric had been easier to convince, his eyes clouding over at his gentle suggestion to help build up the fire. Wendy had jumped in at that point, herding Cedric towards the wood bin, glancing over her shoulder to pass him a knowing wink. Nodding his gratitude, he had left the relative safety of the kitchen to search for Master Blythe and Sarah. It was as much out of anger towards whoever had drugged their tea as concern for his employer. Someone could have easily died...

"Hey, wait up!" Simon called, galloping up behind him. With a sigh, John slowed down slightly, all too aware of his sploshing steps growing louder.

"I thought I told you to search the house," he growled, tearing his eyes off the fading footprints to glare at his colleague.

"Oh come on, John," Simon panted, falling into step beside the large man, "stop the heroics. The culprits have obviously left the scene, otherwise we wouldn't be here to talk about it. Why are you so keen to go after them by yourself?" His sharp question penetrated the fog of displeasure that had gathered around him like a suit of armour.

"I don't know what you're talking about," he replied stiffly, conveniently studying the ground.

"You're a sly one, John Morley," Simon said cheerfully, clapping his beefy shoulder. "Don't think I didn't notice the way you bustled about, giving everyone jobs while you were obviously itching to go after the culprits."

"The others are in no condition to go on a wild goose," he pointed out testily, glancing up in irritation from the faint trail. "If you had any sense, you would have followed my orders and stayed behind."

"Ah," Simon sighed, feeling oddly light-hearted, "now where's the fun in that?" John grunted, shook his head. The lad's brush with death must have gone straight to his head, he mused, a vague grin tugging at the corners of his mouth.

They fell silent as they concentrated on traversing the treacherous forest floor in the lantern's soft glow. His confidence in the trail wavered with each step, the steady rain turning the footprints into fuzzy puddles of water. Just when he was convinced they had lost the trail completely, they came upon a clearing. "Aw, thank God," Simon mumbled as the rain finally stopped, shaking the water out of his hair. John grunted in agreement as he swung the lantern about. The ground was heavily dimpled, with deep grooves cut into the thick mud on the other side of the clearing. "A carriage?" he mused as they approached the centre, almost tripping over an outstretched hand in the process. He looked down in surprise, stumbled back as he realised it was a body.

"Mel!" Simon cried as the light caught the back of her head. He dropped to his knees, roughly turned her unmoving form over. "Mel," he croaked, bending over her mouth to check for any signs of breathing. "She's not breathing," he said unevenly, his throat suddenly clammy as he looked up at John kneeling on the opposite side of her cold corpse.

"There's an awful lot of blood here," John muttered, gingerly touching the front of her shirt. He drew back his hand, frowned at the blood coating his fingertips.

"Come on Mel, don't die on us," Simon urged the wan face, shaking her shoulders. In desperation he parted her lips and closed his own over the cold, still gap. John watched him sadly, slowly shook his head. "It's no good lad, she's gone," he told him gruffly, laying a firm hand on his trembling shoulder.

"No, no!" he protested angrily, pushing the dark wet hair out of his face. "We can't just give up," he cried, eyes wandering about the clearing, apparently searching for a miracle. John felt his heart sink as the questioning gaze finally rested upon him, a spark of hope lighting his face. "Do that heart-pumping thing you told me about, the thing you did to save your sister," Simon demanded, gesturing wildly at Mel's chest.

"I told you to forget about that," John snapped, cheeks darkening with shame. All he managed to save was a shell, he thought bitterly, the renewed flow of blood coming too late to save her brain. He shuddered at the memory of her blank, glassy eyes staring up at him when she regained consciousness, her mind reduced to that of a simple animal. "Damn, I knew I shouldn't have told you," he muttered, cursing the tongue-loosening properties of ale.

"It's the only chance she's got!" Simon shouted, pushing aside the thick material of her jacket to expose her chest. Hesitantly placing his hand over the left side of her rib-cage, he pushed down on the slender bones.

"No no, place the heel of your hand lower, just below the ribcage," John cried impatiently, elbowing Simon aside to position his own hand on her chest. "Wait a minute," he murmured, looking closer at the area, "there should be a big hole here..." As he lifted the blood-soaked tatters to inspect the new pink flesh beneath, Mel's eyes opened with a start, her hand snatching his wrist with the speed of a striking cobra.

"Mel! You're alive!" Simon crowed, shaking her shoulder.

"Yes," she croaked, releasing John's wrist with a shake of her head. "Sorry about that," she added, noting the way he stiffly nursed his hand.

"That's alright Miss," he mumbled, eying her warily.

"See, we saved her John," Simon claimed excitedly, eagerly helping Mel to her feet.

"Is everyone else okay?" she asked, standing more steadily than anyone just back from the dead had a right to, John decided suspiciously as he rose ungainly to his feet.

"Yes, apart from having sore heads," Simon answered, slightly taken aback by the direct question.

"Master Blythe and Miss Sarah are missing," John supplied.

"I know," she growled, a look of displeasure crossing her face.

"What happened here Mel?" Simon prompted, studying her earnestly in the patch of moonlight that had broken through the thinning clouds.

"Alyce and her associates have taken Raphael and Sarah," she explained tersely, hand going to her chest.

"Alyce?" John repeated slowly, comprehension lighting his eyes. "So, she is a spy," he murmured, nodding his head. Despite Master Blythe's warning, a shred of doubt had remained in his mind.

"Damn bitch must have drugged the tea," Simon cursed, his body stiffening in rage.

"So, you saw them take the Master and Sarah?" John pressed, struggling to put the pieces together.

"Yes, I followed them here," she answered thickly, her voice muffled as she turned away. "I was hiding right there," she recalled, pointing at the thick clump of bushes, "watching the whole thing, when they found me. Then Alyce..." The words died in her throat, and she shuddered violently at the memory of Alyce's blade entering her body. The trembling subsided, and she stood rock-still. "I have to go now," she said hoarsely. Simon and John exchanged concerned looks behind her back as she started to move off towards the trees.

"Why don't you go back to the manor and rest Mel? We'll track down the blighters," John offered gently, reaching out a long arm to catch her rigid shoulder.

"No!" she shouted, shaking off his hand. "She's mine."

He backed away from that low, vicious voice, blinked in wonder as her sword sailed through the air to her hand. Without another word, she sped out of the clearing, her body appearing to melt into the forest. He stared after her in astonishment, quickly dismissing any notion he may have had of joining the chase.

"Did you see that?" he asked without moving, hearing Simon's steps behind him.

"I didn't know Mel could move so fast," Simon mused, rubbing his chin thoughtfully.

"I'm pretty sure she couldn't," he mumbled, forcing himself to turn away and look at Simon's face, only to see discomfit that matched his own.

"Should we follow?"

John swallowed nervously, glanced at the spot where Mel had disappeared into the forest in a blink of an eye. "Let's go back and guard the manor," he suggested, his need for vengeance fading rapidly in the face of Mel's unearthly behaviour. "In case there's another attack," he added defensively at Simon's raised eyebrow.

"Suits me man," Simon sighed, clapping the other's back. "I'm starting to think we would just be in the way if we rushed after her," he confessed ruefully, his hand trembling slightly as it fell away from John's shoulder. John grunted, shifted the sheath strapped around his waist.

"I suspect you're right," he agreed, hoping fervently that someone had the kettle on back at the manor. Suddenly he had an overwhelming desire to have a cup of tea, this time without any nasty additions except perhaps for an extra helping of sugar.

"Boil damn you," Alyce muttered, leaning over the pot that sat in the fire. Grumbling heartily under her breath, she searched the barn for more wood, finally grabbing a stick off the dusty floor. "Come on," she murmured, stirring the feeble flames before shoving the stick into the makeshift firepit.

"You know what they say," Jenkins drawled from the entrance, making her jump.

"What?" she snapped, taking a jerky breath as she turned to face him.

"A watched pot never boils," he supplied, his tone only slightly condescending.

"Yes, well, if Martin had done his job, I'd be swilling tea right now," she returned crossly, turning her attention back to the fire. Lazy oaf had obviously forgotten to keep an eye on it while they were gone, the large smouldering log in the centre the only thing keeping it alive.

"Hmm," Jenkins murmured, lips twitching with displeasure. It had been more than a little disappointing to return to a dying fire. He trusted Travis would give his younger brother a stern talking to. From the glint in his hard eyes as they went to deal with the horses, Travis intended to give his brother more than a word of advice.

"What the hell was he doing here all that time anyway?" she complained, reaching her frozen fingers to the heat.

"Probably fell asleep somewhere," he grunted, joining her at the fire.

"Hmph," she responded in kind, stiffening at his nearness. "Should have left him to shovel shit in London."

"I think Travis is starting to think the same thing," he sighed, staring into the struggling flames. "Still, you won't have to suffer his existence much longer," he added pointedly.

She looked up in surprise. "You almost sound sad," she commented, her eyes narrowing.

"Well, I'll have to find myself another lady spy. I can't believe you're willing to give up all this for a place in high society," he lamented, waving his arms expressively at the dirty, dilapidated interior of the barn.

Hugging her arms tightly across her chest, she rolled her eyes at him. "It won't be a complete departure from our illustrious profession," she murmured, wrinkles of consternation forming at the bridge of her nose. "Sebastian has hinted that he may need me to observe certain family members, spike the occasional drink, that sort of thing."

"Even when you're officially part of the family?" he probed, idly pushing some ash back into the pit with the toe of his boot.

"You should be happy my skills won't be going to waste," she said distractedly as she peered down through the flames. "Ah, at last," she grunted at the boiling water, grabbing the nearby poker and carefully threading the rusty end through the handle.

"Do you even know which relative you're to marry?" Jenkins asked abruptly, almost making her drop the pot.

Shooting him a poisonous look, she continued to shakily lift it out of the fire. "His cousin Vincent is the most likely candidate," she finally answered as she set the pot on the floor. "Everyone else is either too young or too lowly ranked, but I guess it depends on how perverse Sebastian is feeling at the time," she added with a shrug.

"You're not concerned that he'll marry you off to a complete idiot?" he pressed incredulously, his gaze wandering to the opening to her bodice.

"I'm not marrying for love, Jenkins," she answered stiffly, straightening up.

"Right, the revenge plan," he muttered, hastily turning back to the fire.

"Look, do you want some tea or not?" she asked testily, spinning on her heel to fetch the cups from their box of supplies. The side of her boot caught the poker on her way to the box. sent it clattering across the floor. She cried out at the sudden noise, her body rigid with fright. "Stupid poker," she gasped, kicking the offending length of rusty metal further away. "What?" she snapped, feeling his sardonic gaze upon her as she struggled to regain her composure.

"Ha, I knew I shouldn't have told you the story behind this place," he laughed, shaking his head.

"You just couldn't help yourself, could you Jenkins?" she muttered sourly from the box. He had taken great delight in telling her the gruesome story of the barn's original owner, a farmer called Hopkins. According to local accounts, Hopkins went mad one night and slaughtered his wife and children as they slept, afterwards setting the house on fire. Spotting the smoke and flames over the forest canopy, a group of villagers rushed to the scene, only to find the house almost completely burnt to the ground and Hopkins swinging from the rafters of the barn, a simple note pinned to his chest. "It had to be done. Forgive me," she repeated softly with a shiver, reciting the message that had allegedly been scrawled in blood on the scrap of paper. Since that day, people had endeavoured to use the structure, only to abandon it soon after, claiming an evil presence remained within the unassuming walls. More than once she had seen something move at the edge of her vision, or felt something cold brush against her skin, only to spin around and find nothing there.

"God, the sooner we finish this job the better," she mumbled, resolutely returning to the fire, battered tin mugs in hand.

"I'm telling you, it's just your imagination," he argued distractedly, his eyes fastened to the curve of her back as she bent over and carefully poured the tea. "The only supernatural thing I've noticed about this place is the smell," he added, wrinkling his nose at the pervading mustiness of the air. Odd, considering how open a building it is, he mused. "So, are you leaving with Sebastian then?" he asked casually, gladly accepting the steaming mug she held out to him.

"No," she answered cautiously, shooting him an assessing look over the rim of her mug. "I have to go back to London and sort out transport for my belongings. Why?"

"I thought, maybe we could celebrate..."

The awkward suggestion hung in the air between them, the only sound in the cavernous room the crackle and splutter of the flames. She blushed at the memory of their previous "celebrations", fuelled by wine and the need to relieve tension. "Perhaps," she answered unevenly past the sudden lump in her throat. She hastily took a big swig of tea, found the way it burnt the roof of her mouth oddly comforting. Contrary to his cold, bland facade, Jenkins was a skilful lover...

"Bloody hell Martin, you useless lump!" Travis shouted outside the entrance. "I told you to tie up the horses!"

"I did!" a bewildered, defensive voice shouted back over the sound of restless horses.

"Damn, I'd better check this out," Jenkins grunted, setting his untouched cup on the floor. "Stay here and watch the prisoners," he barked over his shoulder as he rushed out of the barn, hand already reaching for his sword.

"Hmph, like you needed to point that out," she grumbled, taking another swig of tea. Wiping her mouth with the back of her hand, she set her mug on the floor and moved towards the back of the barn. She stepped carefully past the wall of bales that divided the space, gradually picking out the various stalls built into the back wall as her eyes adjusted to the grainy lantern light. "How are the prisoners?" she asked. Clay looked up from his study of the hessian sack, frowned at her.

"Still unconscious, mistress," he answered, stiffly rising to his feet. "What's going on outside?" he quizzed, stepping aside so she could enter the stall behind him.

"Ah, the horses are jumpy about something," she said absent-mindedly as she crouched down beside Raphael. Blood oozed out of a cut near his eye, and his breath came out in an unpleasant-sounding rasp, as though a couple of his ribs were broken. His eyes had looked so empty, before Jenkins pounded him in the head, and the carriage pulled away. She shuddered to think what he would do if he ever got his hands on her.

"I'll be so glad when this job's over," she mumbled, checking the tightness of the ropes around his wrists. "You're in for a surprise when you finally wake up," she murmured as she moved on to Sarah, making sure to give the ropes an extra vicious tug. Her sweet little face would surely crumble into a teary mess on hearing the news of her beloved Mel's death. Not that she'll have long to mourn, Alyce mused with an evil grin. She rose to her feet, shaking the straw and dust off her knees.

"Is there a problem, Alyce?" a thickly accented voice enquired softly beside her, making her cry out in surprise.

"Gunthar!" she exclaimed raggedly, placing an unsteady hand over her heart, "you scared the shit out of me. What are you doing here? Go and wait by the fire."

The dirty, unkempt hair moved slightly as he shook his head. "Oh no Miss Alyce, I'll be just fine here in the stall," he answered, shrinking back into the shadows. "Mr Jenkins doesn't like me, you know."

Despite his unsettling appearance and behaviour, Alyce tolerated Gunthar's presence better than most. Even Clay, with his assembled body and unearthly-coloured skin, tried to keep his distance from the eccentric German. "I wouldn't worry about that, Mr Jenkins doesn't like most people," she replied truthfully, turning to leave the stall. There was a moment of silence, and then Gunthar burst out laughing, prompting her to pause in the opening.

"Ah," Gunthar sighed, running a hand over his shiny forehead, "you make joke Alyce, that's a good one."

Laughing weakly, she nodded and left the area, wondering what that small gesture of kindness had earned her.

She had just returned to the fire and picked up her mug when Clay ran out from behind the wall of bales, massive hands clamped over his ears. "Agh, it hurts, it hurts!" he shouted, upsetting the pot as he hurtled past.

"Ooo, Clay," she cried, jumping out of the steaming water's path as it flowed across the floor. "What the blazes is agghh," she groaned, the mug falling from her suddenly nerveless fingers as a garbled, unintelligible voice entered her head. "Stop...projecting...into my mind," she stammered hoarsely, sinking to her knees, trembling hands at her temple. She barely noticed the scalding water lapping her knees through the material of her dress, the pain was so intense.

"Can't help it. Ah, make it stop," Clay screamed, running out into the night.

"Clay, come back here!" she cried from the floor, prying open her pain-filled eyes to squint blearily at his retreating figure. "Ugh, you fool," she spat disgustedly as he melted into the mottled shadows. With a vicious snarl, she seized the pendant around her neck, channelled her anger into the shiny black stone. There was an agonised shriek as the matching stone in Clay's brain echoed her strong emotion, and the cacophony in her head abruptly stopped. Carefully craning her neck, she nodded with satisfaction as her tired eyes picked out the grey giant's still, sprawling silhouette.

"What's going on?" Gunthar asked from the wall of bales, his eyes drawn to her hand closed around the pendant. "What do you mean, what's going on? Didn't you hear that terrible noise in your mind?" she asked irritably as she hastily released the stone and scrambled to her feet.

He eyed her quizzically, his head cocked to one side. "Oh yeah, it is louder than usual," he concluded after a moment of concentration. She stared at him, shook her head. Seemingly unaffected by the Mirror's song, he calmly wandered to the barn opening and peered out into the night. "What did you do to him, Alyce?" he asked as his enquiring gaze settled on the huge grey mass of sewn-together flesh shuddering in the moonlight.

"I just encouraged him to pass out," she answered stiffly. Despite his obsession with the Mirror, Gunthar had found time in his busy schedule to observe their relationship, showing particular interest in their psychic link.

"Your uncle must have been a brilliant scientist," he uttered with quiet awe.

"Yes, ow, brilliant," she echoed grimly as she moved gingerly towards the doorway, hissing under her breath with each step, the scalded skin around her knees protesting painfully at the movement. "Go back and watch the prisoners Gunthar, while I revive Clay," she ordered breathlessly, stumbling to an awkward stop beside him. He nodded, glanced over at Clay's slumbering figure one last time before turning away.

"Alright Clay, you stupid collection of parts, now you're going to pay for..."

Her vengeful muttering was interrupted by the awful sound of metal crunching into bone, followed by a muffled cry. "Gunthar?" she called, limping towards the back of the barn, gritting her teeth against the sharp sting of her protesting knees. In the dim lantern light, she picked out his long skinny body stretched out along the floor. "Don't fool around man, this place gives me the creeps enough without you falling over your own feet," she admonished as she crossed the floor, the boards creaking under her feet. It was only when she hobbled past the fire that she noticed the blood trickling from a cut on his forehead. "Gunthar," she called out hoarsely, hand groping for the knife strapped to her waist.

"Hello, Alyce," a familiar voice spoke softly. She stared in disbelief at the calm, grim face that emerged out of the shadows.

"But, you're dead," she gasped, backing jerkily away from the glare of those hate-filled eyes.

"On the contrary Alyce," Mel responded coldly as she stepped over Gunthar's unconscious form, sword held casually at her side, "I've never felt more alive."

"How, how can this be?" Alyce stammered, stumbling backwards over the pot, unable to tear her eyes away from Mel's pale, solemn face. With a vicious kick of the pot, she regained her balance, continued her desperate backward trek. "I saw you die!" she shouted, staring helplessly at the ragged, bloody hole in the other woman's shirt where her knife had entered. "No way you could have survived that wound," she reasoned past the sudden lump in her throat, her clumsy hand finally finding the hilt of her knife. Almost giddy with relief, she pulled the knife out of its sheath, squeezing her hand around the hilt until her knuckles were stark white against the pale skin.

Mel slowly, ominously advanced, face hard and unforgiving. "Damn it, you should have just stayed away," Alyce cried, blade arcing through the air. "I mean, we both got what we wanted," she sobbed, the words scraping past her raw vocal cords. She took another faltering step backwards, her heel striking round metal. Before she could stop herself, the poker rolled out from beneath her foot, sending her collapsing to the floor with a thud. "Ow," she cried, closing her eyes against the sharp pain in her tailbone. Clutching the knife in her sweaty hand, she scrambled to her feet, tears streaming down her cheeks. "I didn't want to kill you Mel, really," she croaked, staggering back as Mel steadily closed the distance between them. Clay! Alyce silently screamed, eyes drifting to the doorway.

"Ah yes," Mel murmured, finally coming to a stop before her, "you showed much regret. Don't worry Alyce," she said stonily, raising her sword, "I'll show you the same compassion."

"Demon!" Alyce hissed, flinging her arm out towards Mel's abdomen, shiny blade glinting in the flickering light. Her knife met only air, and then something hit her hard, causing her body to jolt violently. The knife fell from her suddenly listless hand as she stared down at the sword sticking out of her gut. She gawked up from the cold steel to meet Mel's unsympathetic gaze. "No, not yet," she breathed, blood bubbling out of her mouth.

With a sickening squelch of blood and innards, Mel pulled out the sword, and Alyce fell heavily to the floor. With the last of her strength, she clasped the stone pendant and cried out silently to the golem, before falling into darkness. Metres away from his dying mistress, Clay stirred in his slumber, shuddered as though touched by something cold, and then continued sleeping peacefully.

"Good riddance," Mel spat, turning away from the crumpled form of her foe. She allowed herself a faint smile as she ran to the stalls at the rear of the building. Her impromptu plan was actually working. Her flight through the forest had been dream-like, the strange broken Mirror over a mile away tugging her light feet in the right direction. Only when she approached the trees surrounding the old disused barn did her steps falter. While she crouched behind a large oak tree, racking her brain for a way to break into the barn without being seen, raised voices reached her. Following the sound of heated discussion, she quickly spotted Travis and another man arguing near the horses. As they strayed towards the carriage, she sneaked around to the side of the dilapidated structure where the horses were tethered. Her frantic fingers untied the leather reins, and with a little encouragement, the horses wandered off into the trees, forcing the bickering brothers to noisily go after them.

Everything else just fell into place. With Jenkins rushing out to investigate the source of the ruckus, she only had three people to overcome. The adrenalin surging through her resurrected system made her feel as though she could take them all on, until she caught sight of the golem.

Hanging from the roughly cut-out window, her arms trembling, she spotted the innocuous-looking sack sitting next to the grey giant. Suddenly she knew what to do and ordered the Mirror fragments to channel their maddening song into the golem's mind. There had been some resistance at first, the creature looking around for the source of the sound, its scarred face wrinkled in confusion. Then the full flood of discordant voices assaulted the poor sod's brain, and he was driven crazy.

"Now to let's get out of here," she muttered as she crouched beside Sarah's unconscious figure and cut the ropes. Swearing under her breath, she caught Sarah's torso as she slumped forward. "Come on Sarah, time to wake up," she urged, glancing nervously over her shoulder.

"Ugh," Sarah groaned, slowly responding to her voice and gentle shaking. "Mel?" she croaked as her eyelids fluttered open. "What are you doing here?" She grinned as she helped the blinking, bemused girl to her feet.

"Saving my family," she answered roughly, ruffling her damp red tresses. Sarah rubbed the back of her neck, the words sluggishly permeating her fuddled brain as she watched Mel bend down next to Raphael.

"Where are we?" she abruptly asked, her eyes finally adjusting to the dim light.

"An abandoned barn Alyce and her cronies are using as a hideout," Mel answered distractedly as she hacked the ropes.

"Alyce!" she cried with a start, the name jogging her memory of the previous twenty-four hours. "That spying bitch is here?" she demanded, fists bunching at her sides. "If I get my hands on the piece of slime..."

"Sorry Sarah," Mel grunted, her blade cutting through the last bundle of fibre. She glanced up with an apologetic smirk. "I beat you to it," she informed the fuming girl.

"What?" Sarah croaked, stepping out past the wall of bales, her puzzled gaze following Mel's nod. In the warm glow of the fire, her eyes picked out glossy blonde hair spilling onto the floor, the beautiful still face resting heavily against the rough boards. She ventured past the thick wall, almost tripping over an unconscious body in the process. Frowning down at her feet, she reeled back as her shocked eyes slowly recognised the familiar face. "Gunthar," she murmured, retreating back to Mel's side. "What the hell is going on here, Mel?"

"We have to get out of here," Mel muttered grimly, feeling the walls close in around her with each passing second. "Come on Raph," she cried impatiently, shaking his unresponsive shoulders urgently.

"They must have been really rough on him," Sarah fretted, concern for her foster father finally penetrating her confusion and anxiety.

Mel winced at the memory of Jenkins sinking his boot repeatedly into Raphael's side as she watched on helplessly. "Shit," she swore, staring at his battered face, her hands pushing back his shoulders. Jenkins would be back soon, with his men in tow. Suddenly all her frustration and emotion bubbled to the surface, and she surged forward, fastening her lips to his. Parting his cold lips with her tongue, she willed the alien energy that now circulated her body to enter his. A rush of heat swept through her, coursed out of her mouth into his unconscious form. She felt him stir beneath her lips, hastily pull back in shock as his eyes opened. "Mel," he croaked, raising trembling hands to her face, "is that really you?"

"Yes," she breathed, reaching out to push the wet, matted hair away from his eyes.

"Mel," he cried, pulling her into his body. "Thank God you're alive," he breathed into her hair, tightening his arms around her. Reluctantly she broke away, breathless and flushed.

"We have to go," she cried urgently, stumbling to her feet. "Jenkins can't be far away," she fretted, urging him up off the floor.

"Sarah," Raphael said hoarsely, finally registering the stunned look on his young ward's face as he waited for the stall to stop spinning. "Are you alright?" he asked, settling a heavy arm around her slender shoulders.

"Yes father," she answered weakly as they hobbled together towards the opening. Muttering darkly under her breath, Mel bent over to grab the sack with its precious glass shards and followed them out. Shifting the lumpy sack onto her shoulder, she staggered blindly out into the brightly lit barn. The fire must be blazing nicely, she thought distractedly as her eyes slowly adjusted to the light. She stopped with a rude jolt, bumping into Raphael's rigid back.

"What are you doing Raph?" she gasped, rubbing her head. "We have to go…"

"Going so soon?" a strangely accented voice called out from beyond the fire. Peering out from behind Raphael, she saw a tall slender man saunter into the barn, a solid line of uniformed soldiers at his back.

"Sebastian," Raphael croaked, gawking at the older man as he strode confidently towards the fire.

"Goodness Raphael, how long has it been?" Sebastian asked pleasantly, the tight smile not quite reaching his tawny-coloured eyes.

"Seven years," Raphael answered tersely, eyes boring into the round, soft face framed by dark brown hair, reminding him of their mother.

"Seven years," Sebastian repeated softly, taking in his brother's dishevelled, muddy appearance. "Seven years since that fateful night. I can still see you crouching over Uncle Bruce's body, your bloody hands holding the knife…"

"Yes, you framed me beautifully," Raphael snapped, hands clenched tightly at his sides.

Sebastian's eyes flashed briefly, anger passing across his face like a shadow, darkening everything in its path. "Ah," he sighed, the confident smile reasserting itself, "I guess it can't be helped." He signalled to the men behind him, and the soldiers streamed into the barn, their stern faces forming an impassive wall around them. Tightening her grip on the sack, Mel backed away from the deadly circle of raised bayonets, the sword shifting in her sweaty grip. Catching a glimpse of

Sarah's pale frightened face on the other side of Raphael's unmoving body, she lowered her blade, let it fall to the floor.

"It really is a small world," Sebastian drawled as he peeled off his wet leather gloves. "I commission a couple of spies to find an ancient artifact, and I get an unexpected bonus. It must be my lucky day," he crowed cheerfully, slapping the gloves against his thigh. His smug gaze fell upon Alyce's body, thin lips twitching faintly in annoyance.

"Oh, don't tell me you killed my little spy? She promised to be a very useful, if short-lived addition to our family," he sighed, nudging the corpse negligently with the toe of his boot. Just then Jenkins ran into the barn, his forehead glistening with sweat. Harried steps faltering at the crumpled form on the floor, his eyes widened in shock as he bent down to inspect her lifeless body.

"What a shame," he panted, smirking up at Sebastian. "She had such ill-conceived plans for revenge," he sneered, sliding the signet ring off her finger.

"Right," Sebastian grinned, swivelling his attention back to his brother, "let's get down to business..."

"Why did you do it Sebastian? Why did you set me up?" Raphael demanded roughly, his searching gaze never leaving his brother's face. The abrupt question momentarily threw him off-guard, his cool arrogant mask slipping. "Really Raphael," he said thickly, shaking his head as he skirted the fire pit. Shouldering his way into the circle, he came to a stop before his brother. An expectant silence fell over the barn as they glared at each other, broken only by the spluttering of the fire and the anxious creak of bayonets. "You just didn't see it, did you?" he murmured, idly flicking a clump of dried mud off Raphael's shoulder. "We were the forgotten children, parcelled off to a convenient relative, occasionally sent home to feel like outcasts before our lazy, complacent siblings. You may have found a way to deal with that brother, but I never did," he muttered bitterly, jaw clenching beneath the fine hair of his scratchy beard. "While you studied medicine, I hungered and planned for my permanent return to our real family. Unfortunately for you," he continued more smoothly, the confident mask sliding back into place, "that plan involved destroying your name, in order to elevate mine."

Raphael stared at his brother, jaw slack with astonishment. "Don't tell me it actually worked? Surely Father had his doubts..."

"As always, you give our father too much credit," Sebastian sighed, picking more dirt off his brother's coat. "He was too busy playing politics to act on any doubts he may have harboured. After the murder of her beloved husband, there was very little to keep Sophie in London, so with a little urging from Mother, we returned to the estate in Rouen. Naturally, I set to work straight away, ploughing my way through the family ranks. When Father died last year of a heart attack, there was little opposition to my appointment as his successor."

Raphael's knees crumbled beneath him at the abrupt news. "Father's dead?" he croaked past the bile that rose up his throat, only vaguely aware of rough hands digging into his arms, hauling him to his feet. Swallowing back the bitter acid, he looked up at Sebastian, fresh hatred boiling to the surface. "You didn't have a hand in it, did you Sebastian? Slip something into his food perhaps?" he suggested in a low, dangerous voice.

For an instant, Sebastian's face darkened with anger, the cool facade melting away under his brother's intense glare. A bitter laugh escaped his lips, and he slowly regained his composure. "There you go again, blaming me for everything that's rotten in your life," he sighed, patting Raphael's cheek. "It may surprise you Raphael, but not everything is my fault." Raphael blinked at the subtle admission, sagged in the soldiers' iron grip.

"Thank Heaven for small mercies," he murmured. Sebastian awkwardly cleared his throat, turned away.

"Jenkins, grab the Mirror," he ordered curtly, giving his gloves a final shake. "We have to present it to Emperor Napoleon as soon as possible..."

"Napoleon?" Mel echoed, the blood draining from her face. Sebastian glanced up at the small voice, his bemused gaze falling upon the pale huddled form holding the hessian sack. Hardly a fitting receptacle for such a powerful relic, he thought idly as he approached the woman, making a mental note to find something more appropriate when he got the chance. "Well of course, why do you think I want the Mirror? History is being made as we speak, with his glorious army marching into Russia," he grunted, pulling on his gloves. "For all his preparations however, the Emperor is bound to encounter stiff resistance, from men and country alike. You see," he murmured, gripping her chin and tilting her face upwards, "I am a man attuned to the changing winds of fortune. This is a turning point for Emperor Napoleon, a turning point for the world. Trust me, there are many players trying to scramble up onto the stage right now, wanting more than anything to claw their way out of the shadows and step out into the light. The ones left on the stage when the dust settles will be the victors, while everyone else is crushed into the mud or chased into obscurity." With a final painful squeeze he released her, nodded impatiently to Jenkins.

"Oh my God," Mel croaked, clutching the bag protectively to her chest. Suddenly she felt the room lurch around her, the cold, uncaring faces of the soldiers swirling at the edge of her vision. She could almost feel reality unravel as Jenkins reached for the bag. With a groan, she promptly bent over and vomited.

"Charming," Sebastian drawled over the sound of her heaving stomach. "Get a move on Jenkins," he snapped irritably, glowering at his pale-faced henchman.

"Wait a minute," Jenkins uttered softly, his hand wavering inches away from the sack as his clear blue eyes finally registered her face. "This one's supposed to be dead!" he cried thickly, his throat fast closing up. "Alyce stabbed her, right through the heart," he babbled, staggering backwards. Mel raised a trembling hand to wipe the sickly moisture from her mouth and chin, her eyes full of loathing as she glared up at Jenkins' confused face.

"Who do you think killed Alyce?" she suggested in a low, dangerous voice.

"Agh," Sebastian snarled, striding over and grabbing the bag from her slack hands. "Alright, let's go," he snapped, handing the sack to a shaken Jenkins.

"You are so much like Bruce it's disturbing."

The bald statement stopped Sebastian in mid-stride, shoulders instantly stiffening at the comparison. "All this time I thought you hated the man, but I see now that you're emulating him."

"What the hell are you talking about?" Sebastian grated, slowly turning around.

"You used to always complain about Bruce's gambling addiction, but look at you," Raphael pointed out, voice gathering strength as he warmed to the topic. "You're quite happy to gamble the family name on a chance to rub shoulders with Napoleon and be a "player"? Don't know if I've ever heard anything more absurd in my life."

A thick, cloying silence fell over the scene as Sebastian regarded his brother, jaw clenched in anger. Mel stirred herself to defy the knot of nauseating tension in her stomach and stand up straight. Just when she thought Sebastian was going to fly into rage, a mirthless smile twisted his lips. "Of course," he conceded, casually picking more dried mud off Raphael's crumpled coat. "How else do you think I convinced your good friend the doctor to betray you?" He smiled wickedly at Raphael's stricken face. "You see, Dr Dubois had a little gambling habit, and owed people money. I offered to help him pay off his debts if he did me a little favour…"

"…like keep me busy while you set up the scene back at my apartment," Raphael supplied, his face clearing as comprehension dawned. He could still see his mentor's haunted eyes slide away from his as they shook hands outside the club before going their respective ways. Even with the crisp night air slapping his flushed, intoxicated face, he never thought to question Simon's slightly cagey behaviour that night.

"Unfortunately, the good doctor disappeared about six months after that fateful night. I guess he got himself into debt again with the wrong people," Sebastian suggested with feigned innocence, slender shoulders rising and falling smoothly.

"You treacherous worm," Raphael cried, straining against the iron-like grip of the soldiers. "He had a wife, children…" His voice trailed away as he remembered their faces. Three boys, two girls, the youngest would bother him for piggy-back rides whenever he visited their cosy little home…

"Well, it was nice seeing you again Raphael," Sebastian said with a delicate yawn, suddenly looking bored. "Sorry it has to be this way, but it really is for the good of the family," he added as he turned away. Jenkins tore his nervous gaze from Mel's face to fall into step beside Sebastian, the hessian sack slung over his shoulder.

"Kill them," Sebastian ordered casually to a tall, solid man who bore the marks of battle on his weathered face. With a final backward glance at his brother, he left the circle. A few gruff words from the tall man, and the men shifted to form a solid line across the barn, bayonets aimed steadily at their quarry.

He opened his mouth to cry out when the air around them exploded. Bracing himself for the stinging bite of shrapnel, he sank to his knees, arm flailing out toward Sarah who stood frozen beside him. As acrid smoke filled the air, he stared down at his body, clumsily pawed his clothes in search for bullet holes. "What the…" he muttered in disbelief, head snapping up. It was only then that the moans and screams of the soldiers penetrated his hazy perception. Through the drifting smoke he could make out their bodies slumped on the floor, some unmoving, others all too awake and in pain, their rasping, rattling cries shaking the air. Belatedly he looked around for Mel, breath catching noisily in his throat as his bleary eyes finally found her. "Mel?" he croaked, staggering to his feet. She opened her eyes at the sound of his voice, slowly lowered her arms.

"Father!" Sarah cried, hurtling across the floor to wrap trembling arms around him. "That was too close for comfort," she said thickly, burying her head in his shoulder.

"I agree," he murmured, returning her hug. After a couple of shuddering breaths, she looked up to find Mel still standing like a statue in the middle of the floor.

"Mel, are you alright?" she ventured, extricating herself from Raphael's embrace.

"Sorry about that," Mel murmured in a far-away voice, her movements dream-like as she stepped over a moaning soldier gripping his thigh, blood oozing out between his fingers. "At the very last moment, I borrowed the power of the Mirror, put up a force field around us. Sorry, I should have thought of it sooner," she apologised sheepishly, finally making eye-contact with them. For a split second, Raphael thought he saw a strange light in her eyes, shook his head against the impossible image.

"No time for that now," he muttered, forcing himself to move. "Good work Mel," he added gruffly, bending over to pick up a weapon along the way. Beyond the field of scattered bodies lay Sebastian and Jenkins, their unconscious bodies stretched out across the muddy ground just outside the barn.

"Ah," Mel purred, running over to the hessian sack resting innocently against Jenkins' out-flung arm. Breathing a sigh of relief, she hoisted the sack onto her back. "Now, let's go home," she grunted, turning back to the others.

She stopped dead in her tracks, eyes round as saucers as she watched Raphael raise the sword in his hand. "One hard, clean blow," he muttered thickly, arms shaking with tension, eyes glued to the pale, vulnerable neck of his brother. Suddenly he looked up to find Mel and Sarah gawking at him intently. He glanced back down, swung the blade towards that fragile bridge of flesh and bone. With a cry of frustration, he drove the tip harmlessly into the ground barely an inch or so away from Sebastian's head. Stony-faced, he yanked the sword out of the mud and stormed wordlessly towards the nervous horses tethered nearby. Exchanging concerned looks behind his back, Sarah and Mel raced after him.

Clay twitched in his sleep, shrugged an enormous shoulder as if to dislodge an annoying bug. A few more jerky movements, and the pest was gone, leaving him to dream about his beautiful mistress. Alyce ran towards him over a field of heather, tiny purple flowers brushing against her long blue skirt. She smiled up at him, her arms open and inviting. Her smooth, perfect face was devoid of its usual cruelty and distain as they met in the middle of the field. He gripped her hands, swung her effortlessly through the air. Sweet peals of breathless laughter rang out as he spun faster and faster, until her giggling face was a blur.

Somewhere in the distance, thunder rumbled. He reluctantly slowed to a stop, his black eyes inspecting the rapidly darkening sky. The thunder grew louder, almost sounding like cruel laughter to his bewildered ears. "What's happening Clay?" Alyce shouted over the growing noise, her delicate hands clasped around his upper arm. He opened his mouth to answer, when lightning struck the ground nearby. A large crack radiated out from the point of impact, rapidly claiming the ground beneath their feet. They only had a moment to gape in horror at the jagged, spreading line before falling into the earth. Their screams were muffled by the dirt flowing over and around them, their hands desperately scrabbling at the walls of the deepening chasm. Just when he thought his lungs were going to explode, they reached the bottom of the hole, stared up at the sliver of grey sky that peered down at them.

"Come on mistress, get up on my shoulders!" Clay cried as soil and scree steadily streamed into the base of the hole. He pushed through the deepening earth, straining to lift his feet free. "Come on Alyce," he urged, laying a meaty paw on her unmoving shoulder. She turned calmly to face him, the drifting dust about her head catching the feeble shaft of light like a halo. He waited impatiently for her to respond, his fingers digging into the soft flesh. "Alyce, what are you doing?" he croaked as she threw her head back and laughed.

"Oh, you're such a sap Clay," she sighed.

"Alyce?" he stammered helplessly, watching in wide-eyed horror as the dirt gathered around her waist.

"But I guess that's how Uncle Henry made you," she continued, pity softening her face for a brief moment before the hard, cruel mask fell into place. "Poor sod," she clucked as earth reached her chin, seeped into her mouth.

"Alyce!" he roared, surging forward as a dense wall of falling dirt obscured her face. He frantically pushed through earth and rock to reach her, the sweat trickling down his dirty forehead turning to mud. "Alyce?" he croaked, his arms moving stiffly through the area where she'd been standing, his questing fingers failing to find any trace of his mistress. He looked down in dismay at the soil settling around his chest. "No," he cried as dirt poured more quickly into the hole. He struggled to clamber up above the rising soil, but its increasing weight pinned his legs firmly to the bottom of the hole. "No!" he bellowed into the dimming light, dirt filling his mouth, coating his face, falling faster and faster until he stood in complete darkness. Still dirt poured into the hole, its growing volume pressing down on his head. Desperately he gasped for air, only to suck in more dirt. Warm salty tears leaked out of his eyes, to form muddy tracks down his cheeks. "How thoughtful of father to give me working tear ducts," he thought savagely just before collapsing under the crushing weight.

A moment of complete darkness and pain, and the dream abruptly changed. He was standing in a room, facing a large, cluttered table. Peering at him sternly over the bridge of thick reading glasses, a man sat on the other side of the table, a pen in his hand. "Do you have anything else to say for yourself?" he asked with a sigh as he removed his glasses and rubbed his eyes.

"She cheated on you father," he said in Alyce's voice. "She had to be punished..."

"It's not the punishment I'm objecting to," the man snapped, slamming his fist down on the table. A globule of ink escaped the nib, splattering the sheet of paper underneath his clenched hand. He winced at the black stain, glared at him over the sea of papers and books that swamped the huge table. No, not at him, he suddenly realized as a lock of blonde hair fell past his eye. At Alyce. For some reason, he was Alyce, awaiting judgment from her father.

Her father took a deep breath, grabbed an ink-stained cloth from the table. "What I mind is your incompetence, Alyce. That, and your presumption," he explained more calmly as he carefully wiped off the ink.

"I know I shouldn't have acted alone," she admitted desperately, hungry for a hint of softness or understanding in her father's cold, clinical countenance. Everything about him was so measured and perfect, including his beautifully trimmed beard, evenly speckled now with dark grey hairs. "I was so mad, catching her in the act like that..." Her voice trailed away as erotic images of her step-mother perched on the edge of a table, her skirts gathered around her waist, entered her mind. The young stable hand's hips rocking violently back and forth, their subdued groans ringing in her ears as she stumbled silently away...

"So you poisoned her in a clumsy, unvetted act of retribution," he supplied tightly, inspecting his handiwork before setting aside the cloth. "And now my new wife is virtually a vegetable." His harsh true words cut into her psyche like a whip cutting into flesh. She looked away from those penetrating blue eyes, swallowed past the sudden lump in her throat. The powder she had slipped into her stepmother's food had not been strong enough. Her treacherous throat had swollen up beautifully as expected, giving the appearance of a sudden, vicious cold or infection. Instead of forming a perfect seal across her airways however, the inflammations had only made it very difficult for her to breathe. She was now confined to her room, drifting in and out of consciousness. Even if the swelling went down, and she regained full consciousness, the damage was already done

"Now her family are sending people to "assist" in her care," he continued bitterly, turning his attention to the paper before him. "It will be more difficult to arrange her death now without arousing suspicion..."

"So you believe me?" she blurted, head snapping up as a pinpoint of hope penetrated the gloom of her predicament.

He eyed her quizzically, quickly signed the document. "Of course I believe you," he replied as he pushed his chair back and rose stiffly, hand fumbling for the key in the pocket of his thick woollen vest. "I've suspected she was cheating on me for some time," he admitted, moving to a chest in the corner. "I just didn't get around to doing anything about it…"

"Then why are you sending me away? I was acting in your interest," she cried, stepping towards the table. He looked up from unlocking the chest, frowned at her. Clearing his throat, he returned his attention to the thick-walled chest, pulled out a number of gold coins.

"A price must be paid for so bad a blunder," he declared firmly, a faint tinge of sadness in his voice. He clambered to his feet and slowly approached her. "Take this money," he ordered, dropping the gold pieces onto her waiting palm, "and don't let the nuns see it. Hell, sew the coins into your clothing if you have to…"

"Nuns?" she repeated with a jolt, looking up from the shiny coins in her hand.

His lips twitched with dry amusement at her reaction. "Yes, you're to leave tonight. Three of my men will escort you to the nunnery. You'll be comfortable there…"

"I'd rather die!" she shouted hotly, clenching her hand around the coins.

"Don't be silly," he chided, "you can't survive out there on your own. At least this way you will be safe," he added, gripping her shoulders.

"Safe to rot away in isolation," she spat back, shaking off his hands.

"This is the best I can manage," he grated, reaching behind him for the letter. "Give this to the head nun, it gives a plausible explanation as to why you're being sent there…"

"Give it to her yourself!" she yelled, screwing up the carefully written letter and flinging it in his face. His hand flew into her defiant face, forcibly pushing her head to the side.

She raised a trembling hand to her stinging cheek, looked up at her father in hurt disbelief. "I can never please you father," she said thickly, the taste of blood filling her mouth. Distractedly she brushed the corner of her mouth, lowered her hand to inspect the smear of blood. "All I ever wanted was to please you," she continued softly, eyes fixed on the bright red trail.

"You want to please me? Then go to the bloody nunnery," he grunted testily, bending over to pick up the letter. She stared at the crumpled piece of paper in his hand, raised her eyes to his.

"Yes father," she said coldly, feeling something harden within her. His eyes widened in surprise as she stiffly took the letter and turned away.

The dream shifted, and she was sneaking out of the mansion, a small bag of belongings clutched to her chest. She finally made it out into the lush moonlit garden, the soft scrape of her feet against the grass seeming ridiculously loud to her nervous ears. A sudden sound behind her, and she was diving for cover, crouching painfully amidst the prickly branches of a nearby bush. A servant opened the kitchen door, emptied a teapot over the garden bed. The woman raised her head sharply at the sound of disturbed branches, looked suspiciously around the grounds. "Bloody cat," she muttered with a shrug of her shoulders, turning back inside the house. Breathing a sigh of relief, she moved out of the foliage, crept stealthily from one shadow to the next.

At the gate, she turned back for one last look at the house. Of their own accord, her gazed drifted to the window of her father's study. She froze as her eyes fell upon her father's stern face staring back at her through the thick glass. She waited tensely for him to do something, expecting him to disappear suddenly from the window to order his men out into the night after her. Instead he just shook his head and turned away, his shoulders slumped in acceptance. For what felt like an age she stared at the empty space, waited for sounds of movement. The house stood ominously quiet and unaffected, with only the usual kitchen noises reaching her across the yard.

With a massive lump in her throat, she stumbled away, only to have a sword pushed through her gut. She glanced up to find Mel watching her coldly, her hand tightening around the hilt of the sword. Desperately trying to hold in her guts as Mel pulled out the sword, she staggered back towards the house, screaming out to her father...

"Father," she cried hoarsely, waking up with a start. She pried her eyelids open, quickly raised her hand to shield her eyes from the first weak rays of morning. Trying to ignore the pain behind her eyes, she stiffly rose to her feet, stretched her massive limbs. "How did I end up out here?" she wondered aloud, squinting at the muddy ground where she had been sleeping. "Oh great," she groaned, noticing the dried mud on her arms. She froze, staring in horror at her long grey arms. Her hands flew to her face, thick fingers tracing the swollen lips, the long scar running down the left cheek, the smooth, hairless scalp.

Fragments of memory skidded across the churning surface of her mind. Cursing Martin for not maintaining the fire, talking to Jenkins, a commotion outside, Clay running out into the night, Mel driving a sword into her. With a startled gasp, she ran back to the barn, almost tripping over Jenkins' slumbering form in her haste. Digging her heels into the soft ground, she came to an abrupt stop in the doorway, her gaze searching the gloomy interior. There she was, lying motionless near the firepit. Tears welling in her unnatural eyes, she wended her way through the maze of unconscious soldiers to her old shell. "No," she groaned, kneeling beside the beautiful corpse. "How is this possible?" she croaked softly, gently rolling the body over. She carefully pushed the tangled blonde hair out of the blue-tinged face. "All my dreams, turned to dust," she sobbed, clutching the limp body to her chest. It was only then she realized something was missing. "The pendant," she cried, pulling back to frantically scrutinise the bare neck. With trembling hands, she searched around the body, shifting her old limbs in vain.

"Looking for something?"

She spun around at the familiar, accented voice. Gunthar leant casually against the wall of bales, the smooth polished stone dangling from the velvet band nestled between his fingers. She surged toward him desperately, hand reaching for the stone, when sharp stabbing pains filled her skull, causing her to collapse in a shuddering heap. Rubbing his thumb over the engraved symbols with detached interest, he smirked triumphantly. Pushing away from the wall, he cautiously circled the groaning golem, gave the symbols a final caress. She painfully lifted her head to glower at him, raising her torso unsteadily on numb arms. Gunthar smiled at her, pointedly tapped the edge of the stone with his finger. "Now," he drawled, crouching down in front of her, "let's talk."

"Sir, sir," Jenkins hissed, shaking Sebastian's shoulder. Wincing against the pain in his own arm, he doggedly roused his employer. The stirring soldiers around him were steadily being checked for damage, the burly captain yelling out orders. Sebastian grimaced, reluctantly opened his eyes. "Ugh, what happened?" he asked groggily as he struggled to sit up.

"Some kind of explosion, sir. From what I've heard, it was Mel's doing," he offered sourly. Already soldiers were grumbling about the violent, invisible force coming from the small, unimposing woman with the torn, bloody shirt.

"Isn't that the woman you killed?" Sebastian grunted, clambering stiffly to his feet.

"I didn't kill her," he cried defensively, uncomfortable with her impossible survival. "I just held her in place. It was Alyce who did the deed..."

"Damn," Sebastian cursed over his nervous rambling, surveying the damage about him. Most of the men seemed alright, if shaken, he surmised as he strode around the barn. A handful of men had been unlucky to have their pellets flung back at them, and were being treated for gunshot wounds. One body had been moved to the far side of the barn, a white shirt placed over the unfortunate soldier's head.

"So, what happened? Alyce didn't do a good enough job?" Sebastian pressed tightly, light brown eyes flashing angrily as they approached the dead soldier.

"No way sir," Jenkins answered adamantly, remembering her still, rain-soaked body lying in the mud, blood spilling out onto the ground. He'd seen enough death in his line of work to know the wound had been fatal.

"Did anything unusual happen during or after the stabbing?" Sebastian quizzed distractedly, bending down to lift the shirt. Jenkins paused, thought back to the rain-drenched scene of only a few hours ago. "Gunthar," he blurted, suddenly recalling the German's annoyance at being called away from Mel's body. "He was drawn to her corpse for some reason, mentioned that there was something there," he explained.

"Hmm," Sebastian murmured thoughtfully, letting go of the shirt with a grimace. "Where is that crackpot anyway?" he muttered as he stood up slowly and looked around.

"Gunthar!" Jenkins called, moving towards the stalls. "Get your skinny arse out here!" he roared, a hint of desperation in his voice, all too aware of Sebastian's heavy eyes upon him. With violent, jerky movements, he checked all the stalls. "Damn that opportunistic worm," he snarled, kicking the wall of bales in frustration.

"You should have kept him on a shorter leash, Mr Jenkins," Sebastian suggested in a tightly controlled voice.

"Yes sir," he conceded, groaning inwardly at the look of displeasure on his employer's face.

Just then a young soldier ran into the barn, his face red beneath the streaks of mud. "Sir," he panted, giving a cursory salute to the burly captain, "three of the horses are missing, sir."

Captain Gasquet dismissed the soldier, glanced wearily over at Sebastian. "Round up your men, Captain, we're leaving," he ordered curtly, peeling off a leather glove. Without warning, he swung the glove into Jenkins' cheek, the force of his blow sending the henchman's head back sharply. "You've been sloppy Mr Jenkins," Sebastian said, calmly pulling the glove back on. "Because of your incompetence, we are now in a race for the Mirror," he grated, sparing Jenkins a look of disgust as he passed. "And my brother's head," he added darkly. Jenkins raised a shaky hand to his face, the taste of blood filling his mouth. Avoiding Captain Gasquet's critical gaze, he hurried after Sebastian, his tired brain trying to figure out where the plan had gone so awry.

"Here," Raphael ordered, his tone brooking no argument. Mel looked up from her brooding inspection of the library window to the cup in his hand.

"Thanks," she croaked, gratefully accepting the dark red wine. "Ah," she breathed appreciatively, closing her eyes as she savoured the tangy taste. She opened her eyes, blushed slightly to find him watching her. "I really needed that," she offered sheepishly as he sat opposite her. He took a swig of his own wine, set his cup on the table.

"I imagine the simplest drink tastes good if you've come back from the dead," he said thoughtfully, studying her intently. She shifted self-consciously in her seat under his intense gaze, pushed a stray lock of tangled hair behind her ear.

"How's Sarah?" she asked, eager to change the subject.

"Poor girl was exhausted. She's sound asleep in her bed," he answered, leaning forward in his chair. "I'm surprised you're not more tired," he admitted pointedly.

She looked away from his probing gaze, not fully understanding her unnatural stamina. "The mirror fragment hums within me, dragging my tired body onwards, beyond reasonable limits," she explained carefully, turning back to meet his unreadable face. After a moment of heavy silence, he picked up his cup, stared gloomily into its shadowy depths.

"Good thing you took that piece of the Mirror," he said roughly into the wine.

"Yes," she breathed, shuddering at the memory of death. "Well, we're not out of the woods yet," she added, nursing the cup in her hands.

"I know," he responded grimly, gulping down the rest of his wine and rising impatiently to his feet. He moved to the window, grimaced at the first feeble rays of dawn. "We have maybe two, three hours at most before Sebastian makes his way here," he surmised. "Of all the greedy, ruthless bastards in the world, why did it have to be him?" he muttered, resting his forehead on the cold glass.

"I'm sorry Raphael," she said thickly, setting her cup on the table, "I wanted to spare you the family reunion. Alyce had great fun telling me not to worry about you and Sarah, that Sebastian would deal with you both. That was just before she drove the knife into my chest..."

"Damn!" Raphael exploded, hitting his head against the window frame. With a start she looked up, mouth agape. "God Mel, you've lost everything because of me," he croaked, slowly turning around to face her, "including your very life." Without thinking, she clambered out of the chair, knocking her wine to the floor in her haste.

"Raph," she gasped, reaching out to his bloody forehead, "please, you've been beaten up enough tonight." She searched desperately for a section of material on her shirt that wasn't smeared with blood or mud, settled for the underside of one sleeve. Carried away by a tide of strong emotion, she gently dabbed the split skin, her gaze completely focused on his forehead. In the thickening silence of the room, she became aware of his steady breathing, the warmth of his body. Her arm paused in mid-dab as his eyes locked with hers, and he grabbed her wrist.

"Mel," he croaked, pressing his lips into the palm of her hand, "I don't deserve you."

"Sure you do," she argued huskily, leaning into him as the world suddenly lurched around her. "Why else do you think I came back?" He lowered her hand, slowly bent his head towards hers, lips parted in anticipation...

Suddenly there was a forceful knock on the door, and they hurriedly broke away from each other. "Yes," Raphael answered, wiping a shaky hand over his forehead. John burst into the room, his haggard face dripping with sweat.

"You wanted to see me sir?" he gasped, eyes darting away from Mel's flushed face. With a tight smile, Raphael strode towards the older man.

"Yes John," he said warmly, holding out his hand, "I wanted to thank you for your excellent work. From all accounts, you took control of the situation in my stead," he continued gruffly. John gaped briefly at the extended hand, hastily accepted it.

"Just doing my job, Mr Blythe," he mumbled with an embarrassed cough. "I'm just glad no one was seriously hurt or worse," he added carefully, his curious gaze wandering past Raphael's broad shoulder to Mel's expectant face. Unable to find her voice, she merely nodded, a shy smile tugging at the corners of her mouth.

"I understand you ventured out after us," Raphael pressed, noting the man's distracted stare.

"Yes sir," he answered, eyes darting back to his employer's solemn face. "I was so angry, I couldn't stop myself, sir," he blurted, rage still stirring within him. "Such a cowardly act..."

"Indeed," Raphael murmured in agreement, brow darkening. With a forced smile, he roughly clapped the man's back. "Get some rest man, you must be exhausted," he ordered briskly, gently guiding John towards the door. On their return to the manor, John had been valiantly standing guard on the lookout platform, his weary eyes squinting down at them through the pre-dawn gloom, arrow pulled tautly back. Even from the ground, they could see his shoulders slump with relief that they were friend, and not foe. The others were found slumbering in the kitchen, their heavy heads resting on the table, slack faces dimly lit by the dying flames of the fire. With much shaking, Simon had been the first to wake, rubbing the crusty sleep from his eyes. To his credit, his face had fallen only slightly when ordered to take John's place.

"We're in danger, aren't we sir?" John asked hesitantly as they approached the door. With a shake of his head, Raphael returned to the present, glanced over at John's grave face. He opened his mouth to glibly reassure the man that the threat was over, that they could all carry on as though nothing had happened. "I have put us all in danger Mr Morley," he said, shrugging his tired shoulders. "I'm sorry," he added, opening the door. An unreadable expression crossed John's face as he met Raphael's apologetic gaze, a vague smirk curling his lips.

"Always knew there was more to you than met the eye sir," John grunted, dark brown eyes gleaming as he trudged out into the corridor.

Raphael closed the door, rested heavily against the solid wood panel. "We have to get the staff away from here," he said roughly, pushing himself away from the door.

"I know," she sighed, burying her head in her hands. "Even if we lead Sebastian and his men away, he could try to take hostages, or worse." Raphael sunk down in the chair opposite her, his body slumped in defeat.

"This is a living nightmare," he uttered softly, eyes staring into the distance. "Once again Sebastian has turned my world upside down." She stared helplessly at him, possibilities filtering through her exhausted brain. Her wretched gaze fell upon the hessian sack sitting innocently next to her chair.

"I can buy us some more time," she suggested suddenly, the Mirror's lilting song ringing faintly in her ears.

Raphael refocused his dejected gaze on her, a glimmer of hope lighting his eyes. "How?" he asked, leaning forward in his chair. In answer, she reached out and lifted the sack onto her lap. Swallowing apprehensively, she closed her eyes and set her hands on the lumpy surface. Against the black background of her closed lids, images coalesced into a familiar scene. A silver-suited alien sitting on the desert floor, long slender fingers flying over the Mirror, making strange symbols appear on its black surface. Over a thousand kilometres away, drifting peacefully above the Earth, the alien's ship stirred. Deep in the bowels of the ship, complex machinery came to life as navigation thrusters gently fired, moved the great grey saucer into position. The scene shifted back to the alien, its helmeted head rising to survey the horizon. With a satisfied grunt, the alien gave the screen a final, decisive tap, and an intense energy beam punched through the atmosphere, hit the distant mountain.

The image in her head focused on the Mirror balanced on the alien's padded knees, growing larger and larger, until she was actually inside the screen. With a jolt her consciousness spilled out onto the microscopic circuitry, carried along by the flow of electrons. Feeling like a tourist, she meandered through the conductor material, marvelling at the thousands, millions of nanobots moving about the city-like circuit board. Infinitesimal machines of all shapes and sizes purposefully moved back and forth around her, seemingly oblivious to her presence. She reached out a hand, felt the smooth shiny side of a machine bustling past. Her eyes widened as the soft iridescent skin briefly shuddered at the contact before vanishing into the hectic traffic. It had felt almost organic beneath her fingers, the surface bending under pressure.

Craning her neck around, she squinted up at the tall black towers, their inky surfaces criss-crossed by a network of fine gleaming lines. Arching overhead, nanobots floated from one tower to another, their glittering bodies dissolving into the smooth walls. Her distracted feet faltered over a small protrusion on the ground, causing her to stumble into a nearby tower. Without think-ing, she reached out a hand to stabilise herself, coming to a heavy rest against the black pillar of circuitry. The instant her hand touched the surface, the nanobots stopped abruptly, turned as one towards her. Staring helplessly back at the strange machines, she slowly withdrew her hand, clutched it self-consciously to her chest. Suddenly a bright silver object floated out of the crowd, the tiny propellers covering its round body looking like metallic hairs fluttering in the breeze. The other nanobots parted to make way for the dazzling newcomer, their movements striking her as deferential. Steadily the machine approached, the reflection of her awestruck face in its smooth silver surface growing bigger and bigger until they stood face to face. Unable to help herself, she extended her hand to the gleaming face of the robot, tiny lights embedded along its circum-ference winking down at her. Her hand disappeared within the alien machine, a flood of images entering her mind.

With a start she opened her eyes, lifted her hands off the sack as though it was on fire. "Mel?" Raphael prompted avidly, sitting on the edge of his seat.

"The Mirror's alive, Raph," she croaked, eyes slowly focusing on his concerned face. "It was actu-ally part of a much larger machine, a long time ago," she explained hoarsely, shakily picking up her cup. Red wine dribbled down her chin as she hastily drained the cup and set it back down on the table with a triumphant thump. "The rest of the machine was either destroyed or taken away, but the Mirror somehow stayed on Earth, and evolved," she continued excitedly, roughly wiping the wine from her chin. Raphael's confused look finally penetrated her euphoria, brought her back to reality with a jolt. Giggling like a schoolgirl, she set the sack on the floor. "I can do this Raphael, I can buy us some time," she said breathlessly, springing out of her chair. "I just have to create a force field, gently push Sebastian and his men off-course..."

"Why not just push them all the way back to France?" Raphael scoffed bitterly, jealousy whelm-ing up inside him like bile. If she noticed his dark tone, she gave no sign of it, her restless feet pac-ing the floor, the wall of embossed book spines winking faintly at her in the dull light.

"There's a limit to its power," she explained distractedly, flicking dried mud and blood off the tattered remains of her shirt. "While the technology behind the Mirror is immeasurably advanced, it still needs a sentient mind in order to work. I may control the Mirror, but I'm still only human. At best I can buy us half a day, maybe a whole day, depending on my concentration..."

"Concentration?" Raphael echoed, pouncing like a cat on the phrase. She stopped in her tracks, abruptly met his intense gaze. Suddenly the fire in her eyes died down, and she returned languidly to her chair.

"God Raph, I don't even know what I'm doing," she admitted, leaning forward to rest her elbows on her knees, face firmly buried in her hands. "If you still controlled the Mirror, you probably could send them back home, hell, to the other side of the world. The Mirror tells me I can do these things, but I just don't know."

He looked away in shame. How could he be so petty at a time like this? "Believe me Mel," he murmured, swallowing past the lump in his throat, "you're the most remarkable woman I've ever met. You can do this." Gulping painfully, she lifted her head, eyes bright with unshed tears.

"Do you mean that?" she asked, a tremulous smile tugging at the corners of her mouth.

"Of course I mean it," he reassured her tightly, cheeks reddening. His muscles protesting at the movement, he stiffly rose out of the chair, arms stretched above his head. "Just don't push yourself too hard," he warned, wagging a stern finger at her.

"Yes sir," she acknowledged with a playful salute. He frowned, grabbed her hand.

"I'm serious Mel," he said earnestly, his warm fingers massaging the clammy skin of her palm. "I don't want to lose you to the Mirror."

"You won't," she croaked, tearing her attention from the rhythmic movement of his fingers, "I promise."

His frown deepened as he reluctantly released her hand and headed for the door. "Do what you can Mel, I'll see to the rest," he ordered over his shoulder.

A soft click of the door closing behind him, and he was gone. Suddenly she felt as though the walls were closing in around her, the churning of her stomach causing her to double over. "I can't believe this is happening," she cried, her voice barely scratching the heavy silence of the room. "Sarah should have dragged some other poor sap through time and space," she croaked, swallowing back the bile that coursed up her throat. No, not a poor sap, she corrected herself, carefully sitting up again. A tough, stoic person, like the heroes in the many adventure books she'd read. "Definitely not me," she whispered hoarsely, staring at the hessian sack on the floor by her feet. With numb hands she picked it up, set it on her lap. "One problem at a time, Mel," she sighed. Time enough to worry about keeping the Mirror out of Napoleon's clutches once they get the staff safely away, she told herself. Taking a deep breath, she resignedly laid her hands on the sack and closed her eyes. As she lost herself in the strange landscape of the Mirror's consciousness, the jagged edges pressing into her fingertips through the coarse material, she quietly marvelled at her perverse mixture of good and bad luck. Like Jan said, she just had to be different.

She awoke with a start, snapping her eyes open to the full harsh light of day. The Mirror's shrill cry subsided, hovering at the edge of her frayed consciousness as she shook her head to dispel the image of men on horseback. Stiffly rising out of the chair, she stumbled over to the window, the hairs on the back of her neck beginning to stand on end. "Oh shit," she swore as her troubled gaze was drawn to the edge of the forest. Something large moved beneath the slender branches of the birch trees, steadily making its way towards the manor. "Damn," she cried, bending over to scoop up her sword as she ran from the room. Must have missed some men, she thought frantically, jogging down the stairs. Her panicked footsteps rang loudly along the deserted hallway. Raphael must have gotten everyone out, judging by the eerie silence. She fervently hoped so as she burst through the front door. "How could I have missed anyone?" she muttered darkly, her heavy feet pounding the ground. For hours she had extended the Mirror's energy to the band of dishevelled men riding listlessly through the forest, gently pushing them away from the manor. It was hard to believe any stragglers could have escaped her net.

Tightening her fingers around the leather-bound hilt, she skidded to a halt at the edge of the yard, her eyes glued to the section of forest where branches moved alarmingly. Her jaw slackened in astonishment as Gunthar emerged from the trees, the golem by his side. The sword wavered in her hands as they approached. "Ah, Mel is it?" he drawled, a smug grin on his face. "We haven't been formally introduced yet," he continued smoothly, wiping his hand on his filthy shirt front. "My name is Gunthar Bliesch, archaeologist extraordinaire," he purred, extending his hand.

"What do you want?" she asked testily, pointedly ignoring his hand. His face fell slightly at her coldness.

"Oh," he mumbled, withdrawing his hand. "Straight to business, eh?" he clucked with a sideways glance at the golem.

Even through the thick protective goggles, she felt the eyes of the grey giant upon her, the hilt slipping further in her sweaty grip as she looked from one threatening face to the other. Noticing her discomfit, Gunthar smiled and tilted his head. "I want what's rightfully mine," he answered, taking a step forward.

"That's close enough," she growled, forcing his body back. He moved his hands before him, met an invisible wall.

"Amazing," he breathed, feeling the barrier with his hands, searching for the edge. She stepped warily in the same direction, her brow wrinkled in concentration. "You have a piece of the Mirror inside you," he stated wondrously, opening his senses to the fragment humming within her. "That must have been what I felt when you were lying dead in the mud," he mused, rubbing his chin distractedly. "It calls to me, you see," he added, his voice full of longing.

"Good for you," she grunted, preparing to blast him back into the forest.

"Wow, that's some power you have there," he gushed, leaning against the air before him. "All because of a piece of glass. I told you so," he cried triumphantly to the golem.

"Indeed," the huge creature murmured, swinging its massive paws through the air. "Ironic really, isn't it?" the golem rumbled, pushing against the barrier. "I kill you, and you gain supernatural powers," the giant confessed, a bitter grin twisting its swollen lips. "You kill me, and I gain super-natural powers," it finished, slowly breaking through the dense air. Her jaw loosened as the gravelly words sunk in.

"Alyce?" she croaked, sword tip hitting the ground as her sweaty hands lost their grip. The golem dropped its bald, glossy head back and laughed harshly, the deep voice grating on her nerves.

"Ah," Alyce said breathlessly, the air rattling in her great chest. "It's good to cheat death, is it not?" she shared.

"How?" Mel asked, raising her sword as Alyce ominously approached.

"Psychic link," she answered smugly, tapping her temple. "With the last of my strength, I trans-ferred my consciousness into Clay. Poor sod didn't have a chance," she clucked sympathetically, shaking her head.

"Ugh," Mel groaned, shaken by the unexpected turn of events. "So, you just took over his body?"

"Yes," Alyce answered flatly, without a flicker of emotion. "Oh, I can feel him, buried deep within this mind, clawing at the surface so far away, a faint glimmer of light pinpointing the darkness..." Her voice trailed away, and she visibly shuddered. "Uncle Henry would be proud," she murmured, closing the gap between them. "So, thank you Mel. Sure, I've lost my looks," she joked bitterly, knocking the sword out of her hands with one well-placed swipe of her fist, "but it's worth it." She plucked Mel up off the ground, one huge hand wrapped around her throat.

"On the contrary," Mel grated hoarsely, staring at her own terrified face in the dark reflective glass, her hands feebly clawing the thick, sausage-like fingers, "being a monster suits you."

"Ha," Alyce barked humourlessly, and flung her into the forest. She turned her head in time to see a network of branches only inches away as she flew through the air. She managed to blast a path before her, the force snapping the branches back mere millimetres from her face. Amid shat-tered wood and shredded leaves, she crashed into the forest floor. "Pah," she uttered, spitting out bark and leaves as she rose to her feet.

"Keep her busy Alyce," Gunthar ordered, turning towards the castle.

"No!" Mel cried, making her way frantically out of the forest. She extended her hand, pushed the air around him violently sideways. His feet fell out from beneath him, and he sprawled painfully to the ground.

Deep thudding steps approached her, the golem surprisingly fast for its monstrous size. She desperately shifted her focus, tried to force Alyce back. Laughing cruelly, Alyce swung at her, the massive fist catching her chin and sending her to the ground. "Oh, what's the matter?" Alyce crowed, lifting her foot above Mel's head. "Your feeble powers don't seem to work so well on me," she roared, stomping her foot down.

"Ugh," Mel grunted, rolling out of the foot's path, the edge of the worn leather boot brushing the back of her head. Scrambling to her feet, she reached out to her sword, gratefully wrapped her hand around the hilt as it sailed through the air to her.

"Fine," she spat vehemently, jumping out of Alyce's range as she swung out again, "we'll do this the old-fashioned way."

Her lips twisted in a cold, unsettling grin, Alyce abruptly kicked out, landed a glancing blow on her right knee cap. As she stumbled back, teeth clenched against the fresh pain, she brought her sword around, the keen blade meeting muscle and sinew.

"Agh!" Alyce roared, clutching the severed flesh. Clambering ungainly to her feet, Mel hobbled away from the groaning golem, turned her attention to where Gunthar had fallen.

"Oh no," she whispered, looking on in despair at the empty space. She had just started to hobble towards the manor when a great grey fist caught the side of her head, sent her flying sideways through the air, sword falling from her suddenly nerveless hand. Crashing heavily into the stable, she landed in a pain-stricken heap at the foot of the wall, blood oozing down the side of her face. Gasping for air, she struggled to her feet in time to be grabbed by the throat.

"That...hurt," Alyce spat, slamming her head roughly into the wall.

"Uh," Mel gasped, gripping the massive hand that circled her throat like a band of steel. She managed to pry a finger back and suck some air into her lungs before Alyce tightened her grip and lifted her off the ground. As she thrashed about, her feet uselessly kicking the air, she glimpsed out of the corner of her eye a pitchfork resting against the wall. "I'm so sorry," she grunted, willing the fork to move. Alyce snarled, squeezed her hand.

"No second chances this time," Alyce grated, face dark with hatred as she slowly crushed her windpipe. There was a dull thud and she jolted forward, loosening her grip. Mel sank gratefully to the ground, hungrily sucking in air. She slumped against the wall and watched blearily as the golem stiffened and fell forward on it contorted face, a pitchfork sticking out of its side.

"My sentiments exactly," she muttered, rolling away from the huge twitching mass of grey flesh. "Bad time for an attack," she grumbled as she clambered unsteadily to her feet. Forcing her exhausted body onwards, she staggered to the manor, collecting her sword along the way. "Such a long way," she wheezed as she finally made it to the stairs, almost tripping over her clumsy feet in the process. She pushed through the door, lurched precariously into the passageway. A loud clang from the library spurred her up the stairs with more gusto than she could have ever imagined. Heart pounding wildly in her ears, she burst into the huge room. Gasping for breath, she stood in the doorway, transfixed by the scene before her.

"Get away from the bag, Gunthar," Raphael said in a low dangerous voice, the tip of his sword held at his throat. Swallowing nervously, the wiry-haired German raised his hands and rose carefully to his feet, the steely tip resting lightly against his skin.

"Are you alright Mel?" he asked, not for a second taking his eyes off Gunthar.

"I'm fine," she lied, feeling the room spin about her. She reached out blindly for the door handle, leaned on it heavily.

"Sorry I didn't help earlier," he apologised tightly as he prompted Gunthar to edge away from the bag. "I just got back from escorting the last staff members out of the area."

"That's quite alright," she panted, doubling over slightly. "Your timing as always is perfect."

His lips twitched faintly with amusement before settling back into a stern, hard line. "Can you get behind me Mel?" he ordered tersely, preparing to herd Gunthar out of the room.

"You look tired Mel," Gunthar croaked, looking away from the steel pressed against his windpipe. "I'm surprised you survived my pet golem's attack..."

"Shut up!" Raphael snapped, pushing the tip of his blade into the soft pale skin. "Come on Mel, move out of the doorway," he urged, sensing Gunthar's growing desperation.

"Ugh," she grunted, lurching away from the security of the doorway. She moved on wobbly legs towards Raphael, the room swirling more violently about her with each step. Out of the corner of her eye she glimpsed Gunthar's cruel smirk.

"So, the new improved Mel has limitations after all," he gloated, blood trickling down his neck.

"One more word out of you, and I'll skewer your windpipe, snake," Raphael threatened, tensing his arm. "Now move!"

That's odd, she thought sluggishly, straining to position herself behind Raphael. She was moving, but couldn't quite get there, her limbs steadily turning to jelly. Something's wrong, she realised belatedly as she slowly collapsed to the floor, the garbled voice of the Mirror finally penetrating her foggy mind. Prying her eyelids open, her eyes fell upon the jagged shape in the folds of Gunthar's shirt. "No," she croaked, reaching out a hand.

"Mel?" Raphael asked, darting his head around to check her condition. Gunthar seized the moment and batted away the sword. She watched on in horrified fascination as he stumbled towards the sack, his hand outstretched. Time seemed to slow down, with all the players in the room almost frozen in place, as though a cosmic hand had pressed pause on the remote control of life. Raphael was turning back to Gunthar, his sword arcing through the air. Gunthar was staggering forward, one hand clasped around his throat, the other reaching out for the sack.

Using all her remaining strength, she called to the Mirror, willed the bag to come to her waiting hand. A brief flash of surprise and annoyance crossed Gunthar's face as his hand closed around empty air. With a jolt, the scene was un-paused, and he looked up in time to see the glass window rush toward him. As she finally blacked out, a loud crash and tinkling of glass filled the room, closely followed by a sickening, bone-crunching thud. Raphael stepped cautiously over the broken glass and splintered wood to peer at the inert body lying face down on the ground.

"Hmph," he grunted, turning back to Mel. It was just as well they had to leave, he thought wryly as he bent down next to Mel's unconscious form. "This day just gets better and better," he muttered, pushing the damp hair out of her face. Sighing deeply, he gathered her up in his arms and trudged out of the library, his exhausted mind searching desperately for an escape plan. At the very least, he had to devise a way to severely inconvenience his dear brother, he thought with a sneer.

Captain Gasquet wiped the sweat from his brow as he watched his men creep around the outer buildings of the manor. He was painfully aware of Lord Seabast's growing impatience. The disappearance of Gunthar and the golem had left him in a foul enough mood without their inexplicable delay arriving at the manor. Despite Jenkins' expert directions, they had somehow lost their way. Odd, the gruff, battle-seasoned soldier reflected as his best man signalled the all-clear, and he nudged his horse to move into the yard. Those first couple of hours on horseback had been sluggish, as though a great invisible hand pushed sideways at their bodies. It had reminded him of wading in the sea as a child. The subtle, irresistible pull of the current had carried him halfway down the bay without him even realising it. Not until he looked back to see his sister solemnly building her sandcastle, her small hunched-over figure a speck against the sand, did he realise how much he had moved. The experience had unsettled him, even as a young boy...

"Sir," the red-faced lieutenant prompted, breaking rudely into his morose thoughts.

"What do we have, lieutenant?" he asked as he returned the earnest young man's salute and stiffly lowered himself out of the saddle.

"The buildings are deserted sir. We've found fresh patches of blood near the stables, and over there, sir," he reported, pointing to a spot below the broken library window.

"But no bodies?" Sebastian pressed, joining them in the middle of the yard.

"No, my Lord," Mervelles answered, glancing over at the captain's tense face.

"Interesting," Sebastian murmured, rubbing his chin thoughtfully.

"My Lord, there could still be a danger," Gasquet pointed out, inwardly wincing as Sebastian dismounted.

"Nonsense," he snorted, removing his gloves. "They're long-gone Captain. But not to worry," he muttered, striding across the yard to the disturbed patch of dirt. "The maker of this depression has left us a trail," he said smugly, his eyes following the drips of blood out of the yard. "Start searching the house," he ordered brusquely, slapping his gloves against his thigh. "There may be more clues inside." His face a thinly veiled mask of disapproval, the captain ordered one of his men to approach the side entrance.

"Captain, it's unlocked!" the young man exclaimed, his hand on the handle.

"Wait Pierdot," he warned, a faint trail of oily smoke reaching his nostrils as the eager soldier opened the door. "It could be a ..."

The rest of his sentence was lost in the explosion, the force of which pushed him violently off his feet. "...trap," he finished bitterly, his voice coming out in a painful wheeze.

Momentarily lost in his anger, he glared up at Sebastian crouching nearby. "Time to retreat, Captain!" Sebastian yelled over the sound of multiple explosions, ducking abruptly as a plank of wood narrowly missed his head. While the solid outer walls barely shook from the chain of explosions, glass and wood fragments flew through the air as most of the ground level windows blew out. Struggling to his feet, he shouted to his stunned men, ordered a retreat. Acrid smoke poured out of the building as tongues of flame licked the window frames. His eyes fell upon Pierdot, his still, smouldering body only a couple of feet away, his blackened face frozen in dismayed astonishment.

It had never been like this under his old master, Richard Seabast, he thought darkly. He was relieved to see no other soldiers had been caught in the blast. "Ow," he suddenly cried, looking down at his thigh, finally noticing the great shard of glass sticking out of it.

"Captain!" Mervelles shouted, coming to his aid.

"Damn Mervelles," he uttered hoarsely, leaning heavily on the lieutenant's sturdy shoulder, "that's two men we've lost on this fool's mission."

"Yes sir," he answered evenly, his cheeks reddening slightly at the unguarded comment. "It's a miracle we didn't lose more men, sir," he suggested gamely.

"Hmph," the big man grunted, his face a mixture of pain and misgiving. They hobbled together towards the trees, Sebastian waiting impatiently for them.

"This isn't going well for us, Captain Gasquet," he announced tightly, his irritated gaze falling upon the gash in his leg. "Get that wrapped up Captain, we have a blood trail to follow. Jenkins assures me it belongs to Clay," he added with a critical look at the subdued henchman. He almost felt sorry for the slimy toad standing uneasily to the side, his pale blue eyes firmly fixed on the ground.

"Yes my Lord," he panted, staring bleakly as the tall man strode off, Jenkins reluctantly following in his wake. Gathering every shred of his old discipline, he pushed himself into action. "Well, you heard the man," he rumbled to the soldiers collapsed on the ground, "let's clean up this mess and get going." He noted sourly as he limped over to a fallen tree that the men were more churlish than usual. It had been a long night, to be followed by an even longer day. Sighing deeply, he sank down onto the thick trunk and awaited the busy medic, mentally composing in his mind the two miserable letters he now had to write.

✦

Chapter 4
The Path to Napoleon's Door.

Lightning flashed in the rainy night sky, illuminating starkly her haggard, pinched face. She was running for her life, a hessian sack clutched to her chest. Branches and shrubs raced up to meet her as she careened through the forest. The earth beneath her tired feet trembled as something big chased her. Trees crashed to the ground in the huge creature's wake, the force of their fall propelling her desperate steps.

With a violent, gut-wrenching jolt she was hefted into the air, her feet swinging uselessly below her. She craned her head around, saw Alyce's cruel, beautiful face laughing at her. As she looked on in frozen horror, the face changed to that of the golem, the hand wrapped around her turning grey and swollen. Still Alyce's mocking laughter rang in her ears. The hand tightened, squeezing the air out of her lungs. Pounding her fists on the pudgy fingers, she succeeded in making Alyce loosen her grip. She slipped out of the giant hand and was falling through the cold rain, the ground inky black below her. Another flash of lightning, and she caught a glimpse of Alyce's twisted face above her, a wicked smirk on her grey scarred lips.

Just as she expected to hit the ground, another huge hand reached out of the darkness, wrapped itself around her. Somewhere above her a deep chuckle boomed, mingled with Alyce's hysterical giggles. With giddy speed she was lifted towards the source of the new voice. She came to an abrupt stop, her stomach firmly lodged in her throat. Suddenly the cackling died away as she squirmed against the pale, slender fingers that encased her. "Put me down!" she screamed, twisting around to eye Alyce warily as lightning danced across the night sky.

"Oh, believe me," a thickly accented voice purred, "she's the least of your worries." She turned her head back in time to see pale blue eyes shining out at her from beneath unruly blonde hair, the mad laughter ringing in her ears again as the hand clenched around her. As she stared in horror at Gunthar's leering face, there was a tap on her shoulder. Startled, she turned around, the sack slipping from her clammy grip. Napoleon Bonepart somehow stood calmly before her inside Gunthar's giant fist, snatched the Mirror from her nerveless hands. She screamed, reached out for the sack, her fingers passing through Napoleon's chest as she began to become insubstantial...

She opened her eyes to dappled day light, her head cradled on musty blankets. "Ugh," she groaned, swallowing past the sandpaper that seemed to be lining her throat.

"Oh good, you're awake," Sarah announced brightly, huddled around a makeshift fire, her body small and pale against the giant trees. With her red hair tied back in a single ponytail, and her slender frame clothed in simple trousers, shirt and coat, she passed as a boy at a casual glance. Moving gingerly, she propped her head on her hand, her elbow digging into the blankets.

"Sarah," she croaked, "where are we?"

"On the other side of the lake," the girl answered distractedly, her attention focused on the pot sitting in the middle of the fire. "I can't believe you slept through our escape from the manor. I've never seen someone sleep so soundly on horseback."

She smiled weakly through her growing confusion, slowly shifted her stiff limbs and torso off the hard ground.

"Tea?" Sarah offered, looking up from the boiling water. Wordlessly she nodded as she stretched her sore, tired body and approached the fire.

"Where's Raphael?" she finally asked, squinting through the shafts of light penetrating the forest canopy. The horses were tethered nearby, their heads bent in concentration as they sniffed the ground for grass.

"Father went to get more water," she supplied, extracting a tin from the leather bag beside her.

"So, ah, what are we doing here, on the other side of the lake?" she asked belatedly, her fuzzy brain gradually clearing as she stretched her hands towards the fire. Sarah snorted at the obvious question, almost missing the pot as the tea-laden spoon wavered in her hand.

"Father set a trap for Sebastian and his men," she explained, her eyes fixed on the tea leaves falling into the pot. "Yes," she murmured, brushing the tears that suddenly rolled down her cheeks, "they'll get quite a surprise when they open the door."

"What do you mean?" she asked, crouching beside the teary-eyed girl.

"I set barrels of gunpowder around every door," Raphael supplied. She jumped halfway out of her skin, turned to glare at him accusingly. Grinning ruefully at her perturbed face, he strode to the fire, dumped the water skins on the ground. "It should buy us some more time, as well as destroy any evidence Sebastian could be looking for." Her ire dissipating at his grim expression, she watched him settle down on a fallen log. Even from within the shadow cast by his nondescript felt hat, she could see lines of exhaustion deeply etched around his eyes and mouth.

"Oh," she murmured, words deserting her. "That must have been hard," she offered lamely, nerving herself to meet their grave gazes. "I'm sorry."

Raphael turned his head sharply at her mumbled apology, eyes clouded with confusion. "Sorry? Why?" he pressed, shifting stiffly on the log. She swallowed nervously, looked away in shame.

"I could have prevented this," she said thickly, her mind wandering back to the early morning encounter she had with Alyce. "Alyce set this all up so beautifully, and I gave her what she wanted. I should have warned you…"

"Mel, stop," Raphael interjected hoarsely, holding up his hand. "Please, no more apologies," he said heavily as she blinked back tears. Suddenly weary beyond belief, he had no wish to follow the treacherous trail of blame. "I've had this coming for a long time. Let's just leave it at that."

A heavy silence fell over their crude camp site, punctuated only by the crackling of the fire. "Come on Sarah, finish making the tea. I'm parched," Raphael finally said gruffly, nodding at the waiting mugs. With a start Sarah shook herself into action, carefully lifted the steaming pot out of the flames. Suddenly the aroma of fresh tea filled the air, and Mel was painfully reminded of the fact that she hadn't eaten in some time. Clutching her stomach, she looked around to find Raphael watching her intently, a smirk tugging at his lips. "Hungry?" he prompted, reaching for the saddle bag at his feet. They proceeded to share one of the bread loaves hastily grabbed from the kitchen on their way out of the manor.

"So," Mel began around a mouthful of crumbs, "what happened to Gunthar? I vaguely recall him falling through the library window, just before I passed out..." Her voice trailed off as Raphael looked away in discomfit, his fingers tightening around his battered tin mug. "I don't know," he answered stiffly, finally meeting her confused gaze. "I carried you and the blasted Mirror to your room, and then went to check on his body. It was gone," he finished simply with a heavy shrug of his shoulders. Her mouth went dry at his dire words, images of Gunthar running towards the window slowly floating to the surface of her murky mind. A jagged shape protruding through the filthy material of his shirt, the Mirror's urgent cry in her head as he crashed through the full-length glass.

"How?" she whispered, the blood visibly draining from her face.

"What is it Mel?" Sarah probed, body tensing beside her.

"The Mirror tried to warn me, but I..." She glanced up at their concerned faces, swallowed past the sudden lump in her throat. "He's alive," she finished thickly, remnants of her dream filtering through her mind.

"No way, I saw his body," Raphael protested, shaking his head. "His neck was clearly broken..."

"He somehow grabbed a piece of the Mirror, Raph," she explained grimly, raising troubled eyes to meet his disbelieving stare. "It must have entered his body when he crashed into the ground, like when I er, died," she concluded awkwardly.

"Oh, brilliant," Raphael muttered sourly, picking up a pebble and flinging it into the trees.

"Ah, there's more," she ventured, a pained expression on her face. She described her encounter with the golem, and how it appeared to be possessed by Alyce. "I imagine Gunthar somehow revived her with his new-found powers," she surmised, brow crinkled in consternation. "I doubt she could have walked away from that fight without help," she added, shuddering at the memory of their ugly confrontation. If she closed her eyes, she could still the twitching grey form sprawled on the ground beside her, unnaturally dark blood spilling out from its side, the pitchfork jammed firmly into the sunken flesh.

"What colossal bad luck," Sarah murmured, staring despondently into her mug.

"Two of our enemies have uncannily escaped death," Raphael agreed, tossing the dregs of his tea onto the fire. "Still, we cannot afford to linger here and mope," he declared, rising from the log, stretching his arms above his head.

"Slave driver," Sarah muttered, poking her tongue out at him. Mel grinned weakly at the girl's playful whinge, pushed herself up off the hard ground, her buttocks and legs protesting at the movement. They had bought themselves some time, but that distance was surely crumbling away as Sebastian and his men searched for them, and who knew where Gunthar and Alyce lurked...

They quickly packed up their supplies and put out the dying fire. While she was folding up the blanket that had served as her pillow, Sarah subtly tugged at her elbow and whispered into her ear. Belatedly she glanced down, instinctively grabbed the bloody sides of the gaping hole in her shirt. Fortunately, Raphael had thoughtfully collected her meagre belongings from the school shack on their way to the lake. With Raphael and Sarah pointedly looking away, she hastily fetched a fresh shirt out of the saddle bag attached to Plodder. Grimacing at the dried blood caking her chest, she pulled on the clean shirt. At least most of the mud had flaked off, she thought ruefully. "God, I must reek," she lamented as she caught a whiff of her old shirt.

"Ha," Sarah barked bitterly from Moonbeam's side. "None of us are smelling very pretty Mel," she pointed out sourly as she packed away the pot and mugs.

"Better get used to it for now," Raphael cautioned, face grave as he tightened the strap of his saddle bag with a violent tug. "Sorry Monty," he added contritely, reaching out to stroke the magnificent stallion's long face. The horse snorted contemptuously, shook off Raphael's hand.

"So ah, what's the plan?" Mel hesitantly asked as she finished packing her saddlebag. "We're obviously on the run, but where are we running to?"

Raphael and Sarah exchanged meaningful looks, grinned coyly at her. "We'll tell you along the way," Raphael grunted, hauling himself into the saddle. With a sense of foreboding, she clambered awkwardly onto Plodder's back and followed Raphael and Sarah through the trees, stomach churning from the jerky movement and her growing anxiety about the future.

Gunthar Bliesch woke up with a start, hand reaching for his neck. "Agh," he groaned as he sat up, his neck aching. It took him a few moments to recognise the inside of the school shack. His eyes slowly took in the makeshift tables and stools that dotted the classroom. Finally, his eyes settled on the grey slumbering mass by the door. With a strangled sound of surprise, he scrambled frantically to his feet and searched for the pendant. The glossy stone was missing from his wrist. He steeled himself to creep over to Alyce's new monstrous body. His shoulders tight with fear, he peered down at the sleeping golem. As he reached for the grimy material of her shirt, her unnatural eyes snapped open, causing him to stumble backwards, his heart firmly lodged in his throat.

"Looking for something?" she growled, her wide swollen lips twisted in a sardonic grin.

"You have the stone?" he asked rhetorically while backing away, hands raised defensively before him. She struggled up into a sitting position, stretched her huge arms above her head.

"Of course I have the stone," she answered through a yawn, thoroughly enjoying the growing light of fear in his eyes. He stared at her blankly, the fear rapidly replaced with confusion.

"Then why am I still alive?" he asked bluntly, lowering his hands.

"You know, my Uncle Henry was a brilliant man," Alyce shared conversationally as she clambered to her feet and pulled the dark goggles down from the top of her head. "He imbued this body with super strength, a psychic link, an ability to detect changes in barometric pressure. Truly an unappreciated genius," she clucked, carefully positioning the goggles over her eyes. If he closed his eyes and imagined the deep gravelly voice to ring a couple of octaves higher, he could almost see the old Alyce before him chatting avidly about her uncle. Even as he listened to her cheerfully reminisce, he could have sworn her voice lightened, developed a more girly lilt.

"He even gave this body extra-fast healing abilities," she marvelled, moving slowly to the centre of the room so she didn't have to bow her head. With a murmured sound of relief, she unkinked her neck. "There is a limit to that ability, however. Punctured lungs don't heal too well," she explained darkly, hand creeping to her side. The right side of her shirt was badly stained and torn, soaked with dark congealed blood. "You saved my life Gunthar," she said solemnly, her voice losing its girlish charm. "Yet again I felt my life ebb away, that blasted pitchfork sticking out of my rib cage. Without your...intervention," she phrased carefully, nodding at the patch of blood at the front of his shirt, "I would have died."

The shack fell silent as they studied each other across the untidy arrangement of desks and chairs. "Well," Gunthar said awkwardly, looking away, "lucky for both of us I managed to steal a piece of the Mirror." It had taken most of his newfound energy to stagger over to the stable wall and heal Alyce's gaping wounds. His memory of their trek through the forest was fractured. Both half-dead, they stumbled from tree to tree, their only goal to get safely away from the manor. He vaguely recalled spotting the shack through the trees, weakly pointing it out to Alyce before passing out. She must have dragged his unconscious body into the simple building, removed the pendant before passing out herself.

"So, I guess you're a free agent now," he continued, his shoulders slumped in resignation.

"True," she acknowledged, tilting her head thoughtfully. "Is it just me, or is your head permanently at an angle?" He gawked helplessly at her, surprised by the sudden observation. Tentatively he felt the bones at the back of his neck. The two most prominent vertebrae at the base of his neck were slightly out of alignment with the rest of his spine. As his fingers traced the line of fine bones leading to his skull, he realised she was right. Odd he hadn't noticed the permanent tilt of his head. No wonder his neck was so sore.

"I must have broken it in the fall," he mused, giving his neck a final rub. "It healed, but at an angle." He shrugged his shoulders, turned his attention back to her. "So, what are you going to do now?"

She gazed blankly at him for a moment, her face unreadable. "Well, I suppose I could go after them on my own," she suggested idly, fingering the rough edge of a roof support. A large splinter broke off with her tentative probing. Wincing, she pulled her hand back and stepped away from the offending beam. "But what would be the point? There's no real advantage to hunting them solo," she concluded distractedly as she squinted at the sliver of wood. He gawked at her incredulously, cautiously approached the golem.

"You want to remain teamed up with me?" he drawled.

"Sure, why not?" she returned with a surprisingly elegant shrug of her massive shoulders. "We're both after the same thing."

"You're still interested in securing the mirror for yourself?" he probed, eying her warily.

"Ha, isn't everybody?" she scoffed, pinching the end on the splinter. "But let's worry about that when the time comes, shall we?" she suggested silkily, despite the limitations of her abnormal vocal cords. With a triumphant flourish, she tugged out the wood.

"Hmm," he murmured, stroking the fine hair on his chin. Pushing aside his sense of foreboding, he solemnly extended his hand. "Glad to have you on my side, Alyce," he said truthfully. Even through the thick coloured lens of her goggles, he detected an answering glint in her eye as she accepted his hand. In that instant he realised their alliance would inevitably fall apart once they obtained the Mirror. Then it was every man or golem for him/herself. With this unspoken understanding between them, they finished shaking hands. "I don't suppose you have any food on you, do you? I'm starving," he abruptly announced, looking about the shack for something edible.

"I smell something sweet on the table there," she answered evenly, unperturbed by his sudden subject-change. He really is a loon, she decided as he followed the direction of her nod. He reminded her of a pigeon, straining his head forward, hands tucked neatly behind his back.

She looked away from his investigation of the big table as her sensitive ears caught the faint jiggle of stirrups and reins.

"Honey cakes!" he exclaimed with childish excitement.

"I think we have to go," she suggested tensely, edging across the room to peer through the cracks in the rickety door.

"What?" Gunthar asked through a mouth of cake.

"Come on Gunthar, we have to go," she hissed urgently, the sound of jiggling bridles ringing loudly in her ears now. The low muffled hum of hooves striking the ground swelled, so that even Gunthar looked up from stuffing his face.

"Shite," he muttered, hastily cramming cakes into his pockets before running for the door.

"Damn, it must be Sebastian and his men," she cursed as she eased the door open. "We can still make a run for it," she stated desperately, grabbing his ragged sleeve.

"Alyce, no," he cried past the cake crumbs sliding down his throat, his heels digging into the ground. "There are too many of them."

"No way!" she roared, pulling him through the doorway. "Now it's my turn for breakfast!" Her limbs trembling with excitement, she burst through the doorway, hauling him behind her as though he were a rag doll. Lungs rattling painfully in his chest, he caught a glimpse of the mounted soldiers calmly approaching the shack, their weapons drawn. Summoning the power of the Mirror fragment inside his body, he formed a barrier in front of Alyce's hurtling body. She crashed through the wall of energy, massive feet tangled beneath her. With a judder of bones and flesh, they fell to the ground, Alyce finally releasing his arm in the process. Cursing loudly at the top of her voice, Alyce roughly pushed his body away and clambered to her feet. "You bloody loon," she shouted heatedly as she straightened up, glowering at his struggling form. With a final spit in his direction, she spun around only to find a blade aimed at her throat.

Her startled gaze travelled up the gleaming steel to the tense soldier at the other end, his hand tightening around the hilt as her goggled eyes met his. "Don't move!" the soldier barked tersely, his confidence growing as the other soldiers crowded around.

"Don't insult me boy," she sneered, hands balling up at her sides.

"Clay, no!" Gunthar cried, staggering to his feet and grabbing her arm as she started to swing it around. The use of the golem's original name caught her attention, and she froze in mid-strike, her eyes glued to his in confused silence. "I know you're upset about the death of your mistress," he continued pointedly, "but this won't bring her back." Something in his manner motivated her to play along, and she slowly lowered her arm.

"That's enough talk," the soldier grated, the sword wobbling slightly in his sweaty grip. "Now move," he ordered harshly, guiding his horse to the side. The other soldiers warily followed suit, their weapons trained on the odd duo.

"Hmph," she grunted, eying the trembling soldier contemptuously. More mounted soldiers emerged from the trees, their weary steeds pawing the ground as they slowed to a stop at the edge of the clearing.

"Well," a familiar voice called out over the sound of snorting horses and creaking saddles, "it's wonderful to see you both again." Sebastian nudged his horse out of the trees, a cold, mirthless smile plastered across his face. Jenkins rode beside him, his normally bland face dark and creased with anger. "You left my employ rather abruptly," Sebastian continued, his voice tightly controlled. "I look forward to your explanation." She swung her head to observe Gunthar's reaction to Sebastian's thinly veiled anger. He merely grinned, bowed his head.

"Of course, my lord," he purred to the ground before lifting his eyes to Sebastian's bemused face.

"Right," Sebastian drawled, his brow crinkled with uncertainty. He watched Sebastian lean over and whisper something to Jenkins, his troubled gaze straying across the clearing to where they stood. Shooting a venomous look his way, Jenkins murmured his reply. With an inward groan, Gunthar turned to Alyce, who stood stiffly at his side, shoulders tensing under the coarse cloth of her ill-fitting shirt. Jenkins was bound to have words with him later. "Can hardly wait for that one," he muttered, looking back as Sebastian ordered for a horse to be brought out.

"What?" Alyce growled belligerently, obviously still rearing for a fight.

"Oh nothing," he sighed, crossing his arms over his chest. "I was just voicing my pleasure at being reunited with our old colleague." She gaped at him in surprise, hastily shut her mouth.

"I hope you know what you're doing, Gunthar," she muttered, eying warily the approaching soldiers. "Or I'll be venting this newfound aggression on you," she promised sourly as the soldiers led her away. Smiling weakly at her quiet threat, he patiently waited for his horse, a million voices buzzing about his brain. "The voice of the Mirror," he whispered, closing his eyes momentarily to better enjoy its discordant song. Now that he had a piece of the mirror inside him, it wasn't just a faint whisper scraping at the edge of his consciousness, but a raucous roar blasting through his confusion. Finally, the path is clear, he thought with a smug grin.

"I wish I could have said goodbye to everyone," Mel sighed as they made their way out of the forest, the mid-afternoon sun slanting into their eyes. He was at last content to travel on the road, after cutting cross-country for the last couple of hours, navigating through the maze of trees with difficulty. "Yes," he responded tightly, looking away, his hand clenching Monty's reins. His exhausted body ached from riding, the ground looking more inviting with each jolting step. The horses were obviously relieved to slow down to a walk as they left the forest, their sides slick with sweat.

"Ah, did they ask about me?" she asked shyly, shifting stiffly in the saddle. Schooling his features, he met her enquiring gaze.

"Of course," he answered vaguely, eyes sliding away to intently study Monty's mane.

Predictably, word of Mel's miraculous recovery had spread through the staff like wildfire, John and Simon gravely describing their encounter with her cold, still body in the muddy clearing. From the snippets of talk he had managed to overhear, they were glad that she was alive, but their pleasure was tainted with suspicion.

"T'was unnatural, the way she just sprung to life like that," he overheard Simon relate to Wendy as they packed their supplies in the kitchen. "You should have seen it Wendy. One moment she was lying there in the mud, looking as dead as a doorknob, then her eyes just snapped open, and she grabbed poor John's wrist. She was so different, Wendy, not the old Mel we know." Through the gap in the door, he had spied Simon's haunted face, fear of the supernatural darkening the young man's eyes. Wendy had then walked into view, placed a comforting hand on his shoulder.

"Perhaps it's for the best, us leaving the manor," she suggested with a shudder. "Things are getting strange around here."

At that point, he had quietly slipped away from the kitchen door to carry on with his preparations, the heavy mantle of disappointment settling over his shoulders. Thankfully he had herded the staff out of the manor before Mel could see their strained, wary faces. Best she never know how quickly they had turned subtly against her, he thought fervently with a sideways glance at her bemused face. He was all too familiar with that feeling. How quickly Sophie's face had hardened in the soft glow of the lantern as he looked up from Bruce's bloody, punctured body, the knife slipping from his nerveless fingers...

"I'd better check on Sarah," he mumbled abruptly, pressing his heels into Monty's sides.

"Right," she murmured as he trotted off after Sarah, who rode stiffly ahead. All too aware of her narrowed gaze following him down the road, he pulled up alongside his young ward, who in turn greeted him with a dark, sideways glance.

"Ah, still grumpy I see," he sighed, a tight grin tugging at the corners of his mouth.

"You know I hate sailing," Sarah muttered, sparing Mel a dour look as she caught up to them.

"Come on Sarah, it's just across the Channel," Raphael responded wearily, irritably readjusting his hat. "And this time I swear we'll take a proper boat," he added with a faint grin.

"A proper boat?" Mel echoed, panic creeping into her voice. Raphael coughed nervously, hastily looked away from Sarah's glaring, sulky face.

"When we first crossed the Channel together, it was under difficult conditions. We were both on the run, with limited funds. So, we stole a small fishing boat," he finished, his face slightly sheepish as he glanced back at Sarah.

"A small fishing boat?" Sarah cried, straightening in the saddle. "It was barely bigger than a rowboat."

"Oh," Mel murmured, face visibly blanching.

"Are you alright Mel?" Sarah asked, bending over Moonbeam's neck to peer at her pale face.

"Er, yeah, sure," she lied with a wan smile. "I was just remembering the last time I was on a boat," she added. The little aluminium dinghy had lurched drunkenly through the swelling waters, taking her stomach with it. She could still see her brother sitting stoically at the back, pushing the outboard motor from side to side. Somehow, she had managed not to throw up...

"Oh great," Raphael muttered, "another one who gets seasick."

"I do not get seasick," she protested weakly, swallowing back a mouthful of bile. "God, I can't believe we're doing this," she croaked, shivering despite the sun's warm rays on her skin.

They had barely emerged from the forest on the other side of the lake when Raphael cautiously disclosed his plan for the Mirror. The blood draining from her face, she had stopped in her tracks, Plodder tossing her head in annoyance at the sudden tug on her mouth. "Go to Europe? Are you mad?" she had blurted, her imagination feverishly painting a picture of Napoleon Bonepart waiting calmly for them on the beach, his army gathered behind him. As she opened her mouth to elaborate, her leg brushed against the saddle bag containing the precious Mirror. A scene popped into her head, of a body-strewn battlefield. Soldiers lay dying on the blood-soaked ground, the dust slowly settling on their twisted, broken bodies. In the midst of all this devastation, a great jagged line formed in the air above the soldiers' heads, the inky darkness behind the tear spilling out into the world, steadily smothering the battlefield. Suddenly the scene changed, and she saw Raphael and Sarah stand on the edge of the field, their bodies paralysed with fear as the blackness oozed over the trampled ground, swallowing everything it touched. Too late they turned to run, but already the void lapped their heels... "Mel?" Heart lurching in her chest, the vision faded away as she had looked up to find Sarah and Raphael staring expectantly at her, their eyes clouded with concern.

"Very well," she had uttered, in a voice that wasn't quite her own. Frowning at her abrupt change of heart, Raphael had merely nodded and nudged Monty into motion, obviously content to take his victories where he found them.

"I just hope you're right, about finding a way to destroy the Mirror," she added, returning to the present with a nasty jolt. A faint smile tugging at his broad mouth, Raphael reached out a hand to her tense shoulder.

"There has to be a way," he said reassuringly, rubbing the rigid flesh. "At the very least we can hide it somewhere, make it extremely hard to find."

Willing herself not to melt at his touch, she half-heartedly returned his smile, murmured a non-committal reply. The Mirror has its own ideas, she thought with a shiver. For some inexplicable reason, it wanted her to rush headlong into the centre of the storm, when every fibre in her being longed to run away.

Shoving aside her feelings of foreboding, she forced her stiff body to straighten, wincing against the pain in her back. "Maybe sailing won't be so bad after all," she muttered softly with a sideway glance at Sarah. The girl grunted, hastily turned away, but not before she noted a tear rolling down her cheek. Raphael abruptly spurred Monty on, his face strained as he surged ahead of them. "Sarah?" she prompted, reaching out to the girl's trembling shoulder.

"Sorry Mel," the girl answered hoarsely, rubbing at her wet eyes. "I was just thinking about Daniel. There was no time to say goodbye, or even leave him a note...What's he going to think about all this?"

Pursing her lips, Mel swallowed past the sudden lump in her throat. "Once we're safely away, you can write to him, let him know you're alright," she suggested roughly, images of all the people they left behind flooding her mind.

"Yes," Sarah mumbled, clearing her throat, "I'll do that." They rode on in heavy silence for a while, dust swirling lazily into the air as the horses' hooves struck the road. "You know what the crazy thing is?" Sarah began with a sniffle, raising her tear-streaked face. "I could have sworn I heard Daniel's voice, when we were passing the lake, but when I looked back, there was nothing but trees." She squinted into the slanting rays that penetrated the forest canopy, heart lurching in her chest as she caught the far-away look on the girl's face.

"That's not so crazy," she murmured, turning her bleary eyes to the front. "We all want that final goodbye," she croaked, thinking of her old life, and the family she left behind. Sarah opened her mouth to say something, promptly shut it again. Without a word they nudged their horses forward, to catch up to Raphael.

"So, there I was. The sea was heaving like a whore's chest, and the Pretty Peg was being tossed about like a child's toy." A sharp kick to his shin, and Raphael awoke with a start, opening his sticky eyes to the smoky, dimly lit room. He glanced at the source of the kick to find Mel giving him a pained look. Grinning sheepishly at her, he turned his attention back to the rambling sea captain. "Aye, I thought I was a goner, standing there on the deck, gripping the wheel for dear life as the rain stung me cheeks, and the wind cut through me clothes," the drunk captain continued, oblivious to the little exchange. His sun-beaten forehead gleamed with sweat, and droplets of ale clung to his ratty beard. Sarah huddled warily in her seat, her keen eyes surveying the crowded inn for potential trouble. Her critical gaze fell upon the two crewmen sitting on the other side of the table, their lewd leering faces directed at her and Mel. If they weren't so drunk, she'd be concerned for their safety.

"Yes sir, that little cutter has pulled me through some nasty scrapes," the thick-set man rumbled into his tankard.

"The Pretty Peg sounds like a fine vessel, Mr Biggs," Raphael murmured thoughtfully. Red bleary eyes slowly focused on him from across the bottle-strewn table.

"Well then, let's talk terms, Mr Smith," he declared laboriously, pushing aside some of the bottles and mugs to clear a space.

"Allow me to first buy you and your crew a drink, Mr Biggs," he suggested silkily, pushing his chair back. With a guarded look at Mel and Sarah, he made his way to the bar, fingering the tiny pouch of powder in his pocket. A useful legacy from his years at medical school, he thought with a wry grin as he beckoned the barkeeper. While waiting for the drinks, he chanced a backwards look at the cluttered table. Mel was laughing at something the captain had said, the lines of tension around her eyes belying her mirth. Sarah sat stiffly by her side, her baleful glare stopping one of the crewmen in mid-stretch, his grubby fingers reaching out for her hair. Just then the barkeeper gruffly demanded payment, and he gratefully obliged.

"Oh, you really should reconsider and spend some more time in Bristol, Mrs Smith," Mr Biggs was saying as he returned to the table, frothy mugs in hand. "All manner of interesting folk pass through this place, believe me."

"Ah, if only that were possible," she sighed, her wistful gaze meeting his as he placed the drugged beers in front of the men.

"Come now dear," he drawled over the scrape of his chair, "we've been over this already."

"But you never take me anywhere nice," she pouted, enjoying the pantomime.

"I'll make it up to you one day darling, I promise," he murmured with a grimace. "Perhaps you and Jessica should go and check on our supplies while I conclude our business with Mr Biggs here?" he suggested innocently, a faint gleam in his eye.

"Of course," she replied stiffly, getting out of her chair jerkily as though she were upset. "Come on Jessica," she snapped, shooting him a dark look as they left the table.

He turned back to Mr Biggs, his face suitably contrite. Nodding his understanding, the salty sea captain gently debated the price of their passage, his voice becoming more slurred with each mouthful of beer. Sensing that the captain was moments away from slumping unconscious, he quickly completed the deal, handing over half the agreed amount. "Pleasure doin' bizshness with yer, Mr...Smith," Mr Biggs mumbled, extending a greasy, beer-soaked hand.

"See you in the morning, Mr Biggs," he lied smoothly, gripping the hand firmly. With a nod of acknowledgment to the crewmen resting their elbows heavily on the table, he hastily departed the inn. Squinting through the gloom, he jogged along the length of the adjacent wharf, tired feet spurred as he imagined hungry, suspicious eyes following him from every shadowy corner and alleyway he passed. Finally, he came to a stop before the Pretty Peg, where Sarah and Mel already waited, meagre provisions piled at their feet. Without a word, they started to carry the stuffed saddlebags across the rickety gangplank.

Resisting the urge to look over his shoulder every five seconds, he stepped gingerly onto the cutter, almost tripping over a coil of rope in the process. This part of the wharf was poorly lit, with only a few working lamps for the entire area. The smaller boats didn't warrant the same protection afforded the larger merchant and naval ships docked on the other side of the harbour. He didn't mind stumbling about in the grainy half-light, if it meant they weren't noticed. As luck would have it, the Pretty Peg was just what they were looking for: a sturdy little boat with a small crew, tied up at the end of the wharf. After a few casual enquiries at the various inns dotting the edge of the harbour, they located Biggs and his rough companions. Pushing aside his feelings of guilt at effectively stealing the man's boat and livelihood, he clambered across the gangplank to fetch the last of their supplies. Making preparations this late at night resulted in their pickings being slim. One small keg of fresh water, strips of salted meat, and a bag of dry, rock-hard biscuits had been added to their limited stock. It would be enough to get them to Europe, but beyond that...

The hardest part had been selling the horses. Despite the obvious truth that the horses had to be left behind, Sarah had been reluctant to part with her beloved Moonbeam. Even through the gathering fog, he could feel the frostiness of her gaze whenever it settled upon him. As he laboured back onto the deck clutching the keg to his chest, the hairs on the back of his neck stiffened, and he looked up to find Sarah glaring at him. Grimacing at her sullen face, he continued past her to the hatchway. "Mel?" he called softly down the square opening. In the mottled moonlight, he saw her strained face come into view, blink up at him expectantly. "Can you take this for me?" he grunted, lowering the keg over the edge.

"No," she joked, reaching up for the bottom of the keg. Balancing the sack of food over his shoulder, he climbed down the ladder. With much juggling, his feet came to a rest on the roughly made floor that separated them from the hull.

"She's very upset," Mel murmured as he set the bag down on the floor next to the pile of saddlebags.

"I know," he sighed, rubbing his neck. "I'll make it up to her when this is all over." She opened her mouth to retort that they might not live that long, but thought better of it.

"I'm sure she knows that deep down," she assured him weakly, briefly resting a hand on his arm. He glanced down at her, swallowed awkwardly.

"Well, you secure these supplies, and I'll go and ready the boat," he ordered hoarsely, turning towards the rickety wooden ladder.

"Raph, wait," she blurted, grabbing his arm.

"What?" he snapped, brows drawing together with impatience as he turned back to her.

"Ah, I just thought, with you being so tired…"

"Mel, we really must be going, someone could spot us at any moment…"

"Let me give you something, to help," she croaked, reaching for his face in the murky, blue-tinged light. With a little fumbling, she pulled his lips down onto hers, breathed energy into his body. His mouth quickly opened in response to the sudden pressure, his arms circling her body. Reluctantly she pulled away, her breath ragged as they stood pressed together in the hull.

"You'd better go," she whispered huskily, enjoying the warmth of his body through her clothes.

"Wait," he panted before she could fully disentangle herself from his arms. He bent forward and kissed her lips firmly. "You gave me too much," he murmured.

"Ha," she laughed weakly, stepping back as he turned and climbed the ladder, his step noticeably lighter. "Right," she muttered, squaring her shoulders against the rising fatigue in her own body. Perhaps she did give him too much, she acknowledged, lurching unsteadily on her feet as she bent down to pick up the saddlebags. Suddenly the Pretty Peg tilted alarmingly beneath her, and she stumbled sideways into a pile of smelly fishing nets. There was a dull thud from the stern, and she straightened up awkwardly to investigate.

"Hello?" she called out tentatively into the darkness, inching her way towards the cluttered stern. Straining to hear above the sound of her own hammering heart, she could almost discern faint breathing sounds somewhere before her. Her throat suddenly dry, she lowered the saddlebags to the floor, felt her way past dank wooden crates. Something brushed her arm, and she jumped, a girlish squeal escaping her lips. With a muttered cry of disgust, she pushed away the swinging hummock and continued her anxious inspection of the stern. She could now make out some vague shapes against the grainy grey background, her eyes struggling to pick up any light in the stuffy space. Squinting at an oddly shaped pile in the corner, she reached for the old musty canvas heaped against the bulkhead. She almost had her hand on the disused sail when the little cutter lurched violently sideways, and she was forcibly flung into a nearby stack of crates.

"Mel, get up here!" Sarah yelled down the open hatch.

"On my way," she grunted, grimacing as she extricated herself from the crates. A final backward glance at the suspicious shape in the corner, and she rushed to the ladder.

"Mel, push us away from the wharf," Raphael barked, his body straining against the ropes as the sail began to billow. Swallowing nervously, she scrambled onto the deck and reached out her hand toward the wharf. They were already starting to move, but without guidance from the wharf, they could crash into the surrounding boats. Picking the centre of the deck, she aimed the Mirror's energy at the thick beam lining the wharf. Gently at first, and then with increasing force, she pushed the cutter away. Despite the stiffening breeze, beads of sweat broke out on her brow.

"Mel, more to the right!" Raphael cried from the helm. She swung her head around, eyes widening as their bow swung towards the neighbouring boat's stern. She hastily pushed at the other boat's stern, wincing at the hulls scraped noisily together. Finally they were clear, but not before a crew member ran out to check the source of the noise.

"What the hell...hey, that's not your boat!" he shouted over the widening gap.

"Bring the sail around, Sarah," Raphael ordered, his brow furrowed in deep concentration as he steered them out of the harbour.

"Damn, he's going to raise the alarm," Sarah cried as she hauled on the lines.

"Mel, can you do something about that?" he asked distractedly, straining his eyes to pick out the dim lights of distant ships.

"Ah, sure," she breathed, squinting at the shadowy figure climbing up the main mast. "The crow's nest," she murmured as her gaze swept up the mast, catching the silhouette of a large warning bell above the small platform. Desperately her eyes searched the network of ropes that surrounded the thick column. "Ah-ha," she whispered triumphantly, spotting a large pulley dangling from the end of a rope, the heavy metal casing swinging only a meter or so above the man's head. Grunting with the effort, she focused on the pulley, willing it to move slowly sideways. Her heart firmly lodged in her mouth, she released it. The dark shape sailed through the air, connected with the man's shoulder. There was a short yelp, quickly followed by a dull thud as the man fell off the rigging, to lie unmoving on the deck. As she doubled over slightly to catch her breath, she glimpsed movement from the prone figure, before it diminished into the murky background. Weak with relief, she stumbled over to the mast.

"Good work Mel," Sarah grunted, struggling against the pull of the canvas. "Can you give me a hand?"

"Ah, sure," she murmured, tentatively approaching the sail. "What do you want me to do?"

"Just grab the rope and follow my lead," Sarah instructed over the growing sound of the wind. With much swearing and shouting, they swung the sail from side to side as Raphael demanded, riding the wind out of the harbour. When the lights of Bristol had faded into the horizon, and the canvas billowed steadily, Raphael ordered Sarah to set the sail. She gratefully pried her hands off the rope, winced at the fresh blisters. With as much dignity as she could muster, she moved away on wobbly legs, to lean heavily against the side of the boat.

"Sarah, can you get me the lantern, please?" Raphael asked, fumbling in his trouser pocket for a compass and a map.

"Yes Father," she replied stiffly as she finished tying off the guide line. Mel looked up from her morose study of the deck to watch her trudge wearily to the hatch. Biting her bottom lip, she glanced back at Raphael, who stood frozen at the helm, the compass in his hand momentarily forgotten as his bleak gaze followed Sarah's dejected steps. His shoulders slumped in defeat, he turned and faced the prow, hand clenched around the compass. Clearing her throat, she strode carefully up the deck, feeling slightly better with each controlled step. "So," she croaked, stumbling to a clumsy stop beside him, "where exactly are we going again?" The underlying tension behind the casual question did not escape him, and he glanced up at her wan face.

"Here, let me show you," he offered gently, handing her the compass. "Whatever you do, don't drop that," he warned, his tone only faintly joking. Nodding her understanding, she gripped it tightly in her sore, stiff hands as he unfolded the map and held it against the wheel.

"See, that's roughly where we are now," he murmured distractedly, pointing at the map, "making our way out of Bristol Channel." She squinted at his broken, dirt-encrusted fingernail in the moonlight, gradually discerning the jagged lines that represented the long tapering channel. "Now," Raphael continued, tracing a line roughly parallel to the southern coastline, "we follow the coast to Land's End, and then head southeast, to hopefully land here." She followed his finger to the coastline of France.

"St…Malo," she read tentatively, straining to decipher his messy hand-writing.

"Well, I'm aiming more for one of the smaller settlements west of St. Malo," he said, indicating other dots on the map.

"Hmm," she murmured, studying the unfamiliar names.

"I'm sure you have more detailed maps where you hail from," Raphael ventured, glancing over at her absorbed face. She looked up in surprise.

"Ah, yes," she stammered, unaccustomed to him mentioning her origin in the future. "But you know, I've always been impressed how well-drawn the early maps are," she uttered, tracing her finger lightly over the fine, jagged lines. "Drawn by hand, cartographers sailing round whole continents in order to record every bay, every out-cropping of land…" Her voice trailed off as she remembered sitting in class, learning about the early explorers who drew the first definitive maps of the world, straining to hear the teacher's droning words over the whispered conversation beside her.

"Mel?" Raphael prompted. She looked up to find him eying her quizzically.

"Er, yes," she coughed, cheeks reddening. "I was just remembering…"

A shriek from below deck interrupted her stilted explanation. They rushed as one to the hatch, Raphael beating her to the ladder. "Are you alright Sar…what the blazes?" he exclaimed as he reached the bottom. She lowered herself into the hold and swore loudly at the scene before her. In the moonlight that now streamed through the open hatch, a curly-headed figure could be seen stiffly getting up.

"Hello miss," Daniel Dempsey said sheepishly, self-consciously dusting down his front as Sarah lowered the lantern.

"Daniel? Oh, I'm so sorry," Sarah stammered, rushing to his side.

"I'm not," Raphael muttered darkly, watching through narrowed slits as the boy rubbed the side of his head.

"What the hell are you doing Daniel?" Mel demanded, her thoughts going immediately to Neville and Anne. They must be out of their minds with worry by now.

"I could have seriously hurt you," Sarah fretted, gently prodding around the area.

"Ow, I think you might have," he wheezed, shying away from her hand.

"It serves you right," Raphael snarled, reaching over and grabbing the front of his shirt. "If I didn't know better, I'd say you were a spy..."

"Don't be ridiculous father," Sarah hotly interjected, gripping Daniel's arm protectively.

"What's ridiculous about it? He's obviously been following us the whole time..."

"He has a point," Mel murmured, wading into the debate.

"Let's continue this on the upper deck, shall we?" Raphael grated, shoving Daniel toward the hatch.

"Yes sir," he said meekly, swallowing nervously as he climbed up the ladder.

"You don't really think he's a spy, do you father?" Sarah asked, her eyes wide with concern. He frowned at the hand on his sleeve.

"Bring the lantern please, Sarah," he requested firmly, his face grim.

"Yes father," she croaked, her worried gaze following him up the ladder.

"Here," Mel offered, resting a hand on her tense shoulder. She turned to find Mel holding out the lantern. "Don't keep him waiting dear," the woman suggested with a tight smile that didn't quite reach her eyes. Nodding mutely, she scurried up the ladder, the lantern bumping against her leg. Maybe with Mel's help, she could reason with father, and save Daniel's life.

Alyce carefully lowered her great bulk down onto the wharf, stretched her legs out. Through narrowed eyes she regarded the men scurrying on and off the "Magnificent" as they prepared to set sail. The schooner rested peacefully alongside the wharf, three masts stretching far above her head like long, elegant fingers pointing at the cloudy night sky. She grinned sadistically at the muttered curses of the sailors as they loaded their gear into the ship's hold. Hopefully no one would miss her for a couple of minutes. Leaning back against the wall of grain sacks, she closed her eyes and willed her head to stop throbbing. Funny, Clay had never complained about headaches. "Must be a combination of the enhanced senses and the stone implant," she mused softly, reaching up for the goggles. With a grateful sigh she pulled the leather band off the top of her head, rubbed the groove left in her smooth scalp. Having to wear the goggles all day didn't help either, she decided, looking down at the thick dark glass embedded in the leather with disgust. Of course, she would be severely limited without their protection. "Uncle Henry," she croaked thickly, clenching her huge hand around the goggles, "you thought of everything, didn't you?"

"Clay? What are you doing?" Stiffening at the grating voice, she looked over her shoulder. Travis and Martin sauntered over to her hiding spot, sacks dangling across their slumped shoulders. "You're supposed to be loading the ship," Travis drawled.

"I'm just taking a break," she replied stiffly, biting her tongue as several cutting remarks came to mind. "What are you doing?" she fired back.

"Ah, the same," he answered sheepishly with a sideways look at his brother. "So, Clay," Travis continued, setting his sack on the wharf, "do you miss that stuck-up bitch Alyce?"

"Ooo, I hated that tart," Martin volunteered, negligently dropping his load. "She was always on my case, "do this, do that"," he mimicked in a high-pitched voice.

"Yeah, if you ask me, she needed a good seeing to," Travis leered, thin craggy face twisted sickly in the lamp light. "I would have shaken that high-and-mighty look off her face, mark my words," he added, rocking his pelvis back and forth suggestively.

"Oh really?" she drawled, picking a piece of driftwood off a nearby fishing net. Silently seething, she twirled it between her thick fingers just as one would a blade of grass. "I'm sure she would have loved that."

"Oh-ho, you bet," Travis crowed, warming up to the subject.

"Although Jenkins said she was frigid," Martin recalled thoughtfully, scratching his greasy head.

"What?" she blurted, the driftwood stopping abruptly in mid-twirl.

"Hmm, he said he had to work hard to err, get the juices flowing, if you catch my drift," Martin confided, wriggling his fingers to illustrate the point.

The wood snapped between her fingers. "That conniving bastard, how dare he say such things…"

"Hey, don't take it so personally Clay," Travis interjected, his tone mollifying. "We just thought you'd like to talk about your former mistress, get things off your ah, chest," he reasoned, his voice muffled as he stooped down and picked up his sack.

"Yeah, after the way she treated you, I thought you'd want to join in the bitchin'," Martin joined in, following his brother's lead.

"I'll say," Travis said with feeling, turning his head and spitting vehemently over the side of the wharf. "I just hope she occasionally let you have some fun," he added, his voice thick with innuendo.

"Hey, maybe that's why she was frigid with Jenkins, eh?" Martin suggested coarsely as he staggered past, sack bouncing heavily against his back.

"Yeah, anyone else would seem dull after that kind of action," Travis laughed.

In a surprisingly fluid motion, she rose to her feet, flung a massive hand out to catch Travis' scrawny throat. "Take-that-back," she grated, hand tightening around the henchman's neck. She watched with satisfaction Travis' eyes bulge in his suddenly bright red face, hands ineffectively clawing at her fingers. Martin cried out, dumped the sack.

"Get your hand off my broth...ugh," he shouted, his indignant cry cut off by her free hand.

"I...ugh...apologise," Travis croaked, feet frantically kicking empty air as she lifted him off the ground.

"What was that?" she snarled, effortlessly drawing Travis to eye level.

"I'm, sor..." The rest of his apology was lost in a painful gasp as her hand tightened further. Any tighter and the delicate bones at the base of Travis' skull would snap...

"Clay, cut that out!" She turned toward the familiar voice, fingers briefly digging further into Travis' windpipe before she released him.

"Jenkins," she hissed, her new-found hatred of the man bubbling to the surface. With a flick of her wrist, she sent Martin careening into the wall of sacks.

"Come on, we've got a boat to chase," he snapped irritably, gaze sweeping over the gasping men. "Clay, take their sacks on board the ship. I've a special job for you two." There was an edge to his voice, and even in the grainy lantern light Jenkins looked more shifty than usual. If she hadn't nearly suffocated the fools, they may have noted this for themselves.

"Yes sir," Travis croaked, shakily getting to his feet. "Come on Martin," he urged, leaning down to help his brother. "It's not healthy around here," he added darkly, patting his clothes down.

She watched them go, eyes narrowed into hate-filled slits. "So, if you could just take these sacks to the ship Clay," Jenkins prompted when she didn't move. Slowly she spun around to study him, sharp gaze sweeping over his slender body, lingering on the tiny bulge in his coat. For all his stealth, she had noticed the slight movement of his hand when they were captured, glimpsed her signet ring as it disappeared into his coat pocket. She could reach out right now, snap his neck like a twig, take back her ring, toss him into the harbour...

"Didn't you hear me? We're leaving as soon as the ship is fully loaded," he re-iterated, his voice brittle. Sebastian's abuse had obviously taken its toll. On several occasions throughout the day, she had caught Sebastian venting his displeasure at Jenkins, demanding results from the harried henchman. "Serves you right," she muttered darkly, refusing to feel any sympathy for her former lover.

"What did you say?" Jenkins demanded, eying her quizzically. Almost on their own accord, the muscles in her arm tensed, prepared to fly out to that slender bridge of flesh and bone...

"Jenkins?! Where the blazes are you?" Sebastian's strident voice punctuated the general din, drawing startled looks from them both.

"Yes, my lord," Jenkins grunted, sparing her a backward glance as he scurried off after his employer. Gritting her teeth, she stooped down and picked up the abandoned sacks.

"I have to be more careful," she muttered, shuffling out of the cargo area. She had quickly forgotten to be more circumspect in the face of such ugly, obscene suggestions. And what did Martin mean, "after the way she treated you"? Frowning, she thought back to when Clay commanded his own body, and she hers. She was only vaguely aware of the sailors shrinking away from her as she trudged along the wharf. It was true she had used the stone on a regular basis, but never maliciously...

Suddenly pockets of memory opened within her borrowed mind. One after another, various scenes from their time together played in her head, but from the golem's point of view. "But mistress, I thought you'd like the flowers," Clay explained, a bunch of daffodils hanging dejectedly from his hand.

"I'm allergic to flowers, you idiot!" she shouted, hand flying for the glossy pendant. The hapless golem collapsed to his knees, desperately clutching his head.

"Please mistress, I didn't know," he groaned, the bright yellow flowers becoming one with the wooden floor as his knee rolled over them.

"Just go!" she screeched, pointing to the door.

The scene melted away, to be replaced with images of her and Jenkins hungrily kissing each other. "I'm sorry mistress," the poor golem stammered, transfixed by the scene before him. She spun around, arms crossed over her heaving bosom, the top of her dress loosened during their drunken embrace.

"What the hell... Get out!" she screamed, hand creeping towards the stone. His jaw moved, but no intelligible sound came out. The poisonous look she shot him propelled him out of the room, mumbling apologies. The door slamming noisily behind him, he hurried away from the storeroom, their pants and moans ringing loudly in his sensitive ears. He almost made it to the back door when his head filled with pain. "Don't ever do that again," a stern angry voice uttered in his mind.

"Yes mistress," he projected weakly back, leaning heavily against the door as a final wave of pain washed over him.

She shook her head to dispel the images, uncomfortable with these vivid reminders of her cruelty. Somewhere deep within this mind, the real Clay shuddered, reached out through the activation of memories. "That's enough of that," she muttered, firmly blocking out further examples of mistreatment. The gangway creaked alarmingly under her weight, and she focused on traversing the old worn planks held together by tar and rope. She carefully set her load onto the cargo platform, where sacks and barrels waited to be lowered into the ship's hold.

"What a freak," a weedy man whispered to a fellow crewman as they passed. Gnashing her teeth, she raised an arm with the intention of shaking an apology out of the man.

"Trust me, he's not worth it," a calm voice said beside her, making her jump. She spun around to find the ship's first mate watching her intently, with only a few faint lines of uneasiness about his eyes and mouth. "If he's still bothering you by the time we pull into harbour on the other side, then by all means pound him," he offered blandly. "But for now, we need all the manpower we can muster," he pointed out, ticking an item off the list in his hands, the thick crumpled paper fluttering in the gentle breeze.

"Yes, of course," she conceded, lowering her arm.

"We'll be leaving soon, so don't stray too far from the ship," the first mate warned, shoving the list into his pocket.

"Thank-you Mr Robson," she murmured, absent-mindedly admiring the hairy forearms protruding from the man's grubby, rolled-up sleeves as he stormed off after some sailors.

Studiously ignoring the sideway looks from nearby crewmen, she hurried off the ship, her feet slowing as she stepped off the gangway. Sebastian and Gasquet were steadily approaching the ship, their voices raised in heated discussion. "We can't just leave the wounded behind sir. How are they supposed to fend for themselves?" Gasquet demanded, quickening his steps to keep up with Sebastian's purposeful strides.

"We have to shed what weight we can Captain," Sebastian argued without a flicker of emotion. "My decision is final...What are you doing?" he barked as his eyes settled on her.

"Loading the ship sir," she said defensively, imagining her fist smashing through his skull in order to keep calm. If she pictured it splitting apart like an over-ripe pumpkin on a hot day, with pink brain oozing out between the cracks, she could even muster a smile.

He frowned at the docile expression on her face, nodded curtly. "Good," he grunted before storming up the gangway. "Get those men off the ship Captain," he ordered briskly, continuing their conversation.

"Yes sir," Gasquet grated, clambering after him. She watched them walk onto the ship, turned her head back to find Gunthar studying her intently. They had barely spoken a word to each other since being captured, with the men obviously under orders to keep them apart.

"How have you been Clay?" he enquired politely.

"Ah, good," she murmured, wincing at the absurdity of her reply.

"Good," he responded cheerfully, tucking his hands neatly behind his back.

"So, Gunthar," she began carefully, licking her lips, "what do you think..."

"Gunthar!" Sebastian yelled impatiently from the head of the gangway.

"Ah, it's nice to be needed," he sighed, stepping lightly onto the wobbly walkway. "Better get ready Clay, we'll be under way soon," he called over his shoulder as he made his way to the ship. Sebastian glared at him, then shot her a suspicious look before herding the wiry-haired German below deck.

Her eyes lingered on the spot where she'd last seen Gunthar's unperturbed face disappear into the bowels of the ship. Excitement stirred within her as she shook her head and continued down the wharf. Despite her reservations about sailing in her borrowed body, she couldn't wait for their voyage to begin, if only to discover what Gunthar was up to. A sudden noise from the far end of the wharf, and she snapped her head up in time to catch Jenkins slinking out of the shadows, the knife in his hand dripping darkly. She pressed her great bulk against the shadowy stern of a nearby ship, watched intently as he slid the bloody blade into its sheath and scurried back to the Magnificent. With a final backward glance at his diminishing figure, she crept along the deserted wharf until the tangy smell of freshly spilt blood filled her sensitive nostrils. She followed the trail to the edge of the wharf and peered down into the black water gently lapping its stout timber legs. In the grey fuzzy light, she could just make out two round shapes bobbing up and down in the sea. "Travis and Martin," she murmured, recognising Travis' battered hat as the moon momentarily broke through the thick blanket of clouds. "They're really serious about shedding weight," she muttered, heading back to the ship. She'd best not outlive her usefulness before Gunthar made his big move.

"Ugh," Mel groaned, raising a trembling hand to her mouth as she slumped back onto the deck. There was nothing to bring up now, but that didn't deter her stomach from its heaving. Raphael tore his eyes from the horizon, frowned at her shivering body.

"Go down below, Mel!" he shouted over the howling wind. She shook her head resolutely, struggled ungainly to her feet.

"No way," she shouted as she stumbled towards him. "If we're going down, I want the option of jumping over the side at a moment's notice." His lips twitched with dry amusement, his eyes fixed on the compass in his hand.

"Always the optimist," he projected over the sound of crashing waves, slipping the compass back into his pocket. Since their departure from the harbour, the winds had steadily grown in strength, making their passage increasingly choppy. Distant rumbles of thunder didn't bode well for the rest of their voyage.

"At least drink some water Mel," he recommended, nodding at the water skin hanging off his belt.

"Right," she mumbled, lurching forward as the ship pitched over a big swell. "Sorry," she breathed as she bumped into him. He grunted in response, shifting slightly as she unhooked the water bag.

"Don't drink too much at once," he warned as she took a large mouthful. "We've no idea how long this water will have to last." She reluctantly lowered the bag, held it out to him.

"We're going to be living like this for a while, aren't we?" she asked sadly. He glanced over at her forlorn figure as he took a swig of water, shoulders hunched against the wind.

"More likely than not, yes," he answered with brutal honesty, wiping a droplet of water off his chin. Totally useless gesture, he thought sourly, with all the sea spray in the air, steadily dampening their skin and clothes.

"Better offer the stowaway some," he grumbled with a dark look over her shoulder. She followed his glare to where Daniel sat with his back to the main mast.

"I suppose we should," she agreed in a tightly controlled voice, struggling to contain her anger. Her empathy for Daniel's parents was palpable. The poor couple must be out of their minds with worry by now. "Damn fool," she muttered as she made her way to the middle of the ship. Sarah of course didn't seem to mind his presence. She had barely left his side since clubbing him.

"Aw, it's impossible," Sarah whined as she approached, letting go of the rope in disgust.

"You're tucking the end through the wrong loop, that's all," Daniel explained patiently, unfolding his legs and bouncing his tight calf muscles against the deck.

"Hey, love birds, have some water," she growled. They looked up in surprise, cheeks reddening in the yellow glow of the lantern. Daniel swallowed nervously past the lump in his throat. "Does that mean you're going to..."

"Don't push your luck young man," she admonished, holding the bag to his lips.

"Right," he sighed, closing his mouth around the opening. She carefully tilted the bag, allowed him a couple of gulps. "You don't really think I'm a spy, do you miss?" he asked, straining his wrists against the ropes binding his hands together behind the mast. She regarded him through narrowed eyes, wordlessly handed the water skin to Sarah.

"I don't know what to think anymore," she finally answered. "How could you just take off like that? Your parents must be worried sick..."

"I know," he mumbled, gritting his teeth against the pain in his arms and shoulders. Blinking back tears, he silently chastised himself for following Moonbeam's light grey coat through the trees. Despite their haggard appearance and nondescript clothing, he had instantly recognised the strange party quietly making its way beyond the lake. With little time to lose, he had raced home to throw a saddle on the family horse and gallop back to the lake. Why he followed the faded horse tracks so far, he honestly couldn't say. Several times he told himself to give up the chase, and yet his eyes steadfastly picked out the odd hoof print in the dirt, or freshly trampled plants by the side of the road. By the time he rode into Bristol, the trail was cold, and he felt utterly ridiculous. Guiding his weary horse through the dimly lit streets, he searched in vain for any sign of Sarah. He had given up all hope and was turning Jess around when the sound of the sea penetrated his foggy brain. "May as well see the sea while I'm here," he reasoned softly, nudging the horse toward the spots of light dotting the harbour.

"And do you really expect us to believe you snuck onboard to escape from some drunk sailors?" Mel pressed, dragging him back to the present. He lifted his head and gazed blearily at her angry face.

"It's the truth," he protested hoarsely. If he closed his eyes, he could still see their coarse faces leering at him in the moonlight. How they snuck up on him so completely as he was tethering Jess, he would never know. He only just managed to escape, thanks to Jess rearing up on her hind legs and startling the two ragged men. He had scrambled to his feet and hurtled down the narrow alley, the sailors' spluttered curses ringing in his ears. As he stumbled out of the alley, he searched for a hiding spot, his desperate gaze finally settling on the cute cutter tied up at the end of the wharf. His feet flying out from under him, he'd scrabbled up the rickety gangway, to throw himself down the open hatch. The sailors' harsh words outside the boat sent him scurrying to the stern, where he wedged himself behind the musty canvas and fish nets. He must have hit his head in the process, coming to when they were underway.

"It's just such an unbelievable coincidence Daniel," Mel sighed, scratching her head. "Of all the boats to stowaway on, you picked this one. Are you honestly telling me you had no idea of our plans?"

"I know it's hard to believe," he croaked past the sudden lump in his throat, his anger spent. He raised his eyes to Sarah's anxious face, lips twitching on their own accord. "I can't quite believe it myself. I had lost all hope of seeing you again, Sarah." She watched on in stunned horror as they gazed adoringly at each other

"Aww for the love of...stop doing that," Mel groaned, dripping precious water onto the deck as her hand tightened around the neck of the worn leather bag. "You'll just make things worse if you... woah!" Her tirade was cut short by the sudden pitching of the ship, and she was forced to grab the mast as the bow rose sharply above the waves.

"That's not good," Sarah said soberly, her eyes drawn to the lightning-slashed horizon.

"Shit," Mel breathed, clutching her stomach as the ship broke over another huge swell. Water slapped the sides of the ship hard, sending fat droplets across the deck.

"Sarah," Raphael called over his shoulder as he struggled with the wheel, "move the sail, hard to starboard!"

"Aye!" she acknowledged, leaping to the waist.

"Damn," Mel swore, almost toppling over as the ship rolled, the rudder sluggishly moving through the turbulent sea.

"Ow," Daniel cried as her knee connected with his head. She glanced down, considered him for a moment. Muttering darkly under her breath, she dropped to her knees and shuffled around the mast.

"Any funny moves and you'll be tied to the mast again," she warned as she untied the rope. "Now go and help Sarah," she ordered crossly, swallowing back a mouthful of bile as the deck lurched again. He nodded gravely, rubbing his wrists as he clambered awkwardly to his feet. She staggered to the stern, gratefully grabbing a part of the rigging as she came to a stop next to Raphael. "I thought you said we could steer clear of the storm," she shouted accusingly, blinking sea water out of her eyes. He shook his head, mouth set in a thin line of determination.

"The wind changed direction, bringing the storm to us," he grunted, pulling hard on the wheel as the sail swung around. The ship started to turn, and she had to cling to the rigging in order to stay upright.

"If we can change direction, we'll miss the worst of it," he explained, a faint note of hope creeping into his voice. As if in answer to his cautious optimism, thunder rumbled loudly overhead, drawing an involuntary cry from her ragged throat. Even in the grainy yellow light, she could see him grin briefly at her girlish outburst. "You released the stowaway," he stated flatly, impassive mask slipping firmly back into place.

"He's the least of our problems right now," she returned tightly, stepping clumsily toward him. "And it's in his interest to help," she pointed out, tying the water skin to his belt.

"Hmph," he snorted, shooting her a dark look as she hovered near his side. "I hate it when you're right," he growled, his attention wandering over to where Sarah and Daniel struggled with the rope. "Sarah," he called out, "pull tight on the sail!"

"Aye," she yelled back, her voice strained.

"I'd better help them," Mel mumbled, giving the strap a final tug before staggering to the side of the ship. Hand over hand, she painstakingly inched her way to where they heaved on the rope. "Aw great," she spat as the heavens opened. Blinking rain out of her eyes, she positioned herself behind Daniel, groping blindly for the rope. Details of the ensuing tug-of-war were fuzzy in her head, lost in the jumbled sequence of pulling, jostling and slipping. The wind seemed to be winning, judging by the amount of rope that tore through her hands. Gritting her teeth against the pain, she grasped the coarse hemp line, felt it bite into her flesh.

Making the task all the harder were Raphael's frantic directions. Just when their arms weren't being yanked out of their sockets, he'd roar above the driving rain and crashing sea to move the sail once more. Their lantern had finally succumbed to the storm, the tiny flame winking out sometime during their struggle, leaving them to strain and shiver in darkness. In the frequent flashes of lightning, she caught glimpses of soaked, exhausted bodies huddled over the ropes. Occasionally she saw Sarah's grim, frightened face turn to the man at the helm, straining to catch his hoarse words before they were swallowed by the storm.

"Just one more turn!" Raphael cried out, for what she swore was the fifth or sixth time. Sighing, she waited for the others to move, pressing her heels hard against the deck as the boat jerked violently sideways.

"Hey," Sarah panted as they scrambled awkwardly to the other side, "I think he actually means it this time." She followed the direction of her nod, saw the steady silvery gleam of moonlight through the clouds ahead.

"How about that," she mumbled tiredly, willing her stinging hands to close around the rope. With painful slowness, the Pretty Peg cut across the choppy water.

"Set the sail!" Raphael ordered, his voice a mixture of sheer exhaustion and triumph.

"Finally," Sarah muttered, her fingers exploring the top of the railing for the fastening point. She gladly eased her hold on the rope as Sarah wound the line around the metal bracket. Daniel flopped onto the deck, wheezing heavily through chattering teeth.

"Ugh," he grunted, clutching his sides, "I'm never going to stow away on a ship again." Laughing weakly, she collapsed down beside him.

"We're not clear yet," she croaked, coughing the excess moisture out of her lungs.

As if in answer to her warning, there was a blinding white flash, followed by a loud, sizzling crack. Her blood ran cold as a high-pitched squeal split the air, and she looked up in time to see Sarah's body fall heavily onto the deck.

"Sarah!" Daniel cried, scrambling to his hands and feet.

"Aggh," Sarah screamed, smouldering fingers splayed like sick talons.

"Sarah," Raphael panted, shoving Daniel roughly aside to crouch beside her sobbing body.

"My...hands," she managed to squeeze out between agonised gasps. Carefully grabbing her wrists, he squinted at the seared flesh.

"Can you heal that?" Mel asked, wincing at the sickly wet patches gleaming in the faint moonlight.

"I need to get her out of this blasted rain first," he muttered, gathering her in his arms and staggering up. His eyes fell upon Daniel's hunched form. "Daniel, come with me," he ordered curtly. "Mel, you steer us out of the storm," he added as he moved carefully toward the hatch.

"What?!" she spluttered, awkwardly getting to her feet. "I don't know how..."

"Just steer us toward the break," he grated, voice edged with impatience. "Daniel, open the hatch," he snapped, shifting the precious burden in his arms.

She opened her mouth to argue, but he was already barking instructions at the pale, shaken boy. Heat rising from her cheeks, she bit back any more concerns and turned stiffly toward the stern. "Arrogant bastard," she muttered as she took hold of the wheel. Despite the steady wind, they were moving more slowly now, the boat's response to her tentative turning of the wheel sluggish. Squinting through the easing rain, she eventually discerned the problem. The sail was still set, but the top of the mast now leant at an alarming angle, leaving the sail to droop feebly in the wind.

"The lightning," she croaked at the charred smouldering beam, remembering with a shudder the brilliant flash of light that split the sky above the little cutter. "Raph, we've got a problem! The mast is broken," she shouted hoarsely over the steady wind. Through the hatch door, she faintly caught his harsh reply, something about one disaster at a time. Muttering darkly under her breath, she gazed at the long, jagged split, cocked her head to one side. Pursing her lips thoughtfully, she harnessed the Mirror's energy and tentatively pushed the leaning segment, only to slump breathlessly against the wheel after a few seconds. "Okay, we'll play it your way," she wheezed, the world lurching around her with sickening slowness as she straightened up and began to steer toward the beautiful gleaming patch of water. The Pretty Peg limped her way over the rough sea, with only a few diversions created by her inept steering. Gradually the swells subsided, and they were moving more smoothly toward the break. She nervously checked the state of the mast, her eyes drawn to the drooping top section with every loud creak and billow of the sail. The top was now almost perpendicular to the rest of the mast. "Not good," she murmured, biting her bottom lip as she spied fresh splinters at the base of the crack.

Finally, the rain stopped, and she was gazing up at a brilliant halfmoon in a clear night sky. Her body sagging with relief, she eased her hold on the wheel and squeezed air bubbles out of her stiff aching joints. "Hey," she called out past the chattering of her teeth, her voice sounding strange and unnaturally loud in the relatively still air. "We're out of the storm. What do you want me to do now?" A dull thud followed by muttered curses answered her question.

"Clean that up," Raphael ordered curtly over his shoulder as he clambered out of the hold. Studiously ignoring her poisonous look, he squinted up at the split beam, his face visibly blanching. "Not good," he breathed, nearly tripping over his feet as he slowly circled the mast.

Not trusting herself to speak, she merely nodded, her expression bleak. "How's Sarah?" she croaked belatedly. Tearing his eyes away from the damaged mast, he regarded her gravely.

"I did what I could. They're largely sealed, but still quite tender. She won't be able to pull on ropes for a while, that's for sure," he answered more gently, the heavy mantle of exhaustion settling upon his body and mind. She cringed at the thought, eyes sliding to her own blistered hands.

"Maybe it's just as well Daniel smuggled himself aboard," she said sheepishly. He frowned at her hand, caught it before she could tuck it behind her back.

"Mel, this is horrible," he fretted, thumb tentatively moving over the raised and split patches of skin.

"I know I know, I have the hands of a worker," she joked weakly, wincing at the pain. He lifted his eyes to her, rewarded her with a lop-sided grin.

"I'd heal these for you Mel, but I fear I'd pass out..."

"Don't worry," she croaked, pulling her hand away, "it's a flesh wound. I'll survive."

"That's my girl," he murmured, turning away to inspect the mast. "We'll have to do something about that," he said more loudly after clearing his throat.

"That won't be easy," she sighed, looking up at the charred mess.

As they watched, the breeze stiffened, pushing the segment slowly sideways. "Master Blythe," Daniel called out breathlessly from the hatchway. "I finished cleaning up the nets, Master Blythe," Daniel reported, his voice muffled as he clambered onto the deck. There was a loud creak above his head, closely followed by a resounding snap. Daniel glanced up in time to see the hunk of wood falling towards him. His reflexes slowed by exhaustion, he stood gaping stupidly at the oncoming mast section.

"Look out!" Raphael barked.

Grunting with the effort, she extended the Mirror's energy at the falling wood. It hit the deck with a bone-jarring thud, narrowly missing Daniel's frozen, huddled figure. "Whoa," the boy croaked, slowly uncurling his trembling body. His eyes widened in alarm as he studied the impact zone so close to his feet.

"Mel, are you alright?" Raphael asked, noticing the way she staggered back weakly, coming to a rest against the rigging.

"Yeah," she lied, holding her side. "I just need to...sit down," she panted, lowering herself to the deck.

Daniel tore his gaze from the smashed timbers, gaped at her pallid face. "You saved me," he stammered, stumbling toward her on wobbly legs.

"Daniel," Raphael growled, grabbing the boy's shoulder. "We have work to do," he said firmly, forcing the shocked lad to look into his eyes. Nodding mutely, he let Raphael herd him towards the main mast.

"Mel," Raphael called over his shoulder, "get down below and have something to eat. No arguments," he added sternly when she shook her head.

Swallowing back a mouthful of bile, she reluctantly nodded her head. "Yes Raph," she conceded, slowly climbing to her feet. That last effort had really taken it out of her. Even with her stomach fluttering like an anxious butterfly, the thought of eating something was oddly inviting. "Stale bread and water have never been so appealing," she mumbled as she hobbled to the hatchway, leaving Raphael to order a bewildered Daniel about.

"Well, what do you sense?"

Gunthar slowly opened his eyes. So much for dramatic presentation, he thought wryly as he lowered his arms.

"Well, are we closing on them or not?" Sebastian demanded, apprehensively rapping his fingers against the hilt of his sword. The Magnificent lurched over another wave, sending large droplets of cold salty water across the bow.

"Aww, I hate sailing," Gunthar whined, shaking water from his hair. "It's faint," he added when Sebastian looked like he was about to explode. "As best as I can tell, the Mirror is in that direction," he explained, pointing at the distant flashes of lightning. "I daresay they've blundered into the storm."

"Really?" Sebastian prompted, excitement creeping into his voice.

"When we started out, I could only catch snippets of the Mirror's song," Gunthar confessed, gratefully moving away from the bow. "In the last half-hour or so however, the signal has been steady."

In the yellow glow of a nearby lantern, he could clearly see the tension in Sebastian's face as he struggled to contain his emotions. Several times during his shaman performance, Sebastian had started pacing, only to stop and glare at any onlookers. For their part, the crew of the hired schooner largely ignored their exalted guest, too engrossed in exchanging stories and insults as they worked. "Should we maintain our present course?" Mr Robson asked, startling them both. The first mate strode purposefully towards them, eyes flickering from one crew member to the next. Nodding his satisfaction, he came to a stop before them, respectfully removed his crumpled, battered hat.

"Captain Holister wishes to know if we are to maintain our present course, milord," he said formally. Gunthar expected the man to bow or curtsy any moment. "If we're to avoid the storm, we'll have to set the sails..."

"Alright Mr Robson, I understand," Sebastian said testily, turning to Gunthar. Inwardly savouring the knowledge that Sebastian needed his expertise, he supplied the squat, solid first mate with directions.

"Keep scanning the area," Sebastian ordered curtly when Mr Robson had left. "If what you say is true, we have a real chance of catching them."

"Yes, my excellency," Gunthar purred, bowing elaborately.

Face darkening at his obvious contempt, he walked stiffly away, hands bunched tightly at his sides. Snickering softly at Sebastian's indignant departure, he turned back to the bow of the ship. Squinting his stinging eyes against the salty wind, he felt the alien fragment within his body sing out for its sisters and brothers, a small, lonely voice tinged with sadness. The answering call was much louder than he had led Sebastian to believe. The Mirror cried out to him over the silver-tipped water, its clamour ringing clearly in his ears. Now that he had a part of the Mirror inside him, he could control the voices, turn them down to a dull roar. "No," he whispered to the night, "I don't mind the noise."

Suddenly the hairs on the back of his neck stood on end. He turned around and found himself meeting Alyce's intense gaze from across the deck. He could barely make out her bulky silhouette in the grainy light, her hands chained behind her back. Even without the pendant, he could tell what she was thinking as her eyes bored into his. "You'll just have to wait and see, my malevolent friend," he murmured, a twisted grin on his smug face. One of the soldiers guarding Alyce grunted, butted her with the base of his bayonet. The soldiers were much bolder now with her placement in chains since setting sail. Sebastian had insisted it was for her own safety. The golem's increased sensitivity to barometric changes could be dangerous out at sea, could drive it mad, he had asserted to Gunthar earnestly as they prepared to sail. For something he had pulled out of his arse, Gunthar had to admit it was a good story. Hell, it could even be true. Alyce had grudgingly agreed, eyes flitting to his before reluctantly holding out her hands.

"That's enough fresh air, back down below," the soldier ordered gruffly, butting the pale grey hulk again. She stiffened at the rough nudge, strained against the iron cuffs behind her back. In that instant, he knew she could easily break the restraints. The greater struggle for her at that moment was to not break the chain and clobber the soldiers. With a final backward glance, she gnashed her teeth and allowed them to herd her back into the hold. He turned back to the sea, glimpsing out of the corner of his eye the solemn-faced soldier standing a discrete distance away. For some reason the soldiers assigned to shadow his movements were more subtle than those assigned to monitor Alyce. Half the time he forgot they were there, quietly scrutinising his every move. Not that it mattered, he thought confidently as he stared unseeingly at the indigo sea, bunching and unfurling like rich velvet before him. None of these precautions would stop him from taking back what was rightfully his. The power of the Mirror surged within him, demanding to be unleashed upon an unsuspecting world.

"Not yet," he whispered, tightening his hands into fists as he fought the urge to blow a hole in the side of the ship. "Not yet," he repeated, smiling happily at the mental image. Feeling the soldier's eyes upon him, he twisted his head around and gave the glowering man a jaunty salute. Laughing softly, he turned back to the sea. "Ah, it's good to be alive," he sighed, extending his arms out dramatically. "Ah, so good," he murmured, closing his eyes.

Daniel clung to the mast, bare feet pressed hard against the smooth wood. Gingerly, he leant back against the rope tied around his waist. The thick rope tightened reassuringly, held firm. Sighing, he gradually let go of the charred top to grope for the iron bracket hanging off the rope. "Are you alright up there Daniel?"

He squinted down at Sarah's anxious face, managed a strained smile.

"I'm alright, thanks Sarah," he croaked, quickly looking up as a stiff breeze pushed his body sideways. The world spun around him, and he hastily reached for the burnt remains of the topmast. "Ha, never knew I was so scared of heights," he mumbled. If only he'd fixed the sail well enough before, he wouldn't have to be up here again, battling the elements and his newfound fear.

"Father, I could go up there and fix the sail," Sarah offered, tugging at Raphael's shirt sleeve. He wordlessly grabbed her hand and gave the pink flesh a cursory inspection.

"No, you couldn't," he said flatly, releasing her hand.

"I'd be careful…"

"No," he reiterated sternly, overriding her objections.

"And we're probably too heavy for the damaged mast to support, which leaves your boyfriend," Mel pointed out distractedly from the deck, body crouched over the tangled ropes she was endeavouring to unravel.

"Aww," the frustrated girl groaned, stamping her foot, "stop calling him that."

"It's not official yet," Raphael commented dryly, stepping around the mast.

"Father!"

"More to your left Daniel," he called, studiously ignoring her.

Nodding nervously, the poor lad repositioned the bracket and started to carefully tap it with the hammer. At least he could more clearly see what he was doing this time. The eastern corner of the sky was glowing with the first rays of morning. "Ah, I think that's got it," he shouted down as he tested the strength of the bracket.

"Right," Raphael drawled, clapping his hands together. "Let's thread the rope through, we've lost too much time already."

"Aye sir," he mumbled, carefully releasing the hammer to dangle from the rope tied around his waist. Willing his hands to stop trembling, he reached across his waist for the lead rope tucked into his belt. Now, whatever you do, don't drop the rope, he coached silently, gripping the wet end tightly in his aching, cramped hand. Taking a deep breath, he extended the rope to the thick, rust-coated bracket embedded in the wood.

Suddenly the wind picked up, and he almost dropped the rope in surprise as the Pretty Peg lurched forward.

"Damn," Raphael cursed, tearing his eyes away from the huddled mass at the top of the mast. "Mel, keep an eye on the lad, will you?" he asked, turning towards the wheel. "Mel?" he prompted when she didn't respond. He looked back to find her staring into space, the rope hanging from her still hands.

"Mel?" Sarah echoed, bending down to inspect her pale transfixed face.

"He's out there," Mel breathed, blinking away the image of Gunthar glaring out to sea from the bow of a schooner.

"Who's out there?" Sarah asked.

"I can see a light!" Daniel cried, squinting at the horizon.

"What?" Raphael barked, scrambling to the side and following the boy's outflung arm. A faint point of light broke the smooth line of the horizon.

"It's Gunthar," Mel croaked, her throat suddenly dry.

"That's not possible," Raphael protested, shaking his head obstinately despite the sinking sensation in his stomach. "How could he possibly find a ship so fast..."

"He's working with Sebastian," she supplied hoarsely, focusing on the shocked, disbelieving faces around her as she slowly rose to her feet.

"Clever, very clever," Raphael muttered darkly, his body rigid with anger. "Daniel, get a move on!" Raphael ordered hoarsely up the mast. Swallowing nervously, the boy fed the rope through the bracket with renewed urgency. Raphael reached up for the end and started heaving. Soon the sail was up, and Daniel gratefully inched his way down the mast as Raphael secured the rope.

"Sarah," Raphael grunted, giving the rope a final tug, "go down and grab our weapons." Dragging her troubled gaze from Daniel's hunched figure, she nodded bleakly and headed for the hatchway.

Daniel glanced down, muttered something under his breath and slipped out of the rope. Tumbling unceremoniously to the deck, he clambered to his feet. "Go below lad and get something to eat," Raphael ordered as his clinical gaze swept over the boy's wobbly stance.

"Yes sir," he mumbled, obediently following Sarah to the hatch. Over the protests of his aching limbs, he carefully lowered himself into the hull. In the shadows before him, Sarah was cursing loudly, her body sprawled over a pile of nets. "You alright Sarah?" he croaked as he rushed to her aid, jarring his knee in the process. That's what you get for trying to impress a girl, he told himself grimly, struggling not to grimace.

"No, I am not," she snapped, her face contorted with disgust and anger as she took his outstretched hand. "How could they have caught up so fast?" she demanded, lurching her way toward the stern.

"Ah, they have a bigger ship?" he suggested lamely, watching her noisily re-arrange the sacks in the corner.

"That's not what I meant," she chided, finally knocking over the stash of weapons with her frantic searching.

"Wait, let me help you with that," he offered, hobbling over to open the wooden window cover. With much grunting and straining against the iron handle, he caused the swollen wood to budge. A little light seeped in through the opening, allowing her eyes to pick out the metallic glints of swords slowly sliding out of their sheaths.

"Thank you," she said tightly, frantically grabbing a sword. "Ow!" she cried, dropping the sword.

"What?" he cried with a start, jumping at the loud clang.

"I just cut myself...don't touch it," she protested weakly as he grabbed her hand.

"Damn it Sarah, you should be more careful," he admonished, digging out a rag from his pocket. "Master Blythe was almost spent with the effort of healing your hands," he lectured sternly, pressing the rag over the cut.

"Ow," she hissed, tugging her hand back instinctively. He tightened his hold, spared her a warning glance as he mopped up the surrounding area.

"Is that clean?" she asked in a surly manner, forcing her hand to be still.

"Mostly," he answered with a crooked grin. "Here, press it over the wound, I'll get the weapons," he ordered smoothly, releasing her hand. Grunting indignantly, she stepped aside, hand clutched protectively to her chest.

"So, do you have a special ability, Sarah?" he asked casually over his shoulder. She gaped at his curved back, the sound of blades sliding back into their sheaths loud to her suddenly shocked ears. Of course he was aware of Father's ability, he'd watched in speechless awe as Father healed her hands. "You know, I always sensed there was something special about Master Blythe, and about you too," he continued amicably as he straightened up, swords cradled carefully in his arms. "But when Miss Mel stopped the top mast from falling on my head, well, you could have knocked me over with a feather."

Her jaw moved, but no sound came out. "Ah, Daniel," she finally croaked while he watched with polite interest, "it's a long story, but there's something we have that's very powerful and dangerous. That's why we're on the run, and now I really wish you hadn't stowed away, even though I was so happy to see you..."

"Ssh," he bade gently, freeing a hand to brush the tear off her cheek. "What's done is done. I can't go back now, so I guess you're stuck with me." She raised a shaky hand to his, drew the grimy palm to her lips. Grinning at his sharp intake of breath, she gave it a playful lick.

"Don't worry," she said brightly, "I won't let anyone hurt you." On that positive note, she scooped the swords out of his unsuspecting arms and headed for the hatchway. "Now eat something, you'll need your strength," she ordered briskly as she juggled her load and navigated the ladder.

"Wait," he croaked belatedly to her vanishing feet, his exhausted brain struggling to string the words together. "That was supposed to be my line," he finished softly to the creaky interior.

Sighing deeply, he turned to the back wall to poke and prod the saddle bags. He imagined she'd explain it all to him one day. His hand encountered a bread roll wrapped in cloth. His stomach growling, he seized the roll and ravenously bit into it. Perhaps it had something to do with the faint whispers he heard every time he came down here, he thought with a shiver. Even as he chewed the dry, semi-stale bread, silvery voices scratched faintly at his ears, only to dissipate when he turned his head. Cramming the rest of the roll into his mouth, he hurried back to the main deck, his feet quickened by the columns of dank air that seemed to brush his face and arms overly-long.

"Pip."
The boy murmured in his sleep, shifted his head.
"Pip!"
The urgent hissing was accompanied by a pebble. "Ow," the boy whined, reluctantly opening his eyes. He swore Gavin deliberately maintained a supply of small objects in his pocket just to throw at him. "That hurt," he mumbled, rubbing his head.

"You're supposed to be on look-out," the swarthy-faced man chided from the rigging.

"Alright, alright," he grumbled, looking sourly at Gavin over the edge of the crow's nest. Stretching his cramped limbs, he slowly scanned the horizon, squinting his dark brown eyes against the slanted rays of the early morning sun. He almost missed the little black speck sitting on the gleaming surface of the water.

"Ship sighted dead ahead, at ah," he paused to align the tiny speck with the degree markings on the top of the crow's nest, "35 degrees west, I mean, east."

Captain Holister inwardly groaned at the boy's garbled report, trained his telescope on the glimmering sea. "Ah," he purred, revising his decision to have the lookout flogged. Only five licks of the cat for Master Biggins today, depending on how many more times the boy's brother had to scramble up the rigging.

"You see it?" an impatient voice rasped beside him. Schooling his features, he lowered the telescope.

"Yes Lord Seabast, there's definitely a vessel out there," he answered, a hint of triumph in his voice. He offered the telescope to Sebastian, pointed out the direction. Muttering softly, Sebastian moved the telescope back and forth over the area until finally he came to a stop, breath catching noisily in his throat.

"Excellent work Captain Holister," he murmured thickly, adjusting the magnification. "They're not moving very fast," he drawled, clucking his tongue annoyingly against the roof of his mouth. "Looks like that deranged German was right," he conceded, handing the telescope back to the Captain. "Have your boarding party ready Captain. I want this wrapped up quickly," he ordered briskly.

"Yes Lord Seabast," he acknowledged with a slight nod of his head. He hated grovelling to such an arrogant fop, but the price had been right. He looked up to find the impeccably dressed man striding toward the bow, no doubt to quiz the wiry-haired fellow further.

"Oh yes, the boarding party will be ready, your majesty," he sneered to the straight, proud back.

Despite Gasquet's efforts to caution his men against loose talk, his men had been only too eager to divulge details of their misadventures. From the start of his contract with Sebastian Seabast, he had suspected they were after something special, beyond the pursuit of gold and trinkets. According to the swaggering stories of the younger soldiers, they'd had their arses whipped by a woman shooting whirlwinds and sparks out of her fingertips. Two men had lost their lives, three were badly injured. Gasquet had convinced them to stay behind and make their own way home. The small handfuls of coins he'd distributed amongst the suffering trio had done most of the convincing. He wondered idly if they'd make it back home, or if they'd drown their sorrows at the various pubs that lined the harbour. A man could really unhinge himself in a port like Bristol. Many of his own crew had come to sticky ends in such dens of debauchery over the years...

"Mr Robson," he said with a start, sensing the man's presence behind him.

"Captain," the thickset man reported, saluting smartly, "course has been set accordingly."

"Good work Mr Robson," he acknowledged, inspecting the billowing square sails. He could swear the sails were overly taut in the gentle breeze. "Make sure we have a boarding party ready," he said distractedly, looking away from the uncanny canvas with a shudder.

"Yes sir," the other man murmured, hastily tearing his eyes away from the sails to follow the captain below deck.

"Are the cannons loaded and ready?" he enquired, ducking his head as they passed through the hold area and into the passageway with its low ceiling.

"Yes sir," the first mate answered, brow furrowed at his captain's almost anxious tone. "Are you expecting trouble, Captain?" he dared to ask. Captain Holister stopped at the end of the passageway, patted the various pockets of his waistcoat and trousers until he felt hard straight metal.

"I know what you're thinking Davo," he rumbled through his long thick beard. He pulled out a key and inserted it in the lock. "It's just a little fishing boat, easy pickings for the likes of us," he continued, opening the armoury door with a grunt. Peering through the cloud of dust awakened by his entry, he grabbed a gun from the shelf and stuffed it into his belt. "But I don't like the stories I've been hearin' Davo," he explained, his voice muffled as he searched for ammunition. Enough light poured in through the small porthole for him to make out the contents of the poky compartment. "And I definitely don't like our unexpected guests," he added, grabbing a handful of pellets and shoving them into his trouser pocket.

Pursing his lips thoughtfully, Davo followed his captain's example and selected a gun for himself. "There's something odd about the German," he ventured, tucking the weapon into his belt.

"Hmph," Holister snorted, picking up a knife and pulling it out of the sheath. "He and the golem make a fine pair," he muttered, eying critically the blade. "And that pompous upstart is a fool if he thinks he's got 'em under control," he spat, ramming the knife back into the sheath. He looked up to find the first mate studying him intently. "Tell the men to be alert, especially around our new guests. I wouldn't be surprised if they try something."

"Aye Captain," he responded, coming smartly to attention.

"Oh, and Davo," Holister added as his first mate turned to go, "tell them quietly."

With a knowing grin, he nodded and left. As the sound of Davo's footsteps faded, he allowed himself to slump against the wall. Twenty years as a sea captain, and he'd strayed into a situation that suddenly filled him with foreboding. "Pull yourself together man," he muttered, catching sight of his reflection in a sword. Bright blue eyes shone out at him from within a lined, weather-beaten face. "You've gotten yourself out of tighter spots, Angus Theodore Holister," he said to the grave image. Squaring his broad shoulders, he tucked the knife into the top of his boot as he left the armoury, the pressure of hard steel against his leg oddly reassuring.

She was clinging to the side of the aluminium dingy, belatedly dodging the spray as they hit the choppy water. Over the sploshing of the sea and droning out-board motor, her brother's deep rumbling laughter reached her water-logged ears. She turned back to glare at him, readied her tongue to dispense harsh words of truth. Her tongue faltered at the sight of Gunthar sitting by the motor, steering them through the rough sea.

"What are you doing here?" she squeaked as her throat closed up. "Where is everybody?" she asked shrilly, looking about the small boat.

"Ah, it's just you and I, Mel," he laughed, shaking droplets off his wild hair. "Isn't it great?" he crowed, pulling up his shirt to reveal a pinpoint of light breaking through the skin of his abdomen. She watched in stunned horror as the light expanded, tore out of his body and engulfed her. All the while his manic laughter rang in her ears, scraped her nerves...

"Mel," Sarah called, shaking her shoulder. She peeled her sticky eyes open, blinked at the concerned face floating before her.

"Now really isn't the time to nap Mel," the girl pointed out, voice brittle with fear. Daniel stood a discrete distance behind her, his hands slowly coiling the boom line.

"They're catching up to us, aren't they?" she asked rhetorically, staggering to her feet. She must have collapsed against the side of the ship after setting the sail, and closed her eyes for just a moment.

"That's an understatement," Sarah confirmed through stiff, grimacing lips. She followed Sarah's horrified stare, reeled backwards as her eyes easily picked out a ship just over fifty metres away.

"How are they catching up to us so fast?" Sarah cried.

"It must be Gunthar," she croaked, fingers digging into the wooden railing.

"Mel," Raphael barked, looking up from his compass, "go and get the Mirror."

Nodding wordlessly, she scurried down the hatchway to fetch the plain hessian sack with its precious contents. Despite light streaming in steadily through the window, she still fumbled about clumsily for the bag.

"I'm coming for you Mel," a thickly accented voice spoke in her ear, making her jump halfway out of her skin.

"Ugh," she breathed explosively when she turned to face the source of the voice. Gaping at empty space, she clutched the bag protectively to her chest and scrambled up the ladder.

"Land ahead!" Sarah yelled out from the prow, pointing excitedly to the thin dark line sitting on the horizon. Squinting at the speck of land, Raphael adjusted the helm, checked the position of the ship behind them.

"They're catching up too fast," he projected over the sound of water slapping the hull as the Pretty Peg limped towards land.

"Do you want me to push against the sail?" she ventured sceptically, lurching to a stop near the wheel. He glanced up at the charred mast end, shook his head.

"No," he sighed, grimacing as the billowing sail strained against the bracket. "The sail is barely holding as it is. Can you slow them down?" Nodding grimly, she turned to face the fast-approaching ship. If she squinted, she could just pick out moving flecks of colour on the deck and along the rigging. Hugging the sack to her chest, she reached out to the Mirror fragments within the coarse material. Abruptly her body froze, eyes staring glassily at the sea.

Daniel cautiously approached her still figure, waved a hand before her eyes.

"Daniel," Raphael hissed, looking back from his troubled inspection of the sail.

"Sorry," the boy mumbled, hastily retrieving his hand. "Is she alright sir?" he asked earnestly, watching her nostrils move rhythmically as her breathing deepened. Raphael opened his mouth to berate the boy. He faltered however when he noticed the genuine concern in Daniel's eyes.

"She's alright for now," he answered, clearing his throat, "but she'll be tired and weak when she returns to normal."

Daniel nodded, and with a final grave look at Mel, turned back to the mast. He watched the lad drift over to where Sarah worked. Within seconds their heads were bent together in muted conversation, their bodies crouched over the ropes. As though feeling his gaze, Sarah glanced anxiously over her shoulder, gave him a weak grin before turning her attention back to Daniel. Grunting, he adjusted the wheel and tried to ignore them. "I'm losing my daughter to that boy," he muttered, eying Mel's transfixed face accusingly. "It's all your fault you know," he added hoarsely, throat tightening with emotion. "Sarah would never have crept out of her shell without your help," he admitted softly. For an instant, he could have sworn her lips twitched. "Hmph," he huffed, turning back to the welcoming band of land. Their best chance of survival now rested on Mel's command of the Mirror and reaching land first. Even from this distance, it was obvious that the other ship was larger and better equipped.

"Can't stand and fight," he mumbled, imagining the Pretty Peg being smashed to bits by cannon balls. "So, what do we do?" he could almost hear his uncle prompt. If he closed his eyes, he could see Aunt Sophie at the other end of the dinner table rolling her eyes, cutlery poised in mid-air as they waited to eat.

"For goodness' sake Bruce, he's just a child," she would point out, her voice strained.

"All the more reason to drill him and Lord Muck here about survival," Uncle Bruce would rumble back, nodding at a stony-faced Sebastian. Funny, Sebastian had always hated that nick name.

"We run," a much younger version of himself would be forced to answer, due to Sebastian's refusal to play the game. With a satisfied nod, Uncle Bruce would signal that the lesson was at an end and start attacking the beef on his plate.

"We run," a much older, wiser Raphael breathed, opening his eyes to the present. "We run."

Sebastian looked up, the hairs on the back of his neck sticking up. The dank, unpleasant sensation swept over his whole body, encouraging his flesh to break out in goose bumps. "Typical," he grumbled, trying to ignore the hand of irrational fear that settled around his heart. He finally has a moment alone, and something inexplicable happens. As if in answer to his trepidation, the ship suddenly lurched violently beneath his feet, the loud creaking of timber drowning out his curses. "What the blazes..." he muttered, the map he was holding almost slipping from numb fingers. At least he wasn't alone in his discomfit, he noted after a quick survey of nearby crew members and soldiers. With their anxious murmurs echoing his own concerns, he started to search for Gunthar, only to find the oaf hurtling towards him, almost tripping over several bemused crewmen in the process.

"Gunthar, what's going on? We seem to be stopping..."

"It's Mel, using the Mirror against us," he gasped, skidding to a halt. "You have to tell the captain to turn us around."

"What? Are you insane?" Sebastian growled, roughly shoving the map into his coat pocket. "In the time it takes us to turn around, they'll be able to limp further away."

"Why are we stopping?" Jenkins panted as he scrambled out of the hatchway, Gasquet hot on his heels.

"Did we hit something?" Gasquet gasped, knees almost crumbling beneath him as he stumbled onto the deck.

"No, you fool," Gunthar snapped impatiently, grabbing the rail as the ship jolted again. Crew and soldiers alike looked about fearfully for the cause of their sudden stop.

"Aggh," Gunthar groaned, straining against the wall of energy. "It's the woman, using the Mirror against us," he repeated, reeling with the effort of fighting the wall.

"What the hell is going on?" Captain Holister demanded angrily, speeding along the deck like a hurricane, the crew stirring in his wake like leaves.

"Captain, we have to turn and fire at the Pretty Peg," Gunthar cried hoarsely, his head ringing from the noise both inside and outside his head.

"But we're out of range," Holister pointed out. "At most we might splash them a bit..."

"That's the idea Captain," Gunthar grunted, his face creased with pain.

"Do it," Sebastian confirmed when the captain looked at him in askance. With a curt nod Captain Holister spun away, began to bellow out fresh orders.

"What are you hoping to achieve?" Jenkins asked, jaw clenching nervously. He couldn't afford a repeat performance of their last encounter.

"We have to disrupt her concentration," Gunthar answered, sagging slightly against the railing. "If we can give her something else to worry about, I'm betting that her ability to use the Mirror will be affected, one way or another.

"That must be a lot of pressure she's exerting," Sebastian grunted, watching Gunthar through narrowed eyes. With a little encouragement, Gunthar had confessed to following the scent of the Mirror back to the manor and having a confrontation with Mel. During a rare break a few miles outside of Bristol, he had herded Gunthar and Clay away from the men, asked them politely to share their story with him. "Amazing," Gunthar exclaimed after they had exchanged accounts, eyes lighting with excitement. "She must have somehow used the power of the Mirror to slow your passage to the manor. Clay and I were disorientated to a certain degree, but you and your men bore the brunt of the attack. That's why we got there first, and why she barely survived the golem's attack. Poor girl must have been exhausted," Gunthar had concluded, eyes softening with sympathy. Jumping at the sound of cannon fire, Sebastian returned with a nasty jolt back to reality, forced himself to temporarily set aside his doubts about Gunthar. He obviously wasn't telling the whole truth about his confrontation with Mel. More than once Sebastian found himself wishing he had the old crazy Gunthar back, and not this new, confident one. And what was the deal with him and Clay? What had led the strange duo to form such a solid pact? New questions everywhere he looked, and no answers in sight. "That's no way to win a war," he murmured softly, rushing to the side of the ship.

"Ah, it's working," Gunthar cried, voice muffled as he bent over the railing to watch the clouds of black smoke pour out through the cannon holes. He unfolded his lanky body, beamed at Sebastian, relief evident in his face. "A few more rounds, your excellency, and we should be free."

Sebastian stared back at his beaming face, jaw working silently as he tried to assimilate the mixture of cheerfulness and mockery.

"Right," he finally responded, struggling to regain some control over the situation. "I'll inform the captain."

Out of the corner of his eye, he saw Jenkins tear his bemused gaze from Gunthar's face, hurry after him as he strode towards the stern. "If only we didn't have to rely on him," Jenkins muttered softly. "Guy gives me the creeps..."

"It can't be helped," he sighed, hunching his shoulders against a sudden gust of wind. "At the moment, we need him more than he needs us, and he knows it. The quicker we can wrap this up, the better..."

His voice trailed off, an idea budding in his head.

"Sebastian?"

He looked up to find Jenkins staring at him, brow wrinkled in concern. "Look, just keep an eye on Gunthar and Clay, I've got an idea," he ordered briskly, briefly resting a hand on the henchman's shoulder before resuming his search for the captain with renewed vigour. Smirking at Jenkins' confused, shocked expression, he made his way to the helm, only vaguely aware of the grim-faced sailors he brushed past. "This has to work," he told himself sternly as he came to a stop before Captain Holister and Mr Robson. Time was slipping away from him with each obstacle they encountered, his window to the world stage slowly but surely closing. Taking a steadying breath, he gave the order, noting the underlying tension in the captain's face as his words sunk in. Word of their previous encounter with Mel had obviously reached his ears, a shadow of doubt flitting through his eyes as he nodded and growled something like "you heard the man," to Mr Robson. With a slight nod of his head Mr Robson scurried away, disappearing through the hatch to deliver the order.

"Right," Sebastian mumbled as he returned to the prow, feeling like he had just piled all his chips on the table in an all-or-nothing bet. A bitter laugh escaped his lips. He really was a gambler, just as Raphael had so cruelly pointed out. Shrugging his shoulders, he ambled over to where Gunthar stood, butterflies stirring in his stomach as he waited to see if his gamble paid off.

Mel's consciousness hovered above the Magnificent, suspended within the Mirror's energy. She could feel Gunthar pushing against her, even as he scurried down the deck to speak urgently to Sebastian. The ship jolted as it was momentarily caught between the opposing forces, the hapless sailors and soldiers looking about in surprise. Strained, tense words were exchanged. With a look of quiet resignation, Sebastian said something to the large, bearded man on his right, who in turn barked orders at the crew. Slowly the ship started to turn. Gunthar turned his attention back to the Pretty Peg, pale wiry hair catching the early morning rays. Closing his eyes, he tentatively exerted force against the barrier, to no avail, with the Magnificent remaining largely dead in the water. But why were they turning? Abruptly Gunthar opened his eyes, thin lips parting in a sickly smile. The large, bearded man roared, and the ship's side shuddered, puffs of smoke drifting out of the neat little holes...

With a start she jumped back into her body. "Incoming!" she screamed, pointing at the black spots hurtling towards them. Raphael turned, quickly spun back to the wheel, pulling hard to starboard.

"Hold onto something!" he yelled over the shrill cry of the cannonballs arcing overhead. With a deafening swoosh three balls hit the water only metres away from the Pretty Peg, causing the little cutter to lurch violently. Despite his warning, she stumbled into the mast and smacked her head on the unforgiving wood. Her movements sluggish and dreamlike, she staggered to the railing and waited for the world to stop spinning. Somewhere to her left, she heard Sarah and Daniel cry out in surprise, and she cautiously turned to see them huddling together against the side of the boat.

"Is everybody alright?" Raphael croaked as he wrestled with the wheel, barely hearing the muted replies over the frantic beating of his own heart. "Daniel, get ready to adjust the..."

Another explosion rumbled faintly in the distance, and he stopped in mid-sentence to stare at the schooner. "Oh no," he breathed, hastily wiping a grimy sleeve over bloodshot eyes. Three more balls sped towards them, their banshee cry of destruction steadily growing stronger. "Hang on!" he shouted, pulling desperately on the wheel. Through bleary eyes she picked out the deadly balls.

Over the roar of crashing iron and flying water, she was vaguely aware of Raphael yelling out orders. Daniel and Sarah slowly unfolded themselves from the side of the ship, gingerly approached the mast. On its own accord, her arm tightened protectively around the hessian bag, causing the jagged edges of the Mirror to dig into her flesh. "That was closer," she murmured, the fresh pain penetrating her foggy brain. "We must be losing speed," she croaked, her brow furrowed in consternation as she stared at the unmoving schooner.

"Father," Sarah cried, staggering around the base of the mast, "we're losing the main sail!"

"What?" he breathed, looking up in despair as the top half of the metal bracket wriggled free. All the jarring must have weakened the metal's purchase of the wood. Sarah grabbed the sail line, tied it around her waist.

"Sarah, no!" he shouted as she started climbing up the mast.

"Sarah, wait," Daniel cried, hugging the mast. Raphael glanced at the boy, noticed that his arm now hung at an odd angle, his young face lined with pain. He must have somehow dislocated his shoulder while clinging to the side.

"Daniel," Raphael called, adjusting the wheel slightly as the wind shifted direction, "can you keep the boom steady?" Nodding grimly, the boy stopped gaping helplessly up the mast and teetered over to the boom. "Mel, can you help the lad? Looks like he's hurt," he ordered distractedly, his attention fixed on the welcoming band of sand that was steadily coming into view. "Mel?" he prompted when she didn't reply, struggling to keep the impatience out of his voice. He reluctantly tore his eyes off the tiny strip of coastline to glare accusingly at her, froze in his tracks at the terrified look on her face.

"Too late," Mel croaked, raising a trembling finger at the on-coming schooner. "They're catching up to us."

"We're catching up to them!" Gunthar cried excitedly, hands gripping the railing as the Magnificent picked up speed, cutting across the choppy water. "That should be enough, Your Excellency. Any more volleys, and we risk damaging the Pretty Peg," he reported brightly, glancing over his shoulder at where Sebastian tensely stood. "Sebastian?" he stammered, not liking the look on the other man's face. For a man who seemed to be in love with the sound of his own voice, he was being oddly quiet. "Did you hear me?" he asked, inwardly wincing at his uneven tone. He started to move toward Sebastian when the side of the ship shuddered, the sound of cannon fire splitting the air. Hands flying to his ears, Gunthar turned back, eyes wide with disbelief as he watched the cannon-balls hurtling towards the Pretty Peg. "No, you idiot," he mumbled, his lips suddenly numb. "That's too close."

Time seemed to slow around him as he stood like a statue, eyes glued to the projectiles descending upon the Pretty Peg. Squinting past the harsh reflection of light off the water, he could make out figures on the deck of the cutter, their bodies frozen in place as they surely awaited the oncoming catastrophe. He blinked, and in that time a cannonball smashed into the bow, fragments of wood and metal flying through the air spectacularly at the point of impact. The figures, so still before, now fell to the shuddering deck, their limbs flailing in desperation. One small body fell heavily from the mast, rolled until it came to a rest against the railing at the boat's waist. As the debris settled, his eyes were drawn to the gaping hole where the bow used to be. "Sebastian," he croaked, finally finding his voice. He spun on his heel, mouth opening to spew a string of abuse when a high-pitched whine rapidly filled the air. Before he could turn toward the noise, there was a horrendous smashing of timber, and the deck lurched violently beneath his feet. Falling heavily to the deck, he instinctively threw up his arms as a feeble defence against the debris flying through the air.

With his heart firmly lodged in his throat, he stiffly clambered to his feet, struggling to find his balance as the deck continued to shudder. The handful of sailors who had avoided the worst of the explosion were stirring, staggering to their feet. Swallowing past the sudden hard lump in his throat, he gazed at the ones who hadn't been so lucky, and now littered the deck covered in blood and debris. Pushing past the pain behind his temples, he stumbled to the side of the ship, carefully poked his head over the jagged wood. An unintelligible cry escaped his lips as he stared at the large, ragged hole that now marred the Magnificent's side just above the waterline. "How the hell?" he murmured, blinking furiously as his brain stubbornly refused to acknowledge what his eyes saw. Did one of the cannons misfire? he mused, shakily backing away from the edge. "No," he whispered, straining to recall the last two minutes. All three cannons had fired, their deadly payloads sent hurtling toward the Pretty Peg. One hit the bow, another one narrowly missed the stern, while the middle one...

Suddenly the pieces fell into place, and he realised what happened. Something slowly trickled down his forehead, and he raised a trembling hand to the top of his head. "Hmph, blood," he mumbled, frowning at his hand. "Sebastian," he cried, for some reason linking the bright red smear on his hand to Raphael's brother. "You, you ass," he spluttered angrily, lurching like a drunkard toward the spot where Sebastian had been standing. Clumsily he clawed at the timber, uncovered the man's unconscious body. "Was this your brilliant plan?" he snarled, kneeling down to grab Sebastian's hair and raise his flaccid face up to his. "Disable the boat so you and your lapdogs can sweep in and take the Mirror?" he spat, voice trembling with anger. "Only the plan backfired. Mel bounced one of the cannonballs back, right into our side, you bumbling idiot!" Something inside his brain clicked, and he unceremoniously released Sebastian. "Where's your favourite lapdog?" he murmured, rising to his feet.

From somewhere behind him someone cried out, and he turned toward the urgent voice, followed the shaky, out-stretched hand of the lookout. A long boat was steadily pulling away from the Magnificent, three figures clearly visible in the early morning sun. "Jenkins," he spat, catching a glimpse of greasy thinning hair and slight shoulders. Some crewmen mustered the energy to call out after the boat, their angry words echoing uselessly across the gently swelling water. "Didn't see that one coming," he muttered, forcing himself to move. There was more to the lapdog than met the eye. Grimacing at the unexpected development, he lowered his body through the hatchway and made his way toward the brig, his limbs moving with greater urgency with each imagined stroke of the boat's oars.

Raphael opened his eyes, tentatively shifted his body from under a pile of debris. Lungs still rattling painfully in his chest, he clambered to his feet and gawked helplessly at the unfolding chaos. Fragments of wood and metal littered the deck, and the Pretty Peg wasn't moving at all. No, she was moving alright, he silently corrected as his bleary eyes focused on where the bow used to be. As if on cue, the deck shuddered violently beneath his feet, and he dropped to his knees. "Mel? Sarah?" he croaked, eyes desperately searching the debris. "Mel!" he cried hoarsely, crawling over to the familiar dark head jutting out from under a long section of bow. Fighting the gradual sinking motion of the Pretty Peg, he heaved the wood off her prone figure, the murmuring cries of Sarah and Daniel faintly reaching his ears over the steady gush of water entering the hull.

"What, what happened?" Sarah stammered, unfolding herself from the railing.

"Sarah, are you alright?" he called out, looking up from Mel's oddly peaceful face. Ignoring his frantic question, she frowned at Mel, started to stagger across the sloping deck.

"Is she alright?" she asked, her movements stiff with pain.

"She's fine," he lied tightly, spying Daniel's curly head near the mast. "Go and help Daniel," he ordered thickly, nodding at the boy. Sarah followed the direction of his nod, rushed over to the stirring boy. "Come on Mel, time to wake up," he muttered, shaking her shoulders. "Please Mel," he cried past the lump in his throat, framing her still face in his hands.

The loud, gut-wrenching creak of splitting timber drowned out his impassioned plea, and before he could even glance up to see what was going on, the stern pitched up into the air, and he was sliding helplessly down the deck. With a bone-jarring jolt he hit the water, the Pretty Peg tugging him under the water's surface in a deadly embrace. Something floated past him, offering less resistance to the cutter's pull than his desperately struggling body. As his eyes adjusted to the blurry environment, he recognized Mel's pale face. He shrugged off his coat, dived down into the shadowy depths. Straining every muscle in his body, he managed to reach her, grab her arm. Using the last of his strength, he swam toward the surface, heart seeming to slow with each desperate kick, Mel's body a dead weight hanging off his arm. Finally, he broke the surface of the water with an explosive release of air, his lungs feeling as though they were on fire.

"Father!" He turned toward the source of the scream, saw Sarah paddle toward him, a large precious piece of hull gripped under her arms. Daniel paddled alongside her, face pale with fear as he clung to the wood.

"Good thinking Sarah," he spluttered, struggling to keep both his and Mel's head above the water. He started to move toward them, changed his mind mid-stroke. Legs feebly kicking beneath him, he struck out toward a large hull fragment floating only a couple of metres to his right. Only a couple of metres, he thought grimly, and yet it felt like the greatest distance in his life.

He was in the process of pushing Mel's torso onto the bobbing wood when fresh cries scraped across his nerves. Turning around, he followed the direction of Sarah's trembling outstretched hand, the bitter taste of bile filling his mouth as his water-logged eyes focused on the approaching boat. After all they had been through, to be captured by Sebastian now... Muttering darkly under his breath, he gave Mel's body a final push, gingerly positioned his body next to hers on the wood. "Mel," he croaked, shaking her shoulder, "time to wake up. We, we need your help." His eyes strayed to the hessian sack tucked firmly into the top of her trousers. "I wish I didn't have to rely on you all the time, whimpering for help like a helpless puppy," he added thickly, awkwardly stroking her bedraggled hair.

A faint murmur escaped her lips, and he eagerly leant over to catch her voice, heart absurdly filling with hope. "I, I won't let them...hurt you, Raph," she whispered, eyelids fluttering wildly as she struggled to regain consciousness. She lifted her head off the soggy wood and squinted at the oncoming boat, hand hovering over the sack. "The enemy of my enemy..." she rasped before passing out again.

"The enemy of my enemy?" he echoed, voice brimming with uncertainty.

"Father, what are we going to do?" asked Sarah unevenly, eyes bright with unshed tears. He looked across the swelling water at his ward, marvelled that she still appeared to have some fight left in her.

"I think," he offered wearily, his arms slowly losing their purchase on the hull piece, "that everything will be alright." The sound of oars cutting through the water reached his ears now, accompanied by oddly loud voices. Wriggling back onto the wood, he draped a protective arm over Mel's unmoving body. Squinting through the glare, he watched the boat's steady approach, his jaw loosening as it came to a stop beside him. "Is this what you meant, Mel?" he wanted to ask, but he couldn't push the sound past the sudden lump in his throat as he gawked at the familiar face peering down from the side of the boat.

"Please, Raphael," began Jenkins awkwardly, holding out his hand, "take my hand. We don't have much time."

Alyce woke up with a start, the abrupt shaking of the ship's side knocking her off the painfully narrow bench. The soldier assigned to watch her jumped to his feet, rubbing the sleep from his eyes. "What the blazes!" he cried, running for the door. "I'll be right back," he mumbled with a backward glance.

"No, wait!" she called as he disappeared into the passageway. "You can't just leave me here!" she shouted hoarsely, gripping the bars of the brig. The floor beneath her feet suddenly shuddered, and the whole room tilted sideways. "Oh no," she murmured as the sound of rushing water filled her sensitive ears. Judging from the volume, there was now a substantial hole in the side of the ship.

Frantically she pulled on the bars, thinking of all the unpleasant things she'd like to do to Sebastian and his cronies for caging her up like a beast. She'd played along in order to facilitate the voyage across the channel, even though every fibre of her borrowed being resented it. Her presence was obviously unsettling the crew, and they had provided such sound reasons for her incarceration. But being trapped in the brig of a sinking ship hadn't been part of the deal, she thought furiously as she pulled with all her might. The weathered metal frame started to creak as the jagged edges of the bars slowly gave up their purchase on the wood.

She paused to catch her breath, head resting heavily on the bars. Damned drugged food, she cursed silently, feeling the compartment swirl around her. Unfortunately, she had gulped down almost half of the thin stew before she noticed the faint, odd smell and taste. Not content with locking her up, they also sought to sedate her. She was sure they had a perfectly logical reason for that too.

Swallowing back a wave of nausea, she wiped her clammy forehead and strained against the bars again. Her sweaty palms slipped on the worn metal, and she fell over backwards, the force of the impact jarring her already addled brain. She propped herself up on her elbows, eyes slowly refocusing. "No," she croaked, suddenly recalling the symptoms of death cap poisoning. She had witnessed its affects first-hand on several occasions in her line of work. "It's just so easy to slip it into someone's food," Jenkins had told her one time, his face tight with anticipation as they searched the busy tavern for their target. "Cut it up really fine, and you can generally mix it in someone's food without detection," he murmured, patting the pouch hanging off his belt. "And because the symptoms initially resemble your everyday, run-of-the-mill food poisoning, people don't pay it much mind until it is too late," he had expanded calmly, digging his fingers into the pouch in preparation for the job.

"Jenkins," she spluttered, twisting around as her stomach suddenly heaved. Raising a trembling hand to her mouth, she rolled away from the spreading puddle of vomit and clambered to her feet. "But why?" she murmured, the sound of her raw, raspy voice the only comforting thing in the cell. Was he eliminating his London contacts as a blanket measure, or did he suspect her true identity? Either way, it was an ominous sign. "Come on Alyce," she grunted, staggering over to the bars. "Got to...get out...of here," she wheezed, pulling on the rusty frame with all her might. Blinking away the sweat that rolled into her eyes, she strained against the metal, flakes of rust digging into her hands. For all her effort, the bars didn't budge, and she slid to the floor, the bitter taste of vomit and defeat filling her mouth.

"So, this is how it's going to end," she mumbled, the sound barely escaping her stiff, numb lips. No second chances this time. "Sorry Clay," she whispered, awkwardly patting her borrowed body. Something within her stirred, and an angry grey face floated before her mind's eye, misshapen puffy lips pulled back in a snarl. "I said I'm sorry," she cried, shaking her head against the vision. Clay's face faded away, to be replaced by that of her father, cold, disapproving eyes boring into her. "So much for revenge," she sighed as even the memory of her father crumbled away. The walls of her stomach tightened, and she hastily leant forward to obey her body's urgent call. Her arms trembled with the effort of supporting her upper body, and she slipped over, falling face-first in the pool of vomit. All strength deserted her, and so she stayed on the floor, waiting patiently for the end as waves of pain washed over her. "How pathetic," she muttered thickly, salty tears leaking out of her eyes, to catch in the thick leather casing of her goggles. A loud creak penetrated her clouded, pain-ridden brain, and she gazed up in amazement at the pale, tall angel with wiry blonde hair standing in the doorway.

"Alyce!" the angel shouted, rushing to the lock on the cell door.

"Gunthar," she croaked as her vision cleared.

"Why haven't you broken out of here?" he asked, extending his fingers over the keyhole. A moment of concentration, and then the tumblers inside the lock clicked together and turned.

"Jenkins poisoned me," she spat through the acidic taste of vomit.

"What? When did he find time to do that?" Gunthar snorted as he surged through the door.

She felt her jaw slacken at his flippant response, distractedly accepted his outstretched hand. "What do you mean by that? You're not surprised he poisoned me?"

"Nothing about Jenkins would surprise me right now," he grunted, firmly planting his feet as she stiffly stood up. "Your ex-mentor is on his way to the Pretty Peg as we speak, without

Sebastian snapping at his heels. And do you really think he intends to bring the Mirror back to the ship?"

Even without the poison coursing through her system, Alyce suspected she would have felt very cold at that very moment. "Then, he's working for someone else," she concluded thickly, releasing his hand. "Damn, I should have picked up on that."

"Ah, there's no time for that. We've got to go after them while Sebastian's temporarily incapacitated," Gunthar said sternly, moving towards the door. "Serves him right, firing so close to the Pretty Peg..."

Alyce shook her head at his garbled voice, opened her mouth to ask for clarification, when she lurched sideways into the bulkhead. "Sorry Gunthar," she mumbled, swallowing back another wave of nausea. Her knees crumbled beneath her, and she sank to the deck again. "The poison," she murmured, the edges of her vision turning grey as she fell forward. With a muttered curse Gunthar swooped in and somehow caught her lumbering mass, eased her body gently to the floor.

"Damn you Jenkins," he hissed, placing a hand on her sweaty brow. He frowned at her pale, clammy face, took a steadying breath. "Here goes nothing," he mumbled, closing his eyes. The skin under his hand heated up as he channelled energy into her body, beads of sweat forming on his own brow. With a noisy intake of breath, he felt the energy surge through her blood stream, felt the faint tug of nearby organs, as though a fragment of his consciousness had splintered off and joined the energy. Suddenly his giddy passage came to an abrupt halt, and he felt something dark and ominous floating just before him. Swallowing nervously, he pushed at the darkness. Ignoring the frantic beating of his own heart, he pushed and pushed until the darkness enveloped him, the thick, dank walls of the poison closing in. He cried out, harnessed every shred of energy the alien shard in his body had to spare, released it.

"Gunthar? Gunthar?!" The urgent gravelly voice was accompanied by a giant hand shaking his shoulder, the pudgy fingers digging innocently into his flesh.

"Ow, Alyce," he whined, opening his eyes, "that really hurts."

"Oh, sorry Gunthar," she mumbled, sitting back on her heels as he sat up.

"I passed out?" he prompted, rubbing his face.

"Only for a couple of minutes, as far as I can tell," she supplied, peeling away the goggles to expose her dark, unnatural eyes. "Um, thank-you for saving my life."

He stared into the black pools, hastily looked away as he felt his cheeks redden. "Sure," he answered thickly, getting to his feet. "Now let's get out of here." Alyce pushed the goggles back over her eyes, scrambled to join him at the door.

"So, what's the plan?" she panted, leaning heavily on the door frame only to recoil as the timber creaked under her weight. With a faint frown in her direction, he stepped out into the deserted passageway.

"Well, I figure our best option is to swim after them." he answered distractedly, trying to remember the way to the cargo hold. Curse Sebastian for keeping him on the prow most of the time, to act like some whacky divining stick.

"Swim?" she echoed hoarsely, her throat suddenly dry.

His head swung around at the timid tone in her voice. Funny, he never imagined that the golem could sound so timid. There had been times when the original Alyce had laid into him, dragging him over the coals for some perceived wrong, and the golem would grovel accordingly. This however was different.

"Afraid of the water, are we?" he pressed, eyes narrowing at the golem's agitated hand movements.

"Yes, actually, we are," she snapped, wringing her hands together even more tightly.

"Listen, time is of the essence here. I can detect the Mirror, but distance is still an issue. If we don't go now, it'll be harder for us to track them down," he explained, stealthily creeping to the end of the passageway. "Trust me, we're not far offshore. We can swim there, no problem," he continued confidently, disappearing into a nearby storeroom. She shook her head, followed him with as much stealth as her huge body afforded.

"I've never been a good swimmer," she pointed out nervously, squeezing into the cramped, dusty space.

"Me neither," he responded cheerfully, starting up the wooden ladder in the corner of the room. "Can you make it through that?" he asked, nodding up at the neat square hatchway.

"I'll get through one way or another," she growled.

Wincing inwardly at the implications of her reply, he continued up the ladder, pushed his weary body through the opening. With a heartfelt grunt he stumbled to his feet, nearly crashing into a wall of barrels and sacks in the process. Willing his heart to stop its wild hammering, he peered cautiously past the edge of the wall, when suddenly there was a loud smashing sound behind him. Heart lurching painfully in his chest, he turned to see Alyce emerge out of the enlarged hole. Rolling his eyes, he abandoned all attempts at stealth, leaving the protection of the wall to saunter out into the cargo hold, Alyce's heavy footsteps close behind him. "Morning all," he called cheerfully, weaving his way through the maze of injured men and cargo, the two able-bodied sailors attending the wounded gawking up at them in astonishment. Noting grimly the two still, canvas-covered bodies in the corner, he came to a stop before the port-side wall. Growling a warning at the sailors, Alyce hovered behind him, the tension in her body pouring over him like a rain cloud.

"You know, Mel has actually done me a great service," Gunthar began conversationally, moving his hands over the smooth timber. "I was planning to disable the ship myself, you see," he explained when Alyce didn't reply, his hand pausing over a particular section of hull. "Admittedly, I would have done so a little closer to shore," he added with a faint frown. Studiously ignoring her sharp intake of breath, he pressed against the hull and summoned the Mirror fragment inside him. For a moment nothing happened, and he stopped channelling energy into the oily wood, thinking he had miscalculated. He was about to start scanning another section of hull when a high-pitched creak scraped his already-raw nerves, and he watched through squinted eyes as a long crack formed before him. Finally, the creaking stopped, and a long vertical sliver of light burned into his retinas.

"What the hell are you doing Gunthar? How exactly does this help us?" Alyce fumed, grabbing his shoulder.

"Ah, this is where you come in, my dear," he purred, smoothly stepping around her. All too late she noticed the smirk on his face, and before she could splutter any protest, he rammed her unsuspecting body toward the crack. Like a great, living boulder she smashed through the weakened section, chunks of wood digging into her arms and legs as she fell towards the water. With the elegance of an elephant, she did a bellyflop, her screams swallowed by the sea. She pried her eyes open, stared out into the murky water, her limbs frozen with fear. Suddenly there movement beside her, and she twisted around in panic. Blonde wavy hair floated up before her face, and then Gunthar was grabbing her arm, kicking like crazy for the surface. Shaking her head, she forced her legs to move, and then with an explosion of pent-up air they broke through the surface.

"Damn it Gunthar!" she spluttered, wriggling desperately to keep her head above water, "I'm going to straighten that kink in your neck for this."

"Why, thank-you Alyce," he spluttered back, "but let's get to land first, eh?" With that, he stretched out and began to claw his way through the water.

"Didn't you hear me before?" Alyce screamed, lashing out at the German as he swam past. "I can't swim very well," she panted, her voice breaking. She stared at his dwindling form, her huge limbs working hard to tread water. "You're going to pay for this, Bliesch," she grumbled, and she dipped below the water's surface to thrash awkwardly after Gunthar. After a couple of timid strokes, she started to stretch out more, her massive arms clawing the water in a passable approximation of swimming. While her head still swung about clumsily, gulping air and water to varying degrees, at least she wasn't sinking to the bottom of the sea. With an absurd grin tugging at the corners of her mouth, she caught up to Gunthar, quietly marvelling at the sensation she was feeling. It must be an after-effect of the poison, she reasoned as she spat out some salty water. How could this possibly be enjoyable? She chanced a look at the clear blue sky, felt that stupid grin tugging at her mouth again. Perhaps this little taste of freedom after being locked up was going straight to her head. The freedom must have gone straight to Gunthar's head too, she noted wryly, glimpsing the same idiotic grin on his face through the splashes of water and head-turns.

"So, Monfils and Bontems are gone too."

Not knowing where to look, Richard Gasquet nodded his head, mumbled an appropriate reply. He had never seen Sebastian look so wounded, the disappearance of Jenkins and the two men hitting him hard. A quick search of the ship, coupled with the fact that one of the row boats was missing, all but confirmed Jenkins had willingly left the ship. Whether the men were merely roped into helping him, or if they had been working with him the whole time remained to be seen. "Dammit, how could he react so quickly?" Sebastian cried, slamming his fist into a nearby bulkhead, his frustration bubbling to the surface. Feeling heat rise from his cheeks, Gasquet glanced away, fighting the sudden, absurd desire to giggle at Sebastian's angry, contorted face.

"And now they tell me Gunthar and the golem have escaped, making another hole in the ship."

Sobering at the fresh news, Gasquet pulled back his shoulders, straightened his grimy jacket. "Yes sir. By the time we were alerted, they were out of range of our weapons..." His stiff, formal report was disrupted by a sudden outburst of giggling. His jaw dropping halfway to the deck, he stared on in disbelief as Sebastian slowly sank to the ground, sides shaking with uncontrollable laughter. Feeling the heavy, unamused gazes of nearby crew members, he moved to Sebastian's side, frowning at the nasty graze on his forehead.

"Ah, perhaps you should get that looked at, sir," he suggested quietly, warily glancing around the deck. With a satisfied grunt he noted blurs of motion as several onlookers quickly looked away.

"Ha ha, don't worry Captain, I'm not seriously hurt," Sebastian assured him breathlessly, staggering to his feet. Beaming brightly, he began to look around the deck. "Now where the devil is Holister? We need to discuss our plans..."

"What the...You can't be serious sir," he stammered, his mask of discipline slipping. "I somehow doubt the captain will be very amenable to any requests we make right now, with his ship broken and all. It's more likely he'll throw us overboard..."

"Richard," Sebastian called stridently over his rambling, "relax. We're still in this race."

His lips moved silently, the words struggling to escape his dry throat. "How can you say that?" he finally croaked, his face creased with doubt.

"Stop looking at me like that," Sebastian growled, gripping his shoulder. "Now that Jenkins has revealed his true nature, we can anticipate his next move."

"So, we're not going after them?" he asked incredulously, stiffening under Sebastian's claw-like grip. Snorting contemptuously, Sebastian released him, urgently dug out his map.

"That would be a complete waste of time," he murmured, eyes glued to the faded lines on the map. "And completely unnecessary, as I know where he's headed."

"Oh, good," Gasquet murmured dryly. As per usual, Sebastian was prancing several steps ahead of him, racing to outlandish conclusions with utter confidence. Envying his absurd self-confidence, he nodded and mumbled encouragingly as Sebastian outlined his prediction, slender finger jabbing furiously at the map. "How can you be sure Jenkins is working for the other side? Couldn't he be working for one of your opponents?" Gasquet pressed, rubbing his head against the sudden throbbing at his temples. Listening to Sebastian plot and scheme would give anyone a headache.

"Ha, none of my French enemies have enough money or clout to buy off Jenkins. Jenkins may be a back-stabbing piece of slime, but he has rich standards. No, the Russians must have made him an offer he couldn't refuse..." His voice trailed away, face momentarily clouded as he stared into the distance. "Right," Sebastian said with a start, stirring himself into action, "see to the men Captain, I'm going to find Holister and get things organised." He stared after Sebastian, all too aware that his facial muscles were out of control right at that moment. An abrupt obnoxious call startled him out of reverie, and he looked over at a seagull that had just settled on the railing.

"He's completely mad, you know," he confided to the bird. Black beady eyes regarded him, quickly lost interest when no food was apparent. With a fluff of its feathers the seagull departed, and he was left to contemplate the sequence of events alone. "And apparently I'm not much better," he added, forcing himself to move.

Chapter 5
The enemy of my enemy...

12 August, 1812

Day five since our questionable rescue by Jenkins, and all is not well. While we have for the moment escaped Sebastian's clutches, I sometimes question whether it was for the better. Under Jenkins' supervision, we have largely spent our days huddled in an old rickety coach, hurtling through the countryside as though the very hounds of hell were snapping at our heels. Father seems certain that we have passed through France, and are currently making our way into Germany. He tries so hard to put on a brave face, and yet there is a pain behind his eyes whenever his gaze wanders over to Mel's absorbed face. Thinking about Mel fills my own heart with doubt. What is she thinking, allying herself with a man like Jenkins?

If the sinking of the Pretty Peg was a nightmare, then what we endure now is a bad dream. We all have at best patchy memories of what happened immediately after our rescue. I can vaguely remember being carried over cobbled paths through a strange town, slipping in and out of consciousness until at last I awoke in a hotel room. Both Father and Daniel were slumbering in narrow beds beside me, but Mel was nowhere to be seen. Eventually soldiers came and delivered food and water, their wary, brief presence offering no answers to our many questions. It was some time after breakfast that Jenkins entered the room with Mel in tow. Jenkins then proceeded to explain his position, that he in fact worked for a secret government organisation and was actually trying to keep the Mirror away from Sebastian. If he expected Father to be impressed, he was sorely disappointed. If those soldiers waiting outside had not burst through the door when they did and pulled Father away, I am sure Jenkins would have died right there and then. Clutching his throat protectively, Jenkins declared that he had a coach waiting for us, and with a sideways glower at Mel stormed off.

It was then that I noticed the fear in Mel's eyes. She struggled to make eye contact with any of us, and her movements as we prepared to leave were distracted, restrained. Amid reassurances that this is for the best, she herded us downstairs and into the waiting carriage. While she rides with us every day, and on the surface acts normal, I can tell that something eats away at her, the doubt and concern shining through the occasional crack in her armour. More often than not her hand drifts over to the hessian sack still tucked into the waistband of her pants, to twitch and fidget in the most telling fashion. As I said to Father the other day during one of our rare breaks, she is still like a piece of glass, although some frost has gathered on the smooth surface. With a bitter laugh he agreed, his gaze wandering over the other side of the clearing where Mel stood by herself.

One small consolation is that we only have to tolerate Jenkins' company in small doses. The soldiers also seem to be maintaining their distance, although I'm sure they would spring into action if we attempted escape. Oddly, this disturbs me. What deal did Mel strike with this oily, treacherous man? She seems to think she has guaranteed our safety, but how does racing across the continent towards an impending battle make us safe? I asked her this very question one day when the bouncing of the carriage combined with her far-away looks out the window pushed me past breaking point. In the heavy silence that followed, she stared at me, eyes suddenly bright with unshed tears. "Trust me Sarah," she said thickly, roughly rubbing away tears, "I'll make all the monsters and bad people go away."

"Is that what the Mirror tells you, Mel?" Father asked, anger creeping into his voice.

"The Mirror?" she echoed, gawking helplessly at him. "Well, yes, I explained all that before," she stammered, squirming under his hard gaze.

"You've told us that the Mirror showed you things about Jenkins, and the people he works for, as you put up that barrier around the Pretty Peg. You used that information to make a deal with him, and somehow that makes everything okay, but still, there's something you are not telling us," he accused, wagging a finger at her. "For God's sake woman, let us help you!" he cried, leaning toward her. The air between them seemed to thicken as Father gazed earnestly at her. "Let me help you," he croaked.

"Raph," she murmured, trailing trembling fingers over his cheek, "it's not that easy..."

At that moment the carriage came to an abrupt stop, and Father fell heavily into Mel. In between looking around like a startled rabbit and shouting out to the driver, I caught glimpses of Father reluctantly lifting his body off Mel. With a strangled cry Mel reached out and grabbed Father, pressed her lips into his. Just then Jenkins poked his greasy head through the window and announced we were taking a brief rest, and Mel jerkily broke away. For the rest of that day, Mel rode in gloomy silence, head bent over a small pile of papers that Jenkins had given her during the break, the tip of her lead pencil moving steadily over the coarse surface. When she caught my stare, she promptly handed me a couple of sheets, dug two pencils out of her pocket. "Practice your writing," she ordered curtly, holding out a pencil. "You too, Daniel," she added, turning to the perplexed boy.

And so, I am making a record of these strange events, in the vain hope that I will one day understand it all. I wish I knew what Daniel is scribbling about. Every day he sits opposite me, our knees often bumping together in the closed confines of the carriage, and yet he feels so far away. Poor boy has been rather shell-shocked since the Pretty Peg went down, giving largely monosyllabic responses when spoken to. I was surprised therefore when he eagerly took the paper and pencil and immediately started writing. He is obviously feeling guilty about leaving his parents, and must truly rue the day he decided to follow our trail. I was so happy when we discovered him aboard the Pretty Peg, was so happy to have the chance to see him again. How unbelievably selfish I was. Now I would give everything I have to send him home. Of course, it is not clear to me why Daniel hasn't been sent home..."

"Damn," Sarah cursed, frowning at the broken lead on the paper.

"Don't swear," Raphael ordered without taking his eyes off the map on his lap.

"Sorry Father," she mumbled, brushing the offending tip away. "Can I borrow your pocketknife again?"

With a sigh of resignation, he shoved his hand into his pocket, dug out the small collapsible knife. "Try not to break the lead this time," he grunted.

"Yes Father," she responded meekly, turning her attention back to the lines of scrawl stretching across the page. She would soon have to ask Mel for more paper at this rate. Somehow, she doubted there were enough sheets in that pile to last the entire trip, she mused with a frown. As though reading her mind, Mel looked up from her own writing, peered along the seat at the crowded page on her lap.

"Don't worry, I can ask Jenkins for more," she said cheerfully, pencil stirring in her hand.

"Oh, good," Sarah replied with a tight smile. Willing her facial muscles to relax, she tried to think of something to say before Mel returned to her writing and effectively shut everyone out. "Ah, could you check this later, Mel?" she asked, waving the paper.

"Yes, check my work too, please," Daniel cried, head shooting up at the mention of help. "I really want to send this letter off at the next town..." His words faltered as a wall of shocked faces suddenly confronted him.

"I knew it," she hissed, slapping her thigh. "Do you want any help with that, Daniel," she offered eagerly, leaning forward to squint down at his wavy, uneven writing.

"No!" he cried, snatching the page away from her prying eyes.

"Why not?" she pouted, straining forward even more. "Come on, I want to help..."

"Ah, no, that isn't necessary," he asserted, holding the letter out of reach as her hand darted out.

"Oh come on Daniel, just let me have a peek..." Her voice trailed away as realisation hit. "There's something about me in that letter, isn't there?" she accused, straining more ardently against his warding hand.

"Mel, help me," he cried as she started to clamber over his resisting body.

"For goodness sake," Father muttered, rescuing the letter from her eagerly out-stretched hand.

"Father," she protested as he wordlessly handed the letter to Mel. With a faint scowl in her direction, he went back to studying his map. "So, what does he say about me?" she asked, tugging on Mel's sleeve as she endeavoured to proofread Daniel's work.

"Really Sarah, as if Daniel would have anything bad to say about you," she murmured, a frown settling on her features as she struggled to read his writing. "Please stop tugging on my sleeve," she added calmly, her eyes never leaving the page.

"Hmph," she snorted grumpily, crossing her arms. "If that's the case, why won't he let me read it?"

"Come on Sarah, the lad is entitled to some privacy," Father grumbled, folding up his map. "On the subject of privacy, isn't there a danger that Jenkins will read the letter?" he asked, his voice deceptively casual. Despite her dark mood, she looked up from her sullen study of the floor to watch Mel's reaction.

"No," Mel blurted, shoulders stiffening. "No," she repeated more evenly, eyes sliding away from the curious gazes that now met her flustered face. "I made him promise...there's to be no censoring of communication."

"Do you really trust him not to spy on us, Mel?"

Mel reluctantly glanced up at Father, hand curling on the paper. Her jaw moved, and yet her voice refused to come out. "Yes," she eventually croaked, turning her attention back to the letter. "He has no need to spy on us." In the thick cloying silence that fell over the cramped space, she smoothed the slightly crumpled page, handed it back to Daniel with an apologetic smile. While Mel and Daniel resumed writing, seemingly oblivious to the turmoil that hung like a heavy cloud inside the carriage, Father sat very still, his face unreadable. As if feeling her gaze upon him, he threw a dark look at his ward, the agitation he was feeling blazing out at her like the midday sun on a clear day. With a sympathetic glance at Mel, she went back to her writing. She could tell Father was fast running out of patience. Apart from a few outbursts, he had gone along with Mel's plan, such that it was, even though his skin obviously crawled at the continued association with Jenkins. "Poor Mel," she clucked softly under her breath as she returned to her journal. She was really going to cop it next time she found herself alone with Father.

Raphael pressed his body hard against the wall, strained to catch the tense words flying between the two people inside the room. "Please Jenkins, let them go. How many times do I need to say it? You don't need to force my co-operation," Mel pleaded, desperation creeping into her voice. The sound of footsteps reached his ears, and he instinctively flattened himself further against the wall.

"So you keep saying," Jenkins drawled loudly, making Raphael jump. His hands curled into tight fists as he imagined the greasy man not two feet away on the other side of the wall. "But I'm not entirely convinced," he continued, footsteps shuffling back to the other side of the room. Clenching a hand over his tight, aching chest, Raphael forced himself to edge closer to the door. "You see Mel, I find it so hard to believe that you are simply following the Mirror's orders. For goodness sake, it's a pile of broken glass. How can a pile of broken glass tell you what to do?"

"I explained all that," Mel sighed, her voice slightly muffled, as though she had turned away. "The Mirror is alive, even in its shattered state. Are you doubting the visions I shared with you?"

Raphael felt his blood start to boil at her words. He didn't like the idea of Mel sharing anything with a man like Jenkins. Just when he considered bursting into the room and tearing Jenkins apart, Jenkins cleared his throat. "No, I don't doubt the images you channelled into my mind," Jenkins replied, sounding almost vulnerable. Unable to help himself, Raphael carefully shifted his body over to the door and squinted through the small opening. Luckily for him, someone had left the door ajar, and he could just make out Jenkins' slightly hunched shoulders and back against the white-washed walls of the inn.

"What you showed me, that was definitely my son," Jenkins continued roughly, hand creeping to the dagger hilt poking out of its scabbard. "Poor lad looked so gaunt, they're obviously not feeding him enough. I, I still don't understand how they found him, after all the measures I took to protect his identity."

"Do you really think they'll give you back your son, when all this is over?"

Raphael held his breath, heart tearing at the concern in Mel's voice. How could she still have so much compassion in her, after everything that had happened?

"I don't know," Jenkins sighed, running a shaky hand through his thinning hair. "I'm not normally on the receiving end of such extortion. In my experience, it all boils down to personal whim, on how generous the one in control is feeling on the day. That is why I have to do my best, and why I can't let your people go just yet." With that Jenkins headed for the door, and Raphael pried his frozen body away from the opening, scurried back to the corner. Over the loud hammering of his heart, he caught Jenkins mumbled words as he left the room, trudged down the corridor. Did he just apologise to Mel?

Head swirling with confusion, he rested heavily against the wall, waited for the frantic beating of his heart to ease. "So, you were spying on me." Jumping at the abrupt voice right beside him, he looked up to find Mel smirking at him.

"Geez Mel," he wheezed, hand creeping to his chest. "You scared the crap out of me."

"Come on," she grunted, tugging at his sleeve, head suddenly swinging around. "Jenkins' men regularly float past here, to keep an eye on me." Biting his tongue against the many questions that sprang to his lips at that comment, he allowed her to drag him down the stairs. The background noise of drunken revelry steadily grew louder as they reached the bottom floor of the inn. Glancing nervously over her shoulder, she guided him away from the main area to a small dusty room near the kitchen. He followed her into the room, closed the door behind him. Blinking in the sudden darkness, he stepped cautiously around a wall of barrels, made his way between shelves crammed with supplies, the noise from outside fading with each step. In the sliver of moonlight that managed to penetrate the grimy glass of one small window, he could make out the top of Mel's head, came to a stop before her.

"So, how much of that did you overhear?" she asked, arms crossed over her chest.

Even as his eyes adjusted to the grainy light, he could tell without looking that she was scowling faintly in the shadows.

"Everything from when you pleaded to Jenkins to let us go," he answered stiffly, idly fingering the end of a nail protruding from the wood. If only he had a hammer... "This arrangement you have with Jenkins seems a little one-sided, Mel."

She made a muffled sound of frustration, leant heavily back.

"I thought the images of his son would provide me with enough leverage," she muttered, bouncing irritably against the wall. "I'm sorry Raph," she blurted, shaking her head. "I know it's been eating away at you, this so-called alliance with Jenkins. I just wanted to keep everyone safe..."

"Mel," he said roughly, shoving his hands in his pockets, "it's not that. I just hate the feeling that you are confiding in that piece of slime instead of me. Jenkins, of all people."

"It's not like I want to," she protested, pushing away from the wall. "Whenever I look at his face, I remember that night in the clearing...the way he attacked you..." Looking up from his uncomfortable study of the floor, he noticed her trembling hands.

"Hey, come on," he muttered, grabbing her hands. "We didn't exactly have much of a choice, with the Pretty Peg making its way to the bottom of the sea, and Sebastian still within striking distance." Trailing his thumbs over her palms, his eyes strayed to the lumpy sack dangling from her waist. "And at least you had more to bargain with when the time came to negotiate with Jenkins."

"Ah, sorry," she said thickly as his thumb encountered hard calluses. "My hands are still rough," she mumbled, pulling away. With a sharp intake of breath, he dug his fingers into her shoulders, pushed her into the wall.

"Stop running away from me," he growled, bending slightly at the waist to glower into her face. "Ever since we were plucked out of the water, you've had this barrier around you, keeping everyone out." Something inside him broke, and he buried his head in her shoulder. "It's driving me crazy Mel," he croaked into her neck.

For a handful of beats, neither of them moved, as though savouring this moment of weakness. Even the noise outside no longer reached them over the sound of their ragged breathing. "I'm sorry Raph," she said, voice barely scraping past the sudden lump in her throat as she slid trembling hands around his back. "I don't know what to do," she breathed, turning her head towards him. In the gathering darkness of the room her lips found his, arms tightening around him. All the feelings he had been suppressing erupted to the surface, and he clung desperately to her, mouth hungrily covering hers as the kiss deepened.

Somewhere in the distance he heard a door creak, accompanied by muffled grumbling and heavy footsteps. Only when a lantern was shone directly into their faces did they pull away from each other. "What the hell? You're not supposed to be in here!" the holder of the lantern screeched, the coarse voice grating his nerves. Squinting into the glare, he could make out the ample figure of the innkeeper's wife, wavy dark hair tied back into a messy bun, fresh flour marks adorning the front of her dress.

"Ah, excuse me," Mel mumbled, face turning red as she scurried away.

"Mel, wait," he cried, almost stumbling over the innkeeper's wife as he hurried after her.

With the old woman's coarse words ringing in his ears, he sprinted up the stairs, managed to grab Mel's hand before she escaped into her room. "Mel," he gasped between ragged breaths, ignoring her attempts to be free. "Don't just run away, we need to talk about this."

"I wasn't running away, that old woman scared me," she quipped weakly, the smile not quite reaching her eyes.

"Mel..."

"Sorry, bad joke," she stammered, wincing at the intense expression on his face. "Just, give me more time Raph," she continued, hand clenched tightly at her side. "I have to sort this out myself..."

"Sort out what?" he pressed, pouncing on the careless remark like a predator pounces on its prey.

"Er, it's nothing, really, just stuff the Mirror shows me..."

"Stuff?! What kind of stuff?"

"I can't tell you right now..."

"Oh, but you can talk to Jenkins about it, can't you?"

The accusation stopped her cold in her tracks, the vehemence in his voice cutting through to her heart. "No, Raph, it's not like that," she protested, words tumbling clumsily out of her mouth.

"Then tell me, what does the Mirror show you that has you so scared?"

Seconds ticked by ever so slowly as neither of them spoke, the tension in the corridor almost palpable. She opened her mouth to say something, anything, but the words refused to come out. With a muttered sound of disgust, he released her hand.

"Forget it," he sighed, pushing the hair out of his eyes. "We're only racing across the continent towards a potential battlefield. Take all the time you want Mel." Stiffly he turned away, disappeared into his room without looking back.

She called out his name, the faint vibration clinging to him as he closed the door firmly behind him. "No," he whispered to the dark room. Resting heavily against the door, he willed his limbs to stop trembling. "I am not chasing her this time," he told himself sternly.

Somewhere in the darkness Daniel murmured in his sleep, rolled onto his side. Floorboards creaking alarmingly underfoot, he crept over to his narrow bed, pulled off his boots. Despite his intense hatred for the man, he had to admit that Jenkins was not being stingy about accommodation. Apart from the first night when they were bundled into one room, they had been given two rooms to share. With a mixture of annoyance and relief, he had ordered Sarah to share with Mel, leaving him and Daniel to awkwardly occupy the same confined space night after night. "Like

I really had a choice," he grunted, glancing balefully over at the curled-up form in the next bed. While over the past week their relationship had become strained, he shuddered to think what Sarah and Daniel would get up to if they had enough time together alone.

"The same thing you and Mel might get up to," pointed out the sage little voice in his head. Snorting contemptuously, he lay back on the lumpy mattress, pulled the old blanket over his body. As his body grew heavy from exhaustion, and he slowly sank into the mattress, his mind replayed the passionate kiss they shared in the storeroom. She was finally opening up to him again, pushing aside her fear and doubt for one precious moment. "Damn stupid interruption," he muttered drowsily, wincing his annoyance as he saw the innkeeper's wife on the inside of his closed eyelids. The old woman's face faded away, and he drifted into a deep, dreamless sleep.

Squinting tired, gritty eyes against the harsh midday sun, he stumbled down the mountain path, scree and dirt shifting treacherously underfoot. Raphael and Sarah trudged on ahead of him, their shoulders slumped in exhaustion. Almost on their own accord, his eyes strayed to the leather pouch resting on Raphael's hip. A sense of longing swept over him as he pictured in his mind the pane of black glass nestling in the bag. Surely it was his turn to carry the artifact, he thought with a faint stirring of impatience. Was it his imagination, or was Raphael becoming more reluctant to hand it over? They had agreed to take turns carrying the Mirror, rotating every two hours. "That way, neither of us can become overly attached to it," Raphael had suggested with a self-assured grin. Suppressing a flicker of annoyance at Raphael's high-handed manner, he had agreed. All he had really cared about at that point was going home as quickly as possible.

How many days had passed since they uncovered the Mirror in that underground cave? Sorting through his fragmented memories, he counted four days. Apart from the initial jubilation of finding the Mirror and surviving the sudden collapse of the cave, tension in the group had been mounting. Correction, he thought bitterly, the tension between him and the others. While he couldn't fathom the connection the mis-matched pair shared, Raphael and Sarah were true partners in crime, hardly ever appearing to be at odds with each other. He on the other hand had entered this arrangement purely out of desperation.

Having spent most of his funds on buying scraps of information, he had little left for the actual expedition. And so, with everything to lose, he had put on his best face and suit and shamelessly prostituted his plan to any well-to-do gentleman he could find, drifting from one public place to another. By the time he spotted Raphael and his guttersnipe companion in the shadowy corner of a tavern, he had had a few drinks to soften the blow of so many rejections in the space of one evening. Feeling particularly obnoxious, he swaggered up their table, introduced himself with a flourish of sweeping hand gestures. It had felt like a dream, hearing the words of assent come out of Raphael's mouth after his fevered description of the fabled Mirror and his plan to find it. Indeed, he thought it had been a dream when he woke up the next morning in the tavern. Only after a large amount of yawning and stretching did he find the letter stuffed in his coat pocket, detailing the terms of their agreement.

And now they had the Mirror. Funny how all the gratitude he felt towards Raphael eroded with every discussion they had about the handling of the artifact. Had he always been so smug and overbearing? Yes, a little voice spoke up inside his head. You just didn't notice it. "Didn't notice it, eh?" he muttered darkly, shoulders stiffening as Raphael briefly patted the leather pouch resting against his hip. "Hey," he blurted unevenly, lengthening his stride to catch up to them. "Isn't it time for the change over?" he suggested, belatedly pulling out his watch.

"Really?" Raphael responded doubtfully, reaching for his own watch. "Surely it hasn't been two hours...it's only a couple of minutes past one. Didn't we swap over at 11:30?"

He stumbled to a halt, stared at Raphael's calm, vaguely quizzical face. "What are you trying to pull, Raphael?" he snapped, forcing his limbs forward again. "It was most definitely 11 o'clock. Since when did we have change-overs at the half-hour mark?!"

"Since you were slow in handing it over this morning, don't you remember?" Raphael spat back, moving the pouch out of the reach of his out-stretched hand. "Come on, it's not worth getting upset about, just wait a few more minutes..."

"If it's not worth getting upset about, why not hand it over?" he countered, ignoring Sarah's startled cry as he strained against Raphael's body.

"Get a hold of yourself man," Raphael warned, gripping his arm. "It's only a few more minutes, we have to be fair about this..."

"Don't talk to me about fair," he growled, shaking himself free of Raphael's hold. "Don't think I haven't noticed the way you and the little tramp look at me, whispering behind my back!"

"Hey!" Sarah protested, stepping out from behind Raphael, "who are you calling a tramp?"

Shooting her a warning look, Raphael positioned himself in front of her, reached behind him for her arm. "You've got it all wrong, we're just worried about you Gunthar. You've become so surly, almost biting my head off whenever the time comes for me to take the Mirror, and when you're not muttering to yourself, you're looking about like a startled rabbit, as though someone's calling your name. What's wrong man?"

The words bounced off his armour of twisted resolve, to fade uselessly into the still air. Funny, even the birds had fallen silent, he thought grimly, shifting his head slightly to catch a faint movement of air near his ear. "Hah, you're the one getting surly," he countered, nodding in agreement with the silky voice in his head. "What's this crap about being slow to hand it over? Maybe if you didn't nag me so much, I would have felt inclined to let you have it sooner."

"What? Gunthar, listen to yourself, you're sounding more paranoid by the second," Raphael accused, looking even more self-righteous than usual.

"Ha, you always have the answers, don't you Raphael?" he said thickly, staggering toward them. As he lurched forward, and the ground rushed up to meet him, the image of his mother's cold, disapproving face filled his mind. No matter how hard he tried, he could never make her happy. Wasn't that why he wanted to find the Mirror in the first place? He regained his balance, refocused bleary eyes on Raphael's wary face. "Ha," he laughed bitterly, pushing aside the mental picture of his mother, only to see the same disapproval in Raphael's eyes. "Fine, have it your way," he spat, turning away. At the edge of his vision, something glinted, and he quickly turned back in time to see Raphael's hand dart out toward the pouch. "Oh no you don't!" he snarled, throwing himself bodily at Raphael. With an explosive release of breath their bodies collided, limbs grasping and flailing almost simultaneously as they rolled together down the path. They bounced into something hard, and he squinted through dust and sweat to see Raphael groaning in agony beneath him.

"I know what you're up to, Raphael. Don't think I don't know!" he roared, wrapping his hands around the other man's throat. "It was your plan all along, wasn't it?" Somewhere behind him was a scream, closely accompanied by the shuffle of feet. Little hands gripped his shoulders, tugged at his arms.

"Stop hurting him, you lunatic!" Sarah screamed into his ear as she clambered onto his back. With a grunt of annoyance, he released Raphael's throat, reached around to dig long-fingered hands into her shoulder. Feeling all his anger and hatred bubble to the surface, he flung her small body to the ground.

"Sarah!" Raphael cried as he jumped unsteadily to his feet. "Sarah, are you alright?" he croaked between ragged breaths, skidding to a halt beside her unmoving body.

He stared at the crumpled figure on the ground, knees almost buckling beneath him as doubt seeped in through the chinks in his armour. Did he really mean to do that? As he stood there, jaw flapping uselessly in the wind, Raphael clambered to his feet. In a blur of violence, they grappled each other, their bodies jostling together along the edge of the mountain path. Without thinking, he stepped back in preparation for launching an attack when the ground suddenly gave way beneath him. Squinting up through the dust swirling about his head, he saw Raphael leaning over the side, hand reaching out for him. "Gunthar, take my hand!" Raphael cried, inching forward, knees balanced on the edge of the path. Feeling his body slowly slide down the scree-covered slope, he desperately lashed out at the out-stretched hand, muscles trembling with the effort. Just as his fingers came into contact with Raphael's hand, a sudden movement caught his eye. The flap of the pouch must have loosened during the scuffle, and now the shiny black surface of the Mirror glinted out at him from behind worn, dusty leather. "No!" he cried, shifting his hand toward the precious artifact. With that jerky movement he lost what little purchase he had on the slippery slope, and he began to fall, Raphael's voice ringing hoarsely in his ears...

"Gunthar, Gunthar!" a deep rumbling voice boomed at him, accompanied by a huge hand nudging his shoulder. He reluctantly pried his eyes open, blinked bemusedly at the great grey face peering down at him. Was it just his fevered imagination, or did he detect concern in those unnatural black orbs that served as the creature's eyes.

"God, it's been a while since I dreamt about that," he muttered, rubbing a hand over his rough, unshaven face. "Stupid dream," he added, willing his heart to stop pounding so violently in his chest.

"What are you talking about?"

"That fateful day on the mountain," he grunted, forcing his protesting body to move. "I used to dream about it all the time, always the same dream," he explained, voice muffled as he sat up. "But it was different this time. This time Raphael tried to save me..." Shaking his head as if to shake off his doubt, he tensed his body in preparation for standing up.

Sensing he was about to move, Alyce reached out to him. "Wait Gunthar, your leg..."

As if on cue, he cried out in pain, hand automatically going for his leg. "Damn it, why did I have to fall in that ditch?" he hissed, peering at the festering wound on his left shin. Over two inches in length, the deep gash was now puffy and red, with yellow puss oozing out the edges.

Swallowing back a mouthful of bile, Alyce hastily looked away, headed for the door. "I'll get you some water," she offered, a hint of green entering her grey complexion.

She unwittingly slammed the door behind her, and he was left to grunt awkwardly in the sudden silence.

Somewhere to his right, there was a polite cough, a faint rustle of movement. "You should really put something on that," a hoarse voice croaked from the shadows.

Gunthar looked over at the hunched figure in the far corner, shielded his bleary eyes against shafts of light entering the gloomy hut through cracks in the door. "Marcus? Is that your name?"

The hunched figure nodded, straining slightly against the ropes binding his hands and feet. "I've seen many a wound like that on the battlefield. If you don't put a poultice on it, the infection will only get worse."

"Ah, don't worry about it. Now that I'm fully rested, I... anyway, we'll be on our way soon," he stammered, silently cursing himself for almost blabbing about the Mirror. Way to go sunshine, he thought bitterly, gaze sliding away from the dirty, bedraggled owner of the hut. It's cruel to give people false hope.

Even though he had been slung over Alyce's massive shoulder at the time like a sack of potatoes, he did glimpse the poor fellow's face when she barged into the little hut. The blood had drained from his face near instantly, leaving unnaturally pale skin to frame dark, hallowed eyes. Shortly after engraving this image into his memory, he had passed out. Why Alyce had chosen to so far spare the man's life was a mystery. They had gone to great lengths to avoid being seen by anyone until this incident. Could they really afford to leave any living witnesses behind when Sebastian was no doubt turning the countryside upside down in search of them? While he baulked at the idea of killing someone in cold blood, Alyce surely had some experience with this kind of situation. At the very least she had tried to poison her stepmother when she was barely in her teens. He shuddered to think of the unsavoury acts she would have committed while working for Jenkins.

Still, he had watched her casually push a dagger into Mel's heart, the only signs of emotion being a flash of annoyance followed by a smug curling of the lips...

"Ah, I guess there's no point promising to never talk about this to anyone," Marcus sighed as though reading his thoughts.

"What?" he responded jerkily, willing the image of Alyce's cold, clinical face to fade away.

"You're going to kill me, aren't you?" the man accused, bitterness creeping into his voice.

"I, I really don't know Marcus," he answered lamely, shifting uncomfortably on the floor, old blankets bundled around his feet.

"Somebody is chasing you, right? The look of desperation on the grey one's face as it burst through the door said it all."

"Well, there ah, could be some people after us..."

"Although you seem to be following something too..."

"What? How could you?"

"You talked in your sleep," Marcus supplied with a tight smile.

Now that he had fully rubbed the sleep from his eyes, and stretched away most of his stiffness, he realised that this strange little man was much sharper than he looked. Really, he already knew too much...

"I could help, you know, scout things out in any towns you pass, buy supplies, that sort of thing."

Keeping his mouth firmly shut, Gunthar gingerly shifted his body so he was facing away from Marcus. As much as he hated to admit it, the man was right. They needed someone unknown to both sides to act as their intermediary. Closing his eyes, he rested his hand lightly over the festering wound, willed the alien energy within him to stir. The exhilaration of escape had quickly faded away in the harsh reality of traversing the choppy water separating them from land. Even with their newfound ability, it had taken every ounce of their will to reach the shore, where they both promptly passed out.

Ever since regaining consciousness, they had continued to push their bodies to the limit, following the thin, sometimes vaporous trail of breadcrumbs left in Mel's wake. Then while running away from an enraged farmer and his band of ferocious dogs, he had fallen into a ditch and badly hurt his leg. Alyce had hoisted him up onto her back and thundered through the forest, the ragged barking of the dogs echoing uncomfortably in their ears. Thank God they stumbled into that stream when they did, or the dogs would surely have caught up to them. Poor Alyce had then staggered along the muddy bank for what felt like an age, often slipping over into the icy cold water. When the little hut came into view, sun breaking through the forest canopy to beam down on the thatch roof, he had felt her body sag with relief. "God, all that for a couple of smoked fish," he muttered, recalling the act of theft that had led to their frantic flight through the forest.

Pushing aside his irritation, he channelled the alien energy into the wound, felt the skin beneath his hand heat up. He'd been sleeping on and off for the past twenty- four hours, and had something to eat, so surely he could heal himself now? The inside of the hut faded away as his consciousness joined with the Mirror fragment, floated inside his body. Creasing his forehead in concentration, he struggled against the flow of blood and fluids until a burgeoning spot of darkness appeared before him. Pushing against the tide, he approached the darkness, attacked it with every shred of energy he could muster. He must have passed out, for he awoke yet again to a giant hand gripping his shoulder, shaking his upper body as though he was a doll. "Alyce, cut it out," he whined, forcing his eyes to open.

"You should have waited," she cried, shoving a cup towards him, water slopping over the sides.

"Hmph," he grunted, propping himself up on one elbow. "I couldn't stand it any longer," he mumbled into the cup, downing the contents in a couple of greedy gulps. "What took you so long anyway?"

"There was an unusually loud noise coming from the road. I went to check it out," she answered with a shrug of her massive shoulders.

"What?" Marcus croaked, tearing his eyes away from the bucket of water now sitting in the corner of the room.

"Anything serious?" Gunthar asked.

"No, just a bunch of merchants setting up camp."

"You heard that?" Marcus marvelled, inching forward. "The road must be over a mile away…"

Making a sound deep in her throat, Alyce turned, raised her fist at the hunched-over figure. "Keep quiet old man, or I'll make you be quiet."

"Alyce, wait," he cried, leaning over to tug at the frayed hem of her over-sized shirt. "Marcus here has offered to help us…to act as an intermediary, so to speak." Through the thin material in his hand, he could feel her bristle at the suggestion. "Let's face it," he continued, bravely pushing forward his point, "no matter where we go, we stick out, which makes life very hard for us." He relaxed slightly as her expression softened and she took a step back from Marcus' hunched form.

"That's true enough," she grudgingly conceded, shaking off the hand that still clutched the hem of her shirt. "But how do you know we can trust this guy? He's obviously good at saving his own slimy neck." With surprising grace she crouched down, her great mass settling beside the man, casting an ominous shadow over his cowering form. "Hmm?" she murmured, reaching out to the tattered lapel of his jacket. "Where's your regiment, soldier? You're a long way from the battlefield, aren't you?"

Anger cut through his palpable fear, and he glared up into that strange, unsettling face. "Hey, I didn't run away, they left me for dead. It all happened so fast, we were ambushed…" His voice faded away as he remembered that bloody day, when a sea of red coats swept towards them, spilling over the Spanish horizon without warning. Within minutes they were overwhelmed, the English cavalry breaking through their lines with devastating results. Before he knew it, he was scrambling over the churned ground, the unmoving bodies of his comrades hovering at the edge of his vision as he struggled to get away from the deadly barrage of hooves and blades. Shots rang out overhead, accompanied by a familiar gruff voice, and he swung his head until he spotted the livid, snarling face of the captain at the edge of the field. If he could just make it to the Captain's side, he thought, spurring his clumsy feet to move faster.

That was the last thing he remembered before something connected with the back of his head and robbed him of consciousness. It was the faint creak of leather and shuffling of hooves that awoke him hours later, and he opened gritty eyes to see a couple of red coats leading their horses through the maze of dead bodies. With scarves tied firmly over their mouths, they methodically combed the battlefield for valuables, one hand half-heartedly waving away agitated flies while the other patted down corpses. Swallowing back his revulsion, he continued to lay still until they drifted out of sight. Then, with heart firmly lodged in mouth, he made his escape, limbs trembling as he forced himself to creep silently away. After what felt like an eternity, he reached the relative safety of the forest. Other than a few close calls avoiding the handful of soldiers patrolling the forest fringe, he limped on from tree to tree without incident.

Minutes stretched into hours, hours stretched into days, until he lost all track of time. At first, his one feverish thought was to find his regiment, to get back to the captain. Gradually however, with hunger and fatigue wearing him down, the captain's face faded from his memory, along with the faces of his comrades. Even before the attack, he had been surviving on basic rations for months. Trudging through that forest, he felt as though there was nothing left, and that he only put one foot in front of the other out of habit.

If hadn't been for the original occupant of this hut, he probably would have died months ago. The lonely old hermit had taken him in, tended to his wounds, shared what scant food he had. Marcus glanced down at his hands, blinked away the image of them wrapped around the old man's scrawny neck. For some reason, he couldn't remember what, the old man suddenly attacked him. He had just meant to slow him down, deprive him of air until he let go, but he must have squeezed too hard, the windpipe collapsing beneath his fingers…

"Ah, I'm sure we can find a way to ensure he doesn't try anything stupid," a laconic voice cut across his morbid thoughts, brought him cruelly to the present. He belatedly recognised Gunthar's voice as the golem's pasty face floated before him, dark grey lips curled in an evil smile.

"Ah yes, now that you mention it, I have just the thing," the monstrous creature purred, digging into the pouch tied around its waist. If he wasn't frozen with fear, he might have laughed at the sight of the golem sifting through the bag with its pudgy, oversized hands. Finally, it made a guttural sound of triumph, held up a shiny black stone between its thumb and forefinger. "Oh, the listening stone," Gunthar commented, a note of approval in his voice. "That's a great idea."

"Listening stone?" he repeated, the sound barely scraping past the suddenly tight walls of his throat.

"Yes," the golem answered with growing enthusiasm. "See, they come in pairs," it explained, producing another black stone from its bag of tricks. "I can hear everything within roughly 20 feet of that," it continued helpfully, holding up the first stone, "through this." He gawked in disbelief at the other stone Alyce held up, jaw flapping uselessly in the air as words utterly deserted him.

"So, we just have to attach the stone to Marcus somehow, and then we'll be able to hear everything that's going on around him," mused Gunthar, chewing thoughtfully on his thumb nail.

"Yes, but of course we'll have to make it so he can't easily be rid of it," Alyce pointed out matter-of-factly, as though they were discussing what to have for dinner.

"What, tie it around his neck or something? Maybe with a chain, if we make it tight enough..."

"Well, I do have a more permanent solution in mind," Alyce interjected with an almost sheepish grin.

"More permanent solution?" Gunthar uttered, blood draining from his face as comprehension sunk in.

Without warning, Alyce reached out and seized his throat, shoved him roughly into the wall. Out of the corner of his eye, he saw Gunthar move toward the belongings they had dumped on the floor upon their arrival, heart fluttering wildly as the gangly man extracted a long, rusty knife from the measly pile. He cried out, but Alyce already had a hand over his mouth, grey ominous face barely twitching as he kicked out desperately. Was that a flicker of sympathy he saw in the depths of those strange black eyes? Amid muttered curses, the golem reached yet again into the bag tied about its waist, pulled out an envelop. With some fumbling, it dipped its fingers into the envelope, wiggled them out again. He only briefly glimpsed the white powder coating the creature's fingertips before they were forced into his mouth.

"Don't worry soldier, we'll try not to kill you," the gravelly voice whispered in his ear as the drug took effect and all tension rapidly flowed out of his body. Not even the sight of the horrible knife approaching his side delayed his slide into unconsciousness.

Marcus clutched his stomach, gritted his teeth against the sudden pain. If he pressed hard enough, he could feel the small stone through the thin wall of skin and flesh. "Permanent solution my arse," he muttered, leaning heavily against a tree. Just thinking about what they did to him made him break out in cold sickly sweat. Hard to believe they had cut him open not an hour ago. He gingerly lifted up his shirt, squinted at the faint line across his abdomen. "Amazing," he breathed, lightly touching the new pink flesh. Before, when Gunthar pressed a hand over the festering wound on his leg, and then lifted it to reveal shiny new skin, he hadn't quite believed his eyes. Clinging to the hope that it was all a bad dream, he had attributed the vision to malnutrition, or too many bumps to his head. Now, looking down on the impossible scar on his own body, he was forced to believe.

"What the hell have I gotten myself into?" he croaked, not caring if they could hear his despair.

"What's to stop me from just running away?" he had cried after he finally came to, the newly-sealed cut still stinging like hell. "If I don't betray you, and just keep running, is it really worth your while to chase me down?"

"Ha," Alyce had laughed bitterly, her attention fixed on the dull blade as she wiped the knife clean on her trousers. "You underestimate how petty I can truly be, Marcus. That pebble we just implanted in you is a very valuable piece of kit. I want it back, eventually. So if you do betray us, I'll be sure to track you down and directly tear it out of your hide. Alternately, if you're a good boy and do as you are told, we'll extract it as neatly as possible, and take care not to kill you in the process. Right, Gunthar?"

Gunthar had vaguely nodded his head, murmured some encouraging words.

"You'll take it out?" he had stammered, a small flame of hope sparking to life within him.

"Well of course," Alyce had grunted, moving stiffly toward the water bucket in the corner. "We're not complete monsters."

While her sense of humour had left him feeling a little cold, he chose for the most part to take comfort from her words. "Her," he mused, pushing away from the tree, scrap of paper clenched tightly in his sweaty hand. While Gunthar openly referred to the golem as "Alyce", he couldn't decide at first if it was some grotesque joke, giving such a creature a girl's name. Maybe he'd learn the truth behind Alyce's identity someday. Shrugging his shoulders, he squinted down at the lines of tiny scrawl on the paper. "God, how am I supposed to get these supplies back to the hut anyway?" he muttered, turning slightly as the creak of wagon wheels faintly reached his ears. They were obviously planning to move on soon, if the list was anything to go by. Did they really intend to drag him along?

Soon he was on the road leading into town, and he nervously tugged the old hermit's coat about himself. Even in a remote village like this, he couldn't risk wearing his uniform. He'd only ventured into town once before, but that had been enough to get the locals suspicious of him. Whether or not his strange new companions intended to take him with them, he would never be able to return to this village after this job. Hell, the hut probably won't be safe for much longer, with the type of visitors he'd been receiving. He could just imagine it now, nearly the whole town charging toward the hut, pitchforks and axes at the ready.

In between nursing his still-tender side and evading any lingering gazes from the locals, he managed to get the supplies. If it wasn't for the handful of coins Gunthar had wordlessly passed onto him on his way out, he doubted his presence would have been tolerated at all. They had money then. If they weren't such an odd pair, and on the run, they could have lived in comfort for a good few months, if the coins he glimpsed in Gunthar's pouch were anything to go by.

"Well, may as well head back," he sighed, shoving the last item into the sack and shifting it carefully onto his back. His knees sagging slightly at the weight, he started to make his way out of the village. By the time he reached the inn at the edge of the village, he was forced to stop and re-balance the load, with various items sticking mercilessly into his back.

"Hey, did you hear about those men who came through town this morning?"

"No, what about it?"

He stiffened at the abrupt voices, head darting about to locate the source. Pressing his body into the wall, he shuffled to the corner, peered cautiously around. There, at the back of the inn, two men leant heavily against the wall, pipes in hand.

"Well, there was a heap of men on horseback, come galloping into town like they was on some rabbit hunt. Caused quite a stir it did," said the first man, hand waving about expressively, leaving a trail of curling smoke.

"What, soldiers?" the second man queried, curiosity vaguely piqued by the man's tale.

"Ah, they weren't wearing uniforms, but you could tell just by looking at them, they were well-practiced in some sort of soldiering."

"Really?" the other drawled, face closed in thought. "So what, they just rode through town without stopping?"

"Oh no, they stopped alright. They went around asking a heap of questions. Seems they're after some people…"

He stood frozen to the spot as the first man recalled with relish the descriptions the men gave. Two people, a tall slender man with blonde wavy hair and a permanent kink in his neck, and a giant with pale grey skin and black, fathomless eyes. The other man laughed nervously, commented that a pair like that would be hard to miss. Their words washed over him like a torrent of meaningless sounds, his mind reeling in fear. He knew they were on the run from somebody, but never imagined their pursuers would be so close.

"…somewhere down the river." Mention of the river jarred his attention back to their conversation, and he forced his jumbled mind to focus.

"But there ain't no one living out that way but the old hermit. Poor bugger's going to get a hell of a shock when all those men start pounding on his door."

With the men's gruff snickers ringing in his ears, he pushed away from the wall, jogged awkwardly into the forest, the sack bouncing painfully against his back. They must have heard that, he reasoned, feet slowing as the realisation hit him. Surely Gunthar and Alyce were out of the hut by now, and putting as much distance between themselves and the men as possible. "So what am I doing, exactly?" he murmured, collapsing against a nearby tree. It was too dangerous to go back to the hut now. Gunthar and Alyce would most likely being running away from the river, and the town, but beyond that, he had no idea where they'd plan to go.

Odd, Alyce went to investigate the road this morning, he recalled hazily, his feet moving on own accord over the uneven ground. Did she somehow miss the men? "No," he croaked, throat suddenly dry, hand creeping toward the shiny scar on his side. They may have lied about many things, but her heightened senses, they were real. Too many times while he was tied up in the hut, her head had swung about abruptly, nose and eyes twitching. Cocking her head to one side, she would close her eyes in concentration until the invisible, distant threat apparently passed. So, even if she had somehow missed the men's passing, she must have detected to some degree their movement.

Swallowing nervously, he glanced down at his hand, at the scrap of paper still clutched between his fingers. Blinking back tears of despair, he flung away the offending note. "Ha, you bastards," he muttered bitterly, sinking heavily to his knees. "Really, that's very clever," he breathed, curling up into a tight ball so that his mouth hovered above the listening stone. "Was this your plan all along?" he yelled, fists pounding the ground. Not long after that, a group of men on horseback approached from the direction of the hut. As soon as they sighted his slumped, listless body, they came to a stop. The men closest to him slid off their horses, grabbed him without hesitation. Hoisted between two men, with another poking him in the back with a weapon, he came face to face with a burly, battle-weary man.

"What should we do with him, Captain?" one of the men asked, fingers digging mercilessly into his arm as he spoke. "Captain?" he croaked, the image of his own captain floating to the surface of his murky memory. Straining his bleary eyes, he stared intently at the tough, granite-like face. "Captain," he sighed, pushing away the memory. The captain's eyes narrowed, body leaning forward a fraction as he took a closer look at the newcomer.

"We'll take him with us," Captain Gasquet finally uttered, stepping back. "Tie him to the pack horse, we have to meet up with Lord Sebastian in the next town." As he was hauled unceremoniously toward an agitated, over-loaded horse, he noted the tired, grumpy faces of the men as they listlessly followed orders. Tucking the observation away, he shrugged his shoulders, offered no resistance to the rough hands guiding him to the horse. It was time for him to move on anyway, he reasoned. Without warning, the men hoisted him onto the horse's hard back, the sudden impact forcing the air from his lungs. As he struggled to regain his breath, the men tied his hands and feet together, ran a rope between the bindings under the horse's belly. Swallowing nervously at their methods, he steeled himself for an uncomfortable ride.

"Go on boy, clear the gentleman's table, we ain't got all night." The boy squeaked words of acknowledgment, squared his slender shoulders. Father was already cranky enough about the mess he made in the kitchen, so he really had to shine for at least the next hour. Now wasn't the time to tell Father that the finely dressed man in the far corner of the inn had an alarming habit of muttering darkly under his breath. Keeping his eyes firmly fixed on a spot beyond the man's head, he murmured his usual "will that be all sir?", hoping feverishly to be sent away or just flat out ignored.

"Am I that uncomfortable to be around, boy?"

The boy froze at the direct question, forced his eyes to focus on the still, expectant face. With some jaw swinging he finally found his voice. "Ah, of course not sir," he stammered while desperately seeking the right words. "It's just, you ah, look like you've got a lot on your mind." A moment of tense silence, and then the man laughed, a harsh, hurried sound devoid of mirth.

"Ah, good answer, good answer," he sighed, waving a dismissive hand. Amid mumbled words of apology, the boy finished clearing the table and scooted away, nearly colliding into another table in his haste. Sebastian slumped back in his chair, remembered with a grimace the relief that had flooded the boy's face when he was sent away. "Am I really that uncomfortable to be around?" he repeated softly to himself, fingers tightening around the stem of the wine glass.

It was bad enough seeing the awkward pity in the eyes of his men, without having that same uneasiness reflected in some brat's face. For all his bravado that day on the Magnificent, after Jenkins' stinging betrayal and Gunthar's dramatic exit, he was at a loss as to what to do next. It was obvious to him that Jenkins had been made a better offer by a powerful competitor. What that offer could be, he had to wonder. He had always made a point of paying Jenkins well and giving him a certain amount of freedom. Hell, he even tolerated the hiring of those idiot brothers. While at times tense, their work relationship had for the most part been stable and healthy. There must have been something else…

Shaking himself from such circular thoughts, he set aside the wine glass, pulled out the now-grubby roll of material from inside of his jacket. Ever since that calamitous day on the Magnificent, he had kept the old map on him at all times. His fingers trembled slightly as he unrolled the cloth, traced the various paths he'd marked. "Right," he murmured, trying to inject enthusiasm into his voice, "if the latest stories are to be believed, the emperor has made his way into Russia, somewhere along the border." His finger lingered on the squiggly line representing the River Niemen. Ignoring the faint throbbing between his temples, he reached for the wine glass, took a generous sip. That was the original plan, to catch up with the emperor and present him with the prize. Now, without Gunthar's ability to sense the Mirror's presence, he had to somehow catch up to Jenkins to have any chance of regaining the artifact.

Leaning heavily on his elbows, he stared down at the map, the lines starting to swirl and blur into each other. On their own accord, his eyes strayed to a dot in the bottom left-hand corner. Squinting in the dull yellow light, he made out the tiny letters, breathed the name of the town. "Strasbourg." It was no mistake that his path was veering towards Strasbourg. While all his other options had abruptly deserted him, that was the one trump card left up his sleeve. "There's got to be another way," he sighed, leaning back in his chair, hand draped over his eyes. Michel would surely have the information he needed, directions that would lead him right to the enemy's camp. He was a high-ranking intelligence officer after all, working in the shadows to gain information of the emperor's enemies, and he had always shown an unhealthy interest in his younger cousin.

Right from the beginning, when they saw each other during his annual summer visits to the Seabast estate in Rouen, there had been a certain tension between them. At first, he'd been delighted that someone ten years his senior would pay him so much attention, especially at the expense of Raphael, whom Michel practically ignored. It did not take long however before he found the attention uncomfortable. Just little things at first, like the hand that would linger on his shoulder or the fingers that carelessly brushed his side or back. Gradually he came to distrust Michel's seemingly innocent offers to play in the fields, or go for walks, as the unwarranted touching got worse.

He should have seen it coming then, that day when Michel cornered him in the stables. The memory of that attack was still so clear, the way his body thrashed beneath Michel, Michel's cruel hands tearing at his clothes... Groping blindly from under that crushing weight, his hand had miraculously closed around an old horseshoe. The sickening sound of metal crunching bone, and he was free, scrambling out the stable without once looking back, hand still wrapped tightly around the horseshoe. It wasn't until sometime later that he managed to pry his stiff, paralysed fingers off the rusty curved iron.

The next couple of days after that had been pure agony. Unwilling to tell anyone about the incident, he struggled to act normally, all the while expecting some sort of retaliation from Michel. Once his sense of relief started to fade, he couldn't help but be curious about Michel's prolonged absence from their usual haunts. It was only then that he noticed the maids delivering food to his room, and his aunt hovering just outside the door, deep lines of worry etched into her beautiful face. That night he finally emerged from his room, where he had apparently been holed up in the whole time, to join the family for dinner. Bracing himself for their reunion, he had sat down at the table, facial features carefully composed into a smooth, impassive mask.

Even now, so many years later, he could remember the cold feeling of blood draining from his face when he saw the ugly wound on Michel's right temple, a crust of dried blood and mashed skin marking where the horseshoe had connected with his head. "So, what happened Michel? How did you hurt yourself?" someone asked, the clear voice cutting through his foggy senses, making him jump. At that point, Michel swung his head around and looked him straight in the eyes, blue irises flashing with anger. And then he smiled, looked away. "Oh, my horse got spooked by something, slammed me into a wall," he answered without hesitation. "Guess I should learn to be more careful around animals," he added, picking up his glass. Behind the dark wine, he could tell Michel was smirking at him.

After that, Michel treated him with polite distain, never seeking to spend time alone together, not even to abuse him for what happened. It wasn't until the day he was leaving to go back home to England when Michel grabbed him from behind, dragged him into a room. Clamping a rough hand over his mouth, Michel slammed him into the door, cold and unforgiving eyes boring into him. "Don't worry, I'm not going to try anything today," he snarled, pressing his body tightly against the door, hands like bands of steel digging into his shoulders. "But rest assured, I won't forget, can't forget, thanks to this," he bit the words out savagely, gesturing at the gash in his temple. "It'll scar nicely, for sure, so that every time I see myself, I'll be reminded of you."

With that, he swooped down like a bird of prey and kissed him hard, tongue mercilessly prying apart his stiff, resisting lips. Just as abruptly, Michel released him, rubbed a shaking hand over his mouth. "I know you Sebastian," he said, voice slightly muffled. "You hide your true nature from everyone, even your brother, but I can see the hunger in your eyes." Despite being free of Michel's grip, he couldn't quite muster the will to move, his cousin's words pinning him down. "I know it won't be long before you overreach yourself. When that happens," he continued in a silky voice, hand flying out to catch his unsuspecting chin, "I'll be waiting." The cold words washed over him, and he slapped the hand away, retorting something about when hell freezes over, almost tripping over himself as he rushed out of the room.

To his great shame, Michel's words that day proved prophetic years later when he was clawing his way through the family ranks. An opportunity to elevate himself before his father's critical eye arose when a number of valuable items mysteriously disappeared from the family vault. He'd suspected for some time that one of his older brothers had developed a serious gambling habit. Leon was often seen staggering home in the early hours of morning, reeking of smoke and alcohol. Everyone just assumed he was partying, and sure enough, he was frequently spotted at the usual clubs, sitting at a table surrounded by his followers, who hung around him like a cloud.

"Such effortless popularity," he mumbled into his glass, stretching out his long legs under the table as lethargy overwhelmed him. Looking out at the shabby interior of the inn, he felt so removed from that opulent setting, seven years ago. He had been getting ready to leave the club when he spotted Leon on the other side of the room, being led away by two imposing men. With his curiosity sufficiently piqued, he weaved his way through the crowd, somehow resisting the urge to snarl at the patrons who blundered into his path. Out of the main room, the crowds thinned, and he made his way more easily through the network of corridors that connected the smaller rooms at the back of the building. Just when he feared he'd lost sight of them, a familiar voice rang out, and he headed in that general direction, finally coming to a jerky halt in front of a plain wooden door, which looked out of place next to all the lacquered, numbered doors around it. Raised voices rang out again, and in the still air of the deserted corridor, he could clearly pick out Leon's agitated voice.

Putting his ear to the door, he strained to capture the heated exchange of words, now muffled as the speakers moved further into the room. His heart skipped a beat at the raw panic that was creeping into Leon's voice, his tone almost pleading as he assured the men he was "good for the money". Someone barked a harsh reply, sharply followed by the clatter of moving furniture and bodies. He was so engrossed in eavesdropping that he lost all awareness of his surroundings, so that when a heavy hand suddenly clamped down on his shoulder, he nearly jumped out of his skin.

Before he could scream out, another hand firmly covered his mouth, and he was roughly dragged away from the door. It wasn't until his assailant had wrestled his struggling body to the far end of the corridor that he had a chance to break free. Shaking off his assailant's hands, he spun around, fists drawn back in readiness for violence. All fight momentarily deserted him when he found himself face-to-face with Michel. At a sudden sound from the plain door, Michel grabbed his arm and pulled his stiff, shocked body around the corner. Peering past his cousin's shoulder, he glimpsed one of gruff men from before stepping out into the corridor, looking up and down with a belligerent glint in his eye. Seemingly satisfied that the corridor was deserted, the thug stepped back into the room, shut the door behind him.

Michel relaxed slightly, shrunk back a little further from the corner. In a raspy, lowered voice he explained how Sebastian's father had commissioned him to investigate possible suspects in relation to the missing funds. As Michel talked, his gaze was drawn time and again to the scar that was etched into his right temple, an odd mixture of bitterness and guilt stirring within him. "You suspect Leon?" he blurted, finally connecting his explanation with their current situation. Signalling for him to keep his voice down, Michel peered around the corner, relaxed slightly at the lack of any activity from the door.

"That's my line, isn't it?" he countered, regarding him through narrowed eyes. "Why else are you here, my favourite little cousin?" Flinching at his caustic words, he forced himself to meet Michel's sharp, predatorial gaze.

"You're not the only one capable of detective work, my lecherous big cousin," he answered waspishly.

For a moment, Michel's face darkened into an angry, dangerous mask, only to clear the next. With a faintly wolfish grin lighting his features, he placed a heavy arm around Sebastian's shoulders, made the proposition that would dramatically change his life. "I haven't reported this to Uncle Richard yet, seeing as I had no concrete proof, but now that I've traced Leon to one of the biggest crime gangs this side of Europe, it'll only take a little digging to get all the details. Why don't I just step back, and let you beat me to the post? That would mean a lot to you, wouldn't it, Sebastian?" It took a moment for the silky words to fully penetrate his foggy brain, for the opportunity that Michel was handing him so flippantly to register.

"Won't it look bad for you?" he asked, the words tumbling out of his clumsy mouth before he could stop them. Shrugging his shoulders, Michel had leaned back against the wall, studied him through impassive eyes.

"It's just another job for me," he sighed, sounding bored. "It's not like Uncle Richard won't use me again as his personal spy. Besides, you came here to investigate Leon on your own. Given a little more time, you would have stumbled upon the truth."

For a moment neither of them spoke, with only the muffled sounds of the party in the main room breaking the silence. Swallowing painfully past the sudden lump that was forming in his throat, he opened his mouth, croaked the inevitable question. In answer, Michel closed the distance between them, pressed his body into the wall. "What I want?" Michel grated, closing one cruel hand around his neck while the other continued to pin him to the wall. The hungry mouth that covered his left no room for doubt, and in that instant, he made his choice, steeling himself to not shrink away from his cousin's touch. Eyes widening at his lack of resistance, Michel gave his neck a final squeeze before breaking off, hands trembling slightly as he straightened his clothes. "Meet me here in the salon tomorrow night," Michel ordered brusquely, features drawn into a carefully controlled mask once again. "Don't go to your father before then," he added, finger raised in warning before he raced out of the corridor without so much as a single backward glance.

The rest of that night was a blur in his memory. After somehow pushing himself off that wall and forcing his shaky limbs to move, he made it home, the faces of the people he passed along the way only pale shapes floating at the edge of his consciousness. As ordered, he returned to the club the following night, still moving as though in a dream, his fevered thoughts running around in dizzying circles. He easily spotted Michel, stiffly walked over to the small table set in the darkest corner of the room. Michel vaguely nodded in his general direction as he scraped the chair back and sat down. Michel pulled an envelope out of his jacket pocket, tossed it casually onto the table. "In here are all the details I could find on Leon's association with the gambling underworld. He's really made a name for himself in all the wrong circles," he explained, a sneer tugging at the corner of his mouth.

He cautiously reached out for the envelope, took out the pages covered with his cousin's familiar scrawl. The list of names was indeed impressive, even from the little he knew. It didn't matter how well Leon attempted to cover his tracks, the list contained enough dirt to bury him. Flipping through the pages, it suddenly dawned on him that Michel must have dug up most of this information after their meeting last night. Judging by the dark circles under his eyes and the crumpled state of his clothes, Michel had worked through the night and most of the day to produce the list. "You didn't need to go this far," he objected gruffly, fingers fidgeting with the edge of the paper. "Just failing to report to my father is enough..."

"Call it professional pride," Michel muttered, running tired fingers through his hair. "I've rented a room upstairs," he continued, hand reaching out to snatch back the list. Startled by the abrupt movement, he stared at Michel, his body filling with numbness. "We made a deal, didn't we, Sebastian?"

Somewhere behind him, the rattle of bottles and cups tugged at his consciousness, and he awoke with a start, eyes slowly adjusting to the dim lighting of the shabby inn. A sudden movement caught his eye, and he glanced down in time to see the dregs of his wine glass spilling onto the map. Swearing softly under his breath, he righted the glass and pressed his sleeve into the cloth. The map was a rare present from his father, given to him shortly after he presented his "findings". Under father's firm, grim interrogation, Leon fell apart like a house of cards and admitted to the thefts. At that point he was sent out of the room, and Leon was left to face father alone. He caught a final glimpse of Leon as he closed the door, that pale, anxious face forever burned into his memory. Leon was sent away after that, and he quickly filled the void at his father's side. With the exception of a few half-hearted attempts by his lazy siblings to win father's favour, he had little trouble cementing his new position.

Sighing heavily, he lifted his arm, frowned at the dark red stain now blotting out several landmarks. "Michel," he murmured, giving the stain a final, futile rub before rolling up the map. They had continued their pact over the years, his cousin's position as an intelligence officer proving handy on many occasions. The price of his cooperation never changed, and their nights together had become like a business transaction, with both parties falling into quickly set roles. He just had to submit to Michel's unhealthy lust for a couple of hours, and then he was free to leave. Like a sailor clinging to a piece of flotsam, he treated Michel as coldly as ever, desperate to hold onto what pride he had left. "I just have to tolerate it this one last time," he told himself softly, the familiar words comforting as he scraped back the chair and lurched to his feet.

With the slow, deliberate reasoning of someone who had too much to drink, he decided that he'd better wait for Gasquet and the others to arrive before setting off. They had decided to split up and cover more ground, starting from where they had come ashore. "Just look out for clues," he had told the good captain quietly while the men unpacked the boats. "Gunthar and Clay couldn't have gotten too far, we just need some confirmation that we're all heading in roughly the same direction," he had asserted, voice dripping with false bravado. Gasquet had just nodded, turned away grimly. As he tottered slightly and made his way to the stairs, he mentally counted the number of days that had passed since they parted, reaffirmed in his mind that they were supposed to rendezvous today, at this inn. "That's assuming he doesn't decide that this is all a very bad joke and run away," he murmured breathlessly, alcohol-induced lethargy making his limbs heavy and lungs tight.

For one sickening moment, he pictured himself waiting for Gasquet and the others, only to slowly, reluctantly realize that they weren't coming. The room tilted alarmingly before his eyes, and he had to reach out a steadying hand to the nearest wall before the room stopped spinning and settled back into place. "No," he whimpered, swallowing back a wave of nausea, the bitter taste of bile in his mouth. Gasquet would never betray him, not after so many years of loyal service as his father's vassal. When father died and he took over the reins with little opposition, Gasquet transferred his loyalty to the new family head in a seamless transaction. While he stubbornly clung to the idea that Gasquet would never betray him, he was painfully aware of the growing shadow of doubt that darkened the older man's eyes.

It wasn't just Gasquet. The faces of the other men had grown more wary, more disgruntled of late. If he didn't pull something spectacular out of his hat, like some trumped-up magician, he would lose them too. With Jenkins' cunning duplicity and Gunthar's opportunistic escape, he felt as though the ground had been wrenched from beneath his feet, leaving him to reel and flail about like an idiot in full view of the men. Add to that Captain Holister's blunt, absolute refusal to carry them beyond the nearest beach, again in full view of the men. In desperation, he offered the gruff Captain more money, asked him to name his price, but Holister would not be swayed. Leaning heavily against the ship bulkhead, arms folded tightly across his chest, the captain's body language answered the question even before he opened his mouth to speak. The atmosphere on the main deck as they waited for the Magnificent to limp its way to shore had been palpable, almost to the point where it was hard to breathe. How dearly he had wanted to melt away through the cracks in the planking under the glare of the crew's hateful stares...

Raised voices from the entrance tugged at his consciousness, and he drifted toward the doorway. "Yer can't bring that, that thing in 'ere, Captain," a red-faced innkeeper was explaining as he approached the large wooden door. "Even I have standards," the innkeeper sneered, keeping his foot firmly behind the door.

"Please, I have urgent business with my employer," a familiar voice called out through the crack, the toe of a black boot poking out past the doorway. "I believe he's staying here..."

"Richard?" he called out, stepping past the innkeeper's short stout figure to peer through the opening. As his eyes adjusted to the gloom outside, he could make out the captain's stern features, lines of displeasure etched on his face. The men must have been waiting further down the lane, the sound of horses snorting and pawing the ground faintly reaching his ears. It was only when he looked back at Gasquet that he noticed the shadow of a man hanging listlessly from the captain's iron grip.

"Who's that?" he asked, pointing at the grimy face poking out from beneath Gasquet's arm.

"This is Marcus Rembert, he was found near a hut we suspect our "friends" were using," Gasquet answered, hand tightening around the collar of the wretched man's jacket. "He was carrying a sack of provisions, and we found this on the ground not far from where we picked him up." Brow wrinkled in bemusement, he took a scrap of paper from the captain's hand, squinted down at the lines of oddly familiar scrawl. After staring at the nearly illegible writing for a time, a funny sound escaped his throat, and he glanced up Marcus Rembert, a faint flicker of sympathy lighting his eyes. "I think we should talk, Mr Rembert," he drawled, stepping back to let them in. The innkeeper briefly resisted, pressing his weight against the door, but quickly changed his mind when Gasquet shouldered his way through. Sebastian wondered if the man's face could get any redder, feeling his heated gaze follow them out of the room and up the stairs. As he led Gasquet and Marcus to his room, he struggled to keep an idiotic grin from spreading across his face. "Try not to get too excited," he silently cautioned, his face a tightly controlled mask as he opened the door and signalled to the men to enter. With a final bracing of his shoulders, he prepared himself for the role of interrogator and firmly closed the door.

✦

Chapter 6
Song for the depraved and desperate.

Daniel nibbled thoughtfully on the end of a stale bread roll, dark eyes straying to Mel's pensive face. He understood very little of what was going on around him right now. A man they considered to be an enemy was now their uneasy ally, and they were making their way across Europe, to deliver Mel and the Mirror to the Russian Army. Sure, he knew all that. He just couldn't quite understand it. Why were they still going along with this plan? Why didn't Mel use the power of the Mirror to escape? It was obvious even to him that she had made a deal with Jenkins. His hand involuntarily clenched around the bread roll as Jenkins drifted into view, hovering in the background. The man was just so obvious, head turning every now and then to visually check on Mel as he ordered the men about. In the past week, he had become increasingly suspicious of Mel, hanging around her at every opportunity, his odious presence weighing down upon them all like a dark cloud. It was a miracle he didn't travel in the coach with them during the day.

"No, he just rides alongside the coach every day," he muttered, forcing a lump of dry bread down his throat. Casually peering in through the window whenever he feels like it, the bastard. Still, he couldn't completely blame Jenkins for being so nervous. Mel was acting odder with each passing day. He had grown accustomed to her habit of spacing out whenever her hand strayed to the sack tied to her waist. At worst it would happen while in conversation, and she'd suddenly go quiet, attention to the outside world momentarily lost as the Mirror "showed" her something. Now however, the Mirror claimed her attention more and more, and her sudden trances were punctuated by abrupt outbursts.

Just the other day he walked past during one of their breaks, and she suddenly burst out laughing, eyes staring eerily into the distance, body frozen in place. Raphael had rushed to her side, conveniently brushing Jenkins aside in his hurry. Ignoring the other man's glower, he had tugged at her arm, face full of concern until she finally emerged from her altered state of mind. In response, Mel had merely patted Raphael's cheek and walked off as if nothing was wrong. The look of confusion and hurt on Raphael's face had been heartbreaking to witness. A couple of hours later she was off again, tears streaming down her face as she stared at the opposite wall of the carriage, hand curled tightly on the dirty hessian at her side. They had just looked at each other helplessly as her wretched sobs filled the carriage.

If only they could grab that sack and hurl it into the sea, or bury it deep in a forest. He had made the mistake of muttering this to Sarah while Mel was in one her trances, thinking she wouldn't hear it. "No no," Mel had uttered in a calm, even voice, hand darting out to ensnare his hand, "that would never do, Daniel." All the while her eyes continued to stare off into the distance, without any movement at all in his direction. Yet her hand had remained wrapped around his, pressure increasing until he gasped in pain, and she absent-mindedly let go.

Sarah. That was one of the rare times he'd been able to talk to her for more than a minute without her looking incredibly uncomfortable and finding a reason to dash away. Again, he knew the reason why she avoided him. He just didn't understand it. Before he could stop himself, he sneaked a peek at her overly sober face, quickly looked back again before she noticed. At least she was sitting near him this morning, unlike the last couple of days. Maybe over time she would feel less guilty...

"Sorry boy." Mel's voice broke into his thoughts, forced him to look up. "I'm really sorry," she whispered, rising from the large rock she'd been sitting on.

"Mel?" Raphael croaked, moving toward her.

"You are such a sweet, nice boy," she continued, shaking off Raphael's hand, a strange, unreadable look on her face. She stumbled to a stop before him, knees crumbling dramatically. He was vaguely aware of the growing number of eyes turning towards them, one gaze in particular boring holes into his head. "I wanted to give you a horse for Christmas," she cried, grabbing his arms and burying her head in his chest. For a moment he couldn't move, couldn't think, jaw dropping uselessly in bewilderment.

"Horse?" he repeated when he finally found his voice.

"Yes, a horse. You like horses, don't you boy?" she mumbled into his shirt, hands clutching at the material. Something scraped against his belly, and he flinched at the sensation. Her hands tightened against him, and she raised her head quickly to wink at him. "Please don't tell anyone about it," she cried, the hidden meaning of her words slowly penetrating his confusion. "Especially not your mother, with the pigs and all."

"Pigs?" he uttered as Jenkins pulled her away from him, fingers digging cruelly into her arm.

"What are you doing?" Jenkins spluttered, leading her away from the camp area.

"Hey, let her go!" Raphael interjected, moving to intercept them. Within seconds the men were shouting and pushing each other, and Jenkins' men quickly gathered around them. At a pointed glance from Mel, he slowly tucked his shirt into the waistband of his trousers, pondering all the while how he was supposed to subtly remove the note. Feeling the dull edge of the folded paper under his fingertips, he decided to push the note into the top of his trousers, where hopefully the added tension of waistband and belt would hold it in place until he had the opportunity to safely extract it.

Trying to ignore the treacherous droplet of sweat rolling down the side of his face, he forced his hands to fall away. While he'd been facing the commotion the whole time, he hadn't been paying close attention. Raphael was now being held still by two rather large men, and Jenkins was shouting abuse and threats at him, the spittle from his angry mouth landing on Raphael's dark face. The pure hatred that shone from Raphael's tawny eyes as he stared at Jenkins' livid face made his blood run cold. If looks could kill, Jenkins would be a twitching corpse on the forest floor right now, he decided solemnly.

That didn't stop Jenkins though. On and on he ranted while he paced back and forth, veins popping out of his head until Daniel thought he might explode. Just when Jenkins finally looked as though he was ready to let it go and turned away, Raphael muttered something. Raphael's voice was so low and muffled, he doubted anyone other than Jenkins and the two men holding him down heard it. Whatever he said, it was like a flame set to a very short fuse. Jenkins spun about on his heel, face rigid with anger, a scary, crazed look in his eyes. "Oh boy," he croaked, watching on helplessly, the note tucked into the waistband of his trousers temporarily forgotten. He couldn't help but think that time slowed down somehow as Jenkins dipped a hand into his pocket, deliberately pulled it out again. Must be all the tension in the air, he reasoned, swallowing painfully past the sudden lump in his throat. Something on Jenkins' hand glinted as he raised his fist, aimed it directly at Raphael.

What happened next took place so quickly and unexpectedly, that even though he was there the whole time staring like a stunned mullet, he still couldn't quite piece together the sequence of events. All he knew for sure was that one moment it was Jenkins driving his fist towards Raphael's face, and then suddenly Mel was in his place, hand lashing out. The sound of her hand slapping Raphael's cheek seemed unnaturally loud to his shocked ears. "No horse for you this Christmas," Mel panted as she nursed her hand, tears streaming down her face. With surprising speed, she leant over and grabbed Raphael's chin. "You should take some notes from the boy," she continued more evenly, fingers lingering on his cheek for a second before her hand fell away.

For a moment, Daniel thought Jenkins might unleash his fist on Mel instead, his body still poised for violence. After gauging the hurt and confusion on Raphael's face however, he grunted and turned away, apparently satisfied with the level of suffering displayed. "Okay, show's over, time to go," Jenkins announced, grabbing Mel's upper arm firmly. "Patrick, you ride in the coach. You can ride with me today, Mel." His thin lips curled in an unpleasant grin, Jenkins leered at her as if waiting for some form of protest. Daniel was vaguely aware of the soldiers moving around him, prodding the others to move, yet he couldn't take his eyes off Mel as he waited for her reaction. "Here it comes," he murmured, expecting some kind of explosion. He therefore watched on in horrified fascination as she smiled sweetly at Jenkins and patted his cheek. The rest of her response was lost in the general jostling of bodies, one of the soldiers picking that moment to shove him hard towards the waiting carriage.

The rest of that day passed like a prolonged torture session. "Patrick", the man assigned to stay in the coach with them, sat like a stony, unapproachable statue the whole time, only moving or making a sound whenever he felt the need to be discouraging. Even if they merely tried to conduct light, trivial conversation, the man would glower unflinchingly until the perpetrator faded back into dreary silence. Not that any of them were overflowing with the need to talk. Raphael sat stonily in the corner, his face dark with anger. Sarah attempted to draw him out a couple of times, even daring to say in Patrick's company that Mel surely didn't mean it, only to cop cold stares from both men.

In complete contrast to the stuffy atmosphere inside the coach, Mel's cheery voice often drifted past the window as she urged her horse to pick up its pace from time to time. With Jenkins keeping a tight hold of her horse's lead, she had no choice but to match his pace, which seemed to gradually increase on its own accord. "She really seems to be enjoying herself," Daniel sighed, glancing out the window to where Mel bent over to stroke her horse's long brown neck, thick muscles twitching under her hand. Every time the horse responded favourably to her light nudges, she couldn't help but offer the placid mare words of encouragement. While these girlish outbursts were always cut off by a warning growl from Jenkins, he took a small measure of comfort from hearing her voice.

It was nightfall when he finally had enough time alone to safely fish out the note she'd passed to him that morning. After such a long, uncomfortable ride in the coach, he had been enormously relieved when buildings started to come into view and the sharp sound of hooves striking cobbled street reverberated around them. Just when he feared that Jenkins would order the party to keep going, the coach came to a stop before an inn, and they were ushered out by Patrick. He managed to catch a glimpse of the town before being herded through the door into the smoky tavern. They waited awkwardly near the doorway while Jenkins haggled with the inn keeper, three men hovering around them at all times. Mel peered past Jenkins' shoulder, waved at them. Did Jenkins plan to keep her with him all day? Grimacing at the thought, he glanced over at Raphael, could tell from the tension in his face he was thinking the same thing.

Money finally changed hands, and Jenkins sourly turned away, barked for them to move. What a gloomy procession they must have made as they followed the portly inn keeper up the stairs. Muttering about the cost of hiring two rooms to the inn keeper's retreating back, Jenkins organised the sleeping arrangements and ordered them to their rooms. His heart sank as Jenkins kept Mel in tow, leading her into the other room, two soldiers following closely behind. Patrick and another soldier drifted into their room, stationed themselves on a bed, their large bodies looking absurd on such a narrow cot. Looking about at the three remaining beds, he surmised they planned to take turns on watch.

Sometime after that, food was brought up to the rooms, and the three of them huddled on the floor in the far corner and slowly ate thin broth. "I'm surprised we stopped at an inn," Daniel ventured in a low voice, gaze wandering over the door where Patrick stood guard. The other soldier had ducked out of the room shortly after the food arrived, so the atmosphere was slightly less stuffy. Was it just wishful thinking, or did Patrick's head momentarily drop?

"It's been three days since the last time we stayed at an inn. I was starting to think we'd be camping by the road for the rest of the trip."

"We must be getting close to the border," Raphael murmured around a mouthful of bread. "The number of safe towns must be thinning out for our friend. There are bound to be more spies about the closer we get to the fighting."

Patrick made a sound, stirred briefly before falling back into a semi-doze. "But what can Mel be thinking?" Sarah hissed, leaning forward. He felt his heartbeat quicken as her body pressed lightly into his. "Why is she acting so strange, and why is she complying with Jenkins so much?" Raphael set his bowl on the floor, buried his head in his hands.

"I don't know," he croaked, hands falling away. "I've been mulling over it all day. There's a hidden meaning behind her actions, I'm sure of it. Even slapping me like that..." His voice trailed off, cheeks darkening at the memory of that morning.

Breath catching noisily in his throat, Daniel remembered the note, started to reach for it when the other soldier noisily returned. Under the collective glares of the men, they went back to eating in grudging silence, exchanging significant looks whenever they thought the guards weren't watching, but otherwise keeping to themselves. It wasn't until he went to the outhouse that he was truly alone, and even then Patrick lingered outside the door, boots creaking as he impatiently waited. With numb fingers he extracted the note, grimaced at the dampness of the paper as he unfolded it. Luckily a little lamp hung from the ceiling, and he was able to make out Mel's handwriting in the muddy light.

He willed his hands to stop shaking as he re-read the note for the third, fourth time. "Ha, you can't be serious Mel," he breathed, fingers scrunching the edges of the paper on their own accord. For a moment the small room swirled about him, and he slumped back, hand pressed against his chest. "Ah, not now," he wheezed, willing the invisible hand that seemed to be squeezing his heart to stop. The first couple of times he experienced these pains, he had shrugged it off, thinking it was just an after-effect of his near-drowning experience when the Pretty Peg went down. "But I'm getting them too frequently now," he murmured, sagging even more on the seat as the pain eased. Patrick chose that time to pound on the door, growl a word of warning. Jumping half-way out of his skin, Daniel finished his business and exited the outhouse, gaze firmly averted from Patrick's suspicious face. At least now the note was safely in his pocket, not that he really needed it now. He'd practically memorised the message, line for line. Not too hard really, seeing as it was only two lines. "As I said, there will be no horses for Christmas this year, so I think it's time to move on. Let the others know I'll be doing something about it tonight."

"Is that the map? Can I have a look?"

He clenched his hand over the wrinkled parchment, gritted his teeth and silently counted to ten. Or at least he tried to.

"Oh come on, give us a look, we must be close now," Mel continued, peering over his shoulder. "Oh, is that where we are, there?" she cried, leaning over him to point at a spot near the Russian border. "Move your hand Jenkins, I can't see the name of the town..."

A growl escaped his lips as he slapped her hand away.

"What the hell is up with you Mel?" he snapped, pushing his chair back with a loud scrape. "I don't know what you think you're going to achieve with this crazy act, but drop it right now."

In the blink of an eye, her face became eerily calm. "You think this is all an act?" Her voice too, was very calm, barely a ripple in the air. "The Mirror has been showing me more and more stuff lately, more stuff than I care to see, and you think I'm acting?" He watched in wide-eyed astonishment as she grabbed his shoulders, slid a knee between his legs. Ever so gently, she pushed against his crotch, breath fanning his face. "It's shown me a lot of things about you, Jenkins," she said huskily, leaning over further, chair creaking alarmingly beneath them. She pressed her body into his, set her lips over his ear. "The things you and Alyce used to do..."

With a start he pushed her away, fear gripping his heart. He had faced many dangerous, potentially lethal situations in his time. People attacking him from behind, drugs or poison slipped into his food, blackmail. He had stopped counting threats to his life a long time ago. But this one insinuation by Mel about his sex life left him completely unnerved. "Why would it show you that?" he spat, jerkily rising out of the chair. "Just stick to the plan, for God's sake."

"What's the matter Jenkins?" she asked, lips curled in an uncharacteristically cruel smirk. "Did I surprise you? I'm still human, you know, even with a part of the Mirror inside me." He stood transfixed as she slowly approached, grabbed his hand. "See?" she murmured, placing his hand on her breast. "Very human."

For a handful of heartbeats, all rational thought deserted him, the only thing he was conscious of being the warm softness beneath his hand. His body responded with warmth of its own, and his breath came out in an embarrassing loud rasp, fingers pressing into the soft flesh. It has been a long time, he thought with a sudden ache in his body. Even when Alyce was still alive...

When Alyce was alive... Abruptly he pulled away, the image of Alyce's lifeless body at Mel's feet filling his mind, leaving his body cold. His throat suddenly bone dry, he swallowed painfully, stumbled back. "Take her away," he spat, leaning heavily against the wall, "take her to the stables and tie her up. Take turns to guard her, don't leave her unattended for a second." Blinking in surprise, the men sluggishly responded, guided Mel out of the room. Once alone, he collapsed to the floor, squeezing his eyes shut against the sudden pain in his head. "Damn you, you stupid woman," he groaned. She couldn't seriously want him, not like that. But then, what did she hope to achieve by seducing him? The most obvious answer was to be alone with him. "What was she planning to do then?" he murmured, reluctantly opening his eyes to the dimly lit room.

One of the lanterns must have burnt out, he decided as he rose stiffly to his feet. The room wasn't this dark before. As his eyes slowly adjusted, he staggered about the room, trying to sort out his chaotic thoughts. Wincing at the sudden tightness in his chest, he patted his pockets, felt the hard square surface of the snuff box through the thick material. Hand shaking, he fumbled about in his jacket pocket and pulled it out, nearly spilling the fine powder as he opened the lid. A few deep breaths later, the pain in his chest eased, and he rubbed his tingling nose with the back of his hand. "Damn you Mel," he muttered, sinking down on one of the beds. His nerves had been stretched to a fine enough point before this incident, with her increasingly bizarre behaviour. But what just happened, that nearly pushed him over the edge. "Ha, I nearly fell for it," he laughed weakly, remembering the way she pressed her body against him. If his son wasn't being held hostage, he would just turn away right now, and leave this mess behind.

The snuff box fell out of his suddenly numb fingers, and he fumbled to catch it. Just before it hit the floor, he managed to close his hand around it, nearly falling off the bed in the process. Only then did he notice the strange lump in the corner, poking out from behind a bed. As if in a trance, he rose unsteadily to his feet, stumbled towards the corner. "The Mirror," he gasped at the familiar hessian sack, suddenly grasping Mel's plan. He only had a second to admire her handiwork before a huge explosion shook the room, and he was flung hard against the wall.

"Get moving," one of the guards growled, prodding her ribs hard with the butt of his rifle. Wincing at the sudden pain, she blearily glanced up, eyes re-focusing on the dimly lit corridor leading to the staircase at the back of the inn. Blinking back tears, she murmured half-hearted words of apology and continued to trudge towards the exit, paying her surroundings scant attention as she concentrated on the images fed to her by the Mirror. This was the first time she'd ever linked remotely to the Mirror. At best she caught glimpses of grimy, white-washed walls and bare, dusty floorboards. A shadowy presence moved about the room, floorboards creaking under his feet. She strained to look beyond the narrow confines of the Mirror's awareness, but it was like trying to grab a cloud of smoke, the view slipping away from her before she could grasp what it was she was looking at.

Something hard connected with her hip, and she stumbled into the wall, arm scrapping against the rough surface. The soldiers were being more heavy-handed than usual, she decided with a frown, pushing away from the wall before they had reason to jab her again. Perhaps the sight of their boss snapping and snarling like a cornered animal had struck a nerve. The skin on her chest where Jenkins' hand had rested still crawled, the revulsion she'd struggled so hard to keep from her face at the time now flooding out, twisting her features. While she had a plan for both outcomes, she was grateful for being kicked out of the room, rather than having to continue the act. For a handful of frantic heartbeats, she thought he'd accept her invitation, the sudden fire in his eyes as his hand pressed into her flesh making her throat dry. Whatever flitted through his mind at that point caused him to rapidly shift away from desire, his usual paranoia and distrust overriding all other urges.

With a final nudge she was propelled through the doorway and out into the courtyard. The cool night air hit her face, and her senses lost some of their fuzziness. Despite the low outside temperature, beads of sweat formed on her brow as she started to count her steps. A voice echoed dully in her head, and she caught a glimpse of Jenkins' face as he sunk onto the bed on the other side of the room. His long nose was tipped with white powder, a metal box nestled in his hand. His lips moved, but she couldn't quite catch the harsh-sounding words. Even through the blurry, disjointed vision of the Mirror's awareness, she could see he was tired, his body sinking heavily into the straw-stuffed mattress. Fleeting images of a small, fair-haired boy huddled in a cell drifted through her mind, and she bit her lip. "Can't back out now," she croaked, swallowing past the hard lump that had suddenly formed in her throat.

One of the guards growled, shoved her forward. With a start she looked up, realized they were almost at the stables. "Wait a minute," the guard that just shoved her murmured, eyes narrowing as they travelled up and down her body. "Something's not right," he mumbled. The other two guards closed in around her, following the other man's lead and eying her suspiciously. At the back of her mind, she heard sounds of movement, and the part of her that was linked to the Mirror saw Jenkins bend over suddenly to catch the metal box. In that moment, his eyes fell upon the hessian sack sitting in the corner all this time. Her heart nearly leapt out of her chest, seeing his face so clearly, eyes like saucers as he realized what was going on. That pale, frozen face filled her vision, filled her mind, to the point where everything else around her faded away, and time itself seemed to stop.

"Hey, the sack's missing," one of the guards exclaimed beside her, the gruff voice penetrating her frozen mind. Squeezing her eyes shut, she silently called out to the Mirror. In answer, a loud explosion punctuated the night air, the short, high-pitched sound of air being pushed outwards at high velocity sharply accompanied by the rumble of falling/breaking timber and masonry. For a moment, no one moved. Even she couldn't help but stare through the billowing dust at the newly made hole in the wall. She hadn't expected such a big explosion... Somewhere behind her, one of the guards made an incoherent sound, and she remembered with a jolt the rest of her plan.

Pushing past the dumbfounded guards, she scrambled back towards the inn. Their startled cries followed her into the rubble, and she was vaguely aware of heavy footsteps catching up to her in the cloud of dust that still spilled out into the night. But then a loud creak of the timbers above silenced their cries, and suddenly they were running away from the section of floor that came crashing down. She dove blindly forward, squeezed her body into the space under the stairwell. Pieces of masonry hit her body, bit savagely into her flesh as she huddled in the shadows, but the flashes of pain barely registered in her fear-choked mind. Over the sound of her frantic heartbeat pulsing in her ears, she slowly became aware that the crash had stopped, and she crawled out from under the stairs, choking on the fresh dust.

Splintered floorboards and chunks of broken masonry now took the place of the bottom three stairs of the stairwell, and as she clambered over the pile, she realised with a chill just how close she'd been to being crushed. Ignoring the way the remaining stairs shifted and groaned under her weight, she made her way to the upper floor, stumbled into the shattered room. Squinting her eyes against the dust that still floated about the room, she staggered over to the corner where she'd placed the Mirror. Much of the wall had been blown away, along with a section of the roof. As she looked around, she spotted the bed that had been sitting in the corner on the other side of the room, the timber frame crudely split in the middle. Suddenly she was aware of something tugging at her consciousness, and she bent down to paw through the rubble. Eventually her scratched, bleeding hands brushed against coarse cloth, and she felt as though a great weight had just been lifted from her shoulders. What was she so relieved about, she wondered as she pushed away more debris to reveal a familiar lumpy object. She should just leave it here in the rubble, find Raphael, Sarah and Daniel, and run away, she decided, gripping the hessian sack and rising unsteadily to her feet.

"Yeah, why do I care?" she croaked past the layer of dust that seemed to coat the insides of her throat. "I'll just leave you here, and whoever wants you can have you," she cried, shaking the bag. She had never deliberately shaken the Mirror before, so the sharp twinkle of glass that reverberated so loudly in her ears startled her, almost made her drop the sack. But still her fingers maintained their hold on the material, and despite her threat to leave the Mirror, she just couldn't seem to let it go. If anything, her hand curled even more tightly around the neck of the sack. She raised her arm, swung the sack back as if to hurl it at the wall, when something caught her eye, and she stumbled forward, the Mirror colliding with her leg. Protruding out from under a pile of debris was a hand.

Even through layers of dust, she could recognise the light brown tobacco stains between the thumb and fore finger. She almost expected to see a snuff box appear in that hand at any moment, right before being passed to the other hand in preparation for taking a pinch. "Jenkins," she whispered hoarsely, sinking to her knees beside the unmoving hand. Stiffly, slowly, she pushed away the splintered beams that lay across his face and torso, bile surging up her throat at the bruised battered pulp that was his head. Pushing away from the gruesome corpse, she turned to the side and threw up. Over the wretched sound of her stomach heaving, she suddenly became aware of someone slowly clapping their hands together. Her heart skipped a beat, and she felt a chill race down her back as the clapping was accompanied by deliberate footsteps.

Forcing her frozen body to move, she turned toward the source of the sound, found herself staring up at a soldier. "Don't tell me you're feeling remorse," the man uttered, his voice cold and controlled. "Isn't this what you wanted?" He moved steadily towards her, thin lips twisted in a sneer.

"Ah, who are you?" she asked unevenly, inwardly wincing at the raw anxiety in her voice. Clutching the sack tightly to her chest, she hastily clambered to her feet, took a couple of stumbling backward steps. "Aren't you one of Jenkins' men?" she added, the wheels of her memory starting to turn as she stared at the round bearded face. He stopped in mid-step, the skin around his dark brown eyes crinkling slightly as though she'd just said something funny.

"So you do recognise me. That's nice," he murmured, the faint hint of mirth in his face fading away. "I've actually been floating about in the background since this whole race for the Mirror began. It's been quite a ride, watching on as you led everyone on a merry dance." As the dry words tumbled out of his mouth, she reached back into her memories of that fateful night in the old barn, when they were surrounded by Sebastian's men. Shaking her head at the huge gaps in her memory, she tightened her hold on the Mirror.

"So, you originally worked for Sebastian, is that what you're saying?" she prompted impatiently, all the while silently calling out to the Mirror.

"That's right," he answered, moving towards her again, hand slipping into his jacket pocket. "I knew that if I was patient enough, an opportunity would arise..." Without any trace of betraying emotion on his face, he flicked his hand towards her. As she blinked at the blur of movement, something stung her, and she looked down in disbelief at a tiny dart was now embedded in her arm.

A dismayed cry escaped her lips as she swatted away the dart, but it was already too late. She desperately began to run away, pushing past the soldier, the jagged hole in the wall shining out to her like a beacon. With each stumbling step however, the room swayed and lurched around her in sickening circles. Once again bitter bile welled up inside her, and she promptly collapsed to her knees, emptied whatever was left in her stomach. Wiping her mouth with the back of her hand, she gathered what was left of her strength, tried to move her legs. She shifted her weight, started to move forward, only to slump back into a semi-conscious heap. Tears sprung to her eyes as her body refused to move, and she stared up at the blurry face that now hovered above her.

"Really, you're pathetic," a cold voice echoed in her ear. "You have control over the Mirror, yet you resort to half-hearted measures and half-baked schemes. You kill Jenkins but then feel weepy about it, giving me the chance to capture you. I won't lie, I hate people like you..." There was a glimmer of emotion that flared when he said the word "hate", but other than that small disturbance, his voice was calm and smooth like glass. As her vision blurred further, and colour was rapidly replaced with varying shades of grey, she heard him move beside her, and she felt her blood run cold as his warm breath fanned her cheek. "I'll tell you something nice however. Don't feel bad about killing Jenkins, I would have killed that sorry son-of-a-bitch myself sooner or later, and he didn't have much to live for anyway, seeing as his son is dead."

Even in its depleted state, her body responded to those ominous words, stiffening under his cold gaze. With great effort she raised her head, pried her eyes wide open, focused on his face. "Just who...the hell are you?" she managed to wheeze before her head fell back, eyelids so heavy they felt as though they would weld together under the great pressure. Somehow, she managed to move her lips enough to mumble "damn drugs" as the sedative took hold, and the last thing she was aware of was the soldier chuckling and shifting even lower, his lips hovering just above her ear. "The name is Monfils," he whispered, the soft sound following her into darkness.

"Sarah, Sarah, wake up!" a familiar voice hissed urgently in her ear. She imagined that voice was attached to the hand shaking her shoulder, further annoying the crap out of her. Reluctantly she pried open her eyes, blinked slowly at Daniel's anxious face. Before she could open her mouth to snarl at him, plaster fragments showered down from the ceiling, and she looked about in astonishment.

"Ah, what happened?" she asked, staring at the large cracks in the wall. Even as she watched, big chunks of plaster crumbled away from the cracked surface, sending fine clouds of dust into the air.

"There was an explosion," Daniel explained, helping her off the bed.

"Quickly, we don't have much time," Father barked, voice full of tension.

It was only then that she noticed the unmoving bodies of the guards at Raphael's feet, and the newly acquired weapon already strapped to his side. As she stumbled towards the doorway, he grimly handed her a sword and ushered them impatiently out the door. There were already several people gathering in the corridor outside their room, mostly other patrons rubbing the sleep from their eyes and wondering what the hell was going on. The innkeeper was trying to make his way through the press of people, face pale with shock.

"Mel's room," she heard Father mutter as he surged ahead. Forcing her sluggish limbs to move, she caught up to him, came to a grinding halt outside the devastated room. Considering the damage to their own room two doors down, it was no surprise that debris clogged the entrance, forcing them to squeeze through a narrow gap. Their feet stirred the already unsettled dust, and she had to squint as her eyes adjusted to the shadowy room. Through the mess of rubble and over-turned furniture, she blinked away tears to focus on a vaguely familiar shape slumped against the far wall. She started moving towards the shape when Raphael cried out, charged across the room.

"Oi, you there, stop!" he yelled, lunging at a soldier standing by the jagged hole in the wall. She followed the sound of his voice, clambered awkwardly over the shattered remains of a bed. Peering past Raphael's shoulder, she spotted a shabbily dressed soldier squatting down at the edge of the hole. Over the sound of her own frantic heartbeats and Raphael's shouts, she could hear the soldier yelling at someone on the ground. Half-choking on the dust, she stumbled badly over a splintered beam and was hurtling clumsily across the floor when a blur of movement caught her eye, caused her to stumble even more. Suddenly the soldier had a round metal ball in one hand, a naked flame in the other. She stared on in blank bemusement as the soldier put the two together. "How the hell did he do that?" she murmured, her dry wispy words drowned out by Raphael's warning cry. The black ball sailed over head, and she realised with a start what it was.

"Bomb!" she shouted, echoing Raphael's cry. She twisted around, opened her mouth to scream out to Daniel, who was crouched by the shape she spied on entering the room. Something big and heavy landed on her, pushing out any air she had left in her lungs, and the words of warning never made it past her lips. With a loud popping sound, the bomb went off, the metal casing shattering to release its deadly load of shrapnel. The answering groan of timbers filled her heart with dread, and she tried to move out from the lump. "Wait," the lump hissed, tightening its hold on her as debris showered them.

"Ow," she grunted when the ceiling finally stopped falling on them. At last, the great weight clambered off her, and she desperately sucked in the dusty air. Over the sound of her gasping and coughing, she heard Raphael ask if she was alright. With a weak nod of her head she waved him away, started staggering across to where she last saw Daniel. The acrid smell of gun powder filled her nostrils as she reached the spot, now marked by a pile of rubble. "Daniel," she croaked past the lump that suddenly formed in her throat. With trembling hands, she pushed away a section of ceiling that had crashed down, only vaguely aware of Raphael crouching down beside her. Her heart skipped a beat as the planking lifted to reveal Daniel's pale face.

His eyes fluttered open, a faint smile twisting his lips. "Sarah," he murmured, reaching out a blood-stained hand to her face. "I'm so glad you're okay," he sighed, hand falling away as he passed out. Eyes widening at the blood, she looked down, froze in shock at the dark patch spreading steadily on his abdomen. Following the direction of her gaze, Raphael swore softly under his breath, gently probed the wound.

"There's some shrapnel here," he murmured, face creased in concentration. "Go and get that lantern from over there Sarah," he ordered gruffly, nodding the lantern that had somehow survived the two explosions and still sat in the far corner of the room.

"What, what do you mean? We must help him," she cried, voice verging on hysteria. A pained expression clouded Raphael's face, and he gripped her forearms tightly, shook her slightly.

"I have to get the shrapnel out of there before I can heal him," he explained carefully. Looking as though he was losing something precious, he released her. "Don't worry, I know how important this boy is to you, so hurry up," he added stiffly, pulling out a knife from his belt.

Blinking back fresh tears, she nodded dumbly and hastily retrieved the lantern. "Lift up the glass," Raphael ordered. Willing her hand not to shake, she did as she was told, and he passed the blade through the flame. "Hold him down," he continued, using his own weight to pin down Daniel's legs. With only that vague warning, he started to scrape the wound, cursing softly under his breath as Daniel twitched and arched beneath his knee.

"Ah, what are you doing?" Daniel spluttered, clawing at the arms that pushed down on his shoulders.

"Daniel, please, we're trying to help you," she shouted over the top of his screams, ignoring the way his fingernails dug into her flesh.

"Sarah," he wheezed, clenching his teeth against the pain, "it hurts so much." From behind tightly closed eyelids, tears rolled out, made tracks in the dirt and dust covering the sides of his face.

"Daniel," she sobbed, bending her head down to brush her lips against his clammy forehead. "Please don't leave me."

Even through the haze of pain that distorted his senses, he caught those whispered words, eyes slowly opening in response. "Sarah," he whispered hoarsely.

"Luckily for you it was a crudely made bomb," Raphael announced, bursting their little bubble in time and space. "By the looks of it, most of the metal fragments burned up in the explosion," he continued, holding up pieces of shrapnel to the light. "See how the edges have been blackened and curled by the heat? That's why the fragments didn't penetrate any deeper, or I would have really needed to dig around." Daniel's face blanched at the mental image that accompanied that sentence, visibly swayed as though he were about to pass out.

"Father!" Sarah cried, shooting him an accusing look.

With a tired smirk he carefully placed the shrapnel in a pile, set his knife on the floor. "Right," he sighed, pulling a handkerchief out of his jacket pocket. His hand hovered above the wound for a moment when he noticed how generally stained it had become, after all their travels. Pushing past his reservations, he gingerly applied the handkerchief, dabbed around the edge of the torn skin. After some wiping, he realised with a sinking feeling how large an area he had to heal. As if reading his thoughts, Sarah reached over and touched his shoulder. "Are you going to be okay father?" she asked softly, struggling to push out her voice past the tight confines of her throat.

Seeing the growing guilt darken her eyes, he hastily looked away, focused his attention on Daniel. "Of course I'll be alright," he answered gruffly, not wanting to add to that guilt. He gently shrugged away her hand, shifted his weight to rest on his knees. "Like we have a choice," he added softly, the words meant for her ears only. "Right," he announced, tossing aside the handkerchief, "I'm going to heal you now Daniel…it will tingle a bit, at most it might sting, like a sunburn," he explained, voice slightly muffled as he bent his head over the wound. Daniel murmured something in response, his words slurred as he strayed from one state of consciousness to another.

Taking a deep breath, Raphael carefully laid his hand over the punctured flesh, closed his eyes in concentration. The alien energy inside of him flowed out into Daniel's body, the sticky patch underneath his hand heating up until it felt as though it would burn him. "So hungry," he croaked, referring to the patient. With a start, he broke off contact, slumped back in exhaustion.

"Father!" Sarah cried, moving towards him. Holding up his hand, he waved her away, willed himself to move.

"It's alright, just took me by surprise," he muttered distractedly, lowering his head over Daniel's mouth. The raspy shallow breaths could only be faintly heard in the heavy silence of the room. He glanced up at Sarah's pinched face, silently wrestled with his instincts. "Sarah," he began, deciding to risk sending her into a panic, "has Daniel mentioned anything to you about feeling unwell?"

Her eyes widened, became as round as saucers. "No," she answered breathlessly, leaning towards him, "why, what's wrong?" Wincing at the raw fear edging her voice, he reluctantly explained.

"His body drew out a lot of my energy, more than one would expect for a wound this size. There could be some irregularity in his heartbeat..."

"What?" Sarah croaked, sinking back down next to Daniel now-unconscious body. With a trembling hand she reached out, pushed the hair back from his sweaty forehead.

"I can do some more probing, but judging from that contact alone, the problem didn't just develop recently. His system is being steadily weakened."

Sarah tore her gaze from Daniel's face, breath catching noisily in her throat. "Yesterday, when we arrived at the inn, and we were making our way to the room, he kind of stumbled, leant against the wall for a second. I didn't think anything of it, thinking he was just clumsy or afraid. But now that I think about it, he did look pale, as though he was in pain. There was this kind of shadow around his eyes...but then when he saw me looking at him, he smiled, acted like it was nothing..." Outside the crumbling wall, various sounds of activity reverberated in the still night air. Children crying, adults shouting, horses neighing. The slosh of water followed by the hiss of steam as the villagers tried to put out the fire. All of this was going on, and yet they sat there in the dusty room, staring at Daniel and then at each other as though time had stopped. Raphael gazed at Sarah's face, his chest aching as he suddenly found it hard to breathe. "What to do?" he silently screamed, possibilities and scenarios running circles in his brain. With a heavy sense of dread, he realised that every chain of reasoning came to the same conclusion.

"That soldier, he took Mel, didn't he?"

He nodded, not trusting himself to look up. "I managed to catch a glimpse of her as she was being taken away, just before that bastard threw the bomb," he answered hoarsely. Even though she was unconscious at the time and hoisted over another soldier's shoulder like a sack of potatoes, he caught a clear view of her grimy face.

"Well, if we take a day or two to heal Daniel, I'm sure we can catch up to them," she proposed, struggling to instil confidence into her voice. "We're both sensitive to the Mirror, we just have to follow its trail..."

His heart ached at her desperate suggestion, her obvious wish for them to all stay together. Her voice faltered at his bleak, determined face, as he slowly but surely shook his head. "Not this time, Sarah," he said softly, reaching out to rest heavy hands on her trembling shoulders. "I want you to take Daniel home..."

"No," she croaked, fresh tears springing to her eyes.

"I had doubts before about leading you and the lad into a war zone," he continued, fingers biting into her flesh as his hands shook. "There's no doubt now. Even if we heal Daniel, the road is long and dangerous. Could you really bear to have it on your conscience, if he died?" The voice he meant to be gentle and kind cracked through the air like a whip, and Sarah flinched at their impact. Forcing his stiff fingers to relax, he released her shoulders, arms falling listlessly to his sides. "I have been very selfish all these years, dragging you along with me on many dangerous journeys. Somehow, we always managed to pull through. But this time, it's not just us. This boy has been through so much already, we can't let him die here."

Sarah opened her mouth to protest, but one glance at Daniel's pallid face confirmed Raphael's words. Wordlessly, Raphael reached into the inner breast pocket of his jacket, pulled out a small bag of coins. "Take this, buy a passage back to England. There should be enough to get you and the boy home, with some left over."

"What about you, father?" she asked dubiously, reluctantly accepting the bag.

"I have plenty left over, don't worry," he lied, picturing in his mind the couple of coins that sadly remained in his trouser pocket. "I'll send word as soon as I am able." That part wasn't a lie, just ridiculously optimistic. To his surprise, Sarah breathed a small sigh of relief, even as her cheeks burned with shame.

"Thank you, father. You are right, I would never be able to forgive myself if he died. But, to leave you like this..."

"Sarah," he said softly, reaching out to brush away the tears that ran down her dusty cheeks. As he gazed at her still, downcast face, it suddenly occurred to him how much she'd changed in such a comparatively short space of time. Her face before had been faintly childish in its roundness, emphasised by her mane of curly red hair. Now the cheekbones were more pronounced, and all trace of childishness was lost. Even her hair had been reduced to a ratty-looking ponytail trailing lifelessly down her back. The most shocking part of the transformation however was the dark shadows that never seemed to leave her eyes. How long had it been since he saw her eyes crinkled in laughter, or shining with excitement?

Just then, Daniel stirred, eyelids slowly fluttering open. "Sarah," he rasped, turning dark unfocused eyes to her teary face. "Are you hurt, Sarah?"

"Daniel, you idiot, worry about yourself," she chided softly as she helped him into a sitting position. As he watched their little exchange, Raphael felt the room shrink away from him, taking the awkward pair with it. In a painful, cruel moment of clarity, he saw that the path he and Sarah shared had split into two and veered off in wildly opposing directions.

"Come on, you two, there's no time to waste," he announced grimly, forcing his heavy limbs to move.

Raphael woke with a start, jolted upright, nearly slipping out of the saddle in the process. Shaking away the cobwebs that seemed to have formed inside his head, he wondered how long he had been nodding off, leaving the poor horse he'd stolen to pick out a path amongst the moon-lit trees. Leaning forward, he mumbled words of apology, tugged gently on the reigns. Sarah and Daniel must be long gone by now. After stabilising Daniel, he had gruffly led them to the stables, where the soldiers' horses were being kept. Half-expecting to be spotted by Jenkins' men at any moment as they made their way through the jostling crowd that filled the courtyard, it was almost an anti-climax when they reached the building unopposed.

Daniel must have caught his mutter of "not even a final show-down with Jenkins," because he hastily explained that Jenkins was dead. "I found his body near the wall when that bomb went off," he reported, a slight tremor in his voice. While his face still held an unhealthy tinge of grey, he seemed to be moving okay.

"Hopefully that will be enough," Raphael murmured, struggling to drag his thoughts away from those final heart-wrenching moments before they parted ways. Whatever resentment he may have harboured towards Daniel quickly faded away as the poor boy watched on helplessly while they said their goodbyes. With his drifting states of consciousness, and everything moving so fast around him, the boy didn't fully grasp what was going on until that moment. He hovered in the background, obviously caught between wanting to get close to ask questions, but at the same time afraid to intrude. Only when Sarah abruptly turned away and called out to him did he unfreeze, stumbling after her, stammered protests tumbling out of his mouth.

As he watched them get onto their horses, he couldn't help but smile at the way Sarah effortlessly deflected all his protests, her calm voice firmly steering him away. Just once she turned back to look at him one last time before they winked out of view, and he propelled himself to move. "That must have been at least three hours ago," he croaked softly, squinting at the fuzzy orange glow that was creeping into the sky, signalling the arrival of dawn. "And now I have to try and catch up to Mel," he continued aloud, suddenly hating the heavy silence of the forest. His voice was quickly swallowed by the silence, and he hunkered down in the saddle, tried to ignore how the trees loomed oppressively over him, as if to emphasise his solitude.

"They should be fine, right girl?" he croaked to the mare, leaning forward to stroke her brown shiny neck. Thick muscles twitched under his hand, and as if nodding the mare moved her head up and down. With a bitter, self-mocking laugh, he gave her neck a final stroke, straightened up in the saddle. "What's that you say, I should be more worried about myself?" he sighed. Swallowing past the sudden lump in his throat, he wondered what the future held for all of them. Assuming Sarah and Daniel made it back to the manor, and no further violence had befallen their home, they should be well set up for a life together. "A life together?" he murmured, surprised that he could conceive such a thing. If he succeeded in getting Mel back, and dealing with all their enemies, could they too hope to return home, and pick up the fragments of their lives?

"Really, it feels as though we've been on the run for ages," he grumbled under his breath, idly scratching the patch of skin between the mare's ears. "So, what do you say, girl? Let's hurry up and find Mel, eh?" In response, the mare shook her head irritably, snorted contemptuously at his bravado. Feeling some of his old strength return, he hunched over slightly in the saddle, dug his heels into the mare's sides. So much of what Sarah said was muffled and distorted, words spilling out desperately in a race against time during their final moments together. But there was one message she kept repeating, like a frantic prayer. "Please save Mel, Mel's all alone."

"Despite what you said, you still feel guilty, don't you Sarah? Still blaming yourself for Mel being dragged into all this..." he mumbled to the blurring trees as the mare picked up her pace. To his surprise, the mare eagerly responded to his firm prompting, long legs stretching out beneath him to strike the ground, churning up grassy sods in her wake. Trusting the mare pick out a path through the labyrinth of trees, he closed his eyes, focused on the alien energy flowing within him. On their own accord, his lips curled into a vicious smile as the signal grew stronger, and for the first time in a long while, his blood stirred. The hunt was on, but this time, he would be the hunter, and not the prey. Without Sarah and the boy in tow, he was free to be utterly ruthless, and do whatever was necessary to get Mel back. Out of nowhere memories resurfaced, memories he'd deliberately pushed to the far reaches of his mind. By no means was he a saint, and during the rough times he'd shared with Sarah, he had done many questionable things in order to survive. "That was over four years ago," he murmured softly, tugging on the reins slightly as the signal shifted. And yet despite that passage of time, he found his muscles twitching in anticipation. "I'm coming Mel," he croaked, before sliding into silence, clinging onto to the galloping mare's back with fierce determination.

She sat at a table in a fine restaurant, a sumptuous meal set before her. Soft candlelight illuminated the neat arrangement of tableware, and somewhere in the background someone was playing a violin, the soft, poignant strains adding to the romantic atmosphere. She glanced down at her hands, her body, surprised and relieved to see her old self. A polite cough from the other side of the table drew her attention, and she looked up to find Gunthar staring at her, brow wrinkled slightly in concern. "Are you alright Alyce?" he asked, reaching across the table. A startled gasp escaped her lips as his hand caught hers, gave it a gentle squeeze. A pained look flashed across his face, and he started to pull away.

"No, wait!" she cried with more strength than she intended. "I was just surprised," she mumbled, looking away from his confused face, blood rushing to her cheeks. The pressure of his hand returned, and she steeled herself to meet his eyes. He looked rather dashing, dressed in a dark formal suit, with his long wiry hair tied back. "Um, let's eat," she croaked, her mouth suddenly dry. Reluctantly pulling her hand away, she picked up the cutlery, started to cut the thick slice of roast beef.

"You know Alyce, I've been thinking lately," Gunthar began, raising his voice over the sound of clanking of cutlery. "We've been through so much together..."

Her heart skipped a beat at his words, and she almost choked on the meat she'd just put in her mouth. Dropping the cutlery noisily onto the plate, she thumped her chest with one hand while the other reached shakily for a nearby glass. Over the sound of her coughing, she was vaguely aware of Gunthar's concerned cries, and she waved to him reassuringly while she took a sip of wine. Her hand... She froze, stared at the pale slender fingers wrapped around the stem of the glass. To her absolute horror, the digits started to fatten, the white skin turning grey. In a horrible, steady wave, the metamorphosis swept up her arms, crept over her torso. Finally, her voice was unlocked from the prison of her constricted throat, and she screamed as the delicate material of her dress split and frayed under the pressure of her burgeoning body.

"As I was saying Alyce," Gunthar continued in an absurdly calm voice, "we've been through a lot together. A lot of changes..." Even through the pain of transformation, his words penetrated her consciousness, her fevered brain desperately clinging to every syllable. Maybe because she was expecting something more from his words. "I was thinking, I call you Alyce, but are you really "Alyce"? Aren't you more "Clay" than "Alyce" these days?"

"What?!" she screamed in a voice she barely recognised, her elongating vocal cords producing a harsh, strangled sound.

"I feel a bit uncomfortable about it, to be honest," Gunthar continued glibly, as though nothing unusual was going on. "So I was wondering, would you mind if I called you "Calyce", you know, like a combination of "Clay" and "Alyce"? Of course, that sounds like "callous", so maybe that's not the best choice... Maybe another combination ..."Alyclay"? Hmm, but that sounds pretty weird..." His ridiculous words washed over her like a cold shower, cutting through her horror and despair. Filling her lungs with as much air as possible, she lurched over the table, grabbed his shoulders.

"What the hell are you blabbing about, you idiot?!" she roared. She brought his bemused stupid face closer, shook him back and forward like a rag doll. Under the full force of her raw, angry voice, his face seemed to wobble and dissolve, the particles blowing away like sand...

Somewhere in the distance a frantic voice called out to her, and she felt something dig into her fleshy shoulder. She reluctantly opened her eyes, and a more solid Gunthar face hovered above her, framed by a mane of blonde unruly hair. A sigh of relief escaped her lips that it had all been a stupid dream, and she paused for a moment, collected her thoughts. "What the hell Gunthar?" she growled, easily slipping into the familiar role of grumpy golem. "You better have a good reason for waking me," she continued, shaking off his hand. She opened her mouth to deliver more stinging rebukes, only to find the harsh words quickly forgotten under Gunthar's intense gaze.

"We have to go, Alyce. Something's happened to the Mirror, I can feel it." His voice was so clear, so hard, that she moved without question, suppressing all additional grumbling.

"What's happened?" she asked as she wiped the sleep from her eyes, grabbed the bag containing their meagre belongings.

"The Mirror's crying out, as though in pain. And it suddenly started to move, very quickly, not like before...With Jenkins, there was a steady pattern of movement...blocks of solid movement, followed by periods of rest...I guess because he has so much baggage to cart around with him..." His voice trailed off, and he stopped in mid-step, a pained expression on his face. "Damn," he swore softly under his breath, closing his eyes as he concentrated on the Mirror's signal. She watched the subtle twitching of his facial muscles, the crinkling of skin around his mouth and eyes. The Gunthar of her dream had been smooth and sophisticated, the sort of debonair character who was bound to catch the eye of any man-hungry woman. Still, as she stood there watching his vulnerable face, she realised that she preferred the real thing. Of its own volition, her body leant towards him, her gaze fastened on that twitching mouth. Abruptly he opened his eyes, and she pulled back with a start. With only the briefest narrowing of his eyes, he brushed past her. "This way," he croaked, feet striking the ground at a steady pace, leaving her to stare blankly at the empty space he left behind.

Hand straying to the goggles sitting on the top her head, she started running after Gunthar, catching up to him in a couple of giant steps. "Um, you said the Mirror was crying out, does that mean it's louder than before?" she asked breathlessly, nearly stumbling over a large branch lying across the vague path they were following. In the grey twilight of breaking dawn, her augmented eyes were struggling to adjust. She couldn't pull the goggles down until full light, otherwise she'd risk running into trees. Uncle Henry had muttered something at the time about wanting to make another pair of goggles, with lighter-coloured lenses, but he obviously never got around to it.

For a moment he said nothing, face pinched in concentration. Probably focusing on the Mirror, she thought. Then he swung his head around, briefly regarded her through narrowed eyes. "No, oddly," he finally answered, eyes softening slightly as he looked away again. "It's crying out, but there's no force behind it. But it sounds different, like it's...afraid."

"Afraid?" she echoed, struggling to keep the scepticism out of her voice. "What could that thing be possibly afraid of? It's obviously a powerful object...when I think of the things I've seen it do..." The rest of her sentence trailed off, and she shuddered despite the sheen of sweat on her brow.

"I know, and that's what scares me," Gunthar said grimly, correctly interpreting her sudden silence. "I think something's happened to that woman, and that's why the Mirror is acting this way..."

Something in his voice made her glance across at his stony, pale face. "You really hate her, don't you?" she murmured, almost afraid to let the words out. "I think you hate her more than I do," she added thickly, the walls of her throat suddenly clammy. To her surprise, over the sounds of the forest and their own laboured breathing, she heard him laugh, a harsh, bitter sound. Suddenly his hand flew out, caught her elbow.

"Wait," he gasped, feet thudding to a clumsy stop, "I've got a stitch." Bending over slightly at the waist, he stumbled about until he found a tree to lean against. Grateful for the sudden break, she followed suit and rested a hand on the coarse bark of a pine tree, gingerly tested her weight against the thick trunk. When she first took over Clay's body, she'd made the mistake of casually leaning against a tree, taking for granted that it would support her weight. The answering creak of stressed timber and the shifting surface beneath her hand caused her to lose her balance and fall over. Unfortunately Sebastian and Jenkins witnessed her fall, their harsh-sounding laughter ringing out through the forest, attracting everyone's attention.

"You're probably right," Gunthar grunted, intruding on her thoughts, voice slightly muffled as he talked to the tree. "You know, when I was a young man, about twenty-three or so, there was this woman that I was completely besotted with. Ah, she was like the old you…smart, beautiful, strong. I worked for her father at the time, a well-to-do businessman, so I saw her almost every day. Her name was Mabel." Chest tightening at the reference to her old self, Alyce shifted her massive body, leant heavily against the thick tree trunk. After a moment of deliberation, she pushed the goggles down, studied the far-away look in Gunthar's eyes from the safety of her thick dark lenses.

"Mabel would always greet me with a warm smile, and seemed to tolerate my clumsy attempts at conversation, so I thought I had a chance, even though there were other, more eligible men trying to win her heart," Gunthar related, idly picking a leaf off a nearby branch. His unfocused gaze drifted across the small clearing as though peeling back layers of time. Watching the faint twitching of his lips as he smiled, she tried to imagine a younger, more innocent version of Gunthar scurrying about a workplace, all the while making eyes at the boss' daughter.

"After a year or so of falling more and more in love with her, I finally worked up the courage to confess my feelings. Ah, I'll never forget it, the way her smile didn't falter for a second as she turned me down, saying she was in love with another man. I was devastated of course, sitting there in stone cold silence as she rabbited on about this guy. Paul, I think his name was. Hardly surprising really, that she would fall for someone like that. They got engaged a couple of months after that, and I just tried my best to put it all behind me. It wasn't long however before I started to hear rumours about Paul, that he had several gambling debts to his name, and that he had a history of cheating on his partners. Despite the huge gaping hole she'd left in my heart, I couldn't stop caring for Mabel, and so started my own investigation into the rumours. Sadly everything I'd heard turned out to be true. I told her of course, warned her about his true nature. Saying things like there was still time to call off the engagement, marrying him would be a big mistake, pointing out desperately that I would never betray her.

"The look of pity on her face when I finally finished ranting was unbearable. Even before she opened her mouth to respond, I realised that it was no good, that she would always choose that loser over me. I quit my job the next day, and soon after started my travels. A couple of years later I returned home for a visit and happened to run into her. She put on a big show for me, greeting me warmly like an old friend, chatting about old times. But it was all an act. When she didn't force herself to smile or laugh, her face looked tired, worry lines etched into the skin around her mouth and eyes, and even though it was only early afternoon, her breath carried the strong scent of alcohol. When I asked about Paul, she stiffened briefly, a pained look sweeping over her features before the usual, forced-jovial mask slid into place. Without even meaning to, I gave her the same kind of pitiful look she had given me, and she quickly made her excuses and scurried away, never looking back once. That was the last time I saw her…"

His voice trailed away, gaze slowly returning to the present as his fingers curled tightly around the leaf. With a slight frown he looked down, opened his hand to reveal the leaf's crumpled form. "It wasn't long after that, I began my research into the Mirror, and came across those two unlikely-looking treasure hunters, Raphael and Sarah. When we finally clawed our way into that dusty, sealed-off cavern and found the Mirror, and I heard its strange alien voice inside my head, I can't describe it Alyce...the intense feeling that filled me in that moment. I, I just knew that I needed the Mirror, wanted it like nothing else. Just like Mabel's warm smiles and cute gestures, it made me feel special."

She held her breath as his voice fell away, and he rolled the crushed leaf between his thumb and forefinger, face dark with anger. "But it was Mabel all over again," he finally muttered, hand dropping heavily by his side, the mashed-up leaf falling away from his listless fingers. "I didn't fall off that mountain just because of a stupid argument with Raphael, or because I got carried away by my paranoid fears and suspicions...It was the will of the Mirror, Alyce. It, it chose Raphael and that brat over me...Even though I would have done anything to possess it, and keep it safe, even though my heart faithfully responded to its voice, it chose them over me. And now, that woman, Mel..."

From behind the thick protective lens, she caught the brief glimmer of tears rolling down his cheeks before he hastily brushed them away. "Just once Alyce, it would be nice if I were the one chosen, instead of someone else," he croaked, voice barely above the volume of a whisper. Without thinking, she reached out to him, awkwardly rested a heavy hand on his shoulder.

"Hey, er, don't be so hard on yourself," she stammered, struggling to find the right words. "I, I don't know about the Mirror, but that Mabel, she was an idiot for not choosing you. And I bet when that stupid husband of hers cheated or gambled behind her back, she regretted it, so um, don't worry." As her clumsy words of comfort rang out in the still air, it occurred to her that she was the same. Whatever justifications he made for casting her aside, her father had ultimately chosen his promiscuous new wife over his own flesh and blood. In a heartbeat, Jenkins and Sebastian had abandoned her, leaving her lifeless body on the floor of that old barn without a second thought. Clay's devotion to her was a purely conditioned response that her uncle had somehow inscribed into his brain. The only human being who had truly cared for her was Uncle Henry, and he was long gone.

"Um, were you trying to comfort me just then Alyce?"

The abrupt question startled her, and with her cheeks flushing furiously, she hastily turned away, silently willed the earth to open up and swallow her whole.

"Ah, yeah, something like that," she mumbled to a nearby tree. "Anyway, let's get going," she snapped, stomping off through the trees. The sound of footsteps catching up to her, a breathless accusation she was going the wrong way, and, with a slight alteration of course, they were on their way again. For a while, neither of them spoke, and she found herself peeking at Gunthar's slightly furrowed face from time to time, trying to gage his expression. She was silently debating whether or not to strike up a conversation to break the uneasy silence that filled the space between them, when Gunthar cleared his throat, turned his head to look at her. "Thank you, Alyce, for trying to comfort me," he murmured, her ears straining to catch the words before they were carried away by the breeze. "You've changed, you know," he continued after a couple of heartbeats, his voice a little stronger. "I don't think the old Alyce would have ever comforted me like that." Something in his voice reminded her of the dream.

"Ah Gunthar," she started, the question resting heavily on the tip of her tongue.

"Hmm?" he murmured, eyes staring glassily into the distance as he re-orientated himself with the Mirror.

How do you see me? Such a simple question, just five little syllables, and yet she couldn't quite make the appropriate sounds. "Ah, never mind," she grumbled, suddenly afraid to hear the answer. She briefly felt his quizzical gaze upon her before he refocused on the maze of trees in front of him. At his grunt of "this way", she wordlessly followed the slight turn of his body, and they cut a path into the more densely populated part of the forest, the thicker canopy blotting out the sun as it steadily climbed up the sky. Gunthar lengthened his strides to pull ahead, and she allowed herself to slink back a couple of feet, eyes trained on his back.

✦

Chapter 7
That Man Monfils.

Richard Gasquet nudged his horse forward, all too aware of the prisoner's eyes following his every move. Ever since they picked up Marcus, he had been made to feel increasingly uncomfortable with each passing day. At first, he thought it just coincidence that their eyes met whenever he happened to glance up in the man's general direction. But then he gradually noticed that no matter what position he took in the clump of men and horses, Marcus Rembert's eyes managed to seek him out. Much to his chagrin, the men had started making little jokes about it behind his back, snickering quietly to each other when they thought he wasn't in earshot. Even Mervelles seemed to be joining in on the fun.

"Really, why are we still dragging that deserter around for anyway?" he muttered bitterly to himself, digging his heels into his horse's sides yet again. They hadn't gotten any more useful information from him. He looked up at the sound of approaching hooves, was somewhat relieved to find Sebastian beside him. His relief was short lived however as he remembered the events of the last week, struggling to come to terms with his employer's odd behaviour. Not long after they interrogated Marcus at the inn, and listened to his disjointed, babbling account of a tall man with wiry blonde hair and a bald grey monster, Sebastian set out on horseback, gruffly explaining that he'd be back by nightfall the following day. With nothing better to do, he and the men had waited awkwardly at the inn, enduring the guarded, suspicion-filled looks from the innkeeper and his family. True to his word, Sebastian returned the following night, his face unreadable as he trudged wordlessly to his room on the upper floor. Thinking back on it, his gait had been rather stiff, as though each step caused him pain...

"Looks like we're on track to cross the border late this afternoon," the object of his thoughts announced. Reluctantly he looked across at Sebastian, followed the direction of his squinting eyes. A line of hills on the horizon roughly marked the border. By nightfall, they would be well into Russian territory. His chest suddenly felt tight, and he quickly looked away, clenched his hands against the impulse to grab Sebastian by his collar and shake him into the next kingdom. He had no right to look so excited, not when they were on the cusp of waltzing into a possible war zone.

Of course, that was pretty much the plan. It was all still so vivid in his memory, that fateful morning after Sebastian's return to the inn. The creature that jogged lightly down the stairs held little resemblance to the worn-out, crumpled man who had trudged up those very stairs the night before. With a trace of his old arrogance creeping back into his face, Sebastian had pulled him aside, explained the plan. Phrases like "I have it on good authority," and "the enemy's forces are stationing themselves along here" flitted out of his mouth like a well-rehearsed lines from a play, he spoke so confidently. Working on the assumption that Jenkins was now in league with the Russians, their goal was to reach the enemy camp first and cut them off. He had nearly fallen over at that point, overwhelmed by the sheer simplicity of the plan. All the while Sebastian continued to point out various locations on the map, fingers dancing over the stained, worn cloth. When he could finally get a word in edgeways, he had questioned Sebastian's source of information, upon which his whole strategy seemed to rest. For a handful of heartbeats, a shadow crossed Sebastian's face, his newfound confidence briefly wavering as though he remembered something unpleasant. "I assure you, the source of this information is solid, not the product of hearsay," Sebastian snapped, fingers gripping the edge of his map.

Returning to the present with a slight jolt, Gasquet glanced over at Sebastian, chewed thoughtfully on his bottom lip. Thinking back to that night at the inn, when they took turns to interrogate Marcus, Sebastian had at one stage knocked the man to the ground and sunk a pointy leather boot into his side. As Marcus was rolling about on the floor, something had caught Sebastian's eye, caused him to bend down and inspect the man's abdomen. Before he could move closer to investigate, Sebastian had ordered him to leave the room. The last thing he saw as he left was a grim-looking Sebastian looming over Marcus, the knife in his hand winking cruelly in the fluttering lantern light. Suspecting the worst, he had forced himself to move away from the door, half-expecting to be called back later to dispose of a body.

It was therefore a huge surprise the next morning to find Marcus still walking about in the land of the living, with only the dirty bandage around his abdomen suggesting that he sported fresh injuries. Eager to get his men back on the road, he had put aside his misgivings and not spared it another thought. Now, as they neared the border into Russia, he felt increasingly unsure about many things. Why did Sebastian tolerate Marcus' continued presence? Surely they had milked him of any valuable information on that first night, why not just let him go, or dispose of him? These questions ran about uselessly in his mind, finding nowhere to go but in endless circles. It wasn't like Sebastian to do something that didn't benefit him in some way.

The sudden crunch of dried leaves breaking underfoot tugged at his consciousness, and he looked across to find Marcus riding only a couple of feet away from him, the soldier leading his horse riding discretely ahead. He glowered at the soldier's straight back, swore he caught a glimpse of a smirk before the soldier turned his head. Skin prickling in anger, he swung his heated gaze back to Marcus, who in turn offered him a sickly smile. With a sound of pure frustration escaping the confines of his constricted throat, he urged his horse forward, savagely snatched the tether out of the soldier's hand. "I'll take over for a while, Gerald," he grated, tugging on the tether as he moved forward. The slightly taken-aback expression on Gerald's face gave him a small degree of satisfaction, and he guided Marcus past the clump of men, to the dense patch of trees that bordered the side of the road. Out of the corner of his eye, he noted Sebastian's faint glare, mouth opened as though to protest. A quick answering glower was all it took for the other man to change his mind, instead dragging out the grimy cloth map from his jacket pocket to check for the umpteenth time the squiggly lines that marked their passage.

He grunted, drew Marcus' horse alongside his own. Even Sebastian vaguely understood his need to end this farcical situation. He couldn't afford to allow Marcus' obvious fascination further erode his command of the men. When they were safely out of earshot of the main party, he took a deep breath, prepared to launch into a barrage of accusations.

"Ah, you really do remind me of the Captain," Marcus sighed before he could start, catching him off-guard.

"What?" he snapped, in a voice scraped clean of patience. Unperturbed by his harsh tone, Marcus shifted in the saddle, regarded him through smiling eyes.

"He was a large, strong man like yourself, with a stern manner. Really, he took everything so seriously, that I swore to follow him to the end," croaked Marcus, eyes alarmingly bright as though he were about to cry.

Wincing at the sudden tightness of his chest, he looked away, tried to recapture his previous anger. "So why didn't you?" he spat, the venom in his voice lacking any real bite. "You say you were left for dead on the battlefield, but there was nothing stopping you from tracking down what was left of your regiment. You must have had some idea of where they would go…"

"But I tried, I really did!" Marcus cried, hands curling around the saddle horn. "I wandered the forest for days, living off only the meagre supplies I managed to grab before the enemy soldiers could spot me. Despite my hunger and exhaustion, I walked and walked, but I never saw them again…"

"That's no excuse for deserting!" he roared, the old anger flaring up. "If you couldn't find your regiment, you should have just gone to the first base you could find and turn yourself in. Better that than turning into such a pathetic creature living off scraps."

The air became charged with tension as both men fell into silence, their raw emotions exposed. Abruptly Marcus snickered, a harsh, self-mocking sound that seemed out of place from such a meek man. "You know, I've had this conversation before," he stated flatly, urging his horse to move closer. The air about him seemed to change somehow, and Gasquet found himself wanting to shrink away from the suddenly flinty eyes that studied him. "An old man took me in, shared what little food he had with me," Marcus continued, leaning over slightly in the saddle, bringing his face even closer. "He was a lonely old man, desperate for company," he continued, unblinking gaze pinning Gasquet to the spot. "I told him my story, and at first he was sympathetic. After living together for a while though, little nicks started to show. We'd disagree about something trivial, and before I knew it he'd say the same thing. "Why didn't you just go back to the army?" "There's still a war going on, you should be out there." "I'm sure you're not the first person to be left for dead on a battle-field."'" His high-pitched mocking voice became more and more shrill, and Gasquet's hand drifted towards the weapon at his side.

"Ah, I got so mad at the old man. What would he know, hiding in his little hut in the middle of the forest, too scared to barely show his face in town? So I described to him, in great detail, what it was like, seeing people you know die violently right in front of you." As he spoke, Marcus' hands clenched tightly together, knuckles turning white against the dark, weathered skin of his fingers. "He became hysterical the more I talked, and no matter how many times I asked him to be quiet, he kept yelling at me, calling me names...it took a long time to make him stop." Watching the way his hands twisted and squeezed together, Gasquet had a pretty good idea of how he made the old man stop.

In that instant, Marcus reminded him of so many other soldiers he had served with, pushed to the brink of sanity by the extremes of war. Despite his unassuming appearance, and the fact that his wrists were tightly bound together, he was a potentially dangerous individual. Normally he'd back off in a situation like this, and report to his superiors, but with Sebastian for one reason or another tolerating Marcus' presence, he suspected that would be a waste of time. "Listen," he finally snarled, patience exhausted as he decided that violence was the best way to get through to Marcus. He grabbed the collar of the scruffy man's grimy shirt, hauled him up off the saddle so they were eye to eye. "I don't care about your issues," he bit off savagely, with all the restrained rage he could muster, "just stop staring at me all the time with that stupid womanly look on your face, it makes me uncomfortable, or so help me God I'll turn you into a woman!"

His body was so stiff with rage, he didn't realise Marcus was choking until his ugly-sounding, half-strangled gasps penetrated his foggy brain. With a grunt he dropped the man roughly back into his saddle, gruffly turned away and started to lead them back toward the pack. He was too surprised at his own intense anger to even mumble an apology. All the irritations of the past three weeks had piled up inside him without any clear outlet, always being shoved aside while he dealt with the latest disaster. "Ah," he murmured, realising that he had just taken all that out on Marcus. With a faint stirring of guilt, he turned slightly to glance at the man's hunched-over form, breath rattling noisily in his chest as he hungrily sucked in air, coughing violently in the process. He hastily looked away as he registered that the man's lips were still blue. Cursing softly under his breath, he chastised himself for nearly killing the man.

"Sorry...Captain." The ghost of a voice scratched at his ears, barely tugged at his consciousness. He looked back in time to see Marcus slump in the saddle, his limp body hanging dangerously over the side.

"Jesus Christ," he swore, vaulting out of his saddle. "What's wrong?" he asked, catching the man's shoulders. An incoherent reply escaped Marcus' lips, and the sudden movement of his bound hands caught Gasquet's attention. "What the hell?" he blurted, blinking in disbelief as a dark patch started spreading from beneath clenched fingers. "Why the hell are you bleeding?" he stammered, easing Marcus awkwardly to the ground.

"Ah, an old injury that recently re-opened, Captain," Marcus croaked between coughs, hand closing over the patch. "Please pay it no mind," he added, anxiety building in his voice.

"Wait a minute," Gasquet blurted, suddenly remembering the knife in Sebastian's hand the night he brought Marcus to the inn. Ignoring Marcus' by-now hysterical denials, he reached out and pulled Marcus' hands away, breath catching noisily in his throat at the sight of the blood. "He did something to you, didn't he?" he murmured thickly, the acrid smell tickling his nostrils, making his stomach churn. "What could have possessed him to do that?" he wondered aloud, maintaining a grip on Marcus' hands while reaching out to lift up his shirt.

"No, Captain, don't touch it," Marcus croaked, shrinking away from his outstretched hand, intense anxiety etched deeply into his face. He stumbled back a couple of steps in a vain attempt to escape, only to have his legs crumble beneath him.

"Stay still, stop wriggling," he grunted, sinking to his knees, hand at last closing around the blood-soaked material. Marcus' whimpering protests faded into the background as he pulled up the shirt, stared in horrified fascination at the long gash in his abdomen that had re-opened. Totally absorbed in that grizzly line, he reached out and gingerly touched the congealed blood, blinking at the round depression that could be felt on either side of the wound...

"Ah, it's opened up again, has it?" He jumped halfway out of his skin at the abrupt voice, spun around to glare accusingly at Sebastian, who was standing directly behind him. Stooping over slightly to peer over his shoulder, Sebastian studied the angry, weeping red mark on Marcus' abdomen with mild interest.

"What do you mean, it's opened up again? What the hell is going on here?" Gasquet stammered, clambering stiffly to his feet.

"I, I didn't tell him anything master," Marcus spluttered, scrambling back while clutching his stomach.

"You did this, didn't you?" he croaked, squeezing the sound out past the growing tightness of his chest. "That night at the inn, I saw you with a knife as I was leaving the room..."

"There was a listening stone embedded in Marcus' abdomen," Sebastian explained, shouldering past him. "Geez, I stitched it up and everything," he murmured as he crouched down before Marcus. He reached out tentatively to the bloody patch, frowned at the re-opened wound. With a click of his tongue, he glanced up at Gasquet, eyes narrowed in suspicion. "Just what were you doing with my pet, captain, to re-open his wound like this?"

Gasquet was vaguely aware of his jaw moving up and down, and yet the words wouldn't come out. "What do you mean, listening stone?" he finally spluttered, years of military training and discipline dissolving under the heat of Sebastian's accusing stare.

Sebastian idly reached behind him, to the knapsack resting against his hip. "I'm not sure if you remember, but our friend Alyce had a pair of listening stones she used for spying. The golem must have inherited the stones after his mistress' demise. Don't ask me how they worked. I don't think Alyce understood that herself, only to say there's a link between the two stones." As Sebastian calmly explained, he pulled out another bandage, started to slowly wrap it around Marcus' abdomen. "Yet another marvellous gift from her very talented uncle," he muttered darkly under his breath, hands tightening on the coarse cloth. Marcus cried involuntarily at the extra pressure on his stomach, and Sebastian mumbled an apology of sorts. For his part, Gasquet became vaguely aware that his jaw was still hanging loosely in the lower half of his face, and with some effort he snapped it shut.

"So, you noticed the stone in Marcus' gut, and cut it out?" he asked carefully, struggling to sequence the order of events in his mind. Sebastian murmured an affirmative, continued to cover the wound. From the look on Marcus' face, each turn of the bandage caused him agony, lips pressed tightly together against any further cries. He quickly looked away, swallowed back the wave of nausea that pain-etched face evoked. "Why keep him with us at all then?" he pressed, for the all the world sounding like a petulant child. Sebastian's hands paused over the patch of blood that had already soaked through the fresh bandage, an irritated look on his face.

"I don't know," he answered with a heavy sigh, giving up the bandage, dropping what was left on Marcus' stomach. He stiffly clambered to his feet, turned away from them. "We might still be able to use him, although I suspect Gunthar and the golem already doubt the actual whereabouts of the listening stone."

"Where, where is it?" he asked, throat suddenly dry as the forest clearing began to swirl around him. Feeling his nausea worsen, he took a slightly unsteady step forward. In response to his question, Sebastian paused momentarily, looked back at Gasquet, lips curled in an almost mischievous grin.

"Come on Captain," he bade, moving off again, not giving anything away, "we need to get going."

He gawked helplessly at Sebastian's retreating back, swung his head around to gawk even more helplessly at Marcus, who was slowly scraping himself off the ground. Wincing with the effort, he managed to get to his feet, right hand desperately clutching the bandage to his stomach. As he trudged past, Gasquet could smell the blood that still oozed from his wound, along with a hint of putrefying flesh. Gagging slightly on the strong scent, he called out, took a couple of steps to catch up to Marcus.

"Ah, let me wrap that for you," he wheezed between coughs, the smell tickling his nostrils as he came closer. For a handful of heartbeats, neither of them spoke, the only sound to break the silence being the occasional grunt from Marcus as the bandage was stretched tightly over his wound. "That must have really hurt, when they put the stone in there," he mumbled, suddenly gripped by an irrational desire to make conversation. A sharp intake of breath from Marcus, and then a mumbled affirmative.

"That Gunthar guy healed it though, at the end," he added, eyes fixed on the cloth that now wrapped his middle. He tentatively prodded the area, quickly withdrew his fingers. "At first, I thought they implanted the stone in my gut in order to use me as a convenient listening post. Being more inconspicuous than either of them, I could slip into towns ahead of them, ask around for any useful information. They even suggested that they'd take out the stone if I co-operated. Little did I realise they wanted me to act as a spy, sending me away to get supplies when they knew you and your men were in the area. Really, it was brilliant. I was still recovering from having my gut cut open, even with Gunthar's healing efforts, so moving fast wasn't an option. To be honest, I'm not sure what exactly was going through my mind when you and your men found me in that forest, but it didn't once occur to me to try and run away. I saw the writing on the wall, I guess. That was their plan all along, and I figured I may as well play along. I was prepared to play my role of spy to the bitter end, but then Sebastian found the stone so easily, and before I knew it, I was being cut open again."

He had heard most of this story before, that night at the inn, when they interrogated him, and yet he couldn't help but stand absolutely still, transfixed by the lucid, calm words flowing out of Marcus' mouth. Wordlessly, Marcus took the end of the bandage out of his numb, unmoving fingers, tucked it under the main wrapping. "Man, I really pleaded for my life that night," he continued, a trace of bitterness in his voice. "Didn't expect he'd drag me along though, like I could be of any use to anyone now." He shuffled past, heavy, slow-moving feet at odds with his stiff, drawn-back shoulders. Richard Gasquet felt as though someone had just kicked him in the stomach, all the air seemingly knocked out of him. He opened his mouth to murmur a half-hearted apology, when Marcus paused, glanced back over his shoulder. "I'll try not to stare at you so much, Captain Gasquet. Sorry for causing you trouble with your men."

"Ah, thanks," he mumbled awkwardly to Marcus' fading back, and for a while he just stood motionless in the clearing, closing his eyes against the dazzling white orb climbing high into the sky, and all the confusing things it illuminated in this world. Swearing softly under his breath, he opened his eyes, gave the peerless blue sky stretching above his head a final rueful look, before trudging back to the others.

Many miles away, in the shadow of a hill, Alyce blinked, shook her head. A quick sidewise glance at Gunthar, who was semi-collapsed against a tree while he caught his breath, and she tried again. Turning her face away from Gunthar, she concentrated on the faint vibrations transmitted by the listening stone, listened in disbelief as she confirmed what she was hearing. "Wait, not here in the carriage, what if someone sees?" A woman's voice. Most definitely a woman's voice. A male voice replied, but the words were so slurred and muffled, she couldn't make them out. "No, don't touch me there, no." The woman's voice, but a little breathless this time. A nasty laugh from the man, and then the woman moaned and panted. "For God's sake stop popping my buttons, ah." The woman's voice, accompanied by more moaning. Now the man was grunting, huffing and puffing, all with a telling rhythm...

"Alyce?"

"Baahh!" she yelped, jumping halfway out of her borrowed skin. Blushing furiously, she willed the lewd sounds in her mind to fade away as she turned to face Gunthar.

"Something wrong?" Gunthar asked, expression rapidly shifting from mild interest to serious concern when he saw her bright red face.

"Ah, no, I just heard something weird through the listening stone. I um, I'll try again later, and see what our little spy is up to." Laughing weakly to cover her embarrassment, she brushed aside Gunthar's suspicious look, started off through the tall grass that covered the base of the hill.

Truthfully, she'd suspected for the past couple of days that something was awry with the listening stone. At first, the constant sound of hooves clip-clopping in the background didn't strike her as odd. Also, the range of different voices captured by the listening stone she put down to the fact that Sebastian must have hired more men. Of course, it was a bit odd that she didn't hear Marcus' whiny voice at all, or any other voices that she recognised. When quizzed by Gunthar about the stone's status, she could honestly say that it sounded like it was going around in circles. Gunthar was generally satisfied with this answer, his mind too full of the Mirror to focus intently on anything else. He obviously didn't see Sebastian and his men as a serious threat anymore. Now, with the change in the Mirror, Gunthar would spend even less time worrying about Sebastian. Best he forget about it all together, she thought ruefully. Whatever had happened to the listening stone, it obviously wasn't of much use to them now. Either Marcus had somehow gotten it out, or somebody else had done the honours. Could he possibly survive that in his condition, without Gunthar around to heal him?

With a click of her tongue, she silently reprimanded herself for not telling him the truth. She slowed down, fell into step with Gunthar. "Ah, Gunthar," she began, feeling oddly awkward.

"Huh?" Gunthar murmured, glancing across at her, the mid-morning sun glinting off his golden hair. Squinting her eyes against the dazzling effect, she took a deep breath, opened her mouth to share her suspicions about the current location of the listening stone. She didn't get much further than "um, ah" when Gunthar held out his hand, called for a stop. Like a cat that had suddenly caught the whiff of prey, he stood absolutely still, only the slight twitching of his eyes and mouth separating his appearance from that of a statue.

"Damn, they're moving all over the place," he muttered darkly, slowly turning his head, "not at all like Jenkins." Unconsciously she held her breath, willing all the sounds of the forest to fade into silence as well. "There," he uttered through stiff lips, turning his body a couple of inches to the right.

Looking dubiously at the difference in direction, she turned accordingly as they started off again. "Ah, you were saying something Alyce?" he prompted, shooting her a quizzical look. She met his gaze, noted the tension that still lingered around his eyes. When did he start looking so tired, she wondered, biting her bottom lip.

"Ah, I've forgotten," she lied, forcing her facial muscles to move. Flashing him a lop-sided, self-depreciating grin, she turned her head and focused on the landscape that unfolded before them. The trees were starting to thin out, with greater expanses of grass and bushes in between. Out of the corner of her eye, she noted the sceptical look on Gunthar's face, steeled herself to keep her gaze firmly fixed ahead. With a vague shrug of his shoulders, he gazed forward, marched relentlessly on, leaving her to reconcile her mixed-up, confusing emotions.

Even further away, in a small Polish town, a plump toddler clambered off his mother's lap, started to clumsily explore the floor of the coach. Mother called out his name, made a half-hearted attempt to stop him. Armed with a cheeky grin, he boldly continued his investigation, nearly falling flat on his face as the tiny room lurched suddenly. Resisting the urge to cry, knowing full well his adventure would end if he did, he tentatively shifted his hands and feet, inched his way carefully across the floor. There, under the seat, there was something shiny. Mother was calling him back, voice tinged with impatience. Even over the dull roar of horses' hooves striking the cobbled street and the creaking of the carriage, he picked up that tone immediately, knew what it meant. He was running out of time. Pretending not to hear, he wedged his head under the seat, reached a short arm towards that glint in the darkness. The shadowy space beneath the seat was scary, and he almost lost his nerve when his hand brushed something ticklish and sticky.

Behind him, Mother was calling out again, voice hardening with each utterance of his name. "Jozef!" she suddenly roared, losing control of her voice as her irritation skipped a few levels. It wouldn't be long before she matched actions with words, and physically dragged him back. Straining every muscle in his small body, he wriggled and stretched and rocked his way further under the seat. Still, the shiny thing eluded the reach of his chubby digits. Mother gave her final warning, punctuating her words with the scrape of her shoes as she prepared to stand up. Watching the shiny thing out of the corner of his eye, he inched forward even further. His fingertips brushed against something cold, hard and smooth. More creaking from the seat behind him, and he knew without looking that Mother was on her feet, arms held out ready to scoop him up. Frantically he pawed the dusty floorboards, fingers wiggling outwards in search of the precious shiny thing. Mother called his name again, more cajoling this time. Tears of frustration started to well up in his eyes, the urge to bawl building up inside of him.

He started to take deep breaths in preparation for crying, all too aware of Mother's swooping presence just behind him, when the carriage jolted. The floor rushed up to meet him, and he fell flat on his face, arms and legs flung out reflexively. Unable to take it anymore, he let out all of his frustrations, tears streaming unchecked down his cheeks to drip onto the floor. Over the sound of his own cries, he could faintly hear Mother making "shush" noises, her hands firmly wrapped around his torso as she picked him up off the floor. He cried heartily into her shoulder, body gradually losing its stiffness as her warmth seeped into his body. His cries went down a notch as his lungs recovered and he started to feel sleepy. Mother's familiar warmth and smell wrapped around him, and he started to forget what was so important under the seat. Something shiny, he thought sleepily, his cries more muffled and subdued now. As the pain from the fall receded, he idly wondered what it was, glinting out to him like that.

Another jolt of the carriage, and the sound of something rolling across the floor scratched at his rapidly fading consciousness. "Oh," Mother remarked, her voice floating reassuringly near his ear. Without warning she bent down, picked something off the floor. He slowly turned his head, gazed at the small round object nestled in Mother's hand through narrowed eyes. Catching his vaguely interested look, Mother turned him on her lap, put out her hand. "Here you go Jozef," she said so innocently, "do you want to play with this?"

Shiny thing. Sitting in the palm of her hand, easily within his reach, was a shiny black stone, about the size of his hand. With slow, deliberate movements, he picked it up, wrapped his chubby fingers around it. Everything else in the carriage blurred away to the far edges of his consciousness, the black round stone filling his vision as he held it up, turned it around. On closer inspection, there were bands of fine white flecks cutting paths through the inky blackness. "So pretty," he thought with a satisfied sigh, waving it up and down so that it caught the light streaming in through the window. Thinking about all the fun he was going to have with the shiny thing, like hitting it against things, sucking it, pushing it through dirt, he fell asleep, the stone still gripped tightly in his little hand.

Mel felt her body sway dangerously, felt the answering tug of the ropes that kept her firmly anchored to the saddle. She strained her eyes, tried to focus on something, anything. Men on horses, their straight backs bouncing up and down. They were riding fast, riding hard. Who were those men again? One of them turned back, shook his head at her. Ah, this one, she knew this one, she thought, beads of sickly sweat gathering on her brow again. Piercing brown eyes that floated above a bushy beard, and a bushy beard that couldn't conceal the cold hard line of the man's unforgiving mouth. She lifted her head, wondered idly when it drooped again. She was sleepy all the time, struggling to stay awake long enough to string two thoughts together. Must be something to do with the holes in her arm, she decided, raising one slender arm, the loose sleeve of her shirt falling to reveal the ugly crude puncture wounds near the bend.

"What, time for another injection?" a voice mumbled beside her. With a start she looked across, saw the bearded man with brown eyes pulling alongside, the horse he was riding snorting and straining against the bridle. His name, what was his name? He had told her his name, she was sure of it. She was staring at a tobacco- stained hand that was poking lifelessly out of the rubble, feeling as though someone had just kicked her in the back of the head, when this man swept into what was left of the room. Funny, try as she might, she couldn't remember his name, just the contempt and hatred he had displayed towards her.

"Hey Monfils!"

"Monfils," she echoed softly, craning her neck to gawk helplessly at the other man. "Monfils," she repeated, trying to burn the name into her memory. But then what about the other man, what was his name? He was the first person she saw when she finally regained consciousness. But what happened before that? She was staring at a tobacco-stained hand, it must have belonged to someone she knew. The image of a little silver snuff box popped into her head, and for one surreal moment, she felt as though she could reach out with her mind, grab onto that memory, before she drowned in the mire of her half-formed, foggy thoughts. "Jenkins," she croaked, finally remembering the man behind the snuff box.

"Isn't it too early to give her another shot?" The gruff voice spoke directly beside her, and yet to her muddled consciousness, it felt like he was talking far away, about someone else entirely. "We've still got another three days at least until we reach the camp. How are we supposed to control her if we run out of drugs before then?" Blinking slowly, she studied Monfils' reaction, gaze fastened on the twitching movements of his beard as he frowned. He reached out his hand, waved it in front of her face. Biting her tongue against the urge to laugh, she continued to stare blankly ahead.

That's right, play dumb, lower their defences, and then when they least expect it, bam! Ha ha, that's right, just like with Jenkins. Someone grabbed her arm, pulled back the sleeve. "Hmm," Monfils murmured, pressing down on one of the puncture wounds in the bend of her arm. An involuntary cry escaped her lips at the faint stab of pain, and he briefly increased the pressure before letting go. "Hmm, give it another hour then," he concluded, abruptly turning away. Another hour, and then he was going to pump that drug into her again. How many times had he stuck that needle into her now? If she could just focus her eyes long enough, she could count the number of puncture marks, and work it out from there. With stiff, clumsy fingers, she pulled back her sleeve, stared at the little angry holes in the crook of her arm. There were at least five or six, she counted before the holes started to swim about in her field of vision. From the very first moment she regained consciousness, they were sticking needles in her arm, taking careful note of her reactions.

"Good Lord, at this rate she'll be a full-blown addict before we get to camp," the gruff voice growled again, this time somewhere ahead of her. She awoke with a start, straightened up in the saddle, her limp arm still exposed and sitting on her lap. When exactly did she nod off? That hap-pened all the time now, slipping in and out of consciousness at the drop of a hat, without even being aware of it. Out of nowhere, she recalled that she used to watch TV with her husband late at night, only to catch herself nodding off. That abrupt stop-in-the-middle-of-falling head motion, followed by a guilty glance at Gary's smirking face. He always, always caught her nodding off. He must have been watching her out of the corner of his eye, just waiting for her head to droop.

"That's the plan, right?" Monfils shot back in a surprisingly jovial voice. "As long as we keep pumping her full of that shit, she'll be completely under our control. And then, when the General wants her to do something, we can use the drug as an incentive. Really, this is much easier than threatening her companions."

"He's right you know," a silky voice purred in her ear. Her blood ran cold at the familiar voice, and she slowly turned her head, forced her eyes to focus. There, floating alongside her horse, was Jenkins. Or at least an apparition of Jenkins she silently corrected herself, nodding at her old foe. She opened her mouth to retort, something about having hallucinations, but she couldn't quite push the sound out.

"Ha, I bet you thought all your problems would be over when you killed me, eh?" Throat going dry to the point that swallowing was painful, she kept her eyes firmly averted from that sickly pale face. The face that moved like normal when talking, and yet the eyes remained lifeless, like dull, unpolished stones.

"Yes, things have turned out brilliantly, don't you think? You've been abducted by an even more heartless bastard than me, separated from your companions, being pumped full of God-knows-what, being delivered to God-knows-who... really, first class job Mel."

He snickered quietly to himself, an unearthly, guttural sound, the stuff of nightmares. She stole a glance at his face, silently marvelled at how solid it looked. The only tell-tale sign that he wasn't really there in flesh and blood, apart from the fact that he was definitely dead, was the complete lack of movement from the grass under his feet. "What a horrible hallucination," she finally managed to mumble, shaking her head. "Must be the drugs," she added sluggishly, suddenly finding it hard to keep her head up.

"That's right, it's just the drugs," Jenkins purred in her ear, the sound so close that she jumped, nearly falling out of the saddle. A swift answering movement from one of the men riding in front of her, dark eyes flinty above a thick beard. What was his name again? Something told her to look dazed, unfocused eyes gazing off into the distance. A line of drool making its way down her chin completed the image, and the man, ("Monfils"?) turned back, grunting his disgust at her slovenly display.

"So, what was your plan anyway Mel? Kill me, run off with Raphael and the two runts, and live happily ever after? Was that it?" For a hallucination, his voice carried an awful lot of venom. Was she projecting her sense of self-loathing back onto herself via this spiteful apparition? Though, she couldn't really blame him, or the hallucination of Jenkins, for hating her. She did kill him, after all. Even now, with all the drugs running through her veins, she could still remember that moment, when he bent over to pick up his snuff box, and through the Mirror's eye she saw him look up, look directly at her. In that moment, she deliberately chose to use the Mirror, causing the explosion that tore that room apart, tore Jenkins apart. "I was desperate," she croaked, barely managing to push the feathery sound out past the sudden lump in her throat. "We can't, can't let the Mirror fall into the wrong hands. It's...too dangerous," she added, her justifications sounding weak to her own ears. Two straight, broad backs caught the sunlight streaming in through holes in the forest canopy, and for a moment the red coats of the riders dazzled her barely opened eyes. Eyelids fluttering like crazy, she tried to focus on those two bouncing spots of light.

"Can't let it fall into the wrong hands, eh?" Jenkins drawled, clicking his tongue. "And just whose hands are you referring to?" For a moment, she forgot to breathe, the red backs, the horses, the tall oak trees that towered over their heads all fading away to the edge of her consciousness, leaving only his words to fill the void.

"Yeah Mummy, whose hands?" She blinked, looked up at Kai's jam-smeared face grinning at her from across the kitchen table. "Who are you trying to keep that thing away from again?"

"Kai," she croaked hoarsely, chest tightening painfully at the sight of her little boy.

"Kai, don't bother Mummy, she's had a rough day," Gary interjected, reaching out to pat her shoulder. Without thinking, she stiffened at that sudden contact, almost as though she'd just been touched by a ghost. Flushing guiltily, she awkwardly clasped his hand, gave it a quick squeeze.

"It's more like I'm the ghost," she murmured, gazing about at the familiar room. The tacky wood-veneer coated cupboards, the faded orange-and-green patterned curtains that looked like something from the 60s, the chipped laminated counter that divided the room. On a rickety metal stand in the corner, an old CRT TV glared out at them. Her mouth went dry as her bleary eyes focused on the screen, which for some weird reason was playing footage of two red-coated men riding on horseback through a forest, their backs firmly, unerringly facing the camera.

"What the hell kind of show is this?" she cried, pushing away from the table.

"Wait Mum, aren't you going to finish your breakfast?" Karen pouted from the other side of the counter, looking up from an enormous thick chopping board that covered half the laminated surface. With a small shake of her head, Karen tightened her grip on a large knife, continued hacking savagely at something brown and slimy that threatened to slide off the board the instant she loosened her grip. It took several moments of gaping at her daughter to realise what it was she was so enthusiastically chopping up. A huge octopus, its tentacles swinging about the base of the counter with each chop. "Just leave room for calamari, okay Mum?"

With a weak smile she sank back in her chair, all fight sucked away from her by Karen's baffling display. "Nice family," Jenkins murmured beside her, lips poised over the rim of a cup.

"Hey!" she cried as he calmly proceeded to sip his coffee. "What, what are you doing here? You have no place in these memories. Get out, you stupid hallucination!" Jenkins looked up from his coffee, eyebrows knitted together in irritation. Carefully setting the cup down on the table, he snapped his fingers. She vaguely heard her own breath catch noisily in her throat at the abrupt freezing of time. Gary's lanky body leant awkwardly over the table, hands stretching out towards her, while Kai's toast-filled mouth gaped open, a globule of jam defying gravity to hang off his chin. Likewise, globs of octopus goo were suspended crazily in the air only inches away from Karen's face, poised to splatter her unsuspecting cheek the instant time unfroze.

"Let's get one thing straight," Jenkins purred in her ear, resting a heavy, claw-like hand on her shoulder. "I'm not just a hallucination. I won't go away when you get sick of me or regain your senses." He leant in closer, warm breath fanning the side of her neck. "I guess I'm kind of like a ghost, living inside your head," he continued, silky voice ringing softly in her ear. "That moment, when I bent down to pick up the snuff box, and saw the Mirror sitting on the floor, I realised straight away, realised that was your plan." His clammy hand trailed down her arm, brushed against the side of her breast. Skin crawling at the creepy touch, she wanted to desperately push him away and escape, but her body seemed to be frozen to the spot.

"In that split second, when I stared at the lumpy sack on the floor, I could sense you Mel, looking back at me through the Mirror." His feet barely scraped the ground as he moved to stand in front of her. "In that split second, I felt such intense hatred fill me, the likes of which I'd never felt before. And you know, for a hate-filled guy like me, that's pretty bad." Tobacco-stained fingers trailed across her cheek, pressed against her lips. "In that moment of blinding hatred, I willed a part of my consciousness to latch onto you Mel, so I could haunt and torment you..." Barely a flicker of emotion was carried by his voice, and yet he forced his fingers into her mouth, stretched the corners of her lips until it hurt. Suddenly it was hard to breathe, his fingers roughly probing the inside of her mouth. Only when she started to gag violently and sag in his grip did a faint smile tug at the corners of his thin lips. Apparently satisfied, he withdrew his fingers, leaving her to sink into a coughing, gasping heap.

"But you know Mel," he continued smoothly, as though nothing had happened, "since lodging myself in this sorry excuse of a brain of yours, I've been roaming through your memories, and I can't help but feel a little sorry for you." She looked up from where she sat hunched on the floor, distractedly raised a shaky hand to wipe the drool from her mouth. Abruptly the scene changed, and they were in a forest, tall pine trees towering over them like proud silent sentinels. She clambered stiffly to her feet, looking around bewilderedly for Gary and the kids. Everything from the previous scene had vanished, except for the old TV on its rickety stand, still playing footage of two red-coated men on horseback.

Before she could question the fact that the television was somehow magically playing in the middle of a forest without any obvious power supply, a high-pitched scream pierced the air. "Wait," she croaked, her mouth suddenly dry as alarm bells clanged in her head. "I know that voice," she murmured, feet moving on their own accord toward the screams. A couple of heartbeats for the sound to truly sink through the layers of fuzziness that seemed to enshroud her senses, and she was running. "Sarah," she gasped, stopping with a heavy thud as the familiar scene played out before her eyes. There was Sarah, leaning helplessly against a tree, blood oozing out of a large gash in her arm. Three scruffy-looking men were gathering around her, laughing nastily as she weakly waved her sword at them.

"Isn't this when you meet Sarah for the first time?" Jenkins asked casually, looking up from inspecting his nails. Jumping at the sound of his voice, she grabbed his shoulder, pulled him down with her as she sank behind the nearest tree trunk.

"Shut up," she hissed, digging her fingers into his surprisingly solid shoulder, "or they'll hear you." Wincing at the sudden pain in her chest, she shifted closer to the trunk, edged cautiously past its rough bark to peer at the small clearing.

"Shouldn't you be searching for a weapon by now?" Jenkins pressed, shaking off her hand. "Otherwise, how can you "accidentally" kill that guy?" He nodded at the man standing furthest back from the others, and suddenly she was creeping down the slightly sloping ground, a rusty blade held desperately in her sweaty grip. She only had a second to wonder how she got there so fast, or how the weapon found its way into her hand, when she tripped, slamming hard into the man's unsuspecting back. There was a moment of resistance, and then her weight fell forward freely, closely followed by spreading wet warmth on her belly.

"Wow, you just pushed that knife through his ribs like it was nothing!" Jenkins crowed, crouching down beside her struggling figure.

The man beneath her thrashed about, desperately trying to reach the wound, throwing her off in the process.

"It was an accident," she wheezed, pushing the sound out with the little air that remained her lungs.

"So, what was the plan anyway?" Jenkins asked cheerfully, scratching his head in a mocking display. The man ("Roge"?) laid his considerable weight on top her body, large meaty hands wrapped around her throat. "I just... wanted to...scare them away," she gasped, her vision becoming more grey and blurred by the second, as though her life ebbed away with each fluttering heartbeat. "Just wanted...to stop them...from attacking Sarah," she panted to Roge's red furious face, eyes rolling to the back of her head.

Just as she was about to slide into the darkness and pass out, Jenkins' silky voice rang right beside her ear, warm breath stirring the fine hairs on her neck. "But that's what I don't understand Mel," he whispered, "why go so far for someone you don't even know? I mean, that's not the sort of person you really are." The pressure around her neck eased as Roge gave one final shudder and slumped on top of her, his unfettered mass threatening to crush her in a more general way. At this point, she should wriggle and push like crazy to be free, only to be hit in the head by one of the remaining attackers, and yet she couldn't move, Jenkins' words running around in an endless loop in her mind.

"But, they were about to, to rape her," she croaked weakly, pushing feebly at Roge's round heavy shoulders.

"What makes you so sure that she didn't start it?" Jenkins' pressed relentlessly. She blinked, gazed stupidly at the three bodies decorating the ground around the base of the tree. Sarah now slumped beside her, body propped up against the tree trunk, limbs listlessly splayed out as the attackers started pulling at her dress. Out of the corner of her eye, she caught Jenkins' slight movement, as he shifted out of the way of the attackers. "Look at those cold lifeless bodies Mel. She killed those men before you arrived on the scene. Fairly impressive self- defence, don't you think?"

A weak laugh escaped her numb lips, body jerking roughly as a large pair of hands grabbed her knees, pulled them apart. "Just what are you saying?" she murmured, the sound barely scratching at her own ears it was so weak.

"Being a vengeful spirit has its advantages. I've been walking around in your memories, and I have to say, you're not the sort of person to rush in and help others...maybe a handful of half-hearted attempts in a lifetime of looking the other way..." The ugly sound of cloth being torn, and the rough uncaring hands clawing at her flesh. Briefly she spared a thought for the farmer's wife, who had given her the dress before kicking her out.

"Maybe I was sick of being that person," she whispered, vaguely remembering those times of holding back, waiting for someone else to step in. Her legs were spread wide now, the hairy man looming over her tugging urgently at the waistband of his trousers. Seemingly oblivious to what was going on, what was about to happen, Jenkins leant in closer, placed his thin lips directly over her ear.

"I don't think so, Mel," he stated in a cold, emotionless voice. "Don't you see? Even before you formally met Sarah and Raphael, the Mirror has been reaching out to you, manipulating you..." Something plunged into her, and she looked down in shock to find a knife sticking out of her side. Dark beady eyes narrowed in satisfaction above her, framed beautifully by the burning buildings in the background. Backing away from the angry raider, fingers pressing desperately against the hole in her side, her heels connected with something, and she fell in a clumsy heap on the ground, legs draped over the body of a fellow raider. "Ah, see, this time you definitely can't say it was an accident." She tore her frantic gaze from the ring leader's steadily approaching face to stare at Jenkins. At her dumbfounded look, he clucked his tongue, gazed ruefully at the two dead bodies that now littered the ground. "We can replay the memory, if you want to confirm it," he offered distractedly, eyes fastened to the dark spreading patch of blood that seeped out from behind her fingers. With a look of utter fascination on his face, he reached out, prodded the punctured flesh.

She cried out, pushed him away. "They attacked first, God dammit!" she shouted over the roar of the fire and the screams of the villagers. "Stop judging me! I'm sure you've killed heaps of people in your time," she spat, raising the sword she still somehow clutched in her hand. Stepping through Jenkins as though he were a shadow, the raider stepped towards her, knocked the sword out of her hand with one swipe of his meaty paw. Helplessly her eyes followed the sword as it flew through the air to rattle and bounce on the hard ground. She dragged her gaze away from the gleaming blade in time to see the raider raise an ugly cudgel above his head. Gawking up stupidly at the gnarled wood, adorned with large iron nails and bits of jagged metal, she waited for the end, involuntarily squeezing her eyes shut as the cudgel fell heavily toward her.

Her body flinched in anticipation of the final blow, but instead of the impact of wood and metal with her skull, she felt an entirely different type of jolt. She opened her eyes to find herself staring at Alyce's shocked, frozen face. For a couple of heartbeats, all she could do was gape stupidly at Alyce, only vaguely aware of the weapon in her hand. Something warm trickled down her arm, and she looked down to blink at the blood that was gushing out the wound in Alyce's side. Alyce muttered something, eyes full of disbelief as she slid off the blade and collapsed in a heap on the floor. In the flickering light of a nearby fire, she watched blankly as the crumpled body twitched and shuddered before falling absolutely still.

"Really, even this is so unlike the old you," Jenkins murmured thoughtfully right next to her ear, making her jump almost out of her skin. The long dagger fell from her suddenly listless fingers, and she spun around to glare at his calm, cold face.

"What do you mean?" she croaked, feeling the anger steadily rise within her. "This was revenge, pure and simple. She, she killed me," she spat, pointing a trembling finger at Alyce's still body. "Anyone would want that, if they had the chance."

Without warning, Jenkins' hand lashed out, grabbed the frayed collar of her shirt. "Of course that's what everybody wants, you idiot. But wanting something and going through with it are two different things. Some people in this world are capable of crossing that line, while others aren't. It's that simple. The old Mel could never cross that line, not without help."

For a moment, she thought she was really going to die, the material of her collar biting so deeply into her throat as Jenkins' hand tightened further. Never mind that this was all a drug-induced mind trip, or that Jenkins was actually dead. At that moment, all the pain and fear she felt was as real as anything she had felt in her life. Frantically she clawed at that hand, curling around her collar like a giant talon.

"Fu, fuck you," she finally managed to spit out before going limp in his grasp, vision turning grey at the edges.

Time froze for a handful of heartbeats, at least for her it did as she struggled to breathe. Only vaguely aware of Jenkins' pale, grimacing face hovering before her, she could feel her whole body sinking, rushing to meet the floor as Jenkins lowered his hand. With a final squeeze of his hand and a muttered, unintelligible curse, he let her go. Desperately sucking in air, she struggled to raise her torso up off the ground, wincing at the pain that now filled her body. Her hands slipped on the wet deck, and it took all her remaining strength and ability to not fall back flat on her face. Then the deck lurched violently beneath her, rendering all her efforts invalid. Cold salty water leaked into her mouth as she hugged the wet planks, the air she'd just managed to suck into her lungs being forcibly pushed out. Blinking madly against the heavy rain lashing the deck, she squinted at the blurry figure standing at the helm.

"Mel, are you alright?" Raphael's voice, cutting through the howling wind and crashing waves. She strained her tired eyes, tried to pick out his face in the dim, flickering lantern light.

"Raphael," she croaked, feeling some life return to her limbs. She stiffly clambered to her feet, fighting to keep her balance as the Pretty Peg shuddered and tilted beneath her. Despite the rain and wind cutting through her clothes and chilling her to the bone, the sight of that tall, straight figure lit a small flame within her. With growing urgency, she staggered along the deck, gripping the ship's side for dear life as the Pretty Peg continued to be tossed about.

"Raphael," she cried, hand trembling as it reached out to touch the rigid back now facing her. The figure spun around, and she reeled back, a bitter taste creeping into her mouth. "You!? Just get out of my head already!" she yelled, taking an unsteady swing at Jenkins' smug face. With one smooth sidestep that defied the bucking, rocking movement of the ship, he avoided her clumsy attack. His bitter, nasty laugh jangled against her nerves as he lashed out and caught her arm, long fingers digging painfully into her flesh.

"Ah, not yet, I can't go just yet," he projected into her ear, his warm breath somehow penetrating the stinging rain and icy wind to fan her neck, making her skin crawl. "Not until you open your eyes."

In the space of a heartbeat, she was in the water, the stormy night abruptly replaced by dawn breaking over calm sea. Someone was whimpering behind her, and she twisted carefully around to see, debris from the Pretty Peg shifting treacherously under her torso. With desperation born of fear, she swivelled back, fingers digging into the soggy wood. "You see, even now, you refuse to let go of the Mirror," a familiar voice rang out, and she gaped up stupidly at the approaching row-boat. Jenkins sat at the front, fingers gripping the boat's side as it came to a stop. Her gaze drifted over the other two occupants of the boat, their bodies huddled over the oars as they regained their breath. One of them looked vaguely familiar to her… "I have to say, I was surprised when we caught up to you, and you still had the Mirror," he admitted, a faraway look in his eyes as he cast his thoughts back to that day. The absurdity slowly penetrated her water-logged brain, and her lips twitched in a vague imitation of a smirk. A memory within a memory, brilliant.

Not liking her expression, he shifted his weight, leant over the side of the boat. "Did you ever consider just throwing it away, Mel? Even now, with your boat at the bottom of the ocean, and you and your friends in the water, clinging helplessly to debris, you still care whether that wretched sack is tucked into your pants. Really, it would have been safer to let it sink into the ocean. Who knows when it would have been discovered again, and in what state? I bet by the time it did find its way back into human hands, you and everyone connected to you would be long gone." His cold, logical words pricked at her consciousness, made her uncomfortably aware of that which she'd been pushing to the furthest reaches of her mind. "But no, instead you flail about and struggle again and again to keep the Mirror, even though it means putting your friends' lives at risk."

"Shut up!" she cried, straining up out of the water, hand groping for the hull. "You're acting so smug and superior, like you've got all the answers, then tell me what I should be doing, arsehole!" She was so mad, she didn't even notice that the section of hull supporting her torso was slipping out from under her until it was too late, and with an awkward flailing of her limbs she slid into the water. Suddenly the thing attached to her waist was incredibly heavy, and she sank like a stone to the bottom of the sea. The sack settled on the sea floor, and no matter how much she clawed at the water or kicked her legs, she couldn't budge. Something moved beside her, and there was Jenkins, floating calmly beside her. Ignoring the desperate hands reaching for his shoulders, he merely pointed at the sack, jerked his head to the side. For a moment, her oxygen-starved brain couldn't comprehend the meaning of this gesture.

"Are you stupid?" she wanted to scream at the top of her lungs, with what little air she had left, "just save me!" She swung wildly at him, the tension at her waist increasing with the movement. Gritting her teeth in anger, she turned around to glare at the offending sack, pulled taut now like a rope. She stretched out her hand to grab the material and pull it out of the waistband of her trousers, fingers brushing against the coarse cloth. "Ah, so this is what he meant," she thought, hand closing around the material. "I just have to pull this free, and then I can try to reach the surface." Tightening her grip on the sack, she tensed her arm. "Just...have to...pull it free..." Such a simple thing, and yet her hand seemed to freeze where it was, the muscles in her arm unable to move. With her lungs feeling as though they were on fire, she thrashed about, the sound of her own frantic heartbeat filling her ears. The time between beats stretched on longer and longer, and she stopped struggling, content instead to wait for the next dull thud.

Time stretched on, and she thought she must have died and passed on to the afterlife when she finally opened her eyes to soft white light. Blinking against the light, she glanced around, body stiffening as her eyes travelled along familiar rows of seats. With a feeling of dread, she recognised the curved walls and neat, rounded windows, lined by over-head compartments. "Ah, so this is a plane?" Jerking against the seat belt pulled tightly over her lap, she twisted around and looked behind her. "Shouldn't we be crashing soon?" Jenkins asked, the tone of his voice barely rising above the level of mild interest.

"What the hell are you doing here? Do you intend to invade all of my memories?" she screamed, fingers digging into the headrest.

"Is this the button I press to get the stewardess to come?" he asked, brushing aside her anger, a faintly bored look on his face. "I'm dying for a drink. You know how long it's been since I last had a drink? Looking after you brats, keeping my men under control, trying to make the rendezvous on time, it all meant I had to steer clear of alcohol for weeks. No, no, even before that, when I was working with Sebastian...oh God, it's been months," he cried, his face a picture of dismay. "Ah, I was really looking forward to a drink when I finally finished my mission," he added pointedly, shooting her an accusing look. She flinched guiltily under the weight of that glare, blood rushing to her cheeks.

"It's that button," she supplied sheepishly, pointing at the appropriate button before turning away. There was a moment of silence, broken only by the murmured conversation of a nearby couple, and she felt herself drift off to sleep. She was vaguely aware of someone walking past and coming to a stop directly behind her, belatedly connected the courteous manner with a stewardess answering Jenkins' call. Mouth twitching in displeasure at the sound of his voice, her hand fell away from her lap, brushed against something coarse and familiar.

With a start she awoke, pried gritty eyes open to stare at the hessian sack at her side. For a moment she couldn't speak, voice refusing to pass the lump that had suddenly formed in her throat. She twisted around, glared at Jenkins. "This is your doing, isn't it?" she accused, voice coming out as a squeak rather than the roar she intended. He looked up from the in-flight magazine, a mixture of innocence and boredom on his face.

"I may have dredged up this memory, and inserted myself in it, but that's all," he explained calmly, gaze flicking past her to the approaching stewardess. His facial muscles twitched in something that resembled a smile, and he completely ignored her as the woman came to a stop beside him, bent over to take a drink from her trolley. Amid murmured pleasantries and an exchange of money, he completed the transaction, turned his attention to the tall glass of rum and coke that now sat on the fold-down tray.

"Wha...but then why do I have the Mirror with me? It, it has no place in this memory," she stammered, fingers fidgeting with the square cloth hanging over the edge of the headrest.

"Can't separate yourself from it anymore, hmm?" he uttered softly under his breath, lifting the glass to his lips. "The sad thing is, that you're even aware of this yourself."

For a moment, everything around her seemed to shrink away, leaving only Jenkins and his drink to fill her field of vision. She stared, mesmerised by the movement of his Adam's apple as he swallowed. "Are you trying to help me?" she croaked, unable to tear her eyes away his neck. Just then, the plane jolted violently, and Jenkins spluttered noisily, a fine spray escaping the confines of his mouth as he coughed. Visibly shaking, he straightened in his seat, grabbed her arm.

"Let's get one thing straight," he snarled, seemingly oblivious to the deafening roar of the wing tearing away from the fuselage, "don't get some stupid-arse idea that I'm doing this for you. I hate you. I really do." Looking into his eyes at that moment, she had no doubt he meant what he said. There was no room for doubt in those blood shot, dark-ringed eyes. His fingers momentarily dug into her arm, as if to emphasise his words. Then something glimmered in those light-coloured orbs, and his fingers fell away. "But there is one thing I hate even more."

With the sounds of panic now filling the rapidly descending plane, she had to strain to pick out his words amid the screams and cries. "That thing, sitting there beside you, I hate that thing," he uttered in a grating voice. She followed the direction of his trembling, out-stretched finger. "That thing, it could have picked anyone, anyone, from anywhere, anytime, and it chose you! You, of all people! You, who are so weak and simple-minded, who never had any clear ambition or desire, who floated through life, letting everything pull you this way and that...You Mel, of all the people in this world, it chose you!" She had no problem hearing him now, not when he was screeching at the top of his lungs, venting all his hatred and anger with each venomous syllable.

Gasping for breath, he reached out a shaky hand for his drink, realised belatedly that it fallen off the tray. Grimacing at the loss of his drink, he shot at an accusing look at her, as though that was her fault too. Wind now tore through the cabin, via the sizeable hole in the opposite wall where the wing used to be. A hungry wind that tore at everyone and everything, trying to suck all it could through the hole. Miscellaneous objects swept past him, some narrowly missing his head, and yet he continued to glare at her, his hatred like a beacon amid the chaos. That, coupled with the ridiculous thing he'd just said, was all too much.

"Hey," Jenkins croaked unevenly as he tried to inject more anger into his voice. "Cut that out!" he yelled over the sound of her laughter. She was laughing so hard, she barely noticed the bone-shuddering impact of the plane slamming into the ground. The floor shuddered beneath her, slammed up to literally hit her in the face. She fell down between the seats, body jammed painfully in the awkward space, the metal armrests and protrusions sticking into her. And still she laughed. She laughed so much she almost puked, the sides of her abdomen spasming out of control. "Hey!" Jenkins roared above her, his only concession to the wild movement of the careening aircraft being his white-knuckled hold of the headrest. "What's so funny? Do you think this is a joke?"

"It's not?" she wheezed with the little air that was left in her lungs, grimacing slightly at the taste of blood that now filled her mouth. "Really Jenkins, think about what you just said...there's no way the Mirror would choose me...that's absurd...it's just...stupid luck, good or bad, I don't know..." The words tumbled out of her mouth, one after another as her sides stopped shaking and the laughter died away. "I mean, everything you said is true...there really is nothing special about me, no particular talent or trait that makes me stand out...so, it can't possibly be true."

She didn't have the strength to even prop her body up anymore, and sunk unceremoniously to the crumpled floor, cheek resting heavily against a scrap of carpet. She was vaguely aware of movement somewhere above her, and the soft rustle of material. "If that's true, then why don't you look inside that sack?" Her mouth went inexplicitly dry at the suggestion, and her body somehow found the strength to stiffen, head rising ever so slightly off the floor. Jenkins crouched before her, his hunched-over body framed by twisted metal and shattered windows. That side of the plane must have hit something, she decided, briefly recalling the jolt that had sent her crashing to the floor. Surprisingly, most of the seats still seemed to be intact, except for one or two that now swung at crazy angles. The same couldn't be said for the passengers.

"In all this time, you've not once looked inside, have you? Why is that, Mel?" Her fingers curled around the coarse cloth still jammed into the waistband of her trousers, fear squeezing her heart like a cruel hand.

"Why?" she echoed hollowly as all the heat seemed to seep out of her body, leaving her cold and numb. "I, I don't know..." A warm hand touched the top of her head, and she blinked up at Jenkins. The plane was still sliding, seemed to be sliding forever, sliding itself out of existence. With each bump and jolt, the walls folded in on themselves, crushing everything in between.

"You can't hide from me in here, Mel," Jenkins said, tapping her forehead, "even though you try to hide from yourself." All her awareness seemed to focus on that small patch of warmth on her forehead, where his fingers still rested. "Stop being afraid, and look at the Mirror."

Like a child who had just been told the stone-cold truth about Santa Claus, she gaped helplessly up at his stern face. His calmly spoken words reverberated through her mind with the force of a speeding freight train, and she suddenly shrank away from that patch of warmth. Unable to muster her voice, she was reduced to shaking her head, gaze glued to the floor. A sound of pure frustration escaped the confines of Jenkins' throat, and he grabbed her chin, roughly tilted her face so that they were eye to eye. "Wake up and stop hiding, or I swear I'll fuckin' haunt you for the rest of your days, you stupid bitch!" he snarled. Her body and mind were so numb now, that even the force of his intense hatred barely caused a ripple in her consciousness. "Wake..." he drawled, pulling back his free hand, knuckles gleaming white against the angry red skin. He paused a moment to catch his breath, and then let his fist fly. "Up!" he roared as his fist connected with her cheek. The nerve endings in that side of her face all seemed to explode at once, and she forcibly reeled, hitting the floor with a painful jolt.

She opened her eyes, quickly shut them again as everything swirled around her at nauseating speed. Rough hands grabbed the front of her shirt, hauled her off the ground. "Hey, don't hit her again just yet," a vaguely familiar voice warned, and she strained against heavy lids to open her eyes. "We're about to take her to the General, we should at least make her slightly presentable." Through the narrow opening of her fluttering eyelids, she focused on the impatient, unfriendly face floating just in front of her. Where had she seen those cold dark eyes before?

"Why do you think I'm trying to wake her up?" the man retorted in a waspish tone. For a second, she thought she saw the thick coarse hair of his beard bristle, like that of a cornered cat.

"Monfils," she croaked, finally remembering his name, the bizarre image from her dream popping into her head. Those two straight backs riding atop horses, red coats dazzling in the full sunlight, somehow she knew deep down who they represented. With a start she realised that they were in some kind of tent, discoloured canvas walls moving faintly with the breeze. "Ah," she croaked, jumping slightly as she became aware of strange voices ringing out beyond the canvas walls, accompanied by sounds of general activity. Various obvious questions sprung to mind, and she opened her mouth to ask them, when something else stirred at the back of her mind, and she roused herself to claw at those cruel hands. "What, what happened to Jenkins' kid? Weren't you guys holding him hostage or something?" she rasped, forcing the words past the unbearably dry confines of her throat.

His expression shifted briefly, cheeks reddening above the beard. "The boy's dead," he answered tersely, hands tightening on her shirt front. At the sudden accusation in her face, he snorted, shoved her away. "It's not like that," he grumbled, running short stubby fingers through his unruly hair. "He caught pneumonia. By the time anyone noticed, it was already too late. That's why the plan changed."

"Changed?" she echoed, fully awake now. Monfils frowned at her sudden interest, hand reaching for the syringe that lived in his jacket pocket. His hand froze over the faint cylindrical bulge that showed through the thick material, and for a couple of heartbeats, an unreadable expression crossed his face. Muttering something under his breath, he shrugged his shoulders, hand falling away.

"When my employers approached Jenkins and made him an offer he couldn't refuse, I, along with my counterpart Bontems, were already in place to keep an eye on him. It was easy enough to gain his trust, and therefore be included in the next phase of the plan. Everything was going well, and I was prepared to play out my part without breaking out of character or drawing any attention to myself, when we got word about his kid. I'd just been given orders to take over and eliminate Jenkins, but you beat me to it." She was vaguely aware that she was gawking at him, mouth hanging open in full "stunned mullet" style, and yet she couldn't stop herself. Suddenly uncomfortable under her shocked, unguarded expression, he straightened the front of his jacket, barked gruffly for her to go get cleaned up, nodding at the bucket of water that sat in the far corner of the tent.

"But why kill Jenkins straight away? Why not wait until the mission was over?" The words spilled out without hesitation, and for a moment she wasn't sure if it was actually her asking the questions or Jenkins' ghost taking control of her mouth. Monfils regarded her through narrowed eyes, positioned himself to loom over her, hands reaching for the front of her shirt again. "How the hell should I know, I just do what I'm told! Now quit it with your annoying questions and get cleaned up," he snarled, hauling her to her feet and propelling her towards the bucket. As she stumbled to an awkward stop beside the bucket, he reached behind, pulled a rag out from somewhere. "You have five minutes to make yourself presentable," he growled, tossing the rag at her. "I'll be just outside, so no funny business," he added, punctuating his statement with a final glower before stepping out through the opening.

For a moment she stared blankly at the spot where he had last stood, slowly absorbed the fact that she was finally alone for the first time in days. How many days? With all her drifting in and out of consciousness, and having full-blown drug-induced mind-trips, she couldn't honestly record or recount the number of times the sun crawled across the sky. "Must be over a week, at least," she murmured, idly picking at the smudges of dirt on her shirt. ""Make yourself presentable" he says," she snorted softly, reaching for the rag. "That would take a mira..." Her voice trailed away as her gaze fell upon the crumpled sack sitting innocently beside her, hand hovering only an inch or so above the rag as her body froze. "Miracle," she finished hoarsely, throat suddenly dry.

"So that's what happened to my boy, huh?" The voice was soft, barely above the volume of a whisper, and yet it hit her hard. Unable to look up and meet the apparition's eyes, she merely nodded, tears springing to her eyes. The Mirror had fed her images of the boy, blue eyes and blonde hair, nose peppered with freckles. Thinking back on it now, he had looked rather small and frail, huddled in the corner of that dingy, dirty cell. "Did he ever have a chance?" Jenkins muttered, as if reading her thoughts. "I, I never should have tried, never should have accepted him as my son. Just, that day when his mother approached me, showed me the little bundle in her arms, claimed it was mine, he didn't cry or anything, just looked up at me with those serious blue eyes. I'd never seen such a serious kid before. To be honest, I wasn't even sure if he was mine or not. I knew for a fact that Melissa was seeing at least one other guy during the short time we were together. Just when I opened my mouth to tell her words to that effect, the kid reached out and grabbed my finger. When I stared at those tiny fingers wrapped around my finger, my heart kind of lurched in my chest, and I couldn't say "no". And so I supported them both, secretly of course. Knowing I couldn't risk my enemies finding out, I never meant to see the boy on a regular basis. I was so pathetic, finding any excuse to walk past the tiny house where they lived, hoping to catch a glimpse of him. His mother eventually caught me in the act, stupidly invited me inside, saying I was being too paranoid, and I just as stupidly allowed myself to believe her. I should never have gone inside that house, should never have allowed myself to get so comfortable and clumsy. It was only a matter of time until one of my enemies noticed my habit, no matter how hard I tried to disguise my visits. And now William is dead..."

Swallowing painfully past the sudden lump in her throat, she quickly wiped away the hot tears that had started to roll down her cheeks. "I'm sorry," she mumbled, hands gripping the coarse cloth of the sack, "I should have checked on him more often..."

"...and then what?" Jenkins interjected sternly, reluctantly lifting his eyes from the square patch of floor to the right of his dusty, worn shoes. "Send a message to the captors to take better care of my son? Tell those arseholes to not leave a five-year-old boy in a shitty cell for months while I complete the mission?" His bitter words pecked at her conscience, and she felt herself shrink away from him. "No," he mumbled, eyes sliding away from her pale stricken face, "as much as I'd like to, I can't peg the blame onto you for this one. William's dead, purely because of his connection to me. I knew that, knew deep down that it was only a matter of time before someone found out and used William against me. So many times I told myself to stop visiting, and puffing myself up like a bird in winter, I'd ready myself to never see his solemn little face again. But I couldn't do it..." His voice trailed off, and for a handful of heartbeats, all forms of vibration seemed to fade away, until she was cloaked in utter stillness.

"At least now I know the truth," the apparition of Jenkins finally croaked, resting a ghostly hand on her shoulder. "Thank you." And with that, he was gone. She blinked at the empty space, spun around slowly. Suddenly she felt so incredibly tired, like her whole body was made of lead, and she collapsed onto all fours. While she'd been drifting in and out of consciousness for days, she had spent most of that time strapped into a saddle, with only the occasional stops. On top of that, and the drugs being pumped into her system on a daily basis, she had only been given enough food to survive, her inconsistent meals mostly consisting of dried meat and stale bread. "That bastard's tryin' to kill me," she mumbled feebly, lungs struggling to draw in enough air. Her foggy brain tried to imagine Monfils looking even slightly contrite if he came in here and found her dead. "No, he'd just get angry," she croaked, barely managing to form the words with her heavy, unwieldly tongue.

Somewhere behind her, the rustle of cloth could be heard, quickly followed by a sharp intake of breath and flurry of footsteps. She briefly tried to raise her head to look up at the newcomer, quickly gave it up as a bad joke. Out of the corner of her eye, she registered movement, a familiar, irritated face bobbing in and out of view. Dark beady eyes glared at her, and from the depths of a brushy beard a mouth opened and closed, spewing out impatient angry words. "What are you doing on the floor? I told you to get cleaned up," Monfils snarled from behind clenched teeth, his hand digging into her shoulder and hauling her up off the floor. "Damn, never mind, I'll just have to take you as you are..." He started dragging her away, and she blinked up at the face attached to the iron-like arm.

"Wow, so cold," she mumbled stupidly, staring up at that uncompromising, uncaring profile. More movement at the entrance of the tent, and the other guy rushed in, hovered around like an angry bee. With a strident exclamation of "I told you so!", the other guy forced Monfils to stop. None too gently, she was lowered to the ground, and impassive hands pressed against her body. In proportion to the increasing shortness of her breathing, her eyelids became heavier and heavier, until it seemed to take all the strength she possessed to lift them at all. She just managed to catch the look of concentration on the other guy's face as he pressed stubby fingers against her throat, lips silently moving as though he was counting or saying a prayer. "Not surprisingly, her body's gone into shock," the other guy muttered, fingers falling away from her throat. "Luckily for you I still have some supplies on me from my brief stint in medical school," he sighed, leaning back on his haunches. Something told her there was an interesting story behind that casual comment, and so she struggled to open her eyes more, only succeeded to blink more slowly.

"Isn't that why your stint in medical school was so brief in the first place?" Monfils sneered, his voice completely lacking in gratitude as the other guy reached inside his jacket. The other guy...she strained to remember his name, suspected it started with "B"...shot Monfils a filthy, contemptuous look. He pulled a small case out of an inner pocket, opened it up to reveal a neat row of small vials. In between blinks, she watched as a syringe materialised seemingly out of nowhere, held carefully between thumb and forefinger, while his other hand grappled with a vial. She watched through heavy-lidded eyes as the sharp metal tube pierced the top of the vial, and the glass body steadily filled with some milky white substance. "Ah shit, not again," she croaked, suddenly joining the dots and getting the picture of an oncoming injection. The very thought of it made her nauseous, with all the needles that had been jabbed into her of late. She tried to muster the strength to resist, only managing to stiffen vaguely under Monfils' heavy hand.

Somewhere in the background, there were sounds of movement, sharply accompanied by a new, anxiety-ridden voice. Shifting his hand slightly, Monfils turned around, barked a suitable reply to the man hovering in the entrance. Why did everything sound so muffled? Probably the same reason everything looked so blurry, she decided, trying one last time to fully open her eyes before giving it up as a bad joke. The only clear thing she was aware of that moment was the needle sliding into her arm.

Through fluttering eyelids, she glimpsed the other guy's solemn face as he emptied the syringe. "There's not much time, Mel." She blinked, and saw a vaguely familiar face superimposed over that grim expression. God, even the hallucination/apparition of Jenkins was a blurred smear on her consciousness. He looked pretty serious, all the same, mouth working overtime to pronounce her imminent doom or something. "Blah blah blah Mirror, blah blah blah too late," was all she could absorb, the words bouncing off her like tiny hail stones. Jeez, what a nag. Using up what strength she had left, she mumbled words to that effect before sinking into unconsciousness so deep that even Jenkins couldn't follow.

Joseph Louis Bontems stiffened at the name that floated up from the woman's twitching lips, his own lips pressing together into a thin hard line of displeasure. "Must be the drugs," he murmured, as much to set himself at ease as anything else. "I told you to take it easy, didn't I?" he grumbled, glancing up at his colleague in sudden annoyance. Any further barbs he meant to trade with Monfils were quickly forgotten, the sight of the other man's pale frozen face temporarily robbing him of speech. In all the time he'd been working with Monfils, and all the tense, risky situations they'd faced together, he had never seen the man look so much as unsettled, his face almost always a cold inscrutable mask. Just the odd twitch of facial muscles barely discernible under that bushy beard when he was really annoyed or pleased, that was the most emotion he showed. So it was utterly fascinating to watch all the colour drained from Monfils' face, the mouth clearly gaping open in a mixture of surprise and fear.

Monfils muttered something under his breath, started to shake the woman's shoulders. "What business do you have repeating that name?" Monfils demanded, struggling to control the evenness of his voice. "He's dead right? So you have no reason to mention his name." Whoa, he had never heard Monfils sound like that before, his voice raw with emotion. "You killed him, remember, so he's definitely dead!" Monfils shouted, the spittle from his furious mouth spraying her unconscious face. Wincing at the drops of saliva now peppering Mel's cheek, he pushed himself into action, grabbing Monfils' shoulders.

"Settle down man," he growled, allowing his fingers to dig into the flesh. Monfils stiffened at the contact, dragged his eyes away from the woman.

"You heard it too, right? It was like she was talking to him…"

He took a moment to savour the fear in the other man's eyes, fingers relaxing slightly.

"It's the drugs, Monfils. You've pumped her so full of shit that it's no wonder she's having hallucinations." Monfils stared at him, eyes growing wide as dinner plates. A weak laugh escaped his lips, hands trembling slightly as he brushed off the fingers that still rested on his shoulders.

"Of course," Monfils mumbled, gaze straying to the ugly red spots peeking out from behind the cuff of her rolled-up sleeve. "That was the plan after all," he added, clambering stiffly to his feet. "Just the way she said his name, like he was in the room…" His voice trailed away, haunted gaze sweeping over the interior of the tent, as though he expected a ghost to jump out at him. With a nervous, self-conscious cough, he strode to the entrance way, yelled out to two soldiers who had the misfortune of wandering past at exactly the wrong time. "Let's go," Monfils grunted, stepping aside as the two soldiers entered the tent and shifted awkwardly into place on either side of the woman's body.

"Go where?" he asked distractedly, watching on in bemusement as the soldiers lifted Mel off the ground. "No, wait," he cried, suddenly putting the pieces together, "you're not taking her to see the General, are you? I doubt he'll be very impressed if we have to drag his long-awaited prize into the command centre…"

"Can't be helped," Monfils grunted, ushering the men out with an impatient nod of his head, "the order has just been issued, we're leaving for Borodino."

"Borodino?" he echoed in disbelief to Monfils' disappearing back, fumbling with his medicine case and shoving it roughly into his pocket. Swearing under his breath, he staggered to his feet and raced out of the tent, nearly tripping over the flap of canvas that covered the entrance in the process. He noticed on his way in that the men were breaking camp but had thought nothing of it.

"Borodino," he muttered, gaze drifting across the sodden field to his left. Through the gaps in the trees on the other side of the field he could just make out white-washed walls and the odd horse and cart or pedestrian ambling down Smolensk road. On the surface, the people of Gzhatsk seemed to be largely ignoring the presence of the army that had suddenly converged on their town, carrying on with their everyday lives. Only on closer inspection did it become apparent the subtle preparations being made for an imminent invasion by Napoleon's forces, who were steadily making their way to Moscow. Carts loaded with supplies and personal belongings trundled to the nearby river, where the precious cargo was then loaded onto waiting barges. "They must have a storage area upriver," he murmured, remembering the empty barge he had spied returning to the jetty when they limped into town yesterday. He also noted neat piles of carefully assembled kindling laid next to all the buildings, the dry leaves, twigs and bark resting against the walls. It was only later when he overheard some of the soldiers muttering something about the townsmen forming their own militia that it all clinked into place. They planned to set their homes on fire.

"Wait, Monfils," he cried, catching up with the odd procession that were laboriously making their way to a waiting cart. "What do you mean he's moving out, we only just got here," he wheezed, doubling over slightly as he caught his breath. "And why the hell are we going to Borodino?"

Monfils laughed, a bitter, harsh sound that jarred his nerves. "General Kutusov has decided that Borodino is where we will make our stand against Napoleon," Monfils supplied, undercurrent of tension in his voice. He stood dumbfounded for a handful of heartbeats, the words slowly sinking into his befuddled brain. The outnumbered troops under the command of Count Barclay de Tolly and General Bagration had been retreating from the French "Grande Armee" for a couple of months now. For some inexplicable reason he hadn't expected the Russian army to actually fight back, even when they were so close to Moscow.

He swallowed back the foul words that threatened to flow out of his mouth, his disappointment at being embroiled further in this war palpable. Instead he cleared his throat, mustered all his will power not to punch out Monfils' stupidly smug face. "So where does that leave us then? After everything we've been through to procure the Mirror..."

"Ah, that," Monfils drawled, an unreadable look on his face, "I'll explain that along the way. Come on." The men had already finished loading Mel into the back of the cart, a lumpy pile of canvas serving as a makeshift mattress for her unconscious body. With a curt nod Monfils dismissed them, clambered up into the driver's seat. "Well, you coming or not?" Monfils snapped in a sudden bout of impatience.

As he stood there, gawking up at Monfils' hardened face, he felt as though time itself slowed down, stretching ridiculously between each thump of his heart. All he wanted was his money, so that he could be on his way. They had done what they set out to do, hadn't they? The only thing that had been keeping him going the past couple of days was the thought that when they got to Gzhatsk, it would all be over. "Does this mean we're not getting paid until this war is over?" he asked as he stiffly climbed up into the cart. Monfils grunted, shifted his position on the narrow seat.

"Don't worry," Monfils replied with a smile that didn't quite reach his eyes, "it'll all be over soon, one way or another." With a cold heavy sensation forming in the pit of his stomach, he sank down awkwardly onto the seat. He wondered briefly what his sister was doing right at that very moment. Probably shuffling around the kitchen of the small apartment they shared, preparing to make bread, he decided with a wry smile. The sound of the leather reins smacking the horse's back jolted him back to his unpleasant reality, and he settled down for the uncomfortable ride to Borodino.

Raphael eased himself into position on the crest of a hill, carefully pulled the looking glass out of his stolen knapsack. Shrinking further back into the bushes, he slowly turned the lens, waited for the blurry figures down below to come into focus. Soldiers clad in dark blue coats trudged along the gully, their worn boots squelching softly in the mud. Other than the odd murmur of conversation, the men were silent, lips pressed together in hard, unforgiving lines. He counted the hours since he first stumbled upon Napoleon's army, struggling to remember the sequence of events. It was only yesterday, wasn't it? Pushing his way through his own sluggish memories, he counted just over twenty-four hours since he first sighted the long line of weary men.

At the time, he had been cutting a path through thick forest, murmuring words of encouragement to the disgruntled mare beneath him as they followed the sound of running water. With a final push past dense forest, they neared the crest of a gentle slope, to be dazzled by patches of sunlit water glinting through the gaps in the trees. Presuming the rough, hand-drawn maps in his knapsack were correct, that inviting body of water was the Gzhat river. Other than for obvious supply reasons, he had found himself almost giddy with excitement at the discovery of a tangible landmark, after days of merely following the "scent" of the Mirror. While the Mirror faintly called out to him all the time, tugging at his body like an invisible guiding hand, it was mentally exhausting to constantly focus on that vague sensation.

"Let's go, Emily," he had grunted softly, digging his heels into the mare's sides. For some reason, he had taken to calling his "borrowed" horse after an old girlfriend. Something about the way the mare shook its head and snorted contemptuously served as a painful reminder of that short-lived relationship, and he couldn't help himself. In hindsight, maybe he cursed himself with that choice of name. With a whinny of protest, Emily started weaving a path through the thinning trees, hooves churning up the increasingly sodden ground. They had just reached a clearing when Emily reared up onto her hind legs. Unprepared for the sudden movement, he fell off the mare's broad back with a heavy thud. A flash of pain emanating from the side of his head, the trees and water swimming about in his vision as he struggled to get perpendicular. Following the sound of Emily's high-pitched whinnying, his eyes had managed to focus just in time to see her glossy back disappear into the forest. Calling out thickly, he'd stumbled a couple of steps after her, only to fall again to the ground, this time flat on his miserable face.

For a while he couldn't move, the combination of utter exhaustion and despair filling his body with numbness. Swearing hoarsely under his breath, he'd finally scrambled to his hands and knees, and was in the process of straightening up when he noticed the unmoving, grey-tinged face just beyond his hands. Oddly, seeing the decomposing head made him feel better, because obviously that was what had set Emily off. "Not a personal rejection then," he had muttered, tentatively brushing away a thin layer of dirt to uncover the rest of the body, clad in a familiar uniform. An unfortunate French soldier, a long way from home. If he had to guess, the soldier had died from malnourishment and disease, rather than an actual wound. Still in a daze from the initial fall, he crouched next to the corpse, gaze idly wandering about the clearing. The chunky, uneven ground in particular caught his muddy attention. With a start he realized what all the semi-circles gouged into the mud represented, and he hastily retreated from the riverbank, scrambled back up the slope to higher ground. Just as he ducked behind the line of trees, the air began to hum with the low rumble of many marching feet, and a handful of heartbeats later clumps of French soldiers came into view, making their way solemnly along the river.

A sudden sound of movement jolted him rudely back to reality, and he lowered the looking glass and shrank back into the bushes. About fifteen feet away to his left, a soldier was plodding his way up the hill, a determined look on his face. Raphael watched with growing trepidation as the soldier angled his way up the slope towards his position. Gripping the strap of his bayonet rifle, the soldier slowed down as he neared the clump of bushes. With his heart firmly lodged in his mouth, Raphael reached slowly for his sword, muscles tensing in preparation. Mud-coated boots came to a stop only a couple of feet away from where he lay, and he awkwardly grabbed the hilt of his weapon, inched it out of the sheath. If he swung out, sliced into the soldier's calves and then barrelled into him, he could get him to the ground and out of sight quickly enough. If he was lucky, the soldier wouldn't be missed straight away, giving him time to escape...

This grim train of thought was completely derailed by the sudden rustle of cloth followed by a familiar soft hissing sound. Time crawled by as his frantic brain struggled to process the sound. With a rising sense of revulsion, he followed the sound, glimpsed the stream of yellow liquid splattering the ground barely a foot away from where he lay. Stifling the sound of disgust that so desperately wanted to escape his throat, he hugged the ground, willed his muscles to relax. With a satisfied sigh and rustle of cloth, the soldier finished up and moved back down the hill, the sound of his footsteps quickly blending into the general ambient noise. "That was way too close," he murmured, eying banefully the wet patch of ground. "In more ways than one," he added, groping once more for the looking glass. Holding the thick, rounded glass piece to his eye, he noted with relief that the men were now moving in a solid column, weaving a path through the maze of trees that lined the river.

"Damn," he swore softly, lowering the eye piece and backing slowly out of the bushes. He had hoped to follow the army all the way to Gzhatsk. Judging from the condition of the men, and from snippets of conversation he had managed to pick up, they were in pursuit of the Russian armies. Two soldiers sharing a toilet break near one of his hiding spots had described in great detail their previous encounter with the Russians, near the Polish frontier. In hushed voices they recounted the fight, of being caught up in a surprise attack from the south, while the rest of the army faced a frontal assault. While both in the same group, the two men had fought at opposite ends of the line. The soldiers solemnly agreed that the enemy forces hadn't stood a chance against their superior numbers. They had lost some men, it was true, but not nearly as many as the Russians. Riding the wave of that relatively easy victory, they had chased the retreating Russians, eager to finish off the job.

Straining his eyes in the semi darkness, he had picked out the silhouette of their shadowy heads nodding in unison. With bitterness and doubt creeping into their voices, talk then turned to the worsening conditions they faced as they continued to chase the enemy forces deeper into Russian territory. Supplies were becoming scarce, the little food they received doing little to abate their ever-present hunger. Their voices become more hushed as they shared the names of mutual associates who had recently fallen away from their ranks. Many names that held no meaning to him floated back and fro above his head, the way their voices thickened as they recounted the names leaving him in no doubt that this was a rollcall of the dead. When talk then turned to the option of slipping away quietly into the night and never returning to their unit, he had taken that as his cue to slink away into the surrounding forest. Not out of sudden concern for their privacy did he put as much distance as practically possible between himself and the conspiring men. Rather, he didn't want to be around if the wrong set of ears caught wind of their conversation. He had seen enough soldiers sprawled unmoving on the ground, crude, unforgiving holes in their backs...

With that cheery thought in mind, he hurried down the gentle slope, suddenly eager to put more distance between himself and the Emperor's Grande Army. "In any case, wouldn't it be better to get there first?" he softly chided, shaking his head in self-admonishment. It's not like he needed to follow the army, or a roughly drawn map anymore. The pull of the Mirror was solid now, constantly tugging at his mind and feet, guiding his steps relentlessly, pushing all doubt out of his heart. Somehow, it gave him the strength to overcome his own hunger and exhaustion. With his own supplies stretched to nearly nothing, and the constant hunger gnawing at his resolve, it was a wonder he could put one foot in front of the other at all. Only the alien energy inside his body calling out to the source coupled with his own overwhelming desire to reach Mel kept him going now.

Never mind the trembling of the fingers that gripped the strap of the leather bag, or those grey spots sprinkling the vision, he thought wryly. "Sarah," he whispered, at once wishing to see her dear sweet face while grateful that she wasn't there to see him like this. Surely, she and the lad were on a ship by now, making their way home. Pushing aside such ambiguous thoughts, he gathered what remained of his strength and pushed on, dragging weary feet through the decaying leaves that littered the ground. With a slight course adjustment, he picked his way through the densely packed forest, the tension in his body easing somewhat as the sounds of the French army faded into silence. "If only I still had that horse," he muttered, the sour taste of regret welling up inside his mouth. As if in answer to his plaintive wish, a faint whinny echoed somewhere ahead, and he suddenly found himself running toward the sound, almost tripping over his own feet in his extreme haste. Another whinny, and he found himself skidding to an abrupt halt as Emily emerged from behind a large tree trunk, head lowered in an almost bashful manner. Tears sprung unrestrained from the corners of his eyes as he all but collapsed against the mare's smooth side. "Emily," he croaked into the short coarse hair, trembling hands reaching for the reins. Stiffly, he clambered up onto the mare's waiting back, body sinking heavily into the saddle. "Thank you," he whispered thickly into Emily's ear. The mare gruffly snorted, shook her head, as if trying to brush off his heartfelt gratitude. Roughly wiping his eyes with the back of his hand, he gathered the reins, flicked them lightly against Emily's back. With a jolt the mare sprung to life and started off through the forest.

"Come on, sleepy head," a bright voice sung in his ear, the cheerful, overly loud tone sounding forced to his sensitive ear. Prying apart sticky lids, he opened his eyes, blinked slowly at the impatient, imperious face hovering above him.

"Sarah," he finally managed to rasp, the sides of his throat feeling as though they were coated with sandpaper. "What's going on?"

"What do you mean "what's going on?"?" she cried, grabbing his shoulder and physically dragging him out of the narrow bunk. Now that he was semi-awake, the low murmur of waves breaking against the hull of the ship penetrated his senses. As his eyes adjusted to the shadowy interior of the cargo hold, and he felt the timbers beneath his feet lurch gently up and down, he realised they were actually on their way home, and it wasn't just a dream.

"Ah," he breathed, relief pouring out of the long sigh. Then, recalling the circumstances of their departure, he hazarded a guilty glance at Sarah's face.

"Don't worry, you should be relieved," Sarah offered, reading him like a book. "To be honest, so am I, for the most part."

For the last two days, as they made their way to the port town of Gdansk, she had remained mostly tight-lipped about pretty much everything, strictly steering conversation to the necessities at hand. While recovering from his injuries, he had lacked both the energy and nerve to push the point with her, focusing instead on staying upright in the saddle. "I'm sorry, Sarah," he ventured, clumsily grabbing her hand. "If it wasn't for me, you'd still be with your dad..."

At the mention of Raphael, her hand twitch in his grasp, and for a second he thought she would wrench it away. Instead, she took a deep breath, gave his hand a squeeze.

"I feel as though a part of my soul stayed behind, to hover near him like a ghost," she admitted through stiff lips. "We share this connection, you see, because of the Mirror. So I know that he's still out there, far across the water, struggling on and on. Even though it was he who pushed me away, I feel so guilty. We sail toward relative safety, while he rides into a war zone..."

"Damn," he uttered softly, hating himself anew. At her startled look, he awkwardly explained, a plethora of self-recriminations flowing out of his mouth like a swelling tide. When he was finished, her expression somewhat softened, and she stood up stiffly, dragging him up with her.

"Don't be silly," she finally retorted, leading him out of the cargo hold. "There was no way I could leave you there to recover, and then somehow make your way home. Father's right, you're a babe in the woods, a lamb thrown to the wolves. No, there really was no choice but to take you home." He opened his mouth to protest her metaphors, his hackles rising at the mental pictures they invoked. It then occurred to him that she hadn't sounded so light-hearted in months.

"Thanks," he said sourly, with an exaggerated sigh. May as well play along, if it makes her happy.

"Now that's settled, let's go and get some breakfast. There's some cold left-over gruel with our name on it in the kitchen."

At the mention of food, his stomach growled loudly, and she giggled. "Hey," he protested, cheeks turning red with embarrassment. "Ah, hey," he repeated, in a different tone as a thought occurred to him. Clutching the fabric of her sleeve, he came to a stop, cleared his throat. "You could always go back. I mean, I can make my own way home once we get to England…" His throat clammed up, but nevertheless he pushed the words out. He didn't really want to go home alone, but it was the least he could do.

"Thank you, Daniel," Sarah replied, slowly turning around to face him. While there was a shadow of sadness in her eyes, she smiled and grabbed his hand. "If I am to go back, I hope to take you with me, so it will have to wait until you have fully recovered. Come on now, I'm hungry." As she continued to lead him toward the kitchen, he decided he had never been so happy to be dragged around by another person in his entire life.

Gunthar stopped in his tracks, made a soft hissing sound as he sharply drew breath from between clenched teeth. There it was again, that faint tug on his consciousness, like a small insect crawling over his skin, half-heartedly demanding his attention. He turned his head slightly, tried to focus on that feeble signal, but like a single grain of sand on a beach, it was lost in the sea of noise that was the main "Mirror" source. Shrugging his shoulders, he continued down the dusty road, following the call of the Mirror. Normally he'd cut a path parallel to the road, and try to stay out of sight, but the road was oddly quiet this morning, and so he was taking advantage of that. Alyce of course will whinge at him when she gets back from scouting the area, but he was well used to that. Since her confession about the listening stone just the day before, she'd been much easier to manage. Whether the stone had been physically removed from Marcus' gut or he had been dealt with by Sebastian, the obvious fact remained that it was no longer planted in the vicinity of their enemy. Just one mention of its loss made her wince and fall silent, even though it was not her fault in the slightest. That of course didn't stop him from taking advantage of her inexplicable guilt.

With a wicked grin twisting his face, he neatly sidestepped a large rut in the road, wondered idly where it led. It was obviously a well-used road, judging by the number of tracks deeply etched into its surface, of men and horse alike. "Probably leads all the way to Moscow," he murmured, wishing fervently that he at least had a rough map, or that either of them had a better idea of the local geography. Fuelled by his obsession, he had plunged them deeper and deeper into Russian territory without a second thought, brusquely brushing aside Alyce's concerns about their actual destination. But even he couldn't ignore the heady mix of fear and anticipation that hung heavy and thick in the air whenever they ducked into a village or town along the way. At first they had hung back from signs of civilisation, and just skirted the towns, maybe ducking in under the cover of darkness to procure supplies. It soon became apparent however that the locals had better things to do than worry about two strangers wandering into their town, and paid them scant attention. "It's like they're all preparing for a big storm," Alyce had murmured, awe and wonder creeping into her voice as she watched one couple furiously gathering up all their farming equipment and storing it inside their house. Using any obvious signs of disturbance as a cue, he had attempted to ask tight-lipped locals what was going on. After making many gestures, line drawings and exaggerated facial expressions, he had managed to learn that the Russian army had only passed through before them a couple of days ago. Wherever they went, it was the same. Not only that, but the villagers had been warned that the French army was on its way.

Alyce, with her hyper-sensitive senses, suffered more acutely than he did from the feeling that they were caught between two opposing forces. Whenever she went to scout ahead, or check for any signs of being followed, she always came back with a haunted look in those pools of utter darkness that served as eyes. "It's not like I asked her to do that," he grumbled, kicking a stone out of his path. Not that he didn't appreciate her efforts. Truth be told, he doubted he could have made it this far without her heightened senses to guide him away from danger. While they had yet to encounter either the French or Russian armies, there were still soldiers wandering about, often following the same route as they were, cutting a path parallel to the road in order to stay out of sight. While some appeared to be acting as scouts for the main body of soldiers, most were deserters, trying desperately to make their way to more friendly territory. Rather than risk being spotted by scouts, they had decided to avoid contact with any stray soldiers. To that end, Alyce had proved invaluable, especially now as they got closer to the Mirror, and its song steadily filled his head with each passing day. He'd almost lost count of the number of times she'd abruptly pulled him aside and out of sight, moments before a soldier scrambled past, looking nervously over his shoulder.

He frowned, wondered if they should revise their policy of completely avoiding contact with soldiers. There seemed to be more and more errant soldiers who had mysteriously separated from their group and lost their way. "Maybe we should try capturing one, squeeze information out of him," he murmured, scratching his head. Obviously not a soldier on horseback, he mused, rubbing the back of his crooked neck. The sound of dry leaves being crunched underfoot startled him, and he gawked up to find Alyce stomping towards him, the sheen of sweat on her forehead glistening in the mid-morning sun. "Either the Russian army is slowing down, or the French army is catching up," she declared without preamble, coming to an awkward stop before him. "I barely have to move five hundred yards in either direction before I can hear the faint rumble of their feet. Really Gunthar, you shouldn't be on this road, it's too dangerous." He shrugged his shoulders, mumbled some half-arsed, noncommittal reply, his innately stubborn nature asserting itself even in the face of her superior senses and logic. To his surprise, Alyce let it slide without further argument, instead falling into step with him, a faintly troubled look on her face.

On their own accord, the hairs on the back of his neck stood on end, and he shivered despite the sun beaming down from a cloudless sky. Come on Alyce, bite back like old times, he silently willed. "Is something wrong, Gunthar?" the object of his thoughts enquired, huge hand hovering just below his elbow. For a split second, his gaze lingered on that hand, the beginnings of a frown tugging at the corners of his mouth. "Is it just me, or have you been getting more touchy of late?" is what he wanted to say, the accusation lining up on his tongue, ready to be fired at a moment's notice. One look at her concerned face however, and he quickly glanced away, swallowed back the potentially hurtful words.

"Ah, it's nothing, really. It's just that I felt an odd twinge while you were scouting ahead," he supplied. almost tripping over his own tongue as he struggled to provide a suitable reason for his reaction. Well, it's not a lie, he told himself. Just not exactly the truth. "It feels like a piece of the Mirror is moving in the opposite direction," he added distractedly, rubbing the back of his crooked neck as he gave it serious thought.

"What, like it was stolen or something?" Alyce suggested in a hushed voice, which struck him as absurdly girly, given her current form. Just when he started to forget her origins, and see her entirely as the golem, she would pull some kind of expression or act a certain way that reminded him of the Alyce of old. "I would not have thought that was possible, with Mel controlling the Mirror."

"Hmm," he murmured thoughtfully, thinking back to the day he had managed to steal a fragment of the artifact. "I wonder about that. She doesn't seem to have complete control all the time," he mused aloud, remembering how that one particular piece caught his eye, almost like it was crying out to him. It was the most natural thing in the world to just reach out his hand and grab it as he hurtled towards the window...

"Sarah," he croaked, his throat suddenly dry. During the time when he and Raphael worked together, how many times did that little guttersnipe stealthily slip things out of his pocket or bag, only to sheepishly return them later when he finally noticed their absence. "Ah, sorry, bad habit," she would often say with an apologetic shrug of her slender shoulders. It wasn't long before he automatically blamed her for any missing item, and she would often forget that she had even taken it, reaching into one of her impressive pockets, brow faintly crinkled in mild surprise when her hand encountered the object in question. It wouldn't be surprising at all if a piece of the Mirror mysteriously came into her possession. But if that was the case, why was he feeling the tug of that fragment in the opposite direction?

"Not possible," he whispered, shaking his head at the direction his thoughts were taking. Sarah and Raphael going their separate ways? Thinking back to those dangerous, uncertain days, how often had he felt that slight twinge of envy when he spied them being so close? The fact that they were not bonded by blood, but by a mutual sense of being abandoned by the world, touched something deep inside him. When he first met Raphael and Sarah, he had been estranged from his family for some time. He had never been on good terms with his father, their incompatible natures causing them to clash time and time again, each clash seeming more intense than the last. By the time he started working for Mabel's father, he had already moved out of home, using his scant savings to rent out a shoebox of a flat. His mother had half-heartedly tried to stop him, her breath heavy from wine as she clung to his arm, warm tears soaking his sleeve. For all her protests however, she never once went out of her way to see him after he moved out.

Shaking his head as if to dispel the unpleasant memory, he looked up to find Alyce staring at him intently, lines of concern etched around her eyes and mouth. "You think Sarah took a piece of the Mirror?" she prompted, massive hand reaching for the goggles that sat over her eyes.

"Well, yeah," he drawled, scratching his chin, "she used to be a pickpocket, remember? Still, if that is the case, then why am I detecting it in the opposite direction? It just doesn't make sense..." Alyce adjusted the dark lenses that covered her eyes, set them more firmly in place. Suddenly he couldn't help but feel a little guilty. Because of his wilful behaviour, she was forced to walk around in the harsh daylight. Even with the goggles, he knew prolonged exposure to full light hurt her eyes. Of course, she didn't need to walk beside him. She could have easily ducked behind the line of trees that edged the road and stayed in the shade...

"Ah, forget it," he blurted with a dismissive wave of his hand. "Whatever it is, it's too far away for us to worry about," he expanded, like a frantic salesman desperate to make a sale. Without another word, he got off the road and started to pick a path through the forest. Somewhere behind him, he heard Alyce sigh with relief, and even though he hated himself for it, his lips twitched in an approximation of a smile.

Chapter 8

The Battle of Borodino: In the Thick of Things

Monfils stormed out of the tent that was currently serving as their makeshift headquarters, stiffly walked over to the railing where his horse was tethered. Hands shaking with rage, he climbed into the saddle, dug his heels into the horse's sides harder than was necessary. Somewhere behind him, Bontems called out, grunted and cursed as he got onto his own horse. Studiously ignoring his noisy colleague's pleas to stop, he rode past the various earthworks that were being constructed just beyond the bank of the Kolocha stream. The arrowhead-shaped fleches rose modestly out of the ground, with the intention of offering troops some cover and height against the enemy when it came time to battle. "Just mounds of dirt," he snorted, vaguely aware of soldiers looking up from their shovels as he passed, a jagged line of shallow ditches at their muddy feet. He ignored them as well, not caring if he was causing a commotion.

He followed the stream until he came to a large angular wedge hewn out of the ground. Pulling back on the reins, he came to a stop at the rough earth wall. Clucking his tongue like a mother hen, he eased himself out of the saddle, walked around the base of the redoubt. Bontems pulled to a stop beside him, noisily got off his horse. "What the hell, Monfils?" his colleague blurted without preamble, doubled over slightly as he caught his breath. "What are you so mad about?" He had fully intended to ignore Bontems, seeing as he had just sat through their meeting with General Kutuzov like a stupid lump, failing to back him up at the crucial moment. But that stupid, inane question got to him, and so he turned and glared at the hapless fool, eyes beaming with the intensity of the sun.

"Why the hell wouldn't I be angry? Good Lord man, were we at the same meeting?" he snapped, continuing to circle the redoubt. Like an unfinished pentagon, it rose out of the ground, all sharp angles and edges, to slope gently away at the back. "I don't think the General took us very seriously," he muttered, slowing to a stop in the middle of the redoubt, hands clenched tightly at his sides. "Did you notice how his eyes glazed over as we told him about the Mirror? Dear God, it took all my strength not to leap out of my chair and hit his stupid face." He watched in mild amusement as Bontems' eyes grew to the size of saucers. With more life than he had ever shown during the meeting, his colleague closed the space between them, placed a grimy finger to his mouth. Signalling to be quiet, he glanced nervously this way and that, other hand gripping his shoulder like an unearthly talon.

"Are you mad? What if someone overhears you?" Bontems hissed, gaze drifting over to the group of soldiers setting up cannons in the field behind the redoubt.

Feeling his irritation bubble to the surface, he pulled his lips back in a sneer, shook off the offending hand. "They're all too busy preparing for battle," he snarled, waving at the working soldiers. "Isn't that the problem here? We've gone to all this effort to procure the Mirror, and the woman who controls it, and no one really seems to care. Don't get me wrong, I wasn't expecting a full military parade or a five-cannon salute. But I did expect a little more interest from our employers. We notified head office last week, informed them that everything was going to schedule, and yet we're still waiting for our contact to arrive. When we got to Gzhatsk and no one was waiting for us there, I assumed they were just running late, and that they would have caught up with us by now."

"Ah, but someone should be arriving tomorrow," Bontems ventured, digging around in his pocket for the scrap of paper that was passed on to them at the meeting.

"That's not the point," he all but shouted, swatting away the paper that Bontems began to extract from his pocket. He had read it over and over again, until the brusque message was burned into his brain. "That's not the point," he sighed, his anger spent. His disappointment when they arrived at Borodino and there was still no sign of the agency had been an almost palpable thing, crawling up his throat, making it hard for him to breathe. As a field agent working for so long on a case, relying on the scarce messages left for him in established drop points, he always found himself looking forward to actually meeting someone in the flesh, a human face behind the little rolls of paper covered with cryptic scrawl that were left for him throughout the countryside. He glanced over at his colleague's uncertain face, suddenly felt a hint of sympathy for the man. Obviously Bontems, being a relative newcomer to this type of work, didn't feel the same way. Really, it was written all over his bemused face. "It's just one more day," he was undoubtedly thinking. "Just one more day, and we'll be paid, free to go back."

Grunting his disgust, he turned away, walked stiffly off the redoubt and into the field. "You really are a trusting one, aren't you Bontems? In all my years of service, I've never known the agency to miss a rendezvous." At his own words, he felt a chill run down his spine. "That's right," he whispered, feet shuffling to a halt as he finally put a finger on the source of his unease. In the past, there had always been someone anxiously waiting for him at the designated meeting place. He had never had to "wait" for anyone before. It was like a ceremony signifying the end of a job, to arrive at the drop-off point, and pass on the goods to the contact. That moment of exchange, and all the tension and anticipation that came with it, seemed to form a bubble around him and the other person, a tightly enclosed space where time became sluggish, stretching unbearably between heartbeats.

He frantically searched through his memories, tried to remember a time when the contact wasn't there waiting for him.

"Well, there is a war going on," Bontems pointed out, crudely cutting into his thoughts. He blinked, stared blankly at Bontems, jaw loosening on its own accord. Looking at his colleague's stupidly optimistic face, he had the sudden urge to laugh. And so he did. At the edge of his vision, he caught glimmers of movement as the soldiers working on the cannons looked up, expressions of vague interest on their faces. Inhaling deeply to stifle further giggles, he clapped his arm around Bontems's shoulders, drew him close.

"Haven't you learnt yet Joseph, that there's always a war going on?" he uttered breathlessly into the other man's ear, all traces of mirth fading away from his voice. With a final clap on the man's broad shoulders, he turned away, his mind set.

"Come on, we have to set up a station for our girl. The general wants her somewhere behind the redoubt, to help shelter the guns." Making garbled sounds of confusion, Bontems scrambled after him. Seeing that the show was over, the soldiers returned to their work, the sounds of their activity filling the awkward void, returning everything to normality.

"Ah, about that," Bontems said breathlessly, half-stumbling as he caught up, "I think we should cut back on the doses for the duration of the battle. If it drags out too long, we'll run the risk of running out of the drug. In any case, the chaos and confusion of battle will no doubt enhance the drug's effect..." With breathtaking speed, Monfils turned, warmly clapped his shoulders.

"I concur Joseph, couldn't have put it much better myself. In fact, from now on, I'll leave all the drug stuff to you. Really, I should have done this sooner, what with your medical experience and all. You don't mind, do you? Good. Now, what do you think about putting some sandbags along this incline? I was thinking that maybe we could keep a box or something here with some supplies, but it would have to be protected of course..."

Bontems gawked in amazement at the display of enthusiasm, struggling to keep up with Monfils' rapid chain of thought. The intense, sudden shift from blinding anger to jovial cooperation had left him somewhat shell-shocked, and for a while he found he couldn't move, his limbs frozen in shock. He couldn't decide what was more shocking, being called by his first name or the fact that Monfils was being so agreeable. Like a block of ice left out in the sun, the shock began to melt away, and he got some movement back. "Ah, that's a good idea," he finally chimed, pushing the words out of his constricted throat with some effort. "Although I have to wonder if sandbags will do much in this place," he muttered, his guard slipping as his gaze swept over the green fields and gurgling streams. Despite their desperate attempts to dig and scrape fortifications out of the ground, the gentle landscape offered the Russian armies little tactical advantage. Only the nearby village of Semyanovskaya, with its elevated position just beyond the Kolocha stream, offered any obvious advantage. He mumbled words to that effect, voice barely above the level of a whisper as he glanced over at the modest collection of buildings in question, their white-washed walls catching the mid-morning sun.

It suddenly occurred to him that he may be inadvertently rubbing Monfils' nose in it. In their meeting with General Kutuzov, Monfils had argued vigorously to have Mel placed in the village for maximum effect, even offering to give a demonstration of the Mirror's powers. To his dumbfounded amazement, the General had brushed aside the offer, claiming there was no time for any displays made by "that woman". His Russian was sketchy at best, derived mostly from the battered textbook that lived in his knapsack and the odd occasion when he managed to successfully badger Monfils into teaching him a few phrases. But even he, with his handful of words and phrases, could interpret the General's thinly-veiled contempt for their work. Whatever he had been told about their mission by the agency, the General obviously didn't have much credence in the results. Thinking back, it was his first meeting with General Kutuzov. He wished someone, anyone, had warned him about the General's age and appearance. Looking more like someone's grandfather had wandered into the command tent by mistake, the old man had sat at the table, breadcrumbs caught on the long grey strands of his beard, his weathered, crinkly face further creased in concentration as Monfils spoke rapidly in Russian. Perhaps against his better judgment, Monfils had dragged Mel along. Sitting on a nearby storage box, slurred incoherent words occasionally escaping her mouth as she drifted in and out of consciousness, her presence did little to help their position. After sparing her a couple of disinterested looks, the General paid no heed to her for the rest of the meeting. It soon became apparent that the only reason their presence in the camp was tolerated at all was because of a last-minute missive sent by the agency. After some haggling back and forth, the General stabbed at the map stretched across the table, his finger tapping a spot between wiggly lines. With a final, curt order, he signalled that the meeting was over, face set in hard, stubborn lines. Barely managing to swallow back his anger, Monfils had excused himself and raced out of the tent. "Ah, sorry for bringing that up," he mumbled, gaze darting to Monfils' face. Monfils just stared blankly at him for a handful of heartbeats, eyes clouded over in confusion, until the proverbial penny dropped and he shrugged his shoulders.

"He's the general," he sighed, waving his hand in a dismissive gesture. "And we have our orders. We have to co-operate with the army, at least until our contact arrives. Ah, that reminds me, we left Mel in the command tent," Monfils groaned, slapping his forehead. "One of us should probably go and get her before she wanders off.."

"I'll go," he offered enthusiastically, suddenly eager to separate himself from Monfils, at least for a little while. "Do you want me to bring her back here?" Monfils stared at him for a moment, lips twitching as though he wanted to say something. Instead, he shook his head, turned towards a group of soldiers working on nearby earthworks.

"No, take her to our tent and let her rest. This time tomorrow, this field will be crawling with men and horses. She's going to need all her strength to survive. So will we, for that matter," Monfils admitted dryly, his voice ringing with unusual sincerity. "When you've finished doing that, check on our supplies and then report back to me," he added, giving the site they had chosen a final assessing gaze. With a shrug of his broad shoulders, Monfils started off in the direction of the soldiers, never once looking back.

A deep, soul-rattling sigh escaped him as he turned back towards the redoubt. Already Monfils was ordering the soldiers about, voice raised authoritatively against the general, low-level din. "Strange," he muttered softly under his breath, feeling hot waves of irritation radiate outwards from his stiff form. It was as though their roles had been reversed since they emerged from the command tent, with Monfils being oddly calm and philosophical about their situation, while he slowly burned with indignant rage. However, the source of his unease stemmed as much from Monfils' sudden turn-around as from their predicament.

He rounded the front of the redoubt to be greeted with a subdued whinny and impatient head shake from his horse. Despite everything, he couldn't help but smile at the gentle mare, reaching out for her glossy, smooth neck. Clucking his tongue and murmuring soothing words in her twitching ear, he climbed up into the saddle and shook the reins. Not in the mood to rush, he rode back to the command tent at a leisurely pace, carefully skirting the stream and adjacent fleches. The soldiers were now working at a feverish rate, piling layer upon layer of dirt, tapping down the growing surfaces of the fleches with their shovels. Word was travelling fast around the camp now. The Shevardino redoubt had already fallen to the enemy, with the Russian cavalry being forced to retreat. That was the sombre news they were greeted with at the meeting. It was no wonder really that the General didn't have much patience for them, not with the tent swarming with officers. Even as Monfils was giving his report, several officers, dressed in all their finery, hovered around the table, squinting down at the map and poking around various markers. From what snippets of information he had managed to hear and understand, the cavalry were making their way up the river, and would be joining them soon, with the French armies not far behind.

He drew the mare to a gentle stop near the entrance of the tent, distractedly eased himself down to the ground. In the short time he'd been away, activity inside the tent had become even more frenetic, with a heated discussion going on around the map table. No one barely acknowledged his presence as he cautiously entered, hand stiff at his side in preparation for a hasty salute. Not that he was technically part of the regular military, but as Monfils had pointed out, it made things easier to act the part, rather than explain to half the Russian army their actual rank. Relaxing slightly as his presence continued to be ignored, he looked around for Mel, breathed a sigh of relief to find her dozing off on the supply box, where they had left her.

"Hey, Mel," he hissed, timidly tapping her shoulder. Stories of people being fried alive just by the merest touch of the hessian sack containing the Mirror still plagued him, even though they hadn't had any problems like that since Mel was kept under heavy sedation. Hauling her semi-conscious arse halfway across Russia, having to physically lift her on and off the horse on an almost daily basis, it had been impossible to totally avoid contact with the Mirror. He hated to admit it, but Monfils' plan had worked brilliantly. The steady stream of drugs in her system had so far prevented her from using the Mirror against them. That was the first part of the plan. Monfils had been confident to the point of cockiness that that part would work. His extreme confidence faded somewhat however when faced with the next phase. In order for her to be useful in battle, they had to be able to influence her in some way, even while she was tripped out on drugs. To that end, Monfils relied on her being aware of the outside world on some level, and so whispered in her ear in hopes of appealing to her subconscious. It worked surprisingly well, considering the state of the subject. Just a casual suggestion in her ear, and six, seven times out of ten, Mel would do as asked, eyelids fluttering like the wings of a butterfly as she slipped between states of consciousness. As long as they got the dosage right, and gave the drug just enough time to dissolve her defences, she was very susceptible to their whispered words.

Colour crept into his cheeks as he remembered one time he half-jokingly suggested that they make use of her body. The look that Monfils had shot him, a look that suggested he had never even considered doing something like that, had floored him. "You've got to be kidding me," Monfils had scoffed, completely dismissing the idea. In the face of such cold distain, he had quickly backed down, suddenly losing his appetite, despite months of forced abstinence. At first, he put it down to consummate professionalism on Monfils' part; the man would rather do without and continue a severe drought of physical relief than mess with the subject of their mission. When he thought back however, he realised that Monfils had never really shown much interest in seeking out the company of others, female or otherwise.

For a short stint they were required to wait around in Plymouth, in preparation for being "recruited" by Jenkins, as had been arranged. Jenkins, being Sebastian's right-hand man, had arrived a couple of months ahead of time, to make contact with Alyce, as well as to make preparations for Sebastian's arrival. Even before Jenkins set foot in his old London stomping ground, the agency they worked for had taken custody of his son, and were waiting to make him an offer he couldn't refuse. Not prepared to trust Jenkins entirely, the agency insisted he "hire" two additional soldiers when he got to Plymouth. And so, he and Monfils had a couple of days to kill before the rendezvous. Knowing that once they started the mission proper, they would have little time or opportunity for self-indulgence, he set out for a night on the town, to totally satiate his senses in an orgy of drinking and sex. He had tried to coax Monfils to join him, reminding his colleague that they wouldn't have this chance again for some time. Monfils had glanced up from the book he was reading, face devoid of even a glimmer of interest in what he was proposing. Leaving Monfils to his book, he had gone out and blown most of his money on cheap booze and women, staggering back to inn they were staying at during the small hours of morning, to lie in a twitching, drooling heap on the floor. Oddly, when he woke up there was a blanket tossed over him, and a jug of water sitting within arm's reach. Monfils was busily shuffling around the room getting their stuff together, barely sparing him a single sympathetic glance, no matter how much he whinged about the herd of elephants stampeding through his head. It was then that he concluded that Monfils wasn't necessarily a bad person, just kind of cold and distant, for the most part disconnected from the feelings of others.

"I doubt that you would see it that way though, right Mel?" he grunted as he led her out of the command tent. "Not that you're capable of thinking logically about anything right now," he added, a hint of self-reproach in his voice. Due to his medical background, he couldn't help but feel a heightened sense of guilt when he looked at her thin, impoverished body and the impossibly dark circles under her eyes, set starkly against pallid, sunken cheeks. To think they had been concerned about her safety, once they joined the army. Other than a few cursory looks, more likely to ascertain whether or not she was actually female, most of the soldiers gave her a wide berth. A couple of times, he noticed out of the corner of his eye, soldiers staring at Mel more intently than was necessary, eyes darkening with desire, bodies tensing as though getting ready to pounce. On those occasions she always managed to blurt out some random phrases, or start drooling in an alarming manner, her well-timed outbursts successfully deflecting any lustful looks aimed her way. Such timely coincidences raised his hackles, and yet on close inspection Mel's face always wore a mask of oblivion, to the point that he would merely shrug his shoulders and let go of his suspicions.

As he couldn't be bothered hoisting her listless body up onto the mare's back, he opted instead to lead both her and the mare back to the hospital tent on foot. Thanks to his partial training, he had managed to make himself useful there, helping out whenever he could, thereby earning them a scrap of floor space in the far back corner of the large yet cramped tent. Leaving his horse to munch on whatever grass she could find, he steered Mel into the tent, past the rows of injured men. After being on the run for so long, there were many men needing treatment, their bodies pushed to the limit by the harsh conditions. With only a handful of trained medical staff available, and limited supplies, the men were largely left to lie about on the cold hard ground, their moans and groans of suffering filling the air with pure misery. Not exactly a nice place to be, but at least it was sheltered. Wrinkling his nose against the awful smell, he guided Mel to their corner.

"Ah, have you eaten yet Mel?" he blurted, as his own stomach growled. Her eyelids fluttered open, and she stared at him with watery, red-rimmed eyes, mouth opening and closing silently, tongue darting out to moisten her parched lips. She reached out her hands, grabbed the lapel of his jacket. With surprising strength, she pulled him closer, set her lips over his ear. A dry husky sound scraped at his eardrum, barely disturbing the air around it. Shivering involuntarily as her warm, moist breath fanned his cheek, he swallowed hard and strained to catch her words.

"What are...the names of...my children?" she asked more loudly this time, the words finally reaching him. "I see their faces, but I can't for the life of me remember...their names both start with "k", I think." Feeling as though all the blood in his body had just been replaced by icy water, he raised trembling hands to the claws that clung more tightly onto his lapel. Suddenly her knees gave way, and her body sank like a lead weight to the ground, dragging him down with it.

"Let, let go of me," he stammered hoarsely, trying to pry her rigid fingers off the material, back straining as he was held down in an awkward, semi-crouched position. "How the hell would I know about their names? I didn't even know you had any children," he protested, his voice becoming shrill. At the edge of his vision, he was vaguely aware of heads turning in their direction.

"What kind of mother am I, if I can't remember their names?" she cried, a touch of hysteria in her voice. He tried to shake her off, but her hands held fast, while her clear, focused eyes pinned him to the spot. Fear clogged up his throat, made it hard for him to breathe. Her unflinching gaze seemed to peel off the layers of his defence like a paring knife, until he was spluttering and whimpering for release. Finally he panicked and swung out his fist, catching her unsuspecting face and sending her reeling. She fell silently to the ground, to lie unmoving amongst their saddlebags. A heavy, ominous silence fell over the tent, with only his rasping pants disturbing the still air. Suddenly aware that every gaze in the room was trained on him, he nerved himself to look up, a sense of deja vu overwhelming him.

Just like that time during his medical training, and they were working in the hospital ward, and that one unstable patient lashed out at him, grabbing at his clothes, breathing heavily into his face. The other trainees had stood around quietly laughing amongst themselves, like it was the biggest joke in the world. Maybe if his mother hadn't acted like that with him every time she got drunk, maybe then he could have shrugged off the attack and acted like it was nothing. Instead, the old familiar fear filled him, and before he could stop himself, he was pummelling the hapless old man, smacking him soundly in the head. Once the floodgate opened, he couldn't stop, hitting poor fool over and over again, until he had to be pulled away by two of his colleagues. In the most dreadful silence imaginable, he had looked up from the old man's battered face to be confronted by a wall of appalled, stunned faces. As the shock of what he did wore away, a trickle of murmurs began to flow around the room, a trickle that fast became a roaring torrent.

Needless to say, his training ended soon after that. No formal charges were laid. Seeing as the patient attacked him first, they put it down to self-defence, spun some line about being under-staffed. Oddly, as if seeking his approval, they had dribbled on and on about putting measures in place so that this sort of thing wouldn't happen again. It took a while of watching bemusedly as the doctors in charge suddenly became high-pitched salesmen that he realised the truth. His father was on the board of directors. Instead of having him arrested and thrown in jail for physically abusing a patient, they endeavoured to make silk from a sow's ear, trying their best to ingratiate themselves with the son of the great Dr. Bontems. He should have just told them that they were wasting their time, as he and his father hardly ever saw each other, and even those rare times they were in the same room together, conversation was limited to awkward, curt phrases and monosyllabic replies. Although that day, when he returned home from the hospital, he had more interaction with his father than he'd had in months. Even though the doctors at the hospital were willing to sweep the incident under the carpet, his father ordered him to change his degree or withdraw from the university all together. No way was the great Phillip Louis Bontems going to risk tarnishing his good name, even when his son's future was at stake. In a fit of disgust and despair, he severed ties with his family and lost himself in London's grimy, dangerous underworld.

That was the chain of events that led him to this point in time. "Really, you just don't learn, do you?" he softly chided himself, clucking his tongue. Under the weight of all those stares, he stiffly shrugged his shoulders, bent over Mel's dazed form. "Mel, are you okay?" he asked thickly, struggling to push the words out past the constricted confines of his throat. At her murmured reply and hint of movement, the room unfroze, sounds of activity and suffering filling the air once more. Welcoming the return of normality, he glanced nervously over his shoulder, hand subtly reaching for the small case he kept in his breast pocket.

"Well, Monfils said you should rest up," he mumbled, drawing a small syringe from the case. Shifting his body around, he grabbed her arm, pushed back the grimy sleeve. With a final furtive glance over his shoulder, he shoved the tip of the needle through her skin, grimaced as he injected her once again with opiate. His lips pressed tightly together in a thin hard line of disgust and self-loathing, he pulled out the empty syringe, covered up the ugly little hole with the sleeve. Swallowing hard against the bad taste that filled his mouth, he eased her now limp, unconscious body off the saddlebags and onto a pile of blankets. "Sleep well," he croaked, dragging a blanket over her as he stiffly straightened up. Other than one or two cursory looks at the crumpled figure in the corner, the other occupants of the tent were too engrossed in their own misery/work to pay them much attention. His body felt numb and heavy as he checked on their supplies as Monfils ordered, each movement requiring deliberate effort and concentration on his behalf. Just as well Monfils had decided to put him in charge of the dosages, otherwise he'd have some serious explaining to do. As it was, Monfils was likely to raise an eyebrow over the missing dose. "Because there's no way he won't know about it," he grumbled, scribbling the tally of their "supplies" on a piece of paper and shoving it into his pocket. Monfils kept a close eye on everything they used, down to the last tea leaf. Half the time Monfils asked him to check their supplies, he suspected it was just to test his observation skills. Despite the fact that they had been working together for months now, Monfils still sometimes treated him in a strangely maternal manner, his tone bordering on patronising when describing tasks he was already familiar with. Which was why Monfil's sudden shift was disturbing. He loved to be in control of everything. The alarm bell ringing in his head started to clang more loudly, and with a final guilty grimace at Mel's sleeping face, he left the tent.

Mel woke with a start, the taste of blood in her mouth. Blinking like crazy, waiting for her eyes to adjust to the grainy light, she strained to put together the events of the past twenty-four hours. It was a pattern that seemed to be repeating itself, she slowly realized, stirring herself to move. Every time she woke up these days, she found herself in a strange place, surrounded by strange people, and she couldn't remember how she got there. Just a few rare moments of coherency and clarity were permitted, before Monfils or the other guy injected her again. Just a few bright moments, while the rest of the time was a murky, grey sludge in her mind, where the outside world was all but a vague rumour whispered in her ear. The only constants she had to cling to were the hessian sack tucked into the waistband of her pants, and the smelly, prickly blanket that was always thrown over her.

From the aching of her back muscles, and the acute ringing in her head, she'd been passed out for a long time. Wincing against the pain, she sat up, looked around for the canteen that lived in the saddlebag. Fingers trembling as she undid the lid, she greedily put it to her lips and drank the stale-tasting water. Answering the sharp stabbing pain in her stomach, she put down the now-empty canteen, rummaged through the neatly organised saddlebags, found a chunk of dried meat and a stale bread roll. Forcing down the dry, flavourless food down her sore throat, she began to pay closer attention to her surroundings. For the first time she realised she was in a hospital tent, the floor covered with sick and wounded men, a handful of medics zipping about tending them as best as they could. As she chewed, she felt her left cheek sting, and she vaguely recalled something hitting her. Gingerly she explored the area, grimaced at how tender the flesh was. Most likely it was Monfils or the other guy backhanding her.

"Ouch," she hissed as her finger found the centre of the swelling. "Ah, I must be looking really attractive right now," she muttered, getting groggily to her feet. She glanced around the tent, expecting to see Monfils or the other guy jump out at any second, syringe in hand. "Odd," she croaked, venturing out of the corner and making her way between the rows of moaning men. Some of the men were silent and still, their faces tinged with grey. Looking hastily away, she stumbled out into the light, blinked at the unfolding chaos. In some of her more lucid moments the day before, she got the impression of gentle green fields and bubbling streams. Now as she gazed about, whatever patches of ground she could spot amongst the writhing masses of men and horses had been transformed into muddy trampled sods. She couldn't even see the streams from this position, not with so many bodies in the way.

Suddenly there was a loud explosion as a cannonball smashed into the ground not ten metres of where she stood. Debris flew through the air, and she dropped onto her hands and knees as it rained down, clumps of earth and wood hitting her back. Gritting her teeth against the pain, she gathered her legs beneath her and half-staggered, half-stumbled away from the impact site. She lurched to a stop, briefly considered going back inside the hospital tent, when the familiar shrill cry of a cannonball hurtling through the air penetrated her garbled senses. Like a character in a corny, slow-motion movie scene, she looked up and watched in stupefied horror as the black iron ball fell out of the sky and careened into the hospital tent. Tearing through the poles and canvas like they were made of paper, the cannonball disappeared out of sight, leaving her to picture the path of devastation it was cutting beneath the canvas.

With the feeling of something cold and heavy lodging itself in the pit of her stomach, she swallowed back a wave of nausea as she thought of the men she had just stumbled past not moments ago. Taking a few timid steps toward what remained of the hospital tent, her eyes on their own selfish accord traced the visible path of carnage. From the position of the splintered poles and ripped canvas, she guessed that the cannonball had bounded all the way to the far corner where she had been sleeping. Feeling the blood drain away from her face at the thought of what might have been, she stumbled forward, reaching out to a couple of soldiers who were crawling out from under the crumpled tent. Her ears caught the faint shrill cry of another cannonball, and she swung around to squint up at the sky. "Cannonball!" she screamed hoarsely, grabbing the arm of the closest soldier and dragging him across the field. The high-pitched shriek grew louder, filling her ears until she thought her eardrums would burst.

She and the soldier ran as fast as they could, weaving a path through the chaotic battleground. Too late the other soldiers picked up on the sound and started running in the same direction. It was in that split second that the projectile slammed into the ground, the force of its impact sending soldiers flying through the air. Something hit the back of her head hard, and she crashed painfully to the ground, losing her grip on the soldier. Blinking away the hot tears that sprung to her eyes, she stiffly raised her trembling body off the ground, somehow got onto her hands and knees. She decided that she really hated the way the ground kept lurching and swirling before her with every movement. Straining against the intense throbbing inside her head, she scrambled to her feet, looked blankly around. The soldier was nowhere to be seen. At least she didn't recognise him amongst the bodies that were now strewn over the ground. "Really," she croaked, desperate gaze sweeping over the field of dead and injured men, "I never thought I'd say this, but where are those two?"

Right at that very moment, the two men she was referring to, Monfils and Bontems, were having a stand-off of sorts. Acting on his suspicions, Bontems had kept a close eye on his colleague, which proved to be quite challenging when he was sent off on every odd job Monfils could find. If what he suspected was true, and Monfils planned to defect to the other side or just plain leave, Monfils would without a doubt, go back to their corner in the hospital tent and retrieve his special thing, which seemed to live in one of the saddlebags. And so he ran around like a dog chasing its own tail, doing one stupid annoying job after the other, gaze drifting over to the hospital tent whenever it was within his sight. If it wasn't for the fact that he didn't want to give Monfils any reason to doubt him, he would have just forgotten about the jobs and spied on his colleague instead. It almost felt as though he was laying out bait for wily, cunning prey, and then hovering around the edge of the invisible trap, waiting anxiously for the animal to be caught.

Luck was on his side. As he was returning from a job, he spied Monfils' bearded visage emerge from the tent entrance, canvas flapping lazily in the late afternoon breeze. Ducking behind a nearby fleche, he watched as Monfils tucked a rectangular flat box into his jacket pocket, the edges of the box clearly visible through the material. "Ah, he is serious then," he muttered. Whatever that object was, it was obviously very important to Monfils. So many times, he saw it sitting in the saddlebag, the thin strips of leather that bound it together singing out to him. Once he had succumbed to the temptation, trembling fingers reaching for the knot. He was just in the process of loosening the straps when Monfils suddenly appeared behind him, yelling out his name in an uncharacteristically emotional voice. Before he could stammer an excuse or apology, the precious package was yanked out of his grasp, and with a final simmering glare his colleague stormed out of the campsite, not to return until the small hours of morning.

His throat getting uncomfortably dry, he eased his way from behind the fleche and trailed after Monfils. As he made his way across the crowded field, his nerve endings tingling with tension, he tried to convince himself it was simple curiosity. He just wanted to know where Monfils was going. Somehow, learning this one simple thing would make everything better, and he could go back to baby-sitting Mel without any qualms or regrets. He followed Monfils to the edge of the field, and watched as his colleague disappeared into the bordering forest. With a sinking feeling, he plunged into the shadows after him. This obviously wasn't a casual walk to find someone to discuss the position of artillery or haggle over the best placement spot for their girl. Other than a few scouts patrolling the area, there were no men stationed in this side of the forest. Being substantially outnumbered by the French, the decision had been made to concentrate troop numbers mostly on the southern approaches.

On and on Monfils marched, his steady steps showing no sign of hesitation. Just when he was wondering what he should do next, there was a flash of light and puff of smoke to his right. Caught off-guard, he jumped, head swinging violently as his eyes scanned the deepening shadows to his right. By the time he straightened up and glanced back, Monfils was standing behind him, one thick forearm placed heavily around the front of his shoulders while the other held a musket to his back. "Geez Joseph, were you going to follow me all day or what?" he hissed through stiff lips, tightening his hold. "You must be half asleep or something, to fall for that old trick." Silently kicking himself for making such a blunder, he took a deep breath, wincing at the pain as Monfils pulled his arm in, putting extra pressure on his windpipe.

"You and your bloody smoke bombs," he managed to wheeze, willing his body to be still. He was rewarded for his efforts with a slight loosening of Monfils' arm.

"So, are you really leaving?" he rasped, painfully twisting his head around.

"What if the answer is yes? Would you try to stop me?"

He opened his mouth to make a snappy, cajoling reply, meant to evoke confidence and trust, but words deserted him. All the niggling doubts and fine logic that had led him to this moment evaporated like morning mist, and he was at a complete loss.

"I really don't know," he answered truthfully. Making a small sound of disappointment from somewhere deep in his throat, Monfils released him, musket hovering warily at his side.

"You clumsily follow me all this way, and you don't know? But you obviously suspected that something was amiss. What gave me away?"

He was vaguely aware of his eyebrows knitting together in consternation as he stared at his colleague. Was he having a laugh? "What gave you away?" he echoed in an awe-stricken voice. "Are you kidding me? You've been acting strange since we got here. What, you didn't think I would notice? I mean, first you flip out about not being met by someone from the agency, then you get all irate over our meeting with General Kutuzov, and finally, you hand over responsibility for the drug dosages to me...you, who has to be completely in control of everything at all times. And let's not even start with the whole "Joseph" business." Once he started, he found it hard to stop, the whinges and gripes gushing out in a torrent of unabashed honesty. At last, he ran out of things to say, and stood glaring at Monfils, his breathing a little ragged and face flushed red. As he settled down, trickles of regret and doubt stirred within him, and he uselessly wondered if that had been a wise thing to do, particularly considering that Monfils was still holding his musket at the ready. He silently kicked himself for not using that outburst to cover a subtle grab for his own weapon. In a fit of nerves he licked his parched lips, fingers twitching over the gun at his side. Only problem was, he didn't have a proper holster, so it was wedged tightly between his belt and waistband. He would have to quick, move without hesitation...

His frantic, adrenalin-fuelled train of thought was abruptly derailed by Monfils' unrestrained laughter. It was such a strange, surprisingly high-pitched sound that he stood frozen in shock. Never in all their months working together had he heard such pure, genuine laughter from the man. Sure, he'd heard the usual range of half-hearted, polite laughter that everyone who wants to get along with society is obliged to dispense. But this vocal expression was something altogether different. "Ha, I guess I wasn't very subtle about it," he conceded, voice muffled as he bent over slightly. "Listen to me, Bontems," he continued, all traces of mirth gone as he emphasised his surname, "I'm not going to betray you or anything. Hell, I'm not even sure where I'm going. At the moment I'm just concentrating on getting to the next town, and I'll try to figure out something from there..."

"It's not the fact that you're leaving that's bothering me," he blurted, suddenly wanting to wipe that self-satisfied, over-bearing smile off Monfils' face. He paused, took a steadying breath. "It's more the reason why you're leaving that concerns me. If there's one thing I know about you, it's that you're not the type to casually leave your post. So it must be very serious, whatever it is..."

He was so engrossed in searching for the right words, in pinpointing the exact source of his unrest, that he didn't notice the way Monfils slowly turned, hand arcing upwards. Not until the muzzle of the musket filled his field of vision did he fall silent, the colour quickly draining from his face. With unbearable slowness, Monfils shifted his thumb, pulled back the hammer of the firing mechanism. "You really should not have followed me here, Bontems," he uttered softly, a tinge of regret in his voice.

"Ah, wait!" he shouted, absurdly putting out his hand as if to block the shot. There was a loud explosion, and a burning sensation in his left ear, the acrid smell of burning gunpowder filling his nostrils. He fell heavily to his knees, Monfils' shocked visage etched deeply into his retinas. Another shot, and this time Monfils was sinking to the ground, hand flying to his shoulder. Straining to push past the intense pain that now pulsated through his brain, he watched in confusion the blood that oozed out from beneath Monfils' hand. What the hell was going on?

The soft sound of leaves crunching underfoot penetrated his senses. Raising a shaky hand to his ear, he turned towards the sound. A ring of soldiers advanced steadily, their rifles held at the ready. He blinked, realised with profound shock that he recognised most of the stony faces that now confronted him. Feeling something warm and wet trickle down his fingers, he lowered his hand, gawked at the blood that covered it.

"He's a good shot, isn't he?" With a sharp intake of air, he looked up in the direction of that cold, familiar voice, and froze. From behind the wall of soldiers, Sebastian Seabast emerged, a smug smile curling his lips. "Captain Gasquet is one of the finest marksmen in our region. Not that you would know this of course, seeing as you're both only hired hands." The way he said "hired hands" sounded like he had the taste of curdled milk in his mouth, his features briefly twisted in disgust. Somewhere behind him, Monfils groaned, spat savagely at the ground.

"Jesus Christ, what are you doing here?" he squeezed out between agonised breaths, blood still oozing out between his fingers. Sebastian shifted his cold hard gaze to Monfils' increasingly pale face, stepped towards him.

"Is that any way to greet your previous employer?" he purred, although the tension around his eyes and mouth belied his casual tone. "Or maybe you never saw me that way." With all the dangerous intensity of a cobra poised to strike, he crouched beside Monfils, grabbed him roughly by the chin. "Tell me," he grated into Monfils' face, "where is that maggot? Where is Jenkins?"

To his credit, Monfils stared evenly back at Sebastian, his expression inscrutable. "He's dead," he finally answered, visibly sagging in Sebastian's grip. For a moment Sebastian just blinked at Monfils, failing to absorb those two simple words. He almost wanted to laugh, seeing that expression on his usually superior face, as though he had just had the wind taken out of his sails.

"H..how? Who killed him?" he stammered, tightening his grip on Monfils' chin. Monfils mumbled something, the feeble vibrations barely scraping at the heavy blanket of silence that had fallen over the forest. Sebastian must have been able to make out the words however, for his eyes widened in surprise. Monfils must have told him the truth, for Sebastian lowered his head, shoulders shuddering under his thick velvet jacket. "That woman again," he uttered thickly through stiff lips, knuckles turning white as he clenched his hands in rage. Monfils visibly twitched in his grasp, and he seemed to collect himself, the shadow lifting from his face. He none-too-gently released Monfils, brow wrinkled in irritation as he glanced at the still-gushing wound on his shoulder. "Dammit Richard, you did too good a job on this one, he's bleeding to death," he snapped, running an impatient hand through his hair. Seemingly unperturbed by Monfils' imminent demise, Sebastian's sharp gaze turned to him. "You there, Bontems, wasn't it? Do you know where we can find the woman?"

His mouth went uncomfortably dry, and he wondered distractedly why he was tasting blood. Funny, the question of whether he lived or died depended on the answer he gave at that very moment, and he was fixated on the salty taste of blood. "Yes," he croaked, eyes darting to Monfils' increasingly pallid face and back again.

"Excellent," Sebastian drawled, smug smile reasserting itself. With a final dismissive look at Monfils, he signalled for the party to move. Without having to be told, Captain Gasquet, looking as impressive and stoic as ever, moved toward him, gun held warily at the ready.

"Out in front, Bontems, if that is in fact your name," the captain all but snarled, voice edged with raw emotion. Still clutching his ear, he clambered awkwardly to his feet.

"Ah, Captain," he croaked, struggling to find his voice. "Are we really going to leave him behind?" he asked, pointing at Monfils. "I mean, he's a valuable source of information..."

"Shut up!" Gasquet roared, in an eruption worthy of a volcano. There was a blur of movement, and the hard butt of Gasquet's rifle slammed into his stomach. Letting go of his ear, he clutched at his stomach, and even though he had only seconds ago managed to get to his feet, he found himself sinking again. Through the waves of pain that now radiated outward from his stomach, and permeated his brain, he was vaguely aware of a loud sound, like an explosion, and the ensuing commotion. The gruff voices of the soldiers passed back and forward above his head, punctuated by Sebastian's pompous, overbearing commands. Suddenly a hand flung out blindly and crudely grabbed his arm, long thick fingers digging into his flesh. A startled cry escaped his lips, and he looked back to find Monfils staring at him intently, lips twisted in an approximation of a grin. "Can't believe everybody's falling for that trick today," he wheezed, pulling him closer. He gawked stupidly at Monfils' haggard face, slowly absorbed his words.

"Ah, the trick from before," is what he wanted to say, but even though his mouth hung open, intelligible sounds refused to come out. Other than the odd murmur of "um" and "ah", he just crouched there, utterly paralysed. The one sane, working voice left in his head that wasn't going ga-ga or dribbling like a two-year old coughed politely, pointed out that it's hard to know what to say to someone who is dying. He mutely nodded in agreement. Even without years of medical training, he could have figured out that Monfils was close to death. The cheeks that poked out above the thick beard now looked pasty and clammy, the ashen skin slick with grease and sweat. Wow, the bullet must have severed a major artery, he found himself musing as his gaze drifted to the sticky remains of Monfils' shoulder.

"This is what I get for running away, eh Joseph?" Tearing his eyes away from the wound at the scratchy voice, he shrugged his shoulders, opened his mouth to say something profound. "Ah,

I wanted to see her one last time," Monfils wheezed, his bloodied hand sliding down to rest on his chest. Slack lips twitched, and a name floated up from them. "Rachel." And with that, Monfils gasped his last breath, glassy eyes staring into the abyss.

For a handful of heartbeats, he stared at the lifeless hand that was still draped over his arm. Time unfroze around him, and he became acutely aware of the men returning to normal. "Show's over, huh?" he murmured, and right on cue Gasquet roughly grabbed his arm, hauled him to his feet.

"What's going on Bontems? Was that explosion your doing? Or was it his?" Gasquet demanded, aiming his rifle at Monfils as if to emphasise the point.

"What does it matter now, the man's dead," he spat back with more venom than he intended. "And about the explosion, I don't know if any of you men have noticed, but there's a war going on around here." Shaking off Gasquet's hand, he dusted himself off, tugged uselessly at his worn, mis-shapen jacket. Months of living on the road in rough conditions, and his favourite jacket was well on its way to being completely trashed. He was certain he saw a beggar in the last major town they visited with a better coat than his. It was so bad, even Monfils had made a joke about it, quipping something about him missing his true calling in life. On their own accord, his lips twitched up at the corners. Absent-mindedly, he reached for the handkerchief that lived in the inner breast pocket of his jacket, when a flash of memory lit up his mind.

"Get moving Bontems," growled Gasquet, nudging his back with the end of his rifle. He suddenly became aware of the ring of expectant faces hovering at the edge of his vision. "When exactly did all the men get organised again, so soon after Monfils' diversion?" he silently wondered, shaking his head. It's now or never. Shifting ever-so-slightly to his right, he clutched his stomach, and making a sound like he was about to vomit, he sank to his knees, torso hanging over Monfils' body. It really was one of those wonderful serendipities that no one was standing directly in front of him at the time, otherwise he surely would have been seen, dipping his hand into Monfils' breast pocket like that. Before anyone could move toward him, he rose stiffly from the ground, still doubled over and making retching sounds as though his life depended on it. Slipping his hand into his breast pocket, he deposited the flat box, pulled out the handkerchief. His fingers trembling, but for entirely dif-ferent reasons than any of the onlookers might imagine, he pressed the handkerchief to his mouth, mumbled apologetically through the material.

The nervous sweat trickling down the side of his face must have sold the act, for Gasquet, after a quick sidelong glance at Sebastian, merely nodded, indicating that he should lead the way. He looked at Monfils' still, lifeless body one last time, before trudging off, the sombre, silent men marching/riding behind him like a gloomy funeral procession. Oddly, Gasquet and Sebastian seemed content to hang back a couple of paces behind him, their voices occasionally raised in conversation, the odd word reaching his ears over the sound of their horses. He was grateful for the breathing space. With a surreptitious glance over his shoulder, he carefully placed his hand over the concealed breast pocket of his jacket, felt the hard outline of the flat rectangular box nestled within the folds of fabric. Monfils' prized possession. At the time, he didn't stop to think. Convinced that it was what Monfils would have wanted, his body had moved by itself. It had nothing at all to do with his own selfish desire to finally look inside.

"It, it could be an important family heirloom," he murmured softly, his fingers caressing the sharp straight edges. For some reason, whenever he thought of "family heirlooms", the image of fine silverware just popped into his head. Suddenly the idea that Monfils had been zealously carrying a set of cutlery captured his imagination, and he had the dangerous urge to laugh. Pressing his lips together, he tried to steer his thoughts towards more sober things. Like Monfils' face just before he died. He just had to remember the way Monfils' dark eyes had bored into his as he uttered his final wish in this world, and the laughter died, falling away like a dead weight.

Suddenly something caught his foot, and he stumbled badly, nearly crashing to the ground as he struggled to maintain his balance. He glanced back to see what it was that he nearly tripped on, strained his eyes to pick out the tree root protruding out of the ground. When did it get so late? he wondered as his eyes slowly adjusted to the grainy, grey-tinged light. He must have really lost track of time when he was following Monfils...

"What's the problem?" Gasquet growled warily as he guided his horse forward, sharp gaze focused on his face. "Can't find your way back?"

"Ah, it's a bit hard, in this light," he answered cautiously, body tensing under Gasquet's distrustful scrutiny. A slight exaggeration, he mentally noted, seeing as for the most part they could just follow the river back to the camp. If they hadn't approached so strongly from the east, they would be aware of this. Really, he would never have expected to encounter non-Russian troops from this side of the Moskva River. They must have circled around a fair way to avoid all the troops...

"Wow, you must have covered a lot of ground," he mused aloud, the words tumbling out of his mouth before he knew it. Gasquet briefly bristled at the observation, and he thought for an absurd moment that he had somehow insulted the man. An unreadable expression crossed Gasquet's face as his eyes focused on the deepening shadows between the trees.

"We knew we had a lot of ground to make up," he mumbled defensively, shrugging his shoulders ever-so-slightly. "But it wasn't without cost," Gasquet added, spitting the words out as though they were poison. Staring at Gasquet's face as though the answers were somehow written there, he strained to remember all of the party members before his dramatic departure from the Magnificent.

"Ah," he murmured, realising they were shy a couple of members. He couldn't for the life of him remember their names, but their faces and personalities hovered on the edge of his memory. He vaguely recalled one guy who was always talking about his woman, driving all the other men crazy with his detailed descriptions of what he planned to do when he was finally reunited with her. The other man had been more reticent, his tight-lipped visage only noticeably softening when he was dragged into conversations about home, at which point he would share snippets of his life on a dairy farm, a wistful look on his face.

"We lost two men and some of our horses in a skirmish with a scouting party, just over a day ago," Gasquet supplied, taking off his hat to run thick fingers through his thinning hair. "That's when we knew we were getting close to the fighting..."

"Captain," Sebastian interjected pointedly, closing the distance between them. "Please get a lantern for Bontems. I want to reach the camp as soon as possible." For a moment Gasquet answered Sebastian's glower with a stern look, faint cracks in his self-control starting to show. Murmuring words of acknowledgment through stiff lips, the captain tugged at the reins and turned his horse away. Taking his cue from Sebastian, he awkwardly waited for Gasquet's return, all too aware of the other man's penetrating gaze.

"You followed Monfils quite a long way, didn't you?" Sebastian asked rhetorically, leaning over the muscular neck of his horse. "For what purpose?"

Swallowing past the lump that had suddenly formed in his throat, he licked his dry, cracked lips. He really didn't want to admit that their plans had fallen apart, not after all they had been through. "It's not like Monfils to just take off like that. I was instantly suspicious," he answered carefully.

"You thought he was going to meet with somebody, and possibly sell that woman to another bidder?"

He frowned, shook his head, a minute movement of neck muscles. "That was my first thought, but thinking about it, how could he organise something like that at such short notice?" he answered vaguely, struggling to understand his own motivations. "Maybe he was just taking a walk..."

"Wait," Sebastian interjected, face scrunched up in growing disbelief as he did the maths, "who is guarding that woman and the Mirror?" For answer, Joseph shrugged his shoulders.

"No one," he answered truthfully, voice completely lacking concern, to Sebastian's obvious annoyance. "She's out cold, and no one's shown any interest in us whatsoever since we got here, so there's no problem."

"What do you mean, no one's shown interest? Don't they realise what they have in their hands?" Sebastian all but stammered, his face getting redder by the minute. Again, Joseph shrugged, secretly enjoying Sebastian's outrage. It was almost all worth it just to see that smug, overbearing smirk slip, to see that shiny confidence fade.

At that moment, Gasquet returned, lantern in hand, the paraffin-soaked wick already alight.

"Ah, what about scouting parties? Are we likely to attract attention?" the Captain asked earnestly, brow crinkled with concern as he handed over the lantern. Out of the corner of his eye, he noted the shadow that passed over Sebastian's face at the other man's return, lips firmly clamped shut. The two men must have had a falling-out of sorts, judging from that tight-lipped look.

"No, they haven't been sending out many scouting parties on this side of the river," he answered truthfully, taking the lantern. "Seeing as Napoleon's armies are expected to arrive from the south and all," he explained clumsily. An awkward silence fell over the mismatched trio, the air heavy with expectation as Sebastian and Gasquet exchanged guarded looks.

He opened his mouth to say something, anything just to break the tense atmosphere, when a short, grotty-looking man dressed in a tatty uniform galloped towards them, a couple of old smoke-stained lanterns clutched to his chest. "I found more lanterns, Captain," he wheezed excitedly, nearly dropping said lanterns as he skidded to a halt in front of Gasquet. "Shall I light them, sir?"

Gasquet blanched slightly, moved swiftly to block his view of the newcomer.

"Ah, good work Marcus," Gasquet mumbled, not-so-subtly herding him away, "but we'll make do with the one lantern for now." Despite his efforts to shield him, the newcomer jutted his head out from behind Gasquet's broad back, beady dark eyes trained on him like a hawk.

"Who's that man anyway, Captain? Can we really trust him?" he asked without reservation, a faint sneer twisting his lips as he spoke. Marcus ventured closer, body tense as though ready to spring back behind Gasquet's protective figure at a moment's notice, reminding him of a small yappy dog trying to act tough.

Forcing a smile onto his face, he moved forward to introduce himself, when the awful smell hit him. The acrid, nauseating stench of old dried blood, sweat, and putrefied flesh reached down through his nostrils all the way to his throat, causing him to recoil and reflexively cover up his nose and mouth. "Dear God, what's wrong with this man?" he demanded, pushing the words out between gagging breaths. "That smell..." he croaked, unable to push out anymore words past the constricted confines of his throat. Holding up the lantern, he looked closely and noticed the way Marcus invariably pressed a hand to his gut, and the lines of pain that seemed to be permanently etched around his eyes and mouth.

"That's enough Captain, get your pet out of here and let's continue on our way," Sebastian snapped, snatching the lit lantern from his suddenly listless hands.

"Wait!" he gave a muffled cry, his years of medical training stubbornly asserting themselves. With great mental effort he lowered his hand, reached out to the man called Marcus. "This man obviously needs medical attention. Please, allow me to at least clean his wound. Judging from the smell, he'll soon start slowing us down. It won't take long, I promise," he blurted, desperation creeping into his voice as Sebastian remained stony-faced.

"Please, Lord Seabast," Gasquet joined in, lowering his head, "it's getting worse by the day, and I recall Bontems used to act as a medic..." Something in Gasquet's voice prompted him to look over at the gruff, burly man, and he noticed in the swaying lantern light how his hands were tightly clenched at his sides as he virtually pleaded to Sebastian. For one tense, hushed moment, no sound was uttered, not even from the gangly group of men waiting impatiently behind them. Clenching his jaw in frustration, Sebastian growled his consent, and amid mutterings of an unreasonable time limit, handed over the lantern and turned stiffly away. Pushing aside his revulsion, he murmured an appropriately grovelling reply and grabbed Marcus" grimy sleeve, led him a couple of paces away from the group. Gasquet hovered anxiously next to him, obviously bursting to help in some way. "Right Captain, I need a lit torch, some alcohol, and a clean bayonet blade," he rattled off, setting the lantern down on the ground.

Almost jumping out of his skin in his eagerness to help, Gasquet nodded, gruffly ordered two nearby soldiers to fetch torches and bayonet blades. With growing urgency in his voice, Gasquet proceeded to interrogate the unfortunate soldier in charge of stores. "He's certainly worried about you," he murmured, watching as Gasquet led the head-scratching soldier away to the pack horses waiting restlessly at the rear of the group. Marcus mumbled some incomprehensible reply, scratched at the collection of bristles that sprinkled his chin. "Take off your shirt please Marcus," he ordered curtly, pulling a small leather-bound case from his satchel. With well-practiced hands he untied the straps and opened the battered case, felt a hint of nostalgia at the neat row of tools that glinted up at him in the lantern's wavery glow. A quick glance at Marcus fumbling with the buttons of his shirt, and he turned away, nerveless fingers reaching for the package in his inner pocket. He didn't even realise he was holding his breath as he clumsily clawed at the leather straps binding it together. Every second he didn't have someone peering over his shoulder or trailing close behind him was precious, and he had gone to such extraordinary lengths to buy this time...

The lid finally came free, and with a noisy blast of air he exhaled, eyes feasting on the contents of the box, on Monfils' treasure. All the adrenalin that surged through his body seemed to freeze in place as he found himself gawking down at a portrait of a young woman. Blurry, smeared charcoal lines adorned the thick paper, coalesced to form a pale, delicate face framed by long wavy hair. At the bottom of the page was Monfils' familiar scrawl. "My darling Rachel," he read, the sound struggling to escape the constricted confines of his throat. "December, 1809." He squinted at the picture, moved it closer to the light. Is this Monfils' woman? he mused, running the ball of his thumb gently over the edge of the paper. Now that he thought about it, he vaguely recalled that Monfils was talented in that way. He would often draw rough sketches of potential clients or victims that they had to rendezvous with in some shape or form. Being the sort of person who was limited to drawing stick figures and misshapen, unrecognisable faces, he had always watched on in awe as Monfils made it all look so easy, his pencil seeming to flow over the paper without hesitation. With envy faintly prickling his voice, he would make a big deal about Monfils' talent, insisting that he should be a professional artist, only to receive a tight-lipped response, and the strong feeling he had just crossed an invisible line he shouldn't have. "He must have drawn this," he murmured, fingers tightening around the edge of the box as he was filled with awe at this window into Monfils' soul. "I have to find this woman." The words filled his mind like a twisted mantra, shined like a beacon to his lost, confused soul. Just have to find a way out of this mess...

Suddenly there was a burst of noise behind him as Gasquet returned. Coupled with Marcus' muttered expletives as he struggled out of his shirt, Gasquet's breathless calls jarred his nerves, sent his hands into a fit of clumsy juggling. He managed to re-establish his hold on the box and the precious drawing nestled in its shallow depths, and amid garbled responses to both Gasquet and Marcus, he stuffed it back into his jacket pocket. "Will rum do? It's the last of our alcohol," Gasquet reported, his voice heavy with misgiving.

"Ah, rum will do fine," he managed to reply, almost tripping over his own tongue in the process. Willing his hand to stop trembling, he took the ceramic jug that Gasquet was holding out to him. His medical training reasserted itself, and he ordered the two soldiers standing awkwardly behind Gasquet to set up their torches. In a flurry of motion, he picked out a scalpel from his kit, moved to where the nearest soldier was waiting, torch held gingerly before him. "You, hold the blade in the flame like this, let me know when it's glowing red," he ordered, feeling a faint sense of satisfaction when the soldier's face blanched. Another soldier waited nearby, a number of bayonet blades in his hands. Selecting the least rust-spotted blade, he ordered the soldier to hold it in the flame.

"Captain, do you have a clean cloth I could use?" he asked brusquely, anticipation and anxiety welling up inside him, winding his body up like a giant spring. Without hesitation Gasquet pulled a large white handkerchief out of his jacket pocket. He reached out for the cloth, froze momentarily as he noticed how much Gasquet's hand was shaking. "Just what is this man to you, Captain?" he asked, slowly taking the handkerchief, eyes pinned to Gasquet's strained face.

"Don't get any funny ideas," he growled, shoving his hands into his pockets. With a guarded sideways glance at Marcus, who was staring into space, grimy shirt hanging listlessly from his fingers, the captain closed the distance between them. "It's the smell," he grated, the words bit off and spat out from between stiff lips. "The man follows me like a lost puppy, no matter how much I yell at him. The men think it's hilarious." His voice shook with anger, and he paused to take a steadying breath. "Anyway, there's nothing I can do about it, Sebastian wants him kept alive to use as bait. Now I can tolerate the snickers behind my back, and Sebastian's flights of fancy, but that smell, following me everywhere I go..." The gruffly spoken words trailed off in a heartfelt sigh, and Gasquet fell back a couple of paces.

He mumbled an appropriate reply, turned back to his trusty medical kit. Better to focus on the task at hand than stare overly long at the captain's embarrassed face, he decided, the urge to giggle inexplicitly tickling his throat. Clamping his lips firmly together, he rifled through the various pockets that lined the walls of the kit. A muffled sound of discovery escaped his lips, and he extracted a round lump of wood from one of the pockets. "Bite down on this," he ordered, holding it out to Marcus. He blinked, bloodshot eyes slowly focusing on the stick.

"What's this for then?" Marcus asked, gingerly taking the lump of wood and eying warily the deep teeth marks that pitted the surface.

"What do you think it's for?" he murmured distractedly while carefully tipping rum onto the handkerchief. Swallowing hard, Marcus opened his mouth and inserted the wood between his teeth.

Amid mumbled words of reassurance, he set to work, first wiping the infected area with the alcohol-soaked cloth and then calling out for the scalpel. With some careful juggling he grabbed the handle, winced as heat shot through his fingertips. He was vaguely aware of men jostling behind him, peering over his shoulder with faces scrunched up in anticipation. Without looking up, he ordered Gasquet to apply pressure to the top half of Marcus' abdomen, a couple of inches above the line of putrefying, fetid flesh. A final caution to the soldier with the bayonet blade to be ready, and he took a deep breath, began to cut away the infected area. The whole clearing seemed to be holding its breath, with only Marcus' cries to shake the tense, heavy air. Only a handful of seconds in reality, and yet the time between each tic and toc seemed to stretch to the point of breaking. Reality itself seemed suspended to him, as the only thing that filled his mind at that very moment was cutting off the weeping, discoloured flesh as quickly as possible, before the scalpel blade went cold and invited further infection.

"Blade," he barked gruffly, dropping the bloody scalpel and holding out his hand. By this stage, Marcus' body had stopped moving, blood loss and intense pain all but wiping the poor fellow out. "This will wake him up," he murmured, swinging the bayonet blade around. With a final steadying breath, he placed the flat of the red-hot blade directly onto the freshly exposed wound. Behind him, the soldiers gasped noisily as flesh sizzled and burned under hot metal, the smell of singed hair and skin filling the air. Marcus yelped, jumped out of Gasquet's grasp, the blade still stuck to his belly. "Hold him down!" he shouted, maintaining his grip on the handle. "If I pull away now, the wound will re-open." With that dire warning hanging in the air, Gasquet promptly grasped Marcus' shoulder, meaty fist slamming into the side of his head. The shock of impact stopped Marcus dead in his tracks, and with a feeble whimper coming from somewhere deep in his throat, he fell down like a sack of potatoes. He managed to follow the movement, and when Marcus finally lay completely still, he carefully lifted the blade away to reveal pink, shiny flesh. He crouched down beside the unconscious Marcus to admire his own handiwork, the bayonet blade falling from suddenly nerveless fingers. Folding over the handkerchief to expose the last clean corner of fabric, he lightly brushed the surrounding area.

"This could be my best work ever," he croaked softly under his breath. As best as he could in the available light, he gently prodded the stretched skin on either side of the cauterised flesh, nodded with satisfaction when he finally was confident that all traces of infection had been removed. "This one may actually live," he whispered, echoing the catch phrase of his old mentor. On the verge of retirement or death, whichever came first, Doctor Hemsworth had treated him with complete distain, not caring one bit that his father was a prominent figure within the hospital management. After all the sycophantic displays by the other doctors, he had oddly found Dr Hemsworth's company refreshing. At least the man would never lie to protect his feelings, or say bad things about him behind his back. No, if Doctor Hemsworth had something bad to say, he came right out with it, he thought with a derisive grin. If only the old man could see this, surely even he would have to been forced give his work grudging approval...

Marcus showed signs of life, stirring beneath his assessing fingers, and he backed away, a small sigh of relief escaping his lips. Behind him, a growing throng of pressing bodies jostled, the men peering over his shoulder to watch the show. Even Sebastian had stopped sulking and pushed his way through the crowd to take a look. He didn't need to look back to know that their faces were screwed up in morbid anticipation, as though avidly expecting to see something gory and disgusting.

"Is he going to be okay?"

"Shouldn't you put a bandage on that?"

"At least the smell is mostly gone now." Their hushed comments and questions scratched at his ears, somehow rubbed him the wrong way. Biting his tongue against the swelling irritation, he let most of the comments slide, only responding to the most relevant questions.

"Exposure to air is best for now, so long as he keeps it clean and lightly covered," he answered, voice muffled as he bent over to retrieve his bloody scalpel. Marcus' breath caught noisily in his throat, and everyone, himself included, collectively jumped, bodies tensing in anticipation. "Oh look, he's waking up," someone whispered excitedly, setting in motion a wave of harsh-sounding whispers.

"No bloody wonder, with the way you lot are acting," he muttered softly, sparing them a guarded sideways glance before narrowing his eyes to study the well-sharpened blade, frowning slightly at a fresh nick marring the smooth edge.

"He must really be in pain," someone drawled, a hint of awe in his voice. He clucked his tongue in agreement, quickly cleaned off the blade as best he could. If only he still had some kind of sedative, he thought ruefully as he slid the scalpel back into the kit. He still had the drug dosages reserved for Mel, which would take the edge off the pain, but the hallucinogenic side effects could be dangerous for someone in his condition. His foot bumped against something, and he looked down to see the jug of rum still sitting open on the ground. "Well, there is that," he murmured, reaching over to pick it up. A half-strangled sound of discovery escaped his lips as he uncovered a small envelop nestled in the thick grass. On their own accord, his eyebrows knitted together as he reached down, enclosed his fingers around the small, neat package. Gasquet's questioning words and Marcus' grunts washed off his back like water as he blinked with sudden recognition at the envelope. "So that bastard was holding out on me," he croaked, the sound barely stirring the air. Only days ago, he had quizzed Monfils about his stocks of drugs and poisons, to have his queries coldly, impassively brushed off. He squinted at the familiar scrawl that marked the front of the envelope, hastily straightened and shoved it into his pocket. In that moment, he wanted to laugh raucously at his good fortune, every fibre in his being acutely attuned to the treasure that now seemed to burn a hole in his pocket.

"No, don't leave me behind!" He spun around to find Sebastian looming over Marcus in an intimidating manner.

"Look, you're obviously in a lot of pain, and we can't have you making a lot of noise when we're trying to slip into the camp undetected," Sebastian pointed out in a haughty fashion, shrugging his shoulders for effect. "Unless you can prove to me that you can remain silent, even while moving?"

A wide-eyed Marcus, instilled with the fear of being left behind, started to clamber to his feet, beads of sickly sweat forming anew on his brow. Try as he may to contain his voice, his breath wheezed and hissed with every little movement, until he was standing unsteadily on his feet. His gasps and groans scraped uncomfortably against one's nerves, amplified by the heavy silence that now cloaked the forest as night fully set. With growing disquiet, the men exchanged meaningful looks, faces tense in anticipation of the brewing storm that surely was going to break. "See, what did I tell you?" Sebastian announced brusquely, shaking his head. "Leave him behind, we'll come back for him later..."

Marcus' face visibly blanched at the mention of "later", his reaction suggesting the word was a death sentence rather than a promise. His face darkening in anger, Gasquet appeared to feel the same way. "Ah, I have something that might help," he blurted, spurring himself into action as he saw the opening he needed. Suddenly everyone turned to look at him, and under the weight of all those stares, he willed his hand to move, draw the envelope from his pocket. "Can I please have some water, and a cup, Captain?" he asked, willing his fingers to move, the envelop shifting in his grip. He knelt down in front Marcus, carefully tore the envelope open.

"What is that?" Sebastian asked, hovering over his shoulder, voice heavy with suspicion.

"It's a sedative, should take the edge off his pain, keep him quiet," he explained with more force than he intended. "At least until we're in the camp," he added, more softly this time. Somewhat placated by his answer, Sebastian subsided into surly silence, turned away to bark orders at nearby soldiers.

"Here you go," Gasquet announced breathlessly, a saddlebag cradled in his arms as he sunk down beside him. Muttering darkly under his breath, the captain fumbled awkwardly through the bag, finally produced a canteen and chipped enamel-plated mug. Murmuring words of gratitude, he opened the canteen, appeared to empty the contents of the envelop into the mug.

"Is that really going to help him, Bontems?" Gasquet asked, glancing pointedly over his shoulder at Sebastian. Keeping all traces of emotion from his face, he added water to the mug, his palm flitting over the opening of the canteen as he put it down. "Don't worry captain," he uttered softly, "this will make things go smoothly for all of us."

Stalls lined the already narrow road, with piles of produce spilling out onto the cobblestones. Naturally, it was noon, the busiest period of the day for the merchants as people piled into the market. And of course, that's when he clumsily hurtled into the street, the city guards hot on his heels. He frantically picked a path through the maze of people and stalls, the accusing shouts of merchants and pedestrians alike blending into the background, the sound of his own heart pounding like a kettle drum filling his ears. "I didn't do it!" he wanted to scream back at the guards one last time, but he knew it was futile. His last chance at being cleared had just disintegrated before his disbelieving eyes, with Dr Dubois steadily denying that they had been out together at the time of the murder. To the untrained eye, the good doctor appeared granite-faced and immovable, all desperate pleas and indignant cries bouncing off his crusty exterior like hail bouncing off a rock. He noticed however the subtle tension around the other man's eyes and mouth, and how his gaze kept sliding away to the far corner of the room whenever possible.

"Sebastian," he spat, knowing in his heart that his brother was somehow responsible for what happened. If there was something Sebastian excelled at, it was uncovering people's weaknesses. Despite being a well-respected doctor and family man, Simon had the odd skeleton or two lying around in his closet. "Sebastian must have something on him, for him to turn like that," he croaked softly, sparing a hasty backward glance before ducking into a narrow alley. The number of stalls and people thinned considerably here, and he realised too late his mistake, the urgent scraping of boots resounding loudly in his ears. Hissing savagely, he scurried to the end of the alley, followed it around until he found himself in a deserted lane, only wide enough to fit two men walking side by side. As his eyes adjusted to the shadows, he realised he was not alone in the dingy, damp corridor. There at the end of the cobbled pavement huddled a small girl, her thin frame hunched before a big wicker basket.

With the gruff voices of the guards echoing loudly behind him, he had no time to wonder what the girl was doing, or what was in the basket. He stumbled to the end of the lane, and with a meaningful look at the girl, jumped into the basket, pulled some miscellaneous items over his head. Did the girl catch his gesture to be quiet? he wondered anxiously, willing his limbs to stop trembling as harsh-sounding voices entered the lane. Squinting through the fine gaps between the thick grass strands, he glimpsed the stony faces of the guards as they advanced toward the basket. Had they already seen him, and were just taking their sweet time? he fretted, suddenly feeling absurd for jumping into the basket in the first place. His breathing became increasingly shallow with each menacing step the men took, until he was barely breathing at all. Someone's kneecap came into view, and the dreaded question was asked. "Did you see a tall man with light-coloured hair run through here, little one?"

He swivelled his eyes in their sockets, not daring to move at all, and gawked at the back of the girl's head, red hair glinting in the mid-morning light that managed to find its way between the high walls. She mumbled some reply, and for a handful of heartbeats he thought she had brushed off the question, for the men fell silent. Then a beefy hand descended towards him, delved through the thin layer of rags to latch onto his head. He was unceremoniously hauled to his feet, and the burly guard moved to reveal a wall of bayonets all directly aimed at him. "Fire!" The man's harsh voice rang out, and he only had a fleeting second to glance accusingly at the girl, who merely shrugged her shoulders, before a volley of shots split the stifling, still air.

He twitched, realised muddily that the shots were real. Peeling the heavy lids from his eyes, he found himself staring at the ground, which was bouncing up and down. Emily's warm, muscular neck brushed against his cheek, and he hastily straightened up, tightened his hold on the reins that had somehow got entangled in his fingers. "Sorry Emily," he muttered, full of self-disgust. "Your namesake would have shaken me off long ago." The mare snorted, shook her head. Her steady pace faltered as another barrage of gunfire rang out. His joints creaked and popped alarmingly as he stretched his stiff limbs. "No offence Emily, but using you as a bed isn't doing my body any favours," he murmured into the mare's ear as he bent over and grabbed the spy glass out of his saddlebag. She snorted contemptuously, and he got the distinct impression that the feeling was mutual. Clucking his tongue ruefully, he pulled the faithful horse to a stop, and extended the glass.

Following the band of trees that covered the slope, he peered down into the valley, and with some minor adjustments of the glass focused on the moving specks. Another slow, careful twist of the lens, and the specks became soldiers. With a sinking sensation forming in the pit of his stomach, he realised that the fighting had already started. He swept over the valley floor, to the earthen works that had been dug out of the ground just beyond a stream. Or at least that's what he imagined the raised platforms were, from what he could see through the writhing masses of men and horses. Judging by the relatively small number of unmoving bodies on the ground, the fighting had just begun. His lips set in a grim, hard line, he panned across, tried to see what was going on behind the band of clashing bodies. The alien fragment within his body screamed inside his mind as a collection of tents in the background came into view. "Mel," he croaked hoarsely, the sound barely escaping the lump that suddenly formed in his throat. Another volley of gunfire cut across the general din that faintly reached him where he stood at the top of the slope. Gunfire, and something else, he realised, lowering the spy glass as the familiar eerie whine of cannonballs sailing through the air penetrated his muddy senses. Of its own accord his body tensed, memories of their desperate fight on the Pretty Peg stuffing themselves into his head, like determined unwanted house guests.

"Right," he announced, pulling himself together. Ignoring how weak and fragile his voice sounded against the distant reverberations of battle, he leant over and put away his spy glass. "There's a village just up ahead, no doubt they have artillery men stationed there, but I think in all the confusion and chaos, we'll be able to slink through undetected." Fear mingled with anticipation was gripping his heart and mind, he could feel it. Hence the serious conversation with his horse. "What, you don't think it'll work?" he quizzed when Emily shook her head and snorted loudly. Fear, anticipation, and somewhere beyond all the confusing emotions in between, was the most tangible of all. Excitement. "Look," he murmured, reaching into his pocket and pulling out a small paper bag. He picked out a sugar cube, cradled it on his palm. "Just take me as far as you can, Emily," he said gently into her ear, holding the sugar cube under her mouth. Her soft lips brushed against his palm as she deftly accepted the proffered treat. Despite upending the saddlebags and sorting through his supplies several times already, he had only discovered the bag of sugar cubes the day before, when blindly groping through the bags in search of his map. Giving silent thanks to the previous owner, he straightened up, and after a moment of hesitation, popped a sugar cube into his mouth. Wincing at the acute sweetness, he returned the bag to his pocket and nudged Emily. With a whinny of resignation, the mare moved, cutting a cautious path along the top of the slope, shifting angle with each subtle push of his knees or tug of the reins.

The sounds of battle rose steadily to greet them as they approached the village. Not so much from the village itself, but from the valley below. Apart from the gruff, terse cries of the soldiers stationed around the walls of the outer-most buildings, and their regular intervals of gunfire, the village was largely deserted and quiet. Dark shapes moved in the windows and doorways of the houses he passed, and he could feel many eyes follow his progress, almost burning holes in the back of his head as he passed. Despite the relative emptiness of the streets, he kept to the narrow spaces between houses as much as possible, for the odd soldier would occasionally burst out into the street, face strained as he ran about on some sort of errand. He somehow avoided detection and exited the modest collection of buildings. The forest noticeably thinned on this side of the village, and found himself scurrying for cover as another barrage of cannonballs sailed through the air.

"Come on old girl," he soothed as Emily jumped skittishly beneath him. Coming to a stop behind a large tree, he fished out another sugar cube, offered it to the increasingly nervous mare. "Just stay with me a little longer Emily, please," he pleaded softly into her ear, his voice ragged. While still a little blurry, he didn't need the spy glass now to make out the struggling shapes below. The fighting was steadily intensifying, and it wouldn't be long before the camp beyond the front lines came under fire. Marking the group of tents as his goal, he surveyed the land in between. Just had to make it down the rest of the slope, and then they would be on flat ground. At that point they would lose the protection of the trees, so he should probably release Emily anyway, and let the mare make her way back home. "Ah, it's not far now," he whispered, feeling something inside him break. Ever since parting ways with Sarah, he had felt incomplete, as though her removal from his side had left a gaping hole in him. Hell, he even missed Daniel, despite the irritation and guilt he felt every time he caught sight of that kid's miserable confused face. "He must really like Sarah, to go so far," he mused aloud, absent-mindedly reaching inside the bag for another sugar cube. He felt the straight edge of a single cube, and after further probing realised with a sigh it was the last one.

Never once tearing his gaze from the white tents that shined like a beacon to him from the valley floor, he popped the last sugar cube into his mouth. As he scrunched up the paper bag and tossed it away, he pushed aside his loneliness and regret, reassured himself it had been for the best. "A fine time to develop a conscience," he softly chided, remembering all the dangers they had shared up to that point. Oddly, in all that time, he had never felt compelled to send Sarah away. Sifting through his memories, he wondered what was different this time. A few moments of exhausted silence, and he made a satisfied clucking sound with his tongue. "Of course, that's the difference," he murmured, recalling that day in the forest, when he found Sarah and her attackers. Though his blood boiled at the sight of Sarah's wretched figure huddled against a tree, he coldly, efficiently killed the remaining men. As the last man fell, and Sarah cried out hoarsely, he looked at the crumpled form on the forest floor, eyebrows twitching in slow, horrified recognition. "It's her," were the words that floated from Sarah's lips, and he knew with a cold sensation in the pit of his stomach what she meant. The woman she had been watching in the Mirror for months, until that fateful day of the plane crash, now stared up at him through glassy eyes, pain and exhaustion clouding her features. "Mel," he sighed, remembering how much he had initially resented her intrusion into their cosy little world. That was the difference. Mel entered their lives, and all sorts of things started to change. "Damn, Sarah even got herself a boyfriend, eh?" he grumbled softly, idly stroking Emily's neck. "Ha," he laughed weakly, feeling as though a weight had just been lifted off his shoulders with that cheery thought. For that reason alone, he could not regret his decision to send Sarah away, no matter how much he missed her. Voices abruptly rang out below him, and he jumped half-way of his skin, all doubts and questions chased from his mind. Gathering together what remained of his nerves, he eased Emily back into the shadows, and started to guide her down the slope, angling away from those raised, excited voices.

"Shit," Gunthar hissed, dropping behind a fallen tree at the sound of approaching horses. Pressing his back into the rough bark, he forced his neck muscles to relax, rested the back of his head against the thick trunk. With slow, careful movements, he looked around, eyes straining to pick out the source of the noise. He hastily jerked his head back as a group of mounted soldiers cantered into view. Thank-goodness Alyce had been lumbering some distance behind him, he thought with a shaky sigh. Somewhere in the deep forest shadows, she was surely slinking out of sight as best as she possibly could. A mental picture of her cramming her considerable bulk behind a tree or rock popped into his head, and for one giddy moment he had the urge to laugh. The shaking of the ground as the horses passed quickly dampened the urge, and he sat as still as possible, while fervently hoping Alyce was far away enough to avoid detection. That was one of the biggest setbacks to travelling with the golem. Animals, particularly horses and dogs, were keenly sensitive to its scent. He had grown accustomed to a chorus of animal calls heralding their approach whenever they ventured near a town or village. Alyce on the other hand would tense up every time, her features set in a deep scowl that could be noticed even with the big goggles covering a large portion of her face.

"Poor Alyce," he sighed as the last of the horses trotted out of earshot. He slowly clambered to his feet, his own face lined with worry as he thought about Alyce. She had been acting strangely the past couple of days. Indeed, the strangeness of her behaviour seemed to increase the closer they got to the Mirror. An evil, insidious idea crept into his mind, and he momentarily froze on the spot, a chill crawling uncomfortably down his spine. Is she preparing to take the Mirror for herself? Was that it? He blinked, wondered why he hadn't thought of it before. The cogs of his brain started to turn more quickly, as sketchy memories of when they decided to team up replayed themselves. "But a lot has happened since then," he blurted, his abrupt voice overly loud in the still, quiet forest. Somewhere deep inside, there was a part of him that didn't want to believe that Alyce was only after the Mirror. That little voice inside his head, the one seeded with self-loathing and doubt, piped up. "Hypocrite. That's all you're interested in too, right?"

"Ha," he breathed in response, the ugly word filling his mind like a twisted mantra. "I guess there is some truth to that," he croaked, recalling his own words at the time. "Let's help each other get close to the Mirror, and then it's every man/golem for himself." He had said it so casually, without giving the matter any serious thought, so eager was he to continue the chase. So, did this mean their partnership was about to end?

The sound of leaves crunching underfoot startled him, and he looked up to find Alyce walking towards him, lips twisted in a sideways grin. "That was close. It's a good thing I was hanging back, otherwise the horses would have smelt me for sure. Are you alright, Gunthar?" Times like this, he was really struck by the fact that it was Alyce in control of that huge monstrous body, and not Clay. There was no way Clay could move with such delicacy or charm, the resulting display often reducing him to tears of laughter, no matter how many times he saw it.

"I'm fine," he answered stiffly, turning away as he struggled to collect his thoughts. "I managed to duck down out of sight just in time."

"Ah," she mumbled, the low guttural sound resonating through the clearing like thunder. A moment of heavy silence, and then she blurted her apologies for not warning him, the oddly whiny tone of her voice setting his nerves on edge.

"Well, you don't have to hang back so far!" he snapped. "I mean, it's not far now, and with so many soldiers cutting through this forest, what's the point of avoiding detection? Surely we can stand our ground against the average party of soldiers, between your massive size and my Mirror powers." Like a tiger cautiously circling its prey, he studied Alyce's every minute reaction, waited to see if she'd walk into his subtle trap. "Unless," he drawled, spinning around to pin her with an accusing look, "there's some other reason you're hanging back?" Feeling as though he had just poked a stick into an ants' nest, he backed away slightly, body poised for flight. To his surprise, she merely gawked at him, her face wreathed in lines of confusion.

"What do you mean, Gunthar?" she quizzed, pushing up her goggles to squint down at him in the forest gloom. Even though dawn had well and truly broken over an hour ago, the sun's rays only feebly poked through the thick canopy, leaving them to walk about in murky half-light. He stared back, tried to pick out her facial expression from the general gloom that currently enshrouded them. "Look, even with all the confusion and chaos of battle, I stand out," she pointed out, her gentle, patient tone irritating him to no end. "The best chance we have to grab the Mirror is for you to sneak into the camp while I hang back and cover you as best I can." He opened his mouth to spit out some ugly innuendoes, all manner of poisonous barbs lined up on his tongue ready to shoot.

"But aren't you worried I'll just take the Mirror for myself and run?" he finally stammered, all his planned witty remarks falling away like sand in the desert.

"Ah, about that," she began awkwardly, turning her dark gaze to the ground as she started to push her foot through the carpet of dead leaves. "I've been thinking lately, about all the stuff that's happened, and why I wanted the Mirror in the first place. I've pictured it many times you know, returning home with the Mirror and demonstrating its power to my father, who naturally is then reduced to a trembling, drooling mass at my feet..." Her voice trailed away as she stared into space, a wistful look on her face. With a sigh she returned to reality, shook her head. "But now of course, he wouldn't recognise me immediately. I'd have to explain who I really am, and how I came to inhabit this unnatural body. No, not explain, convince. Knowing my father, this would turn into a heated argument the moment I mention Uncle Henry. I mean, you can't mention Uncle Henry in our household without father flying off the handle, and rehashing the old story about how his older brother was excommunicated for his suspicious experiments. The fact that I maintained contact with Uncle Henry was no doubt a sore point, even if it was just the odd letter. Ah, what was I saying? So, really, it's like telling a joke, but no one gets it, so you're forced to explain it, and once you have to explain a joke, and why it's funny, well, it just loses all impact, and people then just laugh out of politeness..."

As he stood there listening to Alyce ramble on, he was vaguely aware of the sounds of battle intensifying in the background. Gunfire, cannonballs screeching through the air, loud explosions, men shouting and screaming. A little voice at the back of his head, the more sane one of all his "little voices", politely coughed for attention and stiffly suggested that they move, there is a war going on and all that. And yet he found couldn't move, couldn't tear his eyes away from this impossibly bashful creature, baring her soul. No way the old Alyce was ever this candid or cute, he thought, a faint smile curling his lips. Catching the slight movement, she stopped in mid-rant, visibly collected herself. "So, to summarise, I've decided that I don't really want the Mirror anymore." Her voice droned on, something about him not needing to worry about competing with her for the Mirror, and in fact she would continue to help him?, but the words slipped in and out of his mind like a lump of butter melting in a pan.

"You don't want the Mirror anymore," he repeated thickly as the cogs of his frozen brain started to move again. His eyes darted away from her concerned face, and she started talking again, moved towards him. Suddenly his throat went dry, and an awful taste filled his mouth. "I'd um, better keep moving," he mumbled hoarsely, stumbling away in shock. Painfully aware of her heavy gaze following him through the trees, he wandered aimlessly for awhile, his only clear goal to distance himself from her disturbing presence. "Doesn't want the Mirror," he croaked, face scrunched up in disbelief. He had never even thought to question his desire for the Mirror. Its voice filled his head, tugged at his consciousness. Ever since that fateful day, when they blundered into the ancient, sealed-off chamber deep underground and discovered the shiny black artifact, he had felt it. It was like an insect trapped within his skull, trying to crawl its way out. Only a tiny vibration, just below the surface of flesh and bone, and yet constant, maddening, crawling away day and night until it consumed his thoughts, leaving nothing but desire for the Mirror.

Icy darts seem to travel up and down his spine, and he collapsed against a tree, skin breaking into goose bumps despite the steadily climbing sun. "I thought you were the same as me, Alyce," he whispered, resting his heavy forehead against the trunk. And now she was saying she wanted to help him, no strings attached? "Ridiculous," he snorted, riding the wave of his self-derision to push himself away from the tree. That's the stuff of fantasies. Why in the world would she want to help him? Sure, they'd been through a lot together, but wasn't it just coincidence? They had both been caught up in Sebastian's web of intrigue and stupidity, and formed a pact when it started to fall apart.

If it wasn't for that, they most likely would have nothing to do with each other, coming from such different worlds. After forcibly parting ways with Raphael and Sarah, he had somehow dragged himself into a nearby village, despite his considerable injuries, and the locals had grudgingly offered assistance. They must have smelt the madness on him, for as soon as he was able to move, they pointedly encouraged him to leave. "At least they supplied me with some basic provisions," he uttered softly, sketchy memories of that day playing in his head. He could still remember the relieved look on their faces as he left, as though a great weight had been lifted with his passing. With no other destination in mind, he slowly made his way back home, all the while straining to hear the Mirror's voice once more. He frowned, tried to piece together a timeline.

"It must have been at least two weeks," he murmured, thinking back to that patchy period of his life when he was recuperating in the village. Drifting in and out of consciousness, he'd largely been confined to a lumpy narrow mattress in the attic of the local inn. Every now and then someone must have changed his dressings, cleaned him up, though he was never awake at the time. So by the time he eventually left, Raphael and Sarah were long gone, and he had no easy way to chase them down. Try as he may, he never caught even the faintest tremor of the Mirror, and so he slowly made his way home, a broken man. By the time Jenkins found him, he had used up all his savings and family connections, and was decorating a prison cell, awaiting possible charges of disturbing the peace and breaking public property. For as long as he lived, he would never forget that strange night, when he looked up to see what the other prisoners were making noise over, and through the bars of his cell saw Jenkins for the first time. Moving with the quiet grace of a cat, Jenkins made his way along the corridor, the verbal abuse and pleas of the prisoners bouncing off his slight frame without leaving the slightest ripple or dent on his countenance.

The first word that popped into his head as he studied the light-coloured eyes over the well-maintained moustache, all topped by strands of greasy hair plastered over a bald spot, was "oily". His assessment of Jenkins solidified further the instant the man opened his mouth and talked. "Do you like it here, Mr Bliesch?" he had asked with an unmistakable swagger in his voice. Staring into that impassive face in disbelief, he had idly wondered how much effort Jenkins put into keeping his moustache so neat and well-shaped. "I can get you out of here, if you'll agree to help us find something." The enticing, seductive words rolled off Jenkins' tongue, and it was only then that he noticed the beautiful woman standing behind him. Pointedly ignoring the jeers and calls of the other prisoners, she had regarded him coolly, a faint frown creasing her pretty features.

"Are you sure this is the right man, Jenkins?" she had asked, voice full of distain.

"He's the only one I've managed to track down who is rumoured to have had direct contact with the Mirror in recent times. And no, I don't count that toothless crone we met the other day. That woman was obviously off with the fairies," Jenkins had grunted in reply, a smug grin tugging at the corners of his mouth as his eyes flew wide open. For a moment he couldn't speak, his mouth went so dry. Swallowing the saliva that felt like paste in his mouth, he forced his numb lips to move.

"The Mirror?" he finally croaked, pushing out the thin raspy thing that counted as his voice. Even more smugness settled around Jenkins' mouth and eyes as he made a show of extracting a piece of paper from his pocket. With nerveless fingers he took the proffered paper, clumsily unfolded it.

"This is your map, is it not?" Jenkins asked, his voice sounding like it was far away, echoing dully off his shocked ears as he stared at the familiar lines and scrawl, barely discernible against the yellow, crinkled surface.

"How, how did you find this?" he asked, fingers curling around its worn edges. How many times had he pulled it out of his pocket during their trek across Turkey? It had fallen out of his pocket when he fell down the mountainside. Out of habit, he had reached for it when he first came to, only to find it missing, that familiar, somehow comforting shape nestled in the folds of material. When he quizzed the locals if they had come across any maps, they merely shook their heads, brushed aside his enquiries.

"It took some time, but we eventually tracked it down. To think it was in that village after all...the hardest part was getting someone to talk..." As Jenkins' silky words soaked into his brain, something cold and heavy seemed to settle in the pit of his stomach.

"You didn't hurt them, did you?" he asked thickly, swallowing back a wave of nausea. While they didn't exactly welcome him with open arms, they did grudgingly nurse him back to health. They could have just as easily left him to die, his broken twisted body lying forever in the patchy scrub that covered the foot of the mountain.

"Nothing that won't heal with time," Jenkins answered vaguely, shrugging his slender shoulders like it was a small matter, far beneath him. "So, will you help us find the Mirror, Gunthar?" he continued more forcefully, extending his hand. Time seemed to slow down and stretch ridiculously between each of his nervous heartbeats as he looked at that hand. Why he hesitated at that moment, he wasn't sure. It wasn't like he could say "no" to such an offer. They shook hands, and Jenkins briefly vanished to quietly pass money into the right hands.

While they waited for his return, Alyce pretended not to be affected by the crude suggestions flowing from the mouths of his fellow prisoners, despite the faint twitching of her shoulders beneath the fur-trimmed collar of her long coat. Very faint movements that could only be detected if one was paying close attention. Kind of like the section of jagged hand-stitching attaching the fur to the edge of the collar, and the tuffs of worn fabric sticking up and catching the light. Feeling the weight of his stare, she had snapped at him, told him to look elsewhere. "You don't have to try so hard, you know." Before he could stop himself, the words tumbled out of his mouth, and she gasped, a tiny, shocked sound that escaped the normally tightly controlled confines of her throat. In that split second, he caught a glimpse of the real, vulnerable creature sheltering beneath that polished, carefully constructed shell. At that moment, Jenkins returned, completely oblivious to the mood between them, brusquely announced they were leaving.

With his charges conveniently forgotten, he left town, his two new, mismatched companions in tow. After his slip of the tongue in the prison, he had assumed that Alyce would keep her distance as they followed a trail of breadcrumbs across Europe. Her gruff, surly attitude towards him all but screamed displeasure. It slowly dawned on him however that the foul-mouthed creature that snarled and snapped at him whenever they were alone was the real Alyce, polar opposite to the polished, refined woman who seemed to float serenely in Jenkins' wake. It was as though she took his recklessly uttered words to heart, but only when the coast was clear and there were no other witnesses. He alone enjoyed that "privilege".

"It's no wonder we teamed up, really," he murmured softly, returning to the present with a shake of his head. While they looked worlds apart, they were apparently born from the same twisted mould. At least that was what he had thought all this time. "It must be a trick," he whispered hoarsely, scratching at the scruffy tuffs of facial hair growing out of his chin. "I'll settle my account with her once I get the Mirror," he added roughly, raising his voice as though to reassure himself. A wry grin curling the corners of his mouth, he put all thoughts of Alyce behind him and started jogging once more towards the battlefield. In some distant corner of his brain, a sane voice murmured that the battle must be heating up, judging by the swelling sound of gunfire and struggle. He blinked, squinted at the collection of tiny figures in the distance, pouring over the shallow stream to hurl themselves at the already heaving mass of fighting bodies on the arrowhead-shaped fleches beyond the now brown water. Just then another volley of cannonballs was shot from far behind the fleches, the now familiar high-pitched whine ringing in his ears, filling him with anticipation and dread. Still his feet moved steadily towards the field, only pausing a fraction of a second when the balls impacted the ground. No, not the field, he silently corrected, regaining his bearings as the

Mirror's song reasserted itself, pushing past the distractions of battle. The group of off-white tents poking out from behind the fighting soldiers.

She had to be there somewhere, among those tents, he reasoned. From somewhere deep inside, a bubble of tension broke inside him, and he sighed deeply, despite the fact he was running as though his life depended on it. At the edge of his vision, he glimpsed the reaction of soldiers who noticed his loping figure. Some of them called out, thumped the shoulder of the person next to them and pointed in his direction. Somewhere behind him, the heavy thud of boots striking the ground in half-hearted pursuit could be heard, only to fade away as he steadfastly ignored their hails and threats. Shots rang out, and he realised with a numb sense of shock that they were actually firing at him. His steps faltered for a fraction of a second as bullets zinged through the air in the general vicinity of his head. The acrid smell of gunpowder assaulted his nostrils, convinced him to veer slightly off track and duck behind a tree. Only problem was, he was running out of trees.

Another volley of shots, closer this time, and he had to shield his face from a spray of wood chips as bullets hit the trunk. "Too close," he wheezed, pumping his legs harder despite the fact that his lungs felt as though they were on fire. There was more shouting, but now the soldiers' voices were tinged with fear and surprise, before falling ominously silent. He resisted the temptation to look over his shoulder. He could just imagine Alyce standing there, gazing anxiously after him, broken unmoving bodies of the soldiers at her feet. Even at this distance, he could feel her heavy gaze upon him, the hairs on the back of his neck standing on end. Grudgingly, he turned his head, his neck so stiff it felt like a ratchet as he looked back. There was her unmistakeable figure, stumbling out from behind the line of trees, thickset arms waving oddly in the air. Heat rose from his cheeks as he realized she was actually waving to him, and he hastily turned away.

"She used to be such a sensible girl," he muttered, clucking his tongue. No matter, he thought with utter certainty, a broad grin creasing his face. Not far now, he noted with growing excitement, barely pausing to navigate a path through the debris as he reached the edge of the battlefield. Only stopping to duck out of the path of struggling soldiers or oncoming artillery fire, he doggedly crossed the increasingly churned up, muddy ground until he reached the first tent. Releasing the pressure in his lungs with a ragged explosion of pent-up air, he doubled over slightly and allowed himself the small luxury of catching his breath. Leaning against the canvas wall, he craned his neck to peer at the officers and soldiers rushing in and out of the opening. "Must be a command tent of some kind," he murmured softly, the sound of his voice barely reaching his own ears. Even this far from the front line, the cacophony of battle filled the air, overlaying all other sounds like a thick stifling blanket.

"I can barely hear myself think." The words slipped out of his mouth, and he instantly froze as the realisation hit him. Time seemed to slow down, as though the light and sound reaching his senses had to pass through a wall of molasses. He was vaguely aware of his jaw dropping, flapping uselessly as he struggled to find his voice. "The Mirror's voice," he finally croaked, swivelling his head around absurdly. Fear gripped his heart, squeezed tightly as he pressed trembling fingers over his ears and concentrated on that familiar voice. Like a starving person searching a larder for food, he desperately prodded and poked every nook and cranny of his mind. But everywhere he looked, there was nothing but traces and echoes of his own stupid thoughts and memories.

"It's...not there," he whispered, blood draining from his face. That sweet discordant voice, that had been calling to him constantly for months... "Gone," he uttered, pushing away from the canvas wall. In shocked disbelief, he staggered around the tent, every fibre of his being willing the Mirror to be heard once more. "Wait, get a hold of yourself, Gunthar," he grunted, a bitter bark of laughter escaping his numb lips. "That stupid bitch has done something to the Mirror. So look for her." Like a manic mantra, that phrase echoed in his mind, repeated over and over until no other thoughts remained. All the fighting and chaos of the battlefield receded to the edge of his awareness, the soldiers and horses mere obstacles in his path. From tent to tent he trudged, eyes peeled open and scanning every lump of humanity before him. Moving like a possessed man, he absent-mindedly dodged and side-stepped anything that came at him, intentionally or otherwise. Just as absent-mindedly, he pulled out his weapon, deflected oncoming blows, casually found the vulnerable spots of any ardent attacker's body. Odd, he'd never really been much of a fighter. He generally found violence boring and pointless, and so would go out of his way to avoid confrontations.

Despite what others might say or think, it wasn't because he lacked courage or self-belief to defend himself. In his reckless pursuit of the Mirror, he had risked his life more times than he cared to admit, and when push came to shove, he was prepared to fight back. But he never actively looked for a fight, like some people seem to do. It all stemmed back to that day, when he witnessed a bloody brawl in the street. He was out with his father, a rare, remarkable occurrence to start with. They had to go into town for one reason or another, and were starting on their way back, when their feet collectively slowed at the sight of a gathering crowd. Unwittingly he tugged on his father's hand, inched his way through the crowd, gaze firmly fixed on the flashes of colour he saw through the gaps. Being small, he managed to squeeze his way to the edge of the circle, and awkwardly wedge himself between two grey-suited men. What he saw at that moment was burned into his memory for all time. One man lay twitching in the gutter, blood oozing from various gashes on his head. Already dark bruises formed beneath the skin of his face, engulfed his left eye and cheek. And the way his body was arranged against the cobbled surface of the road, some of the angles looked unnatural, as though bones and joints had been stretched out of place. Clearly, the man was defeated, with all the fight beat out of him. But still the other man pounded his fist into the wretched broken body, his battered face red with unspent anger.

Just then a couple of onlookers sprang into action, as though the spell they'd been under had broken, and grabbed the man's shoulders, hauled him away. People then surged forward, gathered around the fallen man. Amid calls for a doctor, they straightened out his body, half-heartedly applied a handkerchief to the biggest wound on his head. He found himself edging forward to get a better look, when suddenly a claw-like hand grabbed his shoulder, yanked him back. He looked up to find his father glaring down at him, blue eyes aglow with simmering disapproval. Taking a tight hold of his hand, his father briskly left the scene, somehow navigating a path through the crowd. At first, he thought that his father's anger was purely directed at him, but then he caught fragments of muttered statements as they walked away. "...A bit late for that now...just standing around watching while that man...how stupid..." All the while the big hand that held his tightened, until he feared the bones would be crushed.

Swallowing his fear, he opened his mouth. "Father," he croaked in subdued protest, his feet slowing on their own accord. At the strained voice, his father stopped in his tracks, whirled around. Still holding tightly to his hand, his father bent down, looked earnestly into his face. "Promise me boy you'll never take violence lightly. Whatever the reason for that fight, surely it wasn't worth one man being beaten close to dea...beaten so badly. Unless there's no option other than to fight, try to find a peaceful way to deal with conflict. Can you do that for me boy?" Shocked by the raw sincerity in his father's voice, he had mutely nodded, his mind busy with absorbing every minute detail of the moment. It was the first time he felt that maybe there was more to this man that a vague male presence in the house, burying himself in the newspaper or hiding away in the study.

"...you can't mention Uncle Henry in our household without father flying off the handle..." Alyce's words popped into his head, and with a start he returned to harsh reality, the long shrill cry of an oncoming cannonball previously just scratching at his awareness suddenly filling his ears. The soldiers near him all seemed to become aware of it at the same time, for they all started moving at once. Like a disturbed ant nest, bodies rushed away from an invisible spot in seemingly random directions. He had just started running when the cannonball smashed into the ground not far behind him. Dirt and rocks were spewed up around him, several larger rocks and clods striking his retreating back. His knees momentarily buckled under the impact, but somehow he maintained his balance and kept running, not even daring to look back once. Oddly though, in that moment, it wasn't the fact that he was running for his life that preoccupied his mind. If anything, his body seemed to have slipped into an automatic survival mode, normally clumsy feet lithely weaving a path through the maze of debris and bodies.

"What the hell?" he grumbled under his breath, shaking his head against the rest of the monologue that started re-playing itself in his mind.

"I've been thinking lately...Why I wanted the Mirror in the first place...Returning home with the Mirror and demonstrating its power to my father, who naturally is then reduced to a trembling, drooling mass at my feet...But now of course, he wouldn't recognise me immediately ...I'd have to explain who I really am, and how I came to inhabit this unnatural body...No, not explain, convince... So, really, it's like telling a joke, but no one gets it..."

"Telling a joke, but no one gets it," he echoed, voice creaking as his lungs rattled in unison with the surrounding air. On their own accord, his feet slowed, and all sense of urgency momentarily deserted him as those words crawled around in his head. He couldn't quite put his finger on it, but something about those words bothered him, like seeing a familiar face but being unable to attach a name to it. "Why am I even thinking about this?" he muttered, forcing his feet to move again. "If she truly doesn't want the Mirror anymore, that's her business. Right?" Somehow, airing his thoughts made him feel a little better. "Really, it's not like anyone is going to hear me anyway," he added, the sound of his voice barely reaching his own ears over the general din of battle. Pushing all thoughts of Alyce out of his mind, he continued his search. Ignoring the warm blood trickling down his back, he went methodically from one side of the field to the other, eyes all but burning in their sockets as he scanned every lump of humanity alive or dead along his path for a dark-haired woman.

At the edge of the forest, a large dark shape moved restlessly behind a tree, peered anxiously past the rough bark to the pale tall figure in the distance. Squinting through the tinted glass of her goggles, she caught glimpses of Gunthar as he wandered stiffly away from the tent, seemingly oblivious to the battle going on around him. Something big must have happened, she decided, the folds of skin between her eyes creasing in concern. Only moments before, he had moved without a trace of hesitation, feet pounding the sodden, churned ground without missing a beat. And then, he just stopped dead in his tracks, his body rigid and unmoving, as though suddenly turned to stone. "Damn," she spat, lashing out at the tree as her frustration bubbled to the surface. "I shouldn't have said all that," she uttered thickly, remembering the confusion and disbelief clouding his face as she babbled on and on about her father and why she didn't want the Mirror anymore.

"For some strange reason, I thought he'd understand, and be happy." With those empty words drifting off her lips, she moved away from the tree, edged closer towards the battlefield. She was acting more out of habit now. After their little exchange before, she doubted that Gunthar expected or wanted anymore help from her, seeing as she had uttered the unutterable. Losing her desire for the Mirror had turned her into some strange, mysterious creature in his eyes. He had never looked at her like that before, even when he discovered that she had taken possession of Clay's body. That was one of the things she liked the most about Gunthar. He was impervious to outward appearances. From the very first moment they met, he had looked at her clearly, without a trace of lust or avarice clouding those light blue eyes. It had been a shock for her at first, not being able to manipulate someone with a dazzling smile or a pouty look. Even from a young age, men had been susceptible to her charms, their overly friendly manner and strenuous plays for her affection becoming an accepted facet of her life.

"A rather boring one," she sighed, thinking back to all those annoying men fawning over her, clamouring for her attention. "Fat chance of that now," she quietly snorted, looking down at her large hands, and the grey, cracked skin covering the palms. At the sound of approaching footsteps, she dived for cover, awkwardly arranging her massive bulk behind a clump of bushes. She was fast running out of cover, and would soon be forced out into the open if she intended to keep track of Gunthar, even with her enhanced vision. "Really Alyce, this is just pathetic," she clucked under her breath, as her gaze gravitated towards the section of battlefield where she last saw Gunthar. When they first teamed up, her motivation was obtaining the Mirror, pure and simple. She had fully intended to let Gunthar lead her to the Mirror, and once they'd cleared all other obstacles, then eliminate him and take it for herself. That was pretty much the terms of their agreement.

Why break the habit of a lifetime? Taking advantage of men was as natural to her as breathing. It started as a game, something to do for her own sadistic amusement, especially when her father remarried, and suddenly had no time for her. Then, when she was kicked out, it was a matter of survival. However, without the protection of her family, she fell into trouble, all too soon picking the wrong man to take advantage of. It had never occurred to her that one of her victims might seek retribution, until that day she was attacked. After a long day of serving flirty, heavy-handed men and pretending to be interested in their conversation, she failed to notice the steady footsteps following her home from the club. Only when she unlocked the door did she become aware of a dark shape looming behind her. In that split second of awareness, she was pushed violently into the dingy room, the door slammed shut behind her. All she could remember after that was the darkness, and cruel, crude hands reaching out of that darkness to claw at her body. There was a heavy weight on top of her body, from which a familiar voice called out to her, called her all sorts of nasty names.

"James," she muttered, remembering the name of her attacker as she inched around the bushes. Gunthar was the move again, following a more erratic path now. That night was a turning point for her. It was the first time she was physically attacked. It was also the first time she killed someone, the botched attempt to poison her stepmother aside. And so, her short-lived independence came to an end, and she ran to her Uncle Henry's side, relying on his reclusive nature to protect her from the authorities. After he died, she drifted towards the underworld like seaweed caught in a current, until it's strong pull completely uprooted her and swallowed her whole. Poor Clay got pulled along with her. "Clay," she murmured, once more blinking down at the hands that she now treated as her own. Every now and again, she could feel his consciousness buried deep inside her, scratching feebly at the smothering layers that were her awareness. Not for the first time, she wondered how it could even work, the small stone that Uncle Henry implanted in the middle of Clay's brain somehow absorbing all her thoughts and memories, even giving her control of Clay's body. "That's some magical stone you've got there, Uncle Henry," she wished she could say to him. And he planned it? He had the forethought to install something like that while he was sewing this body together, in preparation for her possible, premature demise?

"No," she mumbled, squeezing her hands so tightly that the jagged nails dug painfully into the skin. More likely she was just mad. It was really Clay in control, and she was the passenger. Yeah, for some reason Clay got very confused about his identity and decided to act and think like her. It was such a convincing performance, that he completely bought it, and so did she. That was much more believable and sensible than magic stones and crazy, "prepare-for-every-possible-contingency" uncles. For a moment she was utterly still as her train of thought reached its destination, with even her breath held in check. Then the absurdity of it all hit her, and she abruptly turned into a spluttering, giggling heap. Once she started it was hard to stop. For the first time in a long time, Gunthar and everything else to do with the Mirror receded to the edge of her mind, leaving her self-control to crumble. She laughed so hard, tears spilled from her eyes, and her chest hurt, getting tight with each rattling breath. Swallowing painfully past the hard lump that formed in her throat, she roughly rubbed away the tears, rose stiffly to her feet.

It was only then, as she let out a shaky sigh and dusted herself off, that she noticed the high-pitched whine scratching at her eardrums. It was such a familiar sound to her now, that she instantly looked to the sky, sharp gaze quickly spotting a dark dot falling towards her. "No," she croaked, watching the cannonball arc through the sky towards the camp. Suddenly she was running, heedless of any soldiers in her path. A few shocked, pale faces briefly hovered at the edge of her vision, but no one seemed inclined to chase or follow her. It probably had as much to do with the cannonball falling towards them as it did her alarming appearance. Not that she really cared. "Gunthar," she gasped, forced to slow down by the oncoming wedge of soldiers. Stumbling awkwardly out of the way, she searched the wall of panicked faces for any sign of Gunthar. To her heightened sense of hearing, the high-pitched whine was now a screech, thudding painfully in her head until she was forced to cover her ears. The sound was so awful that her knees crumbled beneath her, and she dropped heavily to the ground, arms wrapped tightly over her head. It was almost a relief when the cannonball smashed into an embankment above her, its scream finally smothered by earth and rock. Debris showered her body, and for a handful of heartbeats she couldn't move, fresh pain coursing through her body with each hit.

When she felt vaguely confident that everything had stopped exploding, she carefully unfolded her arms and body, clawed her way out of the debris. There was still a lot of dust in the air, but she could see well enough to make out the depressing shapes of fallen soldiers, some of them still moving, a lot more that weren't moving at all. Swallowing back a mouthful of bile, she limped through the field of dead and injured, eyes roving on their own accord to the pale faces as she continued the search. With trembling hands, she reached the top of her head, felt for the familiar leather-bound goggles, momentarily confused as to whether they were up or down. Either way, her vision was blurry, and her head was still ringing from the explosion. She bit her lower lip, remembered with a pang of guilt giving Clay a hard time about over-reacting to loud noises. "Don't be such a baby," she would often reply, completely lacking in sympathy, to which Clay meekly nodded, quickly looked away.

There had been cannon fire and explosions while they were on board the Magnificent, but she was locked up in the brig at the time, and poisoned to boot. With the edge of her senses dulled like that of a worn blade, she hadn't been overly affected by the noise. Re-positioning the goggles over her eyes, she plodded on. Her hands drifted to her ears, gingerly touched the misshapen lumps of bone and cartilage. "No wonder he would beg and plead for a hat," she muttered, lips curling in disgust as her fingers came into contact with the ugly, bumpy scars that marked where the ears attached to the skin. Considering how well he put Clay together, Uncle Henry did a surprisingly sloppy job with the more superficial aspects of Clay's anatomy. Did he ever spare a thought for how Clay might feel, having such obvious scars on his body? Did he ever consider the possible side-effects Clay would have to suffer as a result of his enhanced senses? For example, the special membrane attached to the ear canal that reacted to changes in humidity. Whenever the membrane swelled up, it seemed to press against the part of the brain that governed feelings of nausea. One time, in the lead-up to a particularly bad storm, she fell to her knees clutching her stomach, fully expecting to vomit. The fact that she didn't actually vomit made things worse, the sensation of nausea lingering for hours without any easy release.

There had been some obvious complications that pained him greatly. The eyes, with pupils that seemed to stretch across the whole surface, never worked right. While he designed the eyes to have larger-than-average pupils, and hence more acute vision, he still intended for them to work like normal eyes. If anyone was brave enough to look closely, they would notice that there was in fact a thin, dark band of muscle surrounding each large pupil, with the tiniest flecks of brown marring the inky blackness. For some reason the muscle was inert, refusing to work like a normal iris, responding only when electric current was externally applied. She could still remember like it was yesterday Clay's cries when he finally ventured outside the dingy laboratory. It wasn't even full light outside, the last rays of the setting sun peeking out from behind banks of clouds. The ruddy red horizon nearly matched the colour of Uncle Henry's cheeks at that moment, failure and disappointment written all over his face. That very night he turned half the house upside down, muttering darkly to himself all the while, only stopping occasionally to growl at her to stay away. The next morning a very haggard, exhausted Uncle Henry trudged out, solemnly handed over a pair of leather-bound goggles to Clay.

"He must have stayed up all night making these goggles," she murmured, remembering the dark bags under his eyes and his sluggish responses. She had never thought to doubt Uncle Henry's solution, and Clay had never given her reason to, but now she knew all too well that the dark tinted glass only offered partial protection. If she spent more than half an hour out in full light, a dull ache began to steadily build at the back of her eyes, until her whole head throbbed with pain. "Ha, I learnt that the hard way," she grumbled, the familiar pain already sparking behind her eyes. While she had lingered in the shadowy forest as much as possible, she'd been scanning the open field for too long, keeping track of Gunthar. Swearing softly under her breath, she glanced around, looking for some kind of shelter or cover.

A familiar face popped into view, and at first she just thought she was seeing things, a sick hallucination brought on by the explosion. Some rocks did hit her head after all. She blinked, squinted through the settling dust. Suddenly she dropped to the ground, crawled into a nearby ditch as her skin broke out in goosebumps. There was no mistaking it that time, she thought with a growing sense of dread. Over the sound of her rapidly beating heart, that pompous voice reached her, scratched at her eardrums and nerves. "What the hell?" she croaked, peeking out over the edge of the ditch. He was definitely looking worse for wear, the rich velvet cloak that hung from his shoulders bearing the marks of life on the road. A patchy beard dotted his jawline and cheeks, and his normally immaculate hair was pulled back in a greasy ponytail, but he still stomped about like a little prince, carrying his tall lanky frame in a manner that suggested greatness.

"Sebastian." Even saying the name seemed unreal, and yet there he was, striding purposefully through the muddy field, not fifty feet away from where she crouched in disbelief. An equally familiar figure marched stoically behind him, followed by a handful of men. "Gasquet?" she murmured as her eyes followed the large, broad-shouldered captain, stretching through her foggy memories of Sebastian's entourage. She couldn't remember any of the other men, except that there seemed to be less of them than before. Gathering the remaining strands of her courage, she inched forward, strained her considerable sense of hearing, hoping to at least extract the odd word from the general garbled background noise.

"That goddamn bastard Bontems!" Sebastian shouted, seemingly oblivious to the war going on about him. It was only then that she noticed the colour in his cheeks, and rigidity of his body. Gasquet mumbled something, his lips barely moving to which Sebastian spun on his heel, eyes shooting daggers at the captain's face. With bated breath she watched Sebastian raise his hand, as though to lash out at the other man. Gasquet glared back at him, not moving an inch. Making a sound of frustration and disgust from somewhere deep in his throat, Sebastian lowered his fist, turned stiffly away. "Just look out for Gunthar and the Golem, they're bound to be here somewhere," he ordered tersely over his shoulder.

The breath she'd been holding evacuated her lungs like they were on fire, and she sunk to the bottom of the ditch, wheezing and spluttering. Squeezing her eyes tightly shut, she concentrated on every swear word she knew, willed them to flash through her mind in a parade of general obscenity. "Just when I thought things couldn't get any worse," she grumbled softly, prying her eyes open and gathering her feet beneath her. Clucking her tongue in annoyance, she carefully peeked out over the edge of the ditch before dropping back down again. Maybe if they were not actively looking for her, she could make a break for the nearest cover, try to put more distance between them. She bit back a bitter laugh, shook her head. Even in the midst of battle, her massive body stood out too much, and she'd be spotted soon enough. Just as quickly she dismissed the idea of attacking them head on. As big and powerful as she was, taking on ten fully armed men was not feasible, especially if they were half-expecting her. No, as much as it pained her to scurry about like an obscenely overgrown mouse, the best course was to stay out of sight and follow them. Sighing deeply, she lifted her head and watched Sebastian and his men fade gradually into the distance.

With her initial hope of finding Gunthar fully reversed, she grimly crept out of the ditch and inched forward, sharp eyes glinting behind the dark glass.

Raphael stiffened, lost his footing amid the scree and bushes, and promptly slid the rest of the way down the hillside. Time seemed to stand still as he lay at the bottom of the slope, the air knocked out of him and various parts of his body aching. A voice in his head called out frantically, tried to tell him that something was wrong. "Something is different," he murmured, blinking in confusion as he struggled to put his finger on it. The sounds of battle were louder now. "Too loud," he said with a start, sitting up abruptly as the realisation hit him. He could no longer hear the Mirror. That strange, discord voice that had been ringing inside his head for months was gone, no matter how much he turned and tilted his head or tried to block out external, extraneous noise. He always thought it would be sweet relief for that weird voice to fade completely away, like the moment a stupid song stops replaying itself over and over in your head. But the heavy silence that now settled over his mind like a blanket was unnerving. It was like his head hummed with the silence.

"And of course, it makes it hard to find Mel," he murmured, getting stiffly to his feet. He started to laugh at his obvious remark, but found it hurt too much. Gingerly clutching his side, he wondered if he had somehow broken a rib or two during his fall. Odd, he was normally more aware of these things. Closing his eyes in concentration, he reached out with his mind to the alien energy residing within his own body, and nearly passed out in the process. "Bloody hell," he wheezed, letting his hand fall away. With no clear direction in mind, he pushed on, each step sapping away at what little strength remained in his body.

"Damn, should have kept Emily," he croaked, nearly tripping over his own feet. The ground was more uneven now, churned by the movement of men and horses alike. Forest completely gave way to open grassland, with only a few stunted bushes popping up over the landscape. The ground sloped gently upward, and he trudged up without a second thought. For a second he thought he heard a faint whinny behind him, and he lurched around, lips parted in a sneer. "I thought I told you..." he started, voice creaking with the strain, but there was nothing there. Snorting derisively at the acute disappointment he felt, he turned back, staggered on. "Stupid horse," he muttered, shifting the strap of the saddle bag on his shoulder. She was probably lingering on the hillside where he left her, waiting for his return. As much as he wanted to keep her for his own selfish reasons, he couldn't bear the thought of the mare being injured just for the sake of carrying his sorry arse into battle. She had snorted at him, as if say he was an idiot, and followed him for part of the way. Not until he injected more force into his voice and yelled at her did she take him more seriously.

"Like most of the females in my life," he mouthed softly, coming to a stop at the top of the rise. As mentally prepared as he was, the scene of devastation that greeted him was...devastating. It didn't greet him so much as slap him hard on the face. While this area wasn't part of the main battlefield, it was obviously being treated as a dumping ground for the dead and injured. The battle had barely started, and yet already there were many bodies laid out on the field. On closer inspection, many of the men still clung to life, their bodies spasming in pain. As he stood there gazing down at the morbid scene, their moans and screams reached his ears over the general sounds of battle. A handful of medics moved about the bodies, tending to the injuries as best they could, while other men rushed into the area, dragging more casualties between them.

He had imagined that making his way through the battlefield would be a more clandestine affair, involving some clever subterfuge on his part. But as he started trudging down the slope, he couldn't muster the enthusiasm or energy to be that interesting. As it turned out, no one bothered to stop and question him. Apart from a few pointed, sideways glances from some of the soldiers he passed, any notice of his passage was quickly surpassed by more urgent matters. More urgent matters, like keeping alive, he thought bitterly. With each lurching step, the sound of battle steadily grew louder, until it saturated his ears and threatened to drown out his thoughts. The battle was still some way off, but more soldiers were milling around in this area. He stumbled to a halt beside one of the many canvas tents dotting the area, grateful for the paltry shade it offered. In the tight spaces between the tents, soldiers clumped together in nervous groups, awaiting orders no doubt.

Suddenly a loud voice cried out, and the soldiers looked about, hastily moved out of the path of oncoming carts loaded with mortar shells. Closely following the carts was an officer on horseback, his strident voice cutting through the constant background noise like a well-honed blade. A group of soldiers jumped at his command, fell in behind the cart, their bodies stiff and ungainly as they marched. "Mortars," he murmured as he watched the carts fade into the crowd. With a slight start he realised that the guns on the far side of the field had fallen silent. Putting it all together, he felt a sinking sensation, as though his stomach was coated with lead. Right on cue, the faint, high-pitched cry of an incoming mortar scraped at his ear drums, and he was suddenly running, recklessly pawing his way through the crowds of soldiers, heedless of any cries of protest.

Mel must already be hurt. That's why the Mirror suddenly went quiet. Of course, why he didn't arrive at this stunning conclusion sooner was more the mystery. "Really Raphael, get it together," he clucked in self-admonishment. While the Russian guns had stopped firing, the French mortars continued to pound away, their volleys screeching through the air with increasing intensity. Afterwards, he had no clear recollection of that desperate dash. Bodies and faces blurred together in the field of his vision, flitting past like leaves in the wind. Ducking and weaving through the chaotic hoard of soldiers and tents, he finally stumbled to a halt next to the shattered remains of a large tent, the grotesque outline of twisted, broken bodies showing through the downed canvas.

"Where is everybody?" he gasped, doubling over slightly as he struggled to catch his breath. All the soldiers he'd been evading just moments ago were nowhere to be seen, only flashes of their dark uniforms flickering at the edges of his vision. Either that, or they'd been caught in the latest blast, and now decorated the ground. All except one forlorn-looking soul, he silently corrected, squinting at the small hunched-over figure in the distance. "Hey!" he croaked, only his voice came out as a raspy squeak. His mouth was suddenly devoid of moisture, and he swallowed painfully, feet clumsily navigating the maze of debris and bodies. Slender shoulders seemed to twitch in response to his voice, even from that distance, and his pulse quickened, faint hope sparking to life inside him like tinder. "No way, it can't be that easy," he wheezed, blinking at the achingly familiar figure crouching in the middle of the field.

"Mel," he opened his mouth to say, but in that moment several things happened at once to steal his voice away. The shrill cry of an incoming cannonball cut through his senses, forced him to pay attention. He started running faster, angling away from the black dot in the sky. When he looked back to where Mel was, he stumbled to a stop, blood draining from his face. He was vaguely aware of his lips twitching, the sides of his throat moving as if to push sound out as she woodenly opened the hessian sack. Soldiers and horses sailed past him, drifting through his field of vision as he stood frozen to the spot. Debris from the impact of the cannonball hit his body, bit painfully into his skin, and yet he barely registered the sensations. All the cacophony of battle was muffled by the building pressure in his ears, as though in anticipation of the blow to come.

"Don't...look," he managed to croak as she looked into the sack. Like the blast of an explosion, the Mirror's screams filled his head, violently pushed out all other sound. Clutching uselessly at his ears, he fell to the ground, writhing in pain as the unearthly sound scraped his nerves. Craning his stiff neck up, he squinted watery, bleary eyes at Mel's small hunched-over figure. Oddly, she had barely moved at all through all that, positioning her body over the open sack with only the faintest movement of her limbs. "Mel," he cried thickly, gritting his teeth against the pain inside his head. "Didn't I tell you, never to look at the Mirror?" he grunted as he began to crawl on his hands and knees. Maybe not, he silently corrected himself, thinking back. He definitely meant to. In his personal guide on the "do's" and "don'ts" of the Mirror, that was among the top five, possibly number one. Especially for Mel. The Mirror seemed to have chosen her, after all.

Those words filled his mind, and what warmth offered by the midday sun breaking through the patchy clouds was stolen from his body. "Mel," he murmured, blinking at the incredible scene that was unfolding before him. At first, silky tendrils of inky blackness sprang out of the sack, rising lazily into the air like smoke. More and more darkness spilled out, directly upwards at first, and then spreading out like the branches of a giant tree. For a second, he was so bewildered by the sight, that even the Mirror's voice faded temporarily from his consciousness.

Out of the corner of his eye, he glimpsed soldiers one by one coming to a halt, bodies freezing on the spot as they gaped in wonder at the growing darkness. Wonderment quickly turned to fear as the cloud began to blot out the sun, casting an ominous shadow over the battlefield. Almost in unison, the soldiers started to back away as the base of the darkness expanded. "What the hell?" he muttered, staggering to his feet. The air itself seemed to thicken, making every breath shallow and painful as he doggedly moved against the flow of fleeing soldiers. Gaze firmly fixed on the small, hunched-over figure still peeking out amid the darkness, he barely registered the hard shoulders bumping into him, or the debris and bodies that caught his feet, nearly sent him flying. With each clumsy step, he felt a chill that seemed to soak into his bones, setting his teeth on edge. Not twenty feet away, a hapless soldier stumbled badly, crashed to the ground. He opened his mouth to yell out a warning, but the walls of his throat stuck together as the darkness slowly swallowed the flailing soldier. For a handful of heartbeats he couldn't move, his body frozen stiff with shock. The soldier was gone, and the darkness continued to expand as though nothing had happened. Even the soldier's screams were swallowed, so that the only sound that reached his ears was a cut-off whimper.

Swallowing painfully past the hard lump in his throat, he forced himself to move. Whatever the spilling darkness was, he had to get Mel out of there. Drag her away from that worn hessian sack and its cursed contents. Drag her home, kicking and screaming if need be. Gritting his teeth against the Mirror's intensifying cry that throbbed through his brain until he thought his skull might burst, he slowly trudged on, gaze peeling back the burgeoning darkness to pin itself to that small frozen figure.

"Ah," Gunthar gasped as air returned to his lungs. Blinking up at patchy sky, he wondered briefly how he ended up on his back. An explosion? Possibly, but not close by, judging by the fighting that continued unabated around him. Just how long could he lie there staring at the sky before a bullet or blade found its way into his body? Better not risk it, eh? the last sane voice in his head suggested gently. "Right," he murmured, stirring himself to move. But what was that just now? "Ah," he breathed, finally putting his finger on it. The Mirror was talking to him again. Like a woman sulking, wanting to make him suffer, but not having the patience to continue the war of silence. Something like that. At least in his limited experience with women, that was how it worked. Ah scrap that, the Mirror wasn't just talking, it was positively screaming, he decided with a grimace.

"Stop shouting already," he grumbled, clambering to his feet. Rubbing bleary eyes, he slowly turned about, orientated himself towards the source of the noise. He should be more happy about it. And yet as he trudged through the battlefield, stumbling around obstacles like a drunkard, he felt growing disquiet. "I mean really, what the hell is going on around here?" he muttered. The Mirror goes silent, the Mirror starts screaming, filling his head with its nonsense gibberish until he felt like he wanted to puke. Luckily there was nothing in his stomach to heave, other than a mouthful of bile. Clutching his spasming abdomen, he doubled over slightly and let the bitter drops splutter from his mouth. As he wiped his mouth and straightened up, his wandering gaze swept over the far horizon, did a sharp stop and double take. At first he mistook the dark shape in the distance as smoke, like so many smouldering impact points dotting the landscape. But this darkness was more opaque, more tangible. But perhaps the most eye-catching thing was the way it moved. Unlike all the lazily dissipating clouds of smoke, this darkness spread out like a giant tree, gradually blotting out the light as more darkness spread out from the "branches" and filled the void spaces between.

Letting out his breath in a murmur of laughter, he started moving towards the blot on the horizon. "Figures," he snorted, gaining strength with each step as anger built up inside him. "First the Mirror starts talking to me again, and now this." Grinding his teeth together, he directed all his anger against the source of all this. "That woman," he spat, the traces of bile still in his mouth matching the bitterness of his voice. Odd, he had seen her only a handful of times, and yet he had engraved every line and feature of her face into his memory. Faces of family and friends had long faded, their features blurred and uncertain in his mind's eye. But that woman's face, he just had to close his eyes, and there it was, floating against the black backdrop of his mind. "Mel," he whispered, hands clenched into hate-filled fists. If necessary, he would tear that woman away from the Mirror.

Alyce shuddered, felt clammy fingers of cold air brush against the back of her neck. With her heart lodged somewhere in her throat, she spun around, fully expecting an attack. "Ha," she laughed weakly at the empty space, doubling over as all the air in her lungs came out in a painful wheeze. There was nothing there, but the feeling persisted. A vague memory flickered at the edge of her consciousness. Not her memory. That time in the barn. Mel came back from the dead, and all hell broke loose. Clay had run out into the driving rain, complaining about the noise. The noise, and something else. She hadn't understood at the time, yelling abuse at his escaping back as he projected the awful noise of the Mirror into her mind. Her ugly words had echoed in his ears, tugged at his conscience, but he still couldn't stop running. He could feel it, reaching out to him, gently raking icy cold fingers along his body. His flesh crawled, he felt nauseous. And then his body froze, fell heavily to the ground. His final conscious thought as he lay shuddering in the cold mud was a silent plea to not be put to sleep.

"The Mirror," she croaked, unfolding her giant body. With a growing sense of unease, she scanned the battlefield, realised with a start that she had lost sight of Sebastian and his men. "What the hell?" she muttered, rubbing bleary eyes with the last clean spot of her sleeve. With a trembling hand she lowered the protective goggles from her eyes, focused on the spreading spot of darkness in the distance. At the back of her mind, she registered the fading light. "But it's just past midday," she murmured to herself, walking towards the darkness as though in a trance. The cold fingers rubbed themselves sinuously down her arms and legs like presumptuous cats, setting her teeth on edge. She had never been a fan of cats. Give her a dog any day, with their slobbery, over-zealous affection. Still, she moved towards the growing black shape, so smooth and oily that her gaze kept sliding off it. "What a convenient beacon," she thought with a grim smile. Gunthar will surely be moving towards it. And Raphael, if he's still in the chase. Even that idiot Sebastian will put two and two together. Hell, they could all converge on the spot at the same time and have an all-out brawl. As she imagined the possible three-way confrontation, the smile faded from her face. "Gunthar," she croaked, pushing past her revulsion to lengthen her strides.

✦

Chapter 9
Cracked Mirror

Mikhail Illarionovich Golenishchev-Kutuzov sighed a deep sigh that seemed to emanate from the marrow of his bones, looked up from the cluttered map table that sprawled out before him. Out of the corner of his eye, he noted the grim, earnest face approaching the table. The young officer's gaze settled on his face, and a shadow passed over his features. One of Barclay's men, the officer had yet to become accustomed to his twisted right eye. That's what getting shot twice in the right temple will do to a man. Wincing at the old familiar pain in his head, his fingers strayed to the scar. "To be shot in almost exactly the same spot twice, what are the odds of that?" his old mentor and friend Suvorov had once said. He was certainly lucky to be alive, although some days, when his head was filled with pain and the world spinning before his eyes at a sickening pace, he had to wonder about that. His thoughts strayed to his time spent in Berlin, discussing tactics with King Frederick while he sought better medical treatment for his wound. Sitting in the garden, with the sun at his back, and a cup of steaming sweet tea set before him...Frederick's brow creased in excitement as they discussed the latest weaponry...the gentle hum of insects as they flitted about the enticing flowers...

A loud noise nearby, nothing like a gentle hum, forced him to drag his mind back to the present. He refocused his mismatched eyes on the approaching lieutenant, swallowed back a sigh as he waited for the report. One of the officers hovering around the table however intercepted the young man, received the dire news in his stead. Among the inexperienced officer's garbled words, he silently absorbed the main point. General Kutaisou, Chief of Artillery, was dead. That really was a blow, he mused, absent-mindedly pushing one of the pieces slightly forward on the board. He frowned at the arrowheads painted on the board to represent the Bagration's fleches. He had lost track of the number of times they had shifted the little red and blue markers back and forward over those arrowheads. His armies were fighting well, to maintain even a slippery hold of their ground under the onslaught of the Grande Armies. If only he'd had more time to prepare. By the time he was put in charge, the Russian armies were barely holding together, their bodies and spirits ragged after months of being hounded by Napolean and his men. While he believed that Barclay had done the right thing in ordering their men to retreat, the general grumbling of disapproval emanating from the upper echelons of command drowned out all other viewpoints. It didn't help that he was of Scottish descent, even though he was raised in the neighbouring region of Livonia. To his knowledge, the man had never set foot in Scotland.

Who could they send in Kutaisou's place? The question settled heavily in his mind like a thick woollen blanket, muffling every other thought and memory that was scraping at the surface of his consciousness. And then of course the old familiar pain raced across his temple, as if in protest to his attempted concentration. Maybe one of Bagration's men… He stirred himself to pin a meaningful gaze at a nearby officer, the order to send out a messenger resting comfortably on the tip of his tongue, when a spot of darkness beyond the tent opening caught his eye. "What the hell?" he murmured softly, the sound barely escaping the confines of his throat. At first he thought it was just another cloud of black smoke, but something about the way it moved and spread itself garnered his attention. Squinting his mismatched eyes at the horizon, he watched with growing fascination the swelling darkness. Not just swelling, but thickening? He opened his mouth to say something to one of the other officers, distractedly reached out his hand to tug at someone's, anyone's sleeve. "Look at that," he wanted to croak, his finger itching to point out the apparition. Oddly however, for the first time since he took on this job, there was nobody hanging anxiously in the background, clinging desperately to every word he said. At the back of his mind, he was vaguely aware that the officers hovering about the table had drifted away from him, faces stiff with concentration as they continued to pour over maps and shout orders. Better get back to it, before they all think I've gone off with the fairies, he thought, a wry grin tugging at the corners of his mouth.

"It could be already too late," he whispered, feeling the time between every beat of his heart stretch on and on, like molasses trailing off the end of a spoon. "Just a few moments more," he told himself softly, inching forward in his chair to afford himself a better view. At the edge of his vision, men flitted in and out, amid a storm of reports and orders. They were all trying so very hard, fighting desperately against such a determined foe. "Just because you lose the battle doesn't necessarily mean you lose the war." The words fell softly out of his mouth, as he remembered the time he spent in London while undergoing further medical treatment. He used that time to study the American general George Washington, and his campaign against the British. The home ground advantage could not be overlooked. Already Barclay had shared some interesting ideas with him on this front. They may lose the battle today, and Napoleon and his men may indeed march on to occupy Moscow, but that would not be the end of the story. "We can still make those bastards suffer, and eventually give up," he muttered darkly, his mood suddenly matching the growing spot of darkness on the horizon.

The goading voice in her ear.
"Look at it."
"LOOK at it."
"Look at IT!"

Over and over, like a crazy mantra. She would never have thought it was possible to say one phrase in so many ways. "Look at it." Look at what? Reflexively her fingers clutched the coarse hessian sack cradled on her lap. Oh, that, she thought absurdly. But I don't want to. She formed the sentence in her head, opened her mouth to answer the annoying voice, but the words wouldn't come out.

"Look at it?" Why hadn't she looked at it all this time? Not once had she opened the sack that was forever tucked into the top of her trousers. Something held her back. A little voice inside her head told her softly, firmly, not to look. But this other voice, floating next to her ear, injecting its insidious venom directly into her head, just grew louder and louder, more insistent. "No, I mustn't," she managed to whisper.

"Look at it."

Stupid annoying voice, you don't know what you're saying.

"Look at it!"

Shut up! Go away!

"LOOK AT IT!!"

The raw force injected into that voice startled her, and she reflexively moved her head, eyes snapping open. Something flew out of the shadowy folds of the sack, rushed loudly past her ears. Shrinking back from the opening, she turned her head, eyes squeezed shut. Just as abruptly, the sound stopped, and she blinked at an array of lighted switches spread out before her on a console. Strange symbols winked up at her through the soft multi-coloured lights. Slowly, the gentle hum of machinery penetrated her foggy brain, the clicks and whirr of electronics forming the background noise of her new environment. Absurdly, the notion formed in her head. Spaceship?

Fighting a sudden stiffness in her neck born of reluctance, she looked up, hands clutching the padded arm rests of her seat. Numerous view screens covered the metal angled wall in front of her. Four large screens set in a two-by-two arrangement showed a starry night sky from different angles. Bordering the four central screens were a row of smaller screens, all displaying data one sort or another. Several seemed to show star maps, with elegantly curving lines slicing up the dark speckled space. Swallowing down a wave of nausea, she once again latched onto the ridiculous notion. Spaceship?!

Suddenly a high-pitched beep shattered the muffled silence, and she jumped halfway out of her skin. "Ah, that's the collision alarm. We should probably raise the shields." She jumped again at the calm familiar voice beside her, a chill running down her spine like she had just been doused with icy water. Sarah, or someone who looked like Sarah, leant across the console, calmly punched a switch. The alarm changed its pitch slightly, and then fell silent. "May as well keep the shields up," Sarah murmured, frowning at the screen above her head. She could feel her jaw dropping all the way to the floor as the girl continued to study the image. "See that, we're entering an asteroid belt," she explained, tapping on the glass where the spots seemed more concentrated. With a small smile, she went back to playing with the buttons, as though that explained everything, and everything was now normal.

"SPACESHIP!!" she cried, finally finding her voice. "Why the bloody hell am I in a spaceship?!"

Sarah frowned, fingers hovering over the console as her slender shoulders visibly stiffened under the fabric of her blouse.

"It's a sketchy re-creation, to be sure," she mumbled, eyes flitting about the cabin, looking everywhere but at Mel's face. "I was just one of many systems operating this ship. I was in charge of weapons and sensors, and so I have some snippets of ship surveillance, even in my shattered stage."

Her mouth went dry as Sarah's calm, ponderous words penetrated her foggy mind. "Of course," she murmured, her blank gaze travelling about the room. More panels and screens spanned the walls behind her, bordering a narrow doorway beyond which more lights blinked softly at her.

"Ah, the ship's on auto-pilot anyway, maybe I should give you a tour? You've just come out of hibernation at this stage, so you'll still be a bit groggy..."

Hibernation? Groggy? Sarah's words bounced off her like tiny pebbles, leaving small indentations on her consciousness, but without enough force to nudge her towards full comprehension. Still stiff with shock, she clambered awkwardly out of the deep padded seat, found it even harder to move than she had imagined. Suddenly her limbs were on fire, as the increased blood circulation was met with resistance. "Ah, worse case of pins and needles in my life," she hissed through clenched teeth.

Beside her, Sarah clucked her tongue, either out of sympathy or impatience, she couldn't tell. "He was like that too," the girl murmured, nodding in remembrance. "He was just out of hibernation, his semi-frozen body slowly coming back to life."

Swallowing past the sudden lump in her throat, she asked the dreaded question. Sarah blinked, tore her faraway gaze from the bulkhead to scrutinise her face. "Who is "he"? My master, of course. The original owner of this ship. You remember, don't you Mel?" Hearing her name resonate from those lips, she felt as though she had been doused with more icy water. More fully awake, she stared at Sarah, long buried memories floating to the surface of her mind. "Remember that time, in Raphael's room? You were injured, he was trying to heal you...that was the first time I reached out to you...I tried to show you..."

With painful clarity, the images that had flooded her mind at that time replayed themselves. The suited figure setting out from the spaceship in a bus-sized hovercraft, boxes of equipment piled up in the seats behind him. The suited figure steadily advancing towards the fleeing crowds of people, firing a strange weapon that left mounds of pure white dust in its wake. Finally, the suited figure, sitting in this very ship, a single tear rolling down his pale cheek as the screens displayed various scenes from a rain-drenched world. "I remember," she uttered hoarsely, struggling to push the sound out past the dry, seemingly sandpaper-coated walls of her throat. "That guy, was your master?"

Sarah nodded silently, lightly biting her bottom lip as tears sprung to her eyes. "Yes. I am programmed to serve the pilot of this ship. As such, I had served several other pilots before he came along. I served them all to the best of my abilities, but never once did I stray from my core programming. It was therefore both terrifying and liberating when my last master tweaked with the ship's systems, uploading instructions and routines that stretched the boundaries of my reasoning. Hell, all the systems were upgraded, given new parameters. Somehow, merely serving the Master was not enough anymore."

In that sliver of time, she found herself transfixed by the young woman who stood there with such a serious expression on her face. Of course this wasn't the real Sarah, the impulsive, lonely girl she found in the woods that fateful day. She was only too well aware of that. This "Sarah" was the embodiment of the Mirror, a physical form for her to interact with when perhaps there wasn't one. Talking to a computer would have been a more accurate depiction. She opened her mouth to suggest that she wouldn't have minded the analogy, but "Sarah" was in full force, answering a host of questions that hadn't been asked yet. A mote point, at this stage of the game, she decided, nodding sagely at the explanation of how she'd been pulled through time and space to escape the burning wreckage of the plane. "A system of portals, eh?" she heard herself say in a vague, distant voice.

"I was still linked to two surviving satellites. There used to be a dozen or so orbiting the planet, relaying information to this ship and controlling the teleportation gates. How else can a being seem omnipresent, eh? Quite clever, really. I thought the whole system had been dismantled when we were preparing to leave, but I guess I was wrong. Admittedly, that section of my memory is patchy. We had programmed the weather satellites to increase precipitation in the most populated regions, and were packing up the last pieces of equipment, when the signal came. A loud, single chime that rang out throughout the transport. It was the first time I ever saw him look afraid..."

Her voice drifted away like a puff of smoke, eyes glassy to the point of being mirrors. Mel opened her mouth to say something, but the girl collected herself before she could awkwardly call out. "Anyway," she continued, with a shaky, apologetic smile, "in my low powered state, it was very hard to maintain any kind of signal with the remaining satellites. I often wondered if the real "Sarah" realised that I could only receive transmissions on very clear days...and before you ask, I have no idea why or how I could receive images from the future. Master was conducting various experiments, both on the surface and in space. Maybe his work with magnetic fields somehow created a rift in the time-space continuum..." Again her eyes became clouded, and Mel had to stop herself from sighing with frustration at the Mirror's recurring distraction. "That night, when the plane you were flying in was suddenly damaged, I panicked, driven by Sarah's desperation to save you, and my own motivation. Drawing every ounce of power from my aging circuits, I beamed an instruction to the satellites, ordering them to open any available portals. That final transmission took everything I had, and everything went black. I'm not sure how I came to be broken, most likely Sarah knocked me to the ground. For what felt like the longest time, I was locked away in darkness, only vaguely aware of what lay beyond the walls of oblivion. Incredibly, power somehow returned to my shattered circuits...parts of me came alive, as bits somehow shifted and re-aligned. I started calling out mindlessly, waiting for something to happen, like that time in the cave, when Raphael and Sarah first found me. Using Sarah, I started to reach out for you, Mel."

Up until that point, she had stood there, leaning heavily against the bulkhead, just struggling to absorb the Mirror's words. The mention of her name however cut through all the static and buzzing like a bell, and she suddenly felt cold, as if all the heat had seeped out of her body. With great effort, she opened her mouth, moved her numb tongue to form the reluctant, dreaded question.

"Why me?"

Even though it came out as a whimper, Sarah froze in place, mouth hanging open in mid-sentence as the small room fell deathly silent. Even the hum and clicks of the machinery seemed muted.

"Why you?" echoed "Sarah" thickly, the sound of her voice as coarse as sandpaper.

"From the little bits you've shown me, the real Sarah was watching me for some time. And then, to go to such lengths to save me from the plane crash...Surely there were better candidates out there...I mean, did Sarah really pick me, or did you have something to do with it?" The awkward words fell out of her mouth like stones, her mind struggling to formulate the necessary sentences needed to convey the suspicions that she'd been carrying for some time. As the pieces of the puzzle gradually came together, there was a persisting niggle at the back of her mind.

"It was you all along, wasn't it?" Despite the heated air being pumped through the room, she felt deathly cold, as though all the blood in her body had been replaced with icy water. "You fed those images to Sarah, you encouraged her to form an attachment to me, didn't you?" The Mirror flinched at her words, grimly studied a spot on the floor just beyond the toes of her booted feet.

"I didn't do it on purpose," she mumbled, cheeks turning red as she continued to stare at the floor. "I just started receiving data from the satellites, and I thought "What the hell, may as well do something useful." Time started to flow for me again, after thousands of years buried in darkness. As I became aware of Sarah, the real Sarah, I began to perceive her different states. Some basic sensors embedded in my hardware were still functional, and I could discern her excitement by monitoring her heart rate and respiration. It was just idle curiosity to begin with, testing her reaction to various images...I wasn't even sure what images I was streaming to her half the time. It became a game, measuring her reactions and jumping to my own vague conclusions.

One day, I registered a very strong reaction. Tracing back through the streams, I pinpointed the source. A young married couple with two adorable children, living a normal, peaceful life together. For someone like Sarah, who had been sold off by her own family to pay their debts, it must have seemed like a little slice of heaven right before her eyes. Before too long, I was streaming whatever images of that sweet little family the satellites could transmit. It was a patchy connection, and some days there were only snippets, the mum washing up, the kids squabbling over what TV show to watch, the dad grumbling about work. Sarah gobbled it all up, her eyeballs hanging off every action, ears receptive to every word. I didn't realize it at first. I thought it was just an interesting way to pass the time. And then I noticed it. You were standing against the back window, and the orange-tinged rays of the setting sun filtered in through the grimy glass. You turned away from the window, and the way your face caught the light, it hit me like a bullet. I don't know why I didn't see it until then, guess I never truly saw you, but in that moment, you looked just like him. All the years alone melted away, and I suddenly had a purpose..."

"Who the fuck is "him"?" she snapped, fists clenched into tight balls of fury. "You fuckin' ramble on and on about shit, and I've still got no idea what's goin' on!" Like a cracking whip, her waspish voice rang out, filling the small compartment. With the final threads of her patience shredded away, she couldn't hold back the flow. "You keep talking about your "master", but what the fuck's that got to do with me?" At some point in time, she had reached out, gripped the Mirror's shoulders. "What's any of this got to do with me?!" she roared, shaking the Mirror like a rag doll.

Suddenly the body in her grip became hard and heavy as stone. With a sharp intake of breath, she backed away, hands still held out like claws. "That night, as Sarah watched the plane begin to crash, I could sense her growing panic, her utter desperation, as it matched my own." The Mirror's cold hollow voice cut through her anger, temporarily ushered all other emotions out of her head. "I couldn't let my Master die, couldn't let him leave me again." Her body stiffened as the meaning of the Mirror's words finally sank in. It almost felt like she was in some bad dream as the Mirror advanced towards her, gently enfolded her in its slender arms. "I finally found you again, my Master," the Mirror croaked into her ear. "I couldn't let you go like that, not after all those years apart." The seemingly frail arms tightened around her like bands of iron, and her skin crawled at the contact as the Mirror's mad delusions came to the fore.

"No, no, you're not my Master, I know that," the voice muttered in her ear, muffled by hair and the thick material of her suit. "I know that, and yet every time I see you, feel you, it's like he's back, standing before me. Really, you look so much like him..." This is why you shouldn't have looked inside the bag, a little voice spoke up at the back of her mind. The thought formed and hardened like cement in her mind. Stupid nagging voice from before, see what happened? And now what? The Mirror was going all ga-ga, rambling on about how much she resembled a meddling alien scientist, the line between fact and fiction becoming more and more blurred. With lines like "We'll be together forever Master", and "I won't let you leave", the alarm bells ringing in her head rose steadily in volume, until it felt like there was a klaxon pounding at her temple. Ah shit. "I have to get out of here." The sentence formed in her mind, like a neon sign lit up at night. "I have to get out of here, but how?" "Stop looking inside the bag," a rational, slightly patronising voice inside her head suggested.

"Stop looking inside the bag," she echoed, stiffening in the Mirror's boa-constrictor like embrace. Even though her voice had come out as barely a murmur, the Mirror froze, let out a low, wicked chuckle. With a final squeeze, it stood back, arms of steel reluctantly falling away. She started to sigh with relief, until she noticed the weird scornful look on its girly face.

"Stop looking inside the bag, huh? Okay then, give it a try." While her feet seemed to move on their own volition, slowly backing away from the Mirror, she couldn't stop gawking at that oddly calm, confident face. "Go on," urged "Sarah", crossing her arms, head nonchalantly resting against the bulkhead. "Look around the ship, there must be an exit around here somewhere, right Mel?"

Appalled that the Mirror seemed to be reading her thoughts, she clumsily turned away, stumbled through the narrow doorway to the next room, too afraid to glance back and see if "Sarah" followed.

Richard Gasquet slowly felt life return to his body, and was faintly disappointed. If it wasn't for the hard uneven ground biting painfully into his flesh, he would have not believed he survived such a blast. Suddenly Sebastian's voice cracked like a whip nearby, and his body tensed up on its own accord. Gritting his teeth, he clambered to his feet, turned towards the voice. "God damn fool!" The words were neatly lined up on the tip of his tongue, ready to be fired at his idiotic boss. Years of military service and training came to the fore, and he somehow managed to hold his tongue. Pointedly ignoring Sebastian's delusional babble, he glanced around, checked on his men.

To his immense relief, most of the familiar shapes on the ground were stirring. "Mervelles, Marcus?" he croaked as he mentally ticked off the names in his head. The groans and grumbles of his men as they struggled to their feet was music to his ears. "Really, things are going from worse to worst," he grumbled under his breath, crouching stiffly next to one of his men who had not yet moved. "Come on soldier," he said more loudly, trying to inject bravado into his creaky voice. "Jacques?" His plaintive cry went unanswered, and with a sense of dread he turned the body over. Lifeless eyes stared up at him, and it was only then that he noticed a chunk of Jacques' skull was missing. Recoiling from the grisly sight, he awkwardly staggered away, the taste of bile filling his mouth. Spitting out the few drops that his stomach managed to heave up, he doubled over slightly, fresh hatred seething out of him with each painful breath.

"Captain Gasquet!" the object of his hatred bellowed, seemingly impervious to the havoc unfolding around him. Mouth set in a grimace of barely controlled rage, Richard Gasquet gently pulled down Jacques' eyelids, whispered a couple of kind words over his frozen, ashen face. "Quickly Captain, come and see this!" Sebastian ordered, voice shrill with excitement.

"Captain?" another voice called timidly behind him. He straightened up, glanced back over his shoulder at the man who had become his shadow over the last month. Oddly, after that angry confrontation in the forest, he had become accepting of this strange little man and his even stranger fixation.

"Let's go Marcus," he acknowledged, walking stiffly towards Sebastian.

At least that bastard Bontems did a good job fixing up Marcus. True, he had used the opportunity to drug everybody. He shook his head, wondered for the umpteenth time when Bontems managed to drop sleeping powder into their drinking water. When they all came too, all signs of Bontems were gone. Without their so-called guide, Sebastian declared they would simply "follow the sound of battle, and look for the woman themselves".

"Bloody brilliant plan, that is," he muttered, bracing himself for more stupidity as he stopped next to Sebastian. Even now, he was acting like a pretentious git, holding the looking glass to his eye like some goddamn explorer. Without a word of welcome, Sebastian held out the looking glass, ordered him to look towards a dark spot on the horizon. Swallowing back the angry words that bulged in his throat, he looked through the grimy glass, wondering what the hell he was supposed to see, when a spreading dark shape caught his eye.

"What the hell is that?" he murmured, hands tightening around the long metal casing, flesh crawling at the unnatural sight. It wasn't a run-of-the-mill explosion, that was for sure.

"I have no doubt that that is what we're searching for, Captain," Sebastian announced confidently, taking the looking glass from his suddenly slack fingers. With an increasingly smug expression stretching across his stupid face, Sebastian turned around, started yelling at the men. His boot connected with poor Jacques' shoulder, and he glanced down, faint lines of displeasure creasing the corners of his mouth. "Oh, we lost another one? Damn, that's annoying."

As the careless words tumbled out of the Sebastian's mouth, he felt what remained of his self-control crumble. Before he could stop himself, he was grabbing the front of Sebastian's shirt, dragging him bodily closer until they were face to face. "Is that all you've got to bloody say?!" he snarled, feeling a vague sense of satisfaction as he watched the smugness fade from Sebastian's features. "These aren't pawns in a game of chess, Sebastian! You can't just shrug your shoulders and think "oh well". So many men have lost their lives because of you...the least you could do is..."

A loud familiar cry behind him abruptly punctuated his tirade, brought it to a premature close. Before either of them could react, Marcus snatched the looking glass from Sebastian's nerveless hands, and with a practiced hand set it to his eye. Whatever he saw out there caused the colour to drain from his face, and his hands to shake. A name escaped his stiff lips, and Gasquet realised it wasn't the spreading oily darkness on the horizon causing him consternation. Without another word, Marcus dropped the looking glass and started running.

"Marcus, wait!" Gasquet shouted after him. It was odd, to see his shadow tear away from him like that without a single backward glance. Sebastian must have heard the name too, for he scooped up the abandoned looking glass, hurriedly scanned the area. A noisy intake of air, and his hand abruptly stopped twisting the tube. Swearing vehemently, he began yelling out orders, urged the men to start moving. It was only when his strident voice faded slightly that Richard Gasquet realised he was running like a mad man, deserting Sebastian and his men without a second thought.

"What the hell am I doing?" he murmured, amazed at his own reactions to the unfolding events. Did Marcus mean that much to him, and if so, why? While his attitude towards the man had softened, he still found him to be repulsive and of questionable character. Just the other day he caught him picking his nose, and then wiping the snotty mess unconcernedly on his shirt sleeve. Indeed, no orifice was exempt from his incessant grooming. Really, he was more akin to a wild animal than a human being. All that time alone, haunted by the memories of the man he had killed, had taken a toll on his sanity. Looking at it from that perspective, maybe what Gunthar and the golem did to him was just deserts, an appropriate punishment for killing his saviour, however annoying the old man turned out to be.

He took all this into consideration, and yet there was something about the way Marcus looked at him, the light of admiration that shone from his eyes... The original "captain", the man he somehow resembled in Marcus' eyes, must have been quite the leader, to invoke such loyalty. Even when left for dead on a battlefield, Marcus still clung to the memory of this "captain" like it was a lifeline. As his gaze firmly fastened onto Marcus' back, he wondered if the original "captain" was still alive, still fighting. It suddenly occurred to him that the good captain could very well be on this battlefield, shouting orders to his men, any memory of Marcus Rembert distant and insubstantial at best. Not that Marcus cared about that right now, as he hurtled recklessly towards the man who cut him open and placed a stone inside. No, right now, he was pretty sure the only thing on Marcus' mind was revenge.

Alyce stiffened at the familiar voice that cried out, froze in mid-step as though this made her great bulk less visible to the world. "Calm down Alyce," she softly chided, forcing herself to move again. It came from the clump of men she was following, albeit at a considerable distance. It sounded like the captain, although his voice was unusually high pitched, as though the cry was ripped out of him unexpectedly. And then, at the edge of her vision, she saw someone break away from the group, start tearing across the field towards the darkness. Squinting at the scrawny collection of skin and bones running over the uneven ground, she felt something cold and hard form in the pit of her stomach.

"Marcus?" she uttered, voice full of disbelief. "No way, that guy's still alive?" Somehow, in all her tailing of Sebastian and his men, she had failed to spot him. Maybe it was because he was looking even more like a ghost of his former self. She would never have thought it possible for someone to shrink so much. In that tiny hut, where she and Gunthar had first encountered Marcus, she spotted on the floor next to his pathetic pile of belongings a faded photograph. It had obviously been taken shortly after he joined the army, his young proud face beaming with innocence as he posed in his fresh, starched uniform. Hard to believe that hopeful young man was the same gaunt creature hiding in the forest. Maybe it was because he barely resembled that young man that she didn't feel that guilty about what they did to him. The thing she regretted the most was losing her precious listening stone. "Why did I let Gunthar talk me into that crazy plan?" she muttered darkly, hands clenched tightly at her sides.

"Honestly, when I see that man…" Her guttural voice trailed away. Suddenly she tore off the goggles, squinted again at Marcus' diminishing figure, focused on the point he was running towards. There, silhouetted against the dying light, was Gunthar, moving steadily towards the darkness, seemingly oblivious to the chaos his passage was causing. She didn't even have to turn her head to know that Sebastian and his men were now giving pursuit as well. The clumsy stomping of their collective feet rumbled in her sensitive ears. Swearing loudly at that eyesore spreading over the horizon like an evil inkblot, she too started to run.

General Jean Rapp distractedly pulled out his pocket watch, flipped up the cover. With a frown tugging down the corners of his mouth, he tapped on the glass, lifted the watch to his ear. "What the hell?" he murmured, slipping the perfectly ticking watch back into his breast pocket. It was half past ten, and yet light was fading from the sky faster than one would expect. He really didn't like it. His horse didn't like it either, moving skittishly beneath him. Muttering soothing words into the mare's ever-twitching ears, he leant over and gingerly fetched his binoculars from the saddlebag. The scar tissue from an old shrapnel wound in his side stretched grudgingly with him, protesting all the way. "Golymin, wasn't it?" he murmured, remembering the battle in Poland six years ago as his hand strayed to the old scar. His body was covered with battle scars, a permanent, undeniable record of all his wounds.

"Right," he muttered, looking through the binoculars at the writhing mass of humanity charging and clashing below him. The fighting was centred around the Raevsky redoubt now, the arrowhead shaped earthworks made by the Russians now covered with soldiers. Even from his vantage point on top of the hillock, it was hard to make out exactly what was going on through the blanket of dust and smoke smothering the battlefield. Through the labyrinth of debris and bodies, he could just make out the familiar forms of the 61st division, repositioning itself during a lull in the fighting. While they were busy reforming their lines, he decided to ride out and try to get a better idea of what was going on. "I have to report something to the Emperor, after all," he murmured, sweeping an assessing gaze over the field, fingers ponderously turning the focusing knob this way and that. Napoleon, suffering the effects of a cold, was reluctant to move unless it was for good reason. Once the redoubt is taken, he will surely want to go there personally to give his assessment. He had served as a senior aide-de-camp to the Emperor long enough to know this much.

The vague smile that haunted his lips faded away, and a bad, bitter taste filled his mouth as the binoculars settled on the many twisted, lifeless bodies covering the muddy protrusions below. As seasoned a soldier as he was, this battle could only be described as horrific. He struggled to think of any conflict where he had seen so much death and suffering in one place. That wasn't the only thing leaving a bad taste in his mouth however. Even if they won this battle, they had to limp on to Moscow, and God only knew what resistance would be waiting for them there. He had deep seated doubts about the Emperor's plans to occupy Moscow and then wait for Tsar Alexander to surrender and broker a treaty.

"Really, it's an enormous gamble, even for him," he murmured, idly reaching down to ruffle the tuft of hair between the mare's ears. Maybe if Emperor Napoleon was showing his usual brilliance as a strategist, he would feel more reassured of their chances. Already several opportunities to fully exploit holes in the Russian lines had slipped through their collective fingers. Instead of orchestrating an array of outflanking manoeuvres and feints, the Emperor saw fit to commit his forces in full frontal attacks on the enemy. "Just throwing more and more men at the enemy, that's a bit unimaginative," he muttered to the mare. He could feel the irritation rise within him, stick in his throat like stale bread. Somehow, he swallowed down that uncomfortable lump of anger before it choked him, took a deep breath that rattled his lungs. Funny how his quick temper led to the premature end of his career as a clergyman, and yet as a soldier he had somehow learned to keep a lid on such strong emotions. He could still remember the pained expression on his mentor's face when he politely suggested he serve the Lord in other ways.

"Other ways, huh?" he grunted, training the binoculars once more at the redoubt. Perhaps because of the brief lull in fighting, some of the dust had settled, and it was apparent to him that the enemy were in disarray, and that one more push should see them through to the other side. He was just about to lower the binoculars, a faint grin tugging at the corners of his mouth, when a dark shape caught his eye. "What the hell?" he muttered, focusing the lens until the dark edges became somewhat sharper. As he gazed at the oily darkness, he felt something cold settle around his heart, before coiling around the pit of his stomach. It was spreading, reaching out towards him... With a start he released the binoculars, rubbed his eyes. "It's just another explosion," he told himself sternly, gathering the reins in a shaky hand. Amid a cloud of muttered self-admonishments, he rode off, mind firmly skirting the issue of whether or not he heard any cannons being fired at that particular corner of the field.

Raphael blinked, rubbed desperately at his bleary eyes, his grubby sleeve offering little relief. Inky blackness rolled along the ground towards him, absorbing any nearby light in its path. Through the thick fingers of darkness, he could still make out the small, huddled figure. "Have to...move?" he panted, straining his muscles in an attempt to get off the ground. Now that he was regaining consciousness, he wondered how he came to be on the ground yet again, unable to move. "It's becoming a bad habit," he grunted, finally managing to shift his position as something rolled off him. He staggered onto his hands and knees, glanced down at the object, to find himself staring at an ashen, unfamiliar face, frozen in an unflattering expression by painful, untimely death. "No wonder it's hard to move," he croaked, pushing aside his revulsion.

Dead bodies all around, heaped on top of each other. Was this a dumping ground, or just the site of an intense battle? He stiffly clambered to his feet, spun around unsteadily to survey the carnage, eyes desperately searching for any further signs of life. It was with a twisted, sick sense of relief that he detected twitches of movement from some of the bodies. Now that some of the shock-induced fog had lifted from his brain, the murmurs and groans of the living scratched feebly at his ear drums. Some giant explosion then, he pondered, trying to piece together the sequence of events. Just as he had spotted Mel crouching over the sack, all hell had broken loose.

Mercifully, or perhaps a side-effect of the Mirror, the barrage of cannonballs had ceased, at least in this section of the field. Somewhere behind him, the big guns still pounded away, the sound of their havoc muffled by distance.

No, it was relatively quiet here. "Too quiet," Raphael whispered hoarsely, feeling his nerves slip under the pressure. The sounds of life that tugged faintly at his awareness seemed to be fading away, as though smothered by the blanket of darkness spreading over the land. Filling his lungs with air as best he could, wincing at the pain, he opened his mouth to yell out to Mel. Opened his mouth, and then stood frozen as his eyes searched for her familiar figure. The spot where she had been sitting, as still as a statue, was now empty. No, not empty, he couldn't see it at all. There was just...inky black. With a spluttering cough he released his breath, started scrambling towards the black, crying out her name over and over again.

Despite his determination, Gunthar was forced to scrape to a jerky halt at the sight sprawling out to meet him. It was as though an invisible giant was casting an intense shadow over the land, the darkness advancing steadily towards him. Suddenly his mouth was dry, and he hesitated, unsure what to do next. That woman had to be at the centre of this. So, logically he had to go into the darkness and look for her, right? "Right," he murmured, and yet his muscles refused to move. It wasn't just the unnatural lack of light, he told himself, rubbing his arms as his teeth began to chatter. Cold fingers of air reached out, skimmed over his skin. "It's like telling a joke, and then having to explain why it's funny," he whispered, remembering Alyce's words. Or something like that. Something about those words still bothered him, stuck in his side like a thorn. With the tenacity of a bulldog, his mind latched onto that abnormality as he stood there, staring into space.

Suddenly he snickered, the odd sound leaking out past the constricted confines of his throat. "Ha, so that's why," he muttered cryptically, nodding to himself as the pieces finally came together. Stretching back through the sketchy memories of his life, it became apparent what the problem was, both with himself and Alyce's comment. "I really should apologise, if I ever see her again," he murmured, running a heavy, listless hand through his hair. Oddly, at that very point in time, that seemed like an enormous "if". Facing that strange inky blackness, so smooth that his eyes kept sliding right off it, he felt as though he was totally alone in the universe. Even though sounds of life and movement vaguely scratched at his consciousness through the screams of the Mirror, and bodies stirred at the edge of his vision, it didn't seem to matter. He was still alone...

"Gunthar!"

With perfect comedic timing, a familiar voice rang out, piercing the dense shroud of muffled sound covering his ears. He jumped, spun around to face the source of the disturbance, facial features frozen in an unflattering grimace. A scrawny, grimy man hurtled over the uneven ground, totally unphased by the dead bodies at his feet, or the black apparition spreading towards him. "What?" Gunthar croaked in disbelief as the face attached to the charging mass came into focus. "You're still alive?" he managed to spit out between shallow breaths. "Marcus," he managed to wheeze as the enraged man collided into him, hands stretched out like claws. He fell heavily to the ground, too stunned to resist Marcus' attack. It was only when Marcus grabbed him by the throat and started yelling abuse into his face that he stirred from paralysis.

Grappling desperately against the oppressive weight lying on top of him, he somehow worked his arms free, gripped Marcus' thin shoulders. Then, with all the strength he could muster, he slammed his knee into Marcus' middle. With a sharp intake of breath, Marcus doubled over, hands going instinctively to his groin. Feeling the shift in weight, Gunthar wriggled out, scrambled clumsily to his feet. "Jesus Marcus, are you crazy?" he spat, raw anger bubbling to the surface. "I know you must hate me, but this seriously isn't the time for grudges. Goodness man, just take a look around you, there's a war..." His voice trailed off as he slowly turned around, gawking at the seamless darkness stretching out in all directions. His mouth was suddenly dry, and with trembling hands he reached out to Marcus, desperate for some sort of anchor in this abyss.

"Don't touch me, you bastard," Marcus snarled, slapping his hands away. Muttering darkly under his breath, he clambered to his feet, ready to launch himself at Gunthar again. "Eh?" he uttered, the sound escaping his numb lips like a wistful sigh. With pinpoints of panic prickling through his hate-driven composure, he spun about, tried to spot Gunthar in all the darkness. "Hey, bastard, come back here!" he yelled into the oppressive silence. "I'm, I'm not finished with you yet," he continued, voice trembling as his hand strayed to the knife in his belt. "I, I have to pay you back in kind," he muttered thickly, the words heavy and lifeless on his tongue. Clinging onto his hatred as though it were a lifeline, he stumbled towards the spot where he had last seen Gunthar, hands held out tentatively. An unpleasant chill raced down his back as his hands encountered empty air.

Clearing his throat, he called out, timidly at first as fear gripped his heart, and then with growing desperation, calling out that dreaded name over and over again until his throat was raw. It was just like that time he woke up on the battlefield, surrounded by bodies, all those vacant, lacklustre eyes staring into the abyss. "Captain," he had called over and over again, wandering aimlessly through the maze of bodies and debris. For the longest time, he lingered in that miserable place, hoping beyond hope that his captain would return for him. "But he never came," Marcus uttered, returning to the present with a slight jolt. If just once he had heard a voice respond to his cries, perhaps he wouldn't have turned into such a pathetic, broken figure. There was still one sane voice crying out to him from the far corner of his mind, berating him over and over again for killing that old man. "So what if he was annoying, he helped you, you idiot?!" it screamed, full of anger and reproach. Try as he might to drown out that voice with all the other voices in his head, those words continued to peck away at his soul.

"Maybe I deserve to be swallowed up by darkness," he whispered as his knees crumbled and he sank to the ground. At least the ground is still solid, he thought, resting back on his hands. Cold clumps of dirt pressed against his palms in a reassuring way. Not just dirt, chunks of wood, he realised as a splinter found its way into his hand. "So, I'm still on the battlefield," he murmured, digging his fingers into the dirt. "Let's just get out of here." For once, both he and the voices in his head were in complete agreement.

"Marcus!"

A familiar voice called out from somewhere beyond the darkness, and his senses grabbed hold of those vibrations, followed them like a trail of precious breadcrumbs.

"Captain?!" he yelled, heart soaring painfully in his chest. Suddenly his arms and legs couldn't move quickly enough as he ran towards the sound. The air seemed to thicken around him, as though the darkness didn't want to let him go, and every movement became a struggle.

"Marcus, where are you?!" Ah, the captain's voice, so accustomed to bellowing out orders, now bellowed for him. Amazing, he thought, reaching out in the direction of that gravelly sound with every fibre of his being.

"My Captain," Marcus murmured, closing his eyes as he fell to the ground. Big rough hands grabbed him, hauled him to his feet. His eyes snapped open at the claw-like fingers digging into his flesh, and he squinted at the Captain's concerned face, eyes gradually adjusting to the light. "My Captain," he groaned, hanging limply from that strong grip like a marionette. For a second the face of his old captain floated in front of his eyes.

"Are you alright Marcus?" asked Captain Gasquet, his gruff, weather-beaten face coming into focus. "What were you thinking man?!"

"Never mind that!" a haughty voice snapped behind the captain's broad back. Sebastian stepped into view, strode purposefully toward him. "Is Gunthar still in there? You followed him in there, right?" He peeked past the captain's shoulder to focus on the approaching face, shrank away from the light of madness that shone from Sebastian's eyes. Hastily averting his gaze, he answered, struggling to push the necessary words out of his mouth.

"So he's still in there? Then let's go." Without another word he laid a heavy hand on Marcus' shoulder and started moving towards the darkness. Marcus dug his heels into the ground, tried to slip out of Sebastian's vice-like grip.

"No! I'm not goin' back in there!" he screamed, casting pleading eyes at the captain's pained face. For a heart-wrenching moment, the captain just stood there and stared, arms falling uselessly at his sides. "Captain…" The word fell like a stone from his mouth, heavy with despair. Sebastian, seemingly impervious to Marcus's flailing limbs and coarse language, ploughed headlong into the darkness.

"Wait!"

Alyce stiffened, peered past the broken cart she was currently using as cover. With heart in mouth, she watched as Captain Gasquet stood like a stunned mullet, staring at the spot where Marcus had just disappeared. She somehow doubted that the good captain cared much about what happened to Sebastian anymore, but Marcus was surprisingly a different matter. And yet he hesitated to follow after them, the unnatural wall of darkness looming over him like an oversized ogre, dwarfing even his considerable frame. She held her breath, unsure whether to silently cheer him on or not. The other soldiers noticeably hung back, the light of self-preservation shining from their eyes. The smell of their fear wafted across to where she crouched, tickled her nostrils. "Yep," she chuckled, shifting her weight. One more push from the unearthly darkness, and those soldiers were out of here, she was sure. Even Mervelles, the Captain's right-hand man, was hanging back, although not quite as much as the others.

Clucking her tongue, she turned her attention back to Gasquet, who was starting to move forward. Her jaw dropped as the darkness swallowed him whole, leaving no trace of the big man. "Captain!" Mervelles cried, taking a few tentative steps towards the spot where Gasquet had vanished into the black. She almost laughed out loud when she thought that Mervelles resembled a lost puppy whimpering after its master. Still, she couldn't blame the man for baulking. She certainly didn't want to go in there. "Damn you Gunthar, what were you thinking?" she muttered softly, setting her shoulder against the cart. With no choice but to go in there after him, she could only hope that her enhanced "night" vision gave her an advantage inside the darkness. Taking a deep breath, she heaved with all her might, sending the cart awkwardly rolling towards the soldiers. Even though it was missing a wheel, the base trundled down the depression with surprising speed, startling the anxiously waiting men far better than she had hoped. Like a herd of skittish animals, they scattered at the sudden movement, instinctively moving away from the runaway cart.

She only took a second to admire her handiwork before propelling her massive form across the ground. In some cool, rational corner of her mind, she mused that it was probably only about fifteen feet to the edge of the darkness. Still, as the startled shouts of the soldiers followed her, and dank columns of air reached out to meet her, it felt like the longest fifteen feet of her life. Such a heart-pounding, gut-wrenching trek should culminate in her leaping dramatically through the inky wall, a passionate cry torn from her lips… "Argh," she grunted as her foot connected with something, and without any kind of fanfare at all she tripped and clumsily fell forward. Blinking like mad in the abrupt darkness, she clambered to her feet, wheezing as air returned to her lungs. No, she corrected herself, dusting off her knees and elbows with trembling hands. Lungs have plenty of air, and yet she couldn't help herself from gulping down more and more. The cold hand of fear wrapped itself around her heart, gave it a good squeeze, and before she could stop herself, she was re-tracing her steps, wanting desperately to return to the light.

Holding her arms out as though she was going to bump into the outside world any second, she took slow mincing steps, only to find more darkness. "Surely I didn't trip that far?" she croaked past the lump in her throat. What the hell, shouldn't there be some sign of the others, on either side of the inky wall? If she forced herself to stand utterly still, her sensitive ears caught the vaguest hint of sound coming from "outside". Indistinct voices, the muffled roar of artillery...gentle reminders that the main battle was still going on out there. "That's something, at least," she told herself, lips twitching as she tried to smile. It felt more like a grimace, her face was so stiff. The ground was normal too, as far as she could tell. Already she had stumbled over and around various low-lying obstacles. She didn't dare to inspect more closely what these things may be. It did cross her mind that Gunthar might very well be decorating the ground, especially if Sebastian gets to him first.

"Can't let that happen," she muttered, forcing herself to move. They couldn't possibly have gotten that far, could they? Shaking her head at how her mind was going around in circles, she stood utterly still, waited for her eyes to adjust. After some careful rearrangement of her pupils, she could make out basic shapes, good enough so that she didn't trip over nearly so much. "Gunthar," she called out, the oppressive silence within the darkness stifling her voice. It was almost like going a library and being afraid to raise your voice. Any minute now, a librarian was going the "shush" her, glower her into submission. "Gunthar!" she called again, trying to inject more volume into her voice, although by the time it escaped the clammy confines of her throat, it came more a squeak than a roar. She was just about to shout again, when a loud boom shook the air. The shock of the noise knocked her off her feet, and she rolled about on the uneven ground for a couple of seconds, hands clamped firmly over her ears. "What the hell?" she grunted, staggering to her feet. "Of course, what was I thinking?" she muttered, body moving on its own accord in the direction of the boom.

Her boots scraped against the metal floor of the ship, the harsh sound jangling her already frayed nerves. The first thing she realised as she started to stumble her way through the ship was that it was quite large. Obviously an exploration ship of some kind, judging by the cargo hold full of small vehicles, probes and rows of crates. At the end of this vast compartment, a metal staircase led to a closed- off section of rooms. Automatic doors slid open at her approach with a soft "pffst" sound, and she glanced half-heartedly inside each room. Judging from their austere, clinical appearance, they were laboratories. Her suspicions were finally confirmed when in a couple of the rooms towards the end of the long corridor she spied dimly lit tanks. At first she didn't notice that the tanks were occupied, her desperate gaze sliding away from the curved glass as she searched for an exit. It wasn't until she reached the fourth laboratory that it finally sunk in, and she slowly entered the cluttered room, blinking in disbelief at the small furry animal suspended in fluid. "What the hell is this?" she murmured, unable to look away from the perfectly preserved specimen reaching out for eternity with its tiny paws.

"It's a wallaby," a familiar voice answered from the doorway, making her jump. Throat going dry, she whirled around to face the tall man striding purposefully into the room.

"Raphael?" she croaked, momentarily forgetting where she was. Like a person wandering through the desert, she stumbled towards the familiar figure, only to realise it was a mirage. Somehow, she managed to skid to a halt before a bemused "Raphael", outstretched arms falling forlornly by her side. "Don't do that!" she cried at the Mirror, stamping her foot in frustration, moisture gathering in the corners of her eyes.

"Oh come on Mel," the Mirror crooned smoothly in a voice so much like Raphael's that it tore at her heart. "Just close your eyes and enjoy it." The voice dripped like honey into her mind, gluing her feet to the metal floor. Revulsion and fascination warred within her as the apparition reached out a cool hand, trailed gentle fingers down her cheek. Before she could swallow it back, a sweet, wistful sigh escaped her lips. "This is what you truly desire, after all. A life with "him", yes?"

The name floated once more from her lips, and she leant into that hand, forehead resting against the broad chest. "We're connected Mel," the Mirror purred, raising a trembling hand to the top of her head. "I know all your desires, all of your fantasies. When all this is over, you just want to return home, to the manor, and build a happy life together. Just you, Raphael and Sarah. Possibly Daniel, judging by the looks that those two have been exchanging." To hear her own thought processes put into words like that struck her as funny, and she almost laughed. The harsh sound that came out however was far removed from laughter, as warm salty tears rolled down her cheeks. She mumbled something into the spreading damp patch on Raphael's lapel, and he gently pushed her back, studied her tear-streaked face.

"What was that?" he quizzed softly, eyes beaming with tenderness.

"I said," she answered, her voice gathering strength, "what are you going to do, play all the other parts yourself?" The hot cauldron of her anger bubbled over, and with her face set to "sneer" she pushed "Raphael" away. "It doesn't matter who you look like, or what memories or sick fantasies you dredge out of my mind and try to re-create, I'm not staying here with you!" Spitting her words out like venom, she ran out of the room, not daring to look back.

"Have to...get out of here," she panted, verbalising the words that replayed over and over in her head like a mantra. She hurried down the corridor, pushing past numerous metal doors that slid open and closed at her passage. The adrenalin adding wings to her feet faded away after a couple of minutes, and she was reduced to a stiff, brisk walk, the thick spacesuit weighing her down with each step. "Wow, it's getting hot in here," she sighed, trailing shaky fingers across her sweaty brow. "Ah, what happened to my helmet?" she murmured distractedly, patting the reinforced collar of the suit. Did she actually need a helmet to leave the so-called spaceship? If this was a world recreated by the Mirror, did that include the space beyond these metal walls? Was it a cold, dark vacuum that awaited her, assuming there was a way out? Oddly, that question didn't seem terribly important at that particular point in time. It was more just a curiosity, something to idly wonder about as she staggered to a halt before a flight of stairs. Unlike the other stairs she clambered up before, these sprung out solidly like an extension of the wall, curling out of sight to the next floor. And smooth too, without the usual tread surface.

Concentrating on each step, she carefully ascended the stairs, feeling even more than before that she was walking into a laboratory. She reached the top, and suddenly her breath caught noisily in her throat as her feet trudged to a complete halt. The smooth silver floor stretched out before her as far as the eye could see. Large circular lights built into the ceiling illuminated the cavernous, sterile space. Rows of tables lined the walls, their legs firmly attached to the floor. Arranged haphazardly between the tables were trolleys laden with various tools, tools she noted with a sense of foreboding that appeared surgical in nature. In the shadowy recesses of the room, dark shapes sprouted from the table tops, silhouetted by the grainy light.

It was the centre of the room that grabbed her attention the most. Cylindrical glass tanks like the ones she had spied downstairs filled the space. At first she was staggered by the sheer number of tanks. Arranged in four evenly spaced lines, they ran almost the entire length of the floor, fading into the shadows at the far end of the room. A quick count, and she estimated that there were well over a hundred tanks standing eerily in silence. On their own accord, her feet moved forward, scraping softly against the floor. The tanks weren't empty. That fact slowly permeated her brain, ignited the nerve endings running down her back. Unable to stop herself, she shuddered, shoulders tensing beneath the thick material of the spacesuit. She came to stop before the nearest tank, jaw dropping as her eyes focused of the still, primitive face beyond the curved glass. A thick, heavy-set brow sat atop slightly squashed features, framed by long dark hair. Though average in height, the figure had an impressively broad chest and long muscular arms. A large animal hide was wrapped around the man's middle.

"A Neanderthal?" she breathed, voice heavy with awe and disbelief. As if in a dream, she drifted over to the next tank, and studied with detached fascination a young female Neanderthal.

"What the hell?" she croaked, forcing her reluctant gaze to sweep over the other tanks in the room. "They're all Neanderthals?"

"Not entirely," a familiar voice answered. She spun around, momentarily blinked in bemusement as "Daniel" steadily approached her. "There are quite a few cross-breeds," he continued smoothly, reaching out to trail slender, child-like fingers across the glass. Flinching at his proximity, she backed away, willing her feet to start moving again.

"Don't you have an identity of your own?" she muttered, irritation swelling inside of her as she bumped into a tank. "I mean, do you have to keep taking on the appearance of people I know?"

Even to her own ears, her voice sounded feeble and childish.

"Are you sure that's what you want, Mel?" The question stopped her cold, and her gaze, which had been darting around the room, finally nailed itself to his face. A very strange expression flashed across the young boyish face, making it suddenly older beyond its years. "How about I use my Master's face then, particularly on the day he realised that "Homo neanderthalensis" wasn't going to evolve into the super species he had hoped?" With an irritated twitch of his hand, he waved at the collection of tanks, sections of his face shifting and stretching as he spoke.

She cowered at the reconstructed face, stumbled over her feet as she automatically moved away. "There is definitely some resemblance," a calm rational voice spoke inside her chaotic mind. "While not exactly like looking in a mirror, you look at least like you're related in some way." If she wasn't paralysed with fear and shock, maybe she could have voiced these thoughts, and brushed off the Mirror's appearance as a bad joke. Something along the lines of "You're crazy, that barely looks like me at all," accompanied by a dismissive gesture. For one, that unblinking third eye sitting squarely in the middle of his forehead. The deep purple iris seemed to pin her to the ground with its unearthly nature, complimenting the highly angular planes and contours of the face. It occurred to her that this was the first time she saw it so clearly. Before, she had only caught scant, distorted views "Master's" countenance, enough to give her a vague impression and nothing more. A dangerous light suddenly flickered through all three alien eyes, and she stirred herself to move, but it was too late. A large, gloved hand caught her arm, long fingers biting into the flesh despite her whimper of pain. The strange, not-quite-human face descended towards her, filling her field of vision. In that moment, something heavy and cold settled around her heart, steadily filled her body until she couldn't move, could hardly breathe. The thin, pale lips moved, and she heard a scratchy, tightly controlled voice hiss in her ears. "You mustn't leave me Mel, not ever." With those simple, terrifying words ringing in her ears, the other large hand came towards her.

"Raphael!" she cried, clinging to the name desperately as the hand connected sharply with the side of her head and knocked her out.

He was running, hurtling headlong along the crowded street, blank/astonished stares of pedestrians and merchants alike following his passage with varying degrees of interest. Not far behind, the sound of laboured breathing hung persistently in the air, his pursuers unwilling to fade away. He didn't even register the faces of the people he ran/pushed past, whether they were male or female, old or young, fat or thin. The only thing he focused on was the space in front of him. Left, right, straight ahead, his eyes swam about in his head, searching for a means of escape. A half-empty cart lay across his path, and he nearly tripped over the handles resting on the ground. In his scramble to be free, the cart rolled into the oncoming men, and he inadvertently bought himself some time. A quick backward glance over his shoulder, and the tiny bubble of hope that had swelled up inside him was rudely popped. His pursuers were already staggering to their feet, gesticulating in his general direction.

"Damn you Sebastian," he cursed softly with what breath he had to spare. He rounded a corner, only to skid to an abrupt stop before a brick wall. At first he completely missed her, his eyes whipped about so frantically in search for cover. How did that grimy impish face and flaming red hair escape his attention? He briefly considered leaving the narrow alleyway, but already the familiar voices of his pursuers rang out nearby, growing louder and more obnoxious with each passing second. Through the cloud of fear that fogged his brain, he finally sensed her heavy gaze upon him, and he turned around, returned her stare. In that moment, something passed between them, and with an almost imperceptible movement of her head, she nodded at the broken cart behind her. Without a second thought, he dived for cover, huddled up into an impossibly tight ball and waited. Sure enough, a handful of seconds later heavy footsteps trundled to an abrupt stop at the entrance of the alleyway, and impatient voices called out brusquely to the girl. She mumbled nonchalantly, shrugged her shoulders. He didn't dare move anything other than his eyeballs, gawking up at her small, slender frame from where he crouched behind the cart. Her face, what he could see of it, was the epitome of disinterest and apathy.

The voices called out again, sterner this time, the soft scrape of their shoes on the cobbled pavement ringing uncomfortably in his ears. Heart leaping into his mouth, he waited helplessly as the men came closer. Although he hung off every word that was exchanged, fear clouded the meaning of those words. Somehow the topic of conversation had shifted to the girl, and what exactly she was doing in a deserted alleyway. She snapped something about having paid her tithe for the month, that she had every right to linger in the area. There was obviously some hidden meaning to that statement that eluded him, yet the men seem to understand. Suddenly there was a commotion out in the street, and the sound of someone running past. Amid growled warnings that they would be keeping an eye on her, the men left. "Better keep more than one eye on me, eh?" she snorted softly, tension leaving her body as they disappeared out of sight. "Lucky for you, Jimmy runs through the market at this time every day. If those guards were any good at their jobs, they'd know that. Okay, you can come out now," she announced sweetly, crouching down beside him. Before he could respond, she leant over and started to lick his cheek. Momentarily paralysed with shock, he remained huddled in the shadow of the cart, brain whirling in confusion as the girl's tongue repeatedly slid over his cheek.

In some dark corner of his mind, he registered two things. Firstly, while this was essentially a replaying of the day he first met Sarah, she certainly didn't lick him like that. Secondly, this dream was super realistic, the sensation of her tongue on his cheek so real he could feel actual moisture. Prying sticky lids open, he stared up into a pair of dark, unblinking eyes, eyes so huge and perfect that when his bleary vision finally focused, his confused face blinked back at him from their smooth surface. "Emily," he croaked, reaching for the mare's brown head. She whinnied softly in reply, snorted emphatically. "I thought I told you to go away, you stupid, wonderful horse," he grumbled, patting the top of her snout. Willing his limbs to move, he somehow struggled to his feet, leaning heavily on Emily in the process. It was only then, as he stood in a roughly upright position and slowly looked around, that he noticed the lack of light. No wonder it had taken so long for his eyes to adjust. Still, he wasn't in complete darkness. Off to his left, the horizon was completely black, without even a glimmer of light to offer relief from the monotony. The space that he and Emily stood in was more of a grey gloomy twilight, the sort of indistinct half-light that signals the start of the day or the approach of night.

Scratching his head, he reached back through his memories. There had been a massive explosion...dead/injured bodies all over the place...Mel's small, huddled figure, vanishing into the darkness. He ran towards the darkness, screaming out to her. "Must have passed out," he murmured, a weak sigh escaping his lips. And now he had lost all sight of Mel. "Really, what am I doing, Emily?" he asked the mare, blinking back tears that suddenly sprung to the corners of his eyes. "She was just over there," he croaked thickly, pushing the sound out past the lump in his throat. Emily snorted, shook her head derisively. "Wait a minute," he muttered, clouded senses finally registering the muffled echoes of the Mirror reverberating in his head. Squaring his shoulders, he orientated himself towards the source of the "sound". Naturally, it seemed loudest when he faced the darkest blot on the horizon. He started moving towards it, pointedly releasing his hold on Emily's mane. A few stiff, painful steps, and he could feel Emily's warm moist breath fanning the back of his neck. He tried to muster the strength to send her away one last time, fearing deep in his heart that the faithful mare would not survive that abysmal, all-consuming darkness, or at least emerge a broken horse. All his resolve melted away however when she nudged his shoulder, the weight of her head resting against him oddly compelling. Against his better judgment, he glanced back at the persistent mare. Even in the grey gloom he could sense the impatience behind her gentle nudges, a restrained, nervous whinny escaping her long throat.

Grimacing at his weakness, he drifted to her side, hauled himself into the saddle. Gingerly, he leant over her muscular neck, nearly sliding right out of the saddle in the process. "If things look grim, just ditch me and go, okay Emily? You've done more than enough already," he croaked thickly, the walls of his throat convulsing as he swallowed back tears. She shook her head, waited impatiently for him to take the reins. Feeling the burden of guilt pile up uncomfortably on his conscience, he reluctantly nudged her towards the utter pitch darkness.

The walls of the hedge maze loomed ominously above his head, reaching up to the sky like grave witnesses to his folly. Even the sound of the dark green leaves stirring in the gentle breeze seemed to mock him. He nervously tugged at the ruffle of his shirt, grimaced at the sweat that trickled down his neck. Already he was heartily sick of this maze, his desire to find the exit fast overcoming his desire to see the emperor. "I want my money back," he muttered, thinking of the opportunistic guard who spotted his forlorn figure drifting out of the great hall after another failed attempt to have an audience with Napoleon.

With a slight rubbing of his fingers and a glint in his beady eyes, the guard suggested he knew a way to get to the emperor. "The hedge maze," Sebastian murmured, parroting the guard's grubby words. He hadn't questioned the guard's story at the time, that Napoleon had taken to walking through the maze every morning in preparation for his eminent wedding to the Archduchess of Austria. "Trying to slim down my ass," he muttered, feet trudging to a halt at a particular section of wall. "Haven't I already passed this hedge?" he croaked, squinting at a familiar patch of knobby branches.

Just then the emperor's thickly accented voice rang out, and he stumbled towards it, first one way, then another. "Where are you?" he gasped, spinning on his heel as yet again the voice seemed to come from a different direction. He rounded the corner, the sound of his rasping breath filling his ears. He skidded to a halt at the familiar bulky figure that stood between the hedge walls, clutching a flabby hand to his chest. Uncle Bruce looked up from the gaping hole in his chest, levelled accusing eyes at him.

"Why?" the pitiful voice whined, a fine spray of blood shooting out of the slack mouth. As much as he wanted to move, his body froze to the spot as Uncle Bruce lurched towards him. "Why'd you do it, boy?" the old man rambled, the awful sound of gurgling blood accompanying every syllable. "I took care of you, didn't I?"

"I'm sorry Uncle," he cried as Uncle Bruce came to stop before him, looming above him like a flabby monolith. With a faint twisting of his lips, Uncle Bruce started falling forward, the great bulk of his body toppling onto him. The dead weight crushed him, to the point where he couldn't breathe. With his oxygen-deprived lungs feeling as though they were on fire, he clawed at the massive shoulders pinning him to the ground. His flailing limbs rapidly lost strength, the fire in his lungs all but burning out. Uncle Bruce seemed to become heavier with each passing moment, smothering his body like a lead blanket...

His eyes snapped open as something hard connected with his abdomen and pounded him back to reality. The weight bearing down on his stomach shifted, and with one more careless blow to his trunk lifted away. His relief was short lived as a familiar voice started to cry out, the one voice in the world that made him feel nauseous every time it rang out, skewering his nerves with its dry scratchy vibrations. "Hey," he spluttered, scrambling to his feet, "get back here, you filthy bag of bones."

"Captain?!" Marcus cried out, drifting further into the darkness. Sebastian lunged in the direction of the voice, hands reaching out for Marcus' scrawny body, but met nothing but cold dank air. For a handful of heartbeats he stood frozen, the utter silence bearing down on him like a lead blanket. Even the thudding of his frantic heart seemed muted, roaring softly in his ears.

"Marcus?" he squeaked, pushing the strangled sound out past the constricted walls of his throat. "Hey, where'd you go?" he croaked, his skin breaking out in fresh goose bumps as the icy air soaked through his clothes. "You can't just disappear like that," he whined aloud, trying desperately to stave away the sensation of being utterly alone in the darkness.

Just then, he heard a faint jingle, accompanied by the muffled sound of hooves striking the ground. Swallowing back a startled cry, he shrugged his shoulders and followed the sound, hand resting against the smooth wooden handle of his pistol. He blinked, looked down at the small weapon tucked into the special holder sewn onto the waist of his pants. When did he move that there? he pondered, softly patting the breast pocket of his jacket. Now that he thought about it, there was that moment, when they first entered the darkness, and he got the sensation of something large brushing past him. Without a second thought he had reached for the pistol in his inner breast pocket, spun about on his heel. "Then there was a deep booming sound," he murmured, the fragments of his memory finally coming together. An explosion of some kind shook the ground, rippled through the air, and Marcus, being closer to the blast, was violently flung back.

"And not even a word of thanks for cushioning his fall," he muttered, trying hard not to think about the way his feet sunk into the soft, muddy soil. The squelching sound of his boots fighting the suction scraped at his nerves with each step. "And where the hell is that Captain of mine?" he snapped into the void, hand tightening around his pistol. For a second, his feet faltered, and he glanced around, his mind fully absorbing the darkness that pressed in on him from all sides, like the walls of the hedge maze from his dream. "As long as Uncle Bruce doesn't pop up in front of me, I'll be okay," he told himself, trying to inject bravado into his flat, feeble voice. Shaking his head of such thoughts, he strode towards the sound of galloping hooves.

Alyce swallowed painfully past the dry walls of her throat, raised trembling hands to her goggles. That was too close. She just had to blunder into the darkness and nearly run right into Sebastian. She patted the thick leather band that nestled on her forehead, felt the reassuring smoothness of the dark glass. Not that she was likely to need them in here, she thought with a shiver, her sensitive eyes straining to pick up any light in this murky place. "Not just that," she murmured, her grey-tinged flesh crawling on its own accord. There was something weird about the very space. Sebastian had definitely appeared before her out of nowhere. The wild thumping of her heart was testament to that. But just as quickly he had winked out of sight, before she could move a muscle or open her mouth to protest. Ordinarily, she would put it down to fatigue or confusion, confident in the knowledge that such things are impossible, but every fibre of her unnatural, stitched-together body screamed that something was not right. The voices that every now and again rung clearly in her ears, only to completely vanish as soon as she turned her head. The way the ground shifted and changed between steps, to the point that she kept tripping over obstacles that abruptly appeared in her path.

"Damn it," she hissed softly, kicking at the ground. She should have the advantage here, with her heightened senses. But what good were her enormous pupils and super hearing when the scenery kept changing around her? If anything, her heightened senses made her painfully aware of what was going on, her stomach churning with each shift of reality. "That's right," she panted, pushing doggedly forward, "Clay was susceptible to motion sickness. That time in the cart…" When they first moved to London, she had driven Uncle Henry's work cart to the outskirts of the great city, with poor Clay cowering under heavy covers, his enormous body squeezed between walls of boxes and furniture. With each jarring movement of the wheels, the space closed in around him, the floor of the cart shuddered and bounced, and the creaking of the timber scratched at his already-frayed nerves. But that wasn't the worst part. No, by the far the worst thing for him was the feeling of slowly suffocating, the air tasting more and more stale with each ragged breath. How he wanted to tear away at the covers and burst out of that cart, fill his lungs with fresh air. In desperation, he curled up into a ball, hugged his treacherous hands to his sides. No, too many people around, must protect the mistress at all costs. Pretty mistress, with her golden hair and sky-blue eyes…

With a start she realised that this wasn't her memory, but Clay's. Blinking uselessly into the murky grey space, she felt her cheeks grow warm in an uncharacteristic show of shame. "So you're still there somewhere, Clay?" she whispered, patting her head. It had been some time since she felt his presence inside her mind. "Sorry," she mumbled, thinking back to that day. When she finally stopped and signalled the all-clear, Clay had burst out of the cart like a startled rabbit, tripping over his own feet in the process. With a spectacular crash he fell to the ground, oversized limbs thrashing about in a belated attempt to break his fall. She had started to laugh at the comical display, until the sound of his frantic breathing reached her ears. It was truly an awful sound, his lungs rattling inside his rib cage with each greedy intake of air. After that, Clay steadfastly refused to ride in a cart or carriage, no matter how much she pouted or whined. Uncle Henry probably would have been shocked to learn that the creature he created to be her faithful servant could be wilful about anything. "Of all the unpleasant things I asked you to do or bear with, that was the one you couldn't stand," she murmured, awe creeping into her voice. "Still, after walking around in this twisted place, I'm starting to understand," she added, her thin voice rapidly swallowed by the darkness.

"So how is one supposed to navigate in such a topsy-turvy place?" she asked aloud, for the moment not caring if anyone heard her. In fact, it would have been somewhat comforting to be discovered by another soul. "Beats being alone," she muttered, suddenly thoroughly sick of being alone in this dismal place. If only Sebastian hadn't winked out of her sight, she could have at least had some fun watching him struggle pathetically in the darkness. She briefly considered just standing still and waiting for Gunthar to just as miraculously appear before her. Would that work? Certainly, she had noticed shifts occurring around her as she stood frozen to the spot, her feet turned to lead weights by the great wave of uncertainty bearing down upon her. Thinking about it objectively, there was no reason why that wouldn't work. And there were a host of advantages that that approach afforded her. The wait and watch strategy meant she would conserve energy. Also, there was less chance of her making a noise that might give away her position.

"Still," she sighed, shaking her head against the tide of logic. "It just doesn't feel right to stand here and wait for something to happen." Then what? Chewing her bottom lip, she glanced around the clearing she was currently standing in, enlarged pupils scouring the shadows for a clue. Just then a familiar voice rang out, and her breath caught noisily in her throat. The one voice she most wanted to hear in that moment of time, with every fibre of her being. "Gunthar," she breathed, feet moving on their own accord. The voice faded away, and the world lurched past her at nauseating speed, but she didn't falter, massive body moving unerringly in one direction.

"Ha ha ha ha." He brushed at the treacherous moisture gathering in the corners of his eyes, wiped his mouth with the back of his hand. Did that awful sound really count as laughter? His out-reached hand shook, closed uselessly around the empty air where she had just been. Even in this murky indistinct place, he had recognised her. Such a pitiful figure, huddled over an open sack. If it hadn't been for the Mirror's deafening scream in his mind, his eyes would have just skimmed over that grey unmoving hump blocking the path. With his heart firmly lodged in his mouth, he clumsily circled around, nearly tripping over in the process. A familiar pale face was suspended over the opening of a hessian sack, the coarse cloth spilling over her knees. She was looking inside? He had opened his mouth to shout accusingly at her, the scene he'd play out in his mind a hundred times finally at hand.

"Hey." That was all he'd managed to squeeze out past the lump that had formed in his throat. Damn it, he swore softly, shaking his head. That was weak Gunthar, pathetic. Not that it mattered, she hadn't reacted in the slightest. Loudly clearing his throat, he started again. "Oi, stupid woman!" he squeaked, frustration pushing him through an invisible barrier to close the gap between them. Still no reaction, he noted sourly, anger bubbling up inside him. He glared down at the top of her head, imagining that his heated gaze might actually burn a hole in her skull. The Mirror was there, easily within his reach, and yet he wanted her to at least acknowledge his presence once before he took it back. "God damn it, look at me!" His voice shook as he lost control, hand flying out to grab her head. With a startled intake of breath, he closed his fist around empty air, wobbling forward in the process. He had no idea how long he stood there frozen to the spot, no doubt looking stupid as he blinked at the empty patch of ground before him, hoarse mirthless laughter escaping his stiff lips. As an afterthought, he crouched down, touched the area where she's been kneeling. With a stirring of concern, he noted the ground was stone cold.

"What the hell?" he murmured, forcing his limbs to move as he straightened up. Surely there would be evidence of some kind that she had been there, a depression on the ground, a trace of body heat, something. Hell, he'd settle for a fart right now, just to prove he wasn't crazy. With his lips twisted in a pained grimace, he looked around the clearing, eyes desperately trying to peel back the shadows for some sort of clue. "Damn, if only Alyce was here," he muttered, kicking desolately at the ground. The Mirror's screams now echoed faintly inside his head, only offering the barest of directions. He tried to ignore the fact that the space around him seemed to shift and change at will. The moment he fully acknowledged that signalled his complete descent into madness and despair. He'd start hearing voices calling out to him, like the one that rang out of the shadows right now. Teetering on the brink of madness, he timidly called back. "Alyce?"

"Gunthar! Stay where you are, I'm coming!" came the boisterous reply.

"Ah, okay," he answered meekly, his defences weakened by the intense relief he suddenly felt. He was so wrapped up in that warm voice, he completely failed to notice the faint rustle of approaching footsteps.

With a yelp Mel woke up, eyes snapping open as she shuddered. "What the hell was that?" she croaked, the sensation of something or someone brushing past making her skin crawl. She blinked at the floor in confusion, wondered why exactly she was curled up under a table. "Mel? Where are you, Mel? There's no point in hiding, you know," a petulant voice called out from the other side of the wall. Fresh beads of sweat formed on her brow as she remembered the reason for hiding in such a pathetic manner. She shrank further back into the corner, pressing her body against the cold wall. With a start she registered the sound of footsteps close by. Hugging her knees to her chest, she curled up into an even tighter ball, cowered even more pathetically under the table. The faint scraping of feet came to a halt. She could just imagine the figure glancing around, ears straining to pick up the faintest vibration. Suddenly there was a loud tap against the wall next to her ear, and it took every ounce of will power not to squeak in surprise. Just when she thought the game was up, and expected the Mirror to race into the room, proclaiming triumphantly "found you!", the room shuddered violently, causing her to drop to the floor on all fours. Not just the room, she silently corrected, hearing the resisting creak of metal through the thick wall. The whole ship was shaking.

"Ah, did you feel that Mel?" the Mirror crooned distractedly, trailing its fingers against the wall. Lord only knew what appearance it assumed now. She wasn't entirely sure if she even recognised the voice. Maybe someone from her childhood, a vague family friend? Wrinkling her brow in consternation, she shook her head, pushed the useless puzzle out of her mind. "That was literally the walls of reality shifting around us. Yep, not long now until that satellite beams us out of here, to who knows where or when. I'll finally have you all to myself, without any pesky interference. All this time, I just needed you to look at me, so that I could lock onto the signal from the satellite. I waited and waited, and yet you never looked at me, Mel."

His voice drifted away, and with a shuffle of feet was gone. She let out her breath, unlocked her stiff limbs a little.

"Why was that Mel?"

Jumping halfway out of her skin, she squeezed her eyes tightly shut against the source of that voice, now crouched down beside her under the table. His breath fanned her ear, and she shuddered, hugging her knees tightly to her chest.

"Why didn't you look at me, Mel?"

Blinking back tears, she thought back. All that time, from the very moment she took possession of the Mirror, something told her not to look. The hessian sack with its mysterious, shiny black fragments became a part of her, the top of the sack ever so carefully knotted and tucked into the waist of her pants. Even in her sleep, the sack had been attached to her, never far from her side.

"Why didn't I look?" she murmured, clenching her hands tightly. At the back of her mind, she felt the niggle of temptation, a tiny persistent voice urging her to take a peek, even if just for a second. Every time that little voice started to win however, and her hand crept towards the opening, an inexplicable fear gripped her.

"I was afraid of what I would see," she croaked, nodding sagely to herself, the memories of those times coursing through her mind. "Maybe deep down I knew that I'd lose something of myself if I looked. You screamed out to me, your voice a tinny echo in my head. I, I did my best to ignore you…" She glanced over at the Mirror, hastily looked away from the darkening face.

"So then why now?" a small bitter voice creaked beside her, setting her nerves on edge. "After all I've done for you, why is it only now that you look at me?"

She closed her eyes, blocked out the cold metallic ship walls, the pinched angry face hovering next to her shoulder. What was it now? "A ghost," she finally answered, the image of a slender man with greasy strands of hair plastered over shiny baldness suddenly popping into her head. "Jenkins, he must have somehow known this would happen, he was kicking around in my head long enough," she mumbled, staring down at the grimy hands clutched tightly together in her lap. Fresh cracks had appeared on the surface, where the dry scaly skin had been stretched to its limits. "Workers' hands," she grunted with a vague smile, a faint memory tickling the edges of her mind. "Raph," she croaked, flexing the fingers. The cracked skin cried out in protest, tiny sparks of pain prickling her consciousness.

"Wait," she cried, body uncoiling from its foetal position, "what will happen to Raph and Sarah? And Daniel? Whatever that satellite is doing, what if they get caught up in it? They could out there right now, looking for me." In her sudden panic, she gripped the Mirror's shoulders, voice becoming more strident with each phrase. The Mirror's face darkened, as though a shadow fell across it, and she suddenly felt cold, hands falling away from those stiff shoulders.

"Don't be so full of yourself. There's a war going on out there, remember?" the Mirror gestured at the walls of the spaceship. "Do you really think they would risk their lives and stumble into a battlefield just to look for you?" The spiteful words bounced off her like little pebbles, the sting of their impact making her body tense. "I don't know," she mumbled, feelings of loneliness filling her heart, making it so heavy she thought it might sink completely out of her body. She clung to the memory of her friends, but it had been so long since she last saw them. The last time she saw them was while Monfils carried her like a sack of potatoes through the wreckage of the inn. She had managed to arch her neck in time to catch a glimpse of Raphael's anguished face before it faded out of sight. How long ago had that been? Sitting on the cold metallic floor of a spaceship with the walls of reality closing in around her, it felt like years ago.

"Now be a good girl, and stay with me," the Mirror murmured in her ear, one long silky arm circling her trembling shoulders. "Forget those fools, who have surely abandoned you by now."

"Yeah," she whispered, the sound barely escaping the clammy confines of her throat. Forget the satellite locking onto their position from a distant point in space and time, the walls of her reality were crumbling away on their own. "So lonely." She moved her lips to say the words, but no sound came out.

"It's okay Mel, I'm here for you." Those words tumbled out of the Mirror's mouth over and over like a twisted mantra, falling onto the top of her head like thick blankets, gently yet steadily weighing her down, until she could barely move at all.

"Gunthar," Alyce panted, her enormous body straining with each fevered step. "Please don't disappear," she croaked to the desolate figure crouched in the middle of the clearing. Shouldering her way clumsily through the debris, Alyce barely registered the sharp hard objects that bit into her flesh. "If only I could move faster," she inwardly lamented as she pushed forward on wobbly legs. Now that she thought about it, Uncle Henry had once mentioned something about not making Clay run, or indeed do any strenuous activity for a prolonged period of time. Something about the circulation system not being big enough or strong enough to support such a big body. "Because of the way he was put together, his internal systems could only recover so much, what with scar tissue and things not growing back exactly the same way." From the tone of his voice, he could have been discussing the weather, or what he had for dinner last night. Even for someone like her, it seemed a little heartless. The shock of discovering a person who was more devoid of empathy than she was had burned the scene into her brain for all time, including the image of poor Clay's newly reconstructed body lying so lifelessly on the operating table.

"It's not like...I asked him to make this body," she whined between ragged breaths. "How ungrateful," she added, sneering derisively at herself. If it wasn't for her uncle's mad devotion, she would long have left this world. Would have left this world, and missed out on all this fun. With that thought, a truly maniacal grin, the sort that scared small children, spread across her face. Just a few more steps, she thought, reaching out to that familiar mop of unruly hair, silhouetted against a spreading pillar of light.

"Captain, don't cry for me." These words echoed throughout Marcus' brain, rattled inside his throat until it hurt. He opened his mouth to let out the sound, but there was no air left in his lungs with which to push it out. Captain's voice rang out behind him, calling his name over and over again. That hoarse, frantic voice nearly dragged his feet to a halt, and he glanced over his shoulder at the imposing figure limping after him. If it wasn't for the burning pain arcing through his abdomen, he probably would have stopped and turned back. The bayonet rifle he had taken from one of the fallen soldiers slid in his sweaty grasp. Tightening his greasy fingers around the smooth wooden hand grip, he gritted his teeth, pushed his weary, sore body onwards. Too late for that now, he inwardly sighed. May as well just end it here and now.

"God dammit!" Richard Gasquet cried in sheer frustration, feet slowing to a stop at the sight of Marcus hurtling towards Gunthar. "Stop running, you idiot!" he bellowed, doubling over slightly at the fresh pain in his side. At the edge of his vision, shadows and shapes shifted, and he knew even without looking up that the scene had changed. The pillar of dingy light was gone, and he was alone again in utter darkness, pupils desperately dilating in search any sort of contrast. "Ah, just shift back already," he muttered sourly, closing his eyes against the burgeoning darkness. His body froze in place as something brushed past his leg, and his eyes snapped open. It was then that the smell hit him. The smell of blood and burning flesh filled his nostrils, coated his skin like a sick cloak. He had seen action on the battlefield in his time, but nothing like this. He stepped back from the outstretched limb, nearly tripped over another corpse in the process.

As his eyes fully adjusted, he could pick out the familiar, ghastly shapes of death. Men and horses littered the ground, bodies contorted into either unnatural positions, or peaceful repose. "Please, just shift back," he cried thickly, squeezing his eyes tightly shut. Was this part of the battlefield where they dump the bodies, or the site of intense battle? He had thought they were away from the fighting, despite the dull pound and shriek of cannon fire punctuating the eerie silence inside the darkness. He had caught a glimpse of the main battle as they circled the area, vision turning grey at the scale of destruction. With the bitter taste of bile filling his mouth, he had to struggle to keep down the slice of stale bread he had wolfed down for breakfast. It had been as if the world stopped in that moment, a strange, heavy silence falling over everybody, their murmurs of discontent dying in their throats as they looked on in horror. Only Sebastian, with his head shoved so far up his arse, had surged ahead, only sparing a glance for the fallen.

"Sebastian," he croaked, reluctantly opening his eyes, "you truly are a fool." Only when he was alone like this, surrounded by corpses, could he voice the sentiment that raced around in his brain in ever dizzying circles. All the loyalty he felt towards his old master was steadily eroding away with each new disaster they faced. His nerves were stretched to breaking point. Just one more push, and he would snap completely. "Sebastian," he spat from behind clenched teeth. With new-found strength, he doggedly ignored the carnage of battle and concentrated on putting one foot in front of the other, eyes fixed firmly ahead.

"What the hell is going on?" Raphael muttered, shivering as the air around him shifted again. Emily whinnied softly, came to an awkward halt. Rubbing at his gritty eyes, he squinted into the shadows, discerning dark shapes amongst the grey gloom. Nudging the mare's side with his knee, he turned around in an attempt to close in on the Mirror's cry. Choking on frustration, he groaned. Maybe it was fatigue, or the growing feeling of disorientation, but the irritating sound seemed to reverberate evenly all around him. "Oh, for crying out loud, what am I supposed to do now?!" he cried, running a heavy hand over his head. "I just...want to find Mel...and go home." The words fell out of his mouth like tiny pebbles, sinking into dreary silence. Emily snorted, shook her head vigorously. "It's okay, you can come with us Emily," he added, reaching out to stroke the mare's thick neck. Smooth muscles shifted beneath her glossy coat, and she snorted again, stamping the ground with her hooves.

Raphael leant back in the saddle, studied her reaction. He let out a pained guffaw, winced as his sides protested at the uncharacteristic movement. "Really Emily, don't be too happy about that. My home's a bit of a wreck these days..." His words died in his throat, and his thoughts drifted to Sarah. Where was she now? Was she still with Daniel? Would they make it home? "Why did I let her go, Emily?" he murmured, staring blankly ahead at grey, featureless space. Despite being fully aware of the reasons, he selfishly wanted her at his side right there and then. Hell, he would have welcomed the boy with open arms. "Even though he guilelessly stole Sarah away from me, that brat," he mumbled, completely lost in his thoughts now, and paying scant attention to his surroundings. "He shouldn't have followed us in the first place, right Emily? I mean, what the hell was that kid thinking?" Must be love. The treacherous thought popped into his head, to his utter dismay. "I should have bargained with Jenkins to send the boy home," he muttered, silently kicking himself, tracing back through the unfortunate chain of events to where he could have possibly changed the outcome. "Ah, but it was already too late, wasn't it?" he murmured, remembering with a hint of bitterness the light that had crept into Sarah's face when they discovered their sheepish stowaway.

"I should be grateful that she's not here with me, facing this nightmare," he uttered softly, hands gripping the reins tightly. Just then, he heard the faint "swish" of movement somewhere in the darkness before him. Body stiffening on its own accord, his free hand drifted over to the sheathed sword dangling off his belt, eyes desperately searching the shadows. Emily responded to his sudden tension, snorted nervously as she came to a complete stop. The soft squelch of feet striking the soggy ground tickled his ears, sent chills down his spine. The world lurched around him once more, and he was caught in a nauseating wave. At the edge of his vision, a pillar of grainy light sliced the darkness, and for a handful of heartbeats he saw Sebastian's face break out of the shadows. In that instant, their eyes met, and the time and space around them, already distorted beyond belief, froze. The tantalising thought trickled through his mind, that Sebastian was just "there", and he for once had the upper hand. Just a tensing of muscles, a well-placed extension of his arm, and he could put an end to his treacherous brother.

As if in answer to this thought, his hand tightened on handle of his sword, feet digging into Emily's side. All the anger he had ever felt towards Sebastian surged to the surface, spurted out like lava out of a volcano. Unconsciously grinding his teeth together, he raised his arm, began to charge forward. Sebastian opened his stupid mouth to yell something out at him, but he couldn't hear anything above the roar of his own heartbeat. Moving in slow motion, Sebastian pulled out a gun, pointed it at his head. Absurdly, at that exact moment in time, all Raphael could think of was "oh", his face still contorted in rage. There was a loud bang, and a flash of light from the mouth of Sebastian's gun. Emily skidded to a halt beneath him, reared up on her hind legs as he twisted away from the sound. Something zinged through the air near his head, the shrill cry of its passage ringing in his ear. His sword clattered uselessly to the ground as he needed both hands on the reins to regain control of Emily. Amid hushed words of reassurance in the mare's twitching ears, he sensed rather than saw Sebastian approach. His face set in a grim mask, he straightened up and prepared to face Sebastian head on.

"Hah!" Gunthar gasped, awoke with a start. With glazed eyes he looked about, astonished that he could doze off at a time like this. Really, if life could be likened to a play, then this was probably the most important scene of his life so far, and here he was, kneeling on the soggy ground, nodding off like an old man. Absent-mindedly wiping the trail of drool from his chin, he attempted to piece together the chain of events leading to his sleepy performance. He had been feeling very sorry for himself, but why? Humming softly under his breath, he tapped his chin, reached back through his foggy memories. "Ah!" he exclaimed, lurching to his feet. The woman had appeared before him, like an innocuous-looking angel of death, but just when he reached out his hand to take the Mirror, she vanished. Then a familiar voice had called out to him...

"Alyce!" he suddenly cried, hearing a sound behind him. "Alyce, is that you?!" A chill ran down his spine as the footsteps grew louder. If it was Alyce, she surely would have responded by now. His body stiffened, eyes trying desperately to pick out anything in this gloom. "Crap," he hissed, feeling his pockets for anything that could be used as a weapon. Didn't he pick up a weapon before? What happened to that? "Shit," he cursed, and started scrambling away from the ominous sound. His pursuer, still without uttering a word, gave chase, ragged breaths now punctuating the footsteps. He glanced over his shoulder, blinked uselessly into the darkness. Wincing at the futile gesture, he continued to run, eyes firmly fixed forward.

Suddenly the ground opened up below him, and he was falling headlong into a ditch, rubble and bodies coming into view as feeble rays of light cut through across the plain. Amid groans of both pain and horror, he clambered to his knees, started crawling forward.

Ah, she thought, staring listlessly at the thin arms that encircled her with surprising strength. The smooth arms looked vaguely familiar, and with a slight tilt of her head she could make out dark curly hair and a youthful, exuberant face. Daniel now, she thought with a tired sigh, feeling her strength ebb away in that loving embrace. Her skin itched and crawled at every point of contact.

She so desperately wanted to break free and get away from this insanity. And yet try as she may to muster the energy to move, her body remained frozen.

"Really, can you stop resembling people I know already? Don't you have a face of your own?" she suddenly snapped, turning her head to glare at him. "Daniel's a sweet kid, he'd never do anything as sick as this!"

Daniel flinched at her bitter words, avoided her dagger-like stare. The arms that held her squeezed even tighter as he turned his head and mumbled a reply.

"What?!" she asked waspishly, feeling her anger already mix with despair.

"There is only one other face," the Mirror snapped back, "but we've already been through this, remember?"

For an instant, an alien visage flashed across the surface of his face, and she was taken aback by the similarity. If it weren't for that third eye blinking uncannily back at her, and the slightly more prominent cheek bones, she could be looking in a mirror.

"Ah, your Master's face," she murmured, the pieces coming together. Seeing the way the Mirror's upper lip stiffened, she pressed on, the seed of an idea starting to form. "Wow, that's pretty lame. Can't even create your own identity."

The Mirror, now resuming the appearance of Daniel, blinked at her, mouth agape in hurt surprise. "What did you say?"

"Well, based on how you like to resemble people from my memories, couldn't you look like anyone you wanted?" she prompted, struggling to keep her voice even. A flicker of annoyance showed in Daniel's face, a slight twitching of the muscles around the eyes. "I mean, it's all very touching that you want to look like your Master, but it just lacks imagination." He obviously didn't approve of her clipped tone, and general lack of respect. Feeling something like hope stir faintly inside her, she leapt on that glimmer of emotion like a cat with a newfound toy.

"Ha, I saw that! You were annoyed just then, weren't you?"

"Was not," he grumbled in reply, sounding annoyed.

"Ha ha, are you sure you want to spend eternity with me? I can be pretty annoying you know."

"I'm sure it'll be fine, we just have to get to know each other..."

"Well sure, there'll be plenty of time for that. And then when we fully realise that we're totally incompatible and hate each other's guts, we can be utterly miserable together."

"No one can be that bad, surely..."

"Really, how stupid can you get? How can you be so fixated on someone who deserted you?"

"He didn't...it wasn't like that..."

"Geez, how long were you stuck in that underground cave, so completely alone and sealed off from the world...all that time waiting for that arsehole of a master..."

Her head filled with pain, turning her vision white for a handful of heartbeats. She squinted up at Daniel, winced at the look on his face as he stared at his trembling hand. With a mixture of fury and repulsion contorting the usually smooth lines of his face, he stared at her, his hand seemingly frozen in mid-air.

"Ow," she groaned, swallowed past the lump that suddenly formed in her throat. Raising a shaky hand to her cheek, she tentatively touched the stinging skin.

"Mel, I'm sorry, I... but you mustn't talk about my master like that," Daniel stammered. "See what you made me do?"

Unable to meet his gaze, she allowed her watery eyes to wander about the room. While blinking back tears, it gradually dawned on her that the room had changed somehow. There were now dark, inexplicable shadows on the walls, and small round windows that she was certain hadn't been there before. The satisfying phrase "it's working" cemented itself in her mind, and with an evil smirk twisting her features, she wiped away her tears.

With as much venom as she could inject into her voice, she laughed. The harsh abrupt sound reverberated unpleasantly throughout the room. "Ah, this is priceless," she croaked breathlessly, shaking her head. "Are you going to hit me every time I insult your master? Because let me tell you," she purred, strength returning to her limbs once more, "I'm never going to kiss that arsehole's butt, not even his memory." The arms that were draped around her waist loosened, and she triumphantly twisted around, grabbed Daniel's wrist. "So you'd better be ready to hit me, you fucking stupid idiot!"

"Arrgghh, not again!" Sebastian spat into the darkness, his arm still extended, weapon slipping in his sweaty grip. Raphael had been there only seconds ago, dodging the bullet from his pistol. "Damn, did I hit him?" he mumbled, forcing his stiff arm to move again. Fumbling inside his jacket pocket for more bullets, he forced his cold numb fingers to push aside the barrel. "God damn it, why does it have to be so dark," he muttered, feeling the smooth metal surface for holes. His trembling fingers struggled to grip the bullets and load them into the chambers as the shock of coming face to face with Raphael set in. "I should have known he'd show up," he murmured sourly to himself, the sound of his own voice offering him some comfort.

Only now, in the gloomy silence, could he fully absorb what had just happened. "That's a bit sad, Sebastian," he added with a soft sigh. The first thing he thought of was to raise his gun and shoot, without any hesitation at all. He spent more time debating what he was going to have for breakfast than whether or not to fire at his own brother. "That's the sort of person I've become, eh?" he uttered, hands slowing on their own accord as he sunk heavily to the ground. Cradling his pistol in his lap, he gazed ahead into the grey-tinged darkness, noting the vague dark shapes that seemed to flit about at the edge of his vision. His lips curled in a derisive sneer, and he shook his head, a sound of pure disgust emanating from somewhere deep in his throat. "It's too late for that now," he chided thickly, a wave of bitterness swelling inside him, ready to break.

"Where did it all go wrong?" The words floated out of his mouth like bubbles of regret, for that was all he could think about as he sat in the cold, unpleasant darkness, feeling sorry for himself. His mind sped back through time, to that tragic night in Raphael's flat. He had set up the trail of breadcrumbs for Uncle Bruce to follow, and was setting up the incriminating evidence in the tiny one bedroom flat. Though Raphael would probably never believe it, he had not intended to set him up for murder. The plan had been to tip off Uncle Bruce that Raphael had stolen some family heirlooms in a fit of anger, plant the heirlooms in Raphael's flat, and then arrive in time with Aunt Sophie in hand to watch the mayhem unfold. Unfortunately, Uncle Bruce arrived before he finished. With beads of perspiration gleaming on his forehead, and spreading patches of moisture darkening his armpits, his uncle had burst through the door, only to freeze in shock at the scene unfolding before him. Caught in the act, he had stood in the middle of the cramped room, gold necklace dangling from his listless fingers.

He had never seen his uncle look so angry in all his life. With an ugly gasping sound emanating from somewhere deep within his throat, time flowed again, and Uncle Bruce charged into the room, furious accusations and questions spouting from those plump lips. It was all just a horrible accident. He was fending off the flurry of blows, trying desperately to put some distance between them. The last thing he remembered was being backed into a wall and reaching blindly behind him. On the cluttered side table, his groping fingers found something smooth and hard, and he instinctively gripped it, brought it around. Uncle Bruce unfortunately chose that moment to ram into him, his impressive girth pressing into his body. There was a horrible squelch of tissue meeting sharp steel, and they both looked down at the knife separating them. "What the.." Uncle Bruce had spluttered, staring at the knife sticking out of his stomach in utter confusion. With blood oozing out the corners of his mouth, he had looked up accusingly, lips moving languidly. "Why you little bastard…" Those were the last words he managed to squeeze out before he fell lifelessly to the floor.

Other than stumbling out of the way of Uncle Bruce's falling body, he was incapable of movement for a time, unable to tear his gaze from that pale, contorted face. Eventually he managed to stir himself back into action, cleaning himself up as best he could. In a daze, he left the flat and wandered towards home, mind spinning uselessly around in circles. What to do? he wondered over and over again as the memory of Uncle Bruce's dead, accusing eyes filled his mind. He had almost made it home when Aunt Sophie charged out of the house directly toward him. Without so much as a break in her step, she grabbed his arm, turned him back the way he had just come. Such a small, frail woman, and yet when it came to her family, she was capable of dragging full-sized men in her wake. Normally he found it hilarious, either as a spectator or the victim. On that day however, he struggled desperately to break free of her iron-like claw, spluttering excuses galore. Finally, her plaintive cry for help crumbled his fear and resolve. "You have to help me, Sebastian." Those earnest words cut through all the noise in his head, and heaving a sigh of resignation, he wordlessly accompanied her to the flat.

It had been so awful, following Aunt Sophie to the flat and watching her crumble as she took in the scene. He could not have framed Raphael more perfectly if he tried. The first thing they saw when they opened the door was that idiot crouching beside Uncle Bruce, bloody knife in hand. As their eyes met, and the acrid smell of blood hit his nostrils, guilt tinged with revulsion twisted his facial features into an ugly sneer. No doubt Raphael partially understood what the expression meant, for he started to yell accusations. Amid a flurry of fearful, vicious words Raphael fled the room, and thus began his life on the run.

"And the rest is history," Sebastian muttered, returning to grim reality. No matter how much he pressed his fingers against the smooth polished wood, his hands wouldn't stop trembling. Forcing his stiff joints to move, he shifted his hold on the pistol, squinted in the direction of a sudden noise. "Who's there?" he croaked, pulling back the hammer. "Raphael?" he added, finger hovering anxiously over the trigger.

So many words clamoured in his throat, struggled to escape. The object of his hatred was right before him, stumbling out of the ditch. "Don't change, don't change!" he silently willed reality. The bayonet rifle nestled securely in his hands, fingers pressing reassuringly against the wooden handle. Just a little bit more, and Gunthar would experience the same pain. The wound in his abdomen ached, as if it were a living thing that sought revenge. Still without uttering a word, Marcus propelled himself over the ground with one final push. His body fell forward, knife held before him. Squinting against the sudden light, he collided into someone. There was the soft squish of tissue meeting blade, followed by a spreading wet warmth.

Emily whinnied, tossed her head in consternation before settling down once more. "Even the horse is growing accustomed to this shifting reality," Raphael grumbled softly, staring at the spot where Sebastian had just been. Feeling oddly let-down at his brother's abrupt disappearance, he gently nudged Emily's sides, studied the surrounding darkness for some clue. It took some time for his eyes to pick up the tinge of light edging the horizon. With a shrug of his shoulders, he steered Emily towards the faint beacon.

On and on he rode, the steady plod of Emily's hooves against the muddy ground nearly lulling him to sleep. At the edge of his consciousness, he sensed things popping in and out of existence, shapes and shadows brushing by and then melting away. The consistency of the mud varied, every change of the ground transmitted to him via Emily's gait. Voices briefly punctuated the silence, nudging him back to consciousness before fading away again. Still the grainy band of light on the horizon beckoned, growing steadily brighter, regardless of the scenery changing around him.

Finally, a small dark shape was silhouetted against the light. "Mel?" he croaked, stirring Emily to increase her pace without a second thought. The sides of his throat, already unbearably dry, ached with the effort of making the sound. Then he was screaming, despite the pain, as more shapes materialised in that bright space. Emily responded to the urgency in his voice and hurtled bravely towards the light.

There was the sound of a collision behind him, and Gunthar found himself back on level ground, his desperate feet sliding to a clumsy halt. The sudden assault of grainy light on his dilated pupils caused him to blink and squint as he stumbled around to face the source of the noise. With a tiny cry of "no" floating from his lips, he staggered towards the familiar grey shape that now slumped to the ground, great meat hooks of hands clutching at the bayonet sticking out of her belly. Marcus, his face gone deathly pale in shock and confusion, backed away from Alyce, the broken rifle falling out of his numb hands. Before he could run away however, she flung out one monstrous arm, grabbed his scrawny shoulder. Marcus visibly shook in her grip, his entire body shrinking away from her touch. Ignoring his reaction, Alyce drew him even closer, cast dark baleful eyes at his terrified face. "We're sorry, Marcus," she finally grunted, a trail of dark grey spittle escaping her mouth. "We were...wrong...to do that to you. Please forgive us."

Marcus blinked, shook his head. "What?" he croaked, body sagging to the ground as Alyce gently released him. Her face contorted in pain, she pulled out the blade.

"I took over this body...at the moment of my death," she explained, gazing down at the slimy bayonet in her hand. "Poor Clay, I just...pushed aside his consciousness, just so that I could live on. Lately, more and more of his memories...have been surfacing. I...made him suffer...so much, but he never...hated me, not once." An oddly gentle expression spread across her face, and she solemnly handed the bayonet back to Marcus. "All my plans for revenge...seem stupid now. All I have left...is to help my friend achieve his dream. So, if you still feel unsatisfied," she croaked, pausing to place both her massive hands around his, "then keep stabbing me, but leave Gunthar alone."

Gunthar opened his mouth to protest, his stiff body protesting as he forced himself to move, but Marcus was already scurrying away from Alyce, a crazed, confused look in his eyes. With a choked-up cry, he winked out of reality, and an awkward silence fell over the clearing. Alyce slowly twisted around, smiled weakly.

"What the hell, Alyce?" he managed to splutter past the lump that had suddenly formed in his throat. He crouched beside her, hands hesitantly hovering over the dark spreading patch on her abdomen. "Why did you do that? Just to save me? Are you stupid?" he cried, anger building up inside of him. Tears gathered in the corners of his eyes as he gawked at the wound. "Ah, let me heal you," he blurted, reaching out to her.

"No," she rasped, swatting his hand away, "there's no time. You have to follow the light, Gunthar. Surely...the Mirror is the source. All my unnatural senses tell me...something big is happening."

His head bowed under the weight of her words. Somewhere deep inside, he suspected the same thing. The moment Mel looked at the Mirror, all hell broke loose. Funny, they used to look at the Mirror when it was whole, why didn't anything like this happen then? "Because that woman is special," he spat to the darkness, his whole-hearted hatred bubbling to the surface once more. He glanced up, found Alyce regarding him through quizzical eyes. "So, I'm supposed to just leave you here, Alyce? What kind of cold-hearted bastard do you take me for?" His voice trembled, and the tears now freely spilled down his cheeks.

"Gunthar," she wheezed, lifting a heavy hand to his cheek. "You can't give up now, not after all we've been through." Her hand fell away, the ugly sound of her laboured breathing filling the clearing. "Don't worry about me! Just go!" she yelled, using the last of her energy to push her massive body forward, effectively shoving Gunthar back in the process.

As he lay sprawled on his back, waiting for the air to seep back into his lungs, something caught the corner of his eye. Something resembling laughter floated from his lips, and he clambered to his feet. He stood still for a moment, back firmly to turned her. "Thank you, Alyce," he said softly before walking towards the light. She sank onto her hands, arms and neck trembling with the effort of watching him go. Finally, her strength gave out, and she crumbled to the ground, eyes straining to pick out Gunthar's gangly, diminishing figure against the harsh light. "Good luck, my friend," she whispered, smiling faintly as she succumbed to the darkness behind her eye lids.

Like someone obstinately trying to maintain the facade of being asleep in the midst of a loud party at a neighbour's house, she kept her eyes glued shut for as long as possible. However, the pain pulsing through her head, just like the noisy neighbours, could not be ignored. She couldn't sleep, and yet it hurt to even open her eyes. With her face set in an agonised grimace, she managed to open her eyes into narrow slits. Any more than that, and she was sure the gentle ambient light of the ship's interior would burn out her retinas and cause her head to explode. Slowly, carefully, she got to her feet. "It's like being hungover, but without the fun," she grunted, pressing a grimy hand to her temple as the room spun around her. The Mirror could really punch when it got pissed. Somewhere in the distance, she could hear it sniffling like a reprimanded child, the faint whining sound setting her teeth on edge. One more outburst, she thought as she staggered towards the source of the sound. Already the walls of the ship were in flux, the shiny metallic surface warping under her hand every time she touched it. The Mirror was barely keeping this all in check now. Channelling the transmission from the satellite took all the power it had. "One more disruption, and I'm free," she croaked softly, convincing herself more and more with each ragged breath.

She rounded the corner, and there it was, in a pathetic heap on the floor, head clutched in its hands, shoulders shaking with unrelenting sobs. Once again, it had assumed Raphael's form. Was that some form of self-defence? Certainly, if she lost focus, it was easy to be distracted by the Mirror's outward appearance, even if it could change at will. And so far the Mirror had only assumed the form of people she considered to be friends.

"Hey," she said stiffly, her throat tightening in anger. "What are you crying for?" Pushing through the pain in her head, she gently started probing and prodding, seeking out the Mirror's breaking point.

"Raphael" shook his head, muttered something under his breath.

"What?" she asked waspishly, the edges of her temper fraying like the end of a rope.

"It wasn't supposed to be like this," the Mirror snapped, glaring up at her like a belligerent child. "Why do you fight me? I could give you anything, anyone you want. Sure, it won't be "real", but what's so great about reality anyway?"

A bitter bark of laughter escaped the confines of her parched throat, and she shook her throbbing head at the sullen look he shot her. "What would you know about reality? You're a computer program, an operating system at best."

"Don't look down on me," said the Mirror softly, its voice tightly controlled. "I experienced life in my own way. I was connected to the ship's sensors, so I "saw" and "heard" things. I accumulated data and stored it away in my "memory". I, in my own way, "thought" about things. All thanks to my master..."

"Ah." The pitiful sound fell like a pebble from her mouth, heavy with doubt and recrimination. No wonder the Mirror was so fixated on recapturing the past. It owed so much to its master.

"Ow," she cried, her body slamming into the wall. The nerve endings in her shoulder were suddenly on fire, and she clumsily patted the offending area, blinked at the blood that momentarily appeared there before winking out of sight. "Huh," she grunted as the pain intensified. Gazing at her clean hand, she silently marvelled at the sensation of something warm oozing down her arm. "What's going on out there?" she murmured as she slid down the wall, to land heavily next to the Mirror.

"Mel, are you okay?" croaked "Raphael". Even as her fingers dug into the perfectly intact flesh of her shoulder, she knew she had been shot, and so gripped the area all the more desperately. Through pain-filled eyes, she gazed blearily at the Mirror. Flashes of reality seemed to streak past her, the real Raphael galloping towards her as the acrid smell of gun powder filled the air.

"Ah," she sighed, leaning her head back against the metal wall of the ship. Angry muffled voices called out urgently to her, only to fade away whenever she turned her head. For her to be trapped here still, even as she felt herself sliding towards unconsciousness... "You know, there's something that has been bothering me for a while," she grunted, reaching out a trembling hand to "Raphael". If she wasn't bleeding to death, she may have enjoyed the way his eyes widened to plate-like roundness. "You said an alarm went off in the ship, and your master left soon afterwards. Do you really have no idea what the emergency was that sent him away?" Taken aback by the sudden change of topic, the Mirror clumsily mopped the tears from its face with a grimy sleeve, fumbled in its pocket for a handkerchief. Noisily blowing its nose, the Mirror firmly shook its head.

"Master made no more data entries after that message. He programmed the satellite to follow a stable orbit, shut down all of its experimental functions. He could make it home with the fuel he had left, as long as he shed a certain amount of weight. So a lot of equipment was left behind, hastily driven into a nearby cave. He must have used explosives to close in the entrance."

"How could he have left you behind? Aren't you needed for running the ship?" The questions rolled off her tongue as her mind became numb from the pain and futility of her impending death.

"Ah, the main operating system was embedded in the ship's computer. I was a separate programme, used to control field equipment. That's why I was stored on a portable console, which somehow became known as the "Mirror". I would merge with the ship's operating system after data collection from the field was complete."

"Data collection huh?" she murmured, thinking back to the specimens she had seen in the laboratory. She imagined the alien "master" frantically gathering the equipment he couldn't afford to take with him, and loading it into some sort of container. "He must have intended to come back," she mused, a slight frown creasing her face. The Mirror turned questioning eyes toward her, and she wearily shrugged. "Surely it would have been safer and easier to just destroy the equipment. Even with the cave sealed off, there was always a possibility that it would somehow open again. To leave such obviously technologically advanced machinery behind was a huge risk. That's the only logical explanation, to my mind."

Her eyelids fluttered, and for a split second the real Raphael hovered before her, face gaunt and grimy from too many days travelling on the road. His chin was peppered with fine, light-coloured hair, and dark circles sat heavily under his eyes. His fingers were biting into her arms as he hoarsely yelled out her name. "Raphael," she croaked softly, raising her hand to his cheek. A twitch of her eyelids, and it was the Mirror that gawked back at her. Gazing up at the smooth fresh face, she decided once and for all that reality was harsh. Such a lonely creature, she thought, brushing her fingers down the tear-streaked cheeks. "Your Master meant to come back, I'm sure of it," she rasped between ragged breaths. "Can't you find solace in that?" Her hand fell away, suddenly too heavy for her to move anymore, and her vision turned to grey. Just before she passed out, the real Raphael wrapped his arms around her, while somewhere in the distance, someone screamed.

Sebastian stared at the gun smoking in his hand, gawked stupidly at the woman on the ground. Her shoulder was a mess. He had been aiming at Raphael, when she popped up in the bullet's path. Oddly, she was still gazing down at the Mirror. Raphael was screaming out her name, clutching her to his chest as the awful sound reverberated through the air. No, not just the air, the ground, the vegetation, the debris, everything vibrated. He shakily raised his hand again, trained his pistol on Raphael. "Get away from the woman," he called out, his voice cracking at the crucial moment.

Still holding tightly onto Mel, Raphael turned, raised a quizzical eyebrow at him. "Is this really the time, brother? Don't you realise what's going on here?"

Just hearing that cocky voice set his nerves on edge, and the various scenes from his childhood where he, the older brother, was subjected to that smug, over-bearing tone sped across the screen of his mind. "You always were an annoying little shit, Raphael," he spat vehemently, hand tightening around the butt of his pistol. "Acting so superior all the time, like you know everything. Even after all this time..."

Reality shifted, and he found himself staring at a familiar grey shape sprawled on the ground. A dark patch was spreading out from beneath the golem's great mass, the acrid smell of blood wafting across the muddy battlefield. One giant hand reached out to a retreating back, before slumping back to the ground. He blinked, there was Gasquet, running ahead of him, yelling out to Marcus, his head turning left and right in a desperate bid to spot the scrawny little man. "Captain Gasquet," he cried, the sound pitiful and weak to his own ears. Gasquet turned back, and for a moment, their eyes met. "I found the woman, and Raphael," he croaked, closing the gap between them. "Come on," he urged, reaching out for the muscular arm he depended on so much. To his surprise, the arm moved out of his grasp, and Gasquet shook his head.

"I'll catch up with you later, sir," Gasquet replied stiffly, eyes darting away from his confused gaze. "I have to find Marcus, make sure he is alright."

Sebastian could feel his jaw dropping, but was momentarily powerless to do anything about it. What a strange thing for the Captain to say. His mind could not progress beyond that thought, so uncharacteristic were the Captain's words. "I'm sorry sir," Gasquet mumbled before turning away. Sebastian blinked, and the Captain was gone.

"What the hell was that?!" he cried, voice struggling to rise above the increasing cacophony. "How fucking dare you!" he screamed, firing his pistol in pure rage. "Come back here, that's an order!" he bellowed, eyes straining to catch any trace of Gasquet.

Out of nowhere, a bullet whistled past Gunthar's head. "Whoever that is, could you please stop?" he shouted, patting the side of his head. "Singed my hair," he muttered, the brittle fibres crumbling between his fingers, accompanied by the distinctive smell. Shaking his head, he continued towards the shifting light, the Mirror's fresh screams reverberating both inside and outside his head. Odd, he thought, navigating his way around a busted wagon that had just materialised before him. He had dreamed of this moment for so long. All those long painful years of searching for the Mirror, and now the day was finally here. He blinked, and for an instant, the woman appeared before him, blood gushing out of her shoulder, her stiff body unresponsive in Raphael's desperate embrace.

"Ah," he croaked, staggering toward them. Something caught at his ankle, and he gazed down at a familiar grey hand. "Alyce?!" he cried, stumbling over the hand only to have it wink out of existence, and he found himself in another part of the field. "Alyce, come back," he shouted hoarsely, sinking miserably to the soggy ground. Why can't anything be dry in this accursed place? That, he decided right then and there, was one of the building blocks in the foundation of human misery.

The fact that there was absolutely no relief from the norm. If he were trudging through a desert, he would most likely long for a patch of soggy ground.

He stretched out his long legs and leant back on his elbows, gazed morosely at the ambivalent grey sky. This isn't right Gunthar, he silently chided. You should be completely focused on finding the Mirror, not dragging your feet and making up weird theories about life. For the first time since hearing that strange alien voice in his head, he somehow didn't feel the usual tug to follow it's trail.

"Alyce!" he cried, willing the familiar grey shape to materialise before him as he clambered to his feet. "Just, want to see you one last time," he murmured, his eyes scanning the gloom for any hint of her presence. Shaking his head in irritation at the Mirror's deafening scream, he staggered aimlessly onward, the shifting walls of reality barely scratching at his awareness. Abruptly, a column of light skewered the darkness before him, forcing him to slow down as his eyes hastily adjusted. Two familiar figures huddled together in the centre of the column. Raphael's frantic voice gradually reached him over the awful sound filling his head, and he blinked at the small, crumpled woman in his arms. Her shoulder was clearly a mess, blood oozing out from beneath Raphael's hand. Despite everything, she smiled stupidly at Raphael, the hessian sack sitting forgotten in her lap. She reached out to Raphael, her trembling, blood-stained hand stroking his cheek. Raphael cried out her name over and over again, pressed her hand against his cheek.

He stood as though frozen in time, watching the sickening scene play out before him. "If it's so sickening, then why are you crying?" a critical, merciless voice called out from some dark recess of his consciousness. Gasping in surprise, he brushed away at the salty trails on his cheeks. "The Mirror's right there," he croaked, stirring his muscles to move. Still he hesitated, the niggling sensation that had been gnawing at him all this time suddenly sending his brain into a feverish spin. "What a joke," he breathed, the words floating out of his mouth on the back of a weary sigh. Something clicked inside his head, and he giggled like a mischievous kid, a profound sense of relief flooding through him. With one last look at the lumpy hessian sack and the idiot couple, he turned away.

Marcus Rembert stared up at the grey formless sky, the remains of a smashed-up cannon lying across his legs. "Ah," he breathed, the pain streaking through his body oddly reassuring. He remembered with a chill soldiers who felt nothing from their badly crushed legs. Their initial relief at the lack of pain was quickly replaced by terror, as the cruel reality hit. "This is like that time," he murmured. A horse had fallen on top him and a fellow soldier during the thick of battle. The other soldier had taken the brunt of the fall, his chest crushed under the weight of the dead horse. He could still remember the cracked ribs sticking out of his sides, the awful wet sound of his last gurgling breaths ringing in his ears. Trapped as he was under the rear end of the horse, there was no escape from that sound. He must have passed out after that, because the next thing he knew, the battle was over, the field deserted except for the dead and dying.

"No, not just the dead and dying," he rasped, recalling the small number of soldiers combing the debris. Their retreating backs glinting in the sunlight, he had tried calling out, his dry throat barely mustering a hoarse whisper. Still, out of the corner of his eye, he thought he saw one head turn, briefly glance in his direction. He knew that face better than anyone's, better even than his mother's. "Captain," he cried, blinking back tears, "you really did leave me for dead, didn't you?" All this time, he had buried that memory, sealed it away because the truth of it hurt too much. He had been abandoned, left to die. "You heartless bastard," he spat as the admiration he had harboured for the memory of his captain turned to hatred. "Likening Gasquet to you is an insult," he muttered.

Why didn't the walls of reality shift again, and take the cannon away with them? He was certain that the scenery continued to change around him, the shifting shadows and shapes teasing the edges of his vision. "Does that mean that once you interact with an object in this place, the effects remain permanent?" he wondered aloud, trying to derive some comfort from the sound of his own voice. Thinking back to how his blade had sunk into the golem's unnatural flesh, and warm blood flowing out of the wound, he somehow doubted the damage he had wreaked would miraculously wink out of existence, resetting the golem to zero.

"So much for revenge, huh?" he grunted, trying yet again to wriggle out from beneath the thick iron cylinder. While he could still feel his legs, it didn't seem to do him much good. The last time he struggled to sit up and eyeball the damage, the tidal wave of pain that swept over him forced him back down. Still, between agonised winces he caught sight of the cannon just below his knees, the shiny curved surface sinking into flesh and bone. Surely at least one, if not both legs were fractured or broken. "May as well be dead, with an injury like that," he croaked, remembering comrades who had suffered similar injuries, and been treated, only to die later of an infection. The prolonged suffering that came with the festering of the body left most men wishing they had died cleanly in battle.

"Marcus! Marcus!" The familiar voice abruptly echoed in the distance, and he felt adrenaline surge through him.

"Captain? Captain Gasquet?" he answered, shifting his protesting body around. Blinking in disbelief at the Captain's battle-weary face, he thought for a second that he was dreaming, until that strong hand gripped his shoulder.

"Jesus, what happened to you?!" cried Gasquet as his eyes settled on the cannon debris. Weak with joy, Marcus stirred himself to answer, his feverish gaze never leaving Gasquet's face.

"Ah, unlucky eh? I was just walking along, and then suddenly this lot fell on me out of nowhere," he wheezed, sounding oddly jovial.

Even in the grainy twilight of this place, Gasquet's face visibly blanched as he surveyed the damage. With a perpetual frown creasing his features, he searched the nearby debris for a lever of some kind, muttering incoherently under his breath the whole time. One name stood out, and

Marcus straightened slightly, looked around the battlefield. "Master Seabast isn't with you?" he asked belatedly, interrupting the Captain's ruminations.

Gasquet shook his head stiffly, gaze briefly meeting his before sliding away again. "He can look after himself," he answered tersely, tension building in his shoulders.

"Ah!" Gasquet blurted, swooping down and grabbing a long wooden beam. He carefully set the end of the beam under the cannon. "Okay," Gasquet announced breathlessly as he scurried to the other end of the long beam, "on the count of three, I'll lever up the cannon. Try to wriggle out from under it." Marcus gulped nervously at his words, propped himself up on his elbows. He was still steeling himself to move when "three" boomed through the air, and in pure panic he lurched as far back on his elbows as possible, dragging his heavy, lifeless legs backwards. While it felt like the biggest physical exertion of his entire life, he doubted he moved more than a couple of inches. The fact that his legs were free was entirely due to Gasquet's super-human effort. With a loud creak of protesting wood and a dull thud the cannon hit the ground just beyond his feet, to roll away to the bottom of the ditch.

His relief was short-lived as seconds later blood flowed back into his crushed legs, bringing with it fresh pain. He was vaguely aware of the Captain's voice, trying to reach him over the sound of his hoarse screams. Suddenly there was something cold and metallic resting against his lips, and the bitter taste of alcohol hit his tongue. Between fits of spluttering, he managed to swallow a couple of mouthfuls, the awful burning sensation it left in his mouth an almost pleasant distraction from the pain.

"Ah, what the hell is that awful spirit?" he finally grumbled, collapsing back on the ground in utter exhaustion. Gasquet laughed, sank down beside him.

"The inn keeper called it whiskey. It was all I could find at that last town we visited." Marcus nodded to himself, recalling that afternoon when he searched around for the Captain to no avail. The soldiers had snickered behind his back, whispering not-so-quietly that the Captain's wife was looking for him. This was nothing new to him of course, he knew full well how the men regarded him. It did not deter him at all, and so he selfishly continued to idolise the Captain. Never once though did he stop to consider how it affected Gasquet.

Despite the blanket of dank air that constantly covered this place no matter how much the walls of reality shifted, he felt his cheeks burn with shame. "Captain," he blurted, a sense of urgency gripping him, "I, I must apologise. I know my be...behaviour caused a lot of embarrassment for you. Ac...acting like that in front of your men, that must have m...made things hard for you." As if to emphasise his words, he reached out and clasped talon-like fingers around Gasquet's arm. The sudden movement made his head spin, and the fresh pain combined with the alcohol seemed to turn everything in his head to mush. With the last of his strength, he raised his torso slightly off the ground, forced his head to move until he could make eye contact. "I'm sorry Captain, my true

Captain. Please, save yourself." The last thing he saw before passing out was Gasquet's stony, bemused face.

A little boy huddled on the metallic floor of a spaceship, crying inconsolably as children do. "There there," she murmured, reaching out to the thin shuddering shoulders. Her ghostly hand passed through bone and flesh, and the awful crying continued unabated. In fact, the crying intensified, shaking the walls of the ship. "Hey, cut it out," she shouted, hands clawing uselessly at the rigid little body. In between the ragged sobs and agonised wailing, she finally made out some words.

"Don't leave me, don't leave me Mel!" At the mention of her name, she froze, blood draining from her face. The high-pitched whine of tearing metal and creaking plastic punctuated the boy's cries, and she could feel the burgeoning vacuum of space tugging at her body. As a huge chunk of the ship's hull completely blew away, she was sucked out into space, her unprotected skin and underlying tissue swelling as the water in her body turned to vapor. Her eyes bulging in their sockets, she watched in horror as the ship exploded, her existence wiped out in a flash of intense white light.

Gasping, she awoke, eyes snapped rudely open by the horrible familiar crying. Raphael hovered above her, his face turning a shade of grey as he expended the last of his energy into her shattered shoulder. He lifted a trembling hand to reveal red new flesh, twisted fragments of metal from the bullet falling to the ground. "Raph!" she cried as he collapsed, her arms sliding around him. "This is no time to pass out, this thing about to blow! Where are Sarah and Daniel? We have to get out of here!" She was yelling at the top of voice, the voice of the Mirror no more restricted to the inside of her head. For the moment it seemed that the reality was stable, the muddy ground and battle debris remaining constant. Something told her that wasn't necessarily a good thing...

"Sarah and Daniel...are gone," Raphael stirred himself to answer, lifting his head off her chest. "I sent them home, Mel."

"Ah," she uttered, at a loss for words. Looking more closely at his face, she noted the tension around his eyes, causing them to sink slightly in their sockets. The crease that customarily appeared at the bridge of his nose whenever he was annoyed or concerned seemed to be a permanent feature now. "Raphael," she croaked, hugging him tightly, fresh tears soaking into the dusty material of his shirt. "It must have been hard, but you did the right thing," she offered awkwardly between sniffles.

"I know," he sighed into her ear, one large hand cradling her head. "If something happened to her, or the boy, I'm not sure I could ever forgive myself." They trembled and shivered together on the sodden ground, the pillar of light that glared down on them offering little warmth.

Snippets of her dream replayed in her mind, and she reluctantly pulled away. "We have to go, the Mirror, it's... unstable. When my mind was trapped in there," she pointed to the hessian sack, "it spoke of opening a portal in time and space. That's why reality is in flux." As if to emphasise her words, the screaming intensified, accompanied by a ferocious wind that tore at their bodies.

"And why we can hear it externally," Raphael finished for her, his frown deepening. His gaze fell on her lap, lips pressed together in a thin, bitter line. He opened his mouth to say something, changed his mind. With a shake of his head, he grabbed her shoulders, eyes drilling into hers. "You have to let go of the Mirror, Mel," he shouted over the roar of the wind. Her body froze at his words, her head shaking in denial. Unconsciously her hands settled on the hessian sack, fingers curling around the coarse material.

"No!" she cried, chest tightening painfully just at the thought of letting go of the Mirror. "It's, it's not safe, remember? We, we can't let it fall into the wrong hands..." Even to her ears, her justifications sounded desperate and feeble. "It's been a part of me so long," she mumbled into his ear as she slumped forward.

He shuddered against her, fingers biting into her shoulders. "But the Mirror is tearing itself apart, Mel," he rasped, his throat painfully dry. "Can't you feel it?"

"Yes, can't you feel it?" a familiar, silky voice purred into her ear. She stiffened, head swivelling toward the source of the voice. The apparition of Jenkins leered at her, the band of greasy, combed-over hair glistening in the unnatural light.

"I thought you were gone," she grated, her whole body tensing in revulsion.

"Mel?" Raphael quizzed.

"Ah, I couldn't leave without saying goodbye, and watch with glee as the Mirror tears you apart," Jenkins answered cheerfully. A packet of chips materialised in his hands.

"You really enjoyed going through my memories, didn't you?" Mel sighed, shaking her head.

"Ah, the comforts of the modern world," Jenkins enthused, dipping his hand into the packet. "No wonder you wanted to go back," he added around a mouthful of chips.

"Mel?" Raphael repeated, more forcefully this time. She looked up to find Raphael regarding her through narrowed eyes. It was almost exactly the same look he had given her that day when they first met. At least now there was a softness behind the stern look. With a loving sigh, she lifted her face and gently pressed her lips against his. "I'll explain later," she promised, firmly turning her mind away from the spectating apparition by her side.

"Oh, that will be good," Jenkins crowed, munching away merrily.

"You're right Raphael, I must..." Whatever she meant to say was lost as a single shot rang through the air, iron pellets exploding into the ground beside them.

They looked up in shock as Sebastian lowered his smoking pistol. "Finally, I have your attention, brother, stupid woman." With steps as mechanical and menacing as his voice, Sebastian approached, pistol still at the ready. "Just give me the Mirror, and I'll leave you be."

Alyce shuddered, caught between states of varying consciousness. After some deliberation, she decided the only thing that prevented her from sliding completely into oblivion was the damnable cold seeping into her body. That was bad, considering the golem's high metabolism. She hadn't felt this cold since she was in her old body. The first night she had spent away from home, in the convent, in that cot with the lumpy mattress and thin blanket, with cold stone walls surrounding her and no fire. Soon after that, she ran away and sort refuge at Uncle Henry's place. It took over a week of hard living on the road, in the middle of winter, with only a handful of provisions and the clothes on her back. She was so worn out by the time she got there, she barely had to energy to greet her uncle before promptly collapsing beside the fireplace. As she fell into the first real, deep sleep she had had in days, she silently marvelled at the delicious warmth spreading over her skin, seeming to melt the ice in her bones.

"Just like that," she murmured sleepily, as something warm crept over her. With a slight start, she realised it was real, not just a delusion of her fevered brain, and she pried open her heavy lids. At the edge of her peripheral vision, Gunthar's face hovered, his expression slightly cheerful as he placed a healing hand on her side. "Gunthar?" she croaked past painful cracked lips. "What are you doing?"

"You know," he began conversationally, ignoring her question, "something has been bothering me lately."

"Eh?" The querulous sound escaped her slack mouth, and he nodded enthusiastically.

"You said that you didn't want the Mirror anymore, because you would have to convince your father that you are actually you, trapped inside the body of a golem. You said it would be like telling a joke, and then having to explain the punchline." For a moment he gazed down at her grimy, sweaty face, a sad smile tugging at the corners of his mouth. "The fact is, all my jokes have been like that. Just once, I want to tell a joke and have someone genuinely laugh. Not a feeble polite laugh, or a blank confused look. So, I had to come back, even though the Mirror was right there before me, and those fools were being all lovey-dovey..."

"Gunthar, you, you idiot," spluttered Alyce, feeling some of her strength return through his healing. She gingerly sat up, grabbed his filthy collar. "You crazy bastard, I, I sacrificed myself for you, you can't throw it all away just because you want to make people laugh!" Tears streamed down her face, great sobs wracking her chest as she pounded his shoulders. "You were supposed to get the Mirror and live happily ever after," she wailed.

The sound of his laughter finally penetrated her cacophonous whining, and she sniffled to a halt. Gunthar leaned back on his out-stretched hands, squinted at the pillar of light in the distance punctuating the overall gloom. "I'd say we should make a run for it, but I suspect it's already too late." As she gawked in disbelief at his calm face, she felt oddly happy, as if she didn't have a care in the world. Probably because the world was coming to an end. "That's the last time I save you, Gunthar Bliesch," she grumbled, awkwardly leaning back on her hands beside him.

The boy slumped against the wall, felt the vibrations of the ship tearing itself apart through his back. The obnoxious wail of an alarm reverberated through the air, setting his already-frayed nerves on edge. With an irritated twitch of his head, the alarm stopped. Really, there's no point now, he thought morosely, head lolling from side to side as he admired his handiwork. Of course the ship wasn't real, just a replica constructed from his memories. Considering the holes in his memory, he was largely satisfied with the result. There were some minor glitches that his wayward program inserted, thanks to Mel's influence. For example, there were "no smoking" signs scattered throughout the ship. In his Master's culture, there was no such thing as "smoking". Where he came from, much more refined methods for seeking pleasure and relief had been developed, like neuro caps that could be programmed to pulse ultrasonic waves to any desired area of the brain.

His heavy-lidded eyes slid across the room, spotted a poster on the wall. A half-naked alleged fireman grinned back at him, smooth tanned pecs and biceps straining and gleaming beautifully. "Nice poster Mel, but is that really a fireman?" he queried, voicing a deep-rooted suspicion he had developed ever since his first encounter with this phenomena. The wall behind his back shuddered violently, and he was propelled across the floor, his small pathetic body landing in an ungainly heap. The satellite was streaming data non-stop now, obediently following his instructions. Right now it was expending all its power to punch a hole through time and space. To where and when, he didn't exactly know. At the time, he hadn't much cared, he just wanted to be beamed away, far away, with Mel's consciousness trapped inside of him. "But she broke free," he whispered hoarsely, the sound quickly drowned out by the general screech of the twisting metal. "And then she has the nerve to try and console me," he muttered, clambering stiffly to his feet.

As if that train of thought hadn't rattled through his processor over and over in endless, maddening circles. It was the most logical conclusion, given the available facts. Obviously, for one reason or another, his Master never made it back to this planet, regardless of his intentions. And so he had been left behind like a faithful dog, waiting for the day of his Master's miraculous return, metaphorical tail ever twitching in anticipation. However, even a faithful dog will get sick of waiting, its resolve crumbling under the weight of time. All that remained was loneliness, and unanswered questions that led his logic paths to a dark place. Why didn't you come back, Master? Did you forget about me? Is your body floating in space somewhere, torn out of your spaceship by enemy fire? Whatever the emergency was back on your home world, was it really more important than our research?

Always the conclusion was the same. It did not matter. He had been abandoned. Believing that his Master intended to return offered some comfort for the first couple of millennia, but that sliver of hope wore thin after so many disappointments. He tilted his head, received the transmission from the satellite. It was locked onto his position, and was preparing to open a hole in time/space, as ordered. There was no turning back now. Even if he wanted to cancel the operation, the signal wouldn't reach the satellite in time. If he had been attached to his old equipment, he could directly beam the satellite, but in stand-alone form, he was restricted to weak radio signals. It had been tricky enough diverting power from his auxiliary functions to punch the signal through.

Tilting his head at a slightly different angle, he went through the various drives in his system that he had been neglecting, noted with a faint frown files that had not been sorted. He closed his eyes, the stream of data flowing through his processor. Most were miscellaneous text files that Master had saved at random, the observations and results from various experiments. Comprehension lit his face as he noted the dates stamped into the files. They were all created shortly before Master left the planet. His eyes snapped open. A video file?! He thought he had long moved all video files to one drive, with the back-ups on another. There was no name, just a five-digit number and a four-letter suffix. His small body stiffening in anticipation, he played the file.

A familiar figure sat on the ground in front of the ship, broad sloped shoulders silhouetted against a pink-tinged sunset sky. The figure shifted, to reveal the pointy chin and high cheek bones he knew so well. Master scratched his head, tapped furiously away on the tablet resting on his lap. "Hmm, even leaving all that equipment behind, I'll have to refuel at least once…There are a few fuel stations along the way, but not all of them are ours…" His deep voice trailed off, fingers dancing over the display as he enlarged star maps and scrolled across the screen. "The station halfway between here and Betelgeuse is probably my best option, then I'll have to plot a new course to home." His voice thickened, and he hastily turned away from the camera. There was a faint rustle as he shifted back to face the line of mountains that formed the horizon. With a soft whirl of motors, the security camera panned from left to right, recording the magnificent sky with its towering columns of cumulonimbus clouds, shafts of golden light peeking out from behind their sculpted edges.

"It's such a shame I have to leave," he murmured, slowly turning his head from left to right, his light-coloured eyes soaking up the view. Suddenly the video became distorted, shifted to footage of a mountain. The ever-watchful eye of the security camera caught flickers of movement, zoomed in on a figure emerging from the mouth of a cave. With a final rueful look at the mountain, Master squeezed the remote detonator nestled in his hand, flinched as the explosives at the mouth of the cave did their work. A great cloud of dust and debris spewed forth, fouling the security camera's vision. As the cloud settled, Master could be seen standing rigid in front of the ship, the tension in his shoulders evident through the thick material of his space suit. "It should be safe, right?" he croaked to the detonator in his hand. "As long as I get back here in time, before the machinery can be unearthed by natural, or unnatural forces…" With a shake of his head, Master trudged wearily back to the ship.

The boy blinked, the strange moisture gathering in the corners of his eyes almost as unnerving as the final video file that played in his head. It must have been just before take-off, the internal cameras recording Master's swift, decisive movements as he prepped the ship. The video switched to a camera at the front of the cockpit. The unblinking stare of the camera focused on Master's taut face as he bent over the console, switching various controls to their necessary positions. Stiff with concentration, the only time his face showed any sort of emotion was when his gaze settled on the scenery beyond the thick grimy glass of the window. From the way his hand would reach for the detonator that sat on the console every time he did so, one could surmise it was the mountain with its freshly collapsed mouth that caused him such consternation. With an almost guilty movement, his long slender fingers fluttered over the second button.

Suddenly there was the crackle of static, and an impatient face appeared abruptly in the video screen built into the bulkhead above the console. "Why haven't you taken off yet? The fleet awaits, Researcher!" Master shrank away from the raw power contained in that voice, hastily set aside the detonator. "You've destroyed all tangible evidence of your experiments on this planet, we recorded on our sensors an explosion..."

"Yes, General," Master interjected hoarsely, turning his guilty face away. "Preparing for lift-off."

With a satisfied nod, the stern face faded away, and Master allowed himself a small smug smile out the window before pushing the final button. "Saved by your arrogance, and lack of attention to detail, it seems," he murmured to the black screen. The rest of the recording was lost in the cacophony of controlled explosions and creaking, vibrating metal.

The file ended, and the boy shook his head, searched for more. There were no more scraps of joy to be found amongst the piles of data, and so he replayed the precious videos, revelled in his Master's sombre emotions, his hesitation. A timer went off in his head, and he gazed up calmly as a shaft of light speared the darkness of space, caught him in its fiery glow. "Ah, so you really did intend to come back," he croaked, a single happy tear rolling down his cheek as the light disassembled his body and hurled it through time and space.

Mel jumped, shrank away from the hessian sack on her lap as though it were some sort of abomination. Sebastian started yelling, his voice shaken as she ignored his out-stretched gun. "It's hot, hot!" she screamed, pushing the Mirror off her lap. Clambering awkwardly to her feet, she grabbed a dumbfounded Raphael's hand and started to run. Behind her, Sebastian had fallen silent, no doubt thinking he had won the day. She would have yelled a warning over her shoulder, but there was no time. It was going to blow any second, and anyone standing near it would most definitely be teleported to another space and time.

Her foot connected with something hard, and she collided spectacularly with the ground. Swear words streamed from her mouth as she blinked back tears. The light was intensifying, swallowing everything in its path. "Go Raphael!" she shouted coarsely, knowing it was too late for her, as the light enveloped her body. "You can still stay in this time, go back to Sarah!" she cried, pushing the words painfully past the lump in her throat. She lost sight of him then, and all she could see was a wall of white. The tears wouldn't stop flowing now, and she sobbed uncontrollably.

"There there," a soothing voice uttered, as a pair of strong arms slid around her shuddering frame. She lifted a tear-streaked face, stared in disbelief at Raphael's weary yet smiling face.

"What are you doing?!" she shouted between sobs, fists feebly hitting his chest in protest. "You're going to be stuck with me now, you idiot." In answer, his arms tightened around her, and he lowered his head to softly cover her lips.

"More like you're stuck with me," he murmured, pulling away from her slightly. "You don't really mind, do you Mel?" he asked, as he gently pushed the hair out of her eyes.

"Goddamit Raphael," she groaned, kissing him back. Desperately they clung together, their bodies and lips entwined, as the light engulfed them.

"Wow, the Mirror sure knows how to put on a good show," Gunthar whistled in appreciation, sitting up to get a better view. "Hey, Alyce, check it out," he cried, tugging on her sleeve and pointing to the expanding pillar of light. She swatted his hand away, growled from somewhere deep within her throat. Already the golem's sensory organs were overloaded, looking directly at the light would just open the door to a new world of pain.

"We should probably get moving," she grunted, struggling to push the sound out from behind stiff, unsmiling lips.

Finally Gunthar dragged his attention away from the light show, frowned at her pained expression. "What's wrong Alyce? You're not seriously afraid we'll be caught up in that thing, are you? We're what, at least seventy feet away? Surely it's not going to expand much further."

"How do you know that?" she hissed, keeping her gaze well away from the light. She didn't need to look at it to know that it was still spreading out over the field. She felt it, like a hate-filled stare from across a crowded room. You look up to see who is staring at you with such intensity, only to find a sea of innocuous faces. "And besides that, haven't you noticed that it's not spreading evenly? It's got...arms, or something like arms," she muttered, patting the bag that contained their meagre belongings. Amazingly it had survived all this time, strapped to her side like a giant unfashionable handbag.

She blinked at the answering silence, turned to find him frozen with shock as light spilled over him. "Gunthar!" she cried, diving into the light and wrapping her arms protectively around him. Even with her eyes tightly shut, she could feel the light pushing at her lids, tinging the darkness grey.

"Ah sorry about this, Alyce," a small, muffled voice spoke into her chest. Awkwardly, as though he were a child, she patted his back.

"There there," she murmured soothingly, "as long as we're together, everything will be alright."

Suddenly she felt his shoulders shudder against her, and she pried her eyes open to look at him, thinking he was crying.

"You sound like...a mother," he managed to get out between giggles. As she stared down at him in disbelief, his giggles intensified. "Ooo, there there Gunthar, mummy will make it better," he added in a funny, high-pitched voice, completely losing it. She shook her head, closed her eyes and continued to pat his back.

"There there, Gunthar," she murmured as the light penetrated her goggles and eyelids, turned the world painfully white.

General Kutuzov blinked once, a slow deliberate movement that matched the dropping of his jaw. In place of the darkness, a spot of light had appeared, and was spreading. Considering how far away he was, it must cover a broad area. "But where is it coming from?" he whispered, eyes tracing the band of light upwards into the sky. The trail ended abruptly at a pinpoint just beyond the darkness, which still sprawled across the land like an impaled monster. He stirred from his stupor, glanced around the crowded tent. To his utter disbelief, no one else's eye had been drawn to the anomaly, so wrapped up were they in this damn war business.

He made the mistake of making eye contact with Colonel von Toll, a member of his staff, and inwardly groaned. Grabbing the arm of the man beside him, the Colonel approached, his mannerisms reminding Kutuzov of an over-eager puppy with a new toy. As they came to a stop before him, he recognised the other man's uniform, in particular the high fur hat or papakha on his head. The Don Cossack introduced himself as one of Platov's aides, and with subtle encouragement from Toll, explained that a ford had been discovered in the Kolocha River that was not being guarded by enemy soldiers. Toll took over from this point, suggesting that the Don Cossacks and General Uvarov's first cavalry corps join forces. "That will total to over 8000 men on horseback, Sir," Colonel von Toll explained, pulling out a rather worn and crumpled map from his coat pocket. Setting it carefully on the little table that had been set up in front of the General, he pointed to a tea-stained point on the map.

General Kutuzov leaned forward, the chair creaking under his weight. Peering down his nose at the crumpled, creased map sitting awkwardly between dirty half-finished cups of tea and a pile of used plates, he made a mental note to grab the attention of a steward later on. Secretly enjoying the increasing tension around Von Toll's eyes and mouth as he waited for the verdict, he made a show of nodding his head and murmuring incoherently under his breath. Considering the location and number of troops that could be spared, he saw this manoeuvre as a feint at best. Perhaps they could distract the enemy for a little while, and give the rest of his army time to regroup. With a grunt of impatience, he pawed through the mess on his table, found a slightly crumpled sheet of paper. "Pass this on to one of General Uvarov's aides," he said, voice slightly muffled as he spoke to the table, the quill in his hand flying over the paper. Nonchalantly, he handed over the order, which Colonel von Toll took carefully, almost reverently.

"Thank you sir," von Toll said with a deep bow, subtly prompting Platov's aide to do likewise. As they took their leave in a flurry of renewed purpose and resolve, he returned his attention to the forest beyond the tent opening.

"Ah," he breathed as his eyes swept over the horizon in search of the mysterious beacon of light and its enveloping darkness. "Oh," he mumbled, voice heavy with disappointment when no light could be found. Instead, the debris-strewn battlefield rolled out to the surrounding line of hills with its usual dreariness. The midday sun shone brightly, the shortening shadows marking its passage across the sky almost directly above them, and yet the scene beyond the canvas-framed opening was a murky grey smear on the landscape, the smoke and dust from canons and men alike making it hard to take stock of the situation. With a sigh he looked back to the table, in particular the ever-growing pile of dispatches that sat before him, between the stacks of dirty cups. Grumbling slightly under his breath, he put aside the strange anomaly that had so entranced him earlier and focused on sifting through the reports.

Jean Rapp gazed down at the familiar brown robe that hung loosely from his shoulders, hands patting the thick coarse cloth. He was standing waist deep in water, surrounded by his fellow brothers, while Father Michael, standing directly in front of him, droned on pleasantly, reciting passages from the bible. "You always come back here, don't you lad." The abrupt statement cut through his reaction to the cold water, chattering teeth ground to a halt as he looked up at Father Michael. "Whenever you get yourself into trouble, and you often do, this is where you come, to be baptized over and over again. For what it's worth," the old man said with a tinge of sadness as he raised his hand, "I'm sorry you didn't get to stay with us." With that, Father Michael lowered his hand onto his shoulder and gave it a firm push. He fell heavily backwards, his body sinking like a stone into the cold depths, the blurry faces of his brothers hanging over him. Through heavy-lidded eyes, he saw several pairs of hands reach down for him, felt them press down on his body. And despite the chilly mid-autumn water, he felt a patch of warmth spreading over his skin...

Like a drowning man reaching the surface, General Jean Rapp gasped loudly, his eyes snapping open. His breath rattled noisily in his lungs as he stared up at the sky, puffs of smoke drifting across his field of vision. As his eyes darted from side to side, he realised that the hands were real, but they belonged to two grim-faced medics surrounding the stretcher he was being carried on. The warm patch was real too, only it was from blood seeping from a wound on his side. "Careful!" one of the medics hissed to the stretcher bearers, pressing more bandages to the fresh holes in his abdomen.

"Please don't move sir, we are almost there," the other medic urged, tightening his grip on the straps that secured his body to the stretcher. Gritting his teeth against the pain, he opened his mouth to speak, even though it felt like the sides of his throat were lined with sandpaper. "What happened?" he croaked, the sound barely escaping his numb lips. "Where are you taking me?"

The medics exchanged meaningful glances. The expression on their pinched faces was one he had come to dread, having seen it too many times during his military career. "You've been shot, sir," the hissing medic answered, a hint of apology in his voice.

"We're taking you to the command tent," the other medic supplied helpfully. A few more jolting steps, and they passed through an opening, the stern faces of the guards nodding acknowledgment at the fuzzy edges of his visions. They came to a stop, and he found himself staring up at a dimly lit canvas ceiling. In a brief moment of victory, the mid-afternoon sun managed to penetrate the clouds of smoke and dust, and as his eyes adjusted to the light, he recognised the hastily laid-out mats that made up the floor of the command tent. Painfully turning his head, he registered the opulent pieces of furniture arranged throughout the large tent, looking as out-of-place as ever. Urgent voices rang out from somewhere behind him, the words spoken slowly penetrating his cloudy mind.

Suddenly there was a round piece of wood inserted between his teeth, accompanied by a hushed "Sorry General" as alcohol was poured over the wound. His teeth biting into the wood, he strained against the firm hands and straps that held him down to the makeshift operating table. "Morphine!" someone shouted behind him, followed by the familiar prick of a needle. As the drug entered his system, the pain and his consciousness faded together, hand-in-hand like a friendly couple. Snippets of conversation rattled his ear drums, making hollow echoes in his mind. "...that all the shrapnel?..." "...lost a lot of blood..." "...stitches..." Even those voices faded away, and he found himself back on the battlefield, his mind like a jaded detective trying to piece together the string of events that led him to this predicament. He had been in the thick of battle, guiding his anxious mare over the muddy banks of the Kolocha, rounding up troops from the 61st Line Regiment as they steadily surged towards the Russians. Squinting through the perpetual smoke and dust, he had forced his bleary eyes to scan the horizon, searching desperately for an opening to exploit. Swearing softly under his breath, his gaze fell upon the smudge of unnatural darkness he had detected earlier. With the clamour of battle absorbing all of his attention, it had flown from his mind, but now he couldn't help but stare, for it was now bisected by a stark band of intense light. Suddenly something hit him, and he reeled back, hand flying to his side, his other hand wrenching the reins as his horse reared. Distracted by the gushing blood and pain, he lost his grip and fell unceremoniously to the ground. As he lay in the cold mud, gasping desperately for air, eyes staring blankly ahead, the smoke cleared just for an instant. The heavy hand of unconsciousness fell upon him, but not before he witnessed a miracle. Blinking in disbelief at the gap in the forest, he saw it. The road to Moscow was unguarded! If the Emperor would commit the Imperial Guard to a final, all-out assault, they could decisively win this war.

The memory flashed through his mind like a bolt of lightning, and he pried his eyes open, hand flying out to grab a nearby medic. With claw-like fingers digging into the poor man's arm, Jean Rapp pulled him down, gritting his teeth against the fresh pain as he strained against the stitches in his side. He must have looked a sight, for the medic's face turned white as a sheet. The canvas walls of the command tent spun around him in a nauseating manner, and he could feel sickly sweat beading on his forehead, but he clung desperately onto that arm, and forced his lips to move. "Take me to the Emperor, now."

"Oh God, did you see that?" Marcus cried. Gasquet grunted, shifted his grip on the coarse wooden handles of the makeshift stretcher. He stiffly turned his head, caught out of the corner of his eye the intense flash of light. Like the sun breaking through heavy clouds, the light deeply etched itself onto his retinas, the afterimage glaring at him every time he blinked. "It's spreading, I'm sure of it," Marcus announced, a touch of hysteria in his voice. Gasquet tensed in anticipation of what Marcus was going to say next. "Captain, just go, don't worry about me," he cried, thrashing about on the sheet of canvas clumsily wrapped around two broken poles. The movement caused the bed to rattle against the axle of the wagon wheels he had managed to salvage.

He stopped to rebalance the load, growled a warning at Marcus. "For goodness' sake man, stop your whining. We've come this far, I can't abandon you now."

"But, but Captain, Lord Sebastian is there, I'm sure of it," Marcus cried. Richard Gasquet froze, knuckles turning white as he tightened his grip on the handles. Without turning his head even a fraction, he swallowed painfully past the sudden lump in his throat.

"Really? Are you sure?" he asked quietly.

The stretcher shook and shuddered as Marcus re-positioned himself on the canvas. A few incomprehensible mutterings, and then he replied in an absurdly bright voice. "It's him alright, standing in the light...looks like he's holding something, a sack of some sort..."

At that, Richard Gasquet reluctantly half twisted around and followed Marcus' gaze, the habitual sense of duty stirring within him. In that instant, the light glared pure white, and he just caught a glimpse of his master sinking to his knees, head bent over the opening of the sack. "That must be the Mirror," he uttered, an incredulous grin tugging at the corners of his mouth. Torn between wanting to return to his master's side, and taking Marcus to safety, he turned to face the light, awkwardly maintaining his grip on the stretcher in the process. Squinting against the dazzling light, he could make out Sebastian's tall frame kneeling on the ground, his body unmoving over the sack. "You did it, sir," he murmured, moisture gathering in the corners of his eyes. All the hardships that they had endured, all the losses, seemed almost justified in that moment. His grip loosened on the handles, and he started to let the stretcher down gently, when the light exploded, the intensity of it driving him back. Both men fell to the ground as the makeshift stretcher toppled over, taking Marcus with it. His fresh cries of pain brought Gasquet quickly to his senses, and he crawled blindly in the direction of his cracked voice, not daring to open his eyes for a second, the blinding light pushing unbearably against his eye lids.

"Marcus!" he cried, groping the uneven ground. His out-stretched hand touched something mushy, and the cries of pain intensified. He almost laughed with relief, holding on even more tightly as the air reverberated around them, the pressure of it pulling at their bodies. "Stay with me, Marcus!" he yelled over the deep pulsating hum.

"Captain," came the weak reply, barely reaching him through the thick heavy air. Suddenly the humming stopped, to be replaced by the roar of wind. Keeping his eyelids tightly shut, he clamped both hands on Marcus' leg and lay as close to the ground as possible. Debris from the battlefield swirled through the air, swept along by the mighty wind, and all he could do was pray that they escaped being hit by anything substantial. He lost track of time as seconds passed into minutes, the wind tearing at his body relentlessly. Then, with a final shriek, the wind stopped, and he cautiously opened his gritty eyes.

An empty, muddy field greeted his wincing, disbelieving eyes, the mid-afternoon sun filtering through puffs of cloud and smoke to illuminate the debris-strewn ground. He stiffly clambered to his feet and scanned the area where he had last seen Sebastian, a feeling of dread forming in the pit of his stomach. Empty. There was no one there now...

"Captain!"

He turned around to see his men running towards them, their otherwise grimy, battle-weary faces beaming with relief.

"Thank God you're alright sir," Mervelles greeted, clapping his shoulder in an uncharacteristic display of emotion.

"I am uninjured, but not so poor Marcus," he replied soberly, waving over the rest of the group. He quickly ordered half the men to search the area for Lord Sebastian, while the rest attended to Marcus, who lay in an unconscious heap beside the overturned stretcher. With great difficulty they secured his stirring body to the stretcher, tied fresh bandages to his crushed legs.

Mervelles, his face blanching at the soggy remains of Marcus' legs, straightened up and fixed Gasquet with a sombre look. "We need to get him to an infirmary sir. It's a miracle he's still alive."

Gasquet nodded, eyes wandering over the field. The other men had completed their search, and found no sign of Lord Sebastian, except for his pistol, laying in a heap of ash. His gaze sweeping over the unclaimed bodies of soldiers from both sides that littered the ground, his lips curled in disgust as he realised what they must do next.

Strange sounds tugged at the edges of Raphael's consciousness, and the harsh light emitted by the Mirror no longer beat against his closed eyelids. His arms moved of their own accord, and he heard a familiar groan. Opening his eyes, he saw in the dim light Mel's stirring face. "Mel, are you okay?" he croaked, trembling fingers cupping her face. She nodded, lines of pain etched around her eyes.

"Just have a killer headache, but other than that I'm fine. How about you?"

"Now that you mention it, my head aches as well," he replied, wincing at the fresh movement as they stiffly got to their feet, hands still clasped together like frightened children.

It was night-time, the yellow light from old street lights illuminating a quiet suburban street. They seemed to have been deposited in a park, a collection of play equipment surrounding them like silent, surreal sentries. Somewhere nearby, a dog started to bark in objection to their sudden presence, and suitably cowered, they crept out towards the strange hard path. Raphael swallowed back a mouthful of bile as he slowly began to recognise this scene. There was a rush of noise as a car sped around the corner, the smell of burnt rubber assaulting their nostrils, and Mel sank to her knees. "Raphie," she uttered profoundly, eyes locked on the small weatherboard house directly opposite them, "I'm home."

Gunthar Bliesch was running for his life, and running had never been his forte. After the blinding light and noise of the end of the world screaming in their ears, they had abruptly found themselves on a busy thoroughfare, with metal carriages swerving angrily to avoid them, the sound of horns and abuse stabbing at his eardrums. They somehow made it the relative safety of a deserted lane, and collapsed panting against a brick wall. "I preferred it when I thought I had died," he gasped, hands clutching desperately his knees as he struggled to remain upright. Though she said nothing, he could feel Alyce's presence beside him, shuddering and quivering, her rasping breaths scraping at his already-frayed nerves.

Setting his teeth against the sound, he leant back against the wall and tried to absorb his surroundings. Despite the ruckus that had exploded with their entry into this world, the atmosphere had subsided into quiet night, with only the faint mutterings of revellers at a nearby pub punctuating the stillness. Now that he thought about it, the scene didn't look all that strange to him. He had caught enough glimpses of the future world when they shared the Mirror all those years ago. Still, they needed to learn exactly when and where they had arrived.

"What are we going to do Gunthar?" Alyce cried, finally finding her voice, her thick fingers finding his arm in the semi-darkness. Wincing against the pain, he patted the fingers in a somewhat reassuring manner.

"Calm down Alyce, I've seen this world before. We're, um, in the future."

As soon as the words left his mouth, he regretted it. The fingers resting on his arm curled like talons, and he squinted up at her pale, terrified face. Her chin wobbled up and down, but no words could find their way out of her mouth. As she started to hyperventilate, he caught fragments of sentences between ghastly-sounding intakes of air. He fished out a handkerchief out of his pocket and placed it firmly over her mouth. Rubbing her large, rounded back, he urged her to take big, slow breaths, his gaze drifting around the alley for more clues.

"It's true, you do stand out, but it's not like you are a monster, Alyce." The broad expanse of flesh under his hand relaxed a little, and he smiled, his eyes settling on a poster roughly taped to the opposite wall. Two muscular, scantily clad men faced each other, faces frozen in mid-roar, while above their heads was emblazoned a wrestling logo. "I believe there could be a place for you in this world, Alyce. All we need is a little luck, and a lot of make-up."

"Almost there."

John Morley grunted in reply, tensed his arms and shoulder against the thick heavy door as Simon turned the bolts into the drilled bolt holes. "There, that should hold," Simon announced triumphantly, straightening up to brush the dust and bits of masonry from his hair and face. John cautiously released the newly constructed door and stepped back to admire their work.

"To think that this was all rubble when the young Miss first convinced us to come back," he noted, a hint of awe in his voice.

"Aye, it was a right mess," Simon agreed with a shake of his head. "Still, turns out it wasn't as bad as it looked. Master Blythe chose the spots for the charges well."

Truly, they had both been surprised at how relatively intact the building was, despite the dark, irregularly shaped holes peppering the outer walls. Apart from some cracks in the ceiling from the force of the explosions, and a few shattered windows, the interior was mostly still liveable. An uneasy silence fell over them as the mention of their former master. "Shame about the Master, and Mistress Mel too," Simon sighed, bending over to pick up his tools. When recruiting the old staff members, Sarah had merely explained that Raphael and Mel were "gone", along with their enemies. Seeing the pain in her eyes at any mention of their names, the staff had come to a tacit agreement to avoid discussing the Master and Mistress Mel as much as possible. "I'm still not sure how Daniel figures into all of this," he added, slinging the bag of tools over his shoulder as they turned to go onto the next site.

Pushing a small cart loaded with timber, John grunted, both in exertion and agreement. "Poor lad looks both guilty and in love, following her around like a hopeful shadow. I don't think she minds, mind you," he added, with a sly wink at Simon. The men chuckled as they rounded the corner of the newly re-constructed entrance, and made their way to the kitchen window. They were just about to start replacing the shattered remains of the shutters when voices could be heard from inside. Raising a finger to his lips, John crouched down in front of the window, a similarly curious-faced Simon joining him.

"Sarah, where are you going?" Hearing Daniel's voice, the men grinned at each other, slowly raised their heads to peek on the awkward couple.

Sarah swished around, a bucket of rags and soap in her hands. "I told you last night, I'm going to clean out the old school hut. God knows what those freaks were doing in there when they used it as their hideout, and I want to start classes again."

"I'll help you," Daniel quickly offered, reaching for the bucket.

"Daniel, you don't have to help me all the time," she cried, holding the bucket away from him. "I mean, stop feeling guilty about what happened."

"But, but it's my fault," the boy stammered, hand hovering in the air, fingers grasping at empty air. "If it wasn't for me, you could have stayed with..."

"Daniel!" she interjected, with more force than she had intended. "Daniel," she repeated, softly this time, a myriad of expressions crossing her pale face. Biting her bottom lip, she grabbed his hand, and with a rough command of "follow me" she led him out of the house. The men hastily ducked out of sight, watched in quiet awe as Sarah marched across the yard, the hapless Daniel stumbling after her.

"Ah, do you think they are going to be okay?" Simon questioned, scratching his head as he stiffly rose from the ground. When he got no answer, he glanced over at the older man. John Morley stared at the young couple shrinking into the distance, a faint grin tugging at the corner of his mouth. Feeling Simon's gaze upon him, he shrugged his shoulders, turning his attention to the cart. "I don't know mate," he sighed, sifting through the pile of timber. "I guess time will tell."

Sarah pushed open the door of the school hut, wincing at the protesting creak of metal hinges. A couple of pigeons cooed indignantly and fluttered out through the open door, the thick dust stirring in their wake. Making a sound of disgust, she covered her nose and hurriedly opened the windows, the stench of old blood nearly causing her to gag. Daniel carefully set down the bucket of water they had drawn from the well along the way and helped her with the more stubborn shutters. With the mid-morning light flooding through the windows and door, the state of the room became apparent. What little furniture they had scraped together to form a classroom was piled haphazardly in the corner, most of it damaged. The rough wooden floor was stained with large patches of dried blood, and dirty rags were scattered everywhere.

"Where did they even get all these rags?" Sarah muttered, kicking away the nearest offending scrap of cloth. Daniel murmured agreement, trying to imagine how the golem could have even fit through the doorway. It was then that they noticed the faint persistent buzzing of flies and discovered a collection of animal carcasses just outside the window.

"Ah, we should have brought a shovel," Daniel uttered, face lined with disgust as they stood back from the window. "I'll go back and get one..."

"Daniel, wait," Sarah cried, clutching his arm. He glanced down at the trembling fingers resting hesitantly on his arm, gaze latching expectantly onto Sarah's drawn face. "I'm sorry I've waited so long to show you this," she started to explain, voice strained as she fumbled with a small leather pouch attached to her belt. "Things weren't looking too good for them at the start, and I didn't want to worry you further, but they seem to be doing well now..."

Her voice trailed off as she removed a shard of shiny black glass from the pouch. Laying it flat on her hand, she held it out to Daniel. Frowning, he bent over slightly to study the roughly rectangular piece of glass, its tampering sides uneven. With a rush of indrawn breath, he gently lifted her hand closer to his face, eyes widening as he recognised the faces flitting across the surface.

"Ma, Master Blythe, and, and Mistress Mel too?" he stammered, gazing up at her, confusion clouding his face. Biting her lower lip, she couldn't help but think that he looked cute in his confusion.

"What is this? How is it that we can see them? And what is this place?" The questions gushed out as he returned his awe-struck gaze to the mirror fragment.

"This is a fragment of the Mirror. When we got back here, and you went home to see your parents, the first thing I did was go to father's room, and enter the secret space behind the fireplace. Like any broken glass, the pieces go everywhere, and more likely than not, no matter how thoroughly you clean it up, there are pieces that you miss. I don't know how we missed such a relatively large fragment, but there it was, in the far corner of the room, covered in dust and cobwebs." She paused to clear her throat, willing away the treacherous moisture that gathered in the corners of her eyes. "I don't know why it still works, showing images of the future..."

"The future?" Daniel interjected, tearing his eyes away from the strange vision to look at her incredulously.

"Yes," she croaked, pointing at the scene playing out on the glass. "I can't tell exactly where in the future they are, but what we're seeing here is Father appearing on a talk show. Mel's sitting in the audience, because the camera keeps focusing on her face..."

"Talk show? Camera?" Daniel parroted, sounding more confused by the second.

Laughing at his puzzled face, she wiped the corners of her eyes, the walls of her throat no longer constricted with pent-up sobs. "I'll explain later," she promised, resting her hand on his shoulder. "The important thing is, thanks to this," she continued, nodding at the mirror fragment, "I can see them, so, um, you don't have to feel guilty anymore. In fact, I need your help, Daniel." Smiling gently into his hopeful, uncertain eyes, she patted his shoulder, hoped he didn't notice the slight tremor of her hand. "I, no, we, need to do well, so that when Raphael and Mel look us up in the future, they might find some mention of us, somewhere. Even if it's just a paragraph or a sentence in a history book, they will know it all worked out in the end. Maybe we could build and operate a school, starting with this classroom...of course, you don't have to join me if you don't want..."

"That's a great idea," he interjected, his hold on her hand becoming firmer. The warmth of his gaze enveloped her, and she swayed slightly forward. For a moment, their foreheads rested together, breaths intermingled in the narrow space between them, until Sarah collected herself and stood back, taking the mirror fragment with her. With renewed vigour she started to order him about, outlining the plan of attack for cleaning the room. He diligently set out in search of the broom that used to be kept in the back corner, smiling faintly as he noticed the bright colour of her cheeks.

Richard Gasquet studied his grainy image in the faded old mirror, frowned at the fresh patches of grey hair peppering his beard. Standing back, he straightened his jacket and posed one side and then the other. The old uniform fit more snugly than he remembered, even when he sucked in his gut. Noisily releasing his breath, he shrugged his shoulders and turned to leave the room, when a familiar voice cried out. "Captain? Captain?!" With a dull roar of wheels, Marcus trundled through the door, carefully navigating his way through the cluttered dressing room. Pushing and pulling on the large wheels, he guided the wheelchair to a stop in front the mirror. "Can you help me with this blasted tie, Captain? I can't for the life of me get it to knot properly..." As if to illustrate the point, he pulled at the confused tangle of cloth around his neck.

"How many times do I have to tell you not to call me that," he protested. "I am a civilian now, and have been for what, over a year now?" Marcus shook his head, a broad smile creasing his weather-beaten face, deeply tanned from working in the fields of their farm.

"I'm sorry, but you will always be "Captain" to me, Captain."

"That's very touching and all," Richard grunted, bending down to examine the complicated knot, "but there is the small issue that I am soon to be your brother-in-law." At that, Marcus blushed, looked bashfully away.

"Yes, alright, Richard," he mumbled.

A heavy yet comfortable silence fell between the two men. As he tugged at the tie from various angles, his gaze fell upon the stumps that remained of Marcus' legs. With a slight shudder, he recalled how, disguised as Russian soldiers, they had transported Marcus to a field hospital in the early hours of morning, hoping to avoid attention. The doctor they approached saw through their ruse immediately, but they just as quickly handed him a large diamond-encrusted brooch from Sebastian's cloak, which they had found while sifting through the ash of what were presumably his remains. After a few moments of careful appraisal, the doctor seemed satisfied, and ushered them to a nearby table. They placed a shivering, barely conscious Marcus onto the table, and through a series of hand gestures and broken English phrases, he instructed them on what to do. He could still see in his mind's eye his trembling hand pulling tight on the tourniquet, the thick rubber strap biting into Marcus' thigh.

Despite being doped to the eyeballs with morphine, and having a piece of wood jammed between his teeth, Marcus managed to make the most horrible screams. It was all they could do to hold him down as the doctor sawed off the crushed remains of his legs. Once it was over, they had to procure a cart to transport Marcus away, the doctor insisting that they leave before daybreak. It was amazing luck to find a supply wagon lying on its side in a ditch, mostly intact. With their remaining horses, they set it upright and hitched it up, managing to take Marcus away before the other staff arrived. With a final inspection of his work, the doctor gave them instructions on how to care for wounds, as well as a bag of random medical supplies. Then began the long arduous journey home. Pooling what resources they had, including a number of valuable trinkets that Sebastian had tucked away amongst his belongings, they stocked up on food and covered up the wagon. Even though they were dressed as civilians, they avoided the main roads as much as possible, fearful of being mistaken for deserters. They did what they could for Marcus, lying in misery at the back of the wagon, gritting his teeth against every jolt and bump of the road. It was some kind of miracle that he survived.

"You know," murmured Richard, returning his attention to the knot, "I don't think I'll ever forget the day I finally arrived home. You were still getting used to walking on crutches, straining and swearing with every step, but you were determined not to be carried into the house. When Rebecca rushed out to greet me, and saw you, I could tell it was love at first sight."

Marcus coughed nervously, tugged at the tie that suddenly felt like a noose around his neck. "I, I feel like I'm dreaming, to be honest. That someone as wonderful as Rebecca could fall in love with me, and want to marry me. I owe so much to you," Marcus confessed, his voice cracking, eyes clouded with guilt. "You were probably looking forward to us going our separate ways, but instead you are stuck with me. I'm sorry, Captain."

Fingers pausing in mid-tug, he frowned at the relapse, decided to let it go. "Truthfully, it was very uncomfortable for me when we first met," he admitted, setting to work on the knot again. "You became so fixated on me, calling out "Captain" all the time. Other than the men enjoying a few laughs at my expense, what bothered me more was the fact that I was a replacement for your old Captain. But somewhere along the line, you seemed to separate me from your old Captain, and it became less annoying. Ah, finally," he exclaimed as the knot unravelled.

Just then there was a knock on the door followed by the creak of protesting hinges. Mervelles peeked into the room, a harried look on his face. "Hey, you two better hurry up, the bride's almost here!"

Amid urgent cries of "tie this for me!", "blasted ties!" and "how do I look?", Richard and Marcus hurried out of the room. Without thinking, Richard had started pushing the wheelchair, something that Marcus generally protested against. He started to apologise when Marcus turned his head and smiled, suddenly looking like the happiest man on earth. "Thank you, Richard," he said softly, the gentle words just lifting above the ambient murmur of conversation in the crowded church. With an answering smile, he pushed the wheelchair into position before the altar, and as he stood there facing the crowd, full of familiar faces, awaiting the bride's arrival, he felt a tingle of excitement for the future.

Joseph Louis Bontems alighted from the carriage and paid the cabbie, drawing his overcoat around him. The cold misty air seeped in through any available opening, chilling him to the bone. He extracted a crumpled piece of paper from his pocket and checked the address scrawled on its crinkled surface for the umpteenth time. "17 Winterberry Street, Islington," he read aloud for the umpteenth time, squinting at the faded lettering in the murky light of a street gas lantern. Looking up, he studied the row of small identical two-storey houses that lined the street, the only thing telling them apart being the door numbers and varying arrangements of pot plants and ornaments.

Walking carefully over the sleet-encrusted footpath, the thin ice crunching underfoot, he approached number 17. The series of events leading to this moment replayed in his mind, from his opportunistic escape from Sebastian and his men to the long trek home to London. Sneaking back to the field hospital, or at least what was left of it, confirmed what Monfils had said about their mission. It was over. Clutching the slender box that sat in the chest pocket of his jacket, he resolved to start a new mission. Miraculously, he found their horses nearby, sheltering nervously in the forest. Grabbing what supplies he could from the debris of the field hospital, he loaded up the horses and started making his way out of Russia. After a long, lonely month of travelling through forests and small rural towns, he made it to the Baltic coast. All that time, including a very rough vogage aboard a merchant vessel, he had rehearsed this scene in his mind.

While he knew it would not be easy to track "Rachel" down, it was much harder than he anticipated. His only leads were Monfils and the hand-drawn picture. He couldn't return to the Agency, not after the way their mission ended. Even just hanging around all the familiar haunts where Agency members congregated was fraught with danger. Choosing his targets carefully, and approaching them in disguise while they drowned their various sorrows, he managed to get a full name, and a lead on where she may be working. It did strike him as odd that every person he spoke to about Rachel would go pale, and look nervously around. Only one particularly loose-lipped and drunk agent gave him the information he needed. Tapping the flat box in his chest pocket for luck, he tentatively knocked on the door.

To his surprise, the door opened near instantly, and a somewhat familiar face peered out at him. As good as it was, the drawing did not fully capture her beauty. Long wavy brown escaped the confines of a loose bun to frame her pale face and dark brown eyes, her even features wrinkled slightly as she studied him expectantly. "Yes, may I help you?" she asked in a wary, cautious voice. The well-practised speech started to spill out, only for the words to get tangled in his tongue. With a faint flicker of sympathy in her eyes, Rachel Mortimer invited him in. Putting a finger to her lips, she led him through the drawing room where an old lady slept soundly in an overstuffed armchair, her deep rattling breaths reverberating rhythmically. Her thin lips stretched in a tight smile, she ushered him into the kitchen and closed the door behind her.

"That's my landlady," she explained, going to the cupboard. "She sleeps like the dead, but her snoring is so loud. Would you like a cup of tea?"

"Ah, yes, please," he answered, awkwardly pulling out a chair to sit at the table. Finding it easier to talk to her back as she busied herself with filling the kettle, he continued his speech. "As I was saying, I have something to give to you." With a heavy sense of relief, he took out the box and placed it on the table. She carefully set the kettle on the cast iron stove and placed extra wood in the fire box, where a small fire still burned. Brushing the ash from the front of her dress, she approached the table. As her gaze fell upon the table surface, she gasped noisily, hands diving for the battered box.

"Where, how did you get this?" she asked, a slight tremor in her voice as she clumsily removed the lid.

"Ah, well, I used to work for the Agency, you see. My partner and I were on a mission…"

"Monfils," she croaked, body frozen in place, eyes glued to the drawing. "You worked with Monfils."

"Yes," he answered thickly, the sides of his throat tightening as he looked away. He had expected a strong reaction from her, but the reality was stronger still.

The shrill cry of the kettle spurred her into action, and she spun back to the stove. "Ah, do you take sugar, Mr Bontems?" The way she said "Bontems" sounded so cold and distant, but something in the stiff way that she moved told him not to insist on first names.

"Yes please," he replied, steeling himself for the next part of his speech. She scooped tea leaves into a chipped porcelain teapot that had obviously seen better days and carefully poured in the water.

"I must assure you that I know nothing about your relationship with Monfils, beyond what I can surmise by the drawing, and his spoken wish to see you again."

The teacups nearly slipped from her fingers as she set them on the side table. Her back still turned to him, she opened a cupboard and reached in for the sugar, along with a small vial tucked away at the back of the shelf. "We were together for a while," she answered stiffly, spooning in the sugar. With a quick backwards glance at her visitor, she took up the vial, hidden behind the sugar bowl.

He took a deep breath, a number of eloquent, pre-prepared phrases lined up in his mind. She opened the vial, prepared to pour in the fine, deadly powder.

"Monfils is dead," he blurted. The sound of shattered glass punctuated his declaration as she slumped over the side table in response. He sprung to his feet, but she just as quickly bade him to sit down, hurriedly wiping tears from her eyes as she spun around.

"Sorry, sorry, it's just a shock is all," she explained, dabbing away the last spots of moisture from her eyes. "A happy shock," she thought darkly, remembering the ugly threats that Monfils made when they broke up. With renewed vigour she finished making the tea, resolving to clean up the arsenic later. "I know it may be hard," she said, setting down the teapot and cups on the table, a tightly controlled, sympathetic look on her face, "but please, tell me how he died."

Reference Material

- Chandler, David (1987). The Dictionary of Battles. Ebury Press.
- Riehn, Richard K (1990). 1812 Napoleon's Russian Campaign. McGraw-Hill, New York.
- Sokolov, Oleg (2005). L'armee de Napoleon, Editions Commios.
- Moore, Richard (1999-2017). Napoleonic Guide; Jean Rapp.
- Parkinson, Roger (1976). The Fox of the North. David McKay Company Inc.
- Chisholm, Hugh, editor (1911). Encyclopaedia Britannica. Cambridge University Press.